S0-BHS-554

THE LOEB CLASSICAL LIBRARY

FOUNDED BY JAMES LOEB

EDITED BY

G. P. GOOLD

XENOPHON

V

LCL 51

XENOPHON

CYROPAEDIA

BOOKS I–IV

WITH AN ENGLISH TRANSLATION BY

WALTER MILLER

HARVARD UNIVERSITY PRESS
CAMBRIDGE, MASSACHUSETTS
LONDON, ENGLAND

First published 1914
Reprinted 1925, 1947, 1960, 1968, 1983, 1994

ISBN 0-674-99057-9

Printed in Great Britain by St Edmundsbury Press Ltd,
Bury St Edmunds, Suffolk, on acid-free paper.
Bound by Hunter & Foulis Ltd, Edinburgh, Scotland.

CONTENTS

INTRODUCTION

Xenophon, the son of a knightly family of Athens—general, historian, philosopher, essayist—was born probably about 429 B.C. But there is a story, not very well authenticated, that his life was saved by Socrates in the battle of Delium (424 B.C.), and that this marked the beginning of his attachment to his great master. If this story be true, the date of his birth can hardly be placed later than 444 B.C.

Our chief interest in his career centres about his participation in the Expedition of the Younger Cyrus (401 B.C.); the *Anabasis*, his own account of that brilliant failure, gives him his chief claim to a high place among the great names in historical literature; and his successful conduct of the Retreat of the Ten Thousand gives him his high rank among the world's great generals and tacticians.

When he arrived once more in a land of Hellenic civilization, he found that his revered master Socrates had been put to death by his purblind countrymen, that the knights, to whose order he belonged, were in great disfavour, that there was no tie left to bind him to his home; and so, with the remnant of the

troops that he had brought safe back to Hellas, he joined the Spartan king Agesilaus as he was starting for the conquest of the East, and with him fought against his own native city at Coronea (394 B.C.). From that date he lived, an exile from Athens, at Scillus, among the hills beyond the Alpheus from Olympia. And there he wrote the *Anabasis*, the *Cyropaedia*, the Essays on *Agesilaus*, *The Spartan Constitution*, *Horsemanship*, *Hunting*, and most of his other books. He died at Corinth some time after 357 B.C.

Xenophon's works have been roughly classified under three categories: history, philosophy, and miscellaneous essays. The *Cyropaedia*, however, can scarcely be made to fit into any one of these three groups. It is historical, but not history; it has much Socratic dialogue, but it is not philosophy; it has discussions of many questions of education, ethics, politics, tactics, etc., but it is not an essay. It is biographical, but it is not biography; it contains also, in the episode of Panthea and Abradatas, one of the most charming love stories in literature. We may best call it an historical romance—the western pioneer in that field of literature.

Like all his followers in the realm of historical fiction, Xenophon allows himself many liberties with the facts of history. The constitution of Persia, as set forth in the *Cyropaedia*, is no oriental reality; it is the constitution of Sparta, which, in his admiration

for Agesilaus and Clearchus and the Spartan discipline, he has transfigured and set up as the model of his idealized constitutional monarchy. His Persians worship heroes, go crowned with garlands into battle, send a watchword up and down the lines as they prepare for battle, sing a paean as they enter the fight, and do many other things that real Persians never, Spartans always, did. The simple fare and dress of the Persians smack much more of the austere life of the Eurotas Valley than of the luxurious East. Even the education of the Persian youth is identically the education of young Spartans; and in the teacher of Tigranes no one can fail to recognize Socrates himself. So, too, Cyrus's invincible battle lines are not the wavering, unwieldy hordes of orientals, easily swept away by the Grecian phalanx like chaff before the strong south-wind, but the heavy, solid masses of Sparta; and his tactics on the march and in the fury of battle are not the tactics of a "barbarian" king, but those of the consummate tactician who led the famous Ten Thousand Greeks from Asia back to Hellas.

Actual violence to historical facts is sometimes committed. For example, Media was subdued by force (and treachery) in the lifetime of Astyages (550 B.C.), not voluntarily ceded to Cyrus by Cyaxares as the dowry of his daughter; Cyaxares himself, the son of Astyages, is unknown, save through Xenophon's story; it seems most probable that he is

wholly unhistorical. The conquest of Egypt, ascribed to Cyrus, was in reality accomplished by his son and successor, Cambyses. The beautiful account of the peaceful passing of Cyrus is wholly out of accord with the well-established record of his violent death in the battle against the Massagetae (529 B.C.).

This exhausts the tale of serious divergences from historical accuracy. There is much, on the other hand, that has been overlooked by the critics, though it is of prime importance for the history and the conditions of the orient in Xenophon's own times. The account he gives us of the Armenians and Chaldaeans, for example, affords us information, more full and more valuable than we have from any other source. Xenophon knew his Herodotus and Ctesias, of course, and probably other earlier historians whom we cannot identify; and he drew at will from those sources such facts as he needed for the earlier history of the East. But of far more value to us is the wealth of material gathered by him on his memorable march through Asia and the flood of light that in the *Cyropaedia* he throws on contemporary peoples and manners and customs in the orient.

As a work of art, the *Cyropaedia* brings together and sums up the results of nearly all of Xenophon's literary activity. The *Anabasis* and the events that led to its composition furnish the background of geography, history, and custom; the *Memorabilia* and the discipleship to Socrates contribute the

Socratic method in the discussions of ethics, tactics, generalship, and statesmanship; the *Agesilaus* and *The Spartan Constitution* afford the basis for the ideal state that might have been constructed on Greek soil after the pattern of the kingdom of Cyrus; the essays on *Horsemanship* and *Hunting* find full illustration in every book of the *Cyropaedia*; the views set forth in the *Oeconomicus* on the social status of women and the ideal relations of married life and the home have their practical realization again in the story of Panthea and Abradatas.

The title of the *Cyropaedia* (*The Education of Cyrus*) is misleading. In its scope it includes the whole life and career of the great conqueror. The first book covers the period of his boyhood and youth, and only one chapter of that has to do strictly with his education. In the remaining seven books the theme is not his own education but his campaigns of conquest and his training of others as soldiers and citizens in his new empire. But the first book, in dealing with the education of Cyrus, really answers the supreme questions of government—how to rule and how to be ruled—and therefore gives its name to the whole; for that problem is the real theme of the work.

The spirit of the book is Hellenic throughout—a picture of the East with a dash of local colour, but dominated by the civilization in which Xenophon was reared and the ideals that he had learned to cherish.

The corner-stone of his idealized Persian constitution, "equality of rights before the law" (I. iii. 18), and the "boasted equal freedom of speech" (I. iii. 10) are transferred bodily from the democracy of Athens to the uncongenial environment of an oriental despotism. And yet his chief purpose in writing the story of Cyrus was to give his people a picture of an ideal monarchy with an ideal monarch, guided by Socratic principles and carrying out the author's political and philosophical ideals. In the *Cyropaedia* the didactic element dominates both the history and the fiction; and the hero is an idealistic composite portrait of Socrates, the younger Cyrus, Clearchus, Agesilaus, and Xenophon himself. However it may have been received at Athens, it is only natural that such a book should have been extremely popular among the Romans, and that Cato and Cicero should have found in it teachings that appealed strongly to them for the upbuilding of an empire founded on the majesty of the law and on justice and righteousness, and that the younger Scipio should have had it "always in his hands" as his *vade mecum.*

In point of literary merit, it stands first among the writings of Xenophon. His hero, though he has been criticised as being a little too good, has the same qualities of greatness, goodness, gentleness, and justice that are given to him by the great prophets of Israel. "The Lord God of heaven" has given him "all the kingdoms of the earth" (II. Chron.

xxxvi. 23; Ezra, i. 1–2); and the greatest of Messianic seers finds in Xenophon's hero "the Lord's anointed" (the Messiah), and makes Jehovah say of him (Is. xliv. 28; xlv. 1): "He is my shepherd and shall perform all my pleasure . . . whose right hand I have holden, to subdue nations before him."

BIBLIOGRAPHICAL ADDENDUM (1983)

Budé series:

Cyropédie, Tome I (1, 2), ed. Marcel Bizos, Paris 1971.

Cyropédie, Tome II (3–5), ed. Marcel Bizos, Paris 1973.

Cyropédie, Tome III (6–8), ed. Edouard Delebecque, Paris 1978.

General:

J. K. Anderson, *Xenophon*, London 1974.

W. E. Higgins, *Xenophon the Athenian*, Albany 1977 (Chapter 3: Cyrus).

BIBLIOGRAPHY

The most important manuscripts of Xenophon are ascribed to three families, x, y, and z. The following are cited in the notes:—

Family	Siglum	Manuscript	Place	Date
x	C	Parisinus C	Paris	Fourteenth century
x	E	Etonensis	Eton	Fifteenth century
y	D	Bodleianus	Oxford	Fifteenth century
y	F	Erlangensis	Erlangen	Fifteenth century
	R	Bremensis	Bremen	Fifteenth century
z	A	Parisinus A	Paris	Fifteenth century
z	G	Guelferbytanus	Wolfenbüttel	Fifteenth century
z	H	Escorialensis	Escorial	Twelfth century
	V	Vaticanus	Rome	Twelfth century
	π_2	Fragmenta Oxyrrhynci		Third century
	m	Ambrosianus (I. v. 7–14; III. iii. 44–45)	Milan	Tenth century

The earliest printed edition of Xenophon is the Latin version of Francis Philelfus, 1476.

The *Princeps* of the Greek text was published by Giunta at Florence in 1516 (second edition, 1527), printed from a good manuscript now lost. The title-page runs: *τάδε ἔνεστιν ἐν τῇδε τῇ βίβλῳ Ξενοφῶντος Κύρου Παιδείας βιβλία ή κ.τ.λ.* Haec in hoc libro continentur: Xenophontis Cyripedias Libri VIII.; Anabaseos Libri VII.; Apomnemoneumaton; de Venatione; de Re Equestri; de Equis Alendis; Lacedaemoniorum Respublica; Atheniensium Respublica; Oeconomica; Hieron; Symposium; de Graecorum Gestis Libri VII. In aedibus P. Juntae: Florentiae, 1516.

Bornemann: Xenophontis Opera Omnia recensita et commentariis instructa. 4 voll. Lipsiae: 1838–1863.

Breitenbach: Xenophons Kyropaedie für den Schulgebrauch erklärt von Ludwig Breitenbach. Leipzig: 1858. 3te Aufl. (I.–IV.) 1875, (V.–VIII.) 1878; 4te Aufl. (I.–IV. Büchsenschütz), 1890.

Dindorf: Xenophontis Institutio Cyri, ex Recensione et cum Annotationibus Ludovici Dindorfii. Oxonii: 1857. (Referred to in the notes as Dindorf or Dindorf[3].)

Dindorf: Xenophontis Institutio Cyri, recensuit et praefatus est Ludovicus Dindorfius. Editio IV. emendatior. Lipsiae: 1875. (Referred to in the notes as Dindorf[4].)

BIBLIOGRAPHY

Gail: Xenophon, Œuvres Complètes, traduites en François et accompagnées du texte Grec, de la version Latine, de notes critiques, des variantes des manuscrits de la Bibliothèque Royale, etc., par J. B. Gail. VII. Tomi. Paris: 1797–1815.

Gemoll: Xenophontis Institutio Cyri, recensuit Gulielmus Gemoll. Editio Maior. Leipzig: 1912.

Hertlein: Xenophons Cyropädie. Erklärt von Friedrich Karl Hertlein. Berlin: 1853; (V.–VII.) 3te Aufl. 1876; (I.–IV. Nitsche) 1886.

Holden: The Cyropaedeia of Xenophon with Introduction and Notes. By the Rev. Hubert A. Holden. 4 voll. Cambridge: 1887–1890.

Hug: Xenophontis Institutio Cyri, recensuit Arnoldus Hug. Lipsiae: 1905. (The basis of the present text.)

Hutchinson: Xenophontis de Cyri Institutione Libri VIII. Graeca recognovit, cum cod. Oxon. et omnibus fere libris editis contulit, pluribus in locis emendavit, versione Latina reformavit, etc., Th. Hutchinson. Ed. VI. Oxonii (Londini): (1727) 1765.

Marchant: Xenophontis Opera Omnia recognovit brevique adnotatione critica instruxit E. C. Marchant. Oxonii: 1910.

Poppo: Xenophon. Cyrus. Denuo recensuit adhibita cod. Medico-Laurent. collatione Ernestus Poppo. Lipsiae: 1819; 1823.

Sauppe: Xenophontis Opera edidit Gustavus Sauppe. 5 voll. Lipsiae: 1865–1867–1870.

Schneider: Xenophontis quae exstant. Ex librorum scriptorum fide et virorum doctorum coniecturis recensuit et interpretatus est Joannes Gottlob Schneider. 6 voll. Lipsiae: 1790–1849.

Stephanus: Ξενοφῶντος ἅπαντα τὰ σωζόμενα βιβλία. Multorum veterum exemplarium opera purgata . . . cum Latina interpretatione F. Filelfi . . . Genevae: 1561; 1581.

Weiske: Xenophontis Scripta, in usum lectorum, Graecis litteris tinctorum ad rerum et verborum intelligentiam illustrata a Beniamin Weiske. 6 voll. Lipsiae: 1798–1804.

Zeune: Xenophontis Opera, ed. I. C. Zeune. 6 voll. Lipsiae: 1778–1782.

XENOPHON'S CYROPAEDIA

BOOK I

THE BOYHOOD OF CYRUS

ΞΕΝΟΦΩΝΤΟΣ ΚΥΡΟΥ ΠΑΙΔΕΙΑ

Α

Ι

1. Ἔννοιά ποθ' ἡμῖν ἐγένετο ὅσαι δημοκρατίαι κατελύθησαν ὑπὸ τῶν ἄλλως πως βουλομένων πολιτεύεσθαι μᾶλλον ἢ ἐν δημοκρατίᾳ, ὅσαι τ' αὖ μοναρχίαι, ὅσαι τε ὀλιγαρχίαι ἀνῄρηνται ἤδη ὑπὸ δήμων, καὶ ὅσοι τυραννεῖν ἐπιχειρήσαντες οἱ μὲν αὐτῶν καὶ ταχὺ πάμπαν κατελύθησαν, οἱ δὲ κἂν ὁποσονοῦν χρόνον ἄρχοντες διαγένωνται, θαυμάζονται ὡς σοφοί τε καὶ εὐτυχεῖς ἄνδρες γεγενημένοι. πολλοὺς δ' ἐδοκοῦμεν καταμεμαθηκέναι καὶ ἐν ἰδίοις οἴκοις τοὺς μὲν ἔχοντας καὶ πλείονας οἰκέτας, τοὺς δὲ καὶ πάνυ[1] ὀλίγους, καὶ ὅμως οὐδὲ τοῖς ὀλίγοις τούτοις πάνυ τι δυναμένους χρῆσθαι πειθομένοις[2] τοὺς δεσπότας.

[1] πάνυ Edd.; πάνυ τι yG; πάντη xAHR.
[2] πειθομένοις found only in FG; [πειθομένοις] Sauppe. Dindorf, Hertlein; πειθομένοις [τοὺς δεσπότας] Hirschig, Gemoll.

XENOPHON'S CYROPAEDIA

BOOK I

I

Preface: the instability of government

1. The thought once occurred to us how many republics have been overthrown by people who preferred to live under any form of government other than a republican, and again, how many monarchies and how many oligarchies in times past have been abolished by the people. We reflected, moreover, how many of those individuals who have aspired to absolute power have either been deposed once for all and that right quickly; or if they have continued in power, no matter for how short a time, they are objects of wonder as having proved to be wise and happy men. Then, too, we had observed, we thought, that even in private homes some people who had rather more than the usual number of servants and some also who had only a very few were nevertheless, though nominally masters, quite unable to assert their authority over even those few.

2. Ἔτι δὲ πρὸς τούτοις ἐνενοοῦμεν ὅτι ἄρχοντες μέν εἰσι καὶ οἱ βουκόλοι τῶν βοῶν καὶ οἱ ἱπποφορβοὶ τῶν ἵππων, καὶ πάντες δὲ οἱ καλούμενοι νομεῖς ὧν ἂν ἐπιστατῶσι ζῴων εἰκότως ἂν ἄρχοντες τούτων νομίζοιντο· πάσας τοίνυν ταύτας τὰς ἀγέλας ἐδοκοῦμεν ὁρᾶν μᾶλλον ἐθελούσας πείθεσθαι τοῖς νομεῦσιν ἢ τοὺς ἀνθρώπους τοῖς ἄρχουσι. πορεύονταί τε γὰρ αἱ ἀγέλαι ᾗ ἂν αὐτὰς εὐθύνωσιν οἱ νομεῖς, νέμονταί τε χωρία ἐφ' ὁποῖα ἂν αὐτὰς ἐπάγωσιν, ἀπέχονταί τε ὧν ἂν αὐτὰς ἀπείργωσι· καὶ τοῖς καρποῖς τοίνυν τοῖς γιγνομένοις ἐξ αὐτῶν ἐῶσι τοὺς νομέας χρῆσθαι οὕτως ὅπως ἂν αὐτοὶ βούλωνται. ἔτι τοίνυν οὐδεμίαν πώποτε ἀγέλην ᾐσθήμεθα συστᾶσαν ἐπὶ τὸν νομέα οὔτε ὡς μὴ πείθεσθαι οὔτε ὡς μὴ ἐπιτρέπειν τῷ καρπῷ χρῆσθαι, ἀλλὰ καὶ χαλεπώτεραί εἰσιν αἱ ἀγέλαι πᾶσι τοῖς ἀλλοφύλοις ἢ τοῖς ἄρχουσί τε καὶ ὠφελουμένοις ἀπ' αὐτῶν· ἄνθρωποι δὲ ἐπ' οὐδένας μᾶλλον συνίστανται ἢ ἐπὶ τούτους οὓς ἂν αἴσθωνται ἄρχειν ἑαυτῶν ἐπιχειροῦντας.

3. Ὅτε μὲν δὴ ταῦτα ἐνεθυμούμεθα, οὕτως ἐγιγνώσκομεν περὶ αὐτῶν, ὡς ἀνθρώπῳ πεφυκότι πάντων τῶν ἄλλων ῥᾷον εἴη ζῴων ἢ ἀνθρώπων ἄρχειν. ἐπειδὴ δὲ ἐνενοήσαμεν ὅτι Κῦρος ἐγένετο Πέρσης, ὃς παμπόλλους μὲν ἀνθρώπους ἐκτήσατο πειθομένους ἑαυτῷ, παμπόλλας δὲ πόλεις, πάμπολλα δὲ ἔθνη, ἐκ τούτου δὴ ἠναγκαζόμεθα μετανοεῖν μὴ οὔτε τῶν ἀδυνάτων οὔτε τῶν χαλεπῶν ἔργων ᾖ τὸ ἀνθρώπων ἄρχειν, ἤν τις ἐπισταμένως τοῦτο πράττῃ. Κύρῳ γοῦν ἴσμεν ἐθελήσαντας πείθεσθαι

2. And in addition to this, we reflected that cowherds are the rulers of their cattle, that grooms are the rulers of their horses, and that all who are called herdsmen might properly be regarded as the rulers of the animals over which they are placed in charge. Now we noticed, as we thought, that all these herds obeyed their keepers more readily than men obey their rulers. For the herds go wherever their keeper directs them and graze in those places to which he leads them and keep out of those from which he excludes them. They allow their keeper, moreover, to enjoy, just as he will, the profits that accrue from them. And then again, we have never known of a herd conspiring against its keeper, either to refuse obedience to him or to deny him the privilege of enjoying the profits that accrue. At the same time, herds are more intractable to strangers than to their rulers and those who derive profit from them. Men, however, conspire against none sooner than against those whom they see attempting to rule over them.

Animals more tractable than men

3. Thus, as we meditated on this analogy, we were inclined to conclude that for man, as he is constituted, it is easier to rule over any and all other creatures than to rule over men. But when we reflected that there was one Cyrus, the Persian, who reduced to obedience a vast number of men and cities and nations, we were then compelled to change our opinion and decide that to rule men might be a task neither impossible nor even difficult, if one should only go about it in an intelligent manner. At all events, we know that people obeyed Cyrus willingly, although some of them were distant from him a

Cyrus a king of men

τοὺς μὲν ἀπέχοντας παμπόλλων ἡμερῶν ὁδόν, τοὺς δὲ καὶ μηνῶν, τοὺς δὲ οὐδ' ἑωρακότας πώποτ' αὐτόν, τοὺς δὲ καὶ εὖ εἰδότας ὅτι οὐδ' ἂν ἴδοιεν, καὶ ὅμως ἤθελον αὐτῷ ὑπακούειν.

4. Καὶ γάρ τοι τοσοῦτον διήνεγκε τῶν ἄλλων βασιλέων, καὶ τῶν πατρίους ἀρχὰς παρειληφότων καὶ τῶν δι' ἑαυτῶν κτησαμένων, ὥσθ' ὁ μὲν Σκύθης καίπερ παμπόλλων[1] ὄντων Σκυθῶν ἄλλου μὲν οὐδενὸς δύναιτ' ἂν ἔθνους ἐπάρξαι, ἀγαπῴη δ' ἂν εἰ τοῦ ἑαυτοῦ ἔθνους ἄρχων διαγένοιτο, καὶ ὁ Θρᾷξ Θρᾳκῶν καὶ ὁ Ἰλλυριὸς Ἰλλυριῶν, καὶ τἄλλα δὲ ὡσαύτως ἔθνη ἀκούομεν· τὰ γοῦν ἐν τῇ Εὐρώπῃ ἔτι καὶ νῦν αὐτόνομα εἶναι λέγεται[2] καὶ λελύσθαι ἀπ' ἀλλήλων· Κῦρος δὲ παραλαβὼν ὡσαύτως οὕτω καὶ τὰ ἐν τῇ Ἀσίᾳ ἔθνη αὐτόνομα ὄντα ὁρμηθεὶς σὺν ὀλίγῃ Περσῶν στρατιᾷ ἑκόντων μὲν ἡγήσατο Μήδων, ἑκόντων δὲ Ὑρκανίων, κατεστρέψατο δὲ Σύρους, Ἀσσυρίους, Ἀραβίους, Καππαδόκας, Φρύγας ἀμφοτέρους, Λυδούς, Κᾶρας, Φοίνικας, Βαβυλωνίους, ἦρξε δὲ Βακτρίων καὶ Ἰνδῶν καὶ Κιλίκων, ὡσαύτως δὲ Σακῶν καὶ Παφλαγόνων καὶ Μαγαδιδῶν, καὶ ἄλλων δὲ παμπόλλων ἐθνῶν, ὧν οὐδ' ἂν τὰ ὀνόματα ἔχοι τις εἰπεῖν, ἐπῆρξε δὲ καὶ Ἑλλήνων τῶν ἐν τῇ Ἀσίᾳ, καταβὰς δ' ἐπὶ θάλατταν καὶ Κυπρίων καὶ Αἰγυπτίων.

[1] παμπόλλων DFG; πολλῶν xAHR.
[2] λέγεται MSS.; [λέγεται] Dindorf, Hug, Marchant, omitting the colon after ἀκούομεν.

journey of many days, and others of many months; others, although they had never seen him, and still others who knew well that they never should see him. Nevertheless they were all willing to be his subjects.

4. But all this is not so surprising after all, so very different was he from all other kings, both those who have inherited their thrones from their fathers and those who have gained their crowns by their own efforts; the Scythian king, for instance, would never be able to extend his rule over any other nation besides his own, although the Scythians are very numerous, but he would be well content if he could maintain himself in power over his own people; so the Thracian king with his Thracians, the Illyrian with his Illyrians, and so also all other nations, we are told. Those in Europe, at any rate, are said to be free and independent of one another even to this day. But Cyrus, finding the nations in Asia also independent in exactly the same way, started out with a little band of Persians and became the leader of the Medes by their full consent and of the Hyrcanians by theirs; he then conquered Syria, Assyria, Arabia, Cappadocia, both Phrygias, Lydia, Caria, Phoenicia, and Babylonia; he ruled also over Bactria, India, and Cilicia; and he was likewise king of the Sacians, Paphlagonians, Magadidae, and very many other nations, of which one could not even tell the names; he brought under his sway the Asiatic Greeks also; and, descending to the sea, he added both Cyprus and Egypt to his empire.

The extent of his kingdom

5. Καὶ τοίνυν τούτων τῶν ἐθνῶν ἦρξεν οὔτε αὐτῷ ὁμογλώττων ὄντων οὔτε ἀλλήλοις, καὶ ὅμως ἐδυνάσθη[1] ἐφικέσθαι μὲν ἐπὶ τοσαύτην γῆν τῷ ἀφ' ἑαυτοῦ φόβῳ, ὥστε καταπλῆξαι πάντας καὶ μηδένα ἐπιχειρεῖν αὐτῷ, ἐδυνάσθη[1] δὲ ἐπιθυμίαν ἐμβαλεῖν τοσαύτην τοῦ[2] αὐτῷ χαρίζεσθαι ὥστε ἀεὶ τῇ αὐτοῦ γνώμῃ ἀξιοῦν κυβερνᾶσθαι, ἀνηρτήσατο δὲ τοσαῦτα φῦλα ὅσα καὶ διελθεῖν ἔργον ἐστίν, ὅποι ἂν ἄρξηταί τις πορεύεσθαι ἀπὸ τῶν βασιλείων, ἤν τε πρὸς ἕω ἤν τε πρὸς ἑσπέραν ἤν τε πρὸς ἄρκτον ἤν τε πρὸς μεσημβρίαν.

6. Ἡμεῖς μὲν δὴ ὡς ἄξιον ὄντα θαυμάζεσθαι τοῦτον τὸν ἄνδρα ἐσκεψάμεθα τίς ποτ' ὢν γενεὰν καὶ ποίαν τινὰ φύσιν ἔχων καὶ ποίᾳ τινὶ παιδείᾳ παιδευθεὶς τοσοῦτον διήνεγκεν εἰς τὸ ἄρχειν ἀνθρώπων. ὅσα οὖν καὶ ἐπυθόμεθα καὶ ᾐσθῆσθαι δοκοῦμεν περὶ αὐτοῦ, ταῦτα πειρασόμεθα διηγήσασθαι.

II

1. Πατρὸς μὲν δὴ ὁ Κῦρος λέγεται γενέσθαι Καμβύσου Περσῶν βασιλέως· ὁ δὲ Καμβύσης οὗτος τοῦ Περσειδῶν γένους ἦν· οἱ δὲ Περσεῖδαι ἀπὸ Περσέως κλῄζονται· μητρὸς δὲ ὁμολογεῖται Μανδάνης γενέσθαι· ἡ δὲ Μανδάνη αὕτη

[1] ἐδυνάσθη MSS., except yR²G, which have ἐδυνήθη.
[2] τοῦ πάντας MSS., except D, which omits πάντας; [πάντας] Gemoll, Marchant.

5. He ruled over these nations, even though they lid not speak the same language as he, nor one ıation the same as another; for all that, he was able o cover so vast a region with the fear which he nspired, that he struck all men with terror and no ›ne tried to withstand him; and he was able to ıwaken in all so lively a desire to please him, that hey always wished to be guided by his will. Moreover, the tribes that he brought into subjection to ıimself were so many that it is a difficult matter ven to travel to them all, in whatever direction one egin one's journey from the palace, whether toward he east or the west, toward the north or the south.

The secret of his powei

6. Believing this man to be deserving of all dmiration, we have therefore investigated who he vas in his origin, what natural endowments he ossessed, and what sort of education he had enjoyed, hat he so greatly excelled in governing men. Accordingly, what we have found out or think we know oncerning him we shall now endeavour to present.

II

1. The father of Cyrus is said to have been Cambyses, king of the Persians: this Cambyses elonged to the stock of the Persidae, and the Persidae derive their name from Perseus. His nother, it is generally agreed, was Mandane; and

His parentage

Ἀστυάγους ἦν θυγάτηρ τοῦ Μήδων γενομένου[1] βασιλέως. φῦναι δὲ ὁ Κῦρος λέγεται καὶ ᾄδεται ἔτι καὶ νῦν ὑπὸ τῶν βαρβάρων εἶδος μὲν κάλλιστος, ψυχὴν δὲ φιλανθρωπότατος καὶ φιλομαθέστατος καὶ φιλοτιμότατος, ὥστε πάντα μὲν πόνον ἀνατλῆναι, πάντα δὲ κίνδυνον ὑπομεῖναι τοῦ ἐπαινεῖσθαι ἕνεκα.

2. Φύσιν μὲν δὴ τῆς μορφῆς καὶ τῆς ψυχῆς τοιαύτην ἔχων διαμνημονεύεται· ἐπαιδεύθη γε μὴν ἐν Περσῶν νόμοις· οὗτοι δὲ δοκοῦσιν οἱ νόμοι ἄρχεσθαι τοῦ κοινοῦ ἀγαθοῦ ἐπιμελόμενοι οὐκ ἔνθενπερ ἐν[2] ταῖς πλείσταις πόλεσιν ἄρχονται. αἱ μὲν γὰρ πλεῖσται πόλεις ἀφεῖσαι παιδεύειν ὅπως τις ἐθέλει τοὺς ἑαυτοῦ παῖδας, καὶ αὐτοὺς τοὺς πρεσβυτέρους ὅπως ἐθέλουσι διάγειν, ἔπειτα προστάττουσιν αὐτοῖς μὴ κλέπτειν μηδὲ ἁρπάζειν, μὴ βίᾳ εἰς οἰκίαν παριέναι, μὴ παίειν ὃν μὴ δίκαιον, μὴ μοιχεύειν, μὴ ἀπειθεῖν ἄρχοντι, καὶ τἆλλα τὰ τοιαῦτα ὡσαύτως· ἢν δέ τις τούτων τι παραβαίνῃ, ζημίαν αὐτοῖς ἐπέθεσαν. 3. οἱ δὲ Περσικοὶ νόμοι προλαβόντες ἐπιμέλονται ὅπως τὴν ἀρχὴν μὴ τοιοῦτοι ἔσονται οἱ πολῖται οἷοι πονηροῦ τινος ἢ αἰσχροῦ ἔργου ἐφίεσθαι. ἐπιμέλονται δὲ ὧδε.

Ἔστιν αὐτοῖς ἐλευθέρα ἀγορὰ καλουμένη, ἔνθα τά τε βασίλεια καὶ τἆλλα ἀρχεῖα πεποίηται. ἐντεῦθεν τὰ μὲν ὤνια καὶ οἱ ἀγοραῖοι καὶ αἱ τούτων φωναὶ καὶ ἀπειροκαλίαι ἀπελήλανται

[1] γενομένου xAHR, Hug, Marchant; not in other MSS., Gemoll, Breitenbach.

[2] οὐκ ἔνθενπερ ἐν Hertlein, Edd.; οὐκ ἔνθεν ὅθενπερ (ὅθεν F) yG; οὐχ ὁμοίως γὰρ xAHRD².

his Mandane was the daughter of Astyages, some-
ime king of the Medes. And even to this day the
)arbarians tell in story and in song that Cyrus was
nost handsome in person, most generous of heart,
nost devoted to learning, and most ambitious, so
hat he endured all sorts of labour and faced all
orts of danger for the sake of praise.

2. Such then were the natural endowments,
)hysical and spiritual, that he is reputed to have
ad; but he was educated in conformity with the
aws of the Persians; and these laws appear in their
are for the common weal not to start from the same
)oint as they do in most states. For most states
)ermit every one to train his own children just as he
vill, and the older people themselves to live as they
lease; and then they command them not to steal
nd not to rob, not to break into anybody's house,
ot to strike a person whom they have no right to
trike, not to commit adultery, not to disobey an
fficer, and so forth; and if a man transgress any
ne of these laws, they punish him. 3. The Persian
aws, however, begin at the beginning and take care
hat from the first their citizens shall not be of such
character as ever to desire anything improper or
mmoral; and the measures they take are as follows.

The Persian system of education

They have their so-called "Free Square," where
he royal palace and other government buildings
re located. The hucksters with their wares, their
ries, and their vulgarities are excluded from this
nd relegated to another part of the city, in order

εἰς ἄλλον τόπον, ὡς μὴ μιγνύηται ἡ τούτων τύρβ
τῇ τῶν πεπαιδευμένων εὐκοσμίᾳ. 4. διῄρηται δ
αὕτη ἡ ἀγορὰ ἡ περὶ τὰ ἀρχεῖα τέτταρα μέρη
τούτων δ' ἔστιν ἓν μὲν παισίν, ἓν δὲ ἐφήβοις
ἄλλο τελείοις ἀνδράσιν, ἄλλο τοῖς ὑπὲρ τ
στρατεύσιμα ἔτη γεγονόσι. νόμῳ δ' εἰς τὰ
ἑαυτῶν χώρας ἕκαστοι τούτων πάρεισιν, οἱ μὲ
παῖδες ἅμα τῇ ἡμέρᾳ καὶ οἱ τέλειοι ἄνδρες, οἱ δ
γεραίτεροι ἡνίκ' ἂν ἑκάστῳ προχωρῇ, πλὴν ἐν ταῖ
τεταγμέναις ἡμέραις, ἐν αἷς αὐτοὺς δεῖ παρεῖναι
οἱ δὲ ἔφηβοι καὶ κοιμῶνται περὶ τὰ ἀρχεῖα σὺ
τοῖς γυμνητικοῖς ὅπλοις πλὴν τῶν γεγαμηκότων
οὗτοι δὲ οὔτε ἐπιζητοῦνται, ἢν μὴ προρρηθ
παρεῖναι, οὔτε πολλάκις ἀπεῖναι καλόν.

5. Ἄρχοντες δ' ἐφ' ἑκάστῳ τούτων τῶν μερῶν εἰσ
δώδεκα· δώδεκα γὰρ καὶ Περσῶν φυλαὶ διῄρηνται
καὶ ἐπὶ μὲν τοῖς παισὶν ἐκ τῶν γεραιτέρων ᾑρη
μένοι εἰσὶν οἳ ἂν δοκῶσι τοὺς παῖδας βελτίστου
ἀποδεικνύναι· ἐπὶ δὲ τοῖς ἐφήβοις ἐκ τῶ
τελείων ἀνδρῶν οἳ ἂν αὖ τοὺς ἐφήβους βελτίστου
δοκῶσι παρέχειν· ἐπὶ δὲ τοῖς τελείοις ἀνδράσι
οἳ ἂν δοκῶσι παρέχειν αὐτοὺς μάλιστα τὰ τεταγ
μένα ποιοῦντας καὶ τὰ παραγγελλόμενα ὑπὸ τῆ
μεγίστης ἀρχῆς· εἰσὶ δὲ καὶ τῶν γεραιτέρω
προστάται ᾑρημένοι, οἳ προστατεύουσιν,[1] ὅπω
καὶ οὗτοι τὰ καθήκοντα ἀποτελῶσιν. ἃ δὲ ἑκάστ
ἡλικίᾳ προστέτακται ποιεῖν διηγησόμεθα, ὡ
μᾶλλον δῆλον γένηται ᾗ ἐπιμέλονται ὡς ἂ
βέλτιστοι εἶεν οἱ πολῖται.

[1] οἳ προστατεύουσιν MSS.; [οἳ προστατεύουσιν] Dindorf, Hug
Sauppe, et al.

that their tumult may not intrude upon the orderly life of the cultured. 4. This square, enclosing the government buildings, is divided into four parts; one of these belongs to the boys, one to the youths, another to the men of mature years, and another to those who are past the age for military service. And the laws require them to come daily to their several quarters—the boys and the full-grown men at daybreak; but the elders may come at whatever time it suits each one's convenience, except that they must present themselves on certain specified days. But the youths pass the night also in light armour about the government buildings—all except those who are married; no inquiry is made for such, unless they be especially ordered in advance to be there, but it is not proper for them to be absent too often.

Its organization

5. Over each of these divisions there are twelve officers, for the Persians are divided into twelve tribes. To have charge of the boys, such are chosen from the ranks of the elders as seem likely to make out of the boys the best men; to have charge of the youths, such are chosen from the ranks of the mature men as seem most likely on their part to develop the youths best; to preside over the mature men, those are selected who seem most likely to fit them best to execute the orders and requirements of the highest authorities[1]; and of the elders also chiefs are selected who act as overseers to see that those of this class also do their duty. And what duties are assigned to each age to perform we shall now set forth, that it may be better understood what pains the Persians take that their citizens may prove to be the very best.

[1] *I.e.* a Council of Elders, under the presidency of the king.

6. Οἱ μὲν δὴ παῖδες εἰς τὰ διδασκαλεῖα φοιτῶντες διάγουσι μανθάνοντες δικαιοσύνην· καὶ λέγουσιν ὅτι ἐπὶ τοῦτο ἔρχονται ὥσπερ παρ' ἡμῖν ὅτι[1] γράμματα μαθησόμενοι. οἱ δ' ἄρχοντες αὐτῶν διατελοῦσι τὸ πλεῖστον τῆς ἡμέρας δικάζοντες αὐτοῖς. γίγνεται γὰρ δὴ καὶ παισὶ πρὸς ἀλλήλους ὥσπερ ἀνδράσιν ἐγκλήματα καὶ κλοπῆς καὶ ἁρπαγῆς καὶ βίας καὶ ἀπάτης καὶ κακολογίας καὶ ἄλλων οἵων δὴ εἰκός. οὓς δ' ἂν γνῶσι τούτων τι ἀδικοῦντας, τιμωροῦνται. 7. κολάζουσι δὲ καὶ ὃν ἂν ἀδίκως ἐγκαλοῦντα εὑρίσκωσι. δικάζουσι δὲ καὶ ἐγκλήματος οὗ ἕνεκα ἄνθρωποι μισοῦσι μὲν ἀλλήλους μάλιστα, δικάζονται δὲ ἥκιστα,[2] ἀχαριστίας, καὶ ὃν ἂν γνῶσι δυνάμενον μὲν χάριν ἀποδιδόναι, μὴ ἀποδιδόντα δέ, κολάζουσι καὶ τοῦτον ἰσχυρῶς. οἴονται γὰρ τοὺς ἀχαρίστους καὶ περὶ θεοὺς ἂν μάλιστα ἀμελῶς ἔχειν καὶ περὶ γονέας καὶ πατρίδα καὶ φίλους. ἕπεσθαι δὲ δοκεῖ μάλιστα τῇ ἀχαριστίᾳ ἡ ἀναισχυντία· καὶ γὰρ αὕτη μεγίστη δοκεῖ εἶναι ἐπὶ πάντα τὰ αἰσχρὰ ἡγεμών.

8. Διδάσκουσι δὲ τοὺς παῖδας καὶ σωφροσύνην· μέγα δὲ συμβάλλεται εἰς τὸ μανθάνειν σωφρονεῖν αὐτοὺς ὅτι καὶ τοὺς πρεσβυτέρους ὁρῶσιν ἀνὰ πᾶσαν ἡμέραν σωφρόνως διάγοντας. διδάσκουσι δὲ αὐτοὺς καὶ πείθεσθαι τοῖς ἄρχουσι· μέγα δὲ καὶ εἰς τοῦτο συμβάλλεται ὅτι ὁρῶσι τοὺς πρεσβυτέρους πειθομένους τοῖς ἄρχουσιν ἰσχυρῶς.[3] διδάσκουσι δὲ καὶ ἐγκράτειαν γαστρὸς καὶ ποτοῦ· μέγα δὲ καὶ εἰς τοῦτο συμβάλλεται ὅτι ὁρῶσι

[1] ὅτι Cobet, Edd.; οἱ τὰ MSS.
[2] δὲ ἥκιστα MSS., except xDGR which have δὲ οὐχ ἥκιστα.
[3] διδάσκουσι . . . ἰσχυρῶς not in xAHR.

6. The boys go to school and spend their time in learning justice; and they say that they go there for this purpose, just as in our country they say that they go to learn to read and write. And their officers spend the greater part of the day in deciding cases for them. For, as a matter of course, boys also prefer charges against one another, just as men do, of theft, robbery, assault, cheating, slander, and other things that naturally come up; and when they discover any one committing any of these crimes, they punish him; 7. and they punish also any one whom they find accusing another falsely. And they bring one another to trial also charged with an offence for which people hate one another most but go to law least, namely, that of ingratitude; and if they know that any one is able to return a favour and fails to do so, they punish him also severely. For they think that the ungrateful are likely to be most neglectful of their duty toward their gods, their parents, their country, and their friends; for it seems that shamelessness goes hand in hand with ingratitude; and it is that, we know, which leads the way to every moral wrong.

Its method and curriculum: *A.* Boys

8. They teach the boys self-control also; and it greatly conduces to their learning self-control that they see their elders also living temperately day by day. And they teach them likewise to obey the officers; and it greatly conduces to this also that they see their elders implicitly obeying their officers. And besides, they teach them self-restraint in eating and drinking; and it greatly conduces to this also that they see that their elders do not leave their

τοὺς πρεσβυτέρους οὐ πρόσθεν ἀπιόντας γαστρὸς ἕνεκα πρὶν ἂν ἀφῶσιν οἱ ἄρχοντες, καὶ ὅτι οὐ παρὰ μητρὶ σιτοῦνται οἱ παῖδες, ἀλλὰ παρὰ τῷ διδασκάλῳ, ὅταν οἱ ἄρχοντες σημήνωσι. φέρονται δὲ οἴκοθεν σῖτον μὲν ἄρτον, ὄψον δὲ κάρδαμον, πιεῖν δέ, ἤν τις διψῇ, κώθωνα, ὡς ἀπὸ τοῦ ποταμοῦ ἀρύσασθαι. πρὸς δὲ τούτοις[1] μανθάνουσι καὶ τοξεύειν καὶ ἀκοντίζειν.

Μέχρι μὲν δὴ ἓξ ἢ ἑπτακαίδεκα ἐτῶν ἀπὸ γενεᾶς οἱ παῖδες ταῦτα πράττουσιν, ἐκ τούτου δὲ εἰς τοὺς ἐφήβους ἐξέρχονται.

9. Οὗτοι δ' αὖ οἱ ἔφηβοι διάγουσιν ὧδε. δέκα ἔτη ἀφ' οὗ ἂν ἐκ παίδων ἐξέλθωσι κοιμῶνται μὲν περὶ τὰ ἀρχεῖα, ὥσπερ προειρήκαμεν, καὶ φυλακῆς ἕνεκα τῆς πόλεως καὶ σωφροσύνης· δοκεῖ γὰρ αὕτη ἡ ἡλικία μάλιστα ἐπιμελείας δεῖσθαι· παρέχουσι δὲ καὶ τὴν ἡμέραν ἑαυτοὺς τοῖς ἄρχουσι χρῆσθαι ἤν τι δέωνται ὑπὲρ τοῦ κοινοῦ. καὶ ὅταν μὲν δέῃ, πάντες μένουσι περὶ τὰ ἀρχεῖα· ὅταν δὲ ἐξίῃ βασιλεὺς ἐπὶ θήραν, ἐξάγει τὴν ἡμίσειαν τῆς φυλακῆς·[2] ποιεῖ δὲ τοῦτο πολλάκις τοῦ μηνός. ἔχειν δὲ δεῖ τοὺς ἐξιόντας τόξα καὶ παρὰ τὴν φαρέτραν ἐν κολεῷ κοπίδα ἢ σάγαριν, ἔτι δὲ γέρρον καὶ παλτὰ δύο, ὥστε τὸ μὲν ἀφεῖναι, τῷ δ', ἐὰν δέῃ, ἐκ χειρὸς χρῆσθαι. 10. διὰ τοῦτο

[1] πρὸς δὲ τούτοις DFGVπ, Edd.; πρὸ δὲ τούτων xAHR.
[2] ἐξάγει . . . φυλακῆς xAHR; τὰς ἡμισείας φυλακὰς καταλείπει DFGV.

posts to satisfy their hunger until the officers dismiss them; and the same end is promoted by the fact that the boys do not eat with their mothers but with their teachers, from the time the officers so direct. Furthermore, they bring from home bread for their food, cress for a relish, and for drinking, if any one is thirsty, a cup to draw water from the river. Besides this, they learn to shoot and to throw the spear.

This, then, is what the boys do until they are sixteen or seventeen years of age, and after this they are promoted from the class of boys and enrolled among the young men.

B. Youths

9. Now the young men in their turn live as follows: for ten years after they are promoted from the class of boys they pass the nights, as we said before, about the government buildings. This they do for the sake of guarding the city and of developing their powers of self-control; for this time of life, it seems, demands the most watchful care. And during the day, too, they put themselves at the disposal of the authorities, if they are needed for any service to the state. Whenever it is necessary, they all remain about the public buildings. But when the king goes out hunting, he takes out half the garrison; and this he does many times a month. Those who go must take bow and arrows and, in addition to the quiver, a sabre or bill [1] in its scabbard; they carry along also a light shield and two spears, one to throw, the other to use in case of necessity in a hand-to-hand encounter. 10. They provide for such hunting out

[1] The oriental bill was a tool or weapon with a curved blade, shorter than a sabre and corresponding very closely to the Spanish-American *machete*.

δὲ δημοσίᾳ τοῦ θηρᾶν ἐπιμέλονται, καὶ βασιλεὺς ὥσπερ καὶ ἐν πολέμῳ ἡγεμών ἐστιν αὐτοῖς καὶ αὐτός τε θηρᾷ καὶ τῶν ἄλλων ἐπιμέλεται[1] ὅπως ἂν θηρῶσιν, ὅτι ἀληθεστάτη αὐτοῖς δοκεῖ εἶναι αὕτη ἡ μελέτη τῶν πρὸς τὸν πόλεμον. καὶ γὰρ πρῴ ἀνίστασθαι ἐθίζει καὶ ψύχη καὶ θάλπη ἀνέχεσθαι, γυμνάζει δὲ καὶ ὁδοιπορίαις καὶ δρόμοις, ἀνάγκη δὲ καὶ τοξεῦσαι θηρίον καὶ ἀκοντίσαι ὅπου ἂν παραπίπτῃ. καὶ τὴν ψυχὴν δὲ πολλάκις ἀνάγκη θήγεσθαι ὅταν τι τῶν ἀλκίμων θηρίων ἀνθιστῆται· παίειν μὲν γὰρ δήπου δεῖ τὸ ὁμόσε γιγνόμενον, φυλάξασθαι δὲ τὸ ἐπιφερόμενον· ὥστε οὐ ῥᾴδιον εὑρεῖν τί ἐν τῇ θήρᾳ ἄπεστι τῶν ἐν πολέμῳ παρόντων.

11. Ἐξέρχονται δὲ ἐπὶ τὴν θήραν ἄριστον ἔχοντες πλεῖον μέν, ὡς τὸ εἰκός, τῶν παίδων, τἆλλα δὲ ὅμοιον. καὶ θηρῶντες μὲν οὐκ ἂν ἀριστήσειαν, ἢν δέ τι δεήσῃ ἢ θηρίου ἕνεκα ἐπικαταμεῖναι ἢ ἄλλως ἐθελήσωσι διατρῖψαι περὶ τὴν θήραν, τὸ οὖν ἄριστον τοῦτο δειπνήσαντες τὴν ὑστεραίαν αὖ θηρῶσι μέχρι δείπνου, καὶ μίαν ἄμφω τούτω τὼ ἡμέρα λογίζονται, ὅτι μιᾶς ἡμέρας σῖτον δαπανῶσι. τοῦτο δὲ ποιοῦσι τοῦ ἐθίζεσθαι ἕνεκα, ἵν᾽ ἐάν τι καὶ ἐν πολέμῳ δεήσῃ, δύνωνται τοῦτο ποιεῖν. καὶ ὄψον δὲ τοῦτο ἔχου-

[1] ἐπιμέλεται Dindorf, Hug; ἐπιμελεῖται MSS., most Edd.

of the public treasury; and as the king is their leader in war, so he not only takes part in the hunt himself but sees to it that the others hunt, too. The state bears the expense of the hunting for the reason that the training it gives seems to be the best preparation for war itself. For it accustoms them to rise early in the morning and to endure both heat and cold, and it gives them practice in taking long tramps and runs, and they have to shoot or spear a wild beast whenever it comes in their way. And they must often whet their courage when one of the fierce beasts shows fight; for, of course, they must strike down the animal that comes to close quarters with them, and they must be on their guard against the one that threatens to attack them. In a word, it is not easy to find any quality required in war that is not required also in the chase.

The chase a school for war

11. When they go out hunting they carry along a lunch,[1] more in quantity than that of the boys, as is proper, but in other respects the same; but they would never think of lunching while they are busy with the chase. If, however, for some reason it is necessary to stay longer on account of the game or if for some other reason they wish to continue longer on the chase, then they make their dinner of this luncheon and hunt again on the following day until dinner time; and these two days they count as one, because they consume but one day's provisions. This they do to harden themselves, in order that, if ever it is necessary in war, they may be able to do the same. Those of this age have for relish the game that they kill;

[1] The Greeks ate but two meals a day: the first (ἄριστον, *déjeuner*) toward midday, the other (δεῖπνον, *dîner*) toward sun-down.

σιν οἱ τηλικοῦτοι ὅ τι ἂν θηράσωσιν· εἰ δὲ μή, τὸ κάρδαμον. εἰ δέ τις αὐτοὺς οἴεται ἢ ἐσθίειν ἀηδῶς, ὅταν κάρδαμον μόνον ἔχωσιν ἐπὶ τῷ σίτῳ, ἢ πίνειν ἀηδῶς, ὅταν ὕδωρ πίνωσιν, ἀναμνησθήτω πῶς μὲν ἡδὺ μᾶζα καὶ ἄρτος πεινῶντι φαγεῖν, πῶς δὲ ἡδὺ ὕδωρ πιεῖν διψῶντι.

12. Αἱ δ' αὖ μένουσαι φυλαὶ διατρίβουσι μελετῶσαι τά τε ἄλλα ἃ παῖδες ὄντες ἔμαθον καὶ τοξεύειν καὶ ἀκοντίζειν, καὶ διαγωνιζόμενοι ταῦτα πρὸς ἀλλήλους διατελοῦσιν. εἰσὶ δὲ καὶ δημόσιοι τούτων ἀγῶνες καὶ ἆθλα προτίθεται· ἐν ᾗ δ' ἂν τῶν φυλῶν πλεῖστοι ὦσι δαημονέστατοι καὶ ἀνδρικώτατοι καὶ εὐπιστότατοι, ἐπαινοῦσιν οἱ πολῖται καὶ τιμῶσιν οὐ μόνον τὸν νῦν ἄρχοντα αὐτῶν, ἀλλὰ καὶ ὅστις αὐτοὺς παῖδας ὄντας ἐπαίδευσε. χρῶνται δὲ τοῖς μένουσι τῶν ἐφήβων αἱ ἀρχαί, ἤν τι ἢ φρουρῆσαι δεήσῃ ἢ κακούργους ἐρευνῆσαι ἢ λῃστὰς ὑποδραμεῖν ἢ καὶ ἄλλο τι ὅσα ἰσχύος ἢ τάχους ἔργα[1] ἐστί.

Ταῦτα μὲν δὴ οἱ ἔφηβοι πράττουσιν. ἐπειδὰν δὲ τὰ δέκα ἔτη διατελέσωσιν, ἐξέρχονται εἰς τοὺς τελείους ἄνδρας. 13. ἀφ' οὗ δ' ἂν ἐξέλθωσι χρόνου[2] οὗτοι αὖ πέντε καὶ εἴκοσιν ἔτη διάγουσιν ὧδε. πρῶτον μὲν ὥσπερ οἱ ἔφηβοι παρέχουσιν ἑαυτοὺς ταῖς ἀρχαῖς χρῆσθαι, ἤν τι δέῃ ὑπὲρ τοῦ κοινοῦ, ὅσα φρονούντων τε ἤδη ἔργα ἐστὶ καὶ ἔτι δυναμένων. ἢν δέ ποι[3] δέῃ στρατεύεσθαι, τόξα

[1] Before ἔργα xAHR have ἄλλα.
[2] After χρόνου yG add ἐκ τῶν ἐφήβων.
[3] ποι Dindorf; που MSS.

f they fail to kill any, then cresses. Now, if any one thinks that they do not enjoy eating, when they have only cresses with their bread, or that they do not enjoy drinking when they drink only water, let him remember how sweet barley bread and wheaten bread taste when one is hungry, and how sweet water is to drink when one is thirsty.

12. The divisions remaining at home, in their turn, pass their time shooting with the bow and hurling the spear and practising all the other arts that they learned when they were boys, and they continually engage in contests of this kind with one another. And there are also public contests of this sort, for which prizes are offered; and whatever division has the greatest number of the most expert, the most manly, and the best disciplined young men, the citizens praise and honour not only its present chief officer but also the one who trained them when they were boys. And of the youths who remain behind, the authorities employ any that they may need, whether for garrison duty or for arresting criminals or for hunting down robbers, or for any other service that demands strength or dispatch.

Such, then, is the occupation of the youths. And when they have completed their ten years, they are promoted and enrolled in the class of the mature men. 13. And these, in turn, for twenty-five years after the time they are there enrolled, are occupied as follows. In the first place, like the youths, they are at the disposal of the authorities, if they are needed in the interest of the commonwealth in any service that requires men who have already attained discretion and are still strong in body. But if it is

C. Mature men

μὲν οἱ οὕτω πεπαιδευμένοι οὐκέτι ἔχοντες οὐδ
παλτὰ στρατεύονται, τὰ δ' ἀγχέμαχα ὅπλ
καλούμενα, θώρακά τε περὶ τοῖς στέρνοις κα
γέρρον ἐν τῇ ἀριστερᾷ, οἷόνπερ γράφονται ο
Πέρσαι ἔχοντες, ἐν δὲ τῇ δεξιᾷ μάχαιραν
κοπίδα. καὶ αἱ ἀρχαὶ δὲ πᾶσαι ἐκ τούτων καθί
στανται πλὴν οἱ τῶν παίδων διδάσκαλοι.

Ἐπειδὰν δὲ τὰ πέντε καὶ εἴκοσιν ἔτη διατελέ
σωσιν, εἴησαν μὲν ἂν οὗτοι πλεῖόν τι γεγονότες
τὰ πεντήκοντα ἔτη ἀπὸ γενεᾶς· ἐξέρχονται δ
τηνικαῦτα εἰς τοὺς γεραιτέρους ὄντας τε κα
καλουμένους.

14. Οἱ δ' αὖ γεραίτεροι οὗτοι στρατεύονται μὲ
οὐκέτι ἔξω τῆς ἑαυτῶν, οἴκοι δὲ μένοντες δικάζουσ
τά τε κοινὰ καὶ τὰ ἴδια πάντα. καὶ θανάτου δ
οὗτοι κρίνουσι, καὶ τὰς ἀρχὰς οὗτοι πάσα
αἱροῦνται· καὶ ἤν τις ἢ ἐν ἐφήβοις ἢ ἐν τελείοι
ἀνδράσιν ἐλλίπῃ τι τῶν νομίμων, φαίνουσι μὲν ο
φύλαρχοι ἕκαστοι καὶ τῶν ἄλλων ὁ βουλόμενος
οἱ δὲ γεραίτεροι ἀκούσαντες ἐκκρίνουσιν· ὁ δ
ἐκκριθεὶς ἄτιμος διατελεῖ τὸν λοιπὸν βίον.

15. Ἵνα δὲ σαφέστερον δηλωθῇ πᾶσα ἡ Περσῶ
πολιτεια, μικρὸν ἐπάνειμι· νῦν γὰρ ἐν βραχυτάτ
ἂν δηλωθείη διὰ τὰ προειρημένα. λέγονται μὲ
γὰρ Πέρσαι ἀμφὶ τὰς δώδεκα μυριάδας εἶναι

necessary to make a military expedition anywhere, those who have been thus educated take the field, no longer with bow and arrows, nor yet with spears, but with what are termed "weapons for close conflict"—a corselet about their breast, a round shield upon their left arm (such as Persians are represented with in art), and in their right hands a sabre or bill. From this division also all the magistrates are selected, except the teachers of the boys.

And when they have completed the five-and-twenty years, they are, as one would expect, somewhat more than fifty years of age; and then they come out and take their places among those who really are, as they are called, the "elders."

D. Elders

14. Now these elders, in their turn, no longer perform military service outside their own country, but they remain at home and try all sorts of cases, both public and private. They try people indicted for capital offences also, and they elect all the officers. And if any one, either among the youths or among the mature men, fail in any one of the duties prescribed by law, the respective officers of that division, or any one else who will, may enter complaint, and the elders, when they have heard the case, expel the guilty party; and the one who has been expelled spends the rest of his life degraded and disfranchised.

The constitutional policy of Persia

15. Now, that the whole constitutional policy of the Persians may be more clearly set forth, I will go back a little; for now, in the light of what has already been said, it can be given in a very few words. It is said that the Persians number about one hundred and twenty thousand men[1];

[1] This number is meant to include the nobility only, the so-called "peers" (ὁμότιμοι), and not the total population of Persia.

τούτων δ᾽ οὐδεὶς ἀπελήλαται νόμῳ τιμῶν καὶ ἀρχῶν, ἀλλ᾽ ἔξεστι πᾶσι Πέρσαις πέμπειν τοὺς ἑαυτῶν παῖδας εἰς τὰ κοινὰ τῆς δικαιοσύνης διδασκαλεῖα. ἀλλ᾽ οἱ μὲν δυνάμενοι τρέφειν τοὺς παῖδας ἀργοῦντας πέμπουσιν, οἱ δὲ μὴ δυνάμενοι οὐ πέμπουσιν.[1] οἳ δ᾽ ἂν παιδευθῶσι παρὰ τοῖς δημοσίοις διδασκάλοις, ἔξεστιν αὐτοῖς ἐν τοῖς ἐφήβοις νεανισκεύεσθαι, τοῖς δὲ μὴ διαπαιδευθεῖσιν οὕτως οὐκ ἔξεστιν. οἳ δ᾽ ἂν αὖ ἐν τοῖς ἐφήβοις διατελέσωσι τὰ νόμιμα ποιοῦντες, ἔξεστι τούτοις εἰς τοὺς τελείους ἄνδρας συναλίζεσθαι[2] καὶ ἀρχῶν καὶ τιμῶν μετέχειν, οἳ δ᾽ ἂν μὴ διαγένωνται[3] ἐν τοῖς ἐφήβοις, οὐκ εἰσέρχονται εἰς τοὺς τελείους. οἳ δ᾽ ἂν αὖ ἐν τοῖς τελείοις διαγένωνται ἀνεπίληπτοι, οὗτοι τῶν γεραιτέρων γίγνονται. οὕτω μὲν δὴ οἱ γεραίτεροι διὰ πάντων τῶν καλῶν ἐληλυθότες καθίστανται· καὶ ἡ πολιτεία αὕτη, ᾗ οἴονται χρώμενοι βέλτιστοι ἂν εἶναι.

16. Καὶ νῦν δὲ ἔτι ἐμμένει μαρτύρια καὶ τῆς μετρίας διαίτης αὐτῶν καὶ τοῦ ἐκπονεῖσθαι τὴν δίαιταν. αἰσχρὸν μὲν γὰρ ἔτι καὶ νῦν ἐστι Πέρσαις καὶ τὸ πτύειν[4] καὶ τὸ ἀπομύττεσθαι καὶ τὸ φύσης μεστοὺς φαίνεσθαι, αἰσχρὸν δέ ἐστι καὶ τὸ ἰόντα ποι[5] φανερὸν γενέσθαι ἢ τοῦ οὐρῆσαι ἕνεκα ἢ καὶ ἄλλου τινὸς τοιούτου. ταῦτα δὲ οὐκ ἂν ἐδύναντο ποιεῖν, εἰ μὴ καὶ διαίτῃ μετρίᾳ ἐχρῶντο

[1] οἱ δὲ . . . πέμπουσιν not in CF.
[2] συναλίζεσθαι yHV; συναυλίζεσθαι (*to associate with*) xAGR.
[3] ἂν μὴ διαγένωνται yEGV; ἂν αὖ ἐν τοῖς παισὶ μὴ (μὴ is not in C) διατελέσωσιν ἢ ἐν CAHR.
[4] πτύειν Cobet, Edd.; ἀποπτύειν MSS.
[5] ποι Heindorf, Edd.; που MSS.

and no one of these is by law excluded from holding offices and positions of honour, but all the Persians may send their children to the common schools of justice. Still, only those do send them who are in a position to maintain their children without work; and those who are not so situated do not. And only to such as are educated by the public teachers is it permitted to pass their young manhood in the class of the youths, while to those who have not completed this course of training it is not so permitted. And only to such among the youths as complete the course required by law is it permitted to join the class of mature men and to fill offices and places of distinction, while those who do not finish their course among the young men are not promoted to the class of the mature men. And again, those who finish their course among the mature men without blame become members of the class of elders. So, we see, the elders are made up of those who have enjoyed all honour and distinction. This is the policy by the observance of which they think that their citizens may become the best.

Each class a prerequisite to the one above it

16. There remains even unto this day evidence of their moderate fare and of their working off by exercise what they eat: for even to the present time it is a breach of decorum for a Persian to spit or to blow his nose or to appear afflicted with flatulence; it is a breach of decorum also to be seen going apart either to make water or for anything else of that kind. And this would not be possible for them, if they did not lead an

καὶ τὸ ὑγρὸν ἐκπονοῦντες ἀνήλισκον, ὥστε ἄλλῃ πῃ ἀποχωρεῖν.

Ταῦτα μὲν δὴ κατὰ πάντων Περσῶν ἔχομεν λεγειν· οὗ δ' ἕνεκα ὁ λόγος ὡρμήθη, νῦν λέξομεν τὰς Κύρου πράξεις ἀρξάμενοι ἀπὸ παιδός.

III

1. Κῦρος γὰρ μέχρι μὲν δώδεκα ἐτῶν ἢ ὀλίγῳ πλεῖον ταύτῃ τῇ παιδείᾳ ἐπαιδεύθη, καὶ πάντων τῶν ἡλίκων διαφέρων ἐφαίνετο καὶ εἰς τὸ ταχὺ μανθάνειν ἃ δέοι καὶ εἰς τὸ καλῶς καὶ ἀνδρείως ἕκαστα ποιεῖν. ἐκ δὲ τούτου τοῦ χρόνου μετεπέμψατο Ἀστυάγης τὴν ἑαυτοῦ θυγατέρα καὶ τὸν παῖδα αὐτῆς· ἰδεῖν γὰρ ἐπεθύμει, ὅτι ἤκουεν αὐτὸν καλὸν κἀγαθὸν εἶναι. ἔρχεται δ' αὐτή τε ἡ Μανδάνη πρὸς τὸν πατέρα καὶ τὸν Κῦρον τὸν υἱὸν ἔχουσα.

2. Ὡς δὲ ἀφίκετο τάχιστα καὶ ἔγνω ὁ Κῦρος τὸν Ἀστυάγην τῆς μητρὸς πατέρα ὄντα, εὐθὺς οἷα δὴ παῖς φύσει φιλόστοργος ὢν ἠσπάζετό τε αὐτὸν ὥσπερ ἂν εἴ τις πάλαι συντεθραμμένος καὶ πάλαι φιλῶν ἀσπάζοιτο, καὶ ὁρῶν δὴ αὐτὸν κεκοσμημένον καὶ ὀφθαλμῶν ὑπογραφῇ καὶ χρώματος ἐντρίψει καὶ κόμαις προσθέτοις, ἃ δὴ νόμιμα ἦν ἐν Μήδοις· ταῦτα γὰρ πάντα Μηδικά ἐστι, καὶ οἱ πορφυροῖ χιτῶνες καὶ οἱ κάνδυες καὶ οἱ στρεπτοὶ οἱ περὶ τῇ δέρῃ καὶ τὰ ψέλια τὰ[1] περὶ ταῖς χερσίν,

[1] τὰ E, Edd.; not in any other MS.

abstemious life and throw off the moisture by hard work, so that it passes off in some other way.

This, then, is what we have to say in regard to the Persians in general. Now, to fulfil the purpose with which our narrative was begun, we shall proceed to relate the history of Cyrus from his childhood on.

III

1. Such was the education that Cyrus received until he was twelve years old or a little more; and he showed himself superior to all the other boys of his age both in mastering his tasks quickly and in doing everything in a thorough and manly fashion. It was at this period of his life that Astyages sent for his daughter and her son; for he was eager to see him, as he had heard from time to time that the child was a handsome boy of rare promise. Accordingly, Mandane herself went to her father and took her son Cyrus with her.

Cyrus goes to visit his grandfather

2. As soon as she arrived and Cyrus had recognized in Astyages his mother's father, being naturally an affectionate boy he at once kissed him, just as a person who had long lived with another and long loved him would do. Then he noticed that his grandfather was adorned with pencillings beneath his eyes, with rouge rubbed on his face, and with a wig of false hair—the common Median fashion. For all this is Median, and so are their purple tunics, and their mantles, the necklaces about their necks, and the bracelets on their wrists,

ἐν Πέρσαις δὲ τοῖς οἴκοι καὶ νῦν ἔτι πολὺ καὶ ἐσθῆτες φαυλότεραι καὶ δίαιται εὐτελέστεραι· ὁρῶν δὴ τὸν κόσμον τοῦ πάππου, ἐμβλέπων αὐτῷ ἔλεγεν, Ὦ μῆτερ, ὡς καλός μοι ὁ πάππος. ἐρωτώσης δὲ αὐτὸν τῆς μητρὸς πότερος καλλίων αὐτῷ δοκεῖ εἶναι, ὁ πατὴρ ἢ οὗτος, ἀπεκρίνατο ἄρα ὁ Κῦρος, Ὦ μῆτερ, Περσῶν μὲν πολὺ κάλλιστος ὁ ἐμὸς πατήρ, Μήδων μέντοι ὅσων ἑώρακα ἐγὼ καὶ ἐν ταῖς ὁδοῖς καὶ ἐπὶ ταῖς θύραις πολὺ οὗτος ὁ ἐμὸς πάππος κάλλιστος.

3. Ἀντασπαζόμενος δὲ ὁ πάππος αὐτὸν καὶ στολὴν καλὴν ἐνέδυσε καὶ στρεπτοῖς καὶ ψελίοις ἐτίμα καὶ ἐκόσμει, καὶ εἴ ποι ἐξελαύνοι, ἐφ᾿ ἵππου χρυσοχαλίνου περιῆγεν, ὥσπερ καὶ αὐτὸς εἰώθει πορεύεσθαι. ὁ δὲ Κῦρος ἅτε παῖς ὢν καὶ φιλόκαλος καὶ φιλότιμος ἥδετο τῇ στολῇ, καὶ ἱππεύειν μανθάνων ὑπερέχαιρεν· ἐν Πέρσαις γὰρ διὰ τὸ χαλεπὸν εἶναι καὶ τρέφειν ἵππους καὶ ἱππεύειν ἐν ὀρεινῇ οὔσῃ τῇ χώρᾳ καὶ ἰδεῖν ἵππον πάνυ σπάνιον ἦν.

4. Δειπνῶν δὲ δὴ ὁ Ἀστυάγης σὺν τῇ θυγατρὶ καὶ τῷ Κύρῳ, βουλόμενος τὸν παῖδα ὡς ἥδιστα δειπνεῖν, ἵνα ἧττον τὰ οἴκαδε ποθοίη, προσῆγεν αὐτῷ καὶ παροψίδας καὶ παντοδαπὰ ἐμβάμματα καὶ βρώματα. τὸν δὲ Κῦρον ἔφασαν λέγειν, Ὦ πάππε, ὅσα πράγματα ἔχεις ἐν τῷ δείπνῳ, εἰ ἀνάγκη σοι ἐπὶ πάντα τὰ λεκάρια ταῦτα διατείνειν τὰς χεῖρας καὶ ἀπογεύεσθαι τούτων τῶν παντοδαπῶν βρωμάτων.

while the Persians at home even to this day have much plainer clothing and a more frugal way of life. So, observing his grandfather's adornment and staring at him, he said: "Oh mother, how handsome my grandfather is!" And when his mother asked him which he thought more handsome, his father or his grandfather, Cyrus answered at once: "Of the Persians, mother, my father is much the handsomest; but of the Medes, as far as I have seen them either on the streets or at court, my grandfather here is the handsomest by far."

3. Then his grandfather kissed him in return and gave him a beautiful dress to wear and, as a mark of royal favour, adorned him with necklaces and bracelets; and if he went out for a ride anywhere, he took the boy along upon a horse with a gold-studded bridle, just as he himself was accustomed to go. And as Cyrus was a boy fond of beautiful things and eager for distinction, he was pleased with his dress and greatly delighted at learning to ride; for in Persia, on account of its being difficult to breed horses and to practise horsemanship because it is a mountainous country, it was a very rare thing even to see a horse.

A Median dinner

4. And then again, when Astyages dined with his daughter and Cyrus, he set before him dainty side-dishes and all sorts of sauces and meats, for he wished the boy to enjoy his dinner as much as possible, in order that he might be less likely to feel homesick. And Cyrus, they say, observed: "How much trouble you have at your dinner, grandfather, if you have to reach out your hands to all these dishes and taste of all these different kinds of food!"

Τί δέ, φάναι τὸν Ἀστυάγην, οὐ γὰρ πολύ σοι δοκεῖ εἶναι κάλλιον τόδε τὸ δεῖπνον τοῦ ἐν Πέρσαις;

Τὸν δὲ Κῦρον πρὸς ταῦτα ἀποκρίνασθαι [λέγεται],[1] Οὔκ, ὦ πάππε, ἀλλὰ πολὺ ἁπλουστέρα καὶ εὐθυτέρα παρ' ἡμῖν ἡ ὁδός ἐστιν ἐπὶ τὸ ἐμπλησθῆναι ἢ παρ' ὑμῖν· ἡμᾶς μὲν γὰρ ἄρτος καὶ κρέα εἰς τοῦτο ἄγει, ὑμεῖς δὲ εἰς μὲν τὸ αὐτὸ ἡμῖν σπεύδετε, πολλοὺς δέ τινας ἑλιγμοὺς ἄνω καὶ κάτω πλανώμενοι μόλις ἀφικνεῖσθε ὅποι ἡμεῖς πάλαι ἥκομεν.

5. Ἀλλ', ὦ παῖ, φάναι τὸν Ἀστυάγην, οὐκ ἀχθόμενοι ταῦτα περιπλανώμεθα· γευόμενος δὲ καὶ σύ, ἔφη, γνώσει ὅτι ἡδέα ἐστίν.

Ἀλλὰ καὶ σέ, φάναι τὸν Κῦρον, ὁρῶ, ὦ πάππε, μυσαττόμενον ταῦτα τὰ βρώματα.

Καὶ τὸν Ἀστυάγην ἐπερέσθαι, Καὶ τίνι δὴ σὺ τεκμαιρόμενος, ὦ παῖ, λέγεις;

Ὅτι σε, φάναι, ὁρῶ, ὅταν μὲν τοῦ ἄρτου ἅψῃ, εἰς οὐδὲν τὴν χεῖρα ἀποψώμενον, ὅταν δὲ τούτων τινὸς θίγῃς, εὐθὺς ἀποκαθαίρει τὴν χεῖρα εἰς τὰ χειρόμακτρα, ὡς πάνυ ἀχθόμενος ὅτι πλέα σοι ἀπ' αὐτῶν ἐγένετο.

6. Πρὸς ταῦτα δὲ τὸν Ἀστυάγην εἰπεῖν, Εἰ τοίνυν οὕτω γιγνώσκεις, ὦ παῖ, ἀλλὰ κρέα γε εὐωχοῦ, ἵνα νεανίας οἴκαδε ἀπέλθῃς. ἅμα δὲ ταῦτα λέγοντα πολλὰ αὐτῷ παραφέρειν καὶ θήρεια[2] καὶ τῶν ἡμέρων.

Καὶ τὸν Κῦρον, ἐπεὶ ἑώρα πολλὰ τὰ κρέα, εἰπεῖν, Ἦ καὶ δίδως, φάναι, ὦ πάππε, πάντα

[1] [λέγεται] Cobet, Edd.; λέγεται MSS.
[2] θήρεια C², Edd.; θηρία all other MSS.

"Why so?" said Astyages. "Really now, don't you think this dinner much finer than your Persian dinners?"

"No, grandfather," Cyrus replied to this; "but the road to satiety is much more simple and direct in our country than with you; for bread and meat take us there; but you, though you make for the same goal as we, go wandering through many a maze, up and down, and only arrive at last at the point that we long since have reached."

5. "But, my boy," said Astyages, "we do not object to this wandering about; and you also," he added, "if you taste, will see that it is pleasant."

"But, grandfather," said Cyrus, "I observe that even you are disgusted with these viands."

"And by what, pray, do you judge, my boy," asked Astyages, "that you say this?"

"Because," said he, "I observe that when you touch bread, you do not wipe your hand on anything; but when you touch any of these other things you at once cleanse your hand upon your napkin, as if you were exceedingly displeased that it had become soiled with them."

6. "Well then, my boy," Astyages replied to this, "if that is your judgment, at least regale yourself with meat, that you may go back home a strong young man." And as he said this, he placed before him an abundance of meat of both wild and domestic animals.

And when Cyrus saw that there was a great quantity of meat, he said: "And do you really

ταῦτά μοι τὰ κρέα ὅ τι ἂν βούλωμαι αὐτοῖς χρῆσθαι;

Νὴ Δία, φάναι, ὦ παῖ, ἔγωγέ σοι.

7. Ἐνταῦθα δὴ τὸν Κῦρον λαβόντα τῶν κρεῶν διαδιδόναι τοῖς ἀμφὶ τὸν πάππον θεραπευταῖς, ἐπιλέγοντα ἑκάστῳ, Σοὶ μὲν τοῦτο ὅτι προθύμως με ἱππεύειν διδάσκεις, σοὶ δ᾽ ὅτι μοι παλτὸν ἔδωκας· νῦν γὰρ τοῦτ᾽ ἔχω· σοὶ δ᾽ ὅτι τὸν πάππον καλῶς θεραπεύεις, σοὶ δ᾽ ὅτι μου τὴν μητέρα τιμᾷς· τοιαῦτα ἐποίει, ἕως διεδίδου πάντα ἃ ἔλαβε κρέα.

8. Σάκᾳ δέ, φάναι τὸν Ἀστυάγην, τῷ οἰνοχόῳ, ὃν ἐγὼ μάλιστα τιμῶ, οὐδὲν δίδως; ὁ δὲ Σάκας ἄρα καλός τε[1] ὢν ἐτύγχανε καὶ τιμὴν ἔχων προσάγειν τοὺς δεομένους Ἀστυάγους καὶ ἀποκωλύειν οὓς μὴ καιρὸς αὐτῷ δοκοίη εἶναι προσάγειν.

Καὶ τὸν Κῦρον ἐπερέσθαι προπετῶς ὡς ἂν παῖς μηδέπω ὑποπτήσσων, Διὰ τί δή, ὦ πάππε, τοῦτον οὕτω τιμᾷς;

Καὶ τὸν Ἀστυάγην σκώψαντα εἰπεῖν, Οὐχ ὁρᾷς, φάναι, ὡς καλῶς οἰνοχοεῖ καὶ εὐσχημόνως; οἱ δὲ τῶν βασιλέων τούτων οἰνοχόοι κομψῶς τε οἰνοχοοῦσι καὶ καθαρείως ἐγχέουσι καὶ διδόασι τοῖς τρισὶ δακτύλοις ὀχοῦντες τὴν φιάλην καὶ προσφέρουσιν ὡς ἂν ἐνδοῖεν τὸ ἔκπωμα εὐληπτότατα τῷ μέλλοντι πίνειν.

9. Κέλευσον δή, φάναι, ὦ πάππε, τὸν Σάκαν καὶ ἐμοὶ δοῦναι τὸ ἔκπωμα, ἵνα κἀγὼ καλῶς σοι πιεῖν ἐγχέας ἀνακτήσωμαί σε, ἢν δύνωμαι.

[1] τε y, Edd.; γε xzR.

mean to give me all this meat, grandfather, to dispose of as I please?"

"Yes, by Zeus," said he, "I do."

7. Thereupon Cyrus took some of the meat and proceeded to distribute it among his grandfather's servants, saying to them in turn: "I give this to you, because you take so much pains to teach me to ride; to you, because you gave me a spear, for at present this is all I have to give; to you, because you serve my grandfather so well; and to you, because you are respectful to my mother." He kept on thus, while he was distributing all the meat that he had received.

Cyrus and the cup-bearer

8. "But," said Astyages, "are you not going to give any to Sacas, my cupbearer, whom I like best of all?" Now Sacas, it seems, chanced to be a handsome fellow who had the office of introducing to Astyages those who had business with him and of keeping out those whom he thought it not expedient to admit.

And Cyrus asked pertly, as a boy might do who was not yet at all shy, "Pray, grandfather, why do you like this fellow so much?"

And Astyages replied with a jest: "Do you not see," said he, "how nicely and gracefully he pours the wine?" Now the cupbearers of those kings perform their office with fine airs; they pour in the wine with neatness and then present the goblet, conveying it with three fingers, and offer it in such a way as to place it most conveniently in the grasp of the one who is to drink.

9. "Well, grandfather," said he, "bid Sacas give me the cup, that I also may deftly pour for you to drink and thus win your favour, if I can."

Καὶ τὸν κελεῦσαι δοῦναι. λαβόντα δὲ τὸν Κῦρον οὕτω μὲν δὴ εὖ κλύσαι τὸ ἔκπωμα ὥσπερ τὸν Σάκαν ἑώρα, οὕτω δὲ στήσαντα τὸ πρόσωπον σπουδαίως καὶ εὐσχημόνως πως προσενεγκεῖν καὶ ἐνδοῦναι τὴν φιάλην τῷ πάππῳ ὥστε τῇ μητρὶ καὶ τῷ Ἀστυάγει πολὺν γέλωτα παρασχεῖν. καὶ αὐτὸν δὲ τὸν Κῦρον ἐκγελάσαντα ἀναπηδῆσαι πρὸς τὸν πάππον καὶ φιλοῦντα ἅμα εἰπεῖν, Ὦ Σάκα, ἀπόλωλας· ἐκβαλῶ σε ἐκ τῆς τιμῆς· τά τε γὰρ ἄλλα, φάναι, σοῦ κάλλιον οἰνοχοήσω καὶ οὐκ ἐκπίομαι αὐτὸς τὸν οἶνον.

Οἱ δ' ἄρα τῶν βασιλέων οἰνοχόοι, ἐπειδὰν διδῶσι τὴν φιάλην, ἀρύσαντες ἀπ' αὐτῆς τῷ κυάθῳ εἰς τὴν ἀριστερὰν χεῖρα ἐγχεάμενοι καταρροφοῦσι, τοῦ δὴ εἰ φάρμακα ἐγχέοιεν[1] μὴ λυσιτελεῖν αὐτοῖς.

10. Ἐκ τούτου δὴ ὁ Ἀστυάγης ἐπισκώπτων, Καὶ τί δή, ἔφη, ὦ Κῦρε, τἆλλα μιμούμενος τὸν Σάκαν οὐκ ἀπερρόφησας τοῦ οἴνου;

Ὅτι, ἔφη, νὴ Δία ἐδεδοίκειν μὴ ἐν τῷ κρατῆρι φάρμακα μεμιγμένα εἴη. καὶ γὰρ ὅτε εἱστίασας σὺ τοὺς φίλους ἐν τοῖς γενεθλίοις, σαφῶς κατέμαθον φάρμακα ὑμῖν αὐτὸν ἐγχέαντα.

Καὶ πῶς δὴ σὺ τοῦτο, ἔφη, ὦ παῖ, κατέγνως;

Ὅτι νὴ Δί' ὑμᾶς ἑώρων καὶ ταῖς γνώμαις καὶ τοῖς σώμασι σφαλλομένους. πρῶτον μὲν γὰρ ἃ οὐκ ἐᾶτε ἡμᾶς τοὺς παῖδας ποιεῖν, ταῦτα αὐτοὶ ἐποιεῖτε. πάντες μὲν γὰρ ἅμα ἐκεκράγειτε, ἐμανθάνετε δὲ οὐδὲν ἀλλήλων, ᾔδετε

[1] ἐγχέοιεν yER; ἐκχέοιεν zC.

And he bade him give it. And Cyrus took the cup and rinsed it out well, exactly as he had often seen Sacas do, and then he brought and presented the goblet to his grandfather, assuming an expression somehow so grave and important, that he made his mother and Astyages laugh heartily. And Cyrus himself also with a laugh sprang up into his grandfather's lap and kissing him said: "Ah, Sacas, you are done for; I shall turn you out of your office; for in other ways," said he, "I shall play the cupbearer better than you and besides I shall not drink up the wine myself."

Now, it is a well known fact that the kings' cupbearers, when they proffer the cup, draw off some of it with the ladle, pour it into their left hand, and swallow it down—so that, if they should put poison in, they may not profit by it.

Cyrus's temperance lecture

10. Thereupon Astyages said in jest: "And why, pray, Cyrus, did you imitate Sacas in everything else but did not sip any of the wine?"

"Because, by Zeus," said he, "I was afraid that poison had been mixed in the bowl. And I had reason to be afraid; for when you entertained your friends on your birthday, I discovered beyond a doubt that he had poured poison into your company's drink."

"And how, pray," said he, "did you discover that, my son?"

"Because, by Zeus," said he, "I saw that you were unsteady both in mind and in body. For in the first place you yourselves kept doing what you never allow us boys to do; for instance, you kept shouting, all at the same time, and none of you heard anything that the

δὲ καὶ μάλα γελοίως, οὐκ ἀκροώμενοι δὲ τοῦ ᾄδοντος ὤμνυτε ἄριστα ᾄδειν· λέγων δὲ ἕκαστος ὑμῶν τὴν ἑαυτοῦ ῥώμην, ἔπειτ᾿ εἰ ἀνασταίητε ὀρχησόμενοι, μὴ ὅπως ὀρχεῖσθαι ἐν ῥυθμῷ, ἀλλ᾿ οὐδ᾿ ὀρθοῦσθαι ἐδύνασθε. ἐπελέλησθε δὲ παντάπασι σύ τε ὅτι βασιλεὺς ἦσθα, οἵ τε ἄλλοι ὅτι σὺ ἄρχων. τότε γὰρ δὴ ἔγωγε καὶ πρῶτον κατέμαθον ὅτι τοῦτ᾿ ἄρ᾿ ἦν ἡ ἰσηγορία ὃ ὑμεῖς τότ᾿ ἐποιεῖτε· οὐδέποτε γοῦν ἐσιωπᾶτε.

11. Καὶ ὁ Ἀστυάγης λέγει, Ὁ δὲ σὸς πατήρ, ὦ παῖ, πίνων οὐ μεθύσκεται;

Οὐ μὰ Δί᾿, ἔφη.

Ἀλλὰ πῶς ποιεῖ;

Διψῶν παύεται, ἄλλο δὲ κακὸν οὐδὲν πάσχει· οὐ γάρ, οἶμαι, ὦ πάππε, Σάκας αὐτῷ οἰνοχοεῖ.

Καὶ ἡ μήτηρ εἶπεν, Ἀλλὰ τί ποτε σύ, ὦ παῖ, τῷ Σάκᾳ οὕτω πολεμεῖς;

Τὸν δὲ Κῦρον εἰπεῖν, Ὅτι νὴ Δία, φάναι, μισῶ αὐτόν· πολλάκις γάρ με πρὸς τὸν πάππον ἐπιθυμοῦντα προσδραμεῖν οὗτος ὁ μιαρώτατος ἀποκωλύει. ἀλλ᾿ ἱκετεύω, φάναι, ὦ πάππε, δός μοι τρεῖς ἡμέρας ἄρξαι αὐτοῦ.

Καὶ τὸν Ἀστυάγην εἰπεῖν, Καὶ πῶς ἂν ἄρξαις αὐτοῦ;

Καὶ τὸν Κῦρον φάναι, Στὰς ἂν ὥσπερ οὗτος ἐπὶ τῇ εἰσόδῳ, ἔπειτα ὁπότε βούλοιτο παριέναι ἐπ᾿ ἄριστον, λέγοιμ᾿ ἂν ὅτι οὔπω δυνατὸν τῷ ἀρίστῳ ἐντυχεῖν· σπουδάζει γὰρ πρός τινας· εἶθ᾿ ὁπότε ἥκοι ἐπὶ τὸ δεῖπνον, λέγοιμ᾿ ἂν ὅτι

others were saying; and you fell to singing, and in a most ridiculous manner at that, and though you did not hear the singer, you swore that he sang most excellently; and though each one of you kept telling stories of his own strength, yet if you stood up to dance, to say nothing of dancing in time, why, you could not even stand up straight. And all of you quite forgot—you, that you were king; and the rest, that you were their sovereign. It was then that I also for my part discovered, and for the first time, that what you were practising was your boasted 'equal freedom of speech'; at any rate, never were any of you silent."

11. "But, my boy," Astyages said, "does not your father get drunk, when he drinks?"

"No, by Zeus," said he.

"Well, how does he manage it?"

"He just quenches his thirst and thus suffers no further harm; for he has, I trow, grandfather, no Sacas to pour wine for him."

"But why in the world, my son," said his mother, "are you so set against Sacas?"

His antipathy toward Sacas

"Because, by Zeus," Cyrus replied, "I don't like him; for oftentimes, when I am eager to run in to see my grandfather, this miserable scoundrel keeps me out. But," he added, "I beg of you, grandfather, allow me for just three days to rule over him."

"And how would you rule over him?" said Astyages.

"I would stand at the door," Cyrus replied, "just as he does, and then when he wished to come in to luncheon, I would say, 'You cannot interview the luncheon yet; for it is engaged with certain persons.' And then when he came to dinner, I would say, 'It

λοῦται· εἰ δὲ πάνυ σπουδάζοι φαγεῖν, εἴποιμ' ἂν ὅτι παρὰ ταῖς γυναιξίν ἐστιν· ἕως παρατείναιμι τοῦτον ὥσπερ οὗτος ἐμὲ παρατείνει ἀπὸ σοῦ κωλύων.

12. Τοσαύτας μὲν αὐτοῖς εὐθυμίας παρεῖχεν ἐπὶ τῷ δείπνῳ· τὰς δ' ἡμέρας, εἴ τινος αἴσθοιτο δεόμενον ἢ τὸν πάππον ἢ τὸν τῆς μητρὸς ἀδελφόν, χαλεπὸν ἦν ἄλλον φθάσαι τοῦτο ποιήσαντα· ὅ τι γὰρ δύναιτο ὁ Κῦρος ὑπερέχαιρεν αὐτοῖς χαριζόμενος.

13. Ἐπεὶ δὲ ἡ Μανδάνη παρεσκευάζετο ὡς ἀπιοῦσα πάλιν πρὸς τὸν ἄνδρα, ἐδεῖτο αὐτῆς ὁ Ἀστυάγης καταλιπεῖν τὸν Κῦρον. ἡ δὲ ἀπεκρίνατο ὅτι βούλοιτο μὲν ἅπαντα τῷ πατρὶ χαρίζεσθαι, ἄκοντα μέντοι τὸν παῖδα χαλεπὸν εἶναι νομίζειν καταλιπεῖν.

14. Ἔνθα δὴ ὁ Ἀστυάγης λέγει πρὸς τὸν Κῦρον, Ὦ παῖ, ἢν μένῃς παρ' ἐμοί, πρῶτον μὲν τῆς παρ' ἐμὲ εἰσόδου σοι οὐ Σάκας ἄρξει, ἀλλ' ὁπόταν βούλῃ εἰσιέναι ὡς ἐμέ, ἐπὶ σοὶ ἔσται· καὶ χάριν σοι εἴσομαι ὅσῳ ἂν πλεονάκις εἰσίῃς ὡς ἐμέ. ἔπειτα δὲ ἵπποις τοῖς ἐμοῖς χρήσει καὶ ἄλλοις ὁπόσοις ἂν βούλῃ, καὶ ὁπόταν ἀπίῃς, ἔχων ἄπει οὓς ἂν αὐτὸς ἐθέλῃς. ἔπειτα δὲ ἐν τῷ δείπνῳ ἐπὶ τὸ μετρίως σοι δοκοῦν ἔχειν ὁποίαν βούλει ὁδὸν πορεύσει. ἔπειτα τά τε νῦν ἐν τῷ παραδείσῳ θηρία δίδωμί σοι καὶ ἄλλα παντοδαπὰ συλλέξω, ἃ σὺ ἐπειδὰν τάχιστα ἱππεύειν μάθῃς, διώξει, καὶ τοξεύων καὶ ἀκοντίζων καταβαλεῖς ὥσπερ οἱ μεγάλοι ἄνδρες. καὶ παῖδας δέ σοι ἐγὼ συμπαίστορας παρέξω, καὶ ἄλλα ὁπόσα ἂν βούλῃ λέγων πρὸς ἐμὲ οὐκ ἀτυχήσεις.

is at the bath.' And if he were very eager to eat, I would say, 'It is with the ladies.' And I would keep that up until I tormented him, just as he torments me by keeping me away from you."

12. Such amusement he furnished them at dinner; and during the day, if he saw that his grandfather or his uncle needed anything, it was difficult for any one else to get ahead of him in supplying the need; for Cyrus was most happy to do them any service that he could.

Mandane leaves Cyrus in Media

13. But when Mandane was making preparations to go back to her husband, Astyages asked her to leave Cyrus behind. And she answered that she desired to do her father's pleasure in everything, but she thought it hard to leave the boy behind against his will.

14. Then Astyages said to Cyrus: "My boy, if you will stay with me, in the first place Sacas shall not control your admission to me, but it shall be in your power to come in to see me whenever you please, and I shall be the more obliged to you the oftener you come to me. And in the second place you shall use my horses and everything else you will; and when you go back home, you shall take with you any of them that you desire. And besides, at dinner you shall go whatever way you please to what seems to you to be temperance. And then, I present to you the animals that are now in the park and I will collect others of every description, and as soon as you learn to ride, you shall hunt and slay them with bow and spear, just as grown-up men do. I will also find some children to be your playfellows; and if you wish anything else, just mention it to me, and you shall not fail to receive it."

15. Ἐπεὶ ταῦτα εἶπεν ὁ Ἀστυάγης, ἡ μήτηρ διηρώτα τὸν Κῦρον πότερον βούλοιτο μένειν ἢ ἀπιέναι. ὁ δὲ οὐκ ἐμέλλησεν, ἀλλὰ ταχὺ εἶπεν ὅτι μένειν βούλοιτο. ἐπερωτηθεὶς δὲ πάλιν ὑπὸ τῆς μητρὸς διὰ τί εἰπεῖν λέγεται, Ὅτι οἴκοι μὲν τῶν ἡλίκων καὶ εἰμὶ καὶ δοκῶ κράτιστος εἶναι, ὦ μῆτερ, καὶ ἀκοντίζων καὶ τοξεύων, ἐνταῦθα δὲ οἶδ' ὅτι ἱππεύων ἥττων εἰμὶ τῶν ἡλίκων· καὶ τοῦτο εὖ ἴσθι, ὦ μῆτερ, ἔφη, ὅτι ἐμὲ πάνυ ἀνιᾷ. ἢν δέ με καταλίπῃς ἐνθάδε καὶ μάθω ἱππεύειν, ὅταν μὲν ἐν Πέρσαις ὦ, οἶμαί σοι ἐκείνους τοὺς ἀγαθοὺς τὰ πεζικὰ ῥᾳδίως νικήσειν, ὅταν δ' εἰς Μήδους ἔλθω, ἐνθάδε πειράσομαι τῷ πάππῳ ἀγαθῶν ἱππέων κράτιστος ὢν ἱππεὺς συμμαχεῖν αὐτῷ.

16. Τὴν δὲ μητέρα εἰπεῖν, Τὴν δὲ δικαιοσύνην, ὦ παῖ, πῶς μαθήσει ἐνθάδε ἐκεῖ ὄντων σοι τῶν διδασκάλων;

Καὶ τὸν Κῦρον φάναι, Ἀλλ', ὦ μῆτερ, ἀκριβῶς ταῦτά γε οἶδα.

Πῶς σὺ οἶσθα; τὴν Μανδάνην εἰπεῖν.

Ὅτι, φάναι, ὁ διδάσκαλός με ὡς ἤδη ἀκριβοῦντα τὴν δικαιοσύνην καὶ ἄλλοις καθίστη δικάζειν. καὶ τοίνυν, φάναι, ἐπὶ μιᾷ ποτε δίκῃ πληγὰς ἔλαβον ὡς οὐκ ὀρθῶς δικάσας. 17. ἦν δὲ ἡ δίκη τοιαύτη. παῖς μέγας μικρὸν ἔχων χιτῶνα παῖδα μικρὸν μέγαν ἔχοντα χιτῶνα ἐκδύσας αὐτὸν τὸν μὲν ἑαυτοῦ ἐκεῖνον ἠμφίεσε, τὸν δ' ἐκείνου αὐτὸς ἐνέδυ. ἐγὼ οὖν τούτοις δικάζων ἔγνων βέλτιον εἶναι ἀμφοτέροις τὸν ἁρμόττοντα ἑκάτερον χιτῶνα ἔχειν. ἐν δὲ τούτῳ

15. When Astyages had said this, his mother asked Cyrus whether he wished to stay or go. And he did not hesitate but said at once that he wished to stay. And when he was asked again by his mother why he wished to stay, he is said to have answered: "Because at home, mother, I am and have the reputation of being the best of those of my years both in throwing the spear and in shooting with the bow; but here I know that I am inferior to my fellows in horsemanship. And let me tell you, mother," said he, "this vexes me exceedingly. But if you leave me here and I learn to ride, I think you will find, when I come back to Persia, that I shall easily surpass the boys over there who are good at exercises on foot, and when I come again to Media, I shall try to be a help to my grandfather by being the best of good horsemen."

Why he wished to stay

16. "But, my boy," said his mother, "how will you learn justice here, while your teachers are over there?"

"Why, mother," Cyrus answered, "that is one thing that I understand thoroughly."

"How so?" said Mandane.

"Because," said he, "my teacher appointed me, on the ground that I was already thoroughly versed in justice, to decide cases for others also. And so, in one case," said he, "I once got a flogging for not deciding correctly. 17. The case was like this: a big boy with a little tunic, finding a little boy with a big tunic on, took it off him and put his own tunic on him, while he himself put on the other's. So, when I tried their case, I decided that it was better for them both that each should keep the tunic that fitted him. And thereupon the master flogged me,

His training in justice

με ἔπαισεν ὁ διδάσκαλος, λέξας[1] ὅτι ὁπότε μὲν τοῦ ἁρμόττοντος εἴην κριτής, οὕτω δέοι ποιεῖν, ὁπότε δὲ κρῖναι δέοι ποτέρου ὁ χιτὼν εἴη, τοῦτ', ἔφη, σκεπτέον εἶναι τίς κτῆσις δικαία ἐστί, πότερα τὸν βίᾳ ἀφελόμενον ἔχειν ἢ τὸν ποιησάμενον ἢ πριάμενον κεκτῆσθαι· ἐπεὶ δ', ἔφη, τὸ μὲν νόμιμον δίκαιον εἶναι, τὸ δὲ ἄνομον βίαιον, σὺν τῷ νόμῳ ἐκέλευεν ἀεὶ τὸν δικαστὴν τὴν ψῆφον τίθεσθαι. οὕτως ἐγώ σοι, ὦ μῆτερ, τά γε δίκαια παντάπασιν ἤδη ἀκριβῶ· ἢν δέ τι ἄρα προσδέωμαι, ὁ πάππος με, ἔφη, οὗτος ἐπιδιδάξει.

18. Ἀλλ' οὐ ταὐτά, ἔφη, ὦ παῖ, παρὰ τῷ πάππῳ καὶ ἐν Πέρσαις δίκαια ὁμολογεῖται. οὗτος μὲν γὰρ τῶν ἐν Μήδοις πάντων ἑαυτὸν δεσπότην πεποίηκεν, ἐν Πέρσαις δὲ τὸ ἴσον ἔχειν δίκαιον νομίζεται. καὶ ὁ σὸς πατὴρ πρῶτος[2] τὰ τεταγμένα μὲν ποιεῖ τῇ πόλει, τὰ τεταγμένα δὲ λαμβάνει, μέτρον δὲ αὐτῷ οὐχ ἡ ψυχὴ ἀλλ' ὁ νόμος ἐστίν. ὅπως οὖν μὴ ἀπολεῖ μαστιγούμενος, ἐπειδὰν οἴκοι ᾖς,[3] ἂν παρὰ τούτου μαθὼν ἥκῃς ἀντὶ τοῦ βασιλικοῦ τὸ τυραννικόν, ἐν ᾧ ἔστι τὸ πλεῖον οἴεσθαι χρῆναι πάντων ἔχειν.

Ἀλλ' ὅ γε σὸς πατήρ, εἶπεν ὁ Κῦρος, δεινότερός ἐστιν, ὦ μῆτερ, διδάσκειν μεῖον ἢ πλεῖον ἔχειν· ἢ οὐχ ὁρᾷς, ἔφη, ὅτι καὶ Μήδους ἅπαντας δεδίδαχεν αὑτοῦ μεῖον ἔχειν;[4] ὥστε θάρρει, ὡς

[1] λέξας zER; λέγων yC².
[2] ὁ σὸς πατὴρ πρῶτος Schneider, Hug; ὁ πρῶτος πατήρ C; ὁ σὸς πρῶτος πατήρ yzER, Marchant; πρῶτος ὁ σὸς πατήρ Gemoll.
[3] ᾖς Heindorf; ἴῃς or εἴης MSS.
[4] ἢ οὐχ . . . ἔχειν not in xz.

saying that when I was a judge of a good fit, I should do as I had done; but when it was my duty to decide whose tunic it was, I had this question, he said, to consider—whose title was the rightful one; whether it was right that he who took it away by force should keep it, or that he who had had it made for himself or had bought it should own it. And since, he said, what is lawful is right and what is unlawful is wrong, he bade the judge always render his verdict on the side of the law. It is in this way, mother, you see, that I already have a thorough understanding of justice in all its bearings; and," he added, "if I do require anything more, my grandfather here will teach me that."

Median vs. Persian ideals of justice

18. "Yes, my son," said she; "but at your grandfather's court they do not recognize the same principles of justice as they do in Persia. For he has made himself master of everything in Media, but in Persia equality of rights is considered justice. And your father is the first one to do what is ordered by the State and to accept what is decreed, and his standard is not his will but the law. Mind, therefore, that you be not flogged within an inch of your life, when you come home, if you return with a knowledge acquired from your grandfather here of the principles not of kingship but of tyranny, one principle of which is that it is right for one to have more than all."

"But your father, at least," said Cyrus, "is more shrewd at teaching people to have less than to have more, mother. Why, do you not see," he went on, "that he has taught all the Medes to have less than himself? So never fear that your father, at any rate,

ὅ γε σὸς πατὴρ οὔτ᾽ ἄλλον οὐδένα οὔτ᾽ ἐμὲ πλεονεκτεῖν μαθόντα ἀποπέμψει.

IV

1. Τοιαῦτα μὲν δὴ πολλὰ ἐλάλει ὁ Κῦρος· τέλος δὲ ἡ μὲν μήτηρ ἀπῆλθε, Κῦρος δὲ κατέμενε καὶ αὐτοῦ ἐτρέφετο. καὶ ταχὺ μὲν τοῖς ἡλικιώταις συνεκέκρατο ὥστε οἰκείως διακεῖσθαι, ταχὺ δὲ τοὺς πατέρας αὐτῶν ἀνήρτητο, προσιὼν καὶ ἔνδηλος ὢν ὅτι ἠσπάζετο αὐτῶν τοὺς υἱεῖς, ὥστε εἴ τι τοῦ βασιλέως δέοιντο, τοὺς παῖδας ἐκέλευον τοῦ Κύρου δεῖσθαι διαπράξασθαι σφίσιν, ὁ δὲ Κῦρος, ὅ τι δέοιντο αὐτοῦ οἱ παῖδες, διὰ τὴν φιλανθρωπίαν καὶ φιλοτιμίαν περὶ παντὸς ἐποιεῖτο διαπράττεσθαι. 2. καὶ ὁ Ἀστυάγης δὲ ὅ τι δέοιτο αὐτοῦ ὁ Κῦρος οὐδὲν ἐδύνατο ἀντέχειν μὴ οὐ χαρίζεσθαι. καὶ γὰρ ἀσθενήσαντος αὐτοῦ οὐδέποτε ἀπέλειπε τὸν πάππον οὐδὲ κλαίων ποτὲ ἐπαύετο, ἀλλὰ δῆλος ἦν πᾶσιν ὅτι ὑπερεφοβεῖτο μή οἱ ὁ πάππος ἀποθάνῃ· καὶ γὰρ ἐκ νυκτὸς εἴ τινος δέοιτο Ἀστυάγης, πρῶτος ᾐσθάνετο Κῦρος καὶ πάντων ἀοκνότατα ἀνεπήδα ὑπηρετήσων ὅ τι οἴοιτο χαριεῖσθαι, ὥστε παντάπασιν ἀνεκτήσατο τὸν Ἀστυάγην.

3. Καὶ ἦν μὲν ἴσως πολυλογώτερος,[1] ἅμα μὲν διὰ τὴν παιδείαν, ὅτι ἠναγκάζετο ὑπὸ τοῦ διδασκάλου καὶ διδόναι λόγον ὧν ἐποίει καὶ λαμβάνειν παρ᾽ ἄλλων, ὁπότε δικάζοι, ἔτι δὲ καὶ διὰ

[1] πολυλογώτερος xzR; π. ἢ παιδίσκος ἔτι ἄνηβος ὢν y.

will turn either me or anybody else out trained under him to have too much."

IV

1. In this way Cyrus often chattered on. At last, however, his mother went away, but Cyrus remained behind and grew up in Media. Soon he had become so intimately associated with other boys of his own years that he was on easy terms with them. And soon he had won their fathers' hearts by visiting them and showing that he loved their sons; so that, if they desired any favour of the king, they bade their sons ask Cyrus to secure it for them. And Cyrus, because of his kindness of heart and his desire for popularity, made every effort to secure for the boys whatever they asked. 2. And Astyages could not refuse any favour that Cyrus asked of him. And this was natural; for, when his grandfather fell sick, Cyrus never left him nor ceased to weep but plainly showed to all that he greatly feared that his grandfather might die. For even at night, if Astyages wanted anything, Cyrus was the first to discover it and with greater alacrity than any one else he would jump up to perform whatever service he thought would give him pleasure, so that he won Astyages's heart completely.

Cyrus's popularity among the Medes

3. He was, perhaps, too talkative, partly on account of his education, because he had always been required by his teacher to render an account of what he was doing and to obtain an account from others whenever he was judge; and partly also because of

His talkativeness

τὸ φιλομαθὴς εἶναι πολλὰ μὲν αὐτὸς ἀεὶ τοὺ παρόντας ἀνηρώτα πῶς ἔχοντα τυγχάνοι, κα ὅσα αὐτὸς ὑπ' ἄλλων ἐρωτῷτο, διὰ τὸ ἀγχίνου εἶναι ταχὺ ἀπεκρίνετο, ὥστ' ἐκ πάντων τούτω ἡ πολυλογία συνελέγετο αὐτῷ· ἀλλ' ὥσπερ γὰ ἐν σώματι, ὅσοι νέοι ὄντες μέγεθος ἔλαβον, ὅμω ἐμφαίνεται τὸ νεαρὸν αὐτοῖς ὃ κατηγορεῖ τὴ ὀλιγοετίαν, οὕτω καὶ Κύρου ἐκ τῆς πολυλογία οὐ θράσος διεφαίνετο, ἀλλ' ἁπλότης καὶ φιλο στοργία, ὥστ' ἐπεθύμει ἄν τις ἔτι πλείω αὐτο ἀκούειν ἢ σιωπῶντι παρεῖναι.

4. Ὡς δὲ προῆγεν αὐτὸν ὁ χρόνος σὺν τῷ μεγέθει εἰς ὥραν τοῦ πρόσηβον γενέσθαι, ἐ τούτῳ δὴ τοῖς μὲν λόγοις μανοτέροις ἐχρῆτ καὶ τῇ φωνῇ ἡσυχαιτέρᾳ, αἰδοῦς δ' ἐνεπίμπλατο ὥστε καὶ ἐρυθραίνεσθαι ὁπότε συντυγχάνοι τοῖ πρεσβυτέροις, καὶ τὸ σκυλακῶδες τὸ πᾶσι ὁμοίως προσπίπτειν οὐκέθ' ὁμοίως προπετὲς[1] εἶχεν. οὕτω δὴ ἡσυχαίτερος μὲν ἦν, ἐν δὲ ταῖς συνουσίαις πάμπαν ἐπίχαρις. καὶ γὰρ ὅσα διαγωνίζονται πολλάκις ἥλικες πρὸς ἀλλήλους, οὐχ ἃ κρείττων ᾔδει ὤν, ταῦτα προυκαλεῖτο τοὺς συνόντας, ἀλλ' ἅπερ εὖ ᾔδει ἑαυτὸν ἥττονα ὄντα, ἐξῆρχε,[2] φάσκων κάλλιον αὐτῶν ποιήσειν, καὶ κατῆρχεν ἤδη ἀναπηδῶν ἐπὶ τοὺς ἵππους ἢ διατοξευσόμενος ἢ διακοντιούμενος ἀπὸ τῶν ἵπ-

[1] προπετές xAHR; προπετῶς yG²; [προπετές] Cobet, Hug.
[2] ἐξῆρχε yR; ταῦτα ἐξῆρχε xz, Gemoll.

is natural curiosity, he was habitually putting many
uestions to those about him why things were thus
nd so; and because of his alertness of mind he
eadily answered questions that others put to him;
o that from all these causes his talkativeness grew
pon him. But it was not unpleasant; for just as in
he body, in the case of those who have attained
heir growth although they are still young, there yet
ppears that freshness which betrays their lack of
ears, so also in Cyrus's case his talkativeness disclosed
ot impertinence but naïveté and an affectionate
lisposition, so that one would be better pleased to
ear still more from his lips than to sit by and have
im keep silent.

4. But as he advanced in stature and in years to
he time of attaining youth's estate, he then came to
se fewer words, his voice was more subdued, and he
ecame so bashful that he actually blushed whenever
e met his elders; and that puppy-like manner of
reaking in upon anybody and everybody alike he no
onger exhibited with so much forwardness. So he
ecame more quiet, to be sure, but in social inter-
ourse altogether charming. The boys liked him,
oo; for in all the contests in which those of the same
ge are wont often to engage with one another he
lid not challenge his mates to those in which he
knew he was superior, but he proposed precisely
those exercises in which he knew he was not their
equal, saying that he would do better than they;
and he would at once take the lead, jumping up upon
the horses to contend on horseback either in archery
or in throwing the spear, although he was not yet a

His spirit of comradeship

πων οὔπω πάνυ ἔποχος ὤν, ἡττώμενος δὲ αὐτὸς ἐφ' ἑαυτῷ μάλιστα ἐγέλα.

5. Ὡς δ' οὐκ ἀπεδίδρασκεν ἐκ τοῦ ἡττᾶσθαι εἰς τὸ μὴ ποιεῖν ὃ ἡττῷτο, ἀλλ' ἐκαλινδεῖτο ἐν τῷ πειρᾶσθαι αὖθις βέλτιον ποιεῖν, ταχὺ μὲν εἰς τὸ ἴσον ἀφίκετο τῇ ἱππικῇ τοῖς ἥλιξι, ταχὺ δὲ παρῄει διὰ τὸ ἐρᾶν τοῦ ἔργου, ταχὺ δὲ τὰ ἐν τῷ παραδείσῳ θηρία ἀνηλώκει διώκων καὶ βάλλων καὶ κατακαίνων, ὥστε ὁ Ἀστυάγης οὐκέτ' εἶχεν αὐτῷ συλλέγειν θηρία. καὶ ὁ Κῦρος αἰσθόμενος ὅτι βουλόμενος οὐ δύναιτό οἱ ζῶντα πολλὰ παρέχειν, ἔλεγε πρὸς αὐτόν, Ὦ πάππε, τί σε δεῖ θηρία ζητοῦντα πράγματ' ἔχειν; ἀλλ' ἐὰν ἐμὲ ἐκπέμπῃς ἐπὶ θήραν σὺν τῷ θείῳ, νομιῶ ὅσα ἂν ἴδω θηρία, ἐμοὶ ταῦτα τρέφεσθαι. 6. ἐπιθυμῶν δὲ σφόδρα ἐξιέναι ἐπὶ τὴν θήραν οὐκέθ' ὁμοίως λιπαρεῖν ἐδύνατο ὥσπερ παῖς ὤν, ἀλλ' ὀκνηρότερον προσῄει. καὶ ἃ πρόσθεν τῷ Σάκᾳ ἐμέμφετο ὅτι οὐ παρίει αὐτὸν πρὸς τὸν πάππον, αὐτὸς ἤδη Σάκας ἑαυτῷ ἐγίγνετο· οὐ γὰρ προσῄει, εἰ μὴ ἴδοι εἰ καιρὸς εἴη, καὶ τοῦ Σάκα ἐδεῖτο πάντως σημαίνειν αὐτῷ ὁπότε ἐγχωροίη [καὶ ὁπότε καιρὸς εἴη].[1] ὥστε ὁ Σάκας ὑπερεφίλει ἤδη καὶ οἱ ἄλλοι πάντες.

7. Ἐπεὶ δ' οὖν ἔγνω ὁ Ἀστυάγης σφόδρα αὐτὸν ἐπιθυμοῦντα ἔξω θηρᾶν, ἐκπέμπει αὐτὸν σὺν τῷ θείῳ καὶ φύλακας συμπέμπει ἐφ' ἵππων

[1] καὶ . . . εἴη bracketed by Zeune, Hug, Gemoll, Marchant.

good rider, and when he was beaten he laughed at himself most heartily.

5. And as he did not shirk being beaten and take refuge in refusing to do that in which he was beaten, but persevered in attempting to do better next time, he speedily became the equal of his fellows in horsemanship and soon on account of his love for the sport he surpassed them; and before long he had exhausted the supply of animals in the park by hunting and shooting and killing them, so that Astyages was no longer able to collect animals for him. And when Cyrus saw that notwithstanding his desire to do so, the king was unable to provide him with many animals alive, he said to him: "Why should you take the trouble, grandfather, to get animals for me? If you will only send me out with my uncle to hunt, I shall consider that all the animals I see were bred for me." 6. But though he was exceedingly eager to go out hunting, he could no longer coax for it as he used to do when he was a boy, but he became more diffident in his approaches. And in the very matter for which he found fault with Sacas before, namely that he would not admit him to his grandfather—he himself now became a Sacas unto himself; for he would not go in unless he saw that it was a proper time, and he asked Sacas by all means to let him know when it was convenient. And so Sacas now came to love him dearly, as did all the rest.

He goes hunting

7. However, when Astyages realized that he was exceedingly eager to hunt out in the wilds, he let him go out with his uncle and he sent along some older men on horseback to look after him, to keep

πρεσβυτέρους, ὅπως ἀπὸ τῶν δυσχωριῶν φυλάττοιεν αὐτὸν καὶ εἰ τῶν ἀγρίων τι φανείη θηρίων. ὁ οὖν Κῦρος τῶν ἑπομένων προθύμως ἐπυνθάνετο ποίοις οὐ χρὴ θηρίοις πελάζειν καὶ ποῖα χρὴ θαρροῦντα διώκειν. οἱ δ' ἔλεγον ὅτι ἄρκτοι τε πολλοὺς ἤδη πλησιάσαντας διέφθειραν καὶ κάπροι καὶ λέοντες καὶ παρδάλεις, αἱ δὲ ἔλαφοι καὶ δορκάδες καὶ οἱ ἄγριοι οἶες καὶ οἱ ὄνοι οἱ ἄγριοι ἀσινεῖς εἰσιν. ἔλεγον δὲ καὶ τοῦτο, τὰς δυσχωρίας ὅτι δέοι φυλάττεσθαι οὐδὲν ἧττον ἢ τὰ θηρία· πολλοὺς γὰρ ἤδη αὐτοῖς τοῖς ἵπποις κατακρημνισθῆναι.

8. Καὶ ὁ Κῦρος πάντα ταῦτα ἐμάνθανε προθύμως· ὡς δὲ εἶδεν ἔλαφον ἐκπηδήσασαν, πάντων ἐπιλαθόμενος ὧν ἤκουσεν ἐδίωκεν οὐδὲν ἄλλο ὁρῶν ἢ ὅπῃ ἔφευγε. καί πως διαπηδῶν αὐτῷ ὁ ἵππος πίπτει εἰς γόνατα, καὶ μικροῦ κἀκεῖνον ἐξετραχήλισεν. οὐ μὴν ἀλλ' ἐπέμεινεν ὁ Κῦρος μόλις πως, καὶ ὁ ἵππος ἐξανέστη. ὡς δ' εἰς τὸ πεδίον ἦλθεν, ἀκοντίσας καταβάλλει τὴν ἔλαφον, καλόν τι χρῆμα καὶ μέγα. καὶ ὁ μὲν δὴ ὑπερέχαιρεν· οἱ δὲ φύλακες προσελάσαντες ἐλοιδόρουν αὐτὸν καὶ ἔλεγον[1] εἰς οἷον κίνδυνον ἔλθοι, καὶ ἔφασαν κατερεῖν αὐτοῦ. ὁ οὖν Κῦρος εἱστήκει καταβεβηκώς, καὶ ἀκούων ταῦτα ἠνιᾶτο. ὡς δ' ᾔσθετο κραυγῆς, ἀνεπήδησεν ἐπὶ τὸν ἵππον ὥσπερ ἐνθουσιῶν, καὶ ὡς εἶδεν ἐκ τοῦ ἀντίου κάπρον προσφερόμενον, ἀντίος ἐλαύνει καὶ διατεινάμενος εὐστόχως[2] βάλλει εἰς τὸ μέτωπον καὶ κατέσχε τὸν κάπρον.

[1] καὶ ἔλεγον bracketed by Cobet, Hug, Marchant.
[2] εὐστόχως yR; εὐτυχῶς (*successfully*) xz.

him away from dangerous places and guard him against wild beasts, in case any should appear. Cyrus, therefore, eagerly inquired of those who attended him what animals one ought not to approach and what animals one might pursue without fear. And they told him that bears and boars and lions and leopards had killed many who came close to them, but that deer and gazelles and wild sheep and wild asses were harmless. And they said this also, that one must be on one's guard against dangerous places no less than against wild beasts; for many riders had been thrown over precipices, horses and all.

8. All these lessons Cyrus eagerly learned. But when he saw a deer spring out from under cover, he forgot everything that he had heard and gave chase, seeing nothing but the direction in which it was making. And somehow his horse in taking a leap fell upon its knees and almost threw him over its head. However, Cyrus managed, with some difficulty, to keep his seat, and his horse got up. And when he came to level ground, he threw his spear and brought down the deer—a fine, large quarry. And he, of course, was greatly delighted; but the guards rode up and scolded him and told him into what danger he had gone and declared that they would tell of him. Now Cyrus stood there, for he had dismounted, and was vexed at being spoken to in this way. But when he heard a halloo, he sprang upon his horse like one possessed and when he saw a boar rushing straight toward him, he rode to meet him and aiming well he struck the boar between the eyes and brought him down.

9. ἐνταῦθα μέντοι ἤδη καὶ ὁ θεῖος αὐτῷ ἐλοιδορεῖτο, τὴν θρασύτητα ὁρῶν. ὁ δ' αὐτοῦ λοιδορουμένου ὅμως ἐδεῖτο ὅσα αὐτὸς ἔλαβε, ταῦτα ἐᾶσαι εἰσκομίσαντα δοῦναι τῷ πάππῳ. τὸν δὲ θεῖον εἰπεῖν φασιν, Ἀλλ' ἢν αἴσθηται ὅτι ἐδίωκες, οὐ σοὶ μόνον λοιδορήσεται, ἀλλὰ καὶ ἐμοί, ὅτι σε εἴων.

Καὶ ἢν βούληται, φάναι αὐτόν, μαστιγωσάτω, ἐπειδάν γε ἐγὼ δῶ αὐτῷ. καὶ σύ γε, ὅ τι βούλει,[1] ἔφη, ὦ θεῖε, τιμωρησάμενος ταῦτα ὅμως χάρισαι μοι.

Καὶ ὁ Κυαξάρης μέντοι τελευτῶν εἶπε, Ποίει ὅπως βούλει· σὺ γὰρ νῦν γε ἡμῶν ἔοικας βασιλεὺς εἶναι.

10. Οὕτω δὴ ὁ Κῦρος εἰσκομίσας τὰ θηρία ἐδίδου τε τῷ πάππῳ καὶ ἔλεγεν ὅτι αὐτὸς ταῦτα θηράσειεν ἐκείνῳ. καὶ τὰ ἀκόντια ἐπεδείκνυ μὲν οὔ, κατέθηκε δὲ ᾑματωμένα ὅπου ᾤετο τὸν πάππον ὄψεσθαι. ὁ δὲ Ἀστυάγης ἄρα εἶπεν, Ἀλλ', ὦ παῖ, δέχομαι μὲν ἔγωγε ἡδέως ὅσα σὺ δίδως, οὐ μέντοι δέομαί γε τούτων οὐδενός, ὥστε σε κινδυνεύειν.

Καὶ ὁ Κῦρος ἔφη, Εἰ τοίνυν μὴ σὺ δέει, ἱκετεύω, ὦ πάππε, ἐμοὶ δὸς αὐτά, ὅπως τοῖς ἡλικιώταις ἐγὼ διαδῶ.

Ἀλλ', ὦ παῖ, ἔφη ὁ Ἀστυάγης, καὶ ταῦτα λαβὼν διαδίδου ὅτῳ σὺ βούλει καὶ τῶν ἄλλων ὁπόσα ἐθέλεις.

11. Καὶ ὁ Κῦρος λαβὼν ἐδίδου τε ἄρας[2] τοῖς

[1] ὅ τι βούλει Hug, Marchant; εἰ βούλει MSS.; but yRC[2] have ὅ τι βούλει after τιμωρησάμενος.
[2] ἄρας xzR, ἄρα y (*accordingly*).

. This time, however, his uncle also reproved him, ɔr he had witnessed his foolhardiness. But for all is scolding, Cyrus nevertheless asked his permission ɔ carry home and present to his grandfather all the ame that he had taken himself. And his uncle, hey say, replied: "But if he finds out that you ave been giving chase, he will chide not only you ut me also for allowing you to do so."

"And if he choose," said Cyrus, "let him flog me, rovided only I may give him the game. And you, ncle," said he, "may punish me in any way you lease—only grant me this favour."

And finally Cyaxares said, though with reluctance: Do as you wish; for now it looks as if it were you ho are our king."

10. So Cyrus carried the animals in and gave hem to his grandfather, saying that he had himself aken this game for him. As for the hunting spears, hough he did not show them to him, he laid them own all blood-stained where he thought his grandather would see them. And then Astyages said: Well, my boy, I am glad to accept what you offer ne; however, I do not need any of these things nough for you to risk your life for them."

He distributes the game among his age-fellows

"Well then, grandfather," said Cyrus, "if you do ot need them, please give them to me, that I may livide them among my boy friends."

"All right, my boy," said Astyages, "take both his and of the rest of the game as much as you wish nd give it to whom you will."

11. So Cyrus received it and took it away and

παισὶ καὶ ἅμα ἔλεγεν, Ὦ παῖδες, ὡς ἄρα ἐφλυα-
ροῦμεν ὅτε τὰ ἐν τῷ παραδείσῳ θηρία ἐθηρῶμεν·
ὅμοιον ἔμοιγε δοκεῖ εἶναι οἷόνπερ εἴ τις δεδεμένα
ζῷα θηρῴη. πρῶτον μὲν γὰρ ἐν μικρῷ χωρίῳ
ἦν, ἔπειτα λεπτὰ καὶ ψωραλέα, καὶ τὸ μὲν
αὐτῶν χωλὸν ἦν, τὸ δὲ κολοβόν· τὰ δ' ἐν τοῖς
ὄρεσι καὶ λειμῶσι θηρία ὡς μὲν καλά, ὡς δὲ
μεγάλα, ὡς δὲ λιπαρὰ ἐφαίνετο. καὶ αἱ μὲν ἔλαφοι
ὥσπερ πτηναὶ ἥλλοντο πρὸς τὸν οὐρανόν, οἱ δὲ
κάπροι ὥσπερ τοὺς ἄνδρας φασὶ τοὺς ἀνδρείους
ὁμόσε ἐφέροντο· ὑπὸ δὲ τῆς πλατύτητος οὐδὲ
ἁμαρτεῖν οἷόν τ' ἦν αὐτῶν· καλλίω δή, ἔφη,
ἔμοιγε δοκεῖ καὶ τεθνηκότα εἶναι ταῦτα ἢ ζῶντα
ἐκεῖνα τὰ περιῳκοδομημένα. ἀλλ' ἆρα ἄν, ἔφη,
ἀφεῖεν καὶ ὑμᾶς οἱ πατέρες ἐπὶ θήραν;

Καὶ ῥᾳδίως γ' ἄν, ἔφασαν, εἰ Ἀστυάγης κελεύοι.

12. Καὶ ὁ Κῦρος εἶπε, Τίς οὖν ἂν ἡμῖν Ἀ-
στυάγει μνησθείη;

Τίς γὰρ ἄν, ἔφασαν, σοῦ γε ἱκανώτερος πεῖσαι;

Ἀλλὰ μὰ τὸν Δία,[1] ἔφη, ἐγὼ μὲν οὐκ οἶδ' ὅστις
ἄνθρωπος γεγένημαι· οὐδὲ γὰρ οἷός τ' εἰμὶ λέγειν
ἔγωγε οὐδ' ἀναβλέπειν πρὸς τὸν πάππον ἐκ τοῦ
ἴσου ἔτι δύναμαι. ἢν δὲ τοσοῦτον ἐπιδιδῶ, δέδοικα, ἔφη, μὴ παντάπασι βλάξ τις καὶ ἠλίθιος
γένωμαι· παιδάριον δ' ὢν δεινότατος[2] λαλεῖν
ἐδόκουν εἶναι.

Καὶ οἱ παῖδες εἶπον, Πονηρὸν λέγεις τὸ πρᾶγμα,
εἰ μηδ' ὑπὲρ ἡμῶν ἄν τι δέῃ δυνήσει πράττειν,

[1] τὸν Δία xzR : τὴν Ἥραν y (the weakling swears *by Hera*).
[2] δεινότατος Leonclavius, Edd.; δεινότατον MSS.

·oceeded to distribute it among the boys, saying as
: did so: "What tomfoolery it was, fellows, when
e used to hunt the animals in the park. To me at
ast, it seems just like hunting animals that were
:d up. For, in the first place, they were in a small
ace; besides, they were lean and mangy; and one
them was lame and another maimed. But the
imals out on the mountains and the plains—how
ie they looked, and large and sleek! And the
:er leaped up skyward as if on wings, and the
ars came charging at one, as they say brave men
in battle. And by reason of their bulk it was
ite impossible to miss them. And to me at least,"
id he, "these seem really more beautiful, when
ad, than those pent up creatures, when alive.
it say," said he, "would not your fathers let you
out hunting, too?"

"Aye, and readily," they said, "if Astyages should
ve the word."

12. "Whom, then, could we find to speak about it
Astyages?" said Cyrus.

The boys lay schemes to go hunting

"Why," said they, "who would be better able to
gain his consent than you yourself?"

"No, by Zeus," said he, "not I; I do not know
hat sort of fellow I have become; for I cannot
eak to my grandfather or even look up at him
y more, as I used to do. And if I keep on at this
te," said he, "I fear I shall become a mere dolt
d ninny. But when I was a little fellow, I was
ought ready enough to chatter."

"That's bad news you're giving us," answered the
ys, "if you are not going to be able to act for us

ἀλλ' ἄλλου τινὸς τὸ ἐπὶ σὲ[1] ἀνάγκη ἔσται δεῖσθ
ἡμᾶς.

13. Ἀκούσας δὲ ταῦτα ὁ Κῦρος ἐδήχθη, καὶ σι
ἀπελθὼν διακελευσάμενος ἑαυτῷ τολμᾶν εἰσῆλθε
ἐπιβουλεύσας ὅπως ἂν ἀλυπότατα εἴποι πρὸς τ
πάππον καὶ διαπράξειεν αὐτῷ τε καὶ τοῖς παισ
ὧν ἐδέοντο. ἤρξατο οὖν ὧδε. Εἰπέ μοι, ἔφη,
πάππε, ἤν τις ἀποδρᾷ σε τῶν οἰκετῶν καὶ λάβ
αὐτόν, τί αὐτῷ χρήσει;

Τί ἄλλο, ἔφη, ἢ δήσας ἐργάζεσθαι ἀναγκάσω;

Ἢν δὲ αὐτόματος πάλιν ἔλθῃ, πῶς ποιήσεις;

Τί δέ, ἔφη, εἰ μὴ μαστιγώσας γε, ἵνα μὴ αὖθ
τοῦτο ποιῇ, ἐξ ἀρχῆς χρήσομαι;

Ὥρα ἄν, ἔφη ὁ Κῦρος, σοὶ παρασκευάζεσθ
εἴη ὅτῳ μαστιγώσεις με, ὡς βουλεύομαί γε ὅπ
σε ἀποδρῶ λαβὼν τοὺς ἡλικιώτας ἐπὶ θήραν.

Καὶ ὁ Ἀστυάγης, Καλῶς, ἔφη, ἐποίησας πρ
ειπών· ἔνδοθεν γάρ, ἔφη, ἀπαγορεύω σοι μ
κινεῖσθαι. χαρίεν γάρ, ἔφη, εἰ ἕνεκα κρεαδίω
τῇ θυγατρὶ τὸν παῖδα ἀποβουκολήσαιμι.

14. Ἀκούσας ταῦτα ὁ Κῦρος ἐπείθετο μὲν κ
ἔμενεν,[2] ἀνιαρὸς δὲ καὶ σκυθρωπὸς ὢν σιωπῇ δι
γεν. ὁ μέντοι Ἀστυάγης ἐπεὶ ἔγνω αὐτὸν λυπο
μενον ἰσχυρῶς, βουλόμενος αὐτῷ χαρίζεσθαι ἐξάγ

[1] ἐπὶ σὲ xz, Edd.; ἐπὶ σοὶ yRC[2] (*in your power*).
[2] ἔμενεν F, Edd.; ἔμεινεν all MSS. except F.

in case of need, and we shall have to ask somebody else to do your part."

13. And Cyrus was nettled at hearing this and went away without a word; and when he had summoned up his courage to make the venture, he went in, after he had laid his plans how he might with the least annoyance broach the subject to his grandfather and accomplish for himself and the other boys what they desired. Accordingly, he began as follows: "Tell me, grandfather," said he, "if one of your servants runs away and you catch him again, what will you do to him?"

"What else," said he, "but put him in chains and make him work?"

"But if he comes back again of his own accord, what will you do?"

"What," said he, "but flog him to prevent his doing it again, and then treat him as before?"

"It may be high time, then," said Cyrus, "for you to be making ready to flog me; for I am planning to run away from you and take my comrades out hunting."

"You have done well to tell me in advance," said Astyages; "for now," he went on, "I forbid you to stir from the palace. For it would be a nice thing, if, for the sake of a few morsels of meat, I should play the careless herdsman and lose my daughter her son."

14. When Cyrus heard this, he obeyed and stayed at home; he said nothing, but continued downcast and sulky. However, when Astyages saw that he was exceedingly disappointed, wishing to give him pleasure, he took him out to hunt; he had got the

They have a great hunt

ἐπὶ θήραν, καὶ πεζοὺς πολλοὺς καὶ ἱππέας συναλίσας καὶ τοὺς παῖδας καὶ συνελάσας εἰς τὰ ἱππάσιμα χωρία τὰ θηρία ἐποίησε μεγάλην θήραν. καὶ βασιλικῶς δὴ παρὼν αὐτὸς ἀπηγόρευε μηδένα βάλλειν, πρὶν Κῦρος ἐμπλησθείη θηρῶν. ὁ δὲ Κῦρος οὐκ εἴα κωλύειν, ἀλλ', Εἰ βούλει, ἔφη, ὦ πάππε, ἡδέως με θηρᾶν, ἄφες τοὺς κατ' ἐμὲ πάντας διώκειν καὶ διαγωνίζεσθαι ὅπως ἕκαστος κράτιστα δύναιτο.

15. Ἐνταῦθα δὴ ὁ Ἀστυάγης ἀφίησι, καὶ στὰς ἐθεᾶτο ἁμιλλωμένους ἐπὶ τὰ θηρία καὶ φιλονικοῦντας καὶ διώκοντας καὶ ἀκοντίζοντας. καὶ Κύρῳ ἥδετο οὐ δυναμένῳ σιγᾶν ὑπὸ τῆς ἡδονῆς, ἀλλ' ὥσπερ σκύλακι γενναίῳ ἀνακλάζοντι, ὁπότε πλησιάζοι θηρίῳ, καὶ παρακαλοῦντι ὀνομαστὶ ἕκαστον. καὶ τοῦ μὲν καταγελῶντα αὐτὸν ὁρῶν ηὐφραίνετο, τὸν δέ τινα καὶ ἐπαινοῦντα [αὐτὸν ᾐσθάνετο][1] οὐδ' ὁπωστιοῦν φθονερῶς. τέλος δ' οὖν πολλὰ θηρία ἔχων ὁ Ἀστυάγης ἀπῄει. καὶ τὸ λοιπὸν οὕτως ἥσθη τῇ τότε θήρᾳ ὥστε ἀεὶ ὁπότε οἷόν τ' εἴη συνεξῄει τῷ Κύρῳ καὶ ἄλλους τε πολλοὺς παρελάμβανε καὶ τοὺς παῖδας, Κύρου ἕνεκα.

Τὸν μὲν δὴ πλεῖστον χρόνον οὕτω διῆγεν ὁ Κῦρος, πᾶσιν ἡδονῆς μὲν καὶ ἀγαθοῦ τινος συναίτιος ὤν, κακοῦ δὲ οὐδενός.[2]

16. Ἀμφὶ δὲ τὰ πέντε ἢ ἑκκαίδεκα ἔτη γενομένου αὐτοῦ ὁ υἱὸς τοῦ Ἀσσυρίων βασιλέως γαμεῖν μέλλων ἐπεθύμησεν αὐτὸς θηρᾶσαι εἰς τοῦτον τὸν χρόνον. ἀκούων οὖν ἐν τοῖς μεθορίοις

[1] **αὐτὸν ᾐσθάνετο** MSS. ; bracketed by Herwerden, Edd.
[2] **οὐδενός** xzR, Marchant ; **οὐδενί** y, Gemoll.

boys together, and a large number of men both on foot and on horseback, and when he had driven the wild animals out into country where riding was practicable, he instituted a great hunt. And as he was present himself, he gave the royal command that no one should throw a spear before Cyrus had his fill of hunting. But Cyrus would not permit him to interfere, but said: "If you wish me to enjoy the hunt, grandfather, let all my comrades give chase and strive to outdo one another, and each do his very best."

15. Thereupon, Astyages gave his consent and from his position he watched them rushing in rivalry upon the beasts and vying eagerly with one another in giving chase and in throwing the spear. And he was pleased to see that Cyrus was unable to keep silence for delight, but, like a well-bred hound, gave tongue whenever he came near an animal and urged on each of his companions by name. And the king was delighted to see him laugh at one and praise another without the least bit of jealousy. At length, then, Astyages went home with a large amount of game; and he was so pleased with that chase, that thenceforth he always went out with Cyrus when it was possible, and he took along with him not only many others but, for Cyrus's sake, the boys as well.

Thus Cyrus passed most of his time, contriving some pleasure and good for all, but responsible for nothing unpleasant to any one.

16. But when Cyrus was about fifteen or sixteen years old, the son of the Assyrian king, on the eve of his marriage, desired in person to get the game for that occasion. Now, hearing that on the frontiers

τοῖς τε αὐτῶν καὶ τοῖς Μήδων πολλὰ θηρία εἶναι ἀθήρευτα διὰ τὸν πόλεμον, ἐνταῦθα ἐπεθύμησεν ἐξελθεῖν. ὅπως οὖν ἀσφαλῶς θηρῴη, ἱππέας τε προσέλαβε πολλοὺς καὶ πελταστάς, οἵτινες ἔμελλον αὐτῷ ἐκ τῶν λασίων τὰ θηρία ἐξελᾶν εἰς τὰ ἐργάσιμά τε καὶ εὐήλατα. ἀφικόμενος δὲ ὅπου ἦν αὐτοῖς τὰ φρούρια καὶ ἡ φυλακή, ἐνταῦθα ἐδειπνοποιεῖτο, ὡς πρῴ τῇ ὑστεραίᾳ θηράσων.

17. Ἤδη δὲ ἑσπέρας γενομένης ἡ διαδοχὴ τῇ πρόσθεν φυλακῇ ἔρχεται ἐκ πόλεως καὶ ἱππεῖς καὶ πεζοί. ἔδοξεν οὖν αὐτῷ πολλὴ στρατιὰ παρεῖναι· δύο γὰρ ὁμοῦ ἦσαν φυλακαί, πολλούς τε αὐτὸς ἧκεν ἔχων ἱππέας καὶ πεζούς. ἐβουλεύσατο οὖν κράτιστον εἶναι λεηλατῆσαι ἐκ τῆς Μηδικῆς, καὶ λαμπρότερόν τ᾽ ἂν φανῆναι τὸ ἔργον τῆς θήρας καὶ ἱερείων ἂν πολλὴν ἀφθονίαν ἐνόμιζε γενέσθαι. οὕτω δὴ πρῴ ἀναστὰς ἦγε τὸ στράτευμα, καὶ τοὺς μὲν πεζοὺς κατέλιπεν ἀθρόους ἐν τοῖς μεθορίοις, αὐτὸς δὲ τοῖς ἵπποις προσελάσας πρὸς τὰ τῶν Μήδων φρούρια, τοὺς μὲν βελτίστους καὶ πλείστους ἔχων μεθ᾽ ἑαυτοῦ ἐνταῦθα κατέμεινεν, ὡς μὴ βοηθοῖεν οἱ φρουροὶ τῶν Μήδων ἐπὶ τοὺς καταθέοντας, τοὺς δ᾽ ἐπιτηδείους ἀφῆκε κατὰ φυλὰς ἄλλους ἄλλοσε καταθεῖν, καὶ ἐκέλευε περιβαλομένους ὅτῳ τις ἐπιτυγχάνοι ἐλαύνειν πρὸς ἑαυτόν.

Οἱ μὲν δὴ ταῦτα ἔπραττον. 18. σημανθέντων δὲ τῷ Ἀστυάγει ὅτι πολέμιοί εἰσιν ἐν τῇ χώρᾳ, ἐξεβοήθει καὶ αὐτὸς πρὸς τὰ ὅρια σὺν τοῖς περὶ

of Assyria and Media there was plenty of game that because of the war had not been hunted, he desired to go out thither. Accordingly, that he might hunt without danger, he took along a large force of cavalry and targeteers, who were to drive the game out of the thickets for him into country that was open and suitable for riding. And when he arrived where their frontier-forts and the garrison were, there he dined, planning to hunt early on the following day.

The Assyrian's foray into Media

17. And now when evening had come, the relief-corps for the former garrison came from the city, both horse and foot. He thought, therefore, that he had a large army at hand; for the two garrisons were there together and he himself had come with a large force of cavalry and infantry. Accordingly, he decided that it was best to make a foray into the Median territory and he thought that thus the exploit of the hunt would appear more brilliant and that the number of animals captured would be immense. And so, rising early, he led his army out; the infantry he left together at the frontier, while he himself, riding up with the horse to the outposts of the Medes, took his stand there with most of his bravest men about him, to prevent the Median guards from coming to the rescue against those who were scouring the country; and he sent out the proper men in divisions, some in one direction, some in another, to scour the country, with orders to capture whatever they came upon and bring it to him.

So they were engaged in these operations. 18. But when word was brought to Astyages that there were enemies in the country, he himself sallied forth to

αὐτὸν καὶ ὁ υἱὸς αὐτοῦ ὡσαύτως σὺν τοῖς παρα-
τυχοῦσιν ἱππόταις, καὶ τοῖς ἄλλοις δὲ ἐσήμαινε
πᾶσιν ἐκβοηθεῖν. ὡς δὲ εἶδον πολλοὺς ἀνθρώπους
τῶν Ἀσσυρίων συντεταγμένους καὶ τοὺς ἱππέας
ἡσυχίαν ἔχοντας, ἔστησαν καὶ οἱ Μῆδοι.

Ὁ δὲ Κῦρος ὁρῶν ἐκβοηθοῦντας καὶ τοὺς
ἄλλους πασσυδί, ἐκβοηθεῖ καὶ αὐτὸς πρῶτον
τότε ὅπλα ἐνδύς, οὔποτε οἰόμενος· οὕτως ἐπεθύμει
αὐτοῖς ἐξοπλίσασθαι· μάλα δὲ καλὰ ἦν καὶ
ἁρμόττοντα αὐτῷ ἃ ὁ πάππος περὶ τὸ σῶμα
ἐπεποίητο. οὕτω δὲ ἐξοπλισάμενος προσήλασε
τῷ ἵππῳ. καὶ ὁ Ἀστυάγης ἐθαύμασε μὲν τίνος
κελεύσαντος ἥκοι, ὅμως δὲ εἶπεν αὐτῷ μένειν παρ'
ἑαυτόν.

19. Ὁ δὲ Κῦρος ὡς εἶδε πολλοὺς ἱππέας
ἀντίους, ἤρετο, Ἦ οὗτοι, ἔφη, ὦ πάππε, πολέμιοί
εἰσιν, οἳ ἐφεστήκασι τοῖς ἵπποις ἠρέμα;

Πολέμιοι μέντοι, ἔφη.

Ἦ καὶ ἐκεῖνοι, ἔφη, οἱ ἐλαύνοντες;

Κἀκεῖνοι μέντοι.

Νὴ τὸν Δί', ἔφη, ὦ πάππε, ἀλλ' οὖν πονηροί
γε φαινόμενοι καὶ ἐπὶ πονηρῶν ἱππαρίων ἄγουσιν
ἡμῶν τὰ χρήματα· οὐκοῦν χρὴ ἐλαύνειν τινὰς
ἡμῶν ἐπ' αὐτούς.

Ἀλλ' οὐχ ὁρᾷς, ἔφη, ὦ παῖ, ὅσον τὸ στῖφος
τῶν ἱππέων ἕστηκε συντεταγμένον; οἳ ἢν ἐπ'

the frontier in person with his body-guard, and likewise his son with the knights that happened to be at hand marched out, while he gave directions to all the others also to come out to his assistance. But when they saw a large number of Assyrian troops drawn up and their cavalry standing still, the Medes also came to a halt.

Cyrus goes to the front

When Cyrus saw the rest marching out with all speed, he put on his armour then for the first time and started out, too; this was an opportunity that he had thought would never come—so eager was he to don his arms; and the armour that his grandfather had had made to order for him was very beautiful and fitted him well. Thus equipped he rode up on his horse. And though Astyages wondered at whose order he had come, he nevertheless told the lad to come and stay by his side.

19. And when Cyrus saw many horsemen over against them, he asked: "Say, grandfather," said he, "are those men enemies who sit there quietly upon their horses?"

"Yes, indeed, they are," said he.

"Are those enemies, too," said Cyrus, "who are riding up and down?"

"Yes, they are enemies, too."

"Well then, by Zeus, grandfather," said he, "at any rate, they are a sorry looking lot on a sorry lot of nags who are raiding our belongings. Why, some of us ought to charge upon them."

"But don't you see, my son," said the king, "what a dense array of cavalry is standing there in

εκείνους ἡμεῖς ἐλαύνωμεν, ὑποτεμοῦνται ἡμᾶς πάλιν [ἐκεῖνοι].[1] ἡμῖν δὲ οὔπω ἡ ἰσχὺς πάρεστιν.

Ἀλλ' ἢν σὺ μένῃς, ἔφη ὁ Κῦρος, καὶ ἀναλαμβάνῃς τοὺς προσβοηθοῦντας, φοβήσονται οὗτοι καὶ οὐ κινήσονται, οἱ δ' ἄγοντες εὐθὺς ἀφήσουσι τὴν λείαν, ἐπειδὰν ἴδωσί τινας ἐπ' αὐτοὺς ἐλαύνοντας.

20. Ταῦτ' εἰπόντος αὐτοῦ ἔδοξέ τι λέγειν τῷ Ἀστυάγει. καὶ ἅμα θαυμάζων ὡς καὶ ἐφρόνει καὶ ἐγρηγόρει κελεύει τὸν υἱὸν λαβόντα τάξιν ἱππέων ἐλαύνειν ἐπὶ τοὺς ἄγοντας τὴν λείαν. Ἐγὼ δέ, ἔφη, ἐπὶ τούσδε, ἢν ἐπὶ σὲ κινῶνται, ἐλῶ,[2] ὥστε ἀναγκασθήσονται ἡμῖν προσέχειν τὸν νοῦν.

Οὕτω δὴ ὁ Κυαξάρης λαβὼν τῶν ἐρρωμένων ἵππων[3] τε καὶ ἀνδρῶν προσελαύνει. καὶ ὁ Κῦρος ὡς εἶδεν ὁρμωμένους, ἐξορμᾷ, καὶ αὐτὸς πρῶτος ἡγεῖτο ταχέως, καὶ ὁ Κυαξάρης μέντοι ἐφείπετο, καὶ οἱ ἄλλοι δὲ οὐκ ἀπελείποντο. ὡς δὲ εἶδον αὐτοὺς πελάζοντας οἱ λεηλατοῦντες, εὐθὺς ἀφέντες τὰ χρήματα ἔφευγον. 21. οἱ δ' ἀμφὶ τὸν Κῦρον ὑπετέμνοντο, καὶ οὓς μὲν κατελάμβανον εὐθὺς ἔπαιον, πρῶτος δὲ ὁ Κῦρος, ὅσοι δὲ παραλλάξαντες αὐτῶν ἔφθασαν, κατόπιν τούτους ἐδίωκον, καὶ οὐκ ἀνίεσαν, ἀλλ' ᾕρουν τινὰς αὐτῶν.

Ὥσπερ δὲ κύων γενναῖος ἄπειρος ἀπρονοήτως φέρεται πρὸς κάπρον, οὕτω καὶ ὁ Κῦρος ἐφέρετο,

[1] ἐκεῖνοι MSS., Dindorf, Sauppe; bracketed by Hug, Marchant; ἐνθένδε Gemoll.

[2] ἐλῶ y, Edd.; ἐλάσω xzR.

[3] ἵππων F, Edd.; ἱππέων xzDR.

line? If we charge upon those over there, these in turn will cut us off; while as for us, the main body of our forces has not yet come."

"But if you stay here," said Cyrus, "and take up the reinforcements that are coming to join us, these fellows will be afraid and will not stir, while the raiders will drop their booty, just as soon as they see some of us charging on them."

20. It seemed to Astyages that there was something in Cyrus's suggestion, when he said this. And while he wondered that the boy was so shrewd and wide-awake, he ordered his son to take a division of the cavalry and charge upon those who were carrying off the spoil. "And if," said he, "these others make a move against you, I will charge upon them, so that they will be forced to turn their attention to us."

His plan for the battle

So then Cyaxares took some of the most powerful horses and men and advanced. And when Cyrus saw them starting, he rushed off and soon took the lead, while Cyaxares followed after, and the rest also were not left behind. And when the foragers saw them approaching, they straightway let go their booty and took to flight. 21. But Cyrus and his followers tried to cut them off, and those whom they caught they at once struck down, Cyrus taking the lead; and they pursued hard after those who succeeded in getting past, and they did not give up but took some of them prisoners.

As a well-bred but untrained hound rushes recklessly upon a boar, so Cyrus rushed on, with regard

His reckless daring

μόνον ὁρῶν τὸ παίειν τὸν ἁλισκόμενον, ἄλλο δ' οὐδὲν προνοῶν.

Οἱ δὲ πολέμιοι ὡς ἑώρων πονοῦντας τοὺς σφετέρους, προυκίνησαν τὸ στῖφος, ὡς παυσομένους τοῦ διωγμοῦ, ἐπεὶ σφᾶς ἴδοιεν προορμήσαντας. 22. ὁ δὲ Κῦρος οὐδὲν μᾶλλον ἀνίει,[1] ἀλλ' ὑπὸ τῆς χαρμονῆς ἀνακαλῶν τὸν θεῖον ἐδίωκε καὶ ἰσχυρὰν τὴν φυγὴν τοῖς πολεμίοις κατέχων ἐποίει, καὶ ὁ Κυαξάρης μέντοι ἐφείπετο, ἴσως καὶ αἰσχυνόμενος τὸν πατέρα, καὶ οἱ ἄλλοι δὲ εἵποντο, προθυμότεροι ὄντες ἐν τῷ τοιούτῳ εἰς τὸ διώκειν καὶ οἱ μὴ πάνυ πρὸς τοὺς ἐναντίους ἄλκιμοι ὄντες.

Ὁ δὲ Ἀστυάγης ὡς ἑώρα τοὺς μὲν ἀπρονοήτως διώκοντας, τοὺς δὲ πολεμίους ἀθρόους τε καὶ τεταγμένους ὑπαντῶντας, δείσας περί τε τοῦ υἱοῦ καὶ τοῦ Κύρου μὴ εἰς παρεσκευασμένους ἀτάκτως ἐμπεσόντες πάθοιέν τι, ἡγεῖτο εὐθὺς πρὸς τοὺς πολεμίους.

23. Οἱ δ' αὖ πολέμιοι ὡς εἶδον τοὺς Μήδους προκινηθέντας, διατεινάμενοι οἱ μὲν τὰ παλτὰ οἱ δὲ τὰ τόξα εἱστήκεσαν, ὡς αὖ, ἐπειδὴ[2] εἰς τόξευμα ἀφίκοιντο, στησομένους, ὥσπερ τὰ πλεῖστα εἰώθεσαν ποιεῖν. μέχρι γὰρ τοσούτου, ὁπότε ἐγγύτατα γένοιντο, προσήλαυνον ἀλλήλοις καὶ ἠκροβολίζοντο πολλάκις μέχρι ἑσπέρας. ἐπεὶ δὲ ἑώρων τοὺς μὲν σφετέρους φυγῇ εἰς ἑαυτοὺς φερομένους, τοὺς δ' ἀμφὶ τὸν Κῦρον ἐπ' αὐτοὺς ὁμοῦ ἀγομένους, τὸν δὲ Ἀστυάγην σὺν τοῖς ἵπποις

[1] ἀνίει y, Edd.; ἀνιεὶς xzR.
[2] ὡς αὖ, ἐπειδὴ Hug; ὡς δή, ἐπειδὴ Marchant, Gemoll; ὡς ἂν ἐπειδὴ yRC²; ἀλλ' xz.

for nothing but to strike down every one he overtook and reckless of anything else.

The enemy, however, when they saw their comrades hard pressed, advanced their column in the hope that the Medes would give up the pursuit on seeing them push forward. 22. But none the more did Cyrus give over, but in his battle-joy he called to his uncle and continued the pursuit; and pressing on he put the enemy to headlong flight, and Cyaxares did not fail to follow, partly perhaps not to be shamed before his father; and the rest likewise followed, for under such circumstances they were more eager for the pursuit, even those who were not so very brave in the face of the enemy.

But when Astyages saw them pursuing recklessly and the enemy advancing in good order to meet them, he was afraid that something might happen to his son and Cyrus, if they fell in disorder upon the enemy in readiness for battle, and straightway he advanced upon the foe.

23. Now the enemy on their part, when they saw the Medes advance, halted, some with spears poised, others with bows drawn, expecting that the other side would also halt, as soon as they came within bow-shot, just as they were accustomed generally to do; for it was their habit to advance only so far against each other, when they came into closest quarters, and to skirmish with missiles, oftentimes till evening. But when they saw their comrades rushing in flight toward them, and Cyrus and his followers bearing down close upon them, and Astyages with his cavalry getting already within

ἐντὸς γιγνόμενον ἤδη τοξεύματος, ἐκκλίνουσι καὶ φεύγουσιν ὁμόθεν διώκοντας ἀνὰ κράτος.

Ἥιρουν δὲ πολλούς· καὶ τοὺς μὲν ἁλισκομένους ἔπαιον καὶ ἵππους καὶ ἄνδρας, τοὺς δὲ πίπτοντας κατέκαινον· καὶ οὐ πρόσθεν ἔστησαν πρὶν[1] πρὸς τοῖς πεζοῖς τῶν Ἀσσυρίων ἐγένοντο. ἐνταῦθα μέντοι δείσαντες μὴ καὶ ἐνέδρα τις μείζων ὑπείη, ἐπέσχον.

24. Ἐκ τούτου δὴ ἀνῆγεν ὁ Ἀστυάγης, μάλα χαίρων καὶ τῇ ἱπποκρατίᾳ, καὶ τὸν Κῦρον οὐκ ἔχων ὅ τι χρὴ λέγειν, αἴτιον μὲν ὄντα εἰδὼς τοῦ ἔργου, μαινόμενον δὲ γιγνώσκων τῇ τόλμῃ. καὶ γὰρ τότε ἀπιόντων οἴκαδε μόνος τῶν ἄλλων ἐκεῖνος οὐδὲν ἄλλο ἢ τοὺς πεπτωκότας περιελαύνων ἐθεᾶτο, καὶ μόλις αὐτὸν ἀφελκύσαντες οἱ ἐπὶ τοῦτο ταχθέντες προσήγαγον τῷ Ἀστυάγει, μάλα ἐπίπροσθεν ποιούμενον τοὺς προσάγοντας, ὅτι ἑώρα τὸ πρόσωπον τοῦ πάππου ἠγριωμένον ἐπὶ τῇ θέᾳ τῇ αὐτοῦ.

25. Ἐν μὲν δὴ Μήδοις ταῦτα ἐγεγένητο, καὶ οἵ τε ἄλλοι πάντες τὸν Κῦρον διὰ στόματος εἶχον καὶ ἐν λόγῳ καὶ ἐν ᾠδαῖς, ὅ τε Ἀστυάγης καὶ πρόσθεν τιμῶν αὐτὸν τότε ὑπερεξεπέπληκτο ἐπ' αὐτῷ. Καμβύσης δὲ ὁ τοῦ Κύρου πατὴρ ἥδετο μὲν πυνθανόμενος ταῦτα, ἐπεὶ δ' ἤκουσεν ἔργα ἀνδρὸς ἤδη διαχειριζόμενον τὸν Κῦρον, ἀπεκάλει δή, ὅπως τὰ ἐν Πέρσαις ἐπιχώρια ἐπιτελοίη. καὶ ὁ Κῦρος δὲ ἐνταῦθα λέγεται εἰπεῖν ὅτι ἀπιέναι βούλοιτο, μὴ ὁ πατήρ τι ἄχθοιτο καὶ ἡ πόλις μέμφοιτο. καὶ τῷ

[1] πρὶν Dindorf, Hug; πρὶν ἢ MSS., Gemoll, Marchant, Breitenbach, et al.

bow-shot, they broke and fled with all their might from the Medes who followed hard after them.

The Medes caught up with many of them; and those whom they overtook they smote, both men and horses; and the fallen they slew. Nor did they stop, until they came up with the Assyrian infantry. Then, however, fearing lest some greater force might be lying in ambush, they came to a halt.

The victory due to him

24. Then Astyages marched back, greatly rejoicing over the victory of his cavalry but not knowing what to say of Cyrus; for though he realized that his grandson was responsible for the outcome, yet he recognized also that he was frenzied with daring. And of this there was further evidence; for, as the rest made their way homeward, he did nothing but ride around alone and gloat upon the slain, and only with difficulty did those who were detailed to do so succeed in dragging him away and taking him to Astyages; and as he came, he set his escort well before him, for he saw that his grandfather's face was angry because of his gloating upon them.

25. Such was his life in Media; and Cyrus was not only on the tongues of all the rest both in story and in song, but Astyages also, while he had esteemed him before, was now highly delighted with him. And Cambyses, Cyrus's father, was pleased to learn this. But when he heard that Cyrus was already performing a man's deeds, he summoned him home to complete the regular curriculum in Persia. And Cyrus also, we are told, said then that he wished to go home, in order that his father might not feel any displeasure nor the state be disposed to

Ἀστυάγει δὲ ἐδόκει εἶναι ἀναγκαῖον ἀποπέμπειν αὐτόν.

Ἔνθα δὴ ἵππους τε αὐτῷ δοὺς οὓς αὐτὸς ἐπεθύμει λαβεῖν καὶ ἄλλα συσκευάσας πολλὰ ἔπεμπε καὶ διὰ τὸ φιλεῖν αὐτὸν καὶ ἅμα ἐλπίδας ἔχων μεγάλας ἐν αὐτῷ ἄνδρα ἔσεσθαι ἱκανὸν καὶ φίλους ὠφελεῖν καὶ ἐχθροὺς ἀνιᾶν. ἀπιόντα δὲ τὸν Κῦρον προὔπεμπον ἅπαντες καὶ παῖδες [καὶ ἥλικες][1] καὶ ἄνδρες καὶ γέροντες ἐφ' ἵππων καὶ Ἀστυάγης αὐτός, καὶ οὐδένα ἔφασαν ὅντιν' οὐ δακρύοντ' ἀποστρέφεσθαι. 26. καὶ Κῦρον δὲ αὐτὸν λέγεται σὺν πολλοῖς δακρύοις ἀποχωρῆσαι. πολλὰ δὲ δῶρα διαδοῦναί φασιν αὐτὸν τοῖς ἡλικιώταις ὧν Ἀστυάγης αὐτῷ ἐδεδώκει, τέλος δὲ καὶ ἣν εἶχε στολὴν τὴν Μηδικὴν ἐκδύντα δοῦναι τινι [δῆλον ὅτι τούτῳ] ὃν[2] μάλιστα ἠσπάζετο. τοὺς μέντοι λαβόντας καὶ δεξαμένους τὰ δῶρα λέγεται Ἀστυάγει ἀπενεγκεῖν, Ἀστυάγην δὲ δεξάμενον Κύρῳ ἀποπέμψαι, τὸν δὲ πάλιν τε ἀποπέμψαι εἰς Μήδους καὶ εἰπεῖν, Εἰ βούλει, ὦ πάππε, ἐμὲ καὶ πάλιν ἰέναι ὡς σὲ μὴ αἰσχυνόμενον, ἔα ἔχειν εἴ τῴ τι ἐγὼ δέδωκα· Ἀστυάγην δὲ ταῦτα ἀκούσαντα ποιῆσαι ὥσπερ Κῦρος ἐπέστειλεν.

27. Εἰ δὲ δεῖ καὶ παιδικοῦ λόγου ἐπιμνησθῆναι, λέγεται, ὅτε Κῦρος ἀπῄει καὶ ἀπηλλάττοντο ἀπ' ἀλλήλων, τοὺς συγγενεῖς φιλοῦντας τῷ στόματι ἀποπέμπεσθαι αὐτὸν νόμῳ Περσικῷ· καὶ γὰρ νῦν ἔτι τοῦτο ποιοῦσι Πέρσαι· ἄνδρα δέ τινα τῶν

[1] [καὶ ἥλικες] Hug; καὶ ἥλικες Gemoll; [καὶ παῖδες] Marchant.

[2] [δῆλον ὅτι τούτῳ] ὃν Hug, Holden; δῆλον ὅτι τούτῳ ὃν y; δηλῶν ὅτι τοῦτον xzR, Dindorf, Breitenbach, et al.; δηλοῦνθ' ὅτι τοῦτον H. J. Müller, Gemoll, Marchant, et al.

riticise; and Astyages, too, thought it expedient to end him home.

So he let him go and not only gave him the horses that he desired to take, but he packed up many other things for him because of his love for him and also because he cherished high hopes that his grandson would be a man able both to help his friends and to give trouble to his enemies. And everybody, both boys and men, young and old, and Astyages himself, escorted him on horseback as he went, and they say that there was no one who turned back without tears. 26. And Cyrus also, it is said, departed very tearfully. And they say that he distributed as presents among his young friends many of the things that Astyages had given to him; and finally he took off the Median robe which he had on and gave it to one whom he loved very dearly. It is said, however, that those who received and accepted his presents carried them to Astyages, and Astyages received them and returned them to Cyrus; but Cyrus sent them back again to Media with this message: "If you wish me ever to come back to you again, grandfather, without having to be ashamed, permit those to whom I have given anything to keep it." And when Astyages heard this, he did as Cyrus's letter bade.

His return to Persia

27. Now, if we may relate a sentimental story, we are told that when Cyrus was going away and they were taking leave of one another, his kinsmen bade him good-bye, after the Persian custom, with a kiss upon his lips. And that custom has survived, for so the Persians do even to this day. Now a certain

A sentimental story

Μήδων μάλα καλὸν κἀγαθὸν ὄντα ἐκπεπλῆχθα
πολύν τινα χρόνον ἐπὶ τῷ κάλλει τοῦ Κύρου
ἡνίκα δὲ ἑώρα τοὺς συγγενεῖς φιλοῦντας αὐτόν
ὑπολειφθῆναι· ἐπεὶ δ' οἱ ἄλλοι ἀπῆλθον, προσελ
θεῖν τῷ Κύρῳ καὶ εἰπεῖν, Ἐμὲ μόνον οὐ γιγνώ
σκεις τῶν συγγενῶν, ὦ Κῦρε;

Τί δέ, εἰπεῖν τὸν Κῦρον, ἦ καὶ σὺ συγγενὴς εἶ;

Μάλιστα, φάναι.

Ταῦτ' ἄρα, εἰπεῖν τὸν Κῦρον, καὶ ἐνεώρας[1] μοι
πολλάκις γὰρ δοκῶ σε γιγνώσκειν τοῦτο ποιοῦντα

Προσελθεῖν γάρ σοι, ἔφη, ἀεὶ βουλόμενος να
μὰ τοὺς θεοὺς ᾐσχυνόμην.

Ἀλλ' οὐκ ἔδει, φάναι τὸν Κῦρον, συγγενῆ γ
ὄντα· ἅμα δὲ προσελθόντα φιλῆσαι αὐτόν.

28. Καὶ τὸν Μῆδον φιληθέντα ἐρέσθαι, Ἦ κα
ἐν Πέρσαις νόμος ἐστὶν οὗτος συγγενεῖς φιλεῖν;

Μάλιστα, φάναι, ὅταν γε ἴδωσιν ἀλλήλους διὰ
χρόνου ἢ ἀπίωσί ποι ἀπ' ἀλλήλων.

Ὥρα ἂν εἴη, ἔφη ὁ Μῆδος, μάλα πάλιν σε
φιλεῖν ἐμέ· ἀπέρχομαι γάρ, ὡς ὁρᾷς, ἤδη.

Οὕτω καὶ τὸν Κῦρον φιλήσαντα πάλιν ἀποπέμπειν καὶ ἀπιέναι. καὶ ὁδόν τε οὔπω πολλὴν
διηνύσθαι[2] αὐτοῖς καὶ τὸν Μῆδον ἥκειν πάλιν

[1] ἐνεώρας y, Edd.; ἐνορᾷς xzR.
[2] διηνύσθαι R, Edd.; διερύσθαι xz; διεληλύσθαι y.

Median gentleman, very noble, had for some considerable time been struck with Cyrus's beauty, and when he saw the boy's kinsmen kissing him, he hung back. But when the rest were gone, he came up to Cyrus and said: "Am I the only one of your kinsmen, Cyrus, whom you do not recognize as such?"

"What," said Cyrus, "do you mean to say that you, too, are a kinsman?"

"Certainly," said he.

"That is the reason, then, it seems," said Cyrus, "why you used to stare at me; for if I am not mistaken, I have often noticed you doing so."

"Yes," said he, "for though I was always desirous of coming to you, by the gods I was too bashful."

"Well, you ought not to have been—at any rate, if you were my kinsman," said Cyrus; and at the same time he went up and kissed him.

28. And when he had been given the kiss, the Mede asked: "Really, is it a custom in Persia to kiss one's kinsfolk?"

"Certainly," said he; "at least, when they see one another after a time of separation, or when they part from one another."

"It may be time, then, for you to kiss me once again," said the Mede; "for, as you see, I am parting from you now."

And so Cyrus kissed him good-bye again and went on his way. But they had not yet gone far, when the Mede came back with his horse in a

ἱδροῦντι τῷ ἵππῳ· καὶ τὸν Κῦρον ἰδόντα, Ἀλλ' ἦ, φάναι, ἐπελάθου τι ὧν ἐβούλου εἰπεῖν;

Μὰ Δία, φάναι, ἀλλ' ἥκω διὰ χρόνου.

Καὶ τὸν Κῦρον εἰπεῖν, Νὴ Δί', ὦ σύγγενες, δι' ὀλίγου γε.

Ποίου ὀλίγου; εἰπεῖν τὸν Μῆδον. οὐκ οἶσθα, φάναι, ὦ Κῦρε, ὅτι καὶ ὅσον σκαρδαμύττω χρόνον, πάνυ πολύς μοι δοκεῖ εἶναι, ὅτι οὐχ ὁρῶ σε τότε τοιοῦτον ὄντα;

Ἐνταῦθα δὴ τὸν Κῦρον γελάσαι τε ἐκ τῶν ἔμπροσθεν δακρύων καὶ εἰπεῖν αὐτῷ θαρρεῖν ἀπιόντι, ὅτι παρέσται αὐτοῖς ὀλίγου χρόνου, ὥστε ὁρᾶν ἐξέσται κἂν βούληται ἀσκαρδαμυκτί.

V

1. Ὁ μὲν δὴ Κῦρος οὕτως ἀπελθὼν ἐν Πέρσαις ἐνιαυτὸν λέγεται ἐν τοῖς παισὶν ἔτι γενέσθαι. καὶ τὸ μὲν πρῶτον οἱ παῖδες ἔσκωπτον αὐτὸν ὡς ἡδυπαθεῖν ἐν Μήδοις μεμαθηκὼς ἥκοι· ἐπεὶ δὲ καὶ ἐσθίοντα αὐτὸν ἑώρων ὥσπερ καὶ αὐτοὶ ἡδέως καὶ πίνοντα, καὶ εἴ ποτ' ἐν ἑορτῇ εὐωχία γένοιτο, ἐπιδιδόντα μᾶλλον αὐτὸν τοῦ ἑαυτοῦ μέρους ᾐσθάνοντο ἢ προσδεόμενον, καὶ πρὸς τούτοις δὲ τἆλλα κρατιστεύοντα αὐτὸν ἑώρων ἑαυτῶν, ἐνταῦθα δὴ πάλιν ὑπέπτησσον αὐτῷ οἱ ἥλικες.

Ἐπεὶ δὲ διελθὼν τὴν παιδείαν ταύτην ἤδη εἰσῆλθεν εἰς τοὺς ἐφήβους, ἐν τούτοις αὖ ἐδόκει

lather. And when Cyrus saw him he said: "Why, how now? Did you forget something that you intended to say?"

"No, by Zeus," said he, "but I have come back after a time of separation."

"By Zeus, cousin," said Cyrus, "a pretty short time."

"Short, is it?" said the Mede; "don't you know, Cyrus," said he, "that even the time it takes me to wink seems an eternity to me, because during that time I do not see you, who are so handsome?"

Then Cyrus laughed through his tears and bade him go and be of good cheer, for in a little while he would come back to them, so that he might soon look at him—without winking, if he chose.

V

1. Now when Cyrus had returned, as before narrated, he is said to have spent one more year in the class of boys in Persia. And at first the boys were inclined to make fun of him, saying that he had come back after having learned to live a life of luxurious ease among the Medes. But when they saw him eating and drinking with no less relish than they themselves, and, if there ever was feasting at any celebration, freely giving away a part of his own share rather than asking for more; and when, in addition to this, they saw him surpassing them in other things as well, then again his comrades began to have proper respect for him.

Cyrus resumes his education in Persia

And when he had passed through this discipline and had now entered the class of the youths, among these

κρατιστεύειν καὶ μελετῶν ἃ χρῆν[1] καὶ καρτερῶν καὶ αἰδούμενος τοὺς πρεσβυτέρους καὶ πειθόμενος τοῖς ἄρχουσι.

2. Προϊόντος δὲ τοῦ χρόνου ὁ μὲν Ἀστυάγης ἐν τοῖς Μήδοις ἀποθνήσκει, ὁ δὲ Κυαξάρης ὁ τοῦ Ἀστυάγους παῖς, τῆς δὲ Κύρου μητρὸς ἀδελφός, τὴν βασιλείαν ἔσχε τὴν Μήδων.

Ὁ δὲ τῶν Ἀσσυρίων βασιλεὺς κατεστραμμένος μὲν πάντας Σύρους, φῦλον πάμπολυ, ὑπήκοον δὲ πεποιημένος τὸν Ἀραβίων βασιλέα, ὑπηκόους δὲ ἔχων ἤδη καὶ Ὑρκανίους, πολιορκῶν δὲ καὶ Βακτρίους, ἐνόμιζεν, εἰ τοὺς Μήδους ἀσθενεῖς ποιήσειε, πάντων γε τῶν πέριξ ῥᾳδίως ἄρξειν· ἰσχυρότατον γὰρ τῶν ἐγγὺς φύλων τοῦτο ἐδόκει εἶναι. 3. οὕτω δὴ διαπέμπει πρός τε τοὺς ὑπ᾿ αὐτὸν πάντας καὶ πρὸς Κροῖσον τὸν Λυδῶν βασιλέα καὶ πρὸς τὸν Καππαδοκῶν καὶ πρὸς Φρύγας ἀμφοτέρους καὶ πρὸς Παφλαγόνας καὶ Ἰνδοὺς καὶ πρὸς Κᾶρας καὶ Κίλικας, τὰ μὲν καὶ διαβάλλων τοὺς Μήδους καὶ Πέρσας, λέγων ὡς μεγάλα τ᾿ εἴη ταῦτα ἔθνη καὶ ἰσχυρὰ καὶ συνεστηκότα εἰς ταὐτό, καὶ ἐπιγαμίας ἀλλήλοις πεποιημένοι εἶεν, καὶ κινδυνεύσοιεν, εἰ μή τις αὐτοὺς φθάσας ἀσθενώσοι, ἐπὶ ἓν ἕκαστον τῶν ἐθνῶν ἰόντες καταστρέψασθαι. οἱ μὲν δὴ καὶ τοῖς λόγοις τούτοις πειθόμενοι συμμαχίαν αὐτῷ ἐποιοῦντο, οἱ δὲ καὶ δώροις καὶ χρήμασιν ἀναπειθόμενοι· πολλὰ γὰρ καὶ τοιαῦτα ἦν αὐτῷ.

4. Κυαξάρης δὲ [ὁ τοῦ Ἀστυάγους παῖς][2] ἐπεὶ ᾐσθάνετο τήν τ᾿ ἐπιβουλὴν καὶ τὴν παρασκευὴν

[1] χρῆν Zeune, Edd.; χρὴ MSS.
[2] ὁ . . . παῖς MSS., Dindorf; bracketed by Hug, Gemoll, Marchant, Breitenbach, et al.

n turn he had the reputation of being the best both n attending to duty and in endurance, in respect oward his elders and in obedience to the officers.

2. In the course of time Astyages died in Media, and Cyaxares, the son of Astyages and brother of Cyrus's mother, succeeded to the Median throne.

Assyria's plans for world-conquest

At that time the king of Assyria had subjugated all Syria, a very large nation, and had made the king of Arabia his vassal; he already had Hyrcania under his dominion and was closely besetting Bactria. So he thought that if he should break the power of the Medes, he should easily obtain dominion over all the nations round about; for he considered the Medes the strongest of the neighbouring tribes. 3. Accordingly, he sent around to all those under his sway and to Croesus, the king of Lydia, to the king of Cappadocia; to both Phrygias, to Paphlagonia, India, Caria, and Cilicia; and to a certain extent also he misrepresented the Medes and Persians, for he said that they were great, powerful nations, that they had intermarried with each other, and were united in common interests, and that unless some one attacked them first and broke their power, they would be likely to make war upon each one of the nations singly and subjugate them. Some, then, entered into an alliance with him because they actually believed what he said; others, because they were bribed with gifts and money, for he had great wealth.

The Medes and Persians

4. Now when Cyaxares heard of the plot and of the warlike preparations of the nations allied against

τῶν συνισταμένων ἐφ' ἑαυτόν, αὐτός τε εὐθέως ὅσα
ἐδύνατο ἀντιπαρεσκευάζετο καὶ εἰς Πέρσας ἔπεμπε
πρός τε τὸ κοινὸν καὶ πρὸς Καμβύσην τὸν τὴν
ἀδελφὴν ἔχοντα καὶ βασιλεύοντα ἐν Πέρσαις·
ἔπεμπε δὲ καὶ πρὸς Κῦρον, δεόμενος αὐτοῦ πειρᾶσθαι ἄρχοντα ἐλθεῖν τῶν ἀνδρῶν, εἴ τινας
πέμποι στρατιώτας τὸ Περσῶν κοινόν. ἤδη γὰρ
καὶ ὁ Κῦρος διατετελεκὼς τὰ ἐν τοῖς ἐφήβοις δέκα
ἔτη ἐν τοῖς τελείοις ἀνδράσιν ἦν.

5. Οὕτω δὴ δεξαμένου τοῦ Κύρου οἱ βουλεύοντες
γεραίτεροι αἱροῦνται αὐτὸν ἄρχοντα τῆς εἰς Μήδους
στρατιᾶς. ἔδοσαν δὲ αὐτῷ καὶ προσελέσθαι διακο-
σίους τῶν ὁμοτίμων, τῶν δ' αὖ διακοσίων ἑκάστῳ
τέτταρας ἔδωκαν προσελέσθαι καὶ τούτους ἐκ τῶν
ὁμοτίμων· γίγνονται μὲν δὴ οὗτοι χίλιοι· τῶν δ'
αὖ χιλίων τούτων ἑκάστῳ ἔταξαν ἐκ τοῦ δήμου
τῶν Περσῶν δέκα μὲν πελταστὰς προσελέσθαι,
δέκα δὲ σφενδονήτας, δέκα δὲ τοξότας· καὶ οὕτως
ἐγένοντο μύριοι μὲν τοξόται, μύριοι δὲ πελτασταί,
μύριοι δὲ σφενδονῆται· χωρὶς δὲ τούτων οἱ χίλιοι
ὑπῆρχον. τοσαύτη μὲν δὴ στρατιὰ τῷ Κύρῳ
ἐδόθη.

6. Ἐπεὶ δὲ ᾑρέθη τάχιστα, ἤρχετο πρῶτον ἀπὸ
τῶν θεῶν· καλλιερησάμενος δὲ τότε προσῃρεῖτο
τοὺς διακοσίους· ἐπεὶ δὲ προσείλοντο καὶ οὗτοι δὴ
τοὺς τέτταρας ἕκαστοι, συνέλεξεν αὐτοὺς καὶ εἶπε
τότε πρῶτον ἐν αὐτοῖς τάδε·

7. Ἄνδρες φίλοι, ἐγὼ προσειλόμην[1] μὲν ὑμᾶς,
οὐ νῦν πρῶτον δοκιμάσας, ἀλλ' ἐκ παίδων ὁρῶν

[1] προσειλόμην yR, Hug; προειλόμην xz, other Edd.

him, without delay he made what counter preparations he could himself and also sent to Persia both to the general assembly and to his brother-in-law, Cambyses, who was king of Persia. And he sent word to Cyrus, too, asking him to try to come as commander of the men, in case the Persian state should send any troops. For Cyrus had by this time completed his ten years among the youths also and was now in the class of mature men.

make counter preparations

5. So Cyrus accepted the invitation, and the elders in council chose him commander of the expedition to Media. And they further permitted him to choose two hundred peers[1] to accompany him, and to each one of the two hundred peers in turn they gave authority to choose four more, these also from the peers. That made a thousand. And each one of the thousand in their turn they bade choose in addition from the common people of the Persians ten targeteers, ten slingers, and ten bowmen. That made ten thousand bowmen, ten thousand targeteers, and ten thousand slingers—not counting the original thousand. So large was the army given to Cyrus.

6. Now as soon as he was chosen, his first act was to consult the gods; and not till he had sacrificed and the omens were propitious, did he proceed to choose his two hundred men. And when these also had chosen each his four, he called them all together and then addressed them for the first time as follows:

7. "My friends, I have chosen you not because I now see your worth for the first time, but because

Cyrus addresses his troops

[1] The "peers," or "equals-in-honour," were so called because they enjoyed equality of rights in matters of education, politics, and offices of honour and distinction. See *Index*, *s.v.*

ὑμᾶς ἃ μὲν καλὰ ἡ πόλις νομίζει, προθύμως ταῦτα
ἐκπονοῦντας, ἃ δὲ αἰσχρὰ ἡγεῖται, παντελῶς τούτων ἀπεχομένους. ὧν δ' ἕνεκα αὐτός τε οὐκ ἄκων
εἰς τόδε τὸ τέλος κατέστην καὶ ὑμᾶς παρεκάλεσα
δηλῶσαι ὑμῖν βούλομαι.

8. Ἐγὼ γὰρ κατενόησα ὅτι οἱ πρόγονοι χείρονες
μὲν ἡμῶν οὐδὲν ἐγένοντο· ἀσκοῦντες γοῦν κἀκεῖνοι
διετέλεσαν ἅπερ ἔργα ἀρετῆς νομίζεται· ὅ τι
μέντοι προσεκτήσαντο τοιοῦτοι ὄντες ἢ τῷ τῶν
Περσῶν κοινῷ ἀγαθὸν ἢ αὐτοῖς, τοῦτ' οὐκέτι
δύναμαι ἰδεῖν. 9. καίτοι ἐγὼ οἶμαι οὐδεμίαν ἀρετὴν
ἀσκεῖσθαι ὑπ' ἀνθρώπων ὡς μηδὲν πλεῖον ἔχωσιν
οἱ ἐσθλοὶ γενόμενοι τῶν πονηρῶν, ἀλλ' οἵ τε τῶν
παραυτίκα ἡδονῶν ἀπεχόμενοι οὐχ ἵνα μηδέποτε
εὐφρανθῶσι, τοῦτο πράττουσιν, ἀλλ' ὡς διὰ ταύτην τὴν ἐγκράτειαν πολλαπλάσια εἰς τὸν ἔπειτα
χρόνον εὐφρανούμενοι οὕτω παρασκευάζονται· οἵ
τε λέγειν προθυμούμενοι δεινοὶ γενέσθαι οὐχ ἵνα
εὖ λέγοντες μηδέποτε παύσωνται, τοῦτο μελετῶ-
σιν, ἀλλ' ἐλπίζοντες τῷ λέγειν εὖ πείθοντες
ἀνθρώπους πολλὰ καὶ μεγάλα ἀγαθὰ διαπράξε-
σθαι·[1] οἵ τε αὖ[2] τὰ πολεμικὰ ἀσκοῦντες οὐχ ὡς
μαχόμενοι μηδέποτε παύσωνται, τοῦτ' ἐκπονοῦσιν,
ἀλλὰ νομίζοντες καὶ οὗτοι τὰ πολεμικὰ ἀγαθοὶ
γενόμενοι πολὺν μὲν ὄλβον, πολλὴν δὲ εὐδαιμο-
νίαν, μεγάλας δὲ τιμὰς καὶ ἑαυτοῖς καὶ πόλει
περιάψειν.

10. Εἰ δέ τινες ταῦτα ἐκπονήσαντες πρίν τινα
καρπὸν ἀπ' αὐτῶν κομίσασθαι περιεῖδον αὐτοὺς
γήρᾳ ἀδυνάτους γενομένους, ὅμοιον ἔμοιγε δοκοῦσι

[1] διαπράξεσθαι my²g²R², Edd.; διαπράξασθαι xyzR.
[2] οἵ τε αὖ m y, Edd.; καὶ οἱ ταῦτα xzR.

I have observed that from your boyhood on you have been zealously following out all that the state considers right and abstaining altogether from all that it regards as wrong. As for myself, I wish to make known to you why I have not hesitated to assume this office and why I have invited you to join me.

8. "I have come to realize that our forefathers were no whit worse than we. At any rate, they also spent their time in practising what are considered the works of virtue. However, what they gained by being what they were, either for the commonwealth of the Persians or for themselves, I can by no means discover. 9. And yet I think that no virtue is practised by men except with the aim that the good, by being such, may have something more than the bad; and I believe that those who abstain from present pleasures do this not that they may never enjoy themselves, but by this self-restraint they prepare themselves to have many times greater enjoyment in time to come. And those who are eager to become able speakers study oratory, not that they may never cease from speaking eloquently, but in the hope that by their eloquence they may persuade men and accomplish great good. And those also who practise military science undergo this labour, not that they may never cease from fighting, but because they think that by gaining proficiency in the arts of war they will secure great wealth and happiness and honour both for themselves and for their country.

The folly of wasting effort

10. "But when men go through all this toil and then allow themselves to become old and feeble before they reap any fruit of their labours, they

πεπονθέναι οἷον εἴ τις γεωργὸς ἀγαθὸς προθυμηθεὶς γενέσθαι καὶ εὖ σπείρων καὶ εὖ φυτεύων, ὁπότε καρποῦσθαι ταῦτα δέοι, ἐῴη τὸν καρπὸν ἀσυγκόμιστον εἰς τὴν γῆν πάλιν καταρρεῖν. καὶ εἴ τίς γε ἀσκητὴς πολλὰ πονήσας καὶ ἀξιόνικος γενόμενος ἀναγώνιστος διατελέσειεν, οὐδ' ἂν οὗτός μοι δοκεῖ δικαίως ἀναίτιος εἶναι ἀφροσύνης. 11. ἀλλ' ἡμεῖς, ὦ ἄνδρες, μὴ πάθωμεν ταῦτα, ἀλλ' ἐπείπερ σύνισμεν ἡμῖν αὐτοῖς ἀπὸ παίδων ἀρξάμενοι ἀσκηταὶ ὄντες τῶν καλῶν κἀγαθῶν ἔργων, ἴωμεν ἐπὶ τοὺς πολεμίους, οὓς ἐγὼ σαφῶς ἐπίσταμαι ἰδιώτας ὄντας ὡς πρὸς ἡμᾶς ἀγωνίζεσθαι. οὐ γάρ πω οὗτοι ἱκανοί εἰσιν ἀγωνισταί, οἳ ἂν τοξεύωσι καὶ ἀκοντίζωσι καὶ ἱππεύωσιν ἐπιστημόνως, ἢν δέ που πονῆσαι δέῃ, τούτῳ λείπωνται, ἀλλ' οὗτοι ἰδιῶταί εἰσι κατὰ τοὺς πόνους· οὐδέ γε οἵτινες ἀγρυπνῆσαι δέον ἡττῶνται τούτου, ἀλλὰ καὶ οὗτοι ἰδιῶται κατὰ τὸν ὕπνον· οὐδέ γε οἱ ταῦτα μὲν ἱκανοί, ἀπαίδευτοι δὲ ὡς χρὴ καὶ συμμάχοις καὶ πολεμίοις χρῆσθαι, ἀλλὰ καὶ οὗτοι δῆλον ὡς τῶν μεγίστων παιδευμάτων ἀπείρως ἔχουσιν.

12. Ὑμεῖς δὲ νυκτὶ μὲν δήπου ὅσαπερ οἱ ἄλλοι ἡμέρᾳ δύναισθ' ἂν[1] χρῆσθαι, πόνους δὲ τοῦ ζῆν ἡδέως ἡγεμόνας νομίζετε, λιμῷ δὲ ὅσαπερ ὄψῳ διαχρῆσθε, ὑδροποσίαν δὲ ῥᾷον τῶν λεόντων φέρετε, κάλλιστον δὲ πάντων καὶ πολεμικώτατον

[1] δύναισθ' ἂν xzR, Edd. ; δύνασθε m y (*you can*).

seem to me at least to be like a man who, anxious to become a good farmer, should sow and plant well but, when harvest-time came, should permit his crop to fall back again to the ground ungathered. And again, if an athlete after long training and after getting himself in condition to win a victory should then persist in refusing to compete, not even he, I ween, would rightly be considered guiltless of folly. 11. But, fellow-soldiers, let us not make this mistake; but, conscious that from our boyhood on we have practised what is good and honourable, let us go against the enemy, who, I am sure, are too untrained to contend against us. For those men are not yet valiant warriors, who, however skilful in the use of bow or spear and in horsemanship, are still found wanting if it is ever necessary to suffer hardship; such persons are mere tiros when it comes to hardships. Nor are those men valiant warriors, who are found wanting when it is necessary to keep awake; but these also are mere tiros in the face of sleep. Nor yet are those men valiant warriors, who have these qualifications but have not been taught how they ought to treat comrades and how to treat enemies, but it is evident that they also are unacquainted with the most important branches of education.

The superior advantages of Persian discipline

12. "Now you, I take it, could make use of the night just as others do of the day; and you consider toil the guide to a happy life; hunger you use regularly as a sauce, and you endure drinking plain water more readily than lions do, while you have stored up in your souls that best

κτῆμα εἰς τὰς ψυχὰς συγκεκόμισθε· ἐπαινούμενο γὰρ μᾶλλον ἢ τοῖς ἄλλοις ἅπασι χαίρετε. τοὺς ἐ ἐπαίνου ἐραστὰς ἀνάγκη[1] διὰ τοῦτο πάντα μὲ πόνον, πάντα δὲ κίνδυνον ἡδέως ὑποδύεσθαι.[2]

13. Εἰ δὲ ταῦτα ἐγὼ λέγω περὶ ὑμῶν ἄλλη γι γνώσκων, ἐμαυτὸν ἐξαπατῶ. ὅ τι γὰρ μὴ τοιοῦτο ἀποβήσεται παρ' ὑμῶν, εἰς ἐμὲ τὸ ἐλλεῖπον ἥξει ἀλλὰ πιστεύω τοι τῇ πείρᾳ καὶ τῇ ὑμῶν εἰς ἐμ εὐνοίᾳ καὶ τῇ τῶν πολεμίων ἀνοίᾳ μὴ ψεύσειν μ ταύτας τὰς ἀγαθὰς ἐλπίδας. ἀλλὰ θαρροῦντες ὁρ μώμεθα, ἐπειδὴ καὶ ἐκποδὼν ἡμῖν γεγένηται τ δόξαι τῶν ἀλλοτρίων ἀδίκως ἐφίεσθαι. νῦν γὰ ἔρχονται μὲν οἱ πολέμιοι ἄρχοντες ἀδίκων χειρῶν καλοῦσι δὲ ἡμᾶς ἐπικούρους οἱ φίλοι· τί οὖν ἐστι ἢ τοῦ ἀλέξασθαι δικαιότερον ἢ τοῦ τοῖς φίλοι ἀρήγειν κάλλιον;

14. Ἀλλὰ μὴν κἀκεῖνο οἶμαι ὑμᾶς θαρρεῖν, τ μὴ παρημεληκότα με τῶν θεῶν τὴν ἔξοδον ποιεῖ σθαι· πολλὰ γάρ μοι συνόντες ἐπίστασθε οὐ μόνο τὰ μεγάλα ἀλλὰ καὶ τὰ μικρὰ πειρώμενον ἀεὶ ἀπ θεῶν ὁρμᾶσθαι.

Τέλος εἶπε, Τί δεῖ ἔτι λέγειν; ἀλλ' ὑμεῖς μὲ τοὺς ἄνδρας ἑλόμενοι καὶ ἀναλαβόντες καὶ τἄλλα παρασκευασάμενοι ἴτε εἰς Μήδους· ἐγὼ δ' ἐπανελ θὼν πρὸς τὸν πατέρα πρόειμι δή, ὅπως τὰ τῶ πολεμίων ὡς τάχιστα μαθὼν οἷά ἐστι παρασκευά

[1] After ἀνάγκη AEGH[2] add κτᾶσθαι τὰ αἴτια.

[2] ὑποδύεσθαι xyR; ὑποδύεσθαι z and ε (above the line) ἀνάγκη κτᾶσθαι τὰ αἴτια. διὰ τοῦτο . . . ὑποδύεσθε Dindorf.

f all possessions and the one most suitable to war: mean, you enjoy praise more than anything else; nd lovers of praise must for this reason gladly ndergo every sort of hardship and every sort of anger.

13. "Now if I say this concerning you while I elieve the contrary to be true, I deceive myself tterly. For if any of these qualities shall fail o be forthcoming in you, the loss will fall on ne. But I feel confident, you see, both from ny own experience and from your good-will toward ne and from the ignorance of the enemy that hese sanguine hopes will not deceive me. So et us set out with good heart, since we are free rom the suspicion of even seeming to aim unjustly t other men's possessions. For, as it is, the enemy re coming, aggressors in wrong, and our friends re calling us to their assistance. What, then, is nore justifiable than to defend oneself, or what nore noble than to assist one's friends?

14. "This, moreover, will, I think, strengthen our confidence: I have not neglected the gods s we embark upon this expedition. For you have een with me enough to know that not only in great things but also in small I always try to begin vith the approval of the gods.

"What more need I add?" he said in closing. "Choose you your men and get them together, and vhen you have made the necessary preparations ome on to Media. As for myself, I will first return o my father and then go on ahead of you, to learn s soon as possible what the plans of the enemy are nd to make what preparations I may require, in

ζωμαι ὅ τι ἂν δέωμαι, ὅπως ὡς κάλλιστα σὺν θε
ἀγωνιζώμεθα.

Οἱ μὲν δὴ ταῦτα ἔπραττον.

VI

1. Κῦρος δὲ ἐλθὼν οἴκαδε καὶ προσευξάμενο
Ἑστίᾳ πατρῴᾳ καὶ Διὶ πατρῴῳ καὶ τοῖς ἄλλοι
θεοῖς ὡρμᾶτο ἐπὶ τὴν στρατείαν, συμπρούπεμπ
δὲ αὐτὸν καὶ ὁ πατήρ. ἐπεὶ δὲ ἔξω τῆς οἰκία
ἐγένοντο, λέγονται ἀστραπαὶ καὶ βρονταὶ αὐτῷ
αἴσιοι γενέσθαι. τούτων δὲ φανέντων οὐδὲν ἄλλ
ἔτι οἰωνιζόμενοι ἐπορεύοντο, ὡς οὐδένα ἂν λύσαντα[1]
τὰ τοῦ μεγίστου θεοῦ σημεῖα. 2. προϊόντι δὲ τῷ
Κύρῳ ὁ πατὴρ ἤρχετο λόγου τοιοῦδε·

Ὦ παῖ, ὅτι μὲν οἱ θεοὶ ἵλεῴ τε καὶ εὐμενεῖ
πέμπουσί σε καὶ ἐν ἱεροῖς δῆλον καὶ ἐν οὐρανίοι
σημείοις· γιγνώσκεις δὲ καὶ αὐτός. ἐγὼ γάρ σ
ταῦτα ἐπίτηδες ἐδιδαξάμην, ὅπως μὴ δι' ἄλλων
ἑρμηνέων τὰς τῶν θεῶν συμβουλίας συνιείης,[2] ἀλλ
αὐτὸς καὶ ὁρῶν τὰ ὁρατὰ καὶ ἀκούων τὰ ἀκουστ
γιγνώσκοις καὶ μὴ ἐπὶ μάντεσιν εἴης, εἰ βούλοιντ
σε ἐξαπατᾶν ἕτερα λέγοντες ἢ τὰ παρὰ τῶν θεῶν
σημαινόμενα, μηδ' αὖ, εἴ ποτε ἄρα ἄνευ μάντεω

[1] οὐδένα ἂν λύσαντα GR, Marchant, Breitenbach; οὐδένα ἂ λήσαντα xAH (*no one would fail to see*); οὐδὲν ἄλλο αὔσαντ D (for ΛΥΣΑΝΤΑ); οὐδένα λήσοντα Dindorf; οὐδένα ἀγνοήσαντ Gemoll (*no one would fail to understand*).

[2] συνιείης Pantazides, Gemoll, Marchant, Breitenbach συν(ε)ίης MSS., Dindorf, et al.

·der that with God's help we may make as good a
ght as possible."

They, for their part, proceeded to do as he had
.id.

VI

1. Now, when Cyrus had gone home and prayed to
ıcestral Hestia, ancestral Zeus, and the rest of the
·ds, he set out upon his expedition; and his father
so joined in escorting him on his way. And when
ıey were out of the house, it is said to have thundered
ıd lightened with happy auspices for him; and when
ıis manifestation had been made, they proceeded,
ithout taking any further auspices, in the convic-
on that no one would make void the signs of the
ıpreme god. 2. Then, as they went on, his father
egan to speak to Cyrus on this wise:

The importance of divine omens

"My son, it is evident both from the sacrifices and
om the signs from the skies that the gods are
nding you forth with their grace and favour; and
ɔu yourself must recognize it, for I had you taught
ıis art on purpose that you might not have to learn
ıe counsels of the gods through others as inter-
reters, but that you yourself, both seeing what is to
e seen and hearing what is to be heard, might
nderstand; for I would not have you at the mercy
f the soothsayers, in case they should wish to
eceive you by saying other things than those
vealed by the gods; and furthermore, if ever you
ıould be without a soothsayer, I would not have
ɔu in doubt as to what to make of the divine

γενοιο, ἀποροῖο θείοις σημειοις ὅ τι χρῷο, ἀλλ
γιγνώσκων διὰ τῆς μαντικῆς τὰ παρὰ τῶν θεῶ
συμβουλευόμενα, τούτοις πείθοιο.

3. Καὶ μὲν δή, ὦ πάτερ, ἔφη ὁ Κῦρος, ὡς ἂ
ἵλεῴ οἱ θεοὶ ὄντες ἡμῖν συμβουλεύειν ἐθέλωσι
ὅσον δύναμαι κατὰ τὸν σὸν λόγον διατελῶ ἐπ
μελόμενος. μέμνημαι γάρ, ἔφη, ἀκούσας πο
σου ὅτι εἰκότως ἂν καὶ παρὰ θεῶν πρακτικώτερ
εἴη ὥσπερ καὶ παρ' ἀνθρώπων ὅστις μὴ ὁπότε
ἀπόροις εἴη, τότε κολακεύοι, ἀλλ' ὅτε τὰ ἄριστ
πράττοι, τότε μάλιστα τῶν θεῶν μεμνῆτο· κ
τῶν φίλων δ' ἔφησθα χρῆναι ὡσαύτως οὕτω
ἐπιμέλεσθαι.

4. Οὐκοῦν νῦν, ἔφη, ὦ παῖ, διά γ' ἐκείνα
τὰς ἐπιμελείας ἥδιον μὲν ἔρχει πρὸς τοὺς θεο
δεησόμενος, ἐλπίζεις δὲ μᾶλλον τεύξεσθαι ὧν ἂ
δέῃ, ὅτι συνειδέναι σαυτῷ δοκεῖς οὐπώποτ' ἀμ
λήσας αὐτῶν;

Πάνυ μὲν οὖν, ἔφη, ὦ πάτερ, ὡς πρὸς φίλου
μοι ὄντας τοὺς θεοὺς οὕτω διάκειμαι.

5. Τί γάρ, ἔφη, ὦ παῖ, μέμνησαι ἐκεῖνα
ποτε ἐδόκει ἡμῖν ὡς ἅπερ δεδώκασιν οἱ θε
μαθόντας ἀνθρώπους βέλτιον πράττειν ἢ ἀνεπ
στήμονας αὐτῶν ὄντας καὶ ἐργαζομένους μᾶλλ
ἀνύτειν ἢ ἀργοῦντας καὶ ἐπιμελομένους ἀσφαλ
στερον διάγειν[1] ἢ ἀφυλακτοῦντας, τούτων πέρ
παρέχοντας οὖν τοιούτους ἑαυτοὺς οἵους δε
οὕτως ἡμῖν ἐδόκει δεῖν καὶ αἰτεῖσθαι τἀγαθὰ παρ
τῶν θεῶν;

6. Ναὶ μὰ Δί', ἔφη ὁ Κῦρος, μέμνημαι μέ

[1] [ἂν] διάγειν Stephanus, Edd.; ἂν διάγειν MSS.
[2] πέρι Madvig, Hug; not in MSS.

revelations, but by your soothsayer's art I would have you understand the counsels of the gods and obey them."

3. "Aye, father," said Cyrus, "as you have taught me, I always try to take care, as far as I can, that the gods may be gracious unto us and willingly give us counsel; for I remember," said he, "having once heard you say that that man would be more likely to have power with the gods, even as with men, who did not fawn upon them when he was in adversity, but remembered the gods most of all when he was in the highest prosperity. And for one's friends also, you said, one ought always to show one's regard in precisely the same way."

The secret of power in prayer

4. "Well, my son," said he, "and owing to that very regard do you not come to the gods with a better heart to pray, and do you not expect more confidently to obtain what you pray for, because you feel conscious of never having neglected them?"

"Yes, indeed, father," said he; "I feel toward the gods as if they were my friends."

5. "To be sure," said his father; "and do you remember the conclusion which once we reached—that as people who know what the gods have granted fare better than those who do not; as people who work accomplish more than those who are idle; as people who are careful live more securely than those who are indifferent; so in this matter it seemed to us that those only who had made themselves what they ought to be had a right to ask for corresponding blessings from the gods?"

God helps those who help themselves

6. "Yes, by Zeus," said Cyrus; "I do indeed

τοι τοιαῦτα ἀκούσας σου· καὶ γὰρ ἀνάγκη με πείθεσθαι τῷ λόγῳ· καὶ γὰρ οἶδά σε λέγοντα ἀεὶ ὡς οὐδὲ θέμις εἴη αἰτεῖσθαι παρὰ τῶν θεῶν οὔτε ἱππεύειν μὴ μαθόντας ἱππομαχοῦντας νικᾶν, οὔτε μὴ ἐπισταμένους τοξεύειν τοξεύοντας κρατεῖν τῶν ἐπισταμένων, οὔτε μὴ ἐπισταμένους κυβερνᾶν σώζειν εὔχεσθαι ναῦς κυβερνῶντας, οὐδὲ μὴ σπείροντάς γε σῖτον εὔχεσθαι καλὸν αὐτοῖς φύεσθαι, οὐδὲ μὴ φυλαττομένους γε ἐν πολέμῳ σωτηρίαν αἰτεῖσθαι· παρὰ γὰρ τοὺς τῶν θεῶν θεσμοὺς πάντα τὰ τοιαῦτα εἶναι· τοὺς δὲ ἀθέμιτα εὐχομένους ὁμοίως ἔφησθα εἰκὸς εἶναι παρὰ θεῶν ἀτυχεῖν ὥσπερ καὶ παρὰ ἀνθρώπων ἀπρακτεῖν τοὺς παράνομα δεομένους.

7. Ἐκείνων δέ, ὦ παῖ, ἐπελάθου ἅ ποτε ἐγὼ καὶ σὺ ἐλογιζόμεθα ὡς ἱκανὸν εἴη καὶ καλὸν ἀνδρὶ ἔργον, εἴ τις δύναιτο ἐπιμεληθῆναι ὅπως ἂν αὐτός τε καλὸς κἀγαθὸς δοκίμως γένοιτο καὶ τἀπιτήδεια αὐτός τε καὶ οἱ οἰκέται ἱκανῶς ἔχοιεν; τὸ δέ, τούτου μεγάλου ἔργου ὄντος, οὕτως ἐπίστασθαι ἀνθρώπων ἄλλων προστατεύειν ὅπως ἕξουσι πάντα τἀπιτήδεια ἔκπλεω καὶ ὅπως ἔσονται πάντες οἵους δεῖ, τοῦτο θαυμαστὸν δήπου ἡμῖν ἐφαίνετο εἶναι.

8. Ναὶ μὰ Δί', ἔφη, ὦ πάτερ, μέμνημαι καὶ τοῦτό σου λέγοντος· συνεδόκει οὖν καὶ ἐμοὶ ὑπερμέγεθες εἶναι ἔργον τὸ καλῶς ἄρχειν· καὶ νῦν γ', ἔφη, ταὐτά μοι δοκεῖ ταῦτα, ὅταν πρὸς αὐτὸ τὸ ἄρχειν σκοπῶν λογίζωμαι. ὅταν μέντοι

remember hearing you say so, and all the more because I could not help but agree with what you said. For I know that you always used to say that those who had not learned to ride had no right to ask the gods to give them victory in a cavalry battle; and those who did not know how to shoot had no right to ask to excel in marksmanship those who did know how; and those who did not know how to steer had no right to pray that they might save ships by taking the helm; neither had those who did not sow at all any right to pray for a fine crop, nor those who were not watchful in war to ask for preservation; for all that is contrary to the ordinances of the gods. You said, moreover, that it was quite as likely that those who prayed for what was not right should fail of success with the gods as that those who asked for what was contrary to human law should be disappointed at the hands of men."

The ruler's task

7. "But, my son, have you forgotten the discussion you and I once had—that it was a great task and one worthy of a man, to do the best he could not only to prove himself a truly good and noble man but also to provide a good living both for himself and his household? And while this was a great task, still, to understand how to govern other people so that they might have all the necessaries of life in abundance and might all become what they ought to be, this seemed to us worthy of all admiration."

8. "Yes, by Zeus, father," said he, "I do remember your saying this also; and I agreed with you, too, that it was an exceedingly difficult task to govern well; and now," said he, "I hold this same opinion still, when I consider the matter and think of the principles of governing. When I look at other people,

γε πρὸς ἄλλους ἀνθρώπους ἰδὼν κατανοήσω οἷοι ὄντες διαγίγνονται ἄρχοντες καὶ οἷοι ὄντες ἀνταγωνισταὶ ἡμῖν ἔσονται, πάνυ μοι δοκεῖ αἰσχρὸν εἶναι τὸ τοιούτους αὐτοὺς ὄντας ὑποπτῆξαι καὶ μὴ ἐθέλειν ἰέναι αὐτοῖς ἀνταγωνιουμένους· οὓς ἔφη, ἐγὼ αἰσθάνομαι ἀρξάμενος ἀπὸ τῶν ἡμετέρων φίλων τούτων ἡγουμένους δεῖν τὸν ἄρχοντα τῶν ἀρχομένων διαφέρειν τῷ καὶ πολυτελέστερον δειπνεῖν καὶ πλέον ἔχειν ἔνδον χρυσίον καὶ πλείονα χρόνον καθεύδειν καὶ πάντα ἀπονώτερον τῶν ἀρχομένων διάγειν. ἐγὼ δὲ οἶμαι, ἔφη, τὸν ἄρχοντα οὐ τῷ ῥᾳδιουργεῖν χρῆναι διαφέρειν τῶν ἀρχομένων, ἀλλὰ τῷ προνοεῖν καὶ φιλοπονεῖν.[1]

9. Ἀλλά τοι, ἔφη, ὦ παῖ, ἔνιά ἐστιν ἃ οὐ πρὸς ἀνθρώπους ἀγωνιστέον, ἀλλὰ πρὸς αὐτὰ τὰ πράγματα, ὧν οὐ ῥᾴδιον εὐπόρως περιγενέσθαι· αὐτίκα δήπου οἶσθα ὅτι εἰ μὴ ἕξει τἀπιτήδεια ἡ στρατιά, καταλελύσεταί[2] σου ἡ ἀρχή.

Οὐκοῦν ταῦτα μέν, ἔφη, ὦ πάτερ, Κυαξάρης φησὶ παρέξειν τοῖς ἐντεῦθεν ἰοῦσι πᾶσιν ὁπόσοι ἂν ὦσι.

Τούτοις δὴ σύ, ἔφη, ὦ παῖ, πιστεύων ἔρχει τοῖς παρὰ Κυαξάρου χρήμασιν;

Ἔγωγ᾽, ἔφη ὁ Κῦρος.

Τί δέ, ἔφη, οἶσθα ὁπόσα αὐτῷ ἔστι;

Μὰ τὸν Δί᾽, ἔφη ὁ Κῦρος, οὐ μὲν δή.

[1] φιλοπονεῖν y, Hug, Gemoll, Marchant, Breitenbach; φιλοπονεῖν προθυμούμενον xzRy², Dindorf.
[2] καταλελύσεται Cobet, Edd.; καταλύσεται MSS.

however, and observe what sort of men those are who, in spite of their character, continue to rule over them, and what sort of opponents we are going to have, it seems to me an utter disgrace to show any respect for such as they are and not to wish to go to fight them. To begin with our own friends here," he continued, "I observe that the Medes consider it necessary for the one who governs them to surpass the governed in greater sumptuousness of fare, in the possession of more money in his palace, in longer hours of sleep, and in a more luxurious manner of life, in every respect, than the governed. But I think," he added, "that the ruler ought to surpass those under his rule not in self-indulgence, but in taking forethought and willingly undergoing toil."

9. "But let me tell you, my boy," said the other, "there are some instances in which we must wrestle not against men but against actual facts, and it is not so easy to get the better of these without trouble. For instance, you doubtless know that if your army does not receive its rations, your authority will soon come to naught."

Supplies essential to success

"Yes, father," said he; "but Cyaxares says that he will furnish supplies for all who come from here, however many they be."

"But, my son," said he, "do you mean to say that you are marching out trusting to the funds at the command of Cyaxares?"

"Yes, I do," said Cyrus.

"But say," said his father, "do you know how much he has?"

"No, by Zeus," said Cyrus, "I know nothing about it."

Ὅμως δὲ τούτοις πιστεύεις τοῖς ἀδήλοις; ὅτι δὲ πολλῶν μὲν σοὶ δεήσει, πολλὰ δὲ καὶ ἄλλα νῦν ἀνάγκη δαπανᾶν ἐκεῖνον, οὐ γιγνώσκεις;[1]

Γιγνώσκω, ἔφη ὁ Κῦρος.

Ἢν οὖν, ἔφη, ἐπιλίπῃ αὐτὸν ἡ δαπάνη ἢ καὶ ἑκὼν ψεύσηται, πῶς σοι ἕξει τὰ τῆς στρατιᾶς;

Δῆλον ὅτι οὐ καλῶς. ἀτάρ, ἔφη, ὦ πάτερ, σὺ εἰ ἐνορᾷς τινα πόρον καὶ ἀπ' ἐμοῦ ἂν προσγενόμενον, ἕως ἔτι ἐν φιλίᾳ ἐσμέν, λέγε.

10. Ἐρωτᾷς, ἔφη, ὦ παῖ, ποῦ ἂν ἀπὸ σοῦ πόρος προσγένοιτο; ἀπὸ τίνος δὲ μᾶλλον εἰκός ἐστι πόρον γενέσθαι ἢ ἀπὸ τοῦ δύναμιν ἔχοντος; σὺ δὲ πεζὴν μὲν δύναμιν ἐνθένδε ἔχων ἔρχει ἀνθ' ἧς οἶδ' ὅτι πολλαπλασίαν ἄλλην οὐκ ἂν δέξαιο, ἱππικὸν δέ σοι, ὅπερ κράτιστον, τὸ Μήδων σύμμαχον ἔσται. ποῖον οὖν ἔθνος τῶν πέριξ οὐ δοκεῖ σοι καὶ χαρίζεσθαι βουλόμενον ὑμῖν ὑπηρετήσειν καὶ φοβούμενον μή τι πάθῃ; ἃ χρή σε κοινῇ σὺν Κυαξάρῃ σκοπεῖσθαι μήποτε ἐπιλίπῃ τι ὑμᾶς ὧν δεῖ ὑπάρχειν, καὶ ἔθους δὲ ἕνεκα μηχανᾶσθαι προσόδου πόρον. τόδε δὲ πάντων μάλιστά μοι μέμνησο μηδέποτε ἀναμένειν τὸ πορίζεσθαι τἀπιτήδεια ἔστ' ἂν ἡ χρεία σε ἀναγκάσῃ· ἀλλ' ὅταν μάλιστα εὐπορῇς, τότε πρὸ τῆς ἀπορίας μηχανῶ. καὶ γὰρ τεύξει

[1] ἐκεῖνον, οὐ γιγνώσκεις H[1], Hug, Marchant, Breitenbach; αὐτόν, οὐ γ., yΠ, Gemoll; ἐκεῖνο οὐ γ. xAGR, Dindorf.

"And do you nevertheless trust to these uncertainties? And do you not know that you will need many things and that he must now have many other expenses?"

"Yes," said Cyrus, "I do."

"Well, then," said he, "if his resources fail or if he play you false on purpose, how will your army fare?"

"Evidently not very well; but father," said he, "if you have in mind any means that I might find at my own command for obtaining supplies, tell me about it, while we are still in a friendly country."

10. "Do you ask me, my son," said he, "where you might yourself find means? Where might you better look to find the means of obtaining supplies than to the one who has an army? Now you are marching out from here with a force of infantry which you would not exchange, I am sure, for any other though many time as large; and you will have for cavalry to support you the Median horse, the best cavalry troops in the world. What nation, then, of those around do you suppose will refuse to serve you, both from the wish to do your side a favour, and for fear of suffering harm? And therefore in common with Cyaxares you should take care that you may never be without any of the things you need to have, and as a matter of habit, too, contrive some means of revenue. And above all I beg you to remember this: never postpone procuring supplies until want compels you to it; but when you have the greatest abundance, then take measures against want. And this is most expedient; for you will obtain more from those upon whom you

μᾶλλον παρ' ὧν ἂν δέῃ μὴ ἄπορος δοκῶν εἶναι, καὶ ἔτι ἀναίτιος ἔσει παρὰ τοῖς σαυτοῦ στρατιώταις· ἐκ τούτου δὲ μᾶλλον καὶ ὑπ' ἄλλων αἰδοῦς τεύξει, καὶ ἤν τινας βούλῃ ἢ εὖ ποιῆσαι τῇ δυνάμει ἢ κακῶς, μᾶλλον ἕως ἂν ἔχωσι τὰ δέοντα οἱ στρατιῶται ὑπηρετήσουσί σοι, καὶ πειστικωτέρους, σάφ' ἴσθι, λόγους δυνήσει τότε λέγειν ὅτανπερ καὶ ἐνδείκνυσθαι μάλιστα δύνῃ καὶ εὖ ποιεῖν ἱκανὸς ὢν καὶ κακῶς.

11. Ἀλλ', ἔφη, ὦ πάτερ, ἄλλως τέ μοι καλῶς δοκεῖς ταῦτα λέγειν πάντα, καὶ ὅτι ὧν μὲν νῦν λέγονται λήψεσθαι οἱ στρατιῶται, οὐδεὶς αὐτῶν ἐμοὶ τούτων χάριν εἴσεται· ἴσασι γὰρ ἐφ' οἷς αὐτοὺς Κυαξάρης ἐπάγεται[1] συμμάχους· ὅ τι δ' ἂν πρὸς τοῖς εἰρημένοις λαμβάνῃ τις, ταῦτα καὶ τιμὴν νομιοῦσι καὶ χάριν τούτων εἰκὸς εἰδέναι τῷ διδόντι. τὸ δ' ἔχοντα δύναμιν ᾗ ἔστι μὲν φίλους εὖ ποιοῦντα ἀντωφελεῖσθαι, ἔστι δὲ ἐχθροὺς [ἔχοντα][2] πειρᾶσθαι τίσασθαι, ἔπειτ' ἀμελεῖν τοῦ πορίζεσθαι, οἴει τι, ἔφη, ἧττόν τι τοῦτο εἶναι αἰσχρὸν ἢ εἴ τις ἔχων μὲν ἀγρούς, ἔχων δὲ ἐργάτας οἷς ἂν ἐργάζοιτο, ἔπειτ' ἐῴη τὴν ἀργοῦσαν ἀνωφέλητον εἶναι; ὥς[3] γ' ἐμοῦ, ἔφη, μηδέποτε ἀμελήσοντος τοῦ τἀπιτήδεια τοῖς στρατιώταις συμμηχανᾶσθαι μήτ' ἐν φιλίᾳ μήτ' ἐν πολεμίᾳ οὕτως ἔχε τὴν γνώμην.

[1] ἐπάγεται Cobet, Hug, Marchant, Gemoll; ἄγεται MSS., Dindorf, Breitenbach, et al.
[2] [ἔχοντα] Madvig, Hug, Gemoll, Marchant; ἔχοντα MSS., Dindorf, Breitenbach.
[3] ὥς MSS.; Ὡς Edd., as if Cambyses spoke here.

make demands, if you do not seem to be in want, and besides you will thus be blameless in the eyes of your own soldiers; in this way, furthermore, you will command more respect from others also, and if you wish to do good or ill to any one with your forces, your soldiers will serve you better as long as they have what they need. And let me assure you that the words you say will have more more power to convince, when you can abundantly prove that you are in a position to do both good and ill."

11. "Well, father," said he, "it seems to me that you are right in all you say, both on other grounds and also because not one of my soldiers will be grateful to me for that which according to the agreement he is to receive; for they know on what terms Cyaxares is having them brought as his allies. But whatever any one receives in addition to what has been agreed upon, that he will consider as a reward, and he will probably be grateful to the giver. But for a man to have an army with which he may do good to his friends and get help in return and try to punish his enemies, and for him then to neglect to make due provision for it, do you think," said he, "that this is in any way less disgraceful than for a man to have fields and labourers to work them and after all to let his land lie idle and unprofitable? But," he added, "I, at any rate, shall not fail to provide supplies for my men, whether in a friendly or in a hostile land —you may be certain of that."

12. Τί γάρ, ἔφη, ὦ παῖ, τῶν ἄλλων, ὧν ἐδόκει ποθ' ἡμῖν ἀναγκαῖον εἶναι μὴ παραμελεῖν, ἦ μέμνησαι;

Εὖ[1] γάρ, ἔφη, μέμνημαι ὅτε ἐγὼ μὲν πρὸς σὲ ἦλθον ἐπ' ἀργύριον, ὅπως ἀποδοίην τῷ φάσκοντι στρατηγεῖν με πεπαιδευκέναι, σὺ δὲ ἅμα διδούς μοι ἐπηρώτας ὧδέ πως, Ἆρά γε, εἶπας, ὦ παῖ, ἐν τοῖς στρατηγικοῖς καὶ οἰκονομίας τί σοι ἐπεμνήσθη ὁ ἀνὴρ ᾧ τὸν μισθὸν φέρεις; οὐδὲν μέντοι ἧττον οἱ στρατιῶται τῶν ἐπιτηδείων δέονται ἢ οἱ ἐν οἴκῳ οἰκέται. ἐπεὶ δ' ἐγώ σοι λέγων τἀληθῆ εἶπον ὅτι οὐδ' ὁτιοῦν περὶ τούτου ἐπεμνήσθη, ἐπήρου με πάλιν εἴ τί μοι ὑγιείας πέρι ἢ ῥώμης ἔλεξεν, ὡς δεῆσον καὶ τούτων ὥσπερ καὶ τῆς στρατηγίας τὸν στρατηγὸν ἐπιμέλεσθαι. 13. ὡς δὲ καὶ ταῦτ' ἀπέφησα, ἐπήρου με αὖ πάλιν εἴ τινας τέχνας ἐδίδαξεν, αἳ[2] τῶν πολεμικῶν ἔργων κράτισται[3] ἂν σύμμαχοι γένοιντο. ἀποφήσαντός δέ μου καὶ τοῦτο ἀνέκρινας αὖ σὺ καὶ τόδε εἴ τί μ' ἐπαίδευσεν ὡς ἂν δυναίμην στρατιᾷ προθυμίαν ἐμβαλεῖν, λέγων ὅτι τὸ πᾶν διαφέρει ἐν παντὶ ἔργῳ προθυμία ἀθυμίας. ἐπεὶ δὲ καὶ τοῦτο ἀνένευον, ἤλεγχες αὖ σὺ εἴ τινα λόγον ποιήσαιτο διδάσκων περὶ τοῦ πείθεσθαι τὴν στρατιάν, ὡς ἄν τις μάλιστα μηχανῷτο. 14. ἐπεὶ δὲ καὶ τοῦτο παντάπασιν ἄρρητον ἐφαίνετο, τέλος δή μ' ἐπήρου ὅ τι ποτὲ διδάσκων

[1] εὖ Jacob, Hug, Gemoll; οὐ MSS. Dindorf, Marchant, Breitenbach.

[2] αἳ Pantazides, most Edd.; αἷς xz, Dindorf, et al.

[3] κράτισται Hertlein, most Edd.; κράτιστοι MSS., Dindorf, et al.

12. "Well then, my boy," said his father, "tell me, do you remember the other points which, we agreed, must not be neglected—eh?"

An incompetent teacher of military science

"Yes," said he, "I remember well when I came to you for money to pay to the man who professed to have taught me to be a general; and you, while you gave it me, asked a question something like this: 'Of course,' you said, 'the man to whom you are taking the pay has given you instruction in domestic economy as a part of the duties of a general, has he not? At any rate, the soldiers need provisions no whit less than the servants in your house.' And when I told you the truth and said that he had given me no instruction whatever in this subject, you asked me further whether he had said anything to me about health or strength, inasmuch as it would be requisite for the general to take thought for these matters as well as for the conduct of his campaign. 13. And when I said 'no' to this also, you asked me once more whether he had taught me any arts that would be the best helps in the business of war. And when I said 'no' to this as well, you put this further question, whether he had put me through any training so that I might be able to inspire my soldiers with enthusiasm, adding that in every project enthusiasm or faintheartedness made all the difference in the world. And when I shook my head in response to this likewise, you questioned me again whether he had given me any lessons to teach me how best to secure obedience on the part of an army. 14. And when this also appeared not to have

στρατηγίαν φαίη με διδάσκειν. κἀγὼ δὴ ἐνταῦθα ἀποκρίνομαι ὅτι τὰ τακτικά. καὶ σὺ γελάσας διῆλθές μοι παρατιθεὶς ἕκαστον τί εἴη ὄφελος στρατιᾷ τακτικῶν ἄνευ τῶν ἐπιτηδείων, τί δ' ἄνευ τοῦ ὑγιαίνειν, τί δ' ἄνευ τοῦ ἐπίστασθαι τὰς ηὑρημένας εἰς πόλεμον τέχνας, . . .[1] τί δ' ἄνευ τοῦ πείθεσθαι. ὡς δέ μοι καταφανὲς ἐποίησας ὅτι μικρόν τι μέρος εἴη στρατηγίας τὰ τακτικά, ἐπερομένου μου εἴ τι τούτων σύ με διδάξαι ἱκανὸς εἴης, ἀπιόντα με ἐκέλευσας τοῖς στρατηγικοῖς νομιζομένοις ἀνδράσι διαλέγεσθαι καὶ πυθέσθαι πῇ ἕκαστα τούτων γίγνεται. 15. ἐκ τούτου δὴ συνῆν τούτοις ἐγώ, οὓς μάλιστα φρονίμους περὶ τούτων ἤκουον εἶναι. καὶ περὶ μὲν τροφῆς ἐπείσθην ἱκανὸν εἶναι ὑπάρχον ὅ τι Κυαξάρης ἔμελλε παρέξειν ἡμῖν, περὶ δὲ ὑγιείας, ἀκούων καὶ ὁρῶν ὅτι καὶ πόλεις αἱ χρῄζουσαι ὑγιαίνειν ἰατροὺς αἱροῦνται καὶ οἱ στρατηγοὶ τῶν στρατιωτῶν ἕνεκεν ἰατροὺς ἐξάγουσιν, οὕτω καὶ ἐγὼ ἐπεὶ ἐν τῷ τέλει τούτῳ ἐγενόμην, εὐθὺς τούτου ἐπεμελήθην, καὶ οἶμαι, ἔφη, ὦ πάτερ, πάνυ ἱκανοὺς τὴν ἰατρικὴν τέχνην ἕξειν μετ' ἐμαυτοῦ ἄνδρας.

16. Πρὸς ταῦτα δὴ ὁ πατὴρ εἶπεν, Ἀλλ', ὦ παῖ, ἔφη, οὗτοι μὲν οὓς λέγεις, ὥσπερ ἱματίων ῥαγέντων εἰσί τινες ἀκεσταί,[2] οὕτω καὶ οἱ ἰατροί, ὅταν τινὲς νοσήσωσι, τότε ἰῶνται τούτους· σοὶ δὲ τούτου μεγαλοπρεπεστέρα ἔσται

[1] A lacuna, from which something like τί δ' ἄνευ τοῦ προθυμίαν ἔχειν is lost, Poppo, Gemoll, Marchant.

[2] ἀκεσταί y, Photius, Cobet, Breitenbach, Gemoll, Marchant; ἠπηταί xzR, Dindorf, et al.

been discussed at all, you finally asked me what in the world he had been teaching me that he professed to have been teaching me generalship. And thereupon I answered, 'tactics.' And you laughed and went through it all, explaining point by point, as you asked of what conceivable use tactics could be to an army, without provisions and health, and of what use it could be without the knowledge of the arts invented for warfare and without obedience. And when you had made it clear to me that tactics was only a small part of generalship, I asked you if you could teach me any of those things, and you bade me go and talk with the men who were reputed to be masters of military science and find out how each one of those problems was to be met. 15. Thereupon I joined myself to those who I heard were most proficient in those branches. And in regard to provisions—I was persuaded that what Cyaxares was to furnish us was enough if it should be forthcoming; and in regard to health—as I had always heard and observed that states that wished to be healthy elected a board of health, and also that generals for the sake of their soldiers took physicians out with them, so also when I was appointed to this position, I immediately took thought for this; and I think," he added, "that you will find that I have with me men eminent in the medical profession."

Practical teaching of military science

16. "Yes, my son," said his father in reply to this, "but just as there are menders of torn garments, so also these physicians whom you mention heal us when we fall sick. But your responsibility for

ἡ τῆς ὑγιείας ἐπιμέλεια· τὸ γὰρ ἀρχὴν μὴ κάμνει[ν]
τὸ στράτευμα, τούτου σοι δεῖ μέλειν.

Καὶ τίνα δὴ ἐγώ, ἔφη, ὦ πάτερ, ὁδὸν ἰὼ[ν]
τοῦτο πράττειν ἱκανὸς ἔσομαι;

Ἢν μὲν δήπου χρόνον τινὰ μέλλῃς ἐν τ[ῷ]
αὐτῷ μένειν, ὑγιεινοῦ πρῶτον δεῖ στρατοπέδο[υ]
μὴ ἀμελῆσαι· τούτου δὲ οὐκ ἂν ἁμάρτοις, ἐάνπε[ρ]
μελήσῃ σοι. καὶ γὰρ λέγοντες οὐδὲν παύοντα[ι]
ἄνθρωποι περί τε τῶν νοσηρῶν χωρίων καὶ περ[ὶ]
τῶν ὑγιεινῶν· μάρτυρες δὲ σαφεῖς ἑκατέροι[ς]
αὐτῶν παρίστανται τά τε σώματα καὶ τ[ὰ]
χρώματα. ἔπειτα δὲ οὐ τὰ χωρία μόνον ἀρκέσε[ι]
σκέψασθαι, ἀλλὰ μνήσθητι σὺ πῶς πειρᾷ σαυτο[ῦ]
ἐπιμέλεσθαι ὅπως ὑγιαίνῃς.

17. Καὶ ὁ Κῦρος εἶπε, Πρῶτον μὲν νὴ Δί[α]
πειρῶμαι μηδέποτε ὑπερπίμπλασθαι· δύσφορο[ν]
γάρ· ἔπειτα δὲ ἐκπονῶ τὰ εἰσιόντα· οὕτω γά[ρ]
μοι δοκεῖ ἥ τε ὑγίεια μᾶλλον παραμένειν κα[ὶ]
ἰσχὺς προσγενέσθαι.

Οὕτω τοίνυν, ἔφη, ὦ παῖ, καὶ τῶν ἄλλων δε[ῖ]
ἐπιμέλεσθαι.

Ἦ καὶ σχολή, ἔφη, ὦ πάτερ, ἔσται σωμα[-]
σκεῖν τοῖς στρατιώταις;

Οὐ μὰ Δί', ἔφη ὁ πατήρ, οὐ μόνον γε, ἀλλ[ὰ]
καὶ ἀνάγκη. δεῖ γὰρ δήπου στρατιάν, εἰ μέλλε[ι]
πράξειν τὰ δέοντα, μηδέποτε παύεσθαι ἢ τοῖ[ς]
πολεμίοις κακὰ πορσύνουσαν ἢ ἑαυτῇ ἀγαθά·
ὡς χαλεπὸν μὲν καὶ ἕνα ἄνθρωπον ἀργὸν τρέ[-]
φεσθαι, πολὺ δ' ἔτι χαλεπώτερον, ὦ παῖ, οἶκο[ν]
ὅλον, πάντων δὲ χαλεπώτατον στρατιὰν ἀργὸ[ν]
τρέφειν. πλεῖστά τε γὰρ τὰ ἐσθίοντα ἐν στρατιᾷ
καὶ ἀπ' ἐλαχίστων ὁρμώμενα καὶ οἷς ἂν λάβ[ῃ]

.ealth will be a larger one than that: you must see ɔ it that your army does not get sick at all."

"And pray what course shall I take, father," said ıe, "that I may be able to accomplish that?"

"In the first place, if you are going to stay for ome time in the same neighbourhood, you must not ıeglect to find a sanitary location for your camp; nd with proper attention you can not fail in this. 'or people are continually talking about unhealthful ocalities and localities that are healthful; and you nay find clear witnesses to either in the physique ınd complexion of the inhabitants; and in the econd place, it is not enough to have regard to the ocalities only, but tell me what means you adopt to ɛeep well yourself."

17. "In the first place, by Zeus," said Cyrus, "I ry never to eat too much, for that is oppressive; and n the second place, I work off by exercise what I ıave eaten, for by so doing health seems more likely o endure and strength to accrue."

"That, then, my son," said he, "is the way in vhich you must take care of the rest also."

"Yes, father," said he; "but will the soldiers find eisure for taking physical exercise?"

"Nay, by Zeus," said his father, "they not only ɛan, but they actually must. For if an army is to do ts duty, it is absolutely necessary that it never ɛease to contrive both evil for the enemy and good 'or itself. What a burden it is to support even one dle man! It is more burdensome still to support a vhole household in idleness; but the worst burden ɔf all is to support an army in idleness. For not ɔnly are the mouths in an army very numerous but the supplies they start with are exceedingly limited,

δαψιλέστατα χρώμενα, ὥστε οὔποτε ἀργεῖ
δεήσει στρατιᾶν.

18. Λέγεις σύ, ἔφη, ὦ πάτερ, ὡς ἐμοὶ δοκε
ὥσπερ οὐδὲ γεωργοῦ ἀργοῦ οὐδὲν ὄφελος, οὕτω
οὐδὲ στρατηγοῦ ἀργοῦντος οὐδὲν ὄφελος εἶναι.

Τὸν δέ γε ἐργάτην στρατηγὸν ἐγώ, ἔφη
ἀναδέχομαι, ἢν μή τις θεὸς βλάπτῃ, ἅμα κα
τἀπιτήδεια μάλιστα ἔχοντας τοὺς στρατιώτα
ἀποδείξειν καὶ τὰ σώματα ἄριστα ἔχοντας παρα
σκευάσειν.

Ἀλλὰ μέντοι, ἔφη, τό γε μελετᾶσθαι ἕκαστ
τῶν πολεμικῶν ἔργων, ἀγῶνας ἄν τίς μοι δοκε
ἔφη, ὦ πάτερ, προειπὼν ἑκάστοις καὶ ἆθλ
προτιθεὶς μάλιστ᾽ ἂν ποιεῖν εὖ ἀσκεῖσθαι ἕκαστ
ὥστε[1] ὁπότε δέοιτο ἔχειν ἂν παρεσκευασμένοι
χρῆσθαι.

Κάλλιστα λέγεις, ἔφη, ὦ παῖ· τοῦτο γὰ
ποιήσας, σάφ᾽ ἴσθι, ὥσπερ χοροὺς τὰς τάξεις ἀ
τὰ προσήκοντα μελετώσας θεάσει.

19. Ἀλλὰ μήν, ὁ Κῦρος ἔφη, εἴς γε τὸ προ
θυμίαν ἐμβαλεῖν στρατιώταις οὐδέν μοι δοκε
ἱκανώτερον εἶναι ἢ τὸ δύνασθαι ἐλπίδας ἐμποιεῖ
ἀνθρώποις.

Ἀλλ᾽, ἔφη, ὦ παῖ, τοῦτό γε τοιοῦτόν ἐστι
οἷόνπερ εἴ τις κύνας ἐν θήρᾳ ἀνακαλοῖτ
ἀεὶ τῇ κλήσει ᾗπερ ὅταν τὸ θηρίον ὁρᾷ. τ
μὲν γὰρ πρῶτον προθύμως εὖ οἶδ᾽ ὅτι ἔχε
ὑπακουούσας· ἢν δὲ πολλάκις ψεύδηται αὐτάς
τελευτῶσαι οὐδ᾽ ὁπόταν ἀληθῶς ὁρῶν καλ
πείθονται αὐτῷ. οὕτω καὶ τὸ περὶ τῶν ἐλπίδω

[1] ἕκαστα, ὥστε y, Dindorf, Gemoll, et al.; ὥστε ἕκαστα xzR
Sauppe.

and they use up most extravagantly whatever they get, so that an army must never be left idle."

18. "Methinks you mean, father," said he, "that just as a lazy farmer is of no account, so also a lazy general is of no account at all."

"But at any rate, as regards the energetic general," said his father, "I can vouch for it that, unless some god do cross him, he will keep his soldiers abundantly supplied with provisions and at the same time in the best physical condition."

Incentives to physical training and to moral enthusiasm

"Yes," said Cyrus; "but at all events, as to practice in the various warlike exercises, it seems to me, father, that by announcing contests in each one and offering prizes you would best secure practice in them, so that you would have everything prepared for use, whenever you might need it."

"Quite right, my son," said he; "for if you do that you may be sure that you will see your companies performing their proper parts like trained sets of dancers."

19. "In the next place," said Cyrus, "for putting enthusiasm into the soldiers nothing seems to be more effectual than the power of inspiring men with hopes."

"Yes, my son," said he; "but that is just as if any one on a hunt should always call up his dogs with the call that he uses when he sees the quarry. For at first, to be sure, he will find them obeying him eagerly; but if he deceives them often, in the end they will not obey him when he calls, even though he really does see a wild beast. So it stands with respect to those hopes also. If any one too

ἔχει· ἣν πολλάκις προσδοκίας ἀγαθῶν ἐμβαλὼν ψεύδηταί τις, οὐδ᾽ ὁπόταν ἀληθεῖς ἐλπίδας λέγῃ ὁ τοιοῦτος πείθειν δύναται. ἀλλὰ τοῦ μὲν αὐτὸν λέγειν ἃ μὴ σαφῶς εἰδείη εἴργεσθαι δεῖ, ὦ παῖ, ἄλλοι δ᾽ ἐνετοὶ[1] λέγοντες ταὔτ᾽ ἂν διαπράττοιεν· τὴν δ᾽ αὑτοῦ παρακέλευσιν εἰς τοὺς μεγίστους κινδύνους δεῖ ὡς μάλιστα ἐν πίστει διασῴζειν.

Ἀλλὰ ναὶ μὰ τὸν Δί᾽, ἔφη ὁ Κῦρος, ὦ πάτερ, καλῶς μοι δοκεῖς λέγειν, καὶ ἐμοὶ οὕτως ἥδιον. 20. τό γε μὴν πειθομένους παρέχεσθαι τοὺς στρατιώτας, οὐκ ἀπείρως μοι δοκῶ αὐτοῦ ἔχειν, ὦ πάτερ· σύ τε γάρ με εὐθὺς τοῦτο ἐκ παιδίου ἐπαίδευες, σαυτῷ πείθεσθαι ἀναγκάζων· ἔπειτα τοῖς διδασκάλοις παρέδωκας, καὶ ἐκεῖνοι αὖ ταὐτὸ τοῦτο ἔπραττον· ἐπεὶ δ᾽ ἐν τοῖς ἐφήβοις ἦμεν, ὁ ἄρχων τοῦ αὐτοῦ τούτου ἰσχυρῶς ἐπεμέλετο· καὶ οἱ νόμοι δέ μοι δοκοῦσιν οἱ πολλοὶ ταῦτα δύο μάλιστα διδάσκειν, ἄρχειν τε καὶ ἄρχεσθαι. καὶ τοίνυν κατανοῶν περὶ τούτων ἐν πᾶσιν ὁρᾶν μοι δοκῶ τὸ προτρέπον πείθεσθαι μάλιστα ὂν τὸ τὸν πειθόμενον ἐπαινεῖν τε καὶ τιμᾶν, τὸν δὲ ἀπειθοῦντα ἀτιμάζειν τε καὶ κολάζειν.

21. Καὶ ἐπὶ μέν γε τὸ ἀνάγκῃ ἕπεσθαι αὕτη, ὦ παῖ, ἡ ὁδός ἐστιν· ἐπὶ δὲ τὸ κρεῖττον τούτου πολύ, τὸ ἑκόντας πείθεσθαι, ἄλλη ἐστὶ συντομωτέρα. ὃν γὰρ ἂν ἡγήσωνται περὶ τοῦ συμφέροντος ἑαυτοῖς φρονιμώτερον ἑαυτῶν εἶναι, τούτῳ οἱ ἄνθρωποι ὑπερηδέως πείθονται. γνοίης δ᾽ ἂν ὅτι τοῦθ᾽ οὕτως ἔχει ἐν ἄλλοις τε πολλοῖς καὶ δὴ

[1] ἐνετοὶ Dindorf, most Edd.; ἐνίοτε xyG; αἴνεται AH; not in R.

often raises false expectations of good things to come, eventually he can gain no credence, even when he holds forth well-grounded hopes. But, my son, you should refrain from saying what you are not perfectly sure of; by making certain others your mouthpiece, however, the desired end may be accomplished; but faith in your own words of encouragement you must keep sacred to the utmost to serve you in the greatest crises."

"Yes, by Zeus, father," said Cyrus; "I think you are right in what you say, and I like your idea better. 20. And then in regard to keeping the soldiers in a state of obedience, I think, father, that I am not inexperienced in that direction; for you instructed me in obedience from my very childhood on, compelling me to obey you. Then you surrendered me to the charge of my teachers, and they pursued the same course; and when we were in the class of young men, the officer in charge paid especial attention to this same point; and most of the laws seem to me to teach these two things above all else, to govern and to be governed. And now, when I think of it, it seems to me that in all things the chief incentive to obedience lies in this: praise and honour for the obedient, punishment and dishonour for the disobedient."

How obedience is best secured

21. "This, my son, is the road to compulsory obedience, indeed, but there is another road, a short cut, to what is much better—namely, to willing obedience. For people are only too glad to obey the man who they believe takes wiser thought for their interests than they themselves do. And you might recognize that this is so in many instances but particularly in the

καὶ ἐν τοῖς κάμνουσιν, ὡς προθύμως τοὺς ἐπιτάξοντας ὅ τι χρὴ ποιεῖν καλοῦσι· καὶ ἐν θαλάττῃ δὲ ὡς προθύμως τοῖς κυβερνήταις οἱ συμπλέοντες πείθονται· καὶ οὕς γ' ἂν νομίσωσί τινες βέλτιον αὑτῶν ὁδοὺς εἰδέναι, ὡς ἰσχυρῶς τούτων οὐδ' ἀπολείπεσθαι ἐθέλουσιν. ὅταν δὲ οἴωνται πειθόμενοι κακόν τι λήψεσθαι, οὔτε ζημίαις πάνυ τι ἐθέλουσιν εἴκειν οὔτε δώροις ἐπαίρεσθαι. οὐδὲ γὰρ δῶρα ἐπὶ τῷ αὑτοῦ κακῷ ἑκὼν οὐδεὶς λαμβάνει.

22. Λέγεις σύ, ὦ πάτερ, εἰς τὸ πειθομένους ἔχειν οὐδὲν εἶναι ἀνυσιμώτερον τοῦ φρονιμώτερον δοκεῖν εἶναι τῶν ἀρχομένων.

Λέγω γὰρ οὖν, ἔφη.

Καὶ πῶς δή τις ἄν, ὦ πάτερ, τοιαύτην δόξαν τάχιστα περὶ αὑτοῦ παρασχέσθαι δύναιτο;

Οὐκ ἔστιν, ἔφη, ὦ παῖ, συντομωτέρα ὁδὸς ἐπὶ τό,[1] περὶ ὧν βούλει, δοκεῖν φρόνιμος εἶναι ἢ τὸ γενέσθαι περὶ τούτων φρόνιμον. καθ' ἓν δ' ἕκαστον σκοπῶν γνώσει ὅτι ἐγὼ ἀληθῆ λέγω. ἢν γὰρ βούλῃ μὴ ὢν ἀγαθὸς γεωργὸς δοκεῖν εἶναι ἀγαθός, ἢ ἱππεὺς ἢ ἰατρὸς ἢ αὐλητὴς ἢ ἄλλ' ὁτιοῦν, ἐννόει πόσα σε δέοι ἂν μηχανᾶσθαι τοῦ δοκεῖν ἕνεκα. καὶ εἰ δὴ πείσαις ἐπαινεῖν τέ σε πολλούς, ὅπως δόξαν λάβοις, καὶ κατασκευὰς καλὰς ἐφ' ἑκάστῳ αὐτῶν κτήσαιο, ἄρτι τε ἐξηπατηκὼς εἴης ἂν καὶ ὀλίγῳ ὕστερον, ὅπου πεῖραν δοίης, ἐξεληλεγμένος ἂν προσέτι καὶ ἀλαζὼν φαίνοιο.

[1] ἐπὶ τό, Hug, Marchant; not in MSS.

case of the sick: how readily they call in those who are to prescribe what they must do; and at sea how cheerfully the passengers obey the captain; and how earnestly travellers desire not to get separated from those who they think are better acquainted with the road than they are. But when people think that they are going to get into trouble if they obey, they will neither yield very much for punishment nor will they be moved by gifts; for no one willingly accepts even a gift at the cost of trouble to himself."

22. "You mean to say, father, that nothing is more effectual toward keeping one's men obedient than to seem to be wiser than they?"

"Yes," said he, "that is just what I mean."

"And how, pray, father, could one most quickly acquire such a reputation for oneself?"

Be what you would seem to be

"There is no shorter road, my son," said he, "than really to be wise in those things in which you wish to seem to be wise; and when you examine concrete instances, you will realize that what I say is true. For example, if you wish to seem to be a good farmer when you are not, or a good rider, doctor, flute-player, or anything else that you are not, just think how many schemes you must invent to keep up your pretensions. And even if you should persuade any number of people to praise you, in order to give yourself a reputation, and if you should procure a fine outfit for each of your professions, you would soon be found to have practised deception; and not long after, when you were giving an exhibition of your skill, you would be shown up and convicted, too, as an impostor."

23. Φρόνιμος δὲ περὶ τοῦ συνοίσειν μέλλοντος πῶς ἄν τις τῷ ὄντι γένοιτο;

Δῆλον, ἔφη, ὦ παῖ, ὅτι ὅσα μὲν ἔστι μαθόντα εἰδέναι, μαθὼν ἄν, ὥσπερ τὰ τακτικὰ ἔμαθες· ὅσα δὲ ἀνθρώποις οὔτε μαθητὰ οὔτε προορατὰ ἀνθρωπίνῃ προνοίᾳ, διὰ μαντικῆς ἂν παρὰ θεῶν πυνθανόμενος φρονιμώτερος ἄλλων εἴης· ὅ τι δὲ γνοίης βέλτιον ὂν πραχθῆναι, ἐπιμελόμενος ἂν τούτου ὡς ἂν πραχθείη. καὶ γὰρ τὸ ἐπιμέλεσθαι οὗ ἂν δέῃ φρονιμωτέρου ἀνδρὸς ἢ τὸ ἀμελεῖν.

24. Ἀλλὰ μέντοι ἐπὶ τὸ φιλεῖσθαι ὑπὸ τῶν ἀρχομένων, ὅπερ ἔμοιγε ἐν τοῖς μεγίστοις δοκεῖ εἶναι, δῆλον ὅτι ἡ αὐτὴ ὁδὸς ἥπερ εἴ τις ὑπὸ τῶν φίλων στέργεσθαι ἐπιθυμοίη· εὖ γὰρ οἶμαι δεῖν ποιοῦντα φανερὸν εἶναι.

Ἀλλὰ τοῦτο μέν, ἔφη, ὦ παῖ, χαλεπὸν τὸ ἀεὶ δύνασθαι εὖ ποιεῖν οὓς ἄν τις ἐθέλῃ· τὸ δὲ συνηδόμενόν τε φαίνεσθαι, ἤν τι ἀγαθὸν αὐτοῖς συμβαίνῃ, καὶ συναχθόμενον, ἤν τι κακόν, καὶ συνεπικουρεῖν προθυμούμενον ταῖς ἀπορίαις αὐτῶν, καὶ φοβούμενον μή τι σφαλῶσι, καὶ προνοεῖν πειρώμενον ὡς μὴ σφάλλωνται, ταῦτά[1] πως δεῖ μᾶλλον συμπαρομαρτεῖν. 25. καὶ ἐπὶ τῶν πράξεων δέ, ἢν μὲν ἐν θέρει ὦσι, τὸν ἄρχοντα δεῖ τοῦ ἡλίου πλεονεκτοῦντα φανερὸν εἶναι· ἢν δὲ ἐν χειμῶνι, τοῦ ψύχους· ἢν δὲ διὰ μόχθων,[2] τῶν

[1] ταῦτα Stobaeus, Edd. ; ἐπὶ ταῦτα MSS.

[2] διὰ μόχθων z, Dindorf, Marchant, Breitenbach; δέῃ μοχθεῖν xyR, Gemoll.

23. "But how could one become really wise in oreseeing that which will prove to be useful?"

"Obviously, my son," said he, "by learning all hat it is possible to acquire by learning, just as you earned tactics. But whatever it is not possible for nan to learn, nor for human wisdom to foresee, that ou may find out from the gods by the soothsayer's rt, and thus prove yourself wiser than others; and f you know anything that it would be best to have lone, you would show yourself wiser than others if ou should exert yourself to get that done; for it is mark of greater wisdom in a man to strive to secure vhat is needful than to neglect it."

The way to win affection

24. "Yes; but as to the love of one's subjects—nd this, it seems to me at least, is one of the most mportant questions—the same course that you would ake if you wished to gain the affection of your riends leads also to that; that is, I think, you must how yourself to be their benefactor."

"Yes, my son," said he; "it is a difficult matter, owever, always to be in a position to do good to vhom you will; but to show that you rejoice with hem if any good befall them, that you sympathize vith them if any ill betide, that you are eager to ielp them in times of distress, that you are anxious hat they be not crossed in any way, and that ou try to prevent their being crossed; it is in these espects somehow that you ought rather to go hand n hand with them. 25. And in his campaigns also, if hey fall in the summer time, the general must show hat he can endure the heat of the sun better than his oldiers can, and that he can endure cold better han they if it be in winter; if the way lead through

πόνων· πάντα γὰρ ταῦτα εἰς τὸ φιλεῖσθαι ὑπ
τῶν ἀρχομένων συλλαμβάνει.

Λέγεις σύ, ἔφη, ὦ πάτερ, ὡς καὶ καρτερώτερο
δεῖ πρὸς πάντα τὸν ἄρχοντα τῶν ἀρχομένων εἶναι

Λέγω γὰρ οὖν, ἔφη. θάρρει μέντοι τοῦτο,
παῖ· εὖ γὰρ ἴσθι ὅτι τῶν ὁμοίων σωμάτων ο
αὐτοὶ πόνοι οὐχ ὁμοίως ἅπτονται ἄρχοντός τε ἀν
δρὸς καὶ ἰδιώτου, ἀλλ' ἐπικουφίζει τι ἡ τιμὴ τοὺ
πόνους τῷ ἄρχοντι καὶ αὐτὸ τὸ εἰδέναι ὅτι οὐ λαν
θάνει ὅ τι ἂν ποιῇ.

26. Ὁπότε δέ, ὦ πάτερ, σοι ἤδη ἔχοιεν μὲ
τἀπιτήδεια οἱ στρατιῶται, ὑγιαίνοιεν δέ, πονεῖ
δὲ δύναιντο, τὰς δὲ πολεμικὰς τέχνας ἠσκηκότε
εἶεν, φιλοτίμως δ' ἔχοιεν πρὸς τὸ ἀγαθοὶ φαίνε
σθαι, τὸ δὲ πείθεσθαι αὐτοῖς ἥδιον εἴη τοῦ ἀπειθεῖν
οὐκ ἂν τηνικαῦτα σωφρονεῖν ἄν τίς σοι δοκοί
διαγωνίζεσθαι βουλόμενος πρὸς τοὺς πολεμίου
ὡς τάχιστα;

Ναὶ μὰ Δί', ἔφη, εἰ μέλλοι γε πλεῖον ἕξειν
εἰ δὲ μή, ἔγωγ' ἂν ὅσῳ οἰοίμην καὶ αὐτὸς βελτίω
εἶναι καὶ τοὺς ἑπομένους βελτίονας ἔχειν, τόσῳ ἂ
μᾶλλον φυλαττοίμην, ὥσπερ καὶ τἄλλα ἂν οἰώ
μεθα πλείστου ἡμῖν ἄξια εἶναι, ταῦτα πειρώμεθ
ὡς ἐν ἐχυρωτάτῳ ποιεῖσθαι.

27. Πλεῖον δ' ἔχειν, ὦ πάτερ, πολεμίων πῶ
ἄν τις δύναιτο μάλιστα;

Οὐ μὰ Δί', ἔφη, οὐκέτι τοῦτο φαῦλον, ὦ
παῖ, οὐδ' ἁπλοῦν ἔργον ἐρωτᾷς· ἀλλ' εὖ ἴσθι ὅτ
δεῖ τὸν μέλλοντα τοῦτο ποιήσειν καὶ ἐπίβουλο
εἶναι καὶ κρυψίνουν καὶ δολερὸν καὶ ἀπατεῶνα

difficulties, that he can endure hardships better. All this contributes to his being loved by his men."

"You mean to say, father," said he, "that in everything the general must show more endurance than his men."

"Yes," said he, "that is just what I mean; however, never fear for that, my son; for bear in mind that the same toils do not affect the general and the private in the same way, though they have the same sort of bodies; but the honour of the general's position and the very consciousness that nothing he does escapes notice lighten the burdens for him."

26. "But, father, when once your soldiers had supplies and were well and able to endure toils, and when they were practised in the arts of war and ambitious to prove themselves brave, and when they were more inclined to obey than to disobey, under such circumstances do you not think it would be wise to desire to engage the enemy at the very first opportunity?"

Taking advantage of the enemy

"Yes, by Zeus," said he; "at any rate, if I expected to gain some advantage by it; otherwise, for my part, the better I thought myself to be and the better my followers, the more should I be on my guard, just as we try to keep other things also which we hold most precious in the greatest possible security."

27. "But, father, what would be the best way to gain an advantage over the enemy?"

"By Zeus," said he, "this is no easy or simple question that you ask now, my son; but, let me tell you, the man who proposes to do that must be designing and cunning, wily and deceitful, a thief

καὶ κλέπτην καὶ ἅρπαγα καὶ ἐν παντὶ πλεονέκτην τῶν πολεμίων.

Καὶ ὁ Κῦρος ἐπιγελάσας εἶπεν, Ὦ Ἡράκλεις, οἷον σὺ λέγεις, ὦ πάτερ, δεῖν ἄνδρα με γενέσθαι.

Οἷος ἂν ὤν,[1] ἔφη, ὦ παῖ, δικαιότατός τε καὶ νομιμώτατος ἀνὴρ εἴης.

28. Πῶς μήν, ἔφη, παῖδας ὄντας ἡμᾶς καὶ ἐφήβους τἀναντία τούτων ἐδιδάσκετε;

Ναὶ μὰ Δί', ἔφη, καὶ νῦν πρὸς τοὺς φίλους τε καὶ πολίτας· ὅπως δέ γε τοὺς πολεμίους δύναισθε κακῶς ποιεῖν οὐκ οἶσθα μανθάνοντας ὑμᾶς πολλὰς κακουργίας;

Οὐ δῆτα, ἔφη, ἔγωγε, ὦ πάτερ.

Τίνος μὴν ἕνεκα, ἔφη, ἐμανθάνετε τοξεύειν; τίνος δ' ἕνεκα ἀκοντίζειν; τίνος δ' ἕνεκα δολοῦν ὗς ἀγρίους καὶ πλέγμασι καὶ ὀρύγμασι; τί δ' ἐλάφους ποδάγραις καὶ ἁρπεδόναις; τί δὲ λέουσι καὶ ἄρκτοις καὶ παρδάλεσιν οὐκ εἰς τὸ ἴσον καθιστάμενοι ἐμάχεσθε, ἀλλὰ μετὰ πλεονεξίας τινὸς ἀεὶ ἐπειρᾶσθε ἀγωνίζεσθαι πρὸς αὐτά; ἢ οὐ πάντα γιγνώσκεις ταῦτα ὅτι κακουργίαι τέ εἰσι καὶ ἀπάται καὶ δολώσεις καὶ πλεονεξίαι;

29. Ναὶ μὰ Δί', ἔφη, θηρίων γε· ἀνθρώπων δὲ εἰ καὶ δόξαιμι βούλεσθαι ἐξαπατῆσαί τινα, πολλὰς πληγὰς οἶδα λαμβάνων.

Οὐδὲ γὰρ τοξεύειν, οἶμαι, οὐδ' ἀκοντίζειν ἄνθρωπον ἐπετρέπομεν ὑμῖν, ἀλλ' ἐπὶ σκοπὸν βάλλειν ἐδιδάσκομεν, ἵνα γε νῦν μὲν μὴ κακουργοίητε

[1] ὤν Hertlein, Edd.; not in MSS.

nd a robber, overreaching the enemy at every oint."

"O Heracles, father," said Cyrus with a laugh, what a man you say I must become!"

"Such, my son," he said, "that you would be at he same time the most righteous and law-abiding nan in the world."

28. "Why then, pray, did you use to teach us the pposite of this when we were boys and youths?"

"Aye, by Zeus," said he; "and so we would have ou still towards your friends and fellow-citizens; ut, that you might be able to hurt your enemies, o you not know that you all were learning many illainies?"

"No, indeed, father," said he; "not I, at any ate."

"Why," said he, "did you learn to shoot, and hy to throw the spear? Why did you learn to nsnare wild boars with nets and pitfalls, and deer ith traps and toils? And why were you not used o confront lions and bears and leopards in a fair ght face to face instead of always trying to contend gainst them with some advantage on your side? Vhy, do you not know that all this is villainy and eceit and trickery and taking unfair advantage?"

29. "Yes, by Zeus," said he, "toward wild animals owever; but if I ever even seemed to wish to eceive a man, I know that I got a good beating for ."

"Yes," said he; "for, methinks, we did not ermit you to shoot at people nor to throw your pear at them; but we taught you to shoot at a ark, in order that you might not for the time at

τοὺς φίλους, εἰ δέ ποτε πόλεμος γένοιτο, δύναισθε καὶ ἀνθρώπων στοχάζεσθαι· καὶ ἐξαπατᾶν δὲ καὶ πλεονεκτεῖν οὐκ ἐν ἀνθρώποις ἐπαιδεύομεν ὑμᾶς, ἀλλ' ἐν θηρίοις, ἵνα μηδ' ἐν τούτοις τοὺς φίλους βλάπτοιτε, εἰ δέ ποτε πόλεμος γένοιτο, μηδὲ τούτων ἀγύμναστοι εἴητε.

30. Οὐκοῦν, ἔφη, ὦ πάτερ, εἴπερ χρήσιμά ἐστιν ἀμφότερα ἐπίστασθαι, εὖ τε ποιεῖν καὶ κακῶς ἀνθρώπους, καὶ διδάσκειν ἀμφότερα ταῦτα ἔδει ἐν[1] ἀνθρώποις.

31. Ἀλλὰ λέγεται, ἔφη, ὦ παῖ, ἐπὶ τῶν ἡμετέρων προγόνων γενέσθαι ποτὲ ἀνὴρ διδάσκαλος τῶν παίδων, ὃς ἐδίδασκεν ἄρα τοὺς παῖδας τὴν δικαιοσύνην, ὥσπερ σὺ κελεύεις, μὴ ψεύδεσθαι καὶ ψεύδεσθαι, καὶ μὴ ἐξαπατᾶν καὶ ἐξαπατᾶν, καὶ μὴ διαβάλλειν καὶ διαβάλλειν, καὶ μὴ πλεονεκτεῖν καὶ πλεονεκτεῖν. διώριζε δὲ τούτων ἅ τε πρὸς τοὺς φίλους ποιητέον καὶ ἃ πρὸς ἐχθρούς. καὶ ἔτι γε[2] ταῦτα ἐδίδασκεν ὡς καὶ τοὺς φίλους δίκαιον εἴη ἐξαπατᾶν ἐπί γε ἀγαθῷ, καὶ κλέπτειν τὰ τῶν φίλων ἐπὶ ἀγαθῷ. 32. ταῦτα δὲ διδάσκοντα ἀνάγκη καὶ γυμνάζειν ἦν πρὸς ἀλλήλους τοὺς παῖδας ταῦτα ποιεῖν, ὥσπερ καὶ ἐν πάλῃ φασὶ τοὺς Ἕλληνας διδάσκειν ἐξαπατᾶν, καὶ γυμνάζειν δὲ τοὺς παῖδας πρὸς ἀλλήλους τοῦτο δύνασθαι ποιεῖν. γενόμενοι οὖν τινες οὕτως εὐφυεῖς καὶ πρὸς τὸ εὖ ἐξαπατᾶν καὶ πρὸς τὸ εὖ πλεονεκτεῖν, ἴσως δὲ καὶ πρὸς τὸ φιλοκερδεῖν οὐκ ἀφυεῖς ὄντες, οὐκ ἀπεί-

[1] ἐν yC², Gemoll, Marchant, Breitenbach; ἐπ' xzR, Dindorf, et al. (*against*).

[2] ἔτι γε Dindorf, most Edd.; ἔτι R; ἔτι δὲ προβὰς y; καὶ ταῦτα δὲ AEC².

least do harm to your friends, but, in case there should ever be a war, that you might be able to aim well at men also. And we instructed you likewise to deceive and to take advantage, not in the case of men but of beasts, in order that you might not injure your friends by so doing, but, if there should ever be a war, that you might not be unpractised in these arts."

Training for taking unfair advantage

30. "Well then, father," said he, "if indeed it is useful to understand both how to do good and how to do evil to men, we ought to have been taught both these branches in the case of men, too."

31. "Yes, my son," said he; "it is said that in the time of our forefathers there was once a teacher of the boys who, it seems, used to teach them justice in the very way that you propose; to lie and not to lie, to cheat and not to cheat, to slander and not to slander, to take and not to take unfair advantage. And he drew the line between what one should do to one's friends and what to one's enemies. And what is more, he used to teach this: that it was right to deceive friends even, provided it were for a good end, and to steal the possessions of a friend for a good purpose. 32. And in teaching these lessons he had also to train the boys to practise them upon one another, just as also in wrestling, the Greeks, they say, teach deception and train the boys to be able to practise it upon one another. When, therefore, some had in this way become expert both in deceiving successfully and in taking unfair advantage and perhaps also not inexpert in avarice, they did not

χοντο οὐδ᾽ ἀπὸ τῶν φίλων τὸ μὴ οὐ πλεονεκτεῖν αὐτῶν πειρᾶσθαι. 33. ἐγένετο οὖν ἐκ τούτων ῥήτρα, ᾗ καὶ νῦν χρώμεθα ἔτι, ἁπλῶς διδάσκειν τοὺς παῖδας ὥσπερ τοὺς οἰκέτας πρὸς ἡμᾶς αὐτοὺς διδάσκομεν ἀληθεύειν καὶ μὴ ἐξαπατᾶν καὶ μὴ πλεονεκτεῖν· εἰ δὲ παρὰ ταῦτα ποιοῖεν, κολάζειν, ὅπως σὺν[1] τοιούτῳ ἔθει ἐθισθέντες πρᾳότεροι πολῖται γένοιντο. 34. ἐπεὶ δὲ ἔχοιεν τὴν ἡλικίαν ἣν σὺ νῦν ἔχεις, ἤδη καὶ τὰ πρὸς τοὺς πολεμίους νόμιμα ἐδόκει ἀσφαλὲς εἶναι διδάσκειν. οὐ γὰρ ἂν ἔτι ἐξενεχθῆναι δοκεῖτε πρὸς τὸ ἄγριοι πολῖται γενέσθαι ἐν τῷ αἰδεῖσθαι ἀλλήλους συντεθραμμένοι· ὥσπερ γε καὶ περὶ ἀφροδισίων οὐ διαλεγόμεθα[2] πρὸς τοὺς ἄγαν νέους, ἵνα μὴ πρὸς τὴν ἰσχυρὰν ἐπιθυμίαν αὐτοῖς ῥᾳδιουργίας προσγενομένης ἀμέτρως αὐτῇ χρῷντο οἱ νέοι.

35. Νὴ Δί᾽, ἔφη· ὡς τοίνυν ὀψιμαθῆ ὄντα ἐμὲ τούτων τῶν πλεονεξιῶν, ὦ πάτερ, μὴ φείδου εἴ τι ἔχεις διδάσκειν ὅπως πλεονεκτήσω ἐγὼ τῶν πολεμίων.

Μηχανῶ τοίνυν, ἔφη, ὁπόση ἐστὶ δύναμις, τεταγμένοις τοῖς σαυτοῦ ἀτάκτους λαμβάνειν τοὺς πολεμίους καὶ ὡπλισμένοις ἀόπλους καὶ ἐγρηγορόσι καθεύδοντας καὶ φανερούς σοι ὄντας ἀφανὴς αὐτὸς ὢν ἐκείνοις καὶ ἐν δυσχωρίᾳ αὐτοὺς γιγνομένους ἐν ἐρυμνῷ αὐτὸς ὢν ὑποδέξει.[3]

[1] σὺν MSS.; ἐν Hug.
[2] διαλεγόμεθα MSS., Dindorf; διελεγόμεθα Sauppe, Hug, Gemoll, et al.
[3] ὑποδέξει MSS., Dindorf, most Edd.; bracketed by Cobet, Hug, et al.

refrain from trying to take an unfair advantage even of their friends. 33. In consequence of that, therefore, an ordinance was passed which obtains even unto this day, simply to teach our boys, just as we teach our servants in their relations toward us, to tell the truth and not to deceive and not to take unfair advantage; and if they should act contrary to this law, the law requires their punishment, in order that, inured to such habits, they may become more refined members of society. 34. But when they came to be as old as you are now, then it seemed to be safe to teach them that also which is lawful toward enemies; for it does not seem likely that you would break away and degenerate into savages after you had been brought up together in mutual respect. In the same way we do not discuss sexual matters in the presence of very young boys, lest in case lax discipline should give a free rein to their passions the young might indulge them to excess."

How to take advantage of the enemy

35. "True, by Zeus," said he; "but seeing that I am late in learning about this art of taking advantage of others, do not neglect to teach me, father, if you can, how I may take advantage of the enemy."

"Contrive, then," said he, "as far as is in your power, with your own men in good order to catch the enemy in disorder, with your own men armed to come upon them unarmed, and with your own men awake to surprise them sleeping, and then you will catch them in an unfavourable position while you yourself are in a strong position, when they are in sight to you and while you yourself are unseen."

36. Καὶ πῶς ἄν, ἔφη, τις τοιαῦτα, ὦ πάτερ, ἁμαρτάνοντας δύναιτ' ἂν τοὺς πολεμίους λαμβάνειν;

Ὅτι, ἔφη, ὦ παῖ, πολλὰ μὲν τούτων ἀνάγκη ἐστὶ καὶ ὑμᾶς καὶ τοὺς πολεμίους παρασχεῖν· σιτοποιεῖσθαί τε γὰρ ἀνάγκη ἀμφοτέρους, κοιμᾶσθαί τε ἀνάγκη ἀμφοτέρους, καὶ ἕωθεν ἐπὶ τἀναγκαῖα σχεδὸν ἅμα πάντας δεῖ ἵεσθαι καὶ ταῖς ὁδοῖς ὁποῖαι ἂν ὦσι τοιαύταις ἀνάγκη χρῆσθαι. ἃ χρή σε πάντα κατανοοῦντα, ἐν ᾧ μὲν ἂν ὑμᾶς γιγνώσκῃς ἀσθενεστάτους γιγνομένους, ἐν τούτῳ μάλιστα φυλάττεσθαι· ἐν ᾧ δ' ἂν τοὺς πολεμίους αἰσθάνῃ εὐχειρωτοτάτους[1] γιγνομένους, ἐν τούτῳ μάλιστα ἐπιτίθεσθαι.

37. Πότερον δ', ἔφη ὁ Κῦρος, ἐν τούτοις μόνον ἔστι πλεονεκτεῖν ἢ καὶ ἐν ἄλλοις τισί;

Καὶ πολύ γε μᾶλλον, ἔφη, ὦ παῖ· ἐν τούτοις μὲν γὰρ ὡς ἐπὶ τὸ πολὺ πάντες ἰσχυρὰς φυλακὰς ποιοῦνται εἰδότες ὅτι δέονται. οἱ δ' ἐξαπατῶντες τοὺς πολεμίους δύνανται καὶ θαρρῆσαι ποιήσαντες ἀφυλάκτους λαμβάνειν καὶ διῶξαι παραδόντες ἑαυτοὺς ἀτάκτους ποιῆσαι καὶ εἰς δυσχωρίαν φυγῇ ὑπαγαγόντες ἐνταῦθα ἐπιτίθεσθαι. 38. δεῖ δή, ἔφη, φιλομαθῆ σε τούτων ἁπάντων ὄντα οὐχ οἷς ἂν μάθῃς τούτοις μόνοις χρῆσθαι, ἀλλὰ καὶ αὐτὸν ποιητὴν εἶναι τῶν πρὸς τοὺς πολεμίους μηχανημάτων, ὥσπερ καὶ οἱ μουσικοὶ οὐχ οἷς ἂν μάθωσι τούτοις μόνον χρῶνται, ἀλλὰ καὶ ἄλλα νέα πειρῶνται ποιεῖν. καὶ σφόδρα μὲν καὶ ἐν τοῖς μουσικοῖς τὰ νέα[2]

[1] εὐχειρωτοτάτους Stephanus, Edd.; εὐχειρο(ωR)τάτους MSS.
[2] νέα zR, most Edd.; νέα μέλη x; μέλη y (*songs*).

36. "And how, father," said he, "could one catch the enemy making such mistakes?"

"Why, my son," said he, "both you and the enemy must necessarily offer many such opportunities; for instance, you must both eat, and you must both sleep, and early in the morning you must almost all at the same time attend to the calls of nature, and you must make use of such roads as you find. All this you must observe, and you must be particularly watchful on the side where you know yourselves to be weaker, and you must attack the enemy above all in that quarter in which you see that they are most vulnerable."

37. "And is it possible to take advantage in these ways only," said Cyrus, "or in other ways also?"

"Aye, far more in other ways, my son," said he; "for in these particulars all men, as a rule, take strict precautions; for they know that they must. But those whose business it is to deceive the enemy can catch them off their guard by inspiring them with over-confidence; and, by offering them the opportunity of pursuit, can get them into disorder; and, by leading them on into unfavourable ground by pretended flight, can there turn and attack them. 38. However, my son," he continued, "since you are desirous of learning all these matters, you must not only utilize what you may learn from others, but you must yourself also be an inventor of stratagems against the enemy, just as musicians render not only those compositions which they have learned but try to compose others also that are new. Now if in

καὶ ἀνθηρὰ εὐδοκιμεῖ, πολὺ δὲ καὶ ἐν τοῖς πολεμικοῖς μᾶλλον τὰ καινὰ μηχανήματα εὐδοκιμεῖ· ταῦτα γὰρ μᾶλλον καὶ ἐξαπατᾶν δύναται τοὺς ὑπεναντίους.

39. Εἰ δὲ σύ γε, ἔφη, ὦ παῖ, μηδὲν ἄλλο ἢ μετενέγκοις ἐπ᾽ ἀνθρώπους τὰς μηχανὰς ἃς καὶ πάνυ ἐπὶ τοῖς μικροῖς θηρίοις ἐμηχανῶ, οὐκ οἴει ἄν, ἔφη, πρόσω πάνυ ἐλάσαι τῆς πρὸς τοὺς πολεμίους πλεονεξίας; σὺ γὰρ ἐπὶ μὲν τὰς ὄρνιθας ἐν τῷ ἰσχυροτάτῳ χειμῶνι ἀνιστάμενος ἐπορεύου νυκτός, καὶ πρὶν κινεῖσθαι τὰς ὄρνιθας ἐπεποίηντό σοι αἱ πάγαι αὐταῖς καὶ τὸ κεκινημένον χωρίον ἐξείκαστο τῷ ἀκινήτῳ· ὄρνιθες δ᾽ ἐπεπαίδευντό σοι ὥστε σοὶ μὲν τὰ συμφέροντα ὑπηρετεῖν, τὰς δὲ ὁμοφύλους ὄρνιθας ἐξαπατᾶν· αὐτὸς δὲ ἐνήδρευες, ὥστε ὁρᾶν μὲν αὐτάς, μὴ ὁρᾶσθαι δὲ ὑπ᾽ αὐτῶν· ἠσκήκεις δὲ φθάνων ἕλκειν ἢ τὰ πτηνὰ φεύγειν. 40. πρὸς δ᾽ αὖ τὸν λαγῶ, ὅτι μὲν ἐν σκότει νέμεται, τὴν δ᾽ ἡμέραν ἀποδιδράσκει, κύνας ἔτρεφες αἳ τῇ ὀσμῇ αὐτὸν ἀνηύρισκον.[1] ὅτι δὲ ταχὺ ἔφευγεν, ἐπεὶ εὑρεθείη, ἄλλας κύνας εἶχες ἐπιτετηδευμένας πρὸς τὸ κατὰ πόδας αἱρεῖν. εἰ δὲ καὶ ταύτας ἀποφύγοι, τοὺς πόρους αὐτῶν ἐκμανθάνων καὶ πρὸς οἷα χωρία φεύγοντες αἱροῦνται[2] οἱ λαγῴ, ἐν τούτοις δίκτυα δυσόρατα ἐνεπετάννυς ἄν, ἵνα ἐν τῷ σφόδρα φεύγειν αὐτὸς ἑαυτὸν ἐμπεσὼν συνέδει. τοῦ δὲ μηδ᾽ ἐντεῦθεν διαφεύγειν σκοποὺς τοῦ γιγνομένου

[1] **ἀνηύρισκον** y, most Edd.; **εὕρισκον** xzR, Sauppe.

[2] **πρὸς . . . αἱροῦνται** MSS., Dindorf, Breitenbach; **[πρὸς] . . . αἱροῦνται** Hug (*places which hares choose in their flight*); **πρὸς . . . ἀεὶ ὁρῶνται** Gemoll; **πρὸς . . .ἀφικνοῦνται** Marchant.

music that which is new and fresh wins applause, new stratagems in warfare also win far greater applause, for such can deceive the enemy even more successfully.

39. "And if you, my son," he went on, "should do nothing more than apply to your dealings with men the tricks that you used to practise so constantly in dealing with small game, do you not think that you would make a very considerable advance in the art of taking advantage of the enemy? For you used to get up in the coldest winter weather and go out before daylight to catch birds, and before the birds were astir you had your snares laid ready for them and the ground disturbed had been made exactly like the ground undisturbed; and your decoy birds had been so trained as to serve your purposes and to deceive the birds of the same species, while you yourself would lie in hiding so as to see them but not to be seen by them; and you had practised drawing your nets before the birds could escape. 40. And again, to catch the hare—because he feeds in the night and hides in the daytime—you used to breed dogs that would find him out by the scent. And because he ran so fast, when he was found, you used to have other dogs trained to catch him by coursing. And in case he escaped even these, you used to find out the runs and the places where hares take refuge and may be caught, and there you would spread out your nets so as to be hardly visible, and the hare in his headlong flight would plunge into them and entangle himself. And lest he escape even from that, you used to station men to watch for what might happen and to pounce

The lessons of the chase applied to the arts of war

καθίστης, οἳ ἐγγύθεν ταχὺ ἔμελλον ἐπιγενήσεσθαι· καὶ αὐτὸς μὲν σὺ ὄπισθεν κραυγῇ οὐδὲν ὑστεριζούσῃ τοῦ λαγῶ βοῶν ἐξέπληττες αὐτὸν ὥστε ἄφρονα[1] ἁλίσκεσθαι, τοὺς δ' ἔμπροσθεν σιγᾶν διδάξας ἐνεδρεύοντας λανθάνειν ἐποίεις.

41. Ὥσπερ οὖν προεῖπον, εἰ τοιαῦτα ἐθελήσαις καὶ ἐπὶ τοῖς ἀνθρώποις μηχανᾶσθαι, οὐκ οἶδ' ἔγωγε εἴ τινος λείποιο[2] ἂν τῶν πολεμίων. ἢν δέ ποτε ἄρα ἀνάγκη γένηται καὶ ἐν τῷ ἰσοπέδῳ καὶ ἐκ τοῦ ἐμφανοῦς καὶ ὡπλισμένους ἀμφοτέρους μάχην συνάπτειν, ἐν τῷ τοιούτῳ δή, ὦ παῖ, αἱ ἐκ πολλοῦ παρεσκευασμέναι πλεονεξίαι μέγα δύνανται. ταύτας δὲ ἐγὼ λέγω εἶναι, ἢν τῶν στρατιωτῶν εὖ μὲν τὰ σώματα ἠσκημένα ᾖ, εὖ δὲ αἱ ψυχαὶ τεθηγμέναι, εὖ δὲ αἱ πολεμικαὶ τέχναι μεμελετημέναι ὦσιν. 42. εὖ δὲ χρὴ καὶ τοῦτο εἰδέναι ὅτι ὁπόσους ἂν ἀξιοῖς σοι πείθεσθαι, καὶ ἐκεῖνοι πάντες ἀξιώσουσι σὲ πρὸ ἑαυτῶν βουλεύεσθαι. μηδέποτ' οὖν ἀφροντίστως ἔχε, ἀλλὰ τῆς μὲν νυκτὸς προσκόπει τί σοι ποιήσουσιν οἱ ἀρχόμενοι, ἐπειδὰν ἡμέρα γένηται, τῆς δ' ἡμέρας ὅπως τὰ εἰς νύκτα κάλλιστα ἕξει. 43. ὅπως δὲ χρὴ τάττειν εἰς μάχην στρατιὰν ἢ ὅπως ἄγειν ἡμέρας ἢ νυκτὸς ἢ στενὰς ἢ πλατείας ὁδοὺς ἢ ὀρεινὰς ἢ πεδινάς, ἢ ὅπως στρατοπεδεύεσθαι, ἢ ὅπως φυλακὰς νυκτερινὰς καὶ ἡμερινὰς καθιστάναι, ἢ ὅπως προσάγειν πρὸς πολεμίους ἢ ἀπάγειν ἀπὸ πολεμίων, ἢ ὅπως παρὰ πόλιν πολεμίαν

[1] ἄφρονα Hertlein, most Edd.; ἀφρ(ἀφθ z)όνως MSS., Dindorf, Sauppe.

[2] τινος λείποιο Hertlein, most Edd.; τινα λείποις yR; τινὰς λίποις z; τινα λίποις ("leave any man alive") Dindorf.

upon him suddenly from a place near by. And you yourself from behind shouting with a cry that kept right up with the hare would frighten him so that he would lose his wits and be taken; those in front, on the other hand, you had instructed to keep silent and made them lie concealed in ambush.

Cambyses's concluding suggestions

41. "As I said before, then, if you would employ such schemes on men also, I am inclined to think that you would not come short of any enemy in the world. But if it is ever necessary—as it may well be—to join battle in the open field, in plain sight, with both armies in full array, why, in such a case, my son, the advantages that have been long since secured are of much avail; by that I mean, if your soldiers are physically in good training, if their hearts are well steeled and the arts of war well studied. 42. Besides, you must remember well that all those from whom you expect obedience to you will, on their part, expect you to take thought for them. So never be careless, but think out at night what your men are to do for you when day comes, and in the daytime think out how the arrangements for the night may best be made. 43. But how you ought to draw up an army in battle array, or how you ought to lead it by day or by night, by narrow ways or broad, over mountains or plains, or how you should pitch camp, or how station your sentinels by night or by day, or how you should advance against the enemy or retreat before them, or how you should lead past a hostile city, or how attack a fortification or withdraw from

ἄγειν ἢ ὅπως πρὸς τεῖχος ἄγειν ἢ ἀπάγειν, ἢ ὅπως νάπη ἢ ποταμοὺς διαβαίνειν, ἢ ὅπως ἱππικὸν φυλάττεσθαι ἢ ὅπως ἀκοντιστὰς ἢ τοξότας, καὶ εἴ γε δή σοι κατὰ κέρας ἄγοντι οἱ πολέμιοι ἐπιφανεῖεν, πῶς χρὴ ἀντικαθιστάναι, καὶ εἴ σοι ἐπὶ φάλαγγος ἄγοντι ἄλλοθέν ποθεν οἱ πολέμιοι φαίνοιντο ἢ κατὰ πρόσωπον, ὅπως χρὴ ἀντιπαράγειν, ἢ ὅπως τὰ τῶν πολεμίων ἄν τις μάλιστα αἰσθάνοιτο, ἢ ὅπως τὰ σὰ οἱ πολέμιοι ἥκιστα εἰδεῖεν, ταῦτα δὲ πάντα[1] τί ἂν ἐγὼ λέγοιμί σοι; ὅσα τε γὰρ ἔγωγε ᾔδειν, πολλάκις ἀκήκοας, ἄλλος τε ὅστις ἐδόκει τι τούτων ἐπίστασθαι, οὐδενὸς αὐτῶν ἠμέληκας οὐδ᾽ ἀδαὴς γεγένησαι. δεῖ οὖν πρὸς τὰ συμβαίνοντα, οἶμαι, τούτοις χρῆσθαι ὁποῖον ἂν συμφέρειν σοι τούτων δοκῇ.

44. Μάθε δέ μου καὶ τάδε, ὦ παῖ, ἔφη, τὰ μέγιστα· παρὰ γὰρ ἱερὰ καὶ οἰωνοὺς μήτε σαυτῷ μηδέποτε μήτε στρατιᾷ κινδυνεύσῃς, κατανοῶν ὡς ἄνθρωποι μὲν αἱροῦνται πράξεις εἰκάζοντες, εἰδότες δὲ οὐδὲν ἀπὸ ποίας ἔσται αὐτοῖς τἀγαθά. 45. γνοίης δ᾽ ἂν ἐξ αὐτῶν τῶν γιγνομένων· πολλοὶ μὲν γὰρ ἤδη πόλεις ἔπεισαν καὶ ταῦτα οἱ δοκοῦντες σοφώτατοι εἶναι πόλεμον ἄρασθαι πρὸς τούτους ὑφ᾽ ὧν οἱ πεισθέντες ἐπιθέσθαι ἀπώλοντο, πολλοὶ δὲ πολλοὺς ηὔξησαν καὶ ἰδιώτας καὶ πόλεις ὑφ᾽ ὧν αὐξηθέντων τὰ μέγιστα κακὰ ἔπαθον, πολλοὶ δὲ οἷς ἐξῆν φίλοις χρῆσθαι καὶ εὖ ποιεῖν καὶ εὖ πάσχειν, τούτοις δούλοις

[1] πάντα y, Edd.; not in xzR.

it, or how you should cross ravines or rivers, or how you should protect yourself against cavalry or spear-men or bowmen, and if the enemy should suddenly come in sight while you are leading on in column, how you should form and take your stand against them, and if they should come in sight from any other quarter than in front as you are marching in phalanx, how you should form and face them, or how any one might best find out the enemy's plans or how the enemy might be least likely to learn his—why should I tell you all these things? For what I, for my part, know, you have often heard; and if any one else had a reputation for understanding anything of that kind, you never neglected to get information from him, nor have you been uninstructed. I think, then, that you should turn this knowledge to account according to circumstances, as each item of it may appear serviceable to you.

Obedience to divine guidance the first rule

44. "Learn this lesson, too, from me, my son," said he; "it is the most important thing of all: never go into any danger either to yourself or to your army contrary to the omens or the auspices, and bear in mind that men choose lines of action by conjecture and do not know in the least from which of them success will come. 45. But you may derive this lesson from the facts of history; for many, and men, too, who seemed most wise, have ere now persuaded states to take up arms against others, and the states thus persuaded to attack have been destroyed. And many have made many others great, both individuals and states; and when they have exalted them, they have suffered the most grievous wrongs at their hands. And many who

μᾶλλον βουληθέντες ἢ φίλοις χρῆσθαι, ὑπ' αὐτῶν τούτων δίκην ἔδοσαν· πολλοῖς δ' οὐκ ἤρκεσεν αὐτοῖς τὸ μέρος ἔχουσι ζῆν ἡδέως, ἐπιθυμήσαντες δὲ πάντων κύριοι εἶναι, διὰ ταῦτα καὶ ὧν εἶχον ἀπέτυχον· πολλοὶ δὲ τὸν πολύευκτον πλοῦτον κατακτησάμενοι, διὰ τοῦτον ἀπώλοντο. 46. οὕτως ἡ ἀνθρωπίνη σοφία οὐδὲν μᾶλλον οἶδε τὸ ἄριστον αἱρεῖσθαι ἢ εἰ κληρούμενος ὅ τι λάχοι τοῦτό τις πράττοι. θεοὶ δέ, ὦ παῖ, ἀεὶ ὄντες πάντα ἴσασι τά τε γεγενημένα καὶ τὰ ὄντα καὶ ὅ τι ἐξ ἑκάστου αὐτῶν ἀποβήσεται, καὶ τῶν συμβουλευομένων ἀνθρώπων οἷς ἂν ἵλεῳ ὦσι, προσημαίνουσιν ἅ τε χρὴ ποιεῖν καὶ ἃ οὐ χρή. εἰ δὲ μὴ πᾶσιν ἐθέλουσι συμβουλεύειν, οὐδὲν θαυμαστόν· οὐ γὰρ ἀνάγκη αὐτοῖς ἐστιν ὧν ἂν μὴ ἐθέλωσιν ἐπιμέλεσθαι.

might have treated people as friends and done them favours and received favours from them, have received their just deserts from these very people because they preferred to treat them like slaves rather than as friends. Many, too, not satisfied to live contentedly in the enjoyment of their own proper share, have lost even that which they had, because they have desired to be lords of everything; and many, when they have gained the much coveted wealth, have been ruined by it. 46. So we see that mere human wisdom does not know how to choose what is best any more than if any one were to cast lots and do as the lot fell. But the gods, my son, the eternal gods, know all things, both what has been and what is and what shall come to pass as a result of each present or past event; and if men consult them, they reveal to those to whom they are propitious what they ought to do and what they ought not to do. But if they are not willing to give counsel to everybody, that is not surprising; for they are under no compulsion to care for any one unless they will."

BOOK II

THE REORGANIZATION OF THE ARMY

B

I

1. Τοιαῦτα μὲν δὴ ἀφίκοντο διαλεγόμενοι μέχρι τῶν ὁρίων τῆς Περσίδος· ἐπεὶ δ' αὐτοῖς ἀετὸς δεξιὸς φανεὶς προηγεῖτο, προσευξάμενοι θεοῖς καὶ ἥρωσι τοῖς Περσίδα γῆν κατέχουσιν ἵλεως καὶ εὐμενεῖς πέμπειν σφᾶς, οὕτω διέβαινον τὰ ὅρια. ἐπειδὴ δὲ διέβησαν, προσηύχοντο αὖθις θεοῖς τοῖς Μηδίαν γῆν κατέχουσιν ἵλεως καὶ εὐμενεῖς δέχεσθαι αὐτούς. ταῦτα δὲ ποιήσαντες, ἀσπασάμενοι ἀλλήλους ὥσπερ εἰκός, ὁ μὲν πατὴρ πάλιν εἰς Πέρσας[1] ἀπῄει, Κῦρος δὲ εἰς Μήδους πρὸς Κυαξάρην ἐπορεύετο.

2. Ἐπεὶ δὲ ἀφίκετο ὁ Κῦρος εἰς Μήδους πρὸς τὸν Κυαξάρην, πρῶτον μὲν ὥσπερ εἰκὸς ἠσπάσαντο ἀλλήλους, ἔπειτα δὲ ἤρετο τὸν Κῦρον ὁ Κυαξάρης πόσον τι ἄγοι τὸ στράτευμα.

Ὁ δὲ ἔφη, Τρισμυρίους[2] μὲν οἷοι καὶ πρόσθεν ἐφοίτων πρὸς ὑμᾶς μισθοφόροι· ἄλλοι δὲ καὶ τῶν οὐδέποτε ἐξελθόντων προσέρχονται τῶν ὁμοτίμων.

Πόσοι τινές; ἔφη ὁ Κυαξάρης.

3. Οὐκ ἂν ὁ ἀριθμός σε, ἔφη ὁ Κῦρος ἀκούσαντα εὐφράνειεν· ἀλλ' ἐκεῖνο ἐννόησον

[1] Πέρσας xy, most Edd.; πόλιν z, Dindorf, Sauppe (*to the capital*). [2] τρισμυρίους Aldus, Edd.; δισμυρίους MSS.

BOOK II

I

1. In such conversation they arrived at the Persian frontier. And when an eagle appeared upon their right and flew on ahead of them, they prayed to the gods and heroes who watch over the land of Persia to conduct them on with grace and favour, and then proceeded to cross the frontier. And when they had crossed, they prayed again to the tutelary gods of the Median land to receive them with grace and favour; and when they had finished their devotions, they embraced one another, as was natural, and the father went back again to Persia, while Cyrus went on to Cyaxares in Media.

Cyrus arrives in Media

2. And when he arrived there, first they embraced one another, as was natural, and then Cyaxares asked Cyrus how large the army was that he was bringing.

Cyrus and Cyaxares discuss the situation

"Thirty thousand," he answered, "of such as have come to you before as mercenaries; but others also, of the peers, who have never before left their country, are coming."

"About how many?" asked Cyaxares.

3. "The number," said Cyrus, "would give you no pleasure, if you were to hear it; but bear this in

ὅτι ὀλίγοι ὄντες οὗτοι οἱ ὁμότιμοι καλούμενοι πολλῶν ὄντων τῶν ἄλλων Περσῶν ῥᾳδίως ἄρχουσιν. ἀτάρ, ἔφη, δέει τι αὐτῶν ἢ μάτην ἐφοβήθης, οἱ δὲ πολέμιοι οὐκ ἔρχονται;

Ναὶ μὰ Δί᾽, ἔφη, καὶ πολλοί γε.

4. Πῶς τοῦτο σαφές;

Ὅτι, ἔφη, πολλοὶ ἥκοντες αὐτόθεν ἄλλος ἄλλον τρόπον πάντες ταὐτὸ λέγουσιν.

Ἀγωνιστέον μὲν ἄρα ἡμῖν πρὸς τοὺς ἄνδρας.

Ἀνάγκη γάρ, ἔφη.

Τί οὖν, ἔφη ὁ Κῦρος, οὐ καὶ τὴν δύναμιν ἔλεξάς μοι, εἰ οἶσθα, πόση τις ἡ προσιοῦσα, καὶ πάλιν τὴν ἡμετέραν, ὅπως εἰδότες ἀμφοτέρας πρὸς ταῦτα βουλευώμεθα ὅπως ἂν ἄριστα ἀγωνιζοίμεθα;

Ἄκουε δή, ἔφη ὁ Κυαξάρης. 5. Κροῖσος μὲν ὁ Λυδὸς ἄγειν λέγεται μυρίους μὲν ἱππέας, πελταστὰς δὲ καὶ τοξότας πλείους ἢ τετρακισμυρίους. Ἀρτακάμαν δὲ τὸν τῆς μεγάλης Φρυγίας ἄρχοντα λέγουσιν ἱππέας μὲν εἰς ὀκτακισχιλίους ἄγειν, λογχοφόρους δὲ σὺν πελτασταῖς οὐ μείους τετρακισμυρίων, Ἀρίβαιον δὲ τὸν τῶν Καππαδοκῶν βασιλέα ἱππέας μὲν ἑξακισχιλίους, τοξότας δὲ καὶ πελταστὰς οὐ μείους τρισμυρίων, τὸν Ἀράβιον δὲ Ἄραγδον ἱππέας τε εἰς μυρίους καὶ ἅρματα εἰς ἑκατὸν καὶ σφενδονητῶν πάμπολύ τι χρῆμα. τοὺς μέντοι Ἕλληνας τοὺς ἐν τῇ Ἀσίᾳ οἰκοῦντας οὐδέν πω σαφὲς λέγεται εἰ ἕπονται. τοὺς δὲ ἀπὸ Φρυγίας τῆς πρὸς Ἑλλησπόντῳ συμβαλεῖν φασι Γάβαιδον ἔχοντα εἰς Καΰστρου Πεδίον ἑξακισχιλίους μὲν ἱππέας, πελταστὰς δὲ

mind, that though the so-called peers are few, they easily rule the rest of the Persians, many though they be. But," he added, "are you in any need of them, or was it a false alarm, and are the enemy not coming?"

"Yes, by Zeus," said he, "they are coming and in great numbers, too."

4. "How is this so certain?"

"Because," said he, "many have come from there, and though one tells the story one way and another another, they all say the same thing."

"We shall have to fight those men, then?"

"Aye," said he; "we must of necessity."

"Well then," said Cyrus, "won't you please tell me, if you know, how great the forces are that are coming against us; and tell me of our own as well, so that with full information about both we may lay our plans accordingly, how best to enter the conflict."

"Listen then," said Cyaxares. 5. "Croesus, the king of Lydia, is said to be coming at the head of 10,000 horsemen and more than 40,000 peltasts and bowmen. And they say that Artacamas, the king of Greater Phrygia, is coming at the head of 8000 horse and not fewer than 40,000 lancers and peltasts; and Aribaeus, the king of Cappadocia, has 6000 horse and not fewer than 30,000 bowmen and peltasts; while the Arabian, Aragdus, has about 10,000 horsemen, about 100 chariots of war, and a great host of slingers. As for the Greeks who dwell in Asia, however, no definite information is as yet received whether they are in the coalition or not. But the contingent from Phrygia on the Hellespont, under Gabaedus, has arrived at Caÿstru-Pedium, it is said, to the number of 6000 horse and 10,000 peltasts.

The probable number of the opposing forces

εἰς μυρίους. Κᾶρας μέντοι καὶ Κίλικας καὶ Παφλαγόνας παρακληθέντας οὔ φασιν ἕπεσθαι. ὁ δὲ Ἀσσύριος ὁ Βαβυλῶνά τε ἔχων καὶ τὴν ἄλλην Ἀσσυρίαν ἐγὼ μὲν οἶμαι ἱππέας μὲν ἄξει οὐκ ἐλάττους δισμυρίων, ἅρματα δ' εὖ οἶδ' οὐ μεῖον διακοσίων, πεζοὺς δὲ οἶμαι παμπόλλους· εἰώθει γοῦν ὁπότε δεῦρ' ἐμβάλλοι.

6. Σύ, ἔφη ὁ Κῦρος, πολεμίους λέγεις ἱππέας μὲν ἑξακισμυρίους εἶναι, πελταστὰς δὲ καὶ τοξότας πλεῖον ἢ εἴκοσι μυριάδας. ἄγε δὴ τῆς σῆς δυνάμεως τί φῂς πλῆθος εἶναι;

Εἰσίν, ἔφη, Μήδων μὲν ἱππεῖς πλείους τῶν μυρίων· πελτασταὶ δὲ καὶ τοξόται γένοιντ' ἂν πως ἐκ[1] τῆς ἡμετέρας κἂν ἑξακισμύριοι. Ἀρμενίων δ', ἔφη, τῶν ὁμόρων ἡμῖν παρέσονται ἱππεῖς μὲν τετρακισχίλιοι, πεζοὶ δὲ δισμύριοι.

Λέγεις σύ, ἔφη ὁ Κῦρος, ἱππέας μὲν ἡμῖν εἶναι μεῖον ἢ τέταρτον[2] μέρος τοῦ τῶν πολεμίων ἱππικοῦ, πεζοὺς δὲ αμφὶ τοὺς ἡμίσεις.

7. Τί οὖν, ἔφη ὁ Κυαξάρης, οὐκ ὀλίγους νομίζεις Περσῶν εἶναι οὓς σὺ φῂς ἄγειν;

Ἀλλ' εἰ μὲν ἀνδρῶν προσδεῖ ἡμῖν, ἔφη ὁ Κῦρος, εἴτε καὶ μή, αὖθις συμβουλευσόμεθα· τὴν δὲ μάχην μοι, ἔφη, λέξον ἑκάστων ἥτις ἐστί.

Σχεδόν, ἔφη ὁ Κυαξάρης, πάντων ἡ αὐτή· τοξόται γάρ εἰσι καὶ ἀκοντισταὶ οἵ τ' ἐκείνων καὶ οἱ ἡμέτεροι.

Οὐκοῦν, ἔφη ὁ Κῦρος, ἀκροβολίζεσθαι ἀνάγκη ἐστὶ τοιούτων γε τῶν ὅπλων ὄντων.

[1] **πως ἐκ** Breitenbach, later Edd.; **ὡς ἐπὶ** MSS., except E which omits **ὡς**.

[2] **τέταρτον** Hug, Gemoll, Marchant, Breitenbach ; **τρίτον** xz Dindorf (*a third*) ; **τὸ τρίτον** y.

he Carians, however, and Cilicians and Paphla-
onians, they say, have not joined the expedition,
.though they have been invited to do so. But the
ssyrians, both those from Babylon and those from
ıe rest of Assyria, will bring, I think, not fewer
ıan 20,000 horse and not fewer, I am sure, than 200
ar-chariots, and a vast number of infantry, I suppose;
; any rate, they used to have as many as that when-
ver they invaded our country."

6. "You mean to say," said Cyrus, "that the
ıemy have 60,000 horse and more than 200,000
eltasts and bowmen. And at how many, pray,
o you estimate the number of your own forces?"

"There are," said he, "of the Medes more than
0,000 horse; and the peltasts and bowmen might
e, from a country like ours, some 60,000; while from
ur neighbours, the Armenians, we shall get 4000
orse and 20,000 foot."

"That is to say," said Cyrus, "we have less than
ne-fourth as many horsemen as the enemy and
bout half as many foot-soldiers."

7. "Tell me, then," said Cyaxares, "do you not
onsider the Persian force small which you say you
re bringing?"

Their method of warfare

"Yes," said Cyrus; "but we will consider later
hether we need more men or not. Now tell me,"
e went on, "what each party's method of fighting
."

"About the same with all," said Cyaxares; "for
here are bowmen and spearmen both on their side
nd on ours."

"Well then," said Cyrus, "as their arms are of
hat sort, we must fight at long range."

8. Ἀνάγκη γὰρ οὖν, ἔφη ὁ Κυαξάρης.

Οὐκοῦν ἐν τούτῳ μὲν τῶν πλειόνων ἡ νίκη πολὺ γὰρ ἂν θᾶττον οἱ ὀλίγοι ὑπὸ τῶν πολλῶ τιτρωσκόμενοι ἀναλωθείησαν ἢ οἱ πολλοὶ ὑπὸ τῶ ὀλίγων.[1]

Εἰ οὖν οὕτως ἔχει, ὦ Κῦρε, τί ἂν ἄλλο τι κρεῖττον εὕροι ἢ πέμπειν εἰς Πέρσας, καὶ ἅμα μὲ διδάσκειν αὐτοὺς ὅτι εἴ τι πείσονται Μῆδοι, εἰ Πέρσας τὸ δεινὸν ἥξει, ἅμα δὲ αἰτεῖν πλεῖο στράτευμα;

Ἀλλὰ τοῦτο μέν, ἔφη ὁ Κῦρος, εὖ ἴσθι ὅτ οὐδ' εἰ πάντες ἔλθοιεν Πέρσαι, πλήθει οὐχ ὑπερ βαλοίμεθ' ἂν τοὺς πολεμίους.

9. Τί μὴν ἄλλο ἐνορᾷς ἄμεινον τούτου;

Ἐγὼ μὲν ἄν, ἔφη ὁ Κῦρος, εἰ σὺ εἴην, ὡ τάχιστα ὅπλα ποιοίμην πᾶσι Πέρσαις τοῖς προσ ιοῦσιν οἷάπερ ἔχοντες ἔρχονται παρ' ἡμῶν ο τῶν ὁμοτίμων καλούμενοι· ταῦτα δ' ἐστὶ θώρα μὲν περὶ τὰ στέρνα, γέρρον δὲ εἰς τὴν ἀριστεράν κοπὶς δὲ ἢ σάγαρις εἰς τὴν δεξιάν· κἂν ταῦτ παρασκευάσῃς, ἡμῖν μὲν ποιήσεις τὸ ὁμόσε τοῖ ἐναντίοις ἰέναι ἀσφαλέστατον, τοῖς πολεμίοις δ τὸ φεύγειν ἢ τὸ μένειν αἱρετώτερον. τάττομεν δ ἔφη, ἡμᾶς μὲν αὐτοὺς ἐπὶ τοὺς μένοντας· οἳ γ μεντἂν αὐτῶν φεύγωσι, τούτους ὑμῖν καὶ τοῖ ἵπποις νέμομεν, ὡς μὴ σχολάζωσι μήτε μένειν[2] μήτε ἀναστρέφεσθαι.

10. Κῦρος μὲν οὕτως ἔλεξε· τῷ δὲ Κυαξάρ

[1] Οὐκοῦν . . . ὀλίγων erroneously given to Cyaxares by Hu Gemoll, Marchant.

[2] μένειν y, most Edd. ; φεύγειν xz, Sauppe (*to make the escape*).

8. "Yes," said Cyaxares, "that will be necessary."
"In that case, then, the victory will be with
ıe side that has the greater numbers; for the few
ould be wounded and killed off by the many sooner
ıan the many by the few."
"If that is so, Cyrus, then what better plan
›uld any one think of than to send to Persia to
.form them that if anything happens to the Medes,
ıe danger will extend to the Persians, and at the
.me time to ask for a larger army?"
"Why," said Cyrus, "let me assure you that even
ıough all the Persians were to come, we should
›t surpass the enemy in point of numbers."
9. "What better plan do you see than this?"
"If I were you," said Cyrus, "I should as quickly
possible have armour made for all the Persians
ho are coming here just like that of the so-called
:ers who are coming from our country—that is, a
›rselet to wear about the breast, a small shield upon
ıe left arm, and a scimitar or sabre in the right
ınd. And if you provide these weapons, you will
ake it the safest procedure for us to fight at close
ıarters with the enemy, while for the enemy flight
ill prove preferable to standing their ground. And
is for us," he continued, "to range ourselves
;ainst those who hold their ground, while those of
ıem who run away we propose to leave to you and
ıe cavalry, that they may have no chance to stand
ıeir ground or to turn back."
10. Thus Cyrus spoke. And to Cyaxares it seemed

Proposed reorganization of the Persian commoners

ἔδοξέ τε εὖ λέγειν, καὶ τοῦ μὲν πλείους μεταπέμπεσθαι οὐκέτι ἐμέμνητο, παρεσκευάζετο δὲ ὅπλ
τὰ προειρημένα. καὶ σχεδόν τε ἕτοιμα ἦν καὶ τά
Περσῶν οἱ ὁμότιμοι παρῆσαν ἔχοντες τὸ ἀπ
Περσῶν στράτευμα.

11. Ἐνταῦθα δὴ εἰπεῖν λέγεται ὁ Κῦρος συν-
αγαγὼν αὐτούς· Ἄνδρες φίλοι, ἐγὼ ὑμᾶς ὁρᾶ
αὐτοὺς μὲν καθωπλισμένους οὕτω καὶ ταῖς ψυχα
παρεσκευασμένους ὡς εἰς χεῖρας συμμίξοντας το
πολεμίοις, τοὺς δὲ ἑπομένους ὑμῖν Πέρσας γιγνώσκων ὅτι οὕτως ὡπλισμένοι εἰσὶν ὡς ὅτι προσω-
τάτω ταχθέντες μάχεσθαι, ἔδεισα μὴ ὀλίγ
καὶ ἔρημοι συμμάχων συμπίπτοντες πολεμίο
πολλοῖς πάθοιτέ τι. νῦν οὖν, ἔφη, σώματα μὲ
ἔχοντες ἀνδρῶν ἥκετε οὐ μεμπτά· ὅπλα δὲ ἔστ
αὐτοῖς ὅμοια τοῖς ἡμετέροις· τάς γε μέντοι ψυχὰ
θήγειν αὐτῶν ἡμέτερον ἔργον. ἄρχοντος γάρ ἐστ
οὐχ ἑαυτὸν μόνον ἀγαθὸν παρέχειν, ἀλλὰ δεῖ κ
τῶν ἀρχομένων ἐπιμέλεσθαι ὅπως ὡς βέλτιστ
ἔσονται.

12. Ὁ μὲν οὕτως εἶπεν· οἱ δ' ἥσθησαν μὲ
πάντες, νομίζοντες μετὰ πλειόνων ἀγωνιεῖσθαι· ε
δ' αὐτῶν καὶ ἔλεξε τοιάδε· 13. Ἀλλὰ θαυμαστ
ἔφη, ἴσως δόξω λέγειν, εἰ Κύρῳ συμβουλεύσ
τι εἰπεῖν ὑπὲρ ἡμῶν, ὅταν τὰ ὅπλα λαμβάνωσ
οἱ ἡμῖν μέλλοντες συμμάχεσθαι· ἀλλὰ γιγνώσκ
γάρ, ἔφη, ὅτι οἱ τῶν ἱκανωτάτων καὶ εὖ κ
κακῶς ποιεῖν λόγοι οὗτοι καὶ μάλιστα ἐνδύοντ
ταῖς ψυχαῖς τῶν ἀκουόντων· καὶ δῶρα ἢν διδῶσ
οἱ τοιοῦτοι, κἂν μείω τυγχάνῃ ὄντα ἢ τὰ παρ
τῶν ὁμοίων, ὅμως μείζονος αὐτὰ τιμῶνται οἱ λαμβάνοντες. καὶ νῦν, ἔφη, οἱ Πέρσαι παραστάτ

hat he spoke to the point; and he no longer talked of sending for reinforcements, but he set about procuring the arms as suggested. And they were almost ready when the Persian peers came with the army from Persia.

11. Thereupon Cyrus is said to have called the peers together and said: "My friends: When I saw you thus equipped and ready in heart to grapple with the enemy in a hand-to-hand encounter, and when I observed that those Persians who follow you are so armed as to do their fighting standing as far off as possible, I was afraid lest, few in number and unaccompanied by others to support you, you might fall in with a large division of the enemy and come to some harm. Now then," said he, "you have brought with you men blameless in bodily strength; and they are to have arms like ours; but to steel their hearts is our task; for it is not the whole duty of an officer to show himself valiant, but he must also take care that his men be as valiant as possible."

Cyrus announces to the peers the proposed change

12. Thus he spoke. And they were all delighted, for they thought they were going into battle with more to support them. And one of them also spoke as follows: 13. "Now," he began, "it will perhaps sound strange if I advise Cyrus to say something on our behalf, when those who are to fight along with us receive their arms. But I venture the suggestion, for I know that when men have most power to do both good and ill, then their words also are the most likely to sink deep into the hearts of the hearers. And if such persons give presents, even though the gifts be of less worth than those given by equals, still the recipients value them more highly. And now," said he, "our Persian comrades will be more

ὑπὸ Κύρου πολὺ μᾶλλον ἡσθήσονται ἢ ὑφ' ἡμῶν παρακαλούμενοι, εἴς τε τοὺς ὁμοτίμους καθιστάμενοι βεβαιοτέρως σφίσιν ἡγήσονται ἔχειν τοῦτο ὑπὸ βασιλέως τε παιδὸς καὶ ὑπὸ στρατηγοῦ γενόμενον ἢ εἰ ὑφ' ἡμῶν τὸ αὐτὸ τοῦτο γίγνοιτο. ἀπεῖναι μέντοι οὐδὲ τὰ ἡμέτερα χρή, ἀλλὰ παντὶ τρόπῳ δεῖ τῶν ἀνδρῶν θήγειν πάντως τὸ φρόνημα. ἡμῖν γὰρ ἔσται τοῦτο χρήσιμον ὅ τι ἂν οὗτοι βελτίονες γένωνται.

14. Οὕτω δὴ ὁ Κῦρος καταθεὶς τὰ ὅπλα εἰς τὸ μέσον καὶ συγκαλέσας πάντας τοὺς Περσῶν στρατιώτας ἔλεξε τοιάδε· 15. Ἄνδρες Πέρσαι, ὑμεῖς καὶ ἔφυτε ἐν τῇ αὐτῇ ἡμῖν καὶ ἐτράφητε, καὶ τὰ σώματά τε οὐδὲν ἡμῶν χείρονα ἔχετε, ψυχάς τε οὐδὲν κακίονας ὑμῖν προσήκει ἡμῶν ἔχειν. τοιοῦτοι δ' ὄντες ἐν μὲν τῇ πατρίδι οὐ μετείχετε τῶν ἴσων ἡμῖν, οὐχ ὑφ' ἡμῶν ἀπελαθέντες ἀλλ' ὑπὸ τοῦ τἀπιτήδεια ἀνάγκην ὑμῖν εἶναι πορίζεσθαι. νῦν δὲ ὅπως μὲν ταῦτα ἕξετε ἐμοὶ μελήσει σὺν τοῖς θεοῖς· ἔξεστι δ' ὑμῖν, εἰ βούλεσθε, λαβόντας ὅπλα οἷάπερ ἡμεῖς ἔχομεν[1] εἰς τὸν αὐτὸν ἡμῖν κίνδυνον ἐμβαίνειν, κἂν τι ἐκ τούτων καλὸν κἀγαθὸν γίγνηται, τῶν ὁμοίων ἡμῖν ἀξιοῦσθαι.

16. Τὸν μὲν οὖν πρόσθεν χρόνον ὑμεῖς τε τοξόται καὶ ἀκοντισταὶ ἦτε καὶ ἡμεῖς, καὶ εἴ τι χείρους ἡμῶν ταῦτα ποιεῖν ἦτε, οὐδὲν θαυμαστόν· οὐ γὰρ ἦν ὑμῖν σχολὴ ὥσπερ ἡμῖν τούτων ἐπιμέλεσθαι· ἐν δὲ ταύτῃ τῇ ὁπλίσει οὐδὲν ἡμεῖς ὑμῶν προέξομεν. θώραξ μέν γε περὶ τὰ στέρνα ἁρμόττων

[1] After ἔχομεν xz and (in the margin) F add καὶ εἴ τι χείρονες ἡμῶν ἐστέ (*although you are somewhat inferior to us*).

ighly pleased to be exhorted by Cyrus than by us; nd when they have taken their place among the eers they will feel that they hold this honour with nore security because conferred by their prince and heir general than if the same honour were bestowed by us. However, our co-operation must not e wanting, but in every way and by all means we nust steel the hearts of our men. For the braver hese men are, the more to our advantage it will be."

14. Accordingly, Cyrus had the arms brought in nd arranged to view, and calling all the Persian oldiers together he spoke as follows: 15. "Fellow-citizens of Persia, you were born and bred upon the ame soil as we; the bodies you have are no whit nferior to ours, and it is not likely that you have earts in the least less brave than our own. In pite of this, in our own country you did not enjoy qual privileges with us, not because you were excluded from them by us, but because you were bliged to earn your own livelihood. Now, however, vith the help of the gods, I shall see to it that you re provided with the necessaries of life; and you re permitted, if you wish, to receive arms like ours, o face the same danger as we, and, if any fair uccess crowns our enterprise, to be counted worthy f an equal share with us.

Cyrus announces the proposed reorganization to the commoners

16. "Now, up to this time you have been bowmen nd lancers, and so have we; and if you were not uite our equals in the use of these arms, there is nothing surprising about that; for you had not the leisure o practise with them that we had. But with this quipment we shall have no advantage over you. In ny case, every man will have a corselet fitted to his

ἑκάστῳ ἔσται, γέρρον δὲ ἐν τῇ ἀριστερᾷ, ὃ πάντε
εἰθίσμεθα φορεῖν, μάχαιρα δὲ ἢ σάγαρις ἐν τ
δεξιᾷ, ᾗ δὴ παίειν τοὺς ἐναντίους δεήσει οὐδὲ
φυλαττομένους μή τι παίοντες ἐξαμάρτωμεν. 17
τί οὖν ἂν ἐν τούτοις ἕτερος ἑτέρου διαφέροι ἡμῶ
πλὴν τόλμῃ; ἣν οὐδὲν ὑμῖν ἧττον προσήκει ἢ ἡμῖ
ὑποτρέφεσθαι. νίκης τε γὰρ ἐπιθυμεῖν, ἣ τ
καλὰ πάντα καὶ τἀγαθὰ κτᾶταί τε καὶ σῴζει, τ
μᾶλλον ἡμῖν ἢ ὑμῖν προσήκει; κράτους τε, ὃ πάντ
τὰ τῶν ἡττόνων τοῖς κρείττοσι δωρεῖται, τί εἰκὸ
ἡμᾶς μᾶλλον ἢ καὶ ὑμᾶς τούτου δεῖσθαι;

18. Τέλος εἶπεν, Ἀκηκόατε πάντα· ὁρᾶτε τ
ὅπλα· ὁ μὲν χρῄζων λαμβανέτω ταῦτα καὶ ἀπο
γραφέσθω πρὸς τὸν ταξίαρχον εἰς τὴν ὁμοία
τάξιν ἡμῖν· ὅτῳ δ᾽ ἀρκεῖ ἐν μισθοφόρου χώρ
εἶναι, καταμενέτω ἐν τοῖς ὑπηρετικοῖς ὅπλοις.

Ὁ μὲν οὕτως εἶπεν. 19. ἀκούσαντες δὲ ο
Πέρσαι ἐνόμισαν, εἰ παρακαλούμενοι ὥστε τ
ὅμοια πονοῦντες τῶν αὐτῶν τυγχάνειν μὴ ἐθελή
σουσι ταῦτα ποιεῖν, δικαίως ἂν διὰ παντὸς το
αἰῶνος ἀμηχανοῦντες βιοτεύειν. οὕτω δὴ ἀπογρά
φονται πάντες ἀνέλαβόν τε τὰ ὅπλα πάντες.

20. Ἐν ᾧ δὲ οἱ πολέμιοι ἐλέγοντο μὲν προσ
ιέναι, παρῆσαν δὲ οὐδέπω, ἐν τούτῳ ἐπειρᾶτο
Κῦρος ἀσκεῖν μὲν τὰ σώματα τῶν μεθ᾽ ἑαυτο
εἰς ἰσχύν, διδάσκειν δὲ τὰ τακτικά, θήγειν δ
τὰς ψυχὰς εἰς τὰ πολεμικά. 21. καὶ πρῶτον μὲ
λαβὼν παρὰ Κυαξάρου ὑπηρέτας προσέταξε

breast, upon his left arm a shield, such as we have all been accustomed to carry, and in his right hand a sabre or scimitar with which, you see, we must strike those opposed to us at such close range that we need not fear to miss our aim when we strike. 17. In this armour, then, how could any one of us have the advantage over another except in courage? And this it is proper for you to cherish in your hearts no less than we. For why is it more proper for us than for you to desire victory, which gains and keeps safe all things beautiful and all things good? And what reason is there that we, any more than you, should desire that superiority in arms which gives to the victors all the belongings of the vanquished?

18. "You have heard all," he said in conclusion. "You see your arms; whosoever will, let him take them and have his name enrolled with the captain in the same companies with us. But whosoever is satisfied to be in the position of a mercenary, let him remain in the armour of the hired soldiery."

The commoners accept

Thus he spoke. 19. And when the Persians heard it, they thought that if they were unwilling to accept, when invited to share the same toils and enjoy the same rewards, they should deserve to live in want through all time. And so they were all enrolled and all took up the arms.

Preliminary drill

20. And while the enemy were said to be approaching but had not yet come, Cyrus tried to develop the physical strength of his men, to teach them tactics, and to steel their hearts for war. 21. And first of all he received quartermasters from Cyaxares and commanded them to furnish ready made

ἑκάστοις τῶν στρατιωτῶν ἱκανῶς[1] ὧν ἐδέοντ πάντα πεποιημένα παρασχεῖν· τοῦτο δὲ παρα σκευάσας οὐδὲν αὐτοῖς ἐλελοίπει ἄλλο ἢ ἀσκεῖ τὰ ἀμφὶ τὸν πόλεμον, ἐκεῖνο δοκῶν καταμεμαθη κέναι ὅτι οὗτοι κράτιστοι ἕκαστα γίγνονται ο ἂν ἀφέμενοι τοῦ πολλοῖς προσέχειν τὸν νοῦ ἐπὶ ἓν ἔργον τράπωνται. καὶ αὐτῶν δὲ τῶ πολεμικῶν περιελὼν καὶ τὸ τόξῳ μελετᾶν κα ἀκοντίῳ κατέλιπε τοῦτο μόνον αὐτοῖς τὸ σὺ μαχαίρᾳ καὶ γέρρῳ καὶ θώρακι μάχεσθαι· ὥστ εὐθὺς αὐτῶν παρεσκεύασε τὰς γνώμας ὡς ὁμόσ ιτέον εἴη τοῖς πολεμίοις, ἢ ὁμολογητέον μηδενὸ εἶναι ἀξίους συμμάχους· τοῦτο δὲ χαλεπὸν ὁμο λογῆσαι οἵτινες ἂν εἰδῶσιν ὅτι οὐδὲ δι' ἓ ἄλλο τρέφονται ἢ ὅπως μαχοῦνται ὑπὲρ τῶ τρεφόντων.

22. Ἔτι δὲ πρὸς τούτοις ἐννοήσας ὅτι περ ὁπόσων ἂν ἐγγένωνται ἀνθρώποις φιλονικίαι, πολὺ μᾶλλον ἐθέλουσι ταῦτ' ἀσκεῖν, ἀγῶνάς τ αὐτοῖς προεῖπεν ἁπάντων ὁπόσα ἐγίγνωσκε ἀσκεῖσθαι ἀγαθὸν εἶναι ὑπὸ στρατιωτῶν κα προεῖπε τάδε, ἰδιώτῃ μὲν ἑαυτὸν παρέχειν εὐπειθ τοῖς ἄρχουσι καὶ ἐθελόπονον καὶ φιλοκίνδυνο μετ' εὐταξίας καὶ ἐπιστήμονα τῶν στρατιωτικῶ καὶ φιλόκαλον περὶ ὅπλα καὶ φιλότιμον ἐπὶ πᾶσ τοῖς τοιούτοις, πεμπαδάρχῳ δ' αὐτὸν ὄντα οἷόνπερ τὸν ἀγαθὸν ἰδιώτην καὶ τὴν πεμπάδα εἰς τ δυνατὸν τοιαύτην παρέχειν, δεκαδάρχῳ δὲ τὴ δεκάδα ὡσαύτως, λοχαγῷ δὲ τὸν λόχον, κα

[1] ἱκανῶς Castalio, Edd.; ἱκανοὺς MSS.
[2] ἐγγένωνται . . . φιλονικίαι Hug, Gemoll, Marchant; ἐγγέ νηται . . . φιλονεικία y; γένωνται . . . φιλονεικίαι xz, Dindorf.

or each of the soldiers a liberal supply of everything hat he needed. And when he had provided for his, he had left them nothing to do but to practise he arts of war, for he thought he had observed hat those became best in any given thing who gave p paying attention to many things and devoted hemselves to that alone. So, in the drill itself he elieved them of even the practice with bow and pear and left them only the drill with sword and hield and breastplate. And so he at once brought ome to them the conviction that they must go into hand-to-hand encounter with the enemy or else dmit that as allies they were good for nothing. ut such an admission is hard for those who know hat they are being maintained for no other purpose han to fight for those who maintain them.

Competitive drill

22. And as, in addition to this, he had further bserved that people are much more willing to ractise those things in which they have rivalry mong themselves, he appointed contests for them everything that he knew it was important for ldiers to practise. What he proposed was as follows: the private soldier, that he show himself bedient to the officers, ready for hardship, eager for anger but subject to good discipline, familiar with he duties required of a soldier, neat in the care f his equipment, and ambitious about all such atters; to the corporal, that, besides being himself ke the good private, he make his squad of five a odel, as far as possible; to the sergeant, that he do kewise with his squad of ten, and the lieutenant

ταξιάρχῳ ἀνεπίκλητον αὐτὸν ὄντα ἐπιμέλεσθα
καὶ τῶν ὑφ' αὐτῷ ἀρχόντων ὅπως ἐκεῖνοι αὖ ἁ
ἂν ἄρχωσι παρέξουσι τὰ δέοντα ποιοῦντας.

23. Ἆθλα δὲ προύφηνε τοῖς μὲν ταξιάρχοις ἁ
τοὺς κρατίστας δόξαντας τὰς τάξεις παρεσκευα
σθαι χιλιάρχους ἔσεσθαι, τῶν δὲ λοχαγῶν ο
κρατίστους δόξειαν τοὺς λόχους ἀποδεικνύνα
εἰς τὰς τῶν ταξιάρχων χώρας ἐπαναβήσεσθα
τῶν δ' αὖ δεκαδάρχων τοὺς κρατίστους εἰς τὰ
τῶν λοχαγῶν χώρας καταστήσεσθαι, τῶν δ' α
πεμπαδάρχων ὡσαύτως εἰς τὰς τῶν δεκαδάρχων
τῶν γε μὴν ἰδιωτῶν τοὺς κρατιστεύοντας εἰς τὰ
τῶν πεμπαδάρχων. ὑπῆρχε δὲ πᾶσι τούτοις τοῖ
ἄρχουσι πρῶτον μὲν θεραπεύεσθαι ὑπὸ τῶ
ἀρχομένων, ἔπειτα δὲ καὶ ἄλλαι τιμαὶ αἱ πρέ
πουσαι ἑκάστοις συμπαρείποντο. ἐπανετείνοντ
δὲ καὶ μείζονες ἐλπίδες τοῖς ἀξίοις ἐπαίνου, ε
τι ἐν τῷ ἐπιόντι χρόνῳ ἀγαθὸν μεῖζον φανοῖτο
24. προεῖπε δὲ νικητήρια καὶ ὅλαις ταῖς τάξεσ
καὶ ὅλοις τοῖς λόχοις, καὶ ταῖς δεκάσιν ὡσαύτω
καὶ ταῖς πεμπάσιν, αἳ ἂν [2] φαίνωνται εὐπιστό

[1] *φανοῖτο* Cobet, most Edd.; *φαίνοιτο* MSS., Dindor
Breitenbach.
[2] *αἳ ἂν* Dindorf, most Edd.; *ἐὰν* MSS., Sauppe.

ith his platoon[1]; and to the captain, that he be nexceptionable himself and see to it that the fficers under him get those whom they command o do their duty.

Rewards of merit

23. As rewards, moreover, he offered the following: the case of captains, those who were thought to ave got their companies into the best condition hould be made colonels; of the lieutenants, those ho were thought to have put their platoons into he best condition should be advanced to the rank of aptains; of the sergeants, those who were the most eritorious should be promoted to the rank of eutenant; in the same way, the best of the corporals hould be promoted to the rank of sergeants; and nally of the privates, the best should be advanced o the rank of corporal. Moreover, all these fficers not only had a right to claim the respect f their subordinates, but other distinctions also ppropriate to each office followed in course. And o those who should deserve praise still greater hopes ere held out, in case in time to come any greater ood fortune should befall. 24. Besides, he offered rizes of victory to whole companies and to whole latoons and to squads of ten and of five likewise, if hey showed themselves implicitly obedient to the

[1] The divisions of Cyrus's army were as follows:—

	Division	*Officer*	*Total*
5 men	= 1 corporal's squad (πεμπάς)	... corporal (πεμπάδαρχος) ...	5
2 corporals' squads	= 1 sergeant's squad (δεκάς)	... sergeant (δεκάδαρχος) ...	10
5 sergeants' squads	= 1 platoon (λόχος)	... lieutenant (λοχαγός) ...	50
2 platoons	= 1 company (τάξις)	... captain (ταξίαρχος) .	100
0 companies	= 1 regiment (χιλιοστύς)	... colonel (χιλίαρχος) ...	1,000
0 regiments	= 1 brigade (μυριοστύς)	... general (μυρίαρχος) ...	10,000

ταται τοῖς ἄρχουσιν οὖσαι καὶ προθυμότατ ἀσκοῦσαι τὰ προειρημένα. ἦν δὲ ταύταις τ νικητήρια οἷα δὴ εἰς πλῆθος πρέπει.

Ταῦτα μὲν δὴ προείρητό τε καὶ ἠσκεῖτο στρατιά.

25. Σκηνὰς δ᾽ αὐτοῖς κατεσκεύασε, πλῆθος μὲ ὅσοι ταξίαρχοι ἦσαν, μέγεθος δὲ ὥστε ἱκανὰ εἶναι τῇ τάξει ἑκάστῃ· ἡ δὲ[1] τάξις ἦν ἑκατὸ ἄνδρες. ἐσκήνουν μὲν δὴ οὕτω κατὰ τάξει ἐν δὲ τῷ ὁμοῦ σκηνοῦν ἐδόκουν μὲν αὐτῷ ὠφε λεῖσθαι πρὸς τὸν μέλλοντα ἀγῶνα τοῦτο ὅτ ἑώρων ἀλλήλους ὁμοίως τρεφομένους καὶ οὐ ἐνῆν πρόφασις μειονεξίας ὥστε ὑφίεσθαί τινας κακίω ἕτερον ἑτέρου εἶναι πρὸς τοὺς πολεμίου ὠφελεῖσθαι δ᾽ ἐδόκουν αὐτῷ καὶ πρὸς τὸ γιγνώ σκειν ἀλλήλους ὁμοῦ σκηνοῦντες. ἐν δὲ τῷ γιγνώ σκεσθαι καὶ τὸ αἰσχύνεσθαι πᾶσι δοκεῖ μᾶλλο ἐγγίγνεσθαι, οἱ δὲ ἀγνοούμενοι ῥᾳδιουργεῖν πω μᾶλλον δοκοῦσιν, ὥσπερ ἐν σκότει ὄντες. 26. ἐδό κουν δ᾽ αὐτῷ καὶ εἰς τὸ τὰς τάξεις ἀκριβοῦ μεγάλα ὠφελεῖσθαι διὰ τὴν συσκηνίαν. εἶχο γὰρ οἱ μὲν ταξίαρχοι ὑφ᾽ ἑαυτοῖς τὰς τάξει κεκοσμημένας ὥσπερ ὁπότε εἰς ἕνα πορεύοιτο τάξις, οἱ δὲ λοχαγοὶ τοὺς λόχους ὡσαύτως, ο δὲ δεκάδαρχοι δεκάδας, πεμπάδαρχοι πεμπάδας 27. τὸ δὲ διακριβοῦν τὰς τάξεις σφόδρα ἐδόκε αὐτῷ ἀγαθὸν εἶναι καὶ εἰς τὸ μὴ ταράττεσθα καὶ εἰ ταραχθεῖεν θᾶττον καταστῆναι, ὥσπε

[1] ἑκάστῃ· ἡ δὲ y, most Edd.; ἑκάστη δ᾽ ἡ z; ἑκάστη δὲ x.
[2] τινας Hug, later Edd.; τινα MSS., earlier Edd.

ficers and very ready in performing the afore
entioned duties. And the prizes of victory for
ese divisions were just such as were appropriate to
roups of men.

Such, then, were the competitions appointed, and
e army began to train for them.

25. Then, he had tents made for them—in number, many as there were captains; in size, large enough accommodate each a company. A company, more-ver, was composed of a hundred men. Accordingly, ey lived in tents each company by itself; for yrus thought that in occupying tents together they ad the following advantages for the coming conflict: ey saw one another provided for in the same ay, and there could be no possible pretext of njust discrimination that could lead any one to low himself to prove less brave than another in the ce of the enemy. And he thought that if they nted together it would help them to get acquainted ith one another. And in getting acquainted with ne another, he thought, a feeling of considerateness as more likely to be engendered in them all, while ose who are unacquainted seem somehow more different—like people when they are in the dark. 6. He thought also that their tenting together elped them not a little to gain a perfect acquaintance ith their positions. For the captains had the com-anies under them in as perfect order as when a ompany was marching single file, and the lieutenants eir platoons, and the sergeants and corporals their uads in the same way. 27. He thought, moreover, at such perfect acquaintance with their places the line was exceedingly helpful both to prevent eir being thrown into confusion and to restore

Tenting by companies

γε καὶ λίθων καὶ ξύλων ἂν δέῃ συναρμοσθῆναι
ἔστι, κἂν ὁπωσοῦν καταβεβλημένα τύχῃ, συναρ
μόσαι αὐτὰ εὐπετῶς, ἢν ἔχῃ γνωρίσματα ὥστ
εὔδηλον εἶναι ἐξ ὁποίας ἕκαστον χώρας αὐτῶ
ἐστιν. 28. ἐδόκουν δ' ὠφελεῖσθαι αὐτῷ ὁμο
τρεφόμενοι καὶ πρὸς τὸ ἧττον ἀλλήλους ἐθέλει
ἀπολείπειν, ὅτι ἑώρα καὶ τὰ θηρία τὰ συντρε
φόμενα δεινὸν ἔχοντα πόθον, ἤν τις αὐτὰ διασπ
ἀπ' ἀλλήλων.

29. Ἐπεμέλετο δὲ καὶ τούτου ὁ Κῦρος ὅπω
μήποτε ἀνίδρωτοι γενόμενοι ἐπὶ τὸ ἄριστον κα
τὸ δεῖπνον εἰσίοιεν. ἢ γὰρ ἐπὶ θήραν ἐξάγω
ἱδρῶτα αὐτοῖς παρεῖχεν, ἢ παιδιὰς τοιαύτα
ἐξηύρισκεν αἳ ἱδρῶτα ἔμελλον παρέχειν, ἢ κα
πρᾶξαι εἴ τι δεόμενος τύχοι, οὕτως ἐξηγεῖτο τῆ
πράξεως ὡς μὴ ἐπανίοιεν ἀνιδρωτί. τοῦτο γὰ
ἡγεῖτο καὶ πρὸς τὸ ἡδέως ἐσθίειν ἀγαθὸν εἶνα
καὶ πρὸς τὸ ὑγιαίνειν καὶ πρὸς τὸ δύνασθα
πονεῖν, καὶ πρὸς τὸ ἀλλήλοις δὲ πρᾳοτέρου
εἶναι ἀγαθὸν ἡγεῖτο τοὺς πόνους εἶναι, ὅτι κα
οἱ ἵπποι συμπονοῦντες ἀλλήλοις πρᾳότεροι συ
εστήκασι. πρός γε μὴν τοὺς πολεμίους μεγα
λοφρονέστεροι γίγνονται οἳ ἂν συνειδῶσιν ἑαυτο
εὖ ἠσκηκότες.

30. Κῦρος δ' ἑαυτῷ σκηνὴν μὲν κατεσκευάσατ
ὥστε ἱκανὴν ἔχειν οἷς καλοίη ἐπὶ δεῖπνον. ἐκάλ
δὲ ὡς τὰ πολλὰ τῶν ταξιάρχων οὓς καιρὸς αὐτ
δοκοίη εἶναι, ἔστι δ' ὅτε καὶ τῶν λοχαγῶν κα

order sooner in case they should be thrown into confusion; just as in the case of stones and timbers which must be fitted together, it is possible to fit them together readily, no matter in how great confusion they may chance to have been thrown down, if they have the guide-marks to make it plain in what place each of them belongs. 28. And finally, he thought that comradeship would be encouraged by their messing together and that they would be less likely to desert one another; for he had often observed that even animals that were fed together had a marvellous yearning for one another, if any one separated them.

Physical culture in Cyrus's discipline

29. Cyrus also took care that they should never come to luncheon or to dinner unless they had had a sweat. For he would get them into a sweat by taking them out hunting; or he would contrive such sports as would make them sweat; or again, if he happened to have some business or other to attend to, he so conducted it that they should not come back without having had a sweat. For this he considered conducive to their enjoying their meals, to their health, and to their being able to endure hardships, and he thought that hardships conduced to their being more reasonable toward one another, for even horses that work together stand more quietly together. At any rate, those who are conscious that they have been well drilled are certainly more courageous in the face of the enemy.

Cyrus's invitations

30. And for himself Cyrus had a tent made big enough to accommodate all whom he might invite to dinner. Now he usually invited as many of the captains as he thought proper, and sometimes also some of the lieutenants and sergeants and corporals;

τῶν δεκαδάρχων τινὰς καὶ τῶν πεμπαδάρχω
ἐκάλει, ἔστι δ' ὅτε καὶ τῶν στρατιωτῶν, ἔστι δ
ὅτε καὶ πεμπάδα ὅλην καὶ δεκάδα ὅλην κα
λόχον ὅλον καὶ τάξιν ὅλην. ἐκάλει δὲ καὶ ἐτίμ
ὁπότε τινὰς ἴδοι τοιοῦτόν τι ποιήσαντας ὃ αὐτὸς
ἐβούλετο ποιεῖν. ἦν δὲ τὰ παρατιθέμενα ἀε
ἴσα αὐτῷ τε καὶ τοῖς καλουμένοις ἐπὶ δεῖπνον.

31. Καὶ τοὺς ἀμφὶ τὸ στράτευμα δὲ ὑπηρέτα
ἰσομοίρους πάντων ἀεὶ ἐποίει· οὐδὲν γὰρ ἧττο
τιμᾶν ἄξιον ἐδόκει αὐτῷ εἶναι τοὺς ἀμφὶ τ
στρατιωτικὰ ὑπηρέτας οὔτε κηρύκων οὔτε πρέσ
βεων. καὶ γὰρ πιστοὺς ἡγεῖτο δεῖν εἶναι τούτου
καὶ ἐπιστήμονας τῶν στρατιωτικῶν καὶ συνετούς
προσέτι δὲ καὶ σφοδροὺς καὶ ταχεῖς καὶ ἀόκνου
καὶ ἀταράκτους. πρὸς δ' ἔτι ἃ οἱ βέλτιστο
νομιζόμενοι ἔχουσιν ἐγίγνωσκεν ὁ Κῦρος δεῖ
τοὺς ὑπηρέτας ἔχειν, καὶ τοῦτο ἀσκεῖν ὡς μηδὲ
ἀναίνοιντο ἔργον, ἀλλὰ πάντα νομίζοιεν πρέπει
αὐτοῖς πράττειν ὅσα ἄρχων προστάττοι.

II

1. Ἀεὶ μὲν οὖν ἐπεμέλετο ὁ Κῦρος, ὁπότε
συσκηνοῖεν, ὅπως εὐχαριστότατοί τε ἅμα λόγοι
ἐμβληθήσονται καὶ παρορμῶντες εἰς τἀγαθόν.
ἀφίκετο δὲ καὶ εἰς τόνδε ποτὲ τὸν λόγον·

Ἆρά γε, ἔφη, ὦ ἄνδρες, ἐνδεέστεροί τι ἡμῶν
διὰ τοῦτο φαίνονται εἶναι οἱ ἑταῖροι ὅτι οὐ
πεπαίδευνται τὸν αὐτὸν τρόπον ἡμῖν, ἢ οὐδὲν ἄρα

[1] αὐτὸς xz, most Edd.; πάντας y, Gemoll.

nd occasionally he invited some of the privates, ometimes a squad of five together, or a squad of ten, or a platoon, or a whole company in a body. And he also used to invite individuals as a mark of honour, whenever he saw that they had done what he himself wished everybody to do. And the same dishes were always placed before those whom he invited to dinner as before himself.

The quartermasters

31. The quartermasters in the army he always allowed an equal share of everything; for he thought that it was fair to show no less regard for the purveyors of the army stores than for heralds or ambassadors. And that was reasonable, for he held that they must be trustworthy, familiar with military affairs, and intelligent, and, in addition to that, energetic, quick, resolute, steady. And still further, Cyrus knew that the quartermasters also must have the qualities which those have who are considered most efficient and that they must train themselves not to refuse any service but to consider that it is their duty to perform whatever the general might require of them.

II

Cyrus's entertainments

1. Whenever Cyrus entertained company at dinner, he always took pains that the conversation introduced should be as entertaining as possible and that it should incite to good. On one occasion he opened the conversation as follows:

"Tell me, men," said he, "do our new comrades seem to be any worse off than we because they have not been educated in the same way as we, or pray do you think that there will be no difference

διοίσειν ἡμῶν οὔτ᾽ ἐν ταῖς συνουσίαις οὔτε ὅται
ἀγωνίζεσθαι πρὸς τοὺς πολεμίους δέῃ;

2. Καὶ Ὑστάσπας ὑπολαβὼν εἶπεν, Ἀλλ
ὁποῖοι μέν τινες ἔσονται εἰς τοὺς πολεμίους οὔπω
ἔγωγε ἐπίσταμαι· ἐν μέντοι τῇ συνουσίᾳ δύσκολο
ναὶ μὰ τοὺς θεοὺς ἔνιοι αὐτῶν φαίνονται. πρῴην
μέν γε, ἔφη, Κυαξάρης ἔπεμψεν εἰς τὴν τάξιν
ἑκάστην ἱερεῖα, καὶ ἐγένετο κρέα ἑκάστῳ ἡμῶν
τρία ἢ καὶ πλείω τὰ περιφερόμενα. καὶ ἤρξατ
μὲν ὁ μάγειρος ἀπ᾽ ἐμοῦ τὴν πρώτην περίοδον
περιφέρων· ὅτε δὲ τὸ δεύτερον εἰσῄει περιοίσων
ἐκέλευσα ἐγὼ ἀπὸ τοῦ τελευταίου ἄρχεσθαι κα
ἀνάπαλιν φέρειν. 3. ἀνακραγὼν οὖν τις τῶν
κατὰ μέσον τὸν κύκλον κατακειμένων στρατιωτῶν
Μὰ Δί᾽, ἔφη, τῶνδε μὲν οὐδὲν ἴσον ἐστίν, εἴγ
ἀφ᾽ ἡμῶν γε τῶν ἐν μέσῳ οὐδεὶς οὐδέποτε ἄρξεται
καὶ ἐγὼ ἀκούσας ἠχθέσθην, εἴ τι μεῖον δοκοῖεν
ἔχειν, καὶ ἐκάλεσα εὐθὺς αὐτὸν πρὸς ἐμέ. ὁ δ
μάλα γε τοῦτο εὐτάκτως ὑπήκουσεν. ὡς δὲ τὰ
περιφερόμενα ἧκε πρὸς ἡμᾶς, ἅτε οἶμαι ὑστάτους
λαμβάνοντας, τὰ μικρότατα λελειμμένα ἦν. ἐν
ταῦθα δὴ ἐκεῖνος πάνυ ἀνιαθεὶς δῆλος ἦν καὶ εἶπε
πρὸς αὐτόν, Τῆς τύχης, τὸ ἐμὲ νῦν κληθέντα δεῦρο
τυχεῖν. 4. καὶ ἐγὼ εἶπον, Ἀλλὰ μὴ φρόντιζε
αὐτίκα γὰρ ἀφ᾽ ἡμῶν ἄρξεται καὶ σὺ πρῶτος
λήψει τὸ μέγιστον. καὶ ἐν τούτῳ περιέφερε τὸ
τρίτον, ὅπερ δὴ λοιπὸν ἦν τῆς περιφορᾶς· κἀκεῖ
νος ἔλαβε, κᾆτ᾽ ἔδοξεν αὐτῷ μεῖον λαβεῖν· κατέ
βαλεν οὖν[1] ὃ ἔλαβεν ὡς ἕτερον ληψόμενος. κα

[1] κᾆτ᾽ . . . οὖν xz, Edd.; μετ᾽ ἐμὲ δεύτερος· ὡς δ᾽ ὁ τρίτο
ἔλαβε καὶ ἔδοξεν αὐτὸν μεῖζον ἑαυτοῦ λαβεῖν καταβάλλει y (*nex
after me; and when the third man was served, and my ma*

between us either in social intercourse or when we shall have to contend with the enemy?"

A story of bad manners

2. "Well," said Hystaspas in reply, "for my part, I cannot tell yet how they will appear in the face of the enemy. But in social intercourse, by the gods, some of them seem ill-mannered enough. The other day, at any rate," he explained, "Cyaxares had meat sent in to each company, and as it was passed around each one of us got three pieces or even more. And the first time round the cook began with me as he passed it around; but when he came in the second time to pass it, I bade him begin with the last and pass it around the other way. 3. Then one of the men sitting in the middle of the circle called out and said, 'By Zeus, this is not fair at all—at any rate, if they are never going to begin with us here in the middle.' And when I heard that, I was vexed that any one should think that he had less than another and I called him to me at once. He obeyed, showing good discipline in this at least. But when that which was being passed came to us, only the smallest pieces were left, as one might expect, for we were the last to be served. Thereupon he was greatly vexed and said to himself: 'Such luck! that I should happen to have been called here just now!' 4. 'Well, never mind,' said I. 'They will begin with us next time, and you, being first, will get the biggest piece.' And at that moment the cook began to pass around the third time what was left of the course; and the man helped himself; and then he thought the piece he had taken too small; so he put back the piece he had, with the intention of taking another. And the cook,

thought his neighbour had got a bigger piece than he, he threw down etc.).

ὁ ἄρταμος οἰόμενος αὐτὸν οὐδέν τι δεῖσθαι ὄψου ᾤχετο παραφέρων πρὶν λαβεῖν αὐτὸν ἕτερον. 5. ἐνταῦθα δὴ οὕτω βαρέως ἤνεγκε τὸ πάθος ὥστε ἀνήλωτο μὲν αὐτῷ ὃ εἰλήφει ὄψον, ὃ δὲ ἔτι αὐτῷ λοιπὸν ἦν τοῦ ἐμβάπτεσθαι, τοῦτό πως ὑπὸ τοῦ ἐκπεπλῆχθαί τε καὶ τῇ τύχῃ ὀργίζεσθαι δυσθετούμενος ἀνέτρεψεν. ὁ μὲν δὴ λοχαγὸς ὁ ἐγγύτατα ἡμῶν ἰδὼν συνεκρότησε τὼ χεῖρε καὶ τῷ γέλωτι ηὐφραίνετο. ἐγὼ μέντοι, ἔφη, προσεποιούμην βήττειν· οὐδὲ γὰρ αὐτὸς ἐδυνάμην τὸν γέλωτα κατασχεῖν. τοιοῦτον μὲν δή σοι ἕνα, ὦ Κῦρε, τῶν ἑταίρων ἐπιδεικνύω.

Ἐπὶ μὲν δὴ τούτῳ ὥσπερ εἰκὸς ἐγέλασαν. 6. ἄλλος δέ τις ἔλεξε τῶν ταξιάρχων, Οὗτος μὲν δή, ὦ Κῦρε, ὡς ἔοικεν, οὕτω δυσκόλῳ ἐπέτυχεν· ἐγὼ δέ, ὡς σὺ διδάξας ἡμᾶς τὰς τάξεις ἀπέπεμψας καὶ ἐκέλευσας διδάσκειν τὴν ἑαυτοῦ ἕκαστον τάξιν ἃ παρὰ σοῦ ἐμάθομεν, οὕτω δὴ καὶ ἐγώ, ὥσπερ καὶ οἱ ἄλλοι ἐποίουν, ἐλθὼν ἐδίδασκον ἕνα λόχον. καὶ στήσας τὸν λοχαγὸν πρῶτον καὶ τάξας δὴ ἐπ' αὐτῷ ἄνδρα νεανίαν καὶ τοὺς ἄλλους ᾗ ᾤμην δεῖν, ἔπειτα στὰς ἐκ τοῦ ἔμπροσθεν βλέπων εἰς τὸν λόχον, ἡνίκα μοι ἐδόκει καιρὸς εἶναι, προϊέναι ἐκέλευσα. 7. καὶ ἀνήρ σοι ὁ νεανίας ἐκεῖνος προελθὼν τοῦ λοχαγοῦ πρότερος ἐπορεύετο. κἀγὼ ἰδὼν εἶπον, Ἄνθρωπε, τί ποιεῖς; καὶ ὃς ἔφη, Προέρχομαι ὥσπερ σὺ κελεύεις. κἀγὼ εἶπον, Ἀλλ' οὐκ ἐγὼ σὲ μόνον ἐκέλευον ἀλλὰ πάντας προϊέναι. καὶ ὃς ἀκούσας τοῦτο μεταστραφεὶς πρὸς τοὺς λοχίτας εἶπεν, Οὐκ ἀκούετε, ἔφη, λοιδορουμένου; προϊέναι πάντας κελεύει. καὶ ἄνδρες πάντες παρελθόντες

thinking that he did not want any more to eat, went on passing it before he got his other piece. 5. Thereupon he took his mishap so to heart that he lost not only the meat he had taken but also what was still left of his sauce; for this last he upset somehow or other in the confusion of his vexation and anger over his hard luck. The lieutenant nearest us saw it and laughed and clapped his hands in amusement. And I," he added, "pretended to cough; for even I could not keep from laughing. Such is one man, Cyrus, that I present to you as one of our comrades."

A comical result of literal obedience

At this they laughed, of course. 6. But another of the captains said: "Our friend here, it seems, Cyrus, has fallen in with a very ill-mannered fellow. But as for me, when you had instructed us about the arrangement of the lines and dismissed us with orders each to teach his own company what we had learned from you, why then I went and proceeded to drill one platoon, just as the others also did. I assigned the lieutenant his place first and arranged next after him a young recruit, and the rest, as I thought proper. Then I took my stand out in front of them facing the platoon, and when it seemed to me to be the proper time, I gave the command to go ahead. 7. And that young recruit, mark you, stepped ahead—of the lieutenant and marched in front of him! And when I saw it, I said: 'Fellow, what are you doing?' 'I am going ahead, as you ordered,' said he. 'Well,' said I, 'I ordered not only you, but all to go ahead.' When he heard this, he turned about to his comrades and said: 'Don't you hear him scolding? He orders us all to go ahead.' Then the men all ran past their lieutenant

τὸν λοχαγὸν ᾖσαν πρὸς ἐμέ. 8. ἐπεὶ δὲ ὁ λοχαγὸ αὐτοὺς ἀνεχώριζεν, ἐδυσφόρουν καὶ ἔλεγον Ποτέρῳ δὴ πείθεσθαι χρή; νῦν γὰρ ὁ μὲν κελεύε προϊέναι, ὁ δ' οὐκ ἐᾷ. ἐγὼ μέντοι ἐνεγκὼν ταῦτα πρᾴως ἐξ ἀρχῆς αὖ καταχωρίσας εἶπον μηδένα τῶν ὄπισθεν κινεῖσθαι πρὶν ἂν ὁ πρόσθεν ἡγῆται ἀλλὰ τοῦτο μόνον ὁρᾶν πάντας, τῷ πρόσθεν ἕπεσθαι. 9. ὡς δ' εἰς Πέρσας τις ἀπιὼν ἦλθε πρὸς ἐμὲ καὶ ἐκέλευσέ με τὴν ἐπιστολὴν ἣν ἔγραψα οἴκαδε δοῦναι, κἀγώ, ὁ γὰρ λοχαγὸς ᾔδει ὅπου ἔκειτο ἡ ἐπιστολή, ἐκέλευσα αὐτὸν δραμόντα ἐνεγκεῖν τὴν ἐπιστολήν, ὁ μὲν δὴ ἔτρεχεν, ὁ δὲ νεανίας ἐκεῖνος εἵπετο τῷ λοχαγῷ σὺν αὐτῷ τῷ θώρακι καὶ τῇ κοπίδι, καὶ ὁ ἄλλος δὲ πᾶς λόχος ἰδὼν ἐκεῖνον συνέτρεχον· καὶ ἧκον οἱ ἄνδρες φέροντες τὴν ἐπιστολήν. οὕτως, ἔφη, ὅ γ' ἐμὸς λόχος σοι ἀκριβοῖ πάντα τὰ παρὰ σοῦ.

10. Οἱ μὲν δὴ ἄλλοι ὡς εἰκὸς ἐγέλων ἐπὶ τῇ δορυφορίᾳ τῆς ἐπιστολῆς· ὁ δὲ Κῦρος εἶπεν, Ὦ Ζεῦ καὶ πάντες θεοί, οἵους ἄρα ἡμεῖς ἔχομεν ἄνδρας ἑταίρους, οἵ γε εὐθεράπευτοι μὲν οὕτως εἰσὶν ὥστ' εἶναι αὐτῶν καὶ μικρῷ ὄψῳ παμπόλλους φίλους ἀνακτήσασθαι, πιθανοὶ δ' οὕτως εἰσί τινες ὥστε πρὶν εἰδέναι τὸ προσταττόμενον πρότερον πείθονται. ἐγὼ μὲν οὐκ οἶδα ποίους τινὰς χρὴ μᾶλλον εὔξασθαι ἢ τοιούτους στρατιώτας ἔχειν.

11. Ὁ μὲν δὴ Κῦρος ἅμα γελῶν οὕτως ἐπῄνεσε τοὺς στρατιώτας. ἐν δὲ τῇ σκηνῇ ἐτύγχανέ τις ὢν τῶν ταξιάρχων Ἀγλαϊτάδας ὄνομα, ἀνὴρ τὸν τρόπον τῶν στρυφνοτέρων ἀνθρώπων, ὃς οὑτωσί

and came toward me. 8. But when the lieutenant ordered them back to their places, they were indignant and said: 'Pray, which one are we to obey? For now the one orders us to go ahead, and the other will not let us.' I took this good-naturedly, however, and when I had got them in position again, I gave instructions that no one of those behind should stir before the one in front led off, but that all should have their attention on this only—to follow the man in front. 9. But when a certain man who was about to start for Persia came up and asked me for the letter which I had written home, I bade the lieutenant run and fetch it, for he knew where it had been placed. So he started off on a run, and that young recruit followed, as he was, breastplate and sword; and then the whole fifty, seeing him run, ran after. And the men came back bringing the letter. So exactly, you see, does my company, at least, carry out all your orders."

10. The rest, of course, laughed over the military escort of the letter, and Cyrus said: "O Zeus and all the gods! What sort of men we have then as our comrades; they are so easily won by kindness that we can make many of them our firm friends with even a little piece of meat; and they are so obedient that they obey even before the orders are given. I, for my part, do not know what sort of soldiers one could ask to have in preference to these!"

11. Thus Cyrus praised his soldiers, laughing at the same time. But one of his captains, Aglaïtadas by name, one of the most austere of men, happened to be in Cyrus's tent at the same time and he spoke somewhat as follows: "You don't mean to say,

Objections raised to both stories

πως εἶπεν· Ἦ γὰρ οἴει, ἔφη, ὦ Κῦρε, τούτους ἀληθῆ λέγειν ταῦτα;

Ἀλλὰ τί μὴν βουλόμενοι, ἔφη ὁ Κῦρος, ψεύδονται;

Τί δ' ἄλλο γ', ἔφη, εἰ μὴ γέλωτα ποιεῖν ἐθέλοντες ὑπὲρ οὗ λέγουσι ταῦτα καὶ ἀλαζονεύονται.

12. Καὶ ὁ Κῦρος, Εὐφήμει, ἔφη, μηδὲ λέγε ἀλαζόνας εἶναι τούτους. ὁ μὲν γὰρ ἀλαζὼν ἔμοιγε δοκεῖ ὄνομα κεῖσθαι ἐπὶ τοῖς προσποιουμένοις καὶ πλουσιωτέροις εἶναι ἢ εἰσὶ καὶ ἀνδρειοτέροις καὶ ποιήσειν ἃ μὴ ἱκανοί εἰσιν ὑπισχνουμένοις, καὶ ταῦτα φανεροῖς γιγνομένοις ὅτι τοῦ λαβεῖν τι ἕνεκα καὶ κερδᾶναι ποιοῦσιν. οἱ δὲ μηχανώμενοι γέλωτα τοῖς συνοῦσι μήτε ἐπὶ τῷ αὑτῶν κέρδει μήτ' ἐπὶ ζημίᾳ τῶν ἀκουόντων μήτε ἐπὶ βλάβῃ μηδεμιᾷ, πῶς οὐχ οὗτοι ἀστεῖοι ἂν καὶ εὐχάριτες δικαιότερον ὀνομάζοιντο μᾶλλον ἢ ἀλαζόνες;

13. Ὁ μὲν δὴ Κῦρος οὕτως ἀπελογήσατο περι τῶν τὸν γέλωτα παρασχόντων· αὐτὸς δὲ ὁ ταξίαρχος[1] ὁ τὴν τοῦ λόχου χαριτίαν διηγησάμενος ἔφη, Ἦπου ἄν, ἔφη, ὦ Ἀγλαϊτάδα, εἴ γε κλαίειν ἐπειρώμεθά σε ποιεῖν, σφόδρ' ἂν ἡμῖν ἐμέμφου, ὥσπερ ἔνιοι καὶ ἐν ᾠδαῖς καὶ ἐν λόγοις οἰκτρά τινα λογοποιοῦντες εἰς δάκρυα πειρῶνται ἄγειν, ὁπότε γε νῦν καὶ αὐτὸς εἰδὼς ὅτι εὐφραίνειν μέν τί σε βουλόμεθα, βλάψαι δ' οὐδέν, ὅμως οὕτως ἐν πολλῇ ἀτιμίᾳ ἡμᾶς ἔχεις.

14. Ναὶ μὰ Δί', ἔφη ὁ Ἀγλαϊτάδας, καὶ δικαίως

[1] ὁ ταξίαρχος Zeune, Dindorf, Gemoll, Breitenbach; ὁ λοχαγός MSS.; [ὁ λοχαγός] Bornemann, Marchant.

Cyrus, that you think what these fellows have been telling is true?"

"Well," said Cyrus, "what object could they have, pray, in telling a lie?"

"What object, indeed," said the other, "except that they wanted to raise a laugh; and so they tell these stories and try to humbug us."

12. "Hush!" said Cyrus. "Don't call these men humbugs. For to me, the name 'humbug' seems to apply to those who pretend that they are richer than they are or braver than they are, and to those who promise to do what they cannot do, and that, too, when it is evident that they do this only for the sake of getting something or making some gain. But those who invent stories to amuse their companions and not for their own gain nor at the expense of their hearers nor to the injury of any one, why should these men not be called 'witty' and 'entertaining' rather than 'humbugs'?"

Is it better to make men laugh than weep?

13. Thus Cyrus defended those who had furnished the fun, and the captain himself who had told the anecdote about his platoon said: "Verily, Aglaïtadas, you might find serious fault with us, if we tried to make you weep, like some authors who invent touching incidents in their poems and stories and try to move us to tears; but now, although you yourself know that we wish to entertain you and not to do you any harm at all, still you heap such reproaches upon us."

14. "Aye, by Zeus," said Aglaïtadas, "and justly,

γε, ἐπεὶ καὶ αὐτοῦ τοῦ κλαίοντας[1] καθίζοντος τοὺς φίλους πολλαχοῦ ἔμοιγε δοκεῖ ἐλάττονος ἄξια διαπράττεσθαι ὁ γέλωτα αὐτοῖς μηχανώμενος. εὑρήσεις δὲ καὶ σύ, ἢν ὀρθῶς λογίζῃ, ἐμὲ ἀληθῆ λέγοντα. κλαύμασι μέν γε καὶ πατέρες υἱοῖς σωφροσύνην μηχανῶνται καὶ διδάσκαλοι παισὶν ἀγαθὰ μαθήματα, καὶ νόμοι γε πολίτας διὰ τοῦ κλαίοντας καθίζειν εἰς δικαιοσύνην προτρέπονται· τοὺς δὲ γέλωτα μηχανωμένους ἔχοις ἂν εἰπεῖν ἢ σώματα ὠφελοῦντας ἢ ψυχὰς οἰκονομικωτέρας τι ποιοῦντας ἢ πολιτικωτέρας;

15. Ἐκ τούτου ὁ Ὑστάσπας ὧδέ πως εἶπε· Σύ, ἔφη, ὦ Ἀγλαϊτάδα, ἢν ἐμοὶ πείθῃ, εἰς μὲν τοὺς πολεμίους θαρρῶν δαπανήσεις τοῦτο τὸ πολλοῦ ἄξιον, καὶ κλαίοντας ἐκείνους πειράσει καθίζειν· ἡμῖν δὲ πάντως, ἔφη, τοῖσδε τοῖς φίλοις τούτου τοῦ ὀλίγου ἀξίου, τοῦ γέλωτος ἐπιδαψιλεύσει. καὶ γὰρ οἶδ' ὅτι πολύς σοί ἐστιν ἀποκείμενος· οὔτε γὰρ αὐτὸς χρώμενος ἀνησίμωκας αὐτόν οὐδὲ μὴν φίλοις οὐδὲ ξένοις ἑκὼν εἶναι γέλωτα παρέχεις. ὥστε οὐδεμία σοι πρόφασίς ἐστιν ὡς οὐ παρεκτέον σοι ἡμῖν γέλωτα.

Καὶ ὁ Ἀγλαϊτάδας εἶπε, Καὶ οἴει γε, ὦ Ὑστάσπα, γέλωτα περιποιεῖν ἐξ ἐμοῦ;

Καὶ ὁ ταξίαρχος[2] εἶπε, Ναὶ μὰ Δί', ἀνόητος ἄρα ἐστίν· ἐπεὶ ἔκ γε σοῦ πῦρ, οἶμαι, ῥᾷον ἄν τις ἐκτρίψειεν ἢ γέλωτα ἐξαγάγοιτο.

16. Ἐπὶ τούτῳ μὲν δὴ οἵ τε ἄλλοι ἐγέλασαν, τὸν τρόπον εἰδότες αὐτοῦ, ὅ τ' Ἀγλαϊτάδας ἐπεμειδίασε. καὶ ὁ Κῦρος ἰδὼν αὐτὸν φαιδρω-

[1] κλάοντας Cobet, Edd.; κλαίειν MSS.
[2] ταξίαρχος Philelphus, Edd.; λοχαγός MSS.

too, since he that makes his friends laugh seems to me to do them much less service than he who makes them weep; and if you will look at it rightly, you, too, will find that I speak the truth. At any rate, fathers develop self-control in their sons by making them weep, and teachers impress good lessons upon their pupils in the same way, and the laws, too, turn the citizens to justice by making them weep. But could you say that those who make us laugh either do good to our bodies or make our minds any more fitted for the management of our private business or of the affairs of state?"

15. Hereupon Hystaspas answered somewhat as follows: "If you will heed me, Aglaïtadas, you will freely expend this very valuable commodity upon your enemies and will try to set them to weeping; but upon us and your friends here you will please to lavish this cheap article, laughter. And you can, for I know you must have a great quantity of it stored up; for you have never spent it upon yourself nor do you ever afford any laughter for your friends or for your enemies if you can help it. So you have no excuse for begrudging us a laugh."

"What!" said Aglaïtadas; "do you really think, Hystaspas, to get a laugh out of me?"

"Well, by Zeus," said the other captain, "he is a very foolish fellow, let me tell you, if he does; for I believe one might rub fire out of you more easily than provoke a laugh from you."

16. At this, of course, the rest laughed; for they knew his character, and Aglaïtadas himself smiled at the sally. And Cyrus seeing him brighten up said:

θέντα, Ἀδικεῖς, ἔφη, ὦ ταξίαρχε,[1] ὅτι ἄνδρα ἡμῖ τὸν σπουδαιότατον διαφθείρεις γελᾶν ἀναπείθωι καὶ ταῦτα, ἔφη, οὕτω πολέμιον ὄντα τῷ γέλωτι.

17. Ταῦτα μὲν δὴ ἐνταῦθα ἔληξεν. ἐκ δ τούτου Χρυσάντας ὧδε ἔλεξεν· 18. Ἀλλ' ἐγώ ἔφη, ὦ Κῦρε καὶ πάντες οἱ παρόντες, ἐννοῶ ὅτ συνεξεληλύθασι μὲν ἡμῖν οἱ μὲν καὶ βελτίονες, ο δὲ καὶ μείονος ἄξιοι· ἢν δέ τι γένηται ἀγαθόν ἀξιώσουσιν οὗτοι πάντες ἰσομοιρεῖν. καίτο ἔγωγε οὐδὲν ἀνισώτερον νομίζω ἐν ἀνθρώποι εἶναι ἢ τοῦ ἴσου τόν τε κακὸν καὶ τὸν ἀγαθὸ ἀξιοῦσθαι.

Καὶ ὁ Κῦρος εἶπε πρὸς τοῦτο, Ἆρ' οὖν, πρὸ τῶν θεῶν, ὦ ἄνδρες, κράτιστον ἡμῖν ἐμβαλεῖν περὶ τούτου βουλὴν εἰς τὸ στράτευμα, πότερα δοκεῖ, ἤν τι ἐκ τῶν πόνων δῷ ὁ θεὸς ἀγαθόν ἰσομοίρους πάντας ποιεῖν, ἢ σκοποῦντας τὰ ἔργα ἑκάστου πρὸς ταῦτα καὶ τὰς τιμὰς ἑκάστῳ προσ-τιθέναι;

19. Καὶ τί δεῖ, ἔφη ὁ Χρυσάντας, ἐμβαλεῖν λόγον περὶ τούτου, ἀλλ' οὐχὶ προειπεῖν ὅτι οὕτω ποιήσεις; οὐ καὶ τοὺς ἀγῶνας οὕτω προεῖπας καὶ τὰ ἆθλα;

Ἀλλὰ μὰ Δί', ἔφη ὁ Κῦρος, οὐχ ὅμοια ταῦτα ἐκείνοις· ἃ μὲν γὰρ ἂν στρατευόμενοι κτήσωνται, κοινὰ οἶμαι ἑαυτῶν ἡγήσονται εἶναι· τὴν δὲ ἀρχὴν τῆς στρατιᾶς ἐμὴν ἴσως ἔτι οἴκοθεν νομίζουσιν εἶναι, ὥστε διατάττοντα ἐμὲ τοὺς ἐπιστάτας οὐδὲν οἶμαι ἀδικεῖν νομίζουσιν.

[1] ταξίαρχε Philelphus, Edd.; λοχαγέ MSS.

"It is not right, captain, for you to corrupt our most serious man by persuading him to laugh, and that, too," said he, "when he is such a foe to laughter."

17. With that, the subject was dropt. But at this point Chrysantas spoke as follows: 18. "Cyrus," said he, "and all you here present, I observe, for my part, that some have come out with us who are of superior merit, others who are less deserving than we. Now, if we meet with success, these will all expect to have share and share alike. And yet I do not believe that anything in the world is more unfair than for the bad and good to be awarded equal shares."

The proper basis for distributing prize money

"Well, then, in the name of the gods, my men," Cyrus replied to this, "will it not be a very good thing for us to suggest to the army a debate on this question: shall we, in case God gives us any success to reward our toils, give to all an equal share or shall we take into consideration each man's services and bestow increased rewards upon him commensurate with them?"

19. "And what is the use," said Chrysantas, "of starting a discussion concerning this matter? Why not rather announce that you propose to do thus and so? Pray, did you not announce the games and offer the prizes that way?"

"Yes, by Zeus," said Cyrus; "but this is not a parallel case. For what the men obtain by fighting, that, I suppose, they will consider their own common property; but the command of the army they still consider fairly to be mine, so that when I appoint the judges, I am sure they think I am within my rights."

20. Ἦ καὶ οἴει, ἔφη ὁ Χρυσάντας, ψηφίσασθα ἂν τὸ πλῆθος συνελθὸν ὥστε μὴ ἴσων ἕκαστοι τυγχάνειν, ἀλλὰ τοὺς κρατίστους καὶ τιμαῖς κα δώροις πλεονεκτεῖν;

Ἔγωγ᾽, ἔφη ὁ Κῦρος, οἶμαι, ἅμα μὲν ἡμῶι συναγορευόντων, ἅμα δὲ καὶ αἰσχρὸν ὂν ἀντι λέγειν τὸ μὴ οὐχὶ τὸν πλεῖστα καὶ πονοῦντα καὶ ὠφελοῦντα τὸ κοινὸν τοῦτον καὶ μεγίστωι ἀξιοῦσθαι. οἶμαι δ᾽, ἔφη, καὶ τοῖς κακίστοι συμφέρον φανεῖσθαι τοὺς ἀγαθοὺς πλεονεκτεῖν.

21. Ὁ δὲ Κῦρος ἐβούλετο καὶ αὐτῶν ἕνεκα τῶι ὁμοτίμων γενέσθαι τοῦτο τὸ ψήφισμα· βελτίου γὰρ ἂν καὶ αὐτοὺς ἡγεῖτο τούτους εἶναι, εἰ εἰδεῖει ὅτι ἐκ τῶν ἔργων καὶ αὐτοὶ κρινόμενοι τῶι ἀξίων τεύξονται. καιρὸς οὖν ἐδόκει αὐτῷ εἶνα νῦν ἐμβαλεῖν περὶ τούτου ψῆφον, ἐν ᾧ καὶ ο ὁμότιμοι ὤκνουν τὴν τοῦ ὄχλου ἰσομοιρίαν. οὕτω δὴ συνεδόκει τοῖς ἐν τῇ σκηνῇ συμβαλέσθαι περ τούτου λόγους καὶ συναγορεύειν ταῦτα ἔφασαι χρῆναι ὅστισπερ ἀνὴρ οἴοιτο εἶναι.

22. Ἐπιγελάσας δὲ τῶν ταξιάρχων τις εἶπεν Ἀλλ᾽ ἐγώ, ἔφη, ἄνδρα οἶδα καὶ τοῦ δήμου ὃς συνερεῖ ὥστε μὴ εἰκῇ οὕτως ἰσομοιρίαν εἶναι.

Ἄλλος δ᾽ ἀντήρετο τοῦτον τίνα λέγοι. ὁ δ ἀπεκρίνατο, Ἔστι νὴ Δί᾽ ἀνὴρ ἡμῖν σύσκηνος, ὃς ἐν παντὶ μαστεύει πλέον ἔχειν.

Ἄλλος δ᾽ ἐπήρετο αὐτόν, Ἦ καὶ τῶν πόνων;

Μὰ Δί᾽, ἔφη, οὐ μὲν δή· ἀλλὰ τοῦτό γε ψευδό-

20. "And do you really believe," said Chrysantas, "that the mass meeting would adopt a resolution that each one should not have an equal share, but that the best should have the preference both in honours and gifts?"

"Yes," said Cyrus, "I do, partly because we recommend it, and partly because it is mean to oppose a proposition that the one who suffers the most and does the most for the state should also receive the highest rewards. And I think," said he, "that even to the worst it will seem proper that the good should have the larger share."

Rewards according to merit

21. Now Cyrus wished for the sake of the peers themselves that this measure should pass; for he thought that even they themselves would be better, if they knew that they also should be judged by their works and should receive according to their deserts. And so it seemed to him to be the proper time to bring this matter to a vote now, while the peers also were questioning the commoners' claims to equality. Accordingly, those in the tent agreed to submit the question to a discussion and they said that whoever thought himself to be a man ought to advocate it.

22. But one of the captains said with a laugh: "Well, I know a man of the commoners, too, who will support the proposition not to have share and share alike in that indiscriminate fashion."

Another asked him whom he meant; and he answered: "By Zeus, he is a messmate of ours, who in everything does his best to get the largest share."

"What! the largest share of hard work, too?" asked another.

"No, by Zeus," said he; "not by any means; but

μενος ἑάλωκα. καὶ γὰρ πόνων καὶ τῶν ἄλλων τῶν τοιούτων ὁρῶ πάνυ θαρραλέως βουλόμενον μεῖον ἔχειν παρ᾽ ὁντιναοῦν.

23. Ἀλλ᾽ ἐγὼ μέν, ἔφη ὁ Κῦρος, ὦ ἄνδρες, γιγνώσκω τοὺς τοιούτους ἀνθρώπους οἷον καὶ οὗτος νῦν λέγει, εἴπερ δεῖ ἐνεργὸν καὶ πειθόμενον ἔχειν τὸ στράτευμα, ἐξαιρετέους[1] εἶναι ἐκ τῆς στρατιᾶς. δοκεῖ γάρ μοι τὸ μὲν πολὺ τῶν στρατιωτῶν εἶναι οἷον ἕπεσθαι ᾗ ἄν τις ἡγῆται· ἄγειν δ᾽ οἶμαι ἐπιχειροῦσιν οἱ μὲν καλοὶ κἀγαθοὶ ἐπὶ τὰ καλὰ κἀγαθά, οἱ δὲ πονηροὶ ἐπὶ τὰ πονηρά. 24. καὶ πολλάκις τοίνυν πλείονας ὁμογνώμονας λαμβάνουσιν οἱ φαῦλοι ἢ οἱ σπουδαῖοι. ἡ γὰρ πονηρία διὰ τῶν παραυτίκα ἡδονῶν πορευομένη ταύτας ἔχει συμπειθούσας πολλοὺς αὐτῇ ὁμογνωμονεῖν· ἡ δ᾽ ἀρετὴ πρὸς ὄρθιον ἄγουσα οὐ πάνυ δεινή ἐστιν ἐν τῷ παραυτίκα εἰκῇ συνεπισπᾶσθαι, ἄλλως τε καὶ ἢν ἄλλοι ὦσιν ἐπὶ τὸ πρανὲς καὶ τὸ μαλακὸν ἀντιπαρακαλοῦντες. 25. καὶ τοίνυν ὅταν μέν τινες βλακείᾳ καὶ ἀπονίᾳ μόνον κακοὶ ὦσι, τούτους ἐγὼ νομίζω ὥσπερ κηφῆνας δαπάνῃ μόνον ζημιοῦν τοὺς κοινῶνας·[2] οἳ δ᾽ ἂν τῶν μὲν πόνων κακοὶ ὦσι κοινωνοί, πρὸς δὲ τὸ πλεονεκτεῖν σφοδροὶ καὶ ἀναίσχυντοι, οὗτοι καὶ ἡγεμονικοί εἰσι πρὸς τὰ πονηρά· πολλάκις γὰρ δύνανται τὴν πονηρίαν πλεονεκτοῦσαν ἀποδεικνύναι· ὥστε παντάπασιν ἐξαιρετέοι ἡμῖν οἱ τοιοῦτοί εἰσι.

[1] *ἐξαιρετέους* Stephanus, Edd.; *ἐξαιρέτους* MSS. (*choice*).

[2] *τοὺς κοινῶνας* Pantazides, Hertlein, most Edd.; *τοὺς κοινωνοὺς* xy; *τῆς κοινωνίας* z, Dindorf, Sauppe.

here I have been caught in a falsehood. For my observation is that he very good-naturedly consents to have a smaller share of hard work and other things of that sort than anybody else.

23. Well, men," said Cyrus, "I am convinced that such fellows as this one of whom our friend has just been telling us must be weeded out of the ranks, if we are to keep our army industrious and obedient. For it seems to me that the majority of the soldiers are the sort to follow wherever any one leads; and the good and noble, I think, try to lead only to what is good and noble, and the vicious to what is vicious. 24. And therefore the base oftentimes find a larger following of congenial spirits than the noble. For since vice makes her appeal through the pleasures of the moment, she has their assistance to persuade many to accept her views; but virtue, leading up hill, is not at all clever at attracting men at first sight and without reflection; and especially is this true, when there are others who call in the opposite direction, to what is downhill and easy. 25. And so, when people are bad only because of laziness and indolence, I believe that they, like drones, damage their associates only by the cost of their keeping. But those who are poor companions in toil, and also extravagant and shameless in their desire for any advantage, these are likely also to lead others to what is vicious; for they are often able to demonstrate that vice does gain some advantage. And so we must weed out such men at any cost.

The vicious and lazy have no place in an army

26. Καὶ μὴ μέντοι[1] σκοπεῖτε ὅπως ἐκ τῶν πολιτῶν ἀντιπληρώσετε τὰς τάξεις, ἀλλ᾽ ὥσπερ ἵπποι οἳ ἂν ἄριστοι ὦσιν, οὐχ οἳ ἂν πατριῶται, τούτους ζητεῖτε, οὕτω καὶ ἀνθρώπους ἐκ πάντων[2] οἳ ἂν ὑμῖν δοκῶσι μάλιστα συνισχυριεῖν τε ὑμᾶς καὶ συγκοσμήσειν, τούτους λαμβάνετε. μαρτυρεῖ δέ μοι καὶ τόδε πρὸς τὸ ἀγαθόν· οὔτε γὰρ ἅρμα δήπου ταχὺ γένοιτ᾽ ἂν βραδέων ἵππων ἐνόντων οὔτε δίκαιον ἀδίκων συνεζευγμένων, οὐδὲ οἶκος δύναιτ᾽ ἂν εὖ οἰκεῖσθαι πονηροῖς οἰκέταις χρώμενος, ἀλλὰ καὶ ἐνδεόμενος οἰκετῶν ἧττον σφάλλεται ἢ ὑπὸ ἀδίκων ταραττόμενος.

27. Εὖ δ᾽ ἴστε, ὦ ἄνδρες, ἔφη, φίλοι, ὅτι οὐδὲ τοῦτο μόνον ὠφελήσουσιν οἱ κακοὶ ἀφαιρεθέντες ὅτι κακοὶ ἀπέσονται, ἀλλὰ καὶ τῶν καταμενόντων οἳ μὲν ἀνεπίμπλαντο ἤδη κακίας, ἀποκαθαροῦνται πάλιν ταύτης, οἱ δὲ ἀγαθοὶ τοὺς κακοὺς ἰδόντες ἀτιμασθέντας πολὺ εὐθυμότερον τῆς ἀρετῆς ἀνθέξονται.

28. Ὁ μὲν οὕτως εἶπε· τοῖς δὲ φίλοις πᾶσι συνέδοξε ταῦτα, καὶ οὕτως ἐποίουν.

Ἐκ δὲ τούτου πάλιν αὐτοῖς σκώμματος ἤρχετο ὁ Κῦρος. κατανοήσας γάρ τινα τῶν λοχαγῶν σύνδειπνον καὶ παρακλίτην πεποιημένον ἄνδρα ὑπέρδασύν τε καὶ ὑπέραισχρον, ἀνακαλέσας τὸν λοχαγὸν ὀνομαστὶ εἶπεν ὧδε· Ὦ Σαμβαύλα, ἔφη, ἀλλ᾽ ἦ καὶ σὺ κατὰ τὸν Ἑλληνικὸν τρόπον, ὅτι

[1] καὶ μὴ μέντοι Hug, Gemoll, Marchant; μηδὲ μέντοι z, Dindorf, Sauppe, Breitenbach; καὶ μηδὲ μέντοι yC; καὶ μέντοι μηδὲ E.

[2] After πάντων Hug omits ἀνθρώπων; Gemoll brackets ἀνθρώπους.

How to fill vacant places in the ranks

26. "Do not, however, endeavour to fill up their places in the ranks with your own countrymen only; but, just as in selecting a team you seek out not horses that are home-bred but those which are best, so also in the case of men, take them from all sources—whoever you think will be most likely to contribute to your strength and to your honour. And I have the following illustrations to prove the worth of my suggestion: a chariot would never go fast, I am sure, if slow horses were attached to it, nor would it be serviceable if horses unfit for service were harnessed to it; nor yet could a house be well managed if it employed vicious servants, but it would suffer less from having no servants at all than from being kept in confusion by incapable servants.

27. "Let me assure you of this, too, my friends," he added, "that the weeding out of the vicious will bring not only this advantage, that the vicious will be out of the way, but also among those who remain the ones that have already been infected with vice will be purged of it, while the virtuous seeing the vicious disgraced will cleave more eagerly to virtue."

28. With that he concluded; and all his friends agreed that what he said was true, and they began to act upon that principle.

The ugly favourite

After that Cyrus began again to jest with them; for he had observed that one of the lieutenants had brought along as a guest and companion at table an exceedingly hairy and exceedingly ill-favoured man; and addressing the lieutenant by name he spoke as follows: "Well, Sambaulas," said he, "so you also have adopted the Greek fashion, have you, and take

καλόν ἐστι, περιάγει[1] τοῦτο τὸ μειράκιον τ
παρακατακείμενόν σοι;

Νὴ τὸν Δί', ἔφη ὁ Σαμβαύλας, ἥδομαι γοῦν κα
ἐγὼ συνών τε καὶ θεώμενος τοῦτον.

29. Ἀκούσαντες ταῦτα οἱ σύσκηνοι προσ
έβλεψαν· ὡς δὲ εἶδον τὸ πρόσωπον τοῦ ἀνδρὸ
ὑπερβάλλον αἴσχει, ἐγέλασαν πάντες. καί τι
εἶπε, Πρὸς τῶν θεῶν, ὦ Σαμβαύλα, ποίῳ ποτ
σε ἔργῳ ὁ ἀνὴρ οὗτος ἀνήρτηται;[2]

30. Καὶ ὃς εἶπεν, Ἐγὼ ὑμῖν νὴ τὸν Δία, ὦ
ἄνδρες, ἐρῶ. ὁποσάκις γὰρ αὐτὸν ἐκάλεσα εἴτ
νυκτὸς εἴτε ἡμέρας, οὐπώποτέ μοι οὔτ' ἀσχολίαι
προυφασίσατο οὔτε βάδην ὑπήκουσεν, ἀλλ' ἀε
τρέχων· ὁποσάκις τε αὐτῷ πρᾶξαί τι προσέ-
ταξα, οὐδὲν ἀνιδρωτί ποτε αὐτὸν εἶδον ποιοῦντα.
πεποίηκε δὲ καὶ τοὺς δεκαδέας πάντας τοιούτους,
οὐ λόγῳ ἀλλ' ἔργῳ ἀποδεικνὺς οἵους δεῖ εἶναι.

31. Καί τις εἶπε, Κἄπειτα τοιοῦτον ὄντα οὐ
φιλεῖς αὐτὸν ὥσπερ τοὺς συγγενεῖς;

Καὶ ὁ αἰσχρὸς ἐκεῖνος πρὸς τοῦτο ἔφη· Μὰ
Δία· οὐ γὰρ φιλόπονός ἐστιν· ἐπεὶ ἤρκει ἂν αὐτῷ,
εἰ ἐμὲ ἤθελε φιλεῖν, τοῦτο ἀντὶ πάντων τῶν[3]
γυμνασίων.

[1] περιάγει Juntine ed., Cobet, most Edd.; περιάγῃ (above the line -ει) F; περιάγεις xzD, Dindorf.
[2] ἀνήρτηται Muretus, Edd.; ἀν(προ-Ε)ήρηται MSS.
[3] τῶν xyGH, Gemoll, Marchant; not in A, Dindorf, et al. (*all kinds of exercises*).

about with you everywhere this youngster who is now beside you, because he is so handsome?"

"Yes, by Zeus," said Sambaulas; "at all events I enjoy both his company and his looks."

29. When his messmates heard this, they looked at the man; and when they saw that his countenance was exceedingly ugly, they all laughed. And one of them said: "In the name of the gods, Sambaulas, what has this fellow done to make such a hit with you?"

30. "By Zeus, fellows," he answered, "I will tell you. Every time that I have called him, whether by day or by night, he has never made any excuse saying that 'he had not time,' nor has he answered my call slowly, but always on a run. And as often as I have bidden him do anything, I have never seen him perform it without sweat; and besides, by showing them not by precept but by example what sort of men they ought to be, he has made his whole squad of ten just like himself."

31. "And yet," said one of the men, "although he is such an excellent fellow, you don't kiss him as you do your relatives?"

And the homely man answered this and said: "No, by Zeus, for he is not fond of hard work; for if he wished to kiss me, that would be an ample substitute for all his drill-work."

III

1. Τοιαῦτα μὲν δὴ καὶ γελοῖα καὶ σπουδαῖ
καὶ ἐλέγετο καὶ ἐπράττετο ἐν τῇ σκηνῇ. τέλο
δὲ τὰς τρίτας σπονδὰς ποιήσαντες καὶ εὐξάμενο
τοῖς θεοῖς τἀγαθὰ τὴν σκηνὴν εἰς κοίτην διέλυοι
τῇ δ' ὑστεραίᾳ ὁ Κῦρος συνέλεξε πάντας τοὺ
στρατιώτας καὶ ἔλεξε τοιάδε·

2. Ἄνδρες φίλοι, ὁ μὲν ἀγὼν ἐγγὺς ἡμῖν
προσέρχονται γὰρ οἱ πολέμιοι. τὰ δ' ἆθλα τῆ
νίκης, ἢν μὲν ἡμεῖς νικῶμεν (τοῦτο γάρ, ἔφη
δεῖ καὶ λέγειν καὶ ποιεῖν), δῆλον ὅτι οἵ τ
πολέμιοι ἡμέτεροι καὶ τὰ τῶν πολεμίων ἀγαθ
πάντα· ἢν δὲ ἡμεῖς αὖ νικώμεθα, καὶ οὕτω τ
τῶν νικωμένων πάντα τοῖς νικῶσιν ἀεὶ ἆθλ
πρόκειται. 3. οὕτω δή, ἔφη, δεῖ ὑμᾶς γιγνώ
σκειν ὡς ὅταν μὲν ἄνθρωποι κοινωνοὶ πολέμο
γενόμενοι ἐν ἑαυτοῖς ἕκαστοι ἔχωσιν ὡς, εἰ μ
αὐτός τις προθυμήσεται, οὐδὲν ἐσόμενον τῶ
δεοντων, ταχὺ πολλὰ καὶ καλὰ διαπράττονται
οὐδὲν γὰρ αὐτοῖς ἀργεῖται τῶν πράττεσθαι δεο
μένων· ὅταν δ' ἕκαστος διανοηθῇ ὡς ἄλλος ἔστα
ὁ πράττων καὶ ὁ μαχόμενος, κἂν αὐτὸς μαλακί
ζηται, τούτοις, ἔφη, εὖ ἴστε ὅτι πᾶσιν ἅμ
πάντα ἥκει τὰ χαλεπὰ φερόμενα. 4. καὶ ὁ θεὸ
οὕτω πως ἐποίησε· τοῖς μὴ θέλουσιν ἑαυτοῖ
προστάττειν ἐκπονεῖν τἀγαθὰ ἄλλους αὐτοῖ
ἐπιτακτῆρας δίδωσι. νῦν οὖν τις, ἔφη, λεγέτω

III

1. THINGS of this sort, both grave and gay, were aid and done at the dinner party. And finally when hey had made the third libation[1] and prayed to the ;ods for their blessings, the party broke up, and hey all went to bed. Then on the morrow, Cyrus alled all his soldiers together and spoke as follows:

The mass meeting

2. "Friends, the conflict is at hand; for the nemy are approaching. As for the prizes of victory, f we are victorious—and we must assume that we hall be and work to that end—it is evident that the nemy and all that is theirs will belong to us. But, n the other hand, if we are defeated—in this case, oo, all the possessions of the vanquished are invari-bly the prizes set for the victors. 3. Accordingly," aid he, "you must realize that when men who are nited as comrades in war are fully persuaded that othing will come out as it should unless each individ-al man exerts himself, then many splendid achieve-nents are speedily accomplished; for nothing that eeds to be done is neglected. But when each one ssumes that there will be some one else to do and o fight, even if he proves a weakling, let me ssure you," said he, "that to such men, all alike, ll that is grievous comes in a flood. 4. And God as ordained it in some such way as this: in the ase of those who will not compel themselves to vork out their own good, he assigns others to be

[1] Xenophon here introduces a Greek custom; the Persians oured no libations. But at the conclusion of a dinner, the reeks poured three libations: the first, to the gods; the econd, to the heroes; the third to Zeus, or to Hermes.

ἐνθάδε ἀναστὰς περὶ αὐτοῦ τούτου ποτέρως ἂν τὴν ἀρετὴν μᾶλλον οἴεται ἀσκεῖσθαι παρ᾽ ἡμῖν εἰ μέλλοι ὁ πλεῖστα καὶ πονεῖν καὶ κινδυνεύειν ἐθέλων πλείστης καὶ τιμῆς τεύξεσθαι, ἢ ἂν εἰδῶμεν ὅτι οὐδὲν διαφέρει κακὸν εἶναι· ὁμοίως γὰρ πάντες τῶν ἴσων τευξόμεθα.

5. Ἐνταῦθα δὴ ἀναστὰς Χρυσάντας, εἷς τῶν ὁμοτίμων, ἀνὴρ οὔτε μέγας οὔτε ἰσχυρὸς ἰδεῖν φρονήσει δὲ διαφέρων, ἔλεξεν, Ἀλλ᾽ οἶμαι μέν, ἔφη, ὦ Κῦρε, οὐδὲ διανοούμενόν σε ὡς δεῖ ἴσον ἔχειν τοὺς κακοὺς τοῖς ἀγαθοῖς ἐμβαλεῖν τοῦτον τὸν λόγον, ἀλλ᾽ ἀποπειρώμενον εἴ τις ἄρα ἔσται ἀνὴρ ὅστις ἐθελήσει ἐπιδεῖξαι ἑαυτὸν ὡς διανοεῖται μηδὲν καλὸν κἀγαθὸν ποιῶν, ἃν ἄλλοι τῇ ἀρετῇ καταπράξωσι, τούτων ἰσομοιρεῖν. 6. ἐγὼ δ᾽, ἔφη, οὔτε ποσίν εἰμι ταχὺς οὔτε χερσὶν ἰσχυρός, γιγνώσκω τε ὅτι ἐξ ὧν ἂν ἐγὼ τῷ ἐμῷ σώματι ποιήσω, οὐ κριθείην οὔτε ἂν πρῶτος οὔτε ἂν δεύτερος, οἶμαι δ᾽ οὐδ᾽ ἂν χιλιοστός, ἴσως δ᾽ οὐδ᾽ ἂν μυριοστός· ἀλλὰ καὶ ἐκεῖνο, ἔφη, σαφῶς ἐπίσταμαι ὅτι εἰ μὲν οἱ δυνατοὶ ἐρρωμένως ἀντιλήψονται τῶν πραγμάτων, ἀγαθοῦ τινός μοι μετέσται τοσοῦτον μέρος ὅσον ἂν δίκαιον ᾖ· εἰ δ᾽ οἱ μὲν κακοὶ μηδὲν ποιήσουσιν, οἱ δ᾽ ἀγαθοὶ καὶ δυνατοὶ ἀθύμως ἕξουσι, δέδοικα, ἔφη, μὴ ἄλλου τινὸς μᾶλλον ἢ τοῦ ἀγαθοῦ μεθέξω πλεῖον μέρος ἢ ἐγὼ βούλομαι.

7. Χρυσάντας μὲν δὴ οὕτως εἶπεν. ἀνέστη δ᾽ ἐπ᾽ αὐτῷ Φεραύλας, Πέρσης τῶν δημοτῶν,

ieir commanders. Now, therefore, let any one stand up and speak to this question before us, whether he thinks that valour would be more cultivated among us, if the one who will do and dare most is also to receive the greatest rewards, or if we know that it makes no difference whether a man be a coward or not, as we shall all share and share alike."

Cyrus proposes rewards on the basis of merit

5. Hereupon Chrysantas, one of the peers, a man neither large nor powerful to look upon, but pre-eminent in understanding, stood up and spoke: "Well, Cyrus," said he, "I think that you are introducing this discussion not because you think that the bad ought to have an equal share with the good, but because you wish to prove whether a single man will really be found who will care to let it be known that he thinks that, even if he himself does nothing good and noble, he should have an equal share of that which others win by their valour. 6. Now I," he went on, "am neither fleet of foot nor strong of arm, and I know that in view of what I shall accomplish by my bodily strength I should not be judged either the first or the second, or even, I suppose, the thousandth, and perhaps not even the ten thousandth. But on this point I am perfectly clear, that if those who are powerful men take matters vigorously in hand, I shall have as large a share of any good fortune that may come as I deserve. But if the bad do nothing and the good and strong lose heart, I am afraid," said he, "that I shall have a larger share than I wish of something other than good."

Chrysantas seconds the proposal

7. Thus spoke Chrysantas. And after him Pheraulas stood up, one of the Persian common-

Pheraulas adds his support

Κύρῳ πως ἔτι οἴκοθεν συνήθης καὶ ἀρεστὸ
ἀνήρ, καὶ τὸ σῶμα[1] καὶ τὴν ψυχὴν οὐκ ἀγεννε
ἀνδρὶ ἐοικώς, καὶ ἔλεξε τοιάδε· 8. Ἐγώ, ἔφη
ὦ Κῦρε καὶ πάντες οἱ παρόντες Πέρσαι, ἡγοῦ
μαι μὲν ἡμᾶς πάντας ἐκ τοῦ ἴσου νῦν ὁρμᾶ
σθαι εἰς τὸ ἀγωνίζεσθαι περὶ ἀρετῆς· ὁρῶ γὰ
ὁμοίᾳ μὲν τροφῇ πάντας ἡμᾶς τὸ σῶμα ἀσκοῦν
τας, ὁμοίας δὲ συνουσίας πάντας ἀξιουμένους
ταὐτὰ δὲ πᾶσιν ἡμῖν πρόκειται. τό τε γὰρ τοῖ
ἄρχουσι πείθεσθαι πᾶσιν ἐν κοινῷ κεῖται, καὶ ὃ
ἂν φανῇ τοῦτο ἀπροφασίστως ποιῶν, τοῦτον ὁρῶ
παρὰ Κύρου τιμῆς τυγχάνοντα· τό τε[2] πρὸς τοὺ
πολεμίους ἄλκιμον εἶναι οὐ τῷ μὲν προσῆκον τῷ
δ' οὔ, ἀλλὰ πᾶσι καὶ τοῦτο προκέκριται κάλ
λιστον εἶναι.

9. Νῦν δ', ἔφη, ἡμῖν καὶ δείκνυται[3] μάχη
ἣν ἐγὼ ὁρῶ πάντας ἀνθρώπους φύσει ἐπιστα
μένους, ὥσπερ γε καὶ τἆλλα ζῷα ἐπίσταταί τιν
μάχην ἕκαστα οὐδὲ παρ' ἑνὸς ἄλλου μαθόντα
παρὰ τῆς φύσεως, οἷον ὁ βοῦς κέρατι παίειν,
ἵππος ὁπλῇ, ὁ κύων στόματι, ὁ κάπρος ὀδόντι
καὶ φυλάττεσθαί γ', ἔφη, ἅπαντα ταῦτα ἐπί
σταται ἀφ' ὧν μάλιστα δεῖ, καὶ ταῦτα εἰς οὐ
δενὸς διδασκάλου πώποτε φοιτήσαντα. 10. κα
ἐγώ, ἔφη, ἐκ παιδίου εὐθὺς προβάλλεσθαι ἠπι
στάμην πρὸ τούτων ὅ τι ᾤμην πληγήσεσθαι· εἰ δ
μὴ ἄλλο μηδὲν ἔχοιμι, τὼ χεῖρε προέχων ἐνεπό

[1] τὸ σῶμα xz, Marchant; τὸ σῶμα οὐκ ἀφυὴς y, most Edd (*not physically unfit*).
[2] τό τε C, Breitenbach, Marchant; τό τ' αὖ yG, Dindorf Gemoll.
[3] δείκνυται x, Marchant, Gemoll; δέδεικται yz, most Edd.

:s, but a man who for some reason or other had
om the beginning won Cyrus's confidence and
fection; besides he was well-favoured in body and
gentleman at heart. His speech was as follows:
. "I think, Cyrus," said he, "and all you Persians
ere assembled, that we are all now starting on an
qual footing in a contest of merit; for I observe
at we are all taking the same bodily exercise, that
e all have the same rations, that we are all considered
orthy to move in the same society, and that the prizes
re offered alike to all. For obedience to the officers
as been enjoined equally upon us all, and whoever
hows himself prompt to comply, I observe that he
eceives honour from Cyrus. Again, to be brave
the face of the enemy is not a thing to be ex-
ected of one and not of another, but it is considered
r the noblest thing for all alike.

9. "And now," he continued, "we have been ini-
iated into a method of fighting, which, I observe, all
en naturally understand, just as in the case of other
reatures each understands some method of fighting
hich it has not learned from any other source than
om instinct: for instance, the bull knows how to
ght with his horns, the horse with his hoofs, the
og with his teeth, the boar with his tusks. And all
now how to protect themselves, too, against that
om which they most need protection, and that, too,
hough they have never gone to school to any teacher.
0. As for myself, I have understood from my very
hildhood how to protect the spot where I thought I
as likely to receive a blow; and if I had nothing
lse I put out my hands to hinder as well as I could

διζον ὅ τι ἐδυνάμην τὸν παίοντα· καὶ τοῦτο ἐποίο
οὐ διδασκόμενος, ἀλλὰ καὶ ἐπ' αὐτῷ τούτῳ παι
μενος, εἰ προβαλοίμην. μάχαιράν γε μὴν εὐθ
παιδίον ὢν ἥρπαζον ὅπου ἴδοιμι, οὐδὲ παρ' ἐνὶ
οὐδὲ τοῦτο μαθὼν ὅπως δεῖ λαμβάνειν ἢ παρ
τῆς φύσεως, ὡς ἐγώ φημι. ἐποίουν γοῦν κα
τοῦτο κωλυόμενος, οὐ διδασκόμενος· ὥσπερ κ
ἄλλα ἔστιν ἃ εἰργόμενος καὶ ὑπὸ μητρὸς καὶ ὑπ
πατρὸς ὑπὸ τῆς φύσεως πράττειν ἠναγκαζόμη
καὶ ναὶ μὰ Δία ἔπαιόν γε τῇ μαχαίρᾳ πᾶν ὅ τ
δυναίμην λανθάνειν. οὐ γὰρ μόνον φύσει ἦ
ὥσπερ τὸ βαδίζειν καὶ τρέχειν, ἀλλὰ καὶ ἡδ
πρὸς τῷ πεφυκέναι τοῦτο ἐδόκει μοι εἶναι.

11. Ἐπεὶ δ' οὖν, ἔφη, αὕτη ἡ μάχη κατα
λείπεται, ἐν ᾗ προθυμίας μᾶλλον ἢ τέχνης ἔργο
ἐστί, πῶς ἡμῖν οὐχ ἡδέως πρὸς τούσδε τοὺ
ὁμοτίμους ἀγωνιστέον; ὅπου γε τὰ μὲν ἆθλα τῆ
ἀρετῆς ἴσα πρόκειται, παραβαλλόμενοι δὲ οὐ
ἴσα εἰς τὸν κίνδυνον ἴμεν, ἀλλ' οὗτοι μὲν ἔντιμο
ὅσπερ μόνος ἥδιστος, βίον, ἡμεῖς δὲ ἐπίπονον μὲ
ἄτιμον δέ, ὅσπερ οἶμαι χαλεπώτατος.

12. Μάλιστα δέ, ὦ ἄνδρες, τοῦτό με [εὐθύ
μως][1] εἰς τὸν ἀγῶνα τὸν πρὸς τούσδε παρορμ
ὅτι Κῦρος ὁ κρίνων ἔσται, ὃς οὐ φθόνῳ κρίνε
ἀλλὰ (σὺν θεῶν ὅρκῳ λέγω) ἦ μὴν ἐμοὶ δοκε
Κῦρος οὕστινας ἂν ὁρᾷ[2] ἀγαθοὺς φιλεῖν οὐδὲ
ἧττον ἑαυτοῦ· τούτοις γοῦν ὁρῶ αὐτὸν ὅ τι ἂν ἔχ

[1] εὐθύμως MSS.; bracketed or omitted by most Edd. εὐθύ πως Gemoll (*straight on*).
[2] ἂν ὁρᾷ y, most Edd.; ὁρᾷ xz, Gemoll.

ıe one who was trying to hit me. And this I did
ıt from having been taught to do so, but even though
was beaten for that very act of putting out my hands.
ırthermore, even when I was a little fellow I used
ı seize a sword wherever I saw one, although, I
eclare, I had never learned, except from instinct,
ven how to take hold of a sword. At any rate, I
ıed to do this, even though they tried to keep me
om it—and certainly they did not teach me so to
ı—just as I was impelled by nature to do certain
her things which my father and mother tried to
eep me away from. And, by Zeus, I used to hack
ith a sword everything that I could without being
ıught at it. For this was not only instinctive, like
alking and running, but I thought it was fun in
ldition to its being natural.

11. "Be that as it may," he went on, "since
ıis method of fighting awaits us, which demands
ıurage more than skill, why should we not gladly
ımpete with the peers here? For the prizes pro-
ısed for excellence are equal, but we shall go into
ıe trial not having at stake interests equal with
ıeirs; for they have at stake a life of honour, which
the most happy of all, while we risk only a life of
ıil unhonoured, which I think is most burdensome.

12. "And this, comrades, gives me the most
ıurage for the competition with these gentlemen,
ıat Cyrus is to be the judge; for he decides not
ith partiality, but (I swear it by the gods) I
erily think that Cyrus loves no less than himself
ıose whom he recognizes as valiant. At any rate,
observe that, whatever he has, he is much
ıore pleased to give it to them than to keep it

ἥδιον[1] διδόντα μᾶλλον ἢ αὐτὸν ἔχοντα. 13. κα
τοι, ἔφη, οἶδα ὅτι οὗτοι μέγα φρονοῦσιν ὅ
πεπαίδευνται δὴ καὶ πρὸς λιμὸν καὶ δίψαν κ
πρὸς ῥῖγος καρτερεῖν, κακῶς εἰδότες ὅτι καὶ ταῦτ
ἡμεῖς ὑπὸ κρείττονος διδασκάλου πεπαιδεύμεθ
ἢ οὗτοι. οὐ γάρ ἐστι διδάσκαλος οὐδεὶς τούτα
κρείττων τῆς ἀνάγκης, ἣ ἡμᾶς καὶ λίαν ταῦ
ἀκριβοῦν ἐδίδαξε. 14. καὶ πονεῖν οὗτοι μὲν τὰ ὅπλ
φέροντες ἐμελέτων, ἅ ἐστιν ἅπασιν ἀνθρώπο
ηὑρημένα ὡς ἂν εὐφορώτατα εἴη, ἡμεῖς δέ γ', ἔφ
ἐν μεγάλοις φορτίοις καὶ βαδίζειν καὶ τρέχει
ἠναγκαζόμεθα, ὥστε νῦν ἐμοὶ δοκεῖν τὸ τῶν ὅπλω
φόρημα πτεροῖς μᾶλλον ἐοικέναι ἢ φορτίῳ.

15. Ὡς οὖν ἐμοῦ γε καὶ ἀγωνιουμένου κα
ὁποῖος ἄν τις ὦ κατὰ τὴν ἀξίαν με τιμᾶ
ἀξιώσοντος, οὕτως, ἔφη, ὦ Κῦρε, γίγνωσκ
καὶ ὑμῖν γ', ἔφη, ὦ ἄνδρες δημόται, παραιν
εἰς ἔριν ὁρμᾶσθαι ταύτης τῆς μάχης πρὸς τοὺ
πεπαιδευμένους τούσδε· νῦν γὰρ ἄνδρες[2] εἰλημ
μένοι εἰσὶν ἐν δημοτικῇ ἀγωνίᾳ.

16. Φεραύλας μὲν δὴ οὕτως εἶπεν. ἀνίσταντ
δὲ καὶ ἄλλοι πολλοὶ ἑκατέρων συναγορεύοντες
ἔδοξε κατὰ τὴν ἀξίαν τιμᾶσθαι ἕκαστον, Κῦρο
δὲ τὸν κρίνοντα εἶναι. ταῦτα μὲν δὴ οὕτ
προυκεχωρήκει.

17. Ἐκάλεσε δ' ἐπὶ δεῖπνον ὁ Κῦρος καὶ ὅλη
ποτὲ τάξιν σὺν τῷ ταξιάρχῳ, ἰδὼν αὐτὸν τοὺ
μὲν ἡμίσεις τῶν ἀνδρῶν τῆς τάξεως ἀντιτάξαντ
ἑκατέρωθεν εἰς ἐμβολήν, θώρακας μὲν ἀμφοτέρου

[1] ἥδιον y, most Edd. ; not in xz, Gemoll.
[2] ἄνδρες Schneider, Edd. ; ἄνδρες MSS.

or himself. 13. And yet I know that these men pride themselves upon having been trained, as they say, to endure hunger and thirst and cold, but they do not know that in this we also have been trained by a better teacher than they have had; for in these branches there is no better teacher than necessity, which has given us exceedingly thorough instruction in them. 14. And they have been in training for hard labour by carrying weapons, which all men have so devised that they may be as easy as possible to bear; while we, on our part, have been obliged to walk and to run with heavy burdens, so that the carrying of arms now seems to me more like having wings than bearing a burden.

15. "Let me inform you, therefore, Cyrus," said he, "that I, for one, shall not only enter this contest, but I shall also expect you to reward me according to my deserts, whatever I am, for better or worse. And you, my fellow-commoners," he concluded, "I recommend you to enter with alacrity into the competition with these gentlemen in this sort of warfare; for now they have been trapped in a contest with commoners."

16. Thus Pheraulas spoke. And many others from both orders rose to speak in favour of the measure. They decided that each one should receive rewards according to his deserts, and that Cyrus should be the judge. Thus, then, the matter was satisfactorily settled.

A sham battle: cudgels *vs.* clods

17. And once Cyrus invited a captain and his whole company to dinner, because he had noticed him drawing up one half of the men of his company against the other half for a sham battle. Both sides

ἔχοντας καὶ γέρρα ἐν ταῖς ἀριστεραῖς, εἰς δὲ τὰς δεξιὰς νάρθηκας παχεῖς τοῖς ἡμίσεσιν ἔδωκε, τοῖς δ' ἑτέροις εἶπεν ὅτι βάλλειν δεήσοι ἀναιρουμένους ταῖς βώλοις.

18. Ἐπεὶ δὲ παρεσκευασμένοι οὕτως ἔστησαν, ἐσήμηνεν αὐτοῖς μάχεσθαι. ἐνταῦθα δὴ οἱ μὲν ἔβαλλον ταῖς βώλοις καὶ ἔστιν οἳ ἐτύγχανον καὶ θωράκων καὶ γέρρων, οἱ δὲ καὶ μηροῦ καὶ κνημῖδος. ἐπεὶ δὲ ὁμοῦ ἐγένοντο, οἱ τοὺς νάρθηκας ἔχοντες ἔπαιον τῶν μὲν μηρούς, τῶν δὲ χεῖρας, τῶν δὲ κνήμας, τῶν δὲ καὶ ἐπικυπτόντων ἐπὶ βώλους ἔπαιον τοὺς τραχήλους καὶ τὰ νῶτα. τέλος δὲ τρεψάμενοι ἐδίωκον οἱ ναρθηκοφόροι παίοντες σὺν πολλῷ γέλωτι καὶ παιδιᾷ. ἐν μέρει γε μὴν οἱ ἕτεροι λαβόντες πάλιν τοὺς νάρθηκας ταὐτὰ ἐποίησαν τοὺς ταῖς βώλοις βάλλοντας.

19. Ταῦτα δ' ἀγασθεὶς ὁ Κῦρος, τοῦ μὲν ταξιάρχου τὴν ἐπίνοιαν, τῶν δὲ τὴν πειθώ, ὅτι ἅμα μὲν ἐγυμνάζοντο, ἅμα δὲ ηὐθυμοῦντο, ἅμα δὲ ἐνίκων οἱ εἰκασθέντες τῇ τῶν Περσῶν ὁπλίσει, τούτοις δὴ ἡσθεὶς ἐκάλεσέ τε ἐπὶ δεῖπνον αὐτοὺς καὶ ἐν τῇ σκηνῇ ἰδών τινας αὐτῶν ἐπιδεδεμένους, τὸν μέν τινα ἀντικνήμιον, τὸν δὲ χεῖρα, ἠρώτα τί πάθοιεν. οἱ δ' ἔλεγον ὅτι πληγεῖεν ταῖς βώλοις. 20. ὁ δὲ πάλιν ἐπηρώτα πότερον ἐπεὶ ὁμοῦ ἐγένοντο ἢ ὅτε πρόσω ἦσαν. οἱ δ' ἔλεγον ὅτε πρόσω ἦσαν. ἐπεὶ δὲ ὁμοῦ ἐγένοντο, παιδιὰν ἔφασαν εἶναι καλλίστην οἱ ναρθηκοφόροι· οἱ δὲ

had breastplates and on their left arms their shields; in the hands of the one side he placed stout cudgels, while he told the other side that they would have to pick up clods to throw.

18. Now when they had taken their stand thus equipped, he gave the order to begin battle. Then those on the one side threw their clods, and some struck the breastplates and shields, others also struck the thighs and greaves of their opponents. But when they came into close quarters, those who had the cudgels struck the others—some upon the thighs, others upon the arms, others upon the shins; and as still others stooped to pick up clods, the cudgels came down upon their necks and backs. And finally, when the cudgel-bearers had put their opponents to flight, they pursued them laying on the blows amid shouts of laughter and merriment. And then again, changing about, the other side took the cudgels with the same result to their opponents, who in turn threw clods.

19. In this Cyrus admired both the captain's cleverness and the men's obedience, and he was pleased to see that they were at the same time having their practice and enjoying themselves and also because that side was victorious which was armed after the fashion of the Persians. Pleased with this he invited them to dinner; and in his tent, observing some of them wearing bandages —one around his leg, another around his arm—he asked them what the matter was; and they answered that they had been hit with the clods. 20. And he inquired further, whether it had happened when they were close together or far apart. And they said it was when they were far apart. But when they came to close quarters, it was capital fun—so

συγκεκομμένοι τοῖς νάρθηξιν ἀνέκραγον ὅτι οὐ σφίσι δοκοίη παιδιὰ εἶναι τὸ ὁμόθεν παίεσθαι· ἅμα δὲ ἐπεδείκνυσαν τῶν ναρθήκων τὰς πληγὰς καὶ ἐν χερσὶ καὶ ἐν τραχήλοις, ἔνιοι δὲ καὶ ἐν προσώποις. καὶ τότε μὲν ὥσπερ εἰκὸς ἐγέλων ἐπ' ἀλλήλοις.

Τῇ δ' ὑστεραίᾳ μεστὸν ἦν τὸ πεδίον πᾶν τῶν[1] τούτους μιμουμένων· καὶ εἰ μὴ ἄλλο τι σπουδαιότερον πράττοιεν, ταύτῃ τῇ παιδιᾷ ἐχρῶντο.

21. Ἄλλον δέ ποτε ἰδὼν ταξίαρχον ἄγοντα τὴν τάξιν ἀπὸ τοῦ ποταμοῦ ἐπὶ τὸ ἀριστερὸν ἐφ' ἑνός, καὶ ὁπότε δοκοίη αὐτῷ καιρὸς εἶναι, παραγγέλλοντα τὸν ὕστερον λόχον παράγειν, καὶ τὸν τρίτον

[1] *πᾶν τῶν* Stephanus, Edd.; *πάντων* MSS.

---

[a] The manœuvre here described is perfectly simple: they are coming up from the river, from the left, thus (letting . stand for private, ‡ for corporal, † for sergeant, * for lieutenant [in command of a division of twenty-five], § for captain):—

⋙→ *First Formation—*

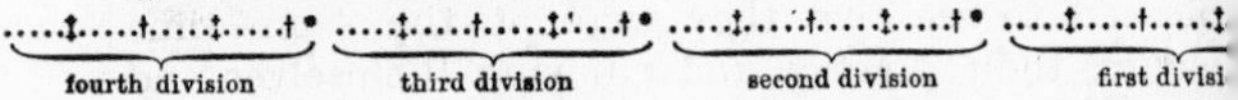

```
....‡....†....‡....†•  ....‡....†....‡....†•  ....‡....†....‡....†•  ....‡....†....‡
   fourth division         third division         second division         first divisi
```

The first division halts, and the other three, in succession, line up abreast with the first; the second formation has the four lieutenants abreast in front and is twenty-five men deep:

⋙→ *Second Formation—*

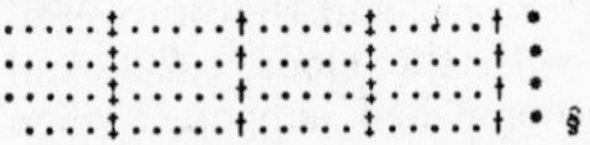

```
.....‡.....†.....‡.....† •
.....‡.....†.....‡.....† •
.....‡.....†.....‡.....† •
 ....‡.....†.....‡.....† • §
```

Then each division doubles up, and the third formation, with the eight sergeants abreast in front, and the eight corporals abreast further back is

he cudgel-bearers said; but those who had been horoughly drubbed with the cudgels cried out hat it did not seem any fun to them to be beaten t close quarters, and at the same time they showed he marks of the cudgels on their arms and their ecks and some also on their faces. And then, as was natural, they laughed at one another.

On the following day the whole plain was full of nen following their example; and if they had nothing nore important to do, they indulged in this sport.

Military drill made pleasant

21. And once he saw another captain leading his company up from the river left about in single file and ordering when he thought it was proper, the second division [a] and then the third and the fourth

Third Formation—

```
....‡.....†
....‡.....† •
....‡.....†
....‡.....† •
....‡.....†
....‡.....† •
....‡.....†
....‡.....† • §
```

With another doubling up of ranks, they assume a front of sixteen men and a depth of six:

Fourth Formation—

```
....‡
....†
....‡
....† •
....‡
....†
....‡
....† •
....‡
....†
....‡
....† •
....‡
....†
....‡
....† • §
```

Finally in these groups of six each, they are led, single file, in to dinner.

καὶ τὸν τέταρτον, εἰς μέτωπον, ἐπεὶ δ' ἐν μετώπῳ οἱ λοχαγοὶ ἐγένοντο, παρηγγύησεν εἰς δύο ἄγειν τὸν λόχον· ἐκ τούτου δὴ παρῆγον οἱ δεκάδαρχοι εἰς μέτωπον· ὁπότε δ' αὖ ἐδόκει αὐτῷ καιρὸς εἶναι, παρήγγειλεν εἰς τέτταρας τὸν λόχον· οὕτω δὴ οἱ πεμπάδαρχοι αὖ παρῆγον εἰς τέτταρας· ἐπεὶ δὲ ἐπὶ θύραις τῆς σκηνῆς ἐγένοντο, παραγγείλας αὖ εἰς ἕνα οὕτως[1] εἰσῆγε τὸν πρῶτον λόχον, καὶ τὸν δεύτερον τούτου κατ' οὐρὰν ἐκέλευσεν ἕπεσθαι, καὶ τὸν τρίτον καὶ τὸν τέταρτον ὡσαύτως παραγγείλας ἡγεῖτο εἴσω· οὕτω δ' εἰσαγαγὼν κατέκλινεν ἐπὶ τὸ δεῖπνον ὥσπερ εἰσεπορεύοντο· τοῦτον οὖν ὁ Κῦρος ἀγασθεὶς τῆς τε πρᾳότητος τῆς διδασκαλίας καὶ τῆς ἐπιμελείας ἐκάλεσε ταύτην τὴν τάξιν ἐπὶ τὸ δεῖπνον σὺν τῷ ταξιάρχῳ.

22. Παρὼν δέ τις ἐπὶ τῷ δείπνῳ κεκλημένος ἄλλος ταξίαρχος, Τὴν δ' ἐμήν, ἔφη, τάξιν, ὦ Κῦρε, οὐ καλεῖς εἰς τὴν σκηνήν; καὶ μὴν ὅταν γε παρίῃ ἐπὶ τὸ δεῖπνον, πάντα ταὐτὰ[2] ποιεῖ· καὶ ὅταν τέλος ἡ σκηνὴ ἔχῃ, ἐξάγει μὲν ὁ οὐραγός, ἔφη, ὁ τοῦ τελευταίου λόχου τὸν λόχον, ὑστάτους ἔχων τοὺς πρώτους τεταγμένους εἰς μάχην· ἔπειτα ὁ δεύτερος τοὺς τοῦ ἑτέρου λόχου ἐπὶ τούτοις, καὶ ὁ τρίτος καὶ ὁ τέταρτος ὡσαύτως, ὅπως, ἔφη, καὶ ὅταν ἀπάγειν δέῃ ἀπὸ πολεμίων, ἐπίστωνται ὡς δεῖ ἀπιέναι. ἐπειδὰν δέ, ἔφη, καταστῶμεν ἐπὶ τὸν δρόμον ἔνθα περιπατοῦμεν, ὅταν μὲν πρὸς ἕω ἴωμεν, ἐγὼ μὲν ἡγοῦμαι,

[1] *οὕτως* Weiske, Breitenbach; *ἰόντων* MSS., Dindorf; [*ἰόντων*] Gemoll, Marchant.
[2] *ταὐτὰ* Dindorf, Edd.; *ταῦτα* MSS.

to advance to the front; and when the lieutenants were in a row in front, he ordered each division to march up in double file. Thus the sergeants came to stand on the front line. Again, when he thought proper, he ordered the divisions to line up four abreast; in this formation, then, the corporals in their turn came to stand four abreast in each division; and when they arrived at the doors of the tent, he commanded them to fall into single file again, and in this order he led the first division into the tent; the second he ordered to fall in line behind the first and follow, and, giving orders in like manner to the third and fourth, he led them inside. And when he had thus led them all in, he gave them their places at dinner in the order in which they came in. Pleased with him for his gentleness of discipline and for his painstaking, Cyrus invited this company also with its captain to dinner.

22. Now there was present another captain who had been invited to the dinner and he said: "Cyrus, will you not invite my company to your tent? My company, too, does all this when we go to mess, and when the meal is finished the rear-guard leader of the last division leads that division out, keeping in the rear those whose place in the battle line is in front; then, next after them, the second rear-guard leader brings out the men of the second division, and the third and the fourth in like manner, in order that," he explained, "they may also know how to withdraw, if ever it is necessary to retreat before the enemy. And when we take our places on the parade-ground, I take the lead, when we march toward the east, and the first division of the company

καὶ ὁ πρῶτος λόχος πρῶτος, καὶ ὁ δεύτερος ὡ
δεῖ, καὶ ὁ τρίτος καὶ ὁ τέταρτος, καὶ αἱ τῶν λό-
χων δεκάδες καὶ πεμπάδες, ἕως ἂν παραγγέλλω
ἐγώ· ὅταν δ', ἔφη, πρὸς ἑσπέραν ἴωμεν, ὁ οὐραγός τε καὶ οἱ τελευταῖοι πρῶτοι ἀφηγοῦνται
ἐμοὶ μέντοι οὕτω πείθονται ὑστέρῳ ἰόντι, ἵνα
ἐθίζωνται καὶ ἕπεσθαι καὶ ἡγεῖσθαι ὁμοίω
πειθόμενοι.

23. Καὶ ὁ Κῦρος ἔφη, Ἦ καὶ ἀεὶ τοῦτο ποιεῖτε;

Ὁποσάκις γε, ἔφη, καὶ δειπνοποιούμεθα, νὴ
Δία.

Καλῶ τοίνυν, ἔφη, ὑμᾶς, ἅμα μὲν ὅτι τὰς
τάξεις μελετᾶτε καὶ προσιόντες καὶ ἀπιόντες,
ἅμα δ' ὅτι καὶ ἡμέρας καὶ νυκτός, ἅμα δ' ὅτι
τά τε σώματα περιπατοῦντες ἀσκεῖτε καὶ τὰς
ψυχὰς ὠφελεῖτε διδάσκοντες. ἐπεὶ οὖν πάντα
διπλᾶ ποιεῖτε, διπλῆν ὑμῖν δίκαιον καὶ τὴν εὐ-
ωχίαν παρέχειν.

24. Μὰ Δί', ἔφη ὁ ταξίαρχος, μήτοι γ' ἐν μιᾷ
ἡμέρᾳ, εἰ μὴ καὶ διπλᾶς ἡμῖν τὰς γαστέρας
παρέξεις.

Καὶ τότε μὲν δὴ οὕτω τὸ τέλος τῆς σκηνῆς
ἐποιήσαντο. τῇ δ' ὑστεραίᾳ ὁ Κῦρος ἐκάλεσεν
ἐκείνην τὴν τάξιν, ὥσπερ ἔφη, καὶ τῇ ἄλλῃ. αἰ-
σθόμενοι δὲ ταῦτα καὶ οἱ ἄλλοι τὸ λοιπὸν πάντες
αὐτοὺς ἐμιμοῦντο.

IV

1. Ἐξέτασιν δέ ποτε πάντων τοῦ Κύρου ποιου-
μένου ἐν τοῖς ὅπλοις καὶ σύνταξιν ἦλθε παρὰ
Κυαξάρου ἄγγελος λέγων ὅτι Ἰνδῶν παρείη πρεσ-

goes first, the second in its proper order, and then the third and the fourth and the squads of ten and five in each division, until I give the order for some change of formation; then," said he, "when we march toward the west, the rear-guard leader and the rear-guard lead off first. Still, even so, they have to look to me for the commands, though I march last, so that they may get into the habit of obeying just the same whether they follow or whether they lead."

23. "Do you always do that way?" asked Cyrus.

"Yes, by Zeus," said he, "as often as we go to dinner."

"Well then," said Cyrus, "I will invite you, because you give your lines practice both in coming and in going, by night and by day, and also because you give your bodies exercise by marching about, and improve your minds by instruction. Since, therefore, you do all this doubly, it is only fair that I should furnish you a double feast also."

24. "No, by Zeus," said the captain, "at any rate not on the same day, unless you will furnish us with double stomachs as well."

Thus they brought that dinner to a close. And on the following day Cyrus invited that company, as he had promised, and again the next day. And when the others heard about it, they all followed, in the future, the example of that company.

IV

An embassy from India

1. Once when Cyrus was holding a general review and parade of all his men under arms, a messenger came from Cyaxares saying that an embassy had

βεία· Κελεύει οὖν σε ἐλθεῖν ὡς τάχιστα. φέρω δέ σοι, ἔφη ὁ ἄγγελος, καὶ στολὴν τὴν καλλίστην παρὰ Κυαξάρου· ἐβούλετο γάρ σε ὡς λαμπρότατα καὶ εὐκοσμότατα προσάγειν, ὡς ὀψομένων τῶν Ἰνδῶν ὅπως ἂν προσίῃς.

2. Ἀκούσας δὲ ταῦτα ὁ Κῦρος παρήγγειλε τῷ πρώτῳ τεταγμένῳ ταξιάρχῳ εἰς μέτωπον στῆναι, ἐφ' ἑνὸς ἄγοντα τὴν τάξιν, ἐν δεξιᾷ ἔχοντα ἑαυτόν, καὶ τῷ δευτέρῳ ἐκέλευσε ταὐτὸ τοῦτο παραγγεῖλαι, καὶ διὰ πάντων οὕτω παραδιδόναι ἐκέλευσεν. οἱ δὲ πειθόμενοι ταχὺ μὲν παρήγγελλον, ταχὺ δὲ τὰ παραγγελλόμενα ἐποίουν, ἐν ὀλίγῳ δὲ χρόνῳ ἐγένοντο τὸ μὲν μέτωπον ἐπὶ τριακοσίων,[1] τοσοῦτοι γὰρ ἦσαν οἱ ταξίαρχοι, τὸ δὲ βάθος ἐφ' ἑκατόν. 3. ἐπεὶ δὲ κατέστησαν, ἕπεσθαι ἐκέλευσεν ὡς ἂν αὐτὸς ἡγῆται· καὶ εὐθὺς τροχάζων ἡγεῖτο. ἐπεὶ δὲ κατενόησε τὴν ἀγυιὰν τὴν πρὸς τὸ βασίλειον φέρουσαν στενοτέραν οὖσαν ἢ ὡς ἐπὶ μετώπου πάντας διιέναι, παραγγείλας τὴν πρώτην χιλιοστὺν ἕπεσθαι κατὰ χώραν, τὴν δὲ δευτέραν κατ' οὐρὰν ταύτης ἀκολουθεῖν, καὶ διὰ παντὸς οὕτως, αὐτὸς μὲν ἡγεῖτο οὐκ ἀναπαυόμενος, αἱ δ' ἄλλαι χιλιοστύες κατ' οὐρὰν ἑκάστη τῆς ἔμπροσθεν εἵποντο.

4. Ἔπεμψε δὲ καὶ ὑπηρέτας δύο ἐπὶ τὸ στόμα τῆς ἀγυιᾶς, ὅπως εἴ τις ἀγνοοίη, σημαίνοιεν τὸ δέον ποιεῖν. ὡς δ' ἀφίκοντο ἐπὶ τὰς Κυαξάρου θύρας, παρήγγειλε τῷ πρώτῳ ταξιάρχῳ τὴν τάξιν

[1] τριακοσίων Muretus, Edd.; διακοσίων MSS. (*two hundred*).

arrived from India. "He therefore bids you come as soon as possible. Moreover," said the messenger, "I am bringing you a very beautiful robe from Cyaxares; for he expressed the wish that you appear as brilliant and splendid as possible when you come, for the Indians will see how you approach him."

2. And when Cyrus heard this, he gave orders to the captain who was stationed first to take his stand at the head of the line, bringing up his company in single file and keeping himself to the right; he told him to transmit the same order to the second captain and to pass it on through all the lines. And they obeyed at once and passed the order on, and they all executed it promptly, and in a little while they were three hundred abreast on the front line, for that was the number of the captains, and a hundred men deep. 3. And when they had got into their places, he ordered them to follow as he himself should lead. And at once he led them off at a double quick step. But when he became aware that the street leading to the king's headquarters was too narrow to admit all his men with such a front, he ordered the first regiment in their present order to follow him, the second to fall in behind the first, and so on through them all, while he himself led on without stopping to rest, and the other regiments followed, each the one before it.

4. And he sent also two adjutants to the entrance of the street, to tell what was to be done, if any one did not understand. And when they arrived at Cyaxares's doors, he ordered the first captain to draw up his company twelve deep, while the sergeants

εἰς δώδεκα τάττειν βάθος, τοὺς δὲ δωδεκάρχους ἐν μετώπῳ καθιστάναι περὶ τὸ βασίλειον, καὶ τῷ δευτέρῳ ταὐτὰ ἐκέλευσε παραγγεῖλαι, καὶ διὰ παντὸς οὕτως. 5. οἱ μὲν δὴ ταῦτ' ἐποίουν· ὁ δ' εἰσῄει πρὸς τὸν Κυαξάρην ἐν τῇ Περσικῇ στολῇ οὐδέν τι ὑβρισμένῃ. ἰδὼν δὲ αὐτὸν ὁ Κυαξάρης τῷ μὲν τάχει ἥσθη, τῇ δὲ φαυλότητι τῆς στολῆς ἠχθέσθη, καὶ εἶπε, Τί τοῦτο, ὦ Κῦρε; οἷον πεποίηκας οὕτω φανεὶς τοῖς Ἰνδοῖς; ἐγὼ δ', ἔφη, ἐβουλόμην σε ὡς λαμπρότατον φανῆναι· καὶ γὰρ ἐμοὶ ἂν κόσμος ἦν τοῦτο, ἐμῆς ὄντα ἀδελφῆς υἱὸν ὅτι μεγαλοπρεπέστατον φαίνεσθαι.

6. Καὶ ὁ Κῦρος πρὸς ταῦτα εἶπε, Καὶ ποτέρως ἄν, ὦ Κυαξάρη, μᾶλλόν σε ἐκόσμουν, εἴπερ πορφυρίδα ἐνδὺς καὶ ψέλια λαβὼν καὶ στρεπτὸν περιθέμενος σχολῇ κελεύοντι ὑπήκουόν σοι, ἢ νῦν ὅτε σὺν τοιαύτῃ καὶ τοσαύτῃ δυνάμει οὕτω σοι ὀξέως ὑπακούω διὰ τὸ σὲ τιμᾶν ἱδρῶτι καὶ σπουδῇ καὶ αὐτὸς κεκοσμημένος καὶ τοὺς ἄλλους ἐπιδεικνύς σοι οὕτω πειθομένους;

Κῦρος μὲν οὖν ταῦτα εἶπεν. ὁ δὲ Κυαξάρης νομίσας αὐτὸν ὀρθῶς λέγειν ἐκάλεσε τοὺς Ἰνδούς. 7. οἱ δὲ Ἰνδοὶ εἰσελθόντες ἔλεξαν ὅτι πέμψειε σφᾶς ὁ Ἰνδῶν βασιλεὺς κελεύων ἐρωτᾶν ἐξ ὅτου ὁ πόλεμος εἴη Μήδοις τε καὶ τῷ Ἀσσυρίῳ· Ἐπεὶ δὲ σοῦ ἀκούσαιμεν, ἐκέλευσεν ἐλθόντας αὖ πρὸς τὸν Ἀσσύριον κἀκείνου ταὐτὰ πυθέσθαι· τέλος δ' ἀμφοτέροις εἰπεῖν ὑμῖν ὅτι ὁ Ἰνδῶν βασιλεύς, τὸ δίκαιον σκεψάμενος, φαίη μετὰ τοῦ ἠδικημένου ἔσεσθαι.

8. Πρὸς ταῦτα ὁ Κυαξάρης εἶπεν, Ἐμοῦ μὲν

were to take their places on the front line about the king's headquarters. He bade him transmit the same orders to the second captain, and so on to all the rest; 5. and they proceeded to do so, while he presented himself before Cyaxares in his Persian dress, which was not at all showy. When Cyaxares saw him, he was pleased at his promptness but displeased with the plainness of his dress and said: "How is this, Cyrus? What do you mean by appearing thus before the Indians? Now I wished you to appear with as much magnificence as possible, for it would have been a mark of respect to me to have my sister's son appear in all possible grandeur."

Cyrus presents himself and his army

6. "Should I be showing you more respect, Cyaxares," Cyrus made reply to this, "if I arrayed myself in purple and adorned myself with bracelets and put on a necklace and at my leisure obeyed your orders, than I have in obeying you with such dispatch and accompanied by so large and so efficient an army? And I have come myself adorned with sweat and marks of haste to honour you and I present the others likewise obedient to you."

Thus Cyrus spoke, and Cyaxares recognizing that he was right summoned the Indians. 7. And when the Indians came in they said that the king of India had sent them with orders to ask on what ground the Medes and the Assyrians had declared war. "And he has ordered us," they said, "when we have heard your statement, to go also to the Assyrian and ask him the same question; and finally, he bade us say to both of you that the king of India declares that when he has weighed the merits of the case, he will side with the party wronged."

The audience

8. "Well, then," Cyaxares made reply to this,

τοίνυν ἀκούετε ὅτι οὐκ ἀδικοῦμεν τὸν Ἀσσύριο
οὐδέν· ἐκείνου δ', εἰ δεῖσθε, ἐλθόντες νῦν πύθεσθ
ὅ τι λέγει.

Παρὼν δὲ ὁ Κῦρος ἤρετο τὸν Κυαξάρην, Ἠ
καὶ ἐγώ, ἔφη, εἴπω ὅ τι γιγνώσκω; καὶ
Κυαξάρης ἐκέλευσεν.

Ὑμεῖς τοίνυν, ἔφη, ἀπαγγείλατε τῷ Ἰνδῶ
βασιλεῖ τάδε, εἰ μή τι ἄλλο Κυαξάρῃ δοκεῖ, ὅτ
φαμὲν ἡμεῖς, εἴ τί φησιν ὑφ' ἡμῶν ἀδικεῖσθαι
Ἀσσύριος, αἱρεῖσθαι αὐτὸν τὸν Ἰνδῶν βασιλέ
δικαστήν.

Οἱ μὲν δὴ ταῦτα ἀκούσαντες ᾤχοντο. 9. ἐπε
δὲ ἐξῆλθον οἱ Ἰνδοί, ὁ Κῦρος πρὸς τὸν Κυαξάρη
ἤρξατο λόγου τοιοῦδε·

Ὦ Κυαξάρη, ἐγὼ μὲν ἦλθον οὐδέν τι πολλ
ἔχων ἴδια χρήματα οἴκοθεν· ὁπόσα δ' ἦν, τούτω
πάνυ ὀλίγα λοιπὰ ἔχω· ἀνήλωκα δέ, ἔφη, εἰ
τοὺς στρατιώτας· καὶ τοῦτο ἴσως, ἔφη, θαυ
μάζεις σὺ πῶς ἐγὼ ἀνήλωκα σοῦ αὐτοὺς τρέφον
τος· εὖ δ' ἴσθι, ἔφη, ὅτι οὐδὲν ἄλλο ποιῶν ἢ
τιμῶν καὶ χαριζόμενος, ὅταν τινὶ ἀγασθῶ τῶν
στρατιωτῶν. 10. δοκεῖ γάρ μοι, ἔφη, πάντα
μὲν οὓς ἄν τις βούληται ἀγαθοὺς συνεργοὺς ποι
εῖσθαι ὁποίου τινὸς οὖν πράγματος, ἥδιον εἶναι εἰ
τε λέγοντα καὶ εὖ ποιοῦντα παρορμᾶν μᾶλλον ἢ
λυποῦντα καὶ ἀναγκάζοντα· οὓς δὲ δὴ τῶν εἰς τὸν
πόλεμον ἔργων ποιήσασθαί τις βούλοιτο συνερ
γοὺς προθύμους, τούτους παντάπασιν ἔμοιγε δοκεῖ
ἀγαθοῖς θηρατέον εἶναι καὶ λόγοις καὶ ἔργοις
φίλους γάρ, οὐκ ἐχθρούς, δεῖ εἶναι τοὺς μέλλοντας
ἀπροφασίστους συμμάχους ἔσεσθαι καὶ μήτε τοῖς
ἀγαθοῖς τοῦ ἄρχοντος φθονήσοντας μήτε ἐν τοῖς

let me tell you that we are not guilty of doing any wrong to the Assyrian ; but go now, if you wish, and ask him what he has to say."

Cyrus, who was present, asked Cyaxares, "May I also tell them what I think ?" And Cyaxares bade him say on.

"Well then," said he, "if Cyaxares has no objection, tell the king of India that we propose, in case the Assyrian says he has been wronged by us, to choose the king of India himself to be our arbitrator."

Upon hearing this, they went away. 9. And when they had gone out, Cyrus addressed Cyaxares as follows:

Cyrus calls upon Cyaxares for funds

"Cyaxares, I came from home without very much money of my own, and of what I had I have very little left. I have spent it," he said, "upon my soldiers. Now you wonder, perhaps, how I have spent it upon them, when you are maintaining them; but I want you to know that it has gone for nothing else than rewards and entertainments, whenever I am pleased with any of my soldiers. 10. For," said he, "in the case of all those whom one wishes to make efficient coadjutors in any enterprise of any sort whatsoever, it seems to me pleasanter to draw them on by kind words and kind services rather than by compulsion and force ; but in the case of those whom one wishes to make enthusiastic followers in his plans of war, one must by all means try to capture them with kind words and kind offices. For those men who are to be trusty comrades, who will not envy their commander in his successes nor betray him in his adversity, must be his friends and

κακοῖς προδώσοντας.[1] 11. ταῦτ' οὖν ἐγὼ οὕτ
προγιγνώσκων χρημάτων δοκῶ προσδεῖσθαι. πρὸ
μὲν οὖν σὲ πάντα ὁρᾶν ὃν αἰσθάνομαι πολλ
δαπανῶντα ἄτοπόν μοι δοκεῖ εἶναι· σκοπεῖν δ
ἀξιῶ κοινῇ καὶ σὲ καὶ ἐμὲ ὅπως σὲ μὴ ἐπιλείψε
χρήματα. ἐὰν γὰρ σὺ ἄφθονα ἔχῃς, οἶδα ὅτι κα
ἐμοὶ ἂν εἴη λαμβάνειν ὁπότε δεοίμην, ἄλλως τ
καὶ εἰ εἰς τοιοῦτόν τι λαμβάνοιμι ὃ μέλλοι καὶ σο
δαπανηθὲν βέλτιον εἶναι.

12. Ἔναγχος οὖν ποτέ σου μέμνημαι ἀκού
σας ὡς ὁ Ἀρμένιος καταφρονοίη σου νῦν, ὅτ
ἀκούει τοὺς πολεμίους προσιόντας ἡμῖν, καὶ οὔτ
τὸ[2] στράτευμα πέμποι οὔτε τὸν δασμὸν ὃν ἔδε
ἀπάγοι.

Ποιεῖ γὰρ ταῦτα, ἔφη, ὦ Κῦρε, ἐκεῖνος· ὥστ
ἔγωγε ἀπορῶ πότερόν μοι κρεῖττον στρατεύεσθα
καὶ πειρᾶσθαι ἀνάγκην αὐτῷ προσθεῖναι ἢ[3] ἐᾶσα
ἐν τῷ παρόντι, μὴ καὶ τοῦτον πολέμιον πρὸς τοῖ
ἄλλοις προσθώμεθα.

13. Καὶ ὁ Κῦρος ἐπήρετο, Αἱ δ' οἰκήσεις αὐτῷ
πότερον ἐν ἐχυροῖς χωρίοις εἰσὶν ἢ καί που ἐ
εὐεφόδοις;

Καὶ ὁ Κυαξάρης εἶπεν, Αἱ μὲν οἰκήσεις οὐ
πάνυ ἐν ἐχυροῖς· ἐγὼ γὰρ τούτου οὐκ ἠμέλουν
ὄρη μέντοι ἔστιν ἔνθα δύναιτ' ἂν ἀπελθὼν ἐν τῷ
παραχρῆμα ἐν ἀσφαλεῖ εἶναι τοῦ μὴ αὐτός γ
ὑποχείριος γενέσθαι, μηδὲ ὅσα ἐνταῦθα δύναιτο

[1] προδώσοντας xAH, Edd.; ὀρρωδήσοντας yG (*shrink in fear*).
[2] τὸ Schneider, Edd.; not in MSS.
[3] ἢ Hug, et al.; ἢ λυσιτελεῖ(-ῆ E) xF, Dindorf; λυσιτελεῖν DG²; νῦν z.

not his enemies. 11. Accordingly, as I recognize this in advance, I think I need more money. However, it seems to me unreasonable for every one to be looking to you, who, I observe, are put to great expense; but I think that you and I should together lay plans that funds may never fail you. For if you have plenty, I am sure it would be possible for me to draw money whenever I needed it, especially if I should take it to spend for something that would be more to your advantage also.

The Armenian defection

12. "Now I remember hearing you say one day recently that the Armenian king despises you now, because he has heard that the enemy are coming against you, and that therefore he is neither sending troops nor paying the tribute which is due."

"Yes, Cyrus," he answered; "that is just what he is doing; and so, for my part, I am in doubt whether it is better to proceed against him and try to enforce allegiance or to let him alone for the present, for fear we bring him also upon us as an enemy, in addition to the others."

13. "But his residences," asked Cyrus, "are they all in fortified places or are perhaps some of them in places easy of approach?"

"His residences," answered Cyaxares, "are in places not very well fortified; I did not fail to attend to that. However, there are mountains where he could take refuge and for a time be safe from falling into our hands himself, and where he could insure the safety of whatever he could have carried up

ὑπεκκομίσασθαι, εἰ μή τις πολιορκοίη προσκαθήμενος, ὥσπερ ὁ ἐμὸς πατὴρ τοῦτο ἐποίησεν.

14. Ἐκ τούτου δὴ ὁ Κῦρος λέγει τάδε· Ἀλλ᾽ εἰ θέλοις, ἔφη, ἐμὲ πέμψαι, ἱππέας μοι προσθεὶς ὁπόσοι δοκοῦσι μέτριοι εἶναι, οἶμαι ἂν σὺν τοῖς θεοῖς ποιῆσαι αὐτὸν καὶ τὸ στράτευμα πέμψαι καὶ ἀποδοῦναι τὸν δασμόν σοι· ἔτι δ᾽ ἐλπίζω καὶ φίλον αὐτὸν μᾶλλον ἡμῖν γενήσεσθαι ἢ νῦν ἐστι.

15. Καὶ ὁ Κυαξάρης εἶπε, Καὶ ἐγώ, ἔφη, ἐλπίζω ἐκείνους ἐλθεῖν ἂν πρὸς σὲ μᾶλλον ἢ πρὸς ἐμέ· ἀκούω γὰρ καὶ συνθηρευτάς τινας τῶν παίδων σοι γενέσθαι αὐτοῦ· ὥστ᾽ ἴσως ἂν καὶ πάλιν ἔλθοιεν πρὸς σέ· ὑποχειρίων δὲ γενομένων αὐτῶν πάντα πραχθείη ἂν ᾗ ἡμεῖς βουλόμεθα.

Οὐκοῦν σοι δοκεῖ, ἔφη ὁ Κῦρος, σύμφορον εἶναι τὸ λεληθέναι ἡμᾶς ταῦτα βουλεύοντας;

Μᾶλλον γὰρ ἄν, ἔφη ὁ Κυαξάρης, καὶ ἔλθοι τις αὐτῶν εἰς χεῖρας, καὶ εἴ τις ὁρμῷτο ἐπ᾽ αὐτούς, ἀπαράσκευοι [1] ἂν λαμβάνοιντο.

16. Ἄκουε τοίνυν, ἔφη ὁ Κῦρος, ἤν τι σοι δόξω λέγειν. ἐγὼ πολλάκις δὴ σὺν πᾶσι τοῖς μετ᾽ ἐμοῦ τεθήρακα ἀμφὶ τὰ ὅρια τῆς τε σῆς χώρας καὶ τῆς τῶν Ἀρμενίων, καὶ ἱππέας τινὰς ἤδη προσλαβὼν τῶν ἐνθένδε ἑταίρων ἀφικόμην.

Τὰ μὲν τοίνυν ὅμοια ποιῶν, ἔφη ὁ Κυαξάρης, οὐκ ἂν ὑποπτεύοιο· εἰ δὲ πολὺ πλείων ἡ δύναμις φαίνοιτο ἧς ἔχων εἴωθας θηρᾶν, τοῦτο ἤδη ὕποπτον ἂν γένοιτο.

[1] ἀπαράσκευοι Dindorf, Breitenbach; ἀπαρασκεύαστοι z, Marchant, Gemoll; ἀπαρασκευαστότεροι y.

there secretly, unless some one should occupy the approaches and hold him in siege, as my father did."

14. "Well," Cyrus then made answer, "if you would give me as many horsemen as you think reasonable and send me there, I think that with the help of the gods I could make him send the troops and pay the tribute to you. And besides, I hope that he will be made a better friend to us than he now is."

15. "I also have hopes," Cyaxares replied, "that they would come to you sooner than to me; for I understand that some of his sons were among your companions in the chase; and so, perhaps, they would join you again. And if they should fall into your hands, everything would be accomplished as we wish."

"Well then," said Cyrus, "do you think it good policy to have this plan of ours kept a secret?"

"Yes, indeed," said Cyaxares; "for then some of them would be more likely to fall into our hands, and besides, if one were to attack them, they would be taken unprepared."

Cyrus's scheme to entrap the Armenian

16. "Listen then," said Cyrus, "and see if you think there is anything in what I say. Now I have often hunted with all my forces near the boundary between your country and the Armenians, and have even gone there with some horsemen from among my companions here."

"And so," said Cyaxares, "if you were to do the same again, you would excite no suspicion; but if they should notice that your force was much larger than that with which you used to hunt, this would at once look suspicious."

17. Ἀλλ᾽ ἔστιν, ἔφη ὁ Κῦρος, καὶ πρόφασιν κατασκευάσαι καὶ ἐνθάδε οὐκ ἄπιστον, καὶ ἤν τις ἐκεῖσε ἐξαγγείλῃ, ὡς ἐγὼ βουλοίμην μεγάλην θήραν ποιῆσαι· καὶ ἱππέας, ἔφη, αἰτοίην ἄν σε ἐκ τοῦ φανεροῦ.

Κάλλιστα λέγεις, ἔφη ὁ Κυαξάρης· ἐγὼ δέ σοι οὐκ ἐθελήσω διδόναι πλὴν μετρίους τινάς, ὡς βουλόμενος πρὸς τὰ φρούρια ἐλθεῖν τὰ πρὸς τῇ Ἀσσυρίᾳ. καὶ γὰρ τῷ ὄντι, ἔφη, βούλομαι ἐλθὼν κατασκευάσαι αὐτὰ ὡς ἐχυρώτατα. ὁπότε δὲ σὺ προεληλυθοίης σὺν ᾗ ἔχοις δυνάμει καὶ θηρῴης καὶ δὴ δύο ἡμέρας, πέμψαιμι ἄν σοι ἱκανοὺς ἱππέας καὶ πεζοὺς τῶν παρ᾽ ἐμοὶ ἠθροισμένων, οὓς σὺ λαβὼν εὐθὺς ἂν ἴοις,[1] καὶ αὐτὸς δ᾽ ἂν ἔχων τὴν ἄλλην δύναμιν πειρῴμην μὴ πρόσω ὑμῶν εἶναι, ἵνα, εἴ που καιρὸς εἴη, ἐπιφανείην.

18. Οὕτω δὴ ὁ μὲν Κυαξάρης εὐθέως πρὸς τὰ φρούρια ἤθροιζεν ἱππέας καὶ πεζούς, καὶ ἁμάξας δὲ σίτου προύπεμπε τὴν ἐπὶ τὰ φρούρια ὁδόν. ὁ δὲ Κῦρος ἐθύετο ἐπὶ τῇ πορείᾳ, καὶ ἅμα πέμπων ἐπὶ τὸν Κυαξάρην ᾔτει τῶν νεωτέρων ἱππέων. ὁ δὲ πάνυ πολλῶν βουλομένων ἕπεσθαι οὐ πολλοὺς ἔδωκεν αὐτῷ.

Προεληλυθότος δ᾽ ἤδη τοῦ Κυαξάρου σὺν δυνάμει πεζῇ καὶ ἱππικῇ τὴν πρὸς τὰ φρούρια ὁδὸν γίγνεται τῷ Κύρῳ τὰ ἱερὰ ἐπὶ τὸν Ἀρμένιον ἰέναι[2] καλά· καὶ οὕτως ἐξάγει δὴ ὡς εἰς θήραν παρεσκευασμένος.

[1] ἂν ἴοις Stephanus, Edd.; ἀνίοις MSS.
[2] ἰέναι xy, Breitenbach, et al.; omitted by Dindorf, et al.; [ἰέναι] Marchant, Gemoll.

17. "But," said Cyrus, "it is possible to devise
ι pretext that will be credited both here and also
here, if some one bring them word that I wish to
nstitute a great hunt; and horsemen I should ask of
ou openly."

"A very clever scheme!" said Cyaxares; "and I
hall refuse to give you more than a reasonable
umber, on the ground that I wish to visit the
utposts on the Assyrian border. And that will be no
ie, for in reality," said he, "I do wish to go there
nd to make them as strong as possible. And when
ou have gone ahead with the forces you have and
ave already been hunting for two days, I will send
ou a sufficient number of the cavalry and infantry
hat are mustered with me, and you may take them
nd make an inroad at once. And I myself, with
he rest of my forces, will try to be not far away
rom you, to make my appearance upon the scene,
hould occasion require it."

18. Thereupon Cyaxares at once proceeded to get
is cavalry and infantry together for visiting the
utposts, and to send out wagon-loads of provisions
n the road to the outposts. But Cyrus proceeded
o offer sacrifice in behalf of his expedition, and at
he same time he sent to Cyaxares and asked for
ome of his younger horsemen. But, although very
nany wished to go along, Cyaxares would not give
im many.

Now after Cyaxares with his forces of cavalry and
nfantry had already started off on the road to the
utposts, Cyrus's sacrifice turned out favourable for
roceeding against the Armenian. Accordingly, he
ed his men out equipped as if for hunting.

19. Πορευομένῳ δ' αὐτῷ εὐθὺς ἐν τῷ πρώτ
χωρίῳ ὑπανίσταται λαγῶς· ἀετὸς δ' ἐπιπτόμενος
αἴσιος, κατιδὼν[2] τὸν λαγῶ φεύγοντα, ἐπιφερό
μενος ἔπαισέ τε αὐτὸν καὶ συναρπάσας ἐξῆρε
κἀπενεγκὼν ἐπὶ λόφον τινὰ οὐ πρόσω ἐχρῆτ
τῇ ἄγρᾳ ὅ τι ἤθελεν. ἰδὼν οὖν ὁ Κῦρος τ
σημεῖον ἥσθη τε καὶ προσεκύνησε Δία βασιλέα
καὶ εἶπε πρὸς τοὺς παρόντας, Ἡ μὲν θήρα καλὴ
ἔσται, ὦ ἄνδρες, ἢν ὁ θεὸς θελήσῃ.

20. Ὡς δὲ πρὸς τοῖς ὁρίοις ἐγένοντο, εὐθὺ
ὥσπερ εἰώθει ἐθήρα· καὶ τὸ μὲν πλῆθος τῶ
πεζῶν καὶ τῶν ἱππέων ὤγμευον αὐτῷ, ὡς ἐπιόντες τὰ θηρία ἐξανισταῖεν· οἱ δὲ ἄριστοι καὶ
πεζοὶ καὶ ἱππεῖς διέστασαν καὶ τἀνιστάμενα
ὑπεδέχοντο καὶ ἐδίωκον· καὶ ᾕρουν πολλοὺς καὶ
σῦς καὶ ἐλάφους καὶ δορκάδας καὶ ὄνους ἀγρίους·
πολλοὶ γὰρ ἐν τούτοις τοῖς τόποις ὄνοι καὶ νῦν
ἔτι γίγνονται.

21. Ἐπεὶ δ' ἔληξε τῆς θήρας, προσμίξας πρὸς
τὰ ὅρια τῶν Ἀρμενίων ἐδειπνοποιήσατο· καὶ
τῇ ὑστεραίᾳ αὖθις ἐθήρα προσελθὼν πρὸς τὰ
ὄρη ὧν ὠρέγετο. ἐπεὶ δ' αὖ ἔληξεν, ἐδειπνοποιεῖτο. τὸ δὲ παρὰ Κυαξάρου στράτευμα ὡς
ᾔσθετο προσιόν, ὑποπέμψας πρὸς αὐτοὺς εἶπεν
ἀπέχοντας αὐτοῦ δειπνοποιεῖσθαι ὡς δύο παρα-
σάγγας, τοῦτο προϊδὼν ὡς συμβαλεῖται πρὸς τὸ
λανθάνειν· ἐπεὶ δὲ δειπνήσειαν,[3] εἶπε τῷ ἄρχοντι
αὐτῶν παρεῖναι πρὸς αὐτόν. μετὰ δὲ τὸ δεῖπνον

[1] ἐπιπτόμενος Cobet, most Edd.; ἐπιπτάμενος MSS., Gemoll.
[2] κατιδὼν Dindorf, Edd.; ὃς κατιδὼν xz; ὡς κατεῖδεν z.
[3] δειπνήσειαν Dindorf, Breitenbach, et al.; δειπνήσαιεν MSS., Marchant, Gemoll.

19. And as he proceeded on his way, in the very irst field a hare started up. And an eagle flying up rom the east[1] caught sight of the hare as it ran and wooping down struck it, seized it, and carried it up, hen bore it away to a hill not far off and disposed of iis prey at his pleasure. Then Cyrus, observing the men, was delighted and did homage to Sovereign 'eus and said to those who were by: "Our hunt, omrades, please God, will be successful."

The hunt on the Armenian frontier

20. When they arrived at the frontier, he at once roceeded to hunt, as he used to do; and the most of iis men, on foot and on horseback, were marching in straight line before him, in order to start up the ;ame as they approached. But the best of his foot ind horse stood at intervals and lay in wait for what vas started up, and pursued it in relays. And they ook many boars, deer, antelope, and wild asses; for nany wild asses breed in those regions even unto his day.

21. And when he stopped hunting, he marched up o the Armenian border and dined; and on the following day, he went up to the mountains toward which ie was aiming and hunted again. And when again ie stopped, he sat down to dinner; but when he saw he army from Cyaxares approaching, he sent to hem secretly and bade them take their dinner at a listance of about two parasangs, for he foresaw that his also would contribute to the secrecy of his lesign; but he ordered their commander to come to iim when they had finished their dinner. Then,

[1] *αἴσιος* means, strictly speaking, "auspicious," "bringing good) omens;" and good omens came from the east, the iome of light.

τοὺς ταξιάρχους παρεκάλει· ἐπεὶ δὲ παρῆσαν ἔλεξεν ὧδε·

22. Ἄνδρες φίλοι, ὁ Ἀρμένιος πρόσθεν μὲ καὶ σύμμαχος ἦν καὶ ὑπήκοος Κυαξάρῃ· νῦν δ ὡς ᾔσθετο τοὺς πολεμίους ἐπιόντας, καταφρονε καὶ οὔτε τὸ στράτευμα πέμπει ἡμῖν οὔτε τὸ δασμὸν ἀποδίδωσι. νῦν οὖν τοῦτον θηρᾶσαι ἢν δυνώμεθα, ἤλθομεν. ὧδ' οὖν, ἔφη, δοκε ποιεῖν. σὺ μέν, ὦ Χρυσάντα, ἐπειδὰν ἀποκοι μηθῇς ὅσον μέτριον, λαβὼν τοὺς ἡμίσεις Περσῶ τῶν σὺν ἡμῖν ἴθι τὴν ὀρεινὴν καὶ κατάλαβε τ ὄρη, εἰς ἅ φασιν αὐτόν, ὅταν τι φοβηθῇ, κατα φεύγειν· ἡγεμόνας δέ σοι ἐγὼ δώσω. 23. φασ μὲν οὖν καὶ δασέα τὰ ὄρη ταῦτα εἶναι, ὥστ ἐλπὶς ὑμᾶς μὴ ὀφθῆναι· ὅμως δὲ εἰ προπέμποι πρὸ τοῦ στρατεύματος εὐζώνους ἄνδρας λῃσταῖ ἐοικότας καὶ τὸ πλῆθος καὶ τὰς στολάς, οὗτο ἄν σοι, εἴ τινι ἐντυγχάνοιεν τῶν Ἀρμενίων τοὺς μὲν ἂν συλλαμβάνοντες αὐτῶν κωλύοιε τῶν ἐξαγγελιῶν, οὓς δὲ μὴ δύναιντο λαμβάνειν ἀποσοβοῦντες ἂν ἐμποδὼν γίγνοιντο τοῦ[1] μὴ ὁρᾶν αὐτοὺς τὸ ὅλον στράτευμά σου, ἀλλ' ὡ περὶ κλωπῶν βουλεύεσθαι. 24. καὶ σὺ μέν, ἔφη, οὕτω ποίει· ἐγὼ δὲ ἅμα τῇ ἡμέρᾳ του ἡμίσεις μὲν τῶν πεζῶν ἔχων, πάντας δὲ τοὺ ἱππέας, πορεύσομαι διὰ τοῦ πεδίου εὐθὺς πρὸ τὰ βασίλεια. καὶ ἢν μὲν ἀνθιστῆται, δῆλον ὅτι μάχεσθαι δεήσει· ἢν δ' αὖ ὑποχωρῇ τοῦ πεδίου, δῆλον ὅτι μεταθεῖν δεήσει· ἢν δ' εἰς τὰ ὄρη φεύγῃ, ἐνταῦθα δή, ἔφη, σὸν ἔργον μηδένα

[1] τοῦ MSS., most Edd.; τὸ Dindorf, Hug.

fter dinner, he called together his captains; and ʼhen they had come he addressed them as follows:

22. "My friends, the Armenian king formerly was oth an ally and a dependent of Cyaxares; but ow since he has seen the enemy coming upon s, he is insolent and neither sends us his comlement of soldiers nor pays his tribute. Now, herefore, he is the game we have come to catch, f we can. And here is the plan that I think ve should pursue: do you, Chrysantas, when you ave had as much rest as you reasonably need, take alf of the Persians who are with us, and following he mountain road take possession of the heights o which they say he flees for refuge when anyhing alarms him. I will furnish you with guides. 3. Now they say that these mountains are thickly vooded, and so I have hopes of your not being seen. Nevertheless, suppose you send ahead of your army ome active men, in the guise of brigands both as to umbers and accoutrements; these, if they met any rmenians, would capture them and so prevent their preading any reports; or, if they failed to capture hem, they would frighten them away and so prevent heir seeing the whole of your army, and would thus ause them to take precautions as against only a and of thieves. 24. Do you, then," said he, "do his; but I, at break of day, with half the infantry nd all the cavalry, will proceed through the plain traight toward the capital. And if he resists, we hall have to fight, of course; and if he abandons the ield, of course we shall have to chase him; but if he lees to the mountain, then it is your business not to et any one of those who come your way escape.

Cyrus lays his real design before his captains

His instructions to Chrysantas

ἀφιέναι τῶν πρὸς σὲ ἀφικνουμένων. 25. νόμι
δὲ ὥσπερ ἐν θήρᾳ ἡμᾶς μὲν τοὺς ἐπιζητοῦντα[1]
ἔσεσθαι, σὲ δὲ τὸν ἐπὶ ταῖς ἄρκυσι· μέμνης
οὖν ἐκεῖνο ὅτι φθάνειν δεῖ πεφραγμένους το
πόρους πρὶν κινεῖσθαι τὴν θήραν. καὶ λεληθέν
δὲ δεῖ τοὺς ἐπὶ τοῖς στόμασιν, εἰ μέλλουσι μ
ἀποτρέψειν τὰ προσφερόμενα. 26. μὴ μέντο
ἔφη, ὦ Χρυσάντα, οὕτως αὖ ποίει ὥσπερ ἐνίο
διὰ τὴν φιλοθηρίαν· πολλάκις γὰρ ὅλην τ
νύκτα ἄυπνος πραγματεύει· ἀλλὰ νῦν ἐᾶσαι χρ
τοὺς ἄνδρας τὸ μέτριον ἀποκοιμηθῆναι, ὡς ἂ
δύνωνται ὑπνομαχεῖν.

27. Μηδέ γε, ὅτι οὐχ ἡγεμόνας ἔχων ἀνθρώπο
πλανᾷ ἀνὰ τὰ ὄρη, ἀλλ' ὅπῃ ἂν τὰ θηρία ὑφηγ
ται, ταύτῃ μεταθεῖς, μήτι καὶ νῦν οὕτω τὰ δύσ
βατα πορεύου, ἀλλὰ κέλευέ σοι τοὺς ἡγεμόνας, ἐὰ
μὴ πολὺ μάσσων ἡ ὁδὸς ᾖ, τὴν ῥᾴστην ἡγεῖσθα
στρατιᾷ γὰρ ἡ ῥᾴστη ταχίστη. 28. μηδέ γε, ὅ
σὺ εἴθισαι τρέχειν ἀνὰ τὰ ὄρη, μήτι δρόμῳ ἡγήσ
ἀλλ' ὡς ἂν δύνηταί σοι ὁ στρατὸς ἕπεσθαι, τ
μέσῳ τῆς σπουδῆς ἡγοῦ. 29. ἀγαθὸν δὲ καὶ τῶ
δυνατωτάτων καὶ προθύμων ὑπομένοντάς τινα
ἐνίοτε παρακελεύεσθαι· ἐπειδὰν δὲ παρέλθῃ τ
κέρας, παροξυντικὸν εἰς τὸ σπεύδειν πάντας παρ
τοὺς βαδίζοντας τρέχοντας ὁρᾶσθαι.

30. Χρυσάντας μὲν δὴ ταῦτα ἀκούσας κα
ἐπιγαυρωθεὶς τῇ ἐντολῇ τοῦ Κύρου, λαβὼν τοὺ
ἡγεμόνας, ἀπελθὼν καὶ παραγγείλας ἃ ἔδει το
ἅμα αὐτῷ μέλλουσι πορεύεσθαι, ἀνεπαύετο. ἐπ

[1] ἐπιζητοῦντας Stephanus, Edd.; ἐπιζητήσοντας MSS.

5. And bear in mind that, just as in hunting, we hall be the ones beating out the game, you the man n charge of the nets. Remember this, then, that the uns must be blocked before the game starts; and hose at the entrance to those runs must keep out of ight, if they are not to turn the animals aside as hey come on. 26. However," he added, "do not in his case do as you sometimes do, Chrysantas, in your ondness for hunting: you often keep yourself busy ll night without sleeping; but now you should let your men rest long enough, so that they may be able to resist drowsiness.

27. "Again, do not, because you personally are accustomed to wander up and down the mountains without following human guides but running after the game wherever it leads you—do not now go into such dangerous and difficult places, but order your guides to lead you by the easiest road, unless it is much too long; for the easiest road is the shortest for an army. 28. And do not lead your men at a run because you are used to running up mountains, but lead with moderate haste, that your army may be able to follow you easily. 29. And it is a good thing for some of the strongest and most zealous to fall back sometimes and encourage the rest; and when the column has passed by them, it is an incentive to all to hasten when these are seen running past them as they walk."

30. On hearing this, Chrysantas was elated with his commission from Cyrus; he took his guides and went away, and after giving what orders he thought necessary to those who were to go with him he went

δὲ ἀπεκοιμήθησαν ὅσον ἐδόκει μέτριον εἶναι, ἐπο
ρεύετο ἐπὶ τὰ ὄρη.

31. Κῦρος δέ, ἐπειδὴ ἡμέρα ἐγένετο, ἄγγελον μὲ
προὔπεμπε πρὸς τὸν Ἀρμένιον, εἰπὼν αὐτῷ λέγει
ὧδε· Κῦρος, ὦ Ἀρμένιε, κελεύει οὕτω ποιεῖν σ
ὅπως ὡς τάχιστα ἔχων οἴσεις[1] καὶ τὸν δασμὸν κα
τὸ στράτευμα. ἢν δ' ἐρωτᾷ ὅπου εἰμί, λέγε τἀληθ
ὅτι ἐπὶ τοῖς ὁρίοις. ἢν δ' ἐρωτᾷ εἰ καὶ αὐτὸ
ἔρχομαι, λέγε κἀνταῦθα τἀληθῆ ὅτι οὐκ οἶσθα
ἐὰν δ' ὁπόσοι ἐσμὲν πυνθάνηται, συμπέμπειν τιν
κέλευε καὶ μαθεῖν.

32. Τὸν μὲν δὴ ἄγγελον ἐπιστείλας ταῦτ
ἔπεμψε, νομίζων φιλικώτερον οὕτως εἶναι ἢ μ
προειπόντα πορεύεσθαι. αὐτὸς δὲ συνταξάμενο
ᾗ ἄριστον καὶ πρὸς τὸ ἀνύτειν τὴν ὁδὸν καὶ πρὸ
τὸ μάχεσθαι, εἴ τι δέοι, ἐπορεύετο. προεῖπε δ
τοῖς στρατιώταις μηδένα ἀδικεῖν, καὶ εἴ τις Ἀρμε
νίων τῳ ἐντυγχάνοι, θαρρεῖν τε παραγγέλλειν κα
ἀγορὰν τὸν θέλοντα ἄγειν ὅπου ἂν ὦσιν, εἴτε σῖτο
εἴτε ποτὰ τυγχάνοι πωλεῖν βουλόμενος.

[1] ἔχων οἴσεις F²G, Dindorf; ἑκὼν οἴσεις Pantazides; ἔχω
οἴσοις AH; ἔχων ἀπίῃς DF¹; ἔχων ἀπίῃς καὶ οἴσεις EC² (ἔχω
ἀπίῃς καὶ οἴσῃς C¹) (*that you go away with and bring*); ἔχω
εἰσίῃς Gemoll (*that you come in with*); ἔχων ἀπίῃ Dindorf⁴
Hug, Marchant, Breitenbach (*that he* [Cyrus] *may retur
with*).

rest. And when they had slept as long as he
ıought reasonable, he started for the mountains.

31. And when it was day, Cyrus sent forward a messenger to the Armenian with instructions to
ɔeak to him as follows: "'King of Armenia, Cyrus
ds you take steps as quickly as possible to deliver
him the tribute and the troops.' And if he asks
here I am, tell the truth and say that I am at the
ontier. And if he asks whether I also am coming
person, tell the truth in that case also and say that
ɔu do not know. But if he inquires how many men
e are, bid him send some one along with you and
nd out."

Cyrus's ultimatum

32. With such instructions he sent the messenger
ff, for he thought that this was a more friendly
ourse than to march upon him without notice. And
e himself set out with his army in the formation
hich he thought best adapted both for covering
istance and for fighting if necessary. He ordered
is soldiers to molest no one, and, if any one met
ny Armenians, to bid them have no fear but to say
ıat if any one of them wished to sell food or drink,
e should feel free to bring it wherever they were
nd open a market.

BOOK III

THE CONQUEST OF ARMENIA AND SCYTHIA

The First Great Battle

Γ

I

1. Ὁ μὲν δὴ Κῦρος ἐν τούτοις ἦν· ὁ δὲ Ἀρμε-
νιος ὡς ἤκουσε τοῦ ἀγγέλου τὰ παρὰ Κύρο
ἐξεπλάγη, ἐννοήσας ὅτι ἀδικοίη καὶ τὸν δασμὸ
λείπων καὶ τὸ στράτευμα οὐ πέμπων, καὶ τ
μέγιστον, ἐφοβεῖτο, ὅτι ὀφθήσεσθαι ἔμελλε τ
βασίλεια οἰκοδομεῖν ἀρχόμενος ὡς ἂν ἱκανὰ ἀπο
μάχεσθαι εἴη. 2. διὰ ταῦτα δὴ πάντα ὀκνῶν ἅμ
μὲν διέπεμπεν ἀθροίζων τὴν ἑαυτοῦ δύναμιν, ἅμ
δ' ἔπεμπεν εἰς τὰ ὄρη τὸν νεώτερον υἱὸν Σάβαρι
καὶ τὰς γυναῖκας, τήν τε ἑαυτοῦ καὶ τὴν τοῦ υἱοῦ
καὶ τὰς θυγατέρας· καὶ κόσμον δὲ καὶ κατασκευ
ἡν τὴν πλείστου ἀξίαν συναπέπεμπε προπομποὺ
δοὺς αὐτοῖς. αὐτὸς δὲ ἅμα μὲν κατασκεψομένου
ἔπεμπε τί πράττοι Κῦρος, ἅμα δὲ συνέταττε τοὺ
παραγιγνομένους τῶν Ἀρμενίων· καὶ ταχὺ παρῆ
σαν ἄλλοι λέγοντες ὅτι καὶ δὴ αὐτὸς ὁμοῦ
3. ἐνταῦθα δὴ οὐκέτι ἔτλη εἰς χεῖρας ἐλθεῖν, ἀλλ
ὑπεχώρει. ὡς δὲ τοῦτ' εἶδον ποιήσαντα αὐτὸν ο
Ἀρμένιοι, διεδίδρασκον ἤδη ἕκαστος ἐπὶ τὰ ἑαυ
τοῦ, βουλόμενοι τὰ ὄντα ἐκποδὼν ποιεῖσθαι.

BOOK III

I

The Armenians hear of Cyrus's approach

1. Cyrus was thus employed; but when the Armenian king heard from the envoy the message of Cyrus, he was alarmed, for he knew that he was doing wrong in withholding the tribute due and in failing to send the troops, and he was afraid most of all because he saw that he was sure to be detected in the act of beginning to build his palace in such a way as to render it strong enough for armed resistance. 2. Disturbed by the consciousness of all these faults, he sent around and collected his forces, and at the same time he sent away to the mountains his younger son, Sabaris, and the women, both his queen and his son's wife, and his daughters. And he sent along with them his most valuable jewels and chattels and gave them an escort. At the same time he sent scouts to spy out what Cyrus was doing, while he went on assigning positions in his service to the Armenians as they came in to him. Presently still others arrived with the news that the man himself was quite near. 3. Then he no longer had the courage to join battle with him but retreated. When the Armenians saw him act thus, they dispersed at once, each to his own possessions, wishing to get their belongings out of the way.

Ὁ δὲ Κῦρος ὡς ἑώρα διαθεόντων καὶ ἐλαυνόντων τὸ πεδίον μεστόν, ὑποπέμπων ἔλεγεν ὅτι οὐδενὶ πολέμιος εἴη τῶν μενόντων. εἰ δέ τινα φεύγοντα λήψοιτο, προηγόρευεν ὅτι ὡς πολεμίῳ χρήσοιτο. οὕτω δὴ οἱ μὲν πολλοὶ κατέμενον, ἦσαν δ' οἳ ὑπεχώρουν σὺν τῷ βασιλεῖ.

4. Ἐπεὶ δ' οἱ σὺν ταῖς γυναιξὶ προϊόντες ἐνέπεσον εἰς τοὺς ἐν τῷ ὄρει, κραυγήν τε εὐθὺς ἐποίουν καὶ φεύγοντες ἡλίσκοντο πολλοί γε αὐτῶν. τέλος δὲ καὶ ὁ παῖς καὶ αἱ γυναῖκες καὶ αἱ θυγατέρες ἑάλωσαν, καὶ τὰ χρήματα ὅσα σὺν αὐτοῖς ἀγόμενα ἔτυχεν.

Ὁ δὲ βασιλεὺς αὐτός,[1] ὡς ᾔσθετο τὰ γιγνόμενα, ἀπορῶν ποῖ τράποιτο ἐπὶ λόφον τινὰ καταφεύγει. 5. ὁ δ' αὖ Κῦρος ταῦτα ἰδὼν περιίσταται τὸν λόφον τῷ παρόντι στρατεύματι, καὶ πρὸς Χρυσάνταν πέμψας ἐκέλευε φυλακὴν τοῦ ὄρους καταλιπόντα ἥκειν. τὸ μὲν δὴ στράτευμα ἠθροίζετο τῷ Κύρῳ.

Ὁ δὲ πέμψας πρὸς τὸν Ἀρμένιον κήρυκα ἤρετο ὧδε· Εἰπέ μοι, ἔφη, ὦ Ἀρμένιε, πότερα βούλει αὐτοῦ μένων τῷ λιμῷ καὶ τῷ δίψει μάχεσθαι ἢ εἰς τὸ ἰσόπεδον καταβὰς ἡμῖν διαμάχεσθαι;

Ἀπεκρίνατο ὁ Ἀρμένιος ὅτι οὐδετέροις βούλοιτο μάχεσθαι. 6. πάλιν ὁ Κῦρος πέμψας ἠρώτα· Τί οὖν κάθησαι ἐνταῦθα καὶ οὐ καταβαίνεις;

Ἀπορῶν, ἔφη, ὅ τι χρὴ ποιεῖν.

[1] αὐτός Pantazides, most Edd.; αὐτῶν MSS., Dindorf, Breitenbach.

And when Cyrus saw the plain full of men running about and driving away, he sent secretly to say that he had no quarrel with any who remained; but he declared that if he caught any one trying to get away, he should treat him as an enemy. Accordingly, the most of them remained, but some retreated with the king.

Chrysantas captures the train of fugitives

4. Now as those with the women in charge went forward they came upon the forces in the mountain. At once they raised a cry and as they tried to escape many of them were caught. And finally the young prince and the wives and daughters were captured and all the treasure that happened to be in the train.

When the king himself learned what was going on, he was in a quandary which way to turn and took refuge upon a certain hill. 5. And when Cyrus saw this he surrounded the hill with the troops he had with him and sent orders to Chrysantas to leave a guard upon the mountains and come. Thus Cyrus's army was being brought together.

The king entrapped

Then he sent a herald to the Armenian to ask him the following question: "Tell me, king of Armenia," he said, "whether you prefer to remain there and fight against hunger and thirst, or to come down into the plain and fight it out with us?"

The Armenian answered that he had no wish to fight against either. 6. Again Cyrus sent to him and asked: "Why then do you sit there and refuse to come down?"

"Because," he answered, "I am in a quandary what to do."

Ἀλλ' οὐδέν, ἔφη ὁ Κῦρος, ἀπορεῖν σε δεῖ· ἔξεστι γάρ σοι ἐπὶ δίκην καταβαίνειν.

Τίς δ', ἔφη, ἔσται ὁ δικάζων;

Δῆλον ὅτι ᾧ ὁ θεὸς ἔδωκε καὶ ἄνευ δίκης χρῆσθαί σοι ὅ τι βούλοιτο.

Ἐνταῦθα δὴ ὁ Ἀρμένιος γιγνώσκων τὴν ἀνάγκην καταβαίνει· καὶ ὁ Κῦρος λαβὼν εἰς τὸ μέσον κἀκεῖνον καὶ τἄλλα πάντα περιεστρατοπεδεύσατο, ὁμοῦ ἤδη πᾶσαν ἔχων τὴν δύναμιν.

7. Ἐν τούτῳ δὲ τῷ χρόνῳ ὁ πρεσβύτερος[1] παῖς τοῦ Ἀρμενίου Τιγράνης ἐξ ἀποδημίας τινὸς προσῄει, ὃς καὶ σύνθηρός ποτε ἐγένετο τῷ Κύρῳ· καὶ ὡς ἤκουσε τὰ γεγενημένα, εὐθὺς πορεύεται ὥσπερ εἶχε πρὸς τὸν Κῦρον. ὡς δ' εἶδε πατέρα τε καὶ μητέρα καὶ ἀδελφοὺς[2] καὶ τὴν ἑαυτοῦ γυναῖκα αἰχμαλώτους γεγενημένους, ἐδάκρυσεν, ὥσπερ εἰκός. 8. ὁ δὲ Κῦρος ἰδὼν αὐτὸν ἄλλο μὲν οὐδὲν ἐφιλοφρονήσατο αὐτῷ, εἶπε δ' ὅτι Εἰς καιρὸν ἥκεις, ἔφη, ὅπως τῆς δίκης ἀκούσῃς[3] παρὼν τῆς ἀμφὶ τοῦ πατρός.

Καὶ εὐθὺς συνεκάλει τοὺς ἡγεμόνας τούς τε τῶν Περσῶν καὶ τοὺς τῶν Μήδων· προσεκάλει δὲ καὶ εἴ τις Ἀρμενίων τῶν ἐντίμων παρῆν. καὶ τὰς γυναῖκας ἐν ταῖς ἁρμαμάξαις παρούσας οὐκ ἀπήλασεν, ἀλλ' εἴα ἀκούειν.

9. Ὁπότε δὲ καλῶς εἶχεν, ἤρχετο τοῦ λόγου, Ὦ Ἀρμένιε, ἔφη, πρῶτον μέν σοι συμβουλεύω ἐν τῇ δίκῃ τἀληθῆ λέγειν, ἵνα σοι ἕν γε

[1] πρεσβύτερος z, Edd.; πρεσβύτατος xy (*oldest*).
[2] ἀδελφοὺς Weiske, later Edd.; τὰς ἀδελφὰς MSS.
[3] ἀκούσῃς xzD, Dindorf[3], Breitenbach, Gemoll, Marchant, et al.; ἀκούσεις F.; ἀκούσει Dindorf[4], Hug.

"But," said Cyrus, "there is no occasion whatever for that; for you are free to come down for trial."

"And who," said he, "will be my judge?"

"He, to be sure, to whom God has given the power to deal with you as he will, even without a trial."

Then the Armenian, recognizing the exigency of his case, came down. And Cyrus received both the king and all that belonged to him into the midst and set his camp round them, for by this time he had all his forces together.

7. Now at this juncture Tigranes, the king's elder son, returned from a journey abroad. He it was who had been Cyrus's companion once on a hunt; and when he heard what had occurred, he came at once, just as he was, to Cyrus. And when he saw his father and mother and brothers and sisters and his own wife all made prisoners, he wept, as might be expected. 8. But Cyrus, when he looked upon him, showed him no token of friendship, but merely remarked: "You have come just in time to attend your father's trial."

The court martial of the king

And immediately he called together the officers of both the Medes and the Persians and all the Armenian nobles who were present. And the women who were there in their carriages he did not exclude but permitted them to attend.

9. When everything was in order, he began his examination: "King of Armenia," said he, "I advise you in the first place in this trial to tell the truth,

ἀπῇ τὸ εὐμισητότατον· τὸ γὰρ ψευδόμενον φα-
νεσθαι εὖ ἴσθι ὅτι καὶ τοῦ συγγνώμης τινὸ
τυγχάνειν ἐμποδὼν μάλιστα ἀνθρώποις γίγνετα
ἔπειτα δ', ἔφη, συνίσασι μέν σοι καὶ οἱ παῖδε
καὶ αἱ γυναῖκες αὗται πάντα ὅσα ἔπραξας, κα
Ἀρμενίων οἱ παρόντες· ἢν δὲ αἰσθάνωνταί σ
ἄλλα ἢ τὰ γενόμενα λέγοντα, νομιοῦσί σε κα
αὐτὸν καταδικάζειν σεαυτοῦ πάντα τὰ ἔσχατ
παθεῖν, ἢν ἐγὼ τἀληθῆ πύθωμαι.

Ἀλλ' ἐρώτα, ἔφη, ὦ Κῦρε, ὅ τι βούλει, ὡ
τἀληθῆ ἐροῦντος. τούτου ἕνεκα καὶ γενέσθω
τι βούλεται.

10. Λέγε δή μοι, ἔφη, ἐπολέμησάς ποτε Ἀστυ
άγει τῷ τῆς ἐμῆς μητρὸς πατρὶ καὶ τοῖς ἄλλοι
Μήδοις;

Ἔγωγ', ἔφη.

Κρατηθεὶς δ' ὑπ' αὐτοῦ συνωμολόγησας δασμὸ
οἴσειν καὶ συστρατεύσεσθαι[1] ὅποι[2] ἐπαγγέλλοι
καὶ ἐρύματα μὴ ἕξειν;

Ἦν ταῦτα.

Νῦν οὖν διὰ τί οὔτε τὸν δασμὸν ἀπῆγε
οὔτε τὸ στράτευμα ἔπεμπες, ἐτείχιζές τε τ
ἐρύματα;

Ἐλευθερίας ἐπεθύμουν· καλὸν γάρ μοι ἐδόκε
εἶναι καὶ αὐτὸν ἐλεύθερον εἶναι καὶ παισὶ
ἐλευθερίαν καταλιπεῖν.

11. Καὶ γάρ ἐστιν, ἔφη ὁ Κῦρος, καλὸ
μάχεσθαι, ὅπως μήποτέ τις δοῦλος μέλλοι γενή-
σεσθαι· ἢν δὲ δὴ ἢ πολέμῳ κρατηθεὶς ἢ κα

[1] συστρατεύσεσθαι Stephanus, Edd.; συστρατεύεσθαι xy συστρατεύσασθαι z.
[2] ὅποι Dindorf, later Edd.; ὅπου MSS.

that you may be guiltless of that offence which is hated more cordially than any other. For let me assure you that being caught in a barefaced lie stands most seriously in the way of a man's receiving any mercy. In the next place," said he, "your children and your wives here and also the Armenians present are cognizant of everything that you have done; and if they hear you telling anything else than the facts, they will think that you are actually condemning your own self to suffer the extreme penalty, if ever I discover the truth."

"Well, Cyrus," said he, "ask what you will, and be assured that I will tell the truth, let happen what will as a result of it."

10. "Tell me then," said the other, "did you ever have a war with Astyages, my mother's father, and with the rest of the Medes?"

"Yes," he answered, "I did."

"And when you were conquered by him, did you agree to pay tribute and to join his army, wherever he should command you to go, and to own no forts?"

"Those are the facts."

"Why, then, have you now failed to pay the tribute and to send the troops, and why have you been building forts?"

"I longed for liberty; for it seemed to me to be a glorious thing both to be free myself and to bequeath liberty to my children."

11. "You are right," said Cyrus; "it is a noble thing to fight that one may never be in danger of becoming a slave. But if any one has been conquered

ἄλλον τινὰ τρόπον δουλωθεὶς ἐπιχειρῶν τις φαίνηται τοὺς δεσπότας ἀποστερεῖν ἑαυτοῦ, τοῦτον σὺ πρῶτος πότερον ὡς ἀγαθὸν ἄνδρα καὶ καλὰ πράττοντα τιμᾷς ἢ ὡς ἀδικοῦντα, ἢν λάβῃς, κολάζεις;

Κολάζω, ἔφη· οὐ γὰρ ἐᾷς σὺ ψεύδεσθαι.

12. Λέγε δὴ σαφῶς, ἔφη ὁ Κῦρος, καθ' ἓν ἕκαστον· ἢν ἄρχων τις τύχῃ σοι καὶ ἁμάρτῃ, πότερον ἐᾷς ἄρχειν ἢ ἄλλον καθίστης ἀντ' αὐτοῦ;

Ἄλλον καθίστημι.

Τί δέ, ἢν χρήματα πολλὰ ἔχῃ, ἐᾷς πλουτεῖν ἢ πένητα ποιεῖς;

Ἀφαιροῦμαι, ἔφη, ἃν ἔχων τυγχάνῃ.

Ἢν δὲ καὶ πρὸς πολεμίους γιγνώσκῃς αὐτὸν ἀφιστάμενον, τί ποιεῖς;

Κατακαίνω, ἔφη· τί γὰρ δεῖ ἐλεγχθέντα ὅτι ψεύδομαι ἀποθανεῖν μᾶλλον ἢ τἀληθῆ λέγοντα;

13. Ἔνθα δὴ ὁ μὲν παῖς αὐτοῦ ὡς ἤκουσε ταῦτα, περιεσπάσατο τὴν τιάραν καὶ τοὺς πέπλους κατερρήξατο, αἱ δὲ γυναῖκες ἀναβοήσασαι ἐδρύπτοντο, ὡς οἰχομένου τοῦ πατρὸς καὶ ἀπολωλότων σφῶν[1] ἤδη. καὶ ὁ Κῦρος σιωπῆσαι κελεύσας εἶπεν,[2] Εἶεν· τὰ μὲν δὴ σὰ δίκαια ταῦτα, ὦ Ἀρμένιε· ἡμῖν δὲ τί συμβουλεύεις ἐκ τούτων ποιεῖν;

Ὁ μὲν δὴ Ἀρμένιος ἐσιώπα ἀπορῶν πότερα

[1] σφῶν C¹G¹F¹, most Edd.; πάντων σφῶν xyz, Dindorf.
[2] εἶπεν z, most Edd.; πάλιν εἶπεν xy, Gemoll.

n war or in any other way reduced to servitude and s then caught attempting to rob his masters of himelf, are you the first man to reward him as an honest nan and one who does right, or do you punish him s a malefactor if you catch him?"

"I punish him," said he; "for you will not let me ell a lie."

The king convicts himself

12. "Answer each of these questions explicitly hen," said Cyrus; "if any one happens to be an fficer under you and does wrong, do you permit him o continue in office or do you put another in his lace?"

"I put another in his place."

"And what if he has great possessions—do you llow him to continue rich, or do you make him oor?"

"I confiscate all that he may happen to possess," aid he.

"And if you find out that he is trying to desert to he enemy, what do you do?"

"I put him to death," said he; "I may as well onfess, for why should I convict myself of lying nd be put to death for that, instead of telling the ruth?"

13. Then his son, when he heard this, stripped off is turban and rent his garments, and the women ried aloud and tore their cheeks, as if it were all ver with their father and they were already lost. But Cyrus bade them be silent and said: "Very vell, king of Armenia; so that is your idea of justice; n accordance with it, then, what do you advise us to lo?"

Then the Armenian was silent, for he was in a

συμβουλεύοι τῷ Κύρῳ κατακαίνειν αὐτὸν ἢ τὰ ναντία διδάσκοι ὧν αὐτὸς ἔφη ποιεῖν. 14. ὁ δ παῖς αὐτοῦ Τιγράνης ἐπήρετο τὸν Κῦρον, Εἰπ μοι, ἔφη, ὦ Κῦρε, ἐπεὶ ὁ πατὴρ ἀπορουντ ἔοικεν, ἦ συμβουλεύσω περὶ αὐτοῦ ἃ οἶμαί σο βέλτιστα εἶναι;

Καὶ ὁ Κῦρος, ᾐσθημένος, ὅτε συνεθήρα αὐτ ὁ Τιγράνης, σοφιστήν τινα αὐτῷ συνόντα κα θαυμαζόμενον ὑπὸ τοῦ Τιγράνου, πάνυ ἐπεθύμε αὐτοῦ ἀκοῦσαι ὅ τι ποτ᾽ ἐροίη· καὶ προθύμω ἐκέλευσε λέγειν ὅ τι γιγνώσκοι.

15. Ἐγὼ τοίνυν, ἔφη ὁ Τιγράνης, εἰ μὲ ἄγασαι τοῦ πατρὸς ἢ ὅσα βεβούλευται ἢ ὅσα πέπραχε, πάνυ σοι συμβουλεύω τοῦτον μιμεῖ σθαι· εἰ μέντοι σοι δοκεῖ πάντα ἡμαρτηκέναι συμβουλεύω τοῦτον μὴ μιμεῖσθαι.

Οὐκοῦν, ἔφη ὁ Κῦρος, τὰ δίκαια ποιῶ ἥκιστ᾽ ἂν τὸν ἁμαρτάνοντα μιμοίμην.

Ἔστιν, ἔφη, ταῦτα.

Κολαστέον ἄρ᾽ ἂν εἴη κατά γε τὸν σὸν λόγο τὸν πατέρα, εἴπερ τὸν ἀδικοῦντα δίκαιον κο λάζειν.

Πότερα δ᾽ ἡγεῖ, ὦ Κῦρε, ἄμεινον εἶναι σὺ τῷ σῷ ἀγαθῷ τὰς τιμωρίας ποιεῖσθαι ἢ σὺν τῇ σῇ ζημίᾳ;

Ἐμαυτὸν ἄρα, ἔφη, οὕτω γ᾽ ἂν τιμωροίμην.

16. Ἀλλὰ μέντοι, ἔφη ὁ Τιγράνης, μεγάλ γ᾽ ἂν ζημιοῖο, εἰ τοὺς σεαυτοῦ κατακαίνοις τότ ὁπότε σοι πλείστου ἄξιοι εἶεν κεκτῆσθαι.

quandary whether to advise Cyrus to put him to death or to propose to him a course opposite to that which he admitted he himself always took. 14. But his son Tigranes put a question to Cyrus, saying: "Tell me, Cyrus, since my father seems to be in doubt, may I advise you in regard to him what I think the best course for you?"

Tigranes pleads his father's case

Now Cyrus had observed when Tigranes used to go hunting with him that there was a certain philosopher with him who was an object of admiration to Tigranes; consequently he was very eager to hear what he would say. So he bade him express his opinion with confidence.

15. "Well," said Tigranes, "if you approve either of my father's theory or his practice, then I advise you by all means to imitate him. But if you think he has done wrong throughout, I advise you not to imitate him."

"Well then," said Cyrus, "if I should do what is right, I should surely not be imitating the one who does wrong."

"That is true," said he.

"Then, according to your reasoning, your father must be punished, if indeed it is right that the one who does wrong should be punished."

"Which do you think is better for you, Cyrus, to mete out your punishments to your benefit or to your own injury?"

"In the latter case, at least," said he, "I should be punishing myself."

16. "Aye, but you would be doing yourself a great injury," said Tigranes, "if you should put your friends to death just at the time when it was of the greatest advantage to you to have them."

Πῶς δ' ἄν, ἔφη ὁ Κῦρος, τότε πλείστου ἄξιοι γίγνοιντο ἄνθρωποι ὁπότε ἀδικοῦντες ἁλίσκοιντο;

Εἰ τότε, οἶμαι, σώφρονες γίγνοιντο. δοκεῖ γάρ μοι, ὦ Κῦρε, οὕτως ἔχειν, ἄνευ μὲν σωφροσύνης οὐδ' ἄλλης ἀρετῆς οὐδὲν ὄφελος εἶναι· τί γὰρ ἄν ἔφη, χρήσαιτ' ἄν τις ἰσχυρῷ ἢ ἀνδρείῳ μὴ σώφρονι [ἢ ἱππικῷ],[1] τί δὲ πλουσίῳ, τί δὲ δυνάστῃ ἐν πόλει; σὺν δὲ σωφροσύνῃ καὶ φίλος πᾶς χρήσιμος καὶ θεράπων πᾶς ἀγαθός.

17. Τοῦτ' οὖν, ἔφη, λέγεις ὡς καὶ ὁ σὸς πατὴρ ἐν τῇδε τῇ μιᾷ ἡμέρᾳ ἐξ ἄφρονος σώφρων γεγένηται;

Πάνυ μὲν οὖν, ἔφη.

Πάθημα ἄρα τῆς ψυχῆς σὺ λέγεις εἶναι τὴν σωφροσύνην, ὥσπερ λύπην, οὐ μάθημα· οὐ γὰρ ἂν δήπου, εἴγε φρόνιμον δεῖ γενέσθαι τὸν μέλλοντα σώφρονα ἔσεσθαι, παραχρῆμα ἐξ ἄφρονος σώφρων ἄν τις γένοιτο.

18. Τί δ', ἔφη, ὦ Κῦρε, οὔπω ᾔσθου καὶ ἕνα ἄνδρα δι' ἀφροσύνην μὲν ἐπιχειροῦντα κρείττονι ἑαυτοῦ μάχεσθαι, ἐπειδὰν δὲ ἡττηθῇ, εὐθὺς πεπαυμένον τῆς πρὸς τοῦτον ἀφροσύνης; πάλιν δ', ἔφη, οὔπω ἑώρακας πόλιν ἀντιταττομένην πρὸς πόλιν ἑτέραν, ἧς ἐπειδὰν ἡττηθῇ παραχρῆμα ταύτῃ ἀντὶ τοῦ μάχεσθαι πείθεσθαι ἐθέλει;

[1] [ἢ ἱππικῷ] Schneider, most Edd.; ἢ ἱππικῷ MSS.; τί δὲ ἱππικῷ Dindorf, Sauppe, et al.

"How," said Cyrus, "could men be of the greatest dvantage to me just at the time when they were aught doing wrong?"

"They would be, I think, if at that time they hould become discreet. For it seems to me to be rue, Cyrus," said he, "that without discretion there s no advantage at all in any other virtue; for what," e continued, "could one do with a strong man or a rave man, or what with a rich man or a man of ower in the state if he lacked discretion? But very friend is useful and every servant good, if he e endowed with discretion."

The acquisition of discretion

17. "Do you mean to say, then," Cyrus answered, that in one day's time your father has become iscreet when he was indiscreet before?"

"Yes," said he, "I do, indeed."

"By that you mean to say that discretion is an ffection of the soul, as sorrow is, and not an cquisition.[1] For I do not suppose that a man could nstantly pass from being indiscreet to being discreet, f indeed the one who is to be discreet must first ave become wise."

18. "What, have you never observed, Cyrus," said e, "that when a man indiscreetly ventures to fight stronger man than himself and has been worsted, he s instantly cured of his indiscretion toward that articular man? And again," he continued, "have ou never seen how when one state is in arms against nother it is at once willing, when defeated, to ubmit to the victor instead of continuing the ight?"

[1] Xenophon makes Cyrus apparently accept the Socratic loctrine that wisdom and the other virtues are matters for earning, the results of study and practice—not a mood, like orrow, anger, or any other emotion.

19. Ποίαν δ', ἔφη ὁ Κῦρος, καὶ σὺ τοῦ πατρὸς ἧτταν λέγων οὕτως ἰσχυρίζει σεσωφρονίσθαι αὐτόν;

Ἣν νὴ Δί', ἔφη, σύνοιδεν ἑαυτῷ ἐλευθερίας μὲν ἐπιθυμήσας, δοῦλος δ' ὡς οὐδεπώποτε γενόμενος, ἃ δὲ ᾠήθη χρῆναι λαθεῖν ἢ φθάσαι ἢ[1] ἀποβιάσασθαι, οὐδὲν τούτων ἱκανὸς γενόμενος διαπράξασθαι. σὲ δὲ οἶδεν, ἃ μὲν ἐβουλήθης ἐξαπατῆσαι αὐτόν, οὕτως ἐξαπατήσαντα ὥσπερ ἄν τις τυφλοὺς καὶ κωφοὺς καὶ μηδ' ὁτιοῦν φρονοῦντας ἐξαπατήσειεν· ἃ δὲ ᾠήθης λαθεῖν χρῆναι, οὕτω σὲ οἶδε λαθόντα ὥστε ἃ ἐνόμιζεν ἑαυτῷ ἐχυρὰ χωρία ἀποκεῖσθαι, ταῦτα σὺ εἱρκτὰς αὐτῷ[2] ἔλαθες προκατασκευάσας· τάχει δὲ τοσοῦτον περιεγένου αὐτοῦ ὥστε πρόσωθεν ἔφθασας ἐλθὼν σὺν πολλῷ στόλῳ πρὶν τοῦτον τὴν παρ' ἑαυτῷ δύναμιν ἀθροίσασθαι.

20. Ἔπειτα δοκεῖ σοι, ἔφη ὁ Κῦρος, καὶ ἡ τοιαύτη ἧττα σωφρονίζειν ἱκανὴ εἶναι ἀνθρώπους, τὸ γνῶναι ἄλλους ἑαυτῶν βελτίονας ὄντας;

Πολύ γε μᾶλλον, ἔφη ὁ Τιγράνης, ἢ ὅταν μάχῃ τις ἡττηθῇ. ὁ μὲν γὰρ ἰσχύι κρατηθεὶς ἔστιν ὅτε ᾠήθη σωμασκήσας ἀναμαχεῖσθαι· καὶ πόλεις γε ἁλοῦσαι συμμάχους προσλαβοῦσαι οἴονται ἀναμαχέσασθαι ἄν· οὓς δ' ἂν βελτίους τινὲς ἑαυτῶν ἡγήσωνται, τούτοις πολλάκις καὶ ἄνευ ἀνάγκης ἐθέλουσι πείθεσθαι.

[1] ἢ xy, most Edd.; not in z, Zeune, Sauppe, Hug.
[2] αὐτῷ xFD², Gemoll; ἑαυτῷ D¹; σοι z (in G marked for erasure); σαυτῷ Ed.; σὺ Sauppe, Dindorf.

19. "To what defeat of your father's do you efer," said Cyrus, "that you are so confident that e has been brought to discretion by it?"

How the king of Armenia learned discretion

"Why that, by Zeus," Tigranes answered, "which e is conscious of having sustained, inasmuch as vhen he aimed at securing liberty he has become nore of a slave than ever, and as he has not been ble to accomplish a single thing of all that he hought he should effect by secrecy or by surprise or y actual force. And he knows that when you lesired to outwit him, you did it as effectually as one ould do who set out to deceive men blind or deaf or leprived of all their senses; and when you thought ou ought to act secretly, you acted with such ecrecy that the fortified places which he thought he ad provided for his own safety you had secretly urned into prisons for him in advance. And so nuch did you surpass him in dispatch, that you came rom a distance with a large army before he could nuster the forces he had at home."

20. "Well," said Cyrus, "do you really think that uch a defeat is adequate to make men discreet—I nean, when they find out that others are their uperiors?"

"Yes," said Tigranes, "much more than when hey are defeated in combat. For the one who is vercome by strength sometimes conceives the idea hat, if he trains his body, he may renew the combat. Even cities too, when captured, think that by taking n new allies they might renew the fight. But if eople are convinced that others are superior to hemselves, they are often ready even without comulsion to submit to them."

21. Σύ, ἔφη, ἔοικας οὐκ οἴεσθαι τοὺς ὑβριστὰ γιγνώσκειν τοὺς ἑαυτῶν σωφρονεστέρους, οὐδ τοὺς κλέπτας τοὺς μὴ κλέπτοντας, οὐδὲ τοὺ ψευδομένους τοὺς τἀληθῆ λέγοντας, οὐδὲ τοὺ ἀδικοῦντας τοὺς τὰ δίκαια ποιοῦντας· οὐκ οἶσθα ἔφη, ὅτι καὶ νῦν ὁ σὸς πατὴρ ἐψεύσατο κα οὐκέτ' ἠμπέδου[1] τὰς πρὸς ἡμᾶς συνθήκας, εἰδὼ ὅτι ἡμεῖς οὐδ' ὁτιοῦν ὧν Ἀστυάγης συνέθετ παραβαίνομεν;

22. Ἀλλ' οὐδ' ἐγὼ τοῦτο λέγω ὡς τὸ γνῶνα μόνον τοὺς βελτίονας σωφρονίζει ἄνευ τοῦ δίκη διδόναι ὑπὸ τῶν βελτιόνων, ὥσπερ ὁ ἐμὸς πατὴ νῦν δίδωσιν.

Ἀλλ', ἔφη ὁ Κῦρος, ὅ γε σὸς πατὴρ πέπονθ μὲν οὐδ' ὁτιοῦν πω κακόν· φοβεῖταί γε μέντο εὖ οἶδ' ὅτι μὴ πάντα τὰ ἔσχατα πάθῃ.

23. Οἴει οὖν τι, ἔφη ὁ Τιγράνης, μᾶλλο καταδουλοῦσθαι ἀνθρώπους τοῦ ἰσχυροῦ φόβου οὐκ οἶσθ' ὅτι οἱ μὲν τῷ ἰσχυροτάτῳ κολασματ νομιζομένῳ σιδήρῳ παιόμενοι ὅμως ἐθέλουσι κα πάλιν μάχεσθαι τοῖς αὐτοῖς; οὓς δ' ἂν σφόδρ φοβηθῶσιν ἄνθρωποι, τούτοις οὐδὲ παραμυθου μένοις ἔτι ἀντιβλέπειν δύνανται;

Λέγεις σύ, ἔφη, ὡς ὁ φόβος τοῦ ἔργῳ κακοῦ σθαι μᾶλλον κολάζει τοὺς ἀνθρώπους.

24. Καὶ σύγε, ἔφη, οἶσθα ὅτι ἀληθῆ λέγω ἐπίστασαι γὰρ ὅτι οἱ μὲν φοβούμενοι μὴ φύγωσ πατρίδα καὶ οἱ μέλλοντες μάχεσθαι δεδιότες μ ἡττηθῶσιν [ἀθύμως διάγουσι, καὶ οἱ πλέοντε μὴ ναυαγήσωσι,][2] καὶ οἱ δουλείαν καὶ δεσμὸ

[1] οὐκέτ' ἠμπέδου Cobet, Edd.; οὐκ ἐξημπέδου MSS.

[2] Bracketed by Madvig and most later Edd. (*are despond*

21. "You seem to think," said the other, "that the insolent do not recognize those more discreet than they, that thieves do not recognize honest men, that liars do not recognize the truthful, and wrong-doers those who do right. Do you not know," he continued, "that even now your father has played false and has not kept his agreement with us, although he knew that we have not been violating any of the agreements made by Astyages?"

22. "Yes; but neither do I mean that simply recognizing their superiors makes people discreet, unless they are punished by those superiors, as my father now is."

"But," said Cyrus, "your father has not yet suffered the least harm; but he is afraid, to be sure, that he will suffer the worst."

Fear of harm worse than the reality

23. "Do you think, then," said Tigranes, "that anything breaks a man's spirit sooner than abject fear? Do you not know that those who are beaten with the sword, which is considered the most potent instrument of correction, are nevertheless ready to fight the same enemy again; but when people really fear anyone very much, then they cannot look him in the face, even when he tries to cheer them?"

"You mean to say," said he, "that fear is a heavier punishment to men than real correction."

24. "And you," said he, "know that what I say is true; for you are aware that, on the one hand, those who are afraid that they are to be exiled from their native land, and those who on the eve of battle are afraid that they shall be defeated,

ent, and those who at sea fear that they are going to be wrecked,); [καὶ . . . ναυαγήσωσι] Gemoll.

φοβούμενοι, οὗτοι μὲν οὔτε σίτου οὔθ' ὕπνου δύνανται λαγχάνειν διὰ τὸν φόβον· οἱ δὲ ἤδη μὲν φυγάδες, ἤδη δ' ἡττημένοι, ἤδη δὲ δουλεύοντες, ἔστιν ὅτε δύνανται καὶ μᾶλλον τῶν εὐδαιμόνων ἐσθίειν τε[1] καὶ καθεύδειν. 25. ἔτι δὲ φανερώτερον καὶ ἐν τοῖσδε οἷον φόρημα ὁ φόβος· ἔνιοι γὰρ φοβούμενοι μὴ ληφθέντες ἀποθάνωσι προαποθνήσκουσιν ὑπὸ τοῦ φόβου, οἱ μὲν ῥιπτοῦντες ἑαυτούς, οἱ δ' ἀπαγχόμενοι, οἱ δ' ἀποσφαττόμενοι· οὕτω πάντων τῶν δεινῶν ὁ φόβος μάλιστα καταπλήττει τὰς ψυχάς. τὸν δ' ἐμὸν πατέρα, ἔφη, νῦν πῶς δοκεῖς διακεῖσθαι τὴν ψυχήν, ὃς οὐ μόνον περὶ ἑαυτοῦ, ἀλλὰ καὶ περὶ ἐμοῦ καὶ περὶ γυναικὸς καὶ περὶ πάντων τῶν τέκνων [δουλείας][2] φοβεῖται;

26. Καὶ ὁ Κῦρος εἶπεν, Ἀλλὰ νῦν μὲν ἔμοιγε οὐδὲν ἄπιστον τοῦτον οὕτω διακεῖσθαι· δοκεῖ μέντοι μοι τοῦ αὐτοῦ ἀνδρὸς εἶναι καὶ εὐτυχοῦντα ἐξυβρίσαι καὶ πταίσαντα ταχὺ πτῆξαι, καὶ ἀνεθέντα γε πάλιν αὖ μέγα φρονῆσαι καὶ πάλιν αὖ πράγματα παρασχεῖν.

27. Ἀλλὰ ναὶ μὰ Δί', ἔφη, ὦ Κῦρε, ἔχει μὲν προφάσεις τὰ ἡμέτερα ἁμαρτήματα ὥστ' ἀπιστεῖν ἡμῖν· ἔξεστι δέ σοι καὶ φρούρια ἐντειχίζειν καὶ τὰ ἐχυρὰ κατέχειν καὶ ἄλλο ὅ τι ἂν βούλῃ πιστὸν λαμβάνειν. καὶ μέντοι, ἔφη, ἡμᾶς μὲν ἕξεις οὐδέν τι τούτοις μέγα λυπουμένους· μεμνησόμεθα γὰρ ὅτι ἡμεῖς αὐτῶν αἴτιοί ἐσμεν· εἰ δέ τινι τῶν ἀναμαρτήτων παραδοὺς τὴν ἀρχὴν

[1] ἐσθίειν τε x, most Edd.; ἐσθίειν τε καὶ πίνειν yz, Gemoll (*both eat and drink*).

[2] δουλείας xyz, Dindorf.; not in Vaticanus 987; [δουλείας] most Edd.

and those who fear slavery or bondage, all such can neither eat nor sleep for fear; whereas those who are already in exile or already defeated or already in slavery can sometimes eat and sleep better than those enjoying a happier lot. 25. And from the following considerations it is still clearer what a burden fear is: some, for fear that they will be caught and put to death, in terror take their own lives before their time—some by hurling themselves over a precipice, other by hanging themselves, others by cutting their own throats; so does fear crush down the soul more than all other terrors. As for my father," he added, "in what a state of mind do you think he is? For he is in dread not only for himself, but also for me, for his wife, and for all of his children."

26. "Well," answered Cyrus, "it is not at all unlikely, I suppose, that he is for the moment in such a state of mind. However, it seems to me that we expect of a man who is insolent in success and abject in failure that, when set on his feet once more, he will again wax arrogant and again cause more trouble."

Tigranes discusses plans for adjustment

27. "Well, by Zeus, Cyrus," said he, "our wrongdoing does, no doubt, give you cause to distrust us; but you may build forts in our country and occupy the strongholds already built and take whatever else you wish as security. And yet," he added, "you will not find us very much aggrieved by your doing so; for we shall remember that we are to blame for it all. But if you hand over our government to some one of those who have done no wrong and yet show

ἀπιστῶν αὐτοῖς φανεῖ, ὅρα μὴ ἅμα τε εὖ ποιήσεις καὶ ἅμα οὐ φίλον νομιοῦσί σε· εἰ δ' αὖ φυλαττόμενος τὸ ἀπεχθάνεσθαι μὴ ἐπιθήσεις αὐτοῖς ζυγὰ τοῦ μὴ ὑβρίσαι, ὅρα μὴ ἐκείνους αὖ δεήσει σε σωφρονίζειν ἔτι μᾶλλον ἢ ἡμᾶς νῦν ἐδέησεν.

28. Ἀλλὰ ναὶ μὰ τοὺς θεούς, ἔφη, τοιούτοις μὲν ἔγωγε ὑπηρέταις, οὓς εἰδείην ἀνάγκῃ ὑπηρετοῦντας, ἀηδῶς ἄν μοι δοκῶ χρῆσθαι· οὓς δὲ γιγνώσκειν δοκοίην ὅτι εὐνοίᾳ καὶ φιλίᾳ τῇ ἐμῇ τὸ δέον συλλαμβάνοιεν, τούτους ἄν μοι δοκῶ καὶ ἁμαρτάνοντας ῥᾷον φέρειν ἢ τοὺς μισοῦντας μέν, ἔκπλεω δὲ πάντα ἀνάγκῃ διαπονουμένους.

Καὶ ὁ Τιγράνης εἶπε πρὸς ταῦτα, Φιλίαν δὲ παρὰ τίνων ἄν ποτε λάβοις τοσαύτην ὅσην σοι παρ' ἡμῶν ἔξεστι κτήσασθαι νῦν;

Παρ' ἐκείνων οἶμαι, ἔφη, [παρὰ] [1] τῶν μηδέποτε πολεμίων γεγενημένων, εἰ ἐθέλοιμι εὐεργετεῖν αὐτοὺς ὥσπερ σὺ νῦν με κελεύεις εὐεργετεῖν ὑμᾶς.

29. Ἦ καὶ δύναιο ἄν, ἔφη, ὦ Κῦρε, ἐν τῷ παρόντι νῦν εὑρεῖν ὅτῳ ἂν χαρίσαιο ὅσαπερ τῷ ἐμῷ πατρί; αὐτίκα, ἔφη, ἤν τινα ἐᾷς ζῆν τῶν σε μηδὲν ἠδικηκότων, τίνα σοι τούτου χάριν οἴει αὐτὸν εἴσεσθαι; τί δ', ἢν αὐτοῦ τέκνα καὶ γυναῖκα μὴ ἀφαιρῇ, τίς σε τούτου ἕνεκα φιλήσει μᾶλλον ἢ ὁ νομίζων προσήκειν αὐτῷ ἀφαιρεθῆναι; τὴν δ' Ἀρμενίων βασιλείαν εἰ μὴ ἕξει, οἶσθά τινα, ἔφη, ἄλλον μᾶλλον λυπούμενον ἢ ἡμᾶς; οὐκοῦν καὶ τοῦτ', ἔφη, δῆλον ὅτι ὁ μάλιστα λυπούμενος εἰ μὴ βασιλεὺς εἴη οὗτος καὶ λαβὼν τὴν ἀρχὴν μεγίστην ἄν σοι χάριν

[1] παρὰ MSS., Dindorf, Hug; [παρὰ] Cobet, Marchant, Gemoll.

hat you distrust them, see to it lest they regard you s no friend, in spite of your favours to them. But if gain, on your guard against incurring their hatred, ou fail to place a check upon them to keep them rom rebellion, see to it lest you need to bring them o discretion even more than you did in our case ıst now."

28. "Nay, by the gods," said he, "I do not think should like to employ servants that I knew served ıe only from compulsion. But if I had servants who thought assisted me, as in duty bound, out of good-vill and friendship toward me, I think I should be etter satisfied with them when they did wrong than vith others who disliked me, when they performed ll their tasks faithfully but from compulsion."

To this Tigranes replied: "From whom could you ver get such friendship as you now can from us?"

"From those, I presume," said he, "who have ever been my enemies, if I would do them such avours as you now bid me do you."

He argues for the continuance of his father's reign

29. "But, Cyrus," said he, "as things now are, ould you find any one to whom you could do as great avours as you can to my father? For example, if you rant any one of those who have done you no wrong is life, what gratitude do you think he will feel oward you for that? And again, who will love you or not depriving him of his wife and children more han he who thinks that it would serve him right to ose them? And do you know of any one who would e more grieved than we, not to have the throne of Armenia? Well, then," he added, "it is evident hat he who would be most grieved not to be king, vould also be most grateful for receiving the throne.

εἰδείη. 30. εἰ δέ τί σοι, ἔφη, μέλει καὶ τ
ὡς ἥκιστα τεταραγμένα τάδε καταλιπεῖν, ὅτι
ἀπίῃς, σκόπει, ἔφη, πότερον ἂν οἴει ἠρεμεστέρ
ἔχειν τὰ ἐνθάδε καινῆς γενομένης ἀρχῆς ἢ τ
εἰωθυίας καταμενούσης· εἰ δέ τί σοι μέλει κ
τοῦ ὡς πλείστην στρατιὰν ἐξάγειν, τίν' ἂν οἴ
μᾶλλον ἐξετάσαι ταύτην ὀρθῶς τοῦ πολλάκ
αὐτῇ κεχρημένου; εἰ δὲ καὶ χρημάτων δεήσε
τίνα ἂν ταῦτα νομίζεις κρεῖττον ἐκπορίσαι τ
καὶ εἰδότος καὶ ἔχοντος πάντα τὰ ὄντα; ὦγαθ
ἔφη, Κῦρε, φύλαξαι μὴ ἡμᾶς ἀποβαλὼν σαυτ
ζημιώσῃς πλείω ἢ ὁ πατὴρ ἐδυνήθη σε βλάψαι.

Ὁ μὲν τοιαῦτα ἔλεγεν. 31. ὁ δὲ Κῦρος ἀκούο
ὑπερήδετο, ὅτι ἐνόμιζε περαίνεσθαι πάντα αὐτ
ὅσαπερ ὑπέσχετο τῷ Κυαξάρῃ πράξειν· ἐμέμνη
γὰρ εἰπὼν ὅτι καὶ φίλον οἴοιτο μᾶλλον ἢ πρόσθ
ποιήσειν.

Καὶ ἐκ τούτου δὴ τὸν Ἀρμένιον ἐρωτᾷ, Ἢ
δὲ δὴ ταῦτα πείθωμαι ὑμῖν, λέγε μοι, ἔφη, σ
ὦ Ἀρμένιε, πόσην μὲν στρατιάν μοι συμπέμψει
πόσα δὲ χρήματα συμβαλεῖ εἰς τὸν πόλεμον;

32. Πρὸς ταῦτα δὴ λέγει ὁ Ἀρμένιος, Οὐδ
ἔχω, ὦ Κῦρε, ἔφη, ἁπλούστερον εἰπεῖν οὐ
δικαιότερον ἢ δεῖξαι μὲν ἐμὲ πᾶσαν τὴν οὖσα
δύναμιν, σὲ δὲ ἰδόντα ὅσην μὲν ἄν σοι δοκ
στρατιὰν ἄγειν, τὴν δὲ καταλιπεῖν τῆς χώρα
φυλακήν. ὡς δ' αὔτως περὶ χρημάτων δηλῶσ
μὲν ἐμὲ δίκαιόν σοι πάντα τὰ ὄντα, σὲ δὲ τούτω
αὐτὸν γνόντα ὁπόσα τε ἂν βούλῃ φέρεσθαι κ
ὁπόσα ἂν βούλῃ καταλιπεῖν.

30. And it you care at all to leave matters here in as little confusion as possible when you go away, consider whether you think the country would be more tranquil under the beginning of a new administration than if the one we are used to should continue. And if you care to take with you as large an army as possible, who do you think would be in a better position to organize the troops properly than he who has often employed them? And if you need money also, who do you think could supply it better than he who knows and commands all the sources of supply? My good Cyrus," he added, "beware lest in casting us aside you do yourself a greater injury than any harm my father has been able to do you."

Thus he spoke. 31. And Cyrus was more than pleased at hearing him, for he thought that everything that he had promised Cyaxares to do was in course of accomplishment; for he remembered having told him that he would make the Armenian more his friend than he was before.

Cyrus takes a conciliatory attitude

"Tell me, king of Armenia," he therefore asked, "if I yield to you in this matter, how large an army will you send with me and how much money will you contribute to the war?"

32. "I have nothing to propose more simple or more fair, Cyrus," the Armenian replied to this, "than for me to show you all the forces I have and for you, when you have seen them, to take as many as you see fit, leaving the rest here to protect the country. And in the same way in regard to the money, it is proper for me to show you all that I have, and for you to decide for yourself and take as much as you please and to leave as much as you please."

33. Καὶ ὁ Κῦρος εἶπεν, Ἴθι δὴ λέξον μοι πόσ
σοι δύναμίς ἐστι, λέξον δὲ καὶ πόσα χρήματα.

Ἐνταῦθα δὴ λέγει ὁ Ἀρμένιος, Ἱππεῖς μὲ
τοίνυν εἰσὶν [Ἀρμενίων][1] εἰς ὀκτακισχιλίους
πεζοὶ δὲ εἰς τέτταρας μυριάδας· χρήματα δ'
ἔφη, σὺν[2] τοῖς θησαυροῖς οἷς ὁ πατὴρ κατέλιπε
ἔστιν εἰς ἀργύριον λογισθέντα τάλαντα πλεί
τῶν τρισχιλίων.

34. Καὶ ὁ Κῦρος οὐκ ἐμέλλησεν, ἀλλ' εἶπε
Τῆς μὲν τοίνυν στρατιᾶς, ἐπεί σοι, ἔφη, οἱ ὅμορο
Χαλδαῖοι πολεμοῦσι, τοὺς ἡμίσεις μοι σύμπεμπε
τῶν δὲ χρημάτων ἀντὶ μὲν τῶν πεντήκοντ
ταλάντων ὧν ἔφερες δασμὸν διπλάσια Κυαξάρ
ἀπόδος, ὅτι ἔλιπες τὴν φοράν· ἐμοὶ δ', ἔφη, ἄλλ
ἑκατὸν δάνεισον· ἐγὼ δέ σοι ὑπισχνοῦμαι, ἢν
θεὸς εὖ διδῷ, ἀνθ' ὧν ἂν ἐμοὶ δανείσῃς ἢ ἄλλ
πλείονος ἄξια εὐεργετήσειν ἢ τὰ χρήματα ἀπα
ριθμήσειν, ἢν δύνωμαι· ἢν δὲ μὴ δύνωμαι, ἀδύ
νατος ἂν φαινοίμην, οἶμαι, ἄδικος δ' οὐκ ἂ
δικαίως κρινοίμην.

35. Καὶ ὁ Ἀρμένιος, Πρὸς τῶν θεῶν, ἔφη
ὦ Κῦρε, μὴ οὕτω λέγε· εἰ δὲ μή, οὐ θαρροῦντ
με ἕξεις· ἀλλὰ νόμιζε, ἔφη, ἂν καταλίπῃς μηδὲ
ἧττον σὰ εἶναι ὧν ἂν ἔχων ἀπίῃς.

Εἶεν, ἔφη ὁ Κῦρος· ὥστε δὲ τὴν γυναῖκα
ἀπολαβεῖν, ἔφη, πόσα ἄν μοι χρήματα δοίης;

Ὁπόσα ἂν δυναίμην, ἔφη.

Τί δέ, ὥστε τοὺς παῖδας;

Καὶ τούτων, ἔφη, ὁπόσα ἂν δυναίμην.

[1] Ἀρμενίων MSS.; bracketed by Hug, Marchant, Gemoll.
[2] σὺν yC¹, Edd.; ἐν C²EHG (*among the treasures*); αὐτοῖς A.

33. "Come then," said Cyrus, "tell me how large 'our forces are and how much money you have."

"Well," the Armenian then answered, "there are bout eight thousand cavalry and about forty thou-and infantry. And the property," said he, "includ-ng the treasures that my father left me, amounts, vhen reduced to cash, to more than three thousand alents."

His demands

34. And without hesitation, Cyrus replied: "Send vith me then," said he, "only half the army, since 'our neighbours, the Chaldaeans, are at war with 'ou. And of the money, instead of the fifty talents vhich you used to pay as tribute, pay Cyaxares double hat sum because you are in arrears with your pay-nents. And lend me personally a hundred more," aid he; "and I promise you that if God prospers ne, I will in return for your loan either do you other avours worth more than that amount or at least pay 'ou back the money, if I can; but if I cannot, I nay seem insolvent, I suppose, but I should not ustly be accounted dishonest."

35. "For heaven's sake, Cyrus," said the Armenian, 'do not talk that way. If you do, you will make me ose heart. But consider," said he, "that what you eave here is no less yours than what you take away."

"Very well," said Cyrus; "now how much money vould you give to get your wife back?"

"As much as I could," said he.

"And how much to get your children?"

"For these also," said he, "as much as I could."

Οὐκοῦν, ἔφη ὁ Κῦρος, ταῦτα μὲν ἤδη διπλάσια τῶν ὄντων. 36. σὺ δέ, ἔφη, ὦ Τιγράνη, λέξον μοι πόσου ἂν πρίαιο ὥστε τὴν γυναῖκα ἀπολαβεῖν.

Ὁ δὲ ἐτύγχανε νεόγαμός τε ὢν καὶ ὑπερφιλῶν τὴν γυναῖκα.

Ἐγὼ μέν, ἔφη, ὦ Κῦρε, κἂν τῆς ψυχῆς πριαίμην ὥστε μήποτε λατρεῦσαι ταύτην.

37. Σὺ μὲν τοίνυν, ἔφη, ἀπάγου τὴν σήν· οὐδὲ γὰρ εἰλῆφθαι ἔγωγε αἰχμάλωτον ταύτην νομίζω σοῦ γε μηπώποτε φυγόντος ἡμᾶς. καὶ σὺ δέ, ὦ Ἀρμένιε, ἀπάγου τὴν γυναῖκα καὶ τοὺς παῖδας μηδὲν αὐτῶν καταθείς, ἵν' εἰδῶσιν ὅτι ἐλεύθεροι πρὸς σὲ ἀπέρχονται. καὶ νῦν μέν, ἔφη, δειπνεῖτε παρ' ἡμῖν· δειπνήσαντες δὲ ἀπελαύνετε ὅποι ὑμῖν θυμός. οὕτω δὴ κατέμειναν.

38. Διασκηνούντων δὲ μετὰ δεῖπνον ἐπήρετο ὁ Κῦρος, Εἰπέ μοι, ἔφη, ὦ Τιγράνη, ποῦ δὴ ἐκεῖνός ἐστιν ὁ ἀνὴρ ὃς συνεθήρα ἡμῖν καὶ σύ μοι μάλα ἐδόκεις θαυμάζειν αὐτόν.

Οὐ γάρ, ἔφη, ἀπέκτεινεν αὐτὸν οὑτοσὶ ὁ ἐμὸς πατήρ;

Τί λαβὼν ἀδικοῦντα;

Διαφθείρειν αὐτὸν ἔφη ἐμέ. καίτοι γ', ἔφη, ὦ Κῦρε, οὕτω καλὸς κἀγαθὸς ἐκεῖνος ἦν ὡς καὶ ὅτε ἀποθνήσκειν ἔμελλε προσκαλέσας με εἶπε, Μή τι σύ, ἔφη, ὦ Τιγράνη, ὅτι ἀποκτείνει με, χαλεπανθῇς τῷ πατρί· οὐ γὰρ κακονοίᾳ τινὶ[1] τοῦτο ποιεῖ, ἀλλ' ἀγνοίᾳ· ὁπόσα δὲ ἀγνοίᾳ ἄνθρωποι ἐξαμαρτάνουσι, πάντ' ἀκούσια ταῦτ' ἔγωγε νομίζω.

[1] τινὶ zED, Dindorf; τῇ σῇ F, most Edd. (*toward you*); τῇ σῇ γε Hug, supposedly after C.

"Well then," said Cyrus, "that makes already
vice as much as you have. 36. And you, Tigranes,"
id he, "tell me how much you would pay to get
our wife back?"

Now it happened that he was newly married and
ved his wife very dearly.

"I would give my life, Cyrus," said he, "to keep
er from slavery."

His generosity

37. "Well then," said he, "take her back; she is
our own. For I, for my part, do not consider that
e has been made a prisoner of war at all, since
u never ran away from us. And you too, king of
rmenia, may take back your wife and children
ithout paying any ransom for them, that they may
now that they return to you free men and women.
nd now," said he, "stay and have dinner with us;
d when you have dined you may drive away
herever you have a mind to go." So they stayed.

A Socrates in Armenia

38. And after dinner, as the party was breaking up,
yrus asked: "Tell me, Tigranes, where is the man
ho used to hunt with us? You seemed to admire
m very much."

"Ah," he replied, "did not my father here have
m put to death?"

"What wrong did he find him doing?"

"He said that he was corrupting me. And yet,
yrus," said he, "he was so noble and so good that
hen he was about to be put to death, he called me
him and said: 'Be not angry with your father,
igranes, for putting me to death; for he does it,
ot from any spirit of malice, but from ignorance,
nd when men do wrong from ignorance, I believe
ey do it quite against their will.'"

39. Ὁ μὲν δὴ Κῦρος ἐπὶ τούτοις εἶπε, Φεῦ το ἀνδρός.

Ὁ δ' Ἀρμένιος ἔλεξεν, Οὔτοι, ἔφη, ὦ Κῦρ οὐδ' οἱ ταῖς ἑαυτῶν γυναιξὶ λαμβάνοντες συνόντα ἀλλοτρίους ἄνδρας οὐ τοῦτο αἰτιώμενοι αὐτοὶ κατακαίνουσιν[1] ὡς ἀφρονεστέρας[2] ποιοῦντας[3] τὰ γυναῖκας, ἀλλὰ νομίζοντες ἀφαιρεῖσθαι αὐτοὺς τὴ πρὸς αὐτοὺς φιλίαν, διὰ τοῦτο ὡς πολεμίοι αὐτοῖς χρῶνται. καὶ ἐγὼ ἐκείνῳ, ἔφη, ἐφθόνου ὅτι μοι ἐδόκει τὸν ἐμὸν υἱὸν ποιεῖν αὐτὸν μᾶλλο θαυμάζειν ἢ ἐμέ.

40. Καὶ ὁ Κῦρος εἶπεν, Ἀλλὰ ναὶ μὰ τοὺ θεούς, ἔφη, ὦ Ἀρμένιε, ἀνθρώπινά μοι δοκεῖ ἁμαρτεῖν· καὶ σύ, ὦ Τιγράνη, συγγίγνωσκε τ πατρί.

Τότε μὲν δὴ τοιαῦτα διαλεχθέντες καὶ φιλοφρο νηθέντες ὥσπερ εἰκὸς ἐκ συναλλαγῆς, ἀναβάντε ἐπὶ τὰς ἁρμαμάξας σὺν ταῖς γυναιξὶν ἀπήλαυνο εὐφραινόμενοι.

41. Ἐπεὶ δ' ἦλθον οἴκαδε, ἔλεγον τοῦ Κύρου μέν τις τὴν σοφίαν, ὁ δὲ τὴν καρτερίαν, ὁ δὲ τὴ πρᾳότητα, ὁ δέ τις καὶ τὸ κάλλος καὶ τὸ μέγεθος.

Ἔνθα δὴ ὁ Τιγράνης ἐπήρετο τὴν γυναῖκα, Ἦ καὶ σοί, ἔφη, ὦ Ἀρμενία, καλὸς ἐδόκει ὁ Κῦρο εἶναι;

Ἀλλὰ μὰ Δί', ἔφη, οὐκ ἐκεῖνον ἐθεώμην.

Ἀλλὰ τίνα μήν; ἔφη ὁ Τιγράνης.

[1] κατακαίνουσιν Cobet, Marchant, Gemoll; κατακτείνουσ MSS., Dindorf, Breitenbach.

[2] ἀφρονεστέρας Stephanus, Dindorf, Breitenbach, Hug; ἀμα θεστέρας yC, Marchant; σωφρονεστέρας zE; ἀκρατεστέρα Gemoll.

[3] ποιοῦντας yC, Edd.; ποιοῦντες zE.

39. "Poor man!" Cyrus exclaimed on hearing his.

Here the Armenian king interrupted: "Do not men who discover strangers in intercourse with their wives kill them, not on the ground that they make their wives more inclined to folly, but in the belief that they alienate from them their wives' affections—for this reason they treat them as enemies. So I was jealous of him because I thought that he made my son regard him more highly than he did me."

40. "Well, by the gods, king of Armenia," said Cyrus, "your sin seems human; and you, Tigranes, must forgive your father."

Then when they had thus conversed and showed their friendly feelings toward one another, as was natural after a reconciliation, they entered their carriages and drove away with their wives, happy.

Armenian appreciation of Cyrus

41. And when they got home they talked, one of Cyrus's wisdom, another of his strength, another of his gentleness, and still another of his beauty and his commanding presence.

Then Tigranes asked his wife: "Tell me, my Armenian princess," said he, "did you, too, think Cyrus handsome?"

"Why, by Zeus," said she, "I did not look at him."

"At whom, then?" asked Tigranes.

Τὸν εἰπόντα νὴ Δία ὡς τῆς αὑτοῦ[1] ψυχῆς ἂν πρίαιτο ὥστε μή με δουλεύειν.

Τότε μὲν δὴ ὥσπερ εἰκὸς ἐκ τοιούτων ἀνεπαύοντο σὺν ἀλλήλοις.

42. Τῇ δ' ὑστεραίᾳ ὁ Ἀρμένιος Κύρῳ μὲν καὶ τῇ στρατιᾷ ἁπάσῃ ξένια ἔπεμπε, προεῖπε δὲ τοῖς ἑαυτοῦ, οὓς δεήσοι στρατεύεσθαι, εἰς τρίτην ἡμέραν παρεῖναι· τὰ δὲ χρήματα ὧν εἶπεν ὁ Κῦρος διπλάσια ἀπηρίθμησεν. ὁ δὲ Κῦρος ὅσα εἶπε λαβὼν τἆλλα ἀπέπεμψεν· ἤρετο δὲ πότερος ἔσται ὁ τὸ στράτευμα ἄγων, ὁ παῖς ἢ αὐτός. εἰπέτην δὲ ἅμα ὁ μὲν πατὴρ οὕτως, Ὁπότερον ἂν σὺ κελεύῃς· ὁ δὲ παῖς οὕτως, Ἐγὼ μὲν οὐκ ἀπολείψομαί σου, ὦ Κῦρε, οὐδ' ἂν σκευοφόρον ἐμὲ δέῃ σοι[2] συνακολουθεῖν.

43. Καὶ ὁ Κῦρος ἐπιγελάσας εἶπε, Καὶ ἐπὶ πόσῳ ἄν, ἔφη, ἐθέλοις τὴν γυναῖκά σου ἀκοῦσαι ὅτι σκευοφορεῖς;

Ἀλλ' οὐδέν, ἔφη, ἀκούειν δεήσει αὐτήν· ἄξω γάρ, ὥστε ὁρᾶν ἐξέσται αὐτῇ ὅ τι ἂν ἐγὼ πράττω.

Ὥρα ἄν, ἔφη, συσκευάζεσθαι ὑμῖν εἴη.

Νόμιζ', ἔφη, συνεσκευασμένους παρέσεσθαι ὅ τι ἂν ὁ πατὴρ δῷ.

Τότε μὲν δὴ ξενισθέντες οἱ στρατιῶται ἐκοιμήθησαν.

[1] αὑτοῦ Edd.; αὐτοῦ MSS.
[2] δέῃ σοι Stephanus, Edd.; δεήσοι yz; δεήσει E; δεήσῃ C.

"At him, by Zeus, who said that he would give his life to keep me from servitude."

Then as might be expected after such experiences, they went to rest together.

42. And on the following day the Armenian king sent guest-presents to Cyrus and all his army, and he commanded those of his men who were to take the field to present themselves on the third day; and he paid Cyrus double the sum of money that he had named. But Cyrus accepted only the amount specified and returned the rest. Then he asked which of the two was to go in command of the forces, the king himself or his son. They both answered at the same instant, the father saying: "Whichever you command"; and the son: "I will never leave you, Cyrus, not even if I have to accompany you as a camp-follower."

Tigranes joins Cyrus's army

43. And Cyrus, laughing, said: "How much would you take to have your wife told that you were a camp-follower?"

"Why," said he, "she will not need to be told anything about it; for I shall take her with me, so that she will be in a position to see whatever I do."

"Then," said he, "it may be high time for you to be getting your things together."

"Be sure," said he, "that we shall be here with everything brought together that my father gives us."

And when the soldiers had received their presents they went to bed.

II

1. Τῇ δ' ὑστεραίᾳ ἀναλαβὼν ὁ Κῦρος τὸν Τιγράνην καὶ τῶν Μήδων ἱππέων τοὺς κρατίστους καὶ τῶν ἑαυτοῦ φίλων ὁπόσους καιρὸς ἐδόκει εἶναι, περιελαύνων τὴν χώραν κατεθεᾶτο, σκοπῶν ποῦ τειχίσειε φρούριον. καὶ ἐπ' ἄκρον τι ἐλθὼν ἐπηρώτα τὸν Τιγράνην ποῖα εἴη τῶν ὀρέων ὁπόθεν οἱ Χαλδαῖοι καταθέοντες λῄζονται. καὶ ὁ Τιγράνης ἐδείκνυ.[1] ὁ δὲ πάλιν ἤρετο, Νῦν δὲ ταῦτα τὰ ὄρη ἔρημά ἐστιν;

Οὐ μὰ Δί', ἔφη, ἀλλ' ἀεὶ σκοποὶ εἰσὶν ἐκείνων οἳ σημαίνουσι τοῖς ἄλλοις ὅ τι ἂν ὁρῶσι.

Τί οὖν, ἔφη, ποιοῦσιν, ἐπὴν αἴσθωνται;

Βοηθοῦσιν, ἔφη, ἐπὶ τὰ ἄκρα, ὡς ἂν ἕκαστος δύνηται.

2. Ταῦτα μὲν δὴ ὁ Κῦρος ἠκηκόει· σκοπῶν δὲ κατενόει πολλὴν τῆς χώρας τοῖς Ἀρμενίοις ἔρημον καὶ ἀργὸν οὖσαν διὰ τὸν πόλεμον. καὶ τότε μὲν ἀπῆλθον ἐπὶ τὸ στρατόπεδον καὶ δειπνήσαντες ἐκοιμήθησαν.

3. Τῇ δ' ὑστεραίᾳ αὐτός τε ὁ Τιγράνης παρῆν συνεσκευασμένος καὶ ἱππεῖς εἰς τοὺς τετρακισχιλίους συνελέγοντο αὐτῷ καὶ τοξόται εἰς τοὺς μυρίους, καὶ πελτασταὶ ἄλλοι τοσοῦτοι.

Ὁ δὲ Κῦρος ἐν ᾧ συνελέγοντο ἐθύετο· ἐπεὶ δὲ καλὰ τὰ ἱερὰ ἦν αὐτῷ, συνεκάλεσε τούς τε τῶν

[1] ἐδείκνυ Dindorf, Hug; ἐδείκνυεν MSS., Breitenbach, Marchant, Gemoll.

II

1. On the morrow Cyrus took with him Tigranes, the best of the Median horsemen, and as many of his own friends as he thought proper, and rode around to inspect the country with a view to finding a place in which to build a fort. And when he had come to a certain eminence he asked Tigranes which were the mountains from which the Chaldaeans were accustomed to descend to make forays into the country. And Tigranes pointed them out. And again he asked: "And are these mountains now unoccupied?"

Preparations for the conquest of Chaldaea

"No, by Zeus," said he; "but they always have scouts up there who signal to the rest whatever they see."

"Then," said he, "what do they do, when they receive the signals?"

"They run out to the heights to help," said he, "each as best he can."

2. Such was the account to which Cyrus listened; and as he looked he observed that a large portion of the Armenians' country was deserted and uncultivated as a result of the war. And then they went back to camp and after they had dined they went to rest.

3. On the following day Tigranes presented himself with his baggage all ready for the start; and under his command were assembled about four thousand horsemen and about ten thousand bowmen and as many peltasts besides.

While they had been coming together, Cyrus had been sacrificing; and when his sacrifice gave favourable omens, he called a meeting of the officers of the

Περσῶν ἡγεμόνας καὶ τοὺς τῶν Μήδων. 4. ἐπεὶ δ' ὁμοῦ ἦσαν, ἔλεξε τοιάδε·

Ἄνδρες φίλοι, ἔστι μὲν τὰ ὄρη ταῦτα ἃ ὁρῶμεν Χαλδαίων· εἰ δὲ ταῦτα καταλάβοιμεν καὶ ἐπ' ἄκρου γένοιτο ἡμέτερον φρούριον, σωφρονεῖν ἀνάγκη ἂν εἴη πρὸς ἡμᾶς ἀμφοτέροις, τοῖς τε Ἀρμενίοις καὶ τοῖς Χαλδαίοις. τὰ μὲν οὖν ἱερὰ καλὰ ἡμῖν· ἀνθρωπίνῃ δὲ προθυμίᾳ εἰς τὸ πραχθῆναι ταῦτα οὐδὲν οὕτω μέγα σύμμαχον ἂν γένοιτο ὡς τάχος. ἢν γὰρ φθάσωμεν πρὶν τοὺς πολεμίους συλλεγῆναι ἀναβάντες, ἢ παντάπασιν ἀμαχεὶ λάβοιμεν ἂν τὸ ἄκρον ἢ ὀλίγοις τε καὶ ἀσθενέσι χρησαίμεθ' ἂν πολεμίοις.

5. Τῶν οὖν πόνων οὐδεὶς ῥᾴων οὐδ' ἀκινδυνότερος, ἔφη, ἐστὶ τοῦ νῦν καρτερῆσαι σπεύδοντας. ἴτε οὖν ἐπὶ τὰ ὅπλα. καὶ . . .[1]

Ὑμεῖς μέν, ὦ Μῆδοι, ἐν ἀριστερᾷ ἡμῶν πορεύεσθε· ὑμεῖς δέ, ὦ Ἀρμένιοι, οἱ μὲν ἡμίσεις ἐν δεξιᾷ, οἱ δ' ἡμίσεις ἔμπροσθεν ἡμῶν ἡγεῖσθε· ὑμεῖς δ', ὦ ἱππεῖς, ὄπισθεν ἕπεσθε παρακελευόμενοι καὶ ὠθοῦντες ἄνω ἡμᾶς, ἢν δέ τις μαλακύνηται, μὴ ἐπιτρέπετε.

6. Ταῦτ' εἰπὼν ὁ Κῦρος ἡγεῖτο ὀρθίους ποιησάμενος τοὺς λόχους. οἱ δὲ Χαλδαῖοι ὡς ἔγνωσαν τὴν ὁρμὴν ἄνω οὖσαν, εὐθὺς ἐσήμαινόν τε τοῖς ἑαυτῶν καὶ συνεβόων ἀλλήλους[2] καὶ συνηθροίζοντο.

Ὁ δὲ Κῦρος παρηγγύα, Ἄνδρες Πέρσαι, ἡμῖν

[1] A lacuna, in which preparations are effected, Hug, Marchant, Gemoll.

[2] ἀλλήλους Schneider, Edd.; ἀλλήλοις MSS.

ersians and of the Medes; 4. and when they
vere come together, he spoke as follows:

"My friends, these mountains which we see
elong to Chaldaea; but if we should seize them and
ave a fort of our own built upon the summit, both
arties—the Armenians, I mean, and the Chaldaeans
—would have to behave with discretion toward us.
Now, the sacrifices give us favourable omens; but, for
he execution of our plan, nothing would be so
trong an ally to human zeal as dispatch. For if we
et up there before the enemy have time to come
ogether, we may gain possession of the heights
ltogether without a battle, or we may at least find
nemies few in number and without strength.

He hurls his army into the Chaldaean mountains

5. "Of the tasks before us, therefore, none is
asier or less fraught with danger," said he, "than
ow bravely to endure the strain of haste. There-
ore, to arms! And . . . .

"You, Medes, march on our left; and you,
Armenians, half keep to our right and half lead on
n front; while you, cavalrymen, shall follow behind,
o encourage and push us on upward; and if any one
s inclined to show weakness, do not allow it."

6. With this command Cyrus brought his companies
to ploy into column and took his place at their head.
And when the Chaldaeans realized that the movement
was directed toward the heights, they immediately
gave the signal to their people, called to one another
to assemble, and began to come together.

And Cyrus gave command: "Fellow-Persians, they

σημαίνουσι σπεύδειν. ἢν γὰρ φθάσωμεν ἄνω
γενόμενοι, οὐδὲν τὰ τῶν πολεμίων δυνήσεται.

7. Εἶχον δ' οἱ Χαλδαῖοι γέρρα τε καὶ παλτ
δύο· καὶ πολεμικώτατοι δὲ λέγονται οὗτοι τῶν περ
ἐκείνην τὴν χώραν εἶναι· καὶ μισθοῦ στρατεύονται
ὁπόταν τις αὐτῶν δέηται, διὰ τὸ πολεμικοί τε κα
πένητες εἶναι· καὶ γὰρ ἡ χώρα αὐτοῖς ὀρεινή τ
ἐστι καὶ ὀλίγη ἡ τὰ χρήματα ἔχουσα.

8. Ὡς δὲ μᾶλλον ἐπλησίαζον οἱ ἀμφὶ τὸν Κῦρο
τῶν ἄκρων, ὁ Τιγράνης σὺν τῷ Κύρῳ πορευόμενο
εἶπεν, Ὦ Κῦρε, ἆρ' οἶσθ', ἔφη, ὅτι αὐτοὺς ἡμᾶ
αὐτίκα μάλα δεήσει μάχεσθαι; ὡς οἵ γε Ἀρμένιο
οὐ μὴ δέξονται τοὺς πολεμίους.

Καὶ ὁ Κῦρος εἰπὼν ὅτι εἰδείη τοῦτο, εὐθὺ
παρηγγύησε τοῖς Πέρσαις παρασκευάζεσθαι, ὡ
αὐτίκα δεῆσον διώκειν, ἐπειδὰν ὑπαγάγωσι τοὺ
πολεμίους ὑποφεύγοντες οἱ Ἀρμένιοι ὥστ' ἐγγὺ
ἡμῖν γενέσθαι.

9. Οὕτω δὴ ἡγοῦντο μὲν οἱ Ἀρμένιοι· τῶ
δὲ Χαλδαίων οἱ παρόντες, ὡς ἐπλησίαζον ο
Ἀρμένιοι, ἀλαλάξαντες ἔθεον, ὥσπερ εἰώθεσαν
εἰς αὐτούς· οἱ δὲ Ἀρμένιοι, ὥσπερ εἰώθεσαν, οὐκ
ἐδέχοντο. 10. ὡς δὲ διώκοντες οἱ Χαλδαῖοι εἶδο
ἐναντίους μαχαιροφόρους ἱεμένους ἄνω, οἱ μὲ
τινες αὐτοῖς πελάσαντες ταχὺ ἀπέθνησκον, ο
δ' ἔφευγον, οἱ δέ τινες καὶ ἑάλωσαν αὐτῶν, ταχὺ
δὲ εἴχετο τὰ ἄκρα. ἐπεὶ δὲ τὰ ἄκρα εἶχον ο
ἀμφὶ τὸν Κῦρον, καθεώρων τε τῶν Χαλδαίων
τὰς οἰκήσεις καὶ ᾐσθάνοντο φεύγοντας αὐτοὺς
ἐκ τῶν ἐγγὺς οἰκήσεων.

11. Ὁ δὲ Κῦρος, ὡς πάντες οἱ στρατιῶται

are signalling us to hasten; for if we get up there first, the enemy's efforts will be of no avail."

7. Now the Chaldaeans carried each a wicker shield and two spears, and they were said to be the most warlike of the peoples in that region. They also serve for hire when any one wants them, for they are fond of war and poor of purse; for their country is mountainous and only a small part of it is productive.

The battle

8. But when Cyrus and his men were getting nearer to the heights, Tigranes, who was marching with Cyrus, said: "Do you know, Cyrus, that we ourselves shall have to do the fighting, and in a very few moments? For the Armenians, I am sure, will never sustain the enemy's attack."

Cyrus answered that he knew that and gave the command to the Persians to make ready, as it would be necessary in a moment to give chase, as soon as the Armenians by pretending flight should decoy the enemy into close quarters.

9. So the Armenians led on. And when they came near, the Chaldaeans already there raised the battle cry, according to their custom, and charged upon them. And the Armenians, according to their custom, failed to sustain the charge. 10. But when the Chaldaeans in pursuit saw before them the swordsmen rushing up against them, some came near and were cut down at once, others fled, and some others of their number were taken prisoners; and soon the heights were taken. And when Cyrus and his men were in possession of the heights, they looked down on the dwellings of the Chaldaeans and saw the people fleeing from their homes near by.

11. Then when the soldiers were all together,

ὁμοῦ ἐγένοντο, ἀριστοποιεῖσθαι παρήγγειλεν. ἐπεὶ δὲ ἠριστήκεσαν, καταμαθὼν ἔνθα αἱ σκοπαὶ ἦσαν αἱ τῶν Χαλδαίων ἐρυμνόν τε ὂν καὶ ἔνυδρον, εὐθὺς ἐτείχιζε φρούριον· καὶ τὸν Τιγράνην ἐκέλευε πέμπειν ἐπὶ τὸν πατέρα καὶ κελεύειν παραγενέσθαι ἔχοντα ὁπόσοι εἶεν τέκτονές τε καὶ λιθοτόμοι.[1] ἐπὶ μὲν δὴ τὸν Ἀρμένιον ᾤχετο ἄγγελος· ὁ δὲ Κῦρος τοῖς παροῦσιν ἐτείχιζεν.

12. Ἐν δὲ τούτῳ προσάγουσι τῷ Κύρῳ τοὺς αἰχμαλώτους δεδεμένους, τοὺς δέ τινας καὶ τετρωμένους· ὡς δὲ εἶδεν, εὐθὺς λύειν μὲν ἐκέλευσε τοὺς δεδεμένους, τοὺς δὲ τετρωμένους ἰατροὺς καλέσας θεραπεύειν ἐκέλευσεν· ἔπειτα δὲ ἔλεξε τοῖς Χαλδαίοις ὅτι ἥκοι οὔτε ἀπολέσαι ἐπιθυμῶν ἐκείνους οὔτε πολεμεῖν δεόμενος, ἀλλ' εἰρήνην βουλόμενος ποιῆσαι Ἀρμενίοις καὶ Χαλδαίοις.

Πρὶν μὲν οὖν ἔχεσθαι τὰ ἄκρα οἶδ' ὅτι οὐδὲν ἐδεῖσθε εἰρήνης· τὰ μὲν γὰρ ὑμέτερα ἀσφαλῶς εἶχε, τὰ δὲ τῶν Ἀρμενίων ἤγετε καὶ ἐφέρετε· νῦν δὲ ὁρᾶτε δὴ ἐν οἵῳ ἐστέ. 13. ἐγὼ οὖν ἀφίημι ὑμᾶς οἴκαδε τοὺς εἰλημμένους, καὶ δίδωμι ὑμῖν σὺν τοῖς ἄλλοις Χαλδαίοις βουλεύσασθαι εἴτε βούλεσθε πολεμεῖν ἡμῖν εἴτε φίλοι εἶναι. καὶ ἢν μὲν πόλεμον αἱρῆσθε, μηκέτι ἥκετε δεῦρο ἄνευ ὅπλων, εἰ σωφρονεῖτε· ἢν δὲ εἰρήνης δοκῆτε

[1] λιθοτόμοι Dindorf, most Edd.; λιθοδόμοι MSS.; λιθολόγοι Valckenaer.

Cyrus bade his men take luncheon; and when they had lunched and he had discovered that the place where the scouts had their posts of observation was strong and well supplied with water, he at once proceeded to build a fort there. He also bade Tigranes send for his father and bid him come with all the carpenters and masons that he had. So a messenger was off to bring the Armenian king, but Cyrus proceeded to build the wall with the men he had at hand.

He releases the prisoners

12. At this juncture they brought to Cyrus the prisoners in chains and also some that had been wounded. And when he saw them he at once ordered that the fetters be taken off, and he sent for surgeons and bade them attend to the wounded men. And then he told the Chaldaeans that he had come with no wish to destroy them and with no desire to make war, but because he wished to make peace between the Armenians and the Chaldaeans.

"Now I know that before the heights were taken you had no wish at all for peace, for everything of yours was secure, while you carried off and plundered the property of the Armenians; but now see in what a predicament you are! 13. Now I am going to let you who have been captured go home and consult with the rest of the Chaldaeans whether you wish to have war with us or to be our friends. And if you choose war, do not come this way again without weapons, if you are wise; but if you decide that you desire peace, come without arms. I shall see to

δεῖσθαι, ἄνευ ὅπλων ἥκετε· ὡς δὲ καλῶς ἕξει τ
ὑμέτερα, ἢν φίλοι γένησθε, ἐμοὶ μελήσει.

14. Ἀκούσαντες δὲ ταῦτα οἱ Χαλδαῖοι, πολλ
μὲν ἐπαινέσαντες, πολλὰ δὲ δεξιωσάμενοι τὸ
Κῦρον ᾤχοντο οἴκαδε.

Ὁ δὲ Ἀρμένιος ὡς ἤκουσε τήν τε κλῆσι
τοῦ Κύρου καὶ τὴν πρᾶξιν, λαβὼν τοὺς τέκτονα
καὶ τἄλλα ὅσων ᾤετο δεῖν, ἧκε πρὸς τὸν Κῦρο
ὡς ἐδύνατο τάχιστα. 15. ἐπεὶ δὲ εἶδε τὸν Κῦρον
ἔλεξεν, Ὦ Κῦρε, ὡς ὀλίγα δυνάμενοι προορᾶ
ἄνθρωποι[1] περὶ τοῦ μέλλοντος πολλὰ ἐπιχει-
ροῦμεν πράττειν. νῦν γὰρ δὴ καὶ ἐγὼ ἐλευθερία
μὲν μηχανᾶσθαι ἐπιχειρήσας δοῦλος ὡς οὐδεπώποτε ἐγενόμην· ἐπεὶ δ᾽ ἑάλωμεν, σαφῶς ἀπολω-
λέναι νομίσαντες νῦν ἀναφαινόμεθα σεσωσμένο
ὡς οὐδεπώποτε. οἳ γὰρ οὐδεπώποτε ἐπαύοντο
πολλὰ κακὰ ἡμᾶς ποιοῦντες, νῦν ὁρῶ τούτους
ἔχοντας ὥσπερ ἐγὼ ηὐχόμην. 16. καὶ τοῦτο
ἐπίστω, ἔφη, ὦ Κῦρε, ὅτι ἐγὼ ὥστε ἀπελάσαι
Χαλδαίους ἀπὸ τούτων τῶν ἄκρων πολλαπλάσια
ἂν ἔδωκα χρήματα ὧν σὺ νῦν ἔχεις παρ᾽ ἐμοῦ·
καὶ ἃ ὑπισχνοῦ ποιήσειν ἀγαθὰ ἡμᾶς ὅτ᾽ ἐλάμ-
βανες τὰ χρήματα, ἀποτετέλεσταί σοι ἤδη, ὥστε
καὶ προσοφείλοντές σοι ἄλλας χάριτας ἀναπε-
φήναμεν, ἃς ἡμεῖς γε, εἰ μὴ κακοί ἐσμεν, αἰσχυ-
νοίμεθ᾽ ἂν σοι μὴ ἀποδιδόντες. 17. ὁ μὲν Ἀρμένιος τοσαῦτ᾽ ἔλεξεν.

Οἱ δὲ Χαλδαῖοι ἧκον δεόμενοι τοῦ Κύρου
εἰρήνην σφίσι ποιῆσαι. καὶ ὁ Κῦρος ἐπήρετο
αὐτούς, Ἄλλο τι, ἔφη, ὦ Χαλδαῖοι, ἢ τούτου

[1] ἅνθρωποι Dindorf, later Edd. ; ἄνθρωποι MSS.

it that you have no cause to complain, if you become our friends."

14. And when the Chaldaeans heard this, they commended Cyrus highly, shook hands with him heartily, and departed for home.

Now, when the king of Armenia received Cyrus's summons and heard of his plans, he came to Cyrus as quickly as he could with the carpenters and all that he thought was necessary. 15. And when he saw Cyrus, he said: "How little of the future, Cyrus, we mortals can foresee, and yet how much we try to accomplish. Why, just now, when I was striving to secure liberty, I became more a slave than ever before; and when we were taken prisoners, we then thought our destruction certain, but we now find that we are saved as never before. For those who never ceased to do us no end of injury I now behold in just the condition that I desired. 16. And believe me, Cyrus," said he, "when I say that to have driven the Chaldaeans from these heights I would have given many times as much money as you now have from me; and the benefit that you promised to do us, when you received the money, you have already conferred so fully that we obviously now owe you a new debt of gratitude besides; and we on our part, if we have not lost all self-respect, should be ashamed if we did not repay it to you." 17. Thus the Armenian king spoke.

The Armenian king expresses his gratification

Now the Chaldaeans had come back with the request that Cyrus should make peace with them. And Cyrus asked them: "Is this the reason that you, Chaldaeans, now desire peace, because you

ἕνεκα εἰρήνης νῦν ἐπιθυμεῖτε ὅτι νομίζετε ἀσφαλέστερον ἂν δύνασθαι ζῆν εἰρήνης γενομένης ἢ πολεμοῦντες, ἐπειδὴ ἡμεῖς τάδ᾽ ἔχομεν;

Ἔφασαν[1] οἱ Χαλδαῖοι.

18. Καὶ ὅς, Τί δ᾽, ἔφη, εἰ καὶ ἄλλα ὑμῖν ἀγαθὰ προσγένοιτο διὰ τὴν εἰρήνην;

Ἔτι ἄν, ἔφασαν, μᾶλλον εὐφραινοίμεθα.

Ἄλλο τι οὖν, ἔφη, ἢ διὰ τὸ γῆς σπανίζειν ἀγαθῆς νῦν πένητες νομίζετ᾽ εἶναι;

Συνέφασαν καὶ τοῦτο.

Τί οὖν; ἔφη ὁ Κῦρος, βούλοισθ᾽ ἂν ἀποτελοῦντες ὅσαπερ οἱ ἄλλοι Ἀρμένιοι ἐξεῖναι ὑμῖν τῆς Ἀρμενίας γῆς ἐργάζεσθαι ὁπόσην ἂν θέλητε;

Ἔφασαν οἱ Χαλδαῖοι, Εἰ πιστεύοιμεν μὴ ἀδικήσεσθαι.

19. Τί δέ, σύ, ἔφη, ὦ Ἀρμένιε, βούλοιο ἄν σοι τὴν νῦν ἀργὸν[2] οὖσαν γῆν ἐνεργὸν γενέσθαι, εἰ μέλλοιεν τὰ νομιζόμενα παρὰ σοὶ ἀποτελεῖν οἱ ἐργαζόμενοι;

Ἔφη ὁ Ἀρμένιος πολλοῦ ἂν τοῦτο πρίασθαι· πολὺ γὰρ ἂν αὐξάνεσθαι τὴν πρόσοδον.

20. Τί δ᾽, ὑμεῖς, ἔφη, ὦ Χαλδαῖοι, ἐπεὶ ὄρη ἀγαθὰ ἔχετε, ἐθέλοιτ᾽ ἂν ἐᾶν νέμειν ταῦτα τοὺς Ἀρμενίους, εἰ ὑμῖν μέλλοιεν οἱ νέμοντες τὰ δίκαια ἀποτελεῖν;

Ἔφασαν οἱ Χαλδαῖοι· πολλὰ γὰρ ἂν ὠφελεῖσθαι οὐδὲν πονοῦντες.

[1] τάδ᾽ ἔχομεν; ἔφασαν z, most Edd.; τὰ ἄκρα ἔχομεν; ἔφασαν Hug; τἄλλ᾽ ἔχομεν ἔφασαν F; τἄλλα ἔφασαν ἔχομεν x; ταῦτ᾽ ἐλέγομεν τἆλλα ἔχομεν ἔφασαν D.

[2] ἀργὸν Stephanus, Edd.; ἀργὴν MSS.

think, that since we are in possession of these heights, you could live in greater security if we had peace than if we were at war?"

The Chaldaeans assented.

18. "And what," said he, "if still other blessings should accrue to you as a result of the proposed peace?"

"We should be still more pleased," they answered.

"Well," said he, "do you think that you are now poor for any other reason than because you have so little fertile land?"

In this also they agreed with him.

"Well then," said Cyrus, "would you avail yourselves of the permission to till as much Armenian land as you wish on condition that you paid in full just as much rental as other tenants in Armenia do?"

"Yes," said the Chaldaeans, "if we could be sure of not being molested."

19. "Tell me, King of Armenia," said he, "would you be willing that that land of yours which now lies uncultivated should be cultivated, if those who cultivate it would pay you the usual rental?"

The Armenian answered that he would give a great deal to have it so; for in this way his revenues would be greatly increased.

20. "And tell me, Chaldaeans," said he, "seeing that you have fine mountains, would you be willing to let the Armenians pasture their herds there, if the herdsmen would pay you what is fair?"

The Chaldaeans said they would; for they would get large profits by it, without any labour on their own part.

Σὺ δέ, ἔφη, ὦ Ἀρμένιε, ἐθέλοις ἂν ταῖς τούτων νομαῖς χρῆσθαι, εἰ μέλλοις μικρὰ ὠφελῶν Χαλδαίους πολὺ πλείω ὠφελήσεσθαι;

Καὶ σφόδρα ἄν, ἔφη, εἴπερ οἰοίμην ἀσφαλῶς νέμειν.

Οὐκοῦν, ἔφη, ἀσφαλῶς ἂν νέμοιτε, εἰ τὰ ἄκρα ἔχοιτε σύμμαχα;

Ἔφη ὁ Ἀρμένιος.

21. Ἀλλὰ μὰ Δί', ἔφασαν οἱ Χαλδαῖοι, οὐκ ἂν ἡμεῖς ἀσφαλῶς ἐργαζοίμεθα μὴ ὅτι τὴν τούτων ἀλλ' οὐδ' ἂν τὴν ἡμετέραν, εἰ οὗτοι τὰ ἄκρα ἔχοιεν.

Εἰ δ' ὑμῖν αὖ, ἔφη, τὰ ἄκρα σύμμαχα εἴη;

Οὕτως ἄν, ἔφασαν, ἡμῖν καλῶς ἔχοι.

Ἀλλὰ μὰ Δί', ἔφη ὁ Ἀρμένιος, οὐκ ἂν ἡμῖν αὖ καλῶς ἔχοι, εἰ οὗτοι παραλήψονται πάλιν τὰ ἄκρα ἄλλως τε καὶ τετειχισμένα.

22. Καὶ ὁ Κῦρος εἶπεν, Οὑτωσὶ τοίνυν, ἔφη, ἐγὼ ποιήσω· οὐδετέροις ὑμῶν τὰ ἄκρα παραδώσω, ἀλλ' ἡμεῖς φυλάξομεν αὐτά· κἂν ἀδικῶσιν ὑμῶν ὁπότεροι, σὺν τοῖς ἀδικουμένοις ἡμεῖς ἐσόμεθα.

23. Ὡς δ' ἤκουσαν ταῦτα ἀμφότεροι, ἐπῄνεσαν καὶ ἔλεγον ὅτι οὕτως ἂν μόνως ἡ εἰρήνη βεβαία γένοιτο. καὶ ἐπὶ τούτοις ἔδοσαν καὶ ἔλαβον πάντες τὰ πιστά, καὶ ἐλευθέρους μὲν ἀμφοτέρους

"And you, King of Armenia," said he, "would you be willing to rent their pasture lands, if by letting the Chaldaeans have a little profit you were to get much greater profit for yourself?"

"Why, of course," said he, "if I thought I could pasture my cattle there in security."

"Well then," said he, "could you pasture them there in security, if the heights were in the possession of your friends?"

"Yes," said the Armenian.

21. "But, by Zeus," said the Chaldaeans, "we could not even work our own farms in security, to say nothing of theirs, if they were to have possession of the heights."

"But," said Cyrus, "suppose on the other hand that the heights were in the possession of your friends?"

"In that case," they answered, "we should be all right."

"But, by Zeus," said the Armenian, "we, on our part, should not be all right, if they are again to get possession of the heights, especially now that they have been fortified."

Cyrus guarantees peace between them

22. "This then," said Cyrus, "is what I shall do: I shall not give possession of the heights to either of you, but we shall keep a garrison there ourselves; and if either of you does wrong, we shall side with the injured party."

23. And when they heard this proposal, both sides gave it their approval and said that only in this way could the peace be effective; and upon these conditions they interchanged assurances of friendship, and agreed that each party should be independent of the other, that there should

ἀπ᾿ ἀλλήλων εἶναι συνετίθεντο, ἐπιγαμίας δ
εἶναι καὶ ἐπεργασίας καὶ ἐπινομίας, καὶ ἐπι
μαχίαν δὲ κοινήν, εἴ τις ἀδικοίη ὁποτέρους.

24. Οὕτω μὲν οὖν τότε διεπράχθη· καὶ νῦ
δὲ ἔτι οὕτω διαμένουσιν αἱ τότε γενόμεναι συνθῆ
και Χαλδαίοις καὶ τῷ τὴν Ἀρμενίαν ἔχοντι
ἐπεὶ δὲ αἱ συνθῆκαι ἐγεγένηντο, εὐθὺς συνετεί
χιζόν τε ἀμφότεροι προθύμως ὡς κοινὸν φρούριο
καὶ τἀπιτήδεια συνεισῆγον.

25. Ἐπεὶ δ᾿ ἑσπέρα προσῄει, συνδείπνους ἔλα
βεν ἀμφοτέρους πρὸς ἑαυτὸν ὡς φίλους ἤδη
συσκηνούντων δὲ εἶπέ τις τῶν Χαλδαίων ὅτ
τοῖς μὲν ἄλλοις σφῶν πᾶσιν εὐκτὰ ταῦτα εἴη
εἰσὶ δέ τινες τῶν Χαλδαίων οἳ λῃζόμενοι ζῶσ
καὶ οὔτ᾿ ἂν ἐπίσταιντο ἐργάζεσθαι οὔτ᾿ ἂν δύ
ναιντο, εἰθισμένοι ἀπὸ πολέμου βιοτεύειν· ἀε
γὰρ ἐλῄζοντο ἢ ἐμισθοφόρουν, πολλάκις μὲν παρ
τῷ Ἰνδῶν βασιλεῖ (καὶ γάρ, ἔφασαν, πολύχρυσο
ἀνήρ) πολλάκις δὲ καὶ παρ᾿ Ἀστυάγει.

26. Καὶ ὁ Κῦρος ἔφη, Τί οὖν οὐ καὶ νῦ
παρ᾿ ἐμοὶ μισθοφοροῦσιν; ἐγὼ γὰρ δώσω ὅσο
τις καὶ ἄλλος πλεῖστον δήποτε ἔδωκε.

Συνέφασαν [οἱ],[1] καὶ πολλούς γε ἔσεσθα
ἔλεγον τοὺς ἐθελήσοντας.

27. Καὶ ταῦτα μὲν δὴ οὕτω συνωμολογεῖτο
ὁ δὲ Κῦρος ὡς ἤκουσεν ὅτι πολλάκις πρὸς τὸ
Ἰνδὸν οἱ Χαλδαῖοι ἐπορεύοντο, ἀναμνησθεὶς ὅτ

[1] [οἱ] omitted by Dindorf and bracketed by later Edd. ; ο
MSS.

e the right of intermarriage and of mutual tillage nd pasturage in each other's territory, and that here should be a defensive alliance, in case any one hould injure either party.

24. Such, then, was the agreement entered into t that time; and to this day the covenants which ere then made between the Chaldaeans and the ing of Armenia still continue in force. And when he treaty was made, they both together began ith enthusiasm at once to build the fort for their ommon protection, and then together they stocked with provisions.

25. When evening was drawing on, he entertained oth sides, now made friends, as his guests at dinner. And while the party was in progress, one of the Chaldaeans said that to all the rest of them this tate of affairs was desirable; but there were some f the Chaldaeans, so they said, who lived by lundering and would not know how to farm nd could not, for they were used to making their iving by the business of war; for they were always naking raids or serving as mercenaries; they were ften in the service of the Indian king (and he paid vell, they said, for he was a very wealthy man) and ften in the service of Astyages.

Chaldaean mercenaries

26. "Then why do they not enter my service now?" asked Cyrus; "I will pay as much as ny one ever did."

They assented and said that the volunteers would e many.

27. These terms were thus agreed upon; and when Cyrus heard that the Chaldaeans made frequent rips to the Indian king, remembering that represen-

Cyrus proposes an embassy to India

ἦλθον παρ' αὐτοῦ κατασκεψόμενοι[1] εἰς Μήδου τὰ αὐτῶν πράγματα καὶ ᾤχοντο πρὸς τοὺ πολεμίους, ὅπως αὖ καὶ τὰ ἐκείνων κατίδωσι ἐβούλετο μαθεῖν τὸν Ἰνδὸν τὰ ἑαυτῷ πεπραγμένα 28. ἤρξατο οὖν λόγου τοιοῦδε·

Ὦ Ἀρμένιε, ἔφη, καὶ ὑμεῖς, ὦ Χαλδαῖοι εἴπατέ μοι, εἴ τινα ἐγὼ νῦν τῶν ἐμῶν ἀποστέλ λοιμι πρὸς τὸν Ἰνδόν, συμπέμψαιτ' ἄν μοι τῶ ὑμετέρων οἵτινες αὐτῷ τήν τε ὁδὸν ἡγοῖντο ἂ καὶ συμπράττοιεν ὥστε γενέσθαι ἡμῖν παρὰ το Ἰνδοῦ ἃ ἐγὼ βούλομαι; ἐγὼ γὰρ χρήματα μὲ προσγενέσθαι ἔτι ἂν βουλοίμην ἡμῖν, ὅπως ἔχ καὶ μισθὸν ἀφθόνως διδόναι οἷς ἂν δέῃ καὶ τιμᾶ καὶ δωρεῖσθαι τῶν συστρατευομένων τοὺς ἀξίους τούτων δὴ ἕνεκα βούλομαι ὡς ἀφθονώτατ χρήματα ἔχειν, δεῖσθαι τούτων νομίζων. τῶ δὲ ὑμετέρων ἡδύ μοι ἀπέχεσθαι· φίλους γὰ ὑμᾶς ἤδη νομίζω· παρὰ δὲ τοῦ Ἰνδοῦ ἡδέως ἂ λάβοιμι, εἰ διδοίη.

29. Ὁ οὖν ἄγγελος, ᾧ κελεύω ὑμᾶς ἡγεμόνα δοῦναι καὶ συμπράκτορας γενέσθαι, ἐλθὼν ἐκεῖσ ὧδε λέξει· Ἔπεμψέ με Κῦρος, ὦ Ἰνδέ, πρὸς σέ φησὶ δὲ προσδεῖσθαι χρημάτων, προσδεχόμενο ἄλλην στρατιὰν οἴκοθεν ἐκ Περσῶν· (καὶ γὰ προσδέχομαι, ἔφη·) ἢν οὖν αὐτῷ πέμψῃς ὁπόσ σοι προχωρεῖ, φησίν, ἢν θεὸς ἀγαθὸν τέλος διδῷ[2] αὐτῷ, πειράσεσθαι ποιῆσαι ὥστε σε νομίζειν κα λῶς βεβουλεῦσθαι χαρισάμενον αὐτῷ. 30. ταῦτ μὲν ὁ παρ' ἐμοῦ λέξει. τοῖς δὲ παρ' ὑμῶν ὑμεῖς α ἐπιστέλλετε ὅ τι ὑμῖν σύμφορον δοκεῖ εἶναι. κα

[1] κατασκεψόμενοι Stephanus, Edd.; κατασκεψάμενοι MSS.
[2] διδῷ MSS., most Edd.; δῷ Hug after Weckherlin.

tatives from him had once come to Media to investigate conditions there and had then visited the enemy to inquire into theirs also, he wished to have him learn what he had done. 28 Accordingly, he began to speak as follows:

"King of Armenia," said he, "and you Chaldaeans, tell me—if I should now send one of my men to the Indian king, would you send along some of yours to conduct him on the way and to co-operate with him in getting what I want from the king of India? Now I should like to have more money, in order to be in a position both to pay generous wages when I ought, and to honour with rewards those of my fellow-soldiers who deserve it; and the reason why I wish to have as generous a supply of money as possible is that I expect to need it, and I shall be glad to spare yours; for I now count you among my friends; but from the Indian king I should be glad to accept a contribution, if he would offer it.

29. "Now, when the messenger, to whom I am asking you to furnish guides and co-workers, arrives there, he will speak on this wise: 'King of India, Cyrus has sent me to you; he says that he needs more funds, for he is expecting another army from his home in Persia'—and that is true," said he, "for I am expecting one—'if, therefore, you will send him as much as you conveniently can, he says that if God will give him good success, he will try to make you think that you were well advised in doing him this favour.' 30. This my envoy will say; do you now, in your turn, give your representatives such instructions as you think expedient for you. And if we get any-

ἢν μὲν λάβωμεν, ἔφη, παρ' αὐτοῦ, ἀφθονωτέροις χρησόμεθα· ἢν δὲ μὴ λάβωμεν, εἰσόμεθα ὅτι οὐδεμίαν αὐτῷ χάριν ὀφείλομεν, ἀλλ' ἐξέσται ἡμῖν ἐκείνου ἕνεκεν πρὸς τὸ ἡμέτερον συμφέρον πάντα τίθεσθαι.

31. Ταῦτ' εἶπεν ὁ Κῦρος, νομίζων τοὺς ἰόντας Ἀρμενίων καὶ Χαλδαίων τοιαῦτα λέξειν περὶ αὐτοῦ οἷα αὐτὸς ἐπεθύμει πάντας ἀνθρώπους καὶ λέγειν καὶ ἀκούειν περὶ αὐτοῦ. καὶ τότε μὲν δή, ὁπότε καλῶς εἶχε, διαλύσαντες τὴν σκηνὴν ἀνεπαύοντο.

III

1. Τῇ δ' ὑστεραίᾳ ὅ τε Κῦρος ἔπεμπε τὸν ἄγγελον ἐπιστείλας ὅσαπερ ἔφη καὶ ὁ Ἀρμένιος καὶ οἱ Χαλδαῖοι συνέπεμπον οὓς ἱκανωτάτους ἐνόμιζον εἶναι καὶ συμπρᾶξαι καὶ εἰπεῖν περὶ Κύρου τὰ προσήκοντα.

Ἐκ δὲ τούτου κατασκευάσας[1] ὁ Κῦρος τὸ φρούριον καὶ φύλαξιν ἱκανοῖς καὶ τοῖς ἐπιτηδείοις πᾶσι καὶ ἄρχοντ' αὐτῶν καταλιπὼν Μῆδον ὃν ᾤετο Κυαξάρῃ ἂν μάλιστα χαρίσασθαι, ἀπῄει συλλαβὼν τὸ στράτευμα ὅσον τε ἦλθεν ἔχων καὶ ὃ παρ' Ἀρμενίων προσέλαβε, καὶ τοὺς παρὰ Χαλδαίων εἰς τετρακισχιλίους, οἳ ᾤοντο καὶ συμπάντων τῶν ἄλλων κρείττονες εἶναι.

2. Ὡς δὲ κατέβη εἰς τὴν οἰκουμένην, οὐδεὶς ἔμεινεν ἔνδον Ἀρμενίων οὔτ' ἀνὴρ οὔτε γυνή,

[1] κατασκευάσας Poppo, most Edd.; παρασκευάσας z (*made ready*); ἐπιτελέσας xy (*completed*).

hing from him, we shall have more abundant funds o use; and if we do not, we shall know that we owe him no thanks, but may, as far as he is conerned, settle everything with a view to our own nterests."

31. Thus Cyrus spoke; and he believed that hose of the Armenians and Chaldaeans who were to go would say such things of him as he desired all nen to say and to hear of him. And then, when it vas time, the banquet came to an end, and they vent to rest.

III

1. On the following day Cyrus gave the envoy the commission of which he had spoken and sent him on his way; and the Armenian king and the Chaldaeans sent along those who they thought would be nost competent to co-operate and to say what was appropriate concerning Cyrus.

Cyrus's departure from Armenia

Then he manned the fort with a competent garrison, supplied it with all things necessary, and left in command a Mede who he thought would be most acceptable to Cyaxares; and then he departed, taking with him not only the army which he had brought with him but also the reinforcements that he had received from the Armenians, and about four thousand Chaldaeans, who considered themselves actually better than all the rest put together.

2. And when he came down into the inhabited part of the country, not one of the Armenians remained indoors, but all, both men and women, in

ἀλλὰ πάντες ὑπήντων ἡδόμενοι τῇ εἰρήνῃ καὶ φέροντες καὶ ἄγοντες ὅ τι ἕκαστος ἄξιον εἶχε. καὶ ὁ Ἀρμένιος τούτοις οὐκ ἤχθετο, οὕτως ἂν νομίζων καὶ τὸν Κῦρον μᾶλλον ἥδεσθαι τῇ ὑπὸ πάντων τιμῇ. τέλος δὲ ὑπήντησε καὶ ἡ γυνὴ τοῦ Ἀρμενίου, τὰς θυγατέρας ἔχουσα καὶ τὸν νεώτερον υἱόν, καὶ σὺν ἄλλοις δώροις τὸ χρυσίον ἐκόμιζεν ὃ πρότερον οὐκ ἤθελε λαβεῖν Κῦρος.

3. Καὶ ὁ Κῦρος ἰδὼν εἶπεν, Ὑμεῖς ἐμὲ οὐ ποιήσετε μισθοῦ περιιόντα εὐεργετεῖν, ἀλλὰ σύ, ὦ γύναι, ἔχουσα ταῦτα τὰ χρήματα ἃ φέρεις ἄπιθι, καὶ τῷ μὲν Ἀρμενίῳ μηκέτι δῷς αὐτὰ κατορύξαι, ἔκπεμψον δὲ τὸν υἱὸν ὡς κάλλιστα ἀπ' αὐτῶν[1] κατασκευάσασα ἐπὶ τὴν στρατιάν· ἀπὸ δὲ τῶν λοιπῶν κτῶ καὶ σαυτῇ καὶ τῷ ἀνδρὶ καὶ ταῖς θυγατράσι καὶ τοῖς υἱοῖς ὅ τι κεκτημένοι καὶ κοσμήσεσθε κάλλιον καὶ ἥδιον τὸν αἰῶνα διάξετε· εἰς δὲ τὴν γῆν, ἔφη, ἀρκείτω τὰ σώματα, ὅταν ἕκαστος τελευτήσῃ, κατακρύπτειν.

4. Ὁ μὲν ταῦτ' εἰπὼν παρήλαυνεν· ὁ δ' Ἀρμένιος συμπρούπεμπε καὶ οἱ ἄλλοι πάντες ἄνθρωποι, ἀνακαλοῦντες τὸν εὐεργέτην, τὸν ἄνδρα τὸν ἀγαθόν· καὶ τοῦτ' ἐποίουν, ἕως ἐκ τῆς χώρας ἀπῆν. συναπέστειλε δ' αὐτῷ ὁ Ἀρμένιος καὶ στρατιὰν πλείονα, ὡς εἰρήνης οἴκοι οὔσης.

5. Οὕτω δὴ[2] ὁ Κῦρος ἀπῄει κεχρηματισμένος οὐχ ἃ ἔλαβε μόνον χρήματα, ἀλλὰ πολὺ πλείονα τούτων ἡτοιμασμένος διὰ τὸν τρόπον, ὥστε λαμβάνειν ὁπότε δέοιτο.

[1] ἀπ' αὐτῶν zD, Edd.; ἁπάντων x; ἀπάντων F.
[2] δὴ MSS., most Edd.; δ' Hug.

their joy at the restoration of peace, came forth to meet him, each one carrying or bringing whatever he had of value. And their king did not disapprove, for he thought that Cyrus would thus be all the better pleased at receiving honour from all. And finally also the queen with her daughters and her younger son came up to him bringing not only the money which before Cyrus had refused to take, but other gifts as well.

3. And when he saw it Cyrus said: "You shall not make me go about doing good for pay! No, good queen; take back home with you this money which you bring; and do not give it to the king again to bury, but with it get your son as fine an outfit as possible and send him to the army; and with what is left get both for yourself and your husband, your daughters and your sons, anything the possession of which will enable you to adorn yourselves more handsomely and spend your days more happily. But let it suffice," he added, "to bury in the earth only our bodies, when the end shall come to each."

4. Thus he spoke and rode past her. And the king of Armenia escorted him on his way, as did all the rest of the people, proclaiming him again and again their benefactor, their valiant hero. And this they continued to do until he had quitted their borders. And as there was now peace at home, the king increased the contingent of troops that he sent with him.

5. Thus Cyrus departed, not only enriched with the ready money that he had received, but also having secured by his conduct far larger funds in reserve, to draw upon in time of need.

Καὶ τότε μὲν ἐστρατοπεδεύσατο ἐν τοῖς μεθορίοις. τῇ δ' ὑστεραίᾳ τὸ μὲν στράτευμα κα τὰ χρήματα ἔπεμψε πρὸς Κυαξάρην· ὁ δὲ πλησίον ἦν, ὥσπερ ἔφησεν· αὐτὸς δὲ σὺν Τιγράνῃ καὶ Περσῶν τοῖς ἀρίστοις ἐθήρα ὅπουπερ ἐπιτυγχάνοιεν θηρίοις καὶ ηὐφραίνετο.

6. Ἐπεὶ δ' ἀφίκετο εἰς Μήδους, τῶν χρημάτων ἔδωκε τοῖς αὑτοῦ ταξιάρχοις ὅσα ἐδόκει ἑκάστῳ ἱκανὰ εἶναι, ὅπως καὶ ἐκεῖνοι ἔχοιεν τιμᾶν, εἰ τινας ἄγαιντο τῶν ὑφ' ἑαυτούς· ἐνόμιζε γάρ, εἰ ἕκαστος τὸ μέρος ἀξιέπαινον ποιήσειε, τὸ ὅλον αὐτῷ καλῶς ἔχειν. καὶ αὐτὸς δὲ ὅ τι που καλὸν ἴδοι ὂν[1] εἰς στρατιάν, ταῦτα κτώμενος διεδωρεῖτο τοῖς ἀεὶ ἀξιωτάτοις, νομίζων ὅ τι καλὸν κἀγαθὸν ἔχοι τὸ στράτευμα, τούτοις ἅπασιν αὐτὸς κεκοσμῆσθαι.

7. Ἡνίκα δὲ αὐτοῖς διεδίδου ὧν ἔλαβεν, ἔλεξεν ὧδέ πως εἰς τὸ μέσον τῶν ταξιάρχων καὶ λοχαγῶν καὶ πάντων ὅσους ἐτίμα· Ἄνδρες φίλοι, δοκεῖ ἡμῖν εὐφροσύνη τις νῦν παρεῖναι, καὶ ὅτι εὐπορία τις προσγεγένηται καὶ ὅτι ἔχομεν ἀφ' ὧν τιμᾶν ἕξομεν οὓς ἂν βουλώμεθα καὶ τιμᾶσθαι ὡς ἂν ἕκαστος ἄξιος ᾖ. 8. πάντως δὴ ἀναμιμνῃσκώμεθα τὰ ποῖ' ἄττ' ἔργα τούτων τῶν ἀγαθῶν ἐστιν αἴτια· σκοπούμενοι γὰρ εὑρήσετε τό τε ἀγρυπνῆσαι ὅπου ἔδει καὶ τὸ πονῆσαι καὶ τὸ σπεῦσαι καὶ τὸ μὴ εἶξαι τοῖς πολεμίοις. οὕτως οὖν χρὴ

[1] ὂν Hug, Breitenbach ; not in MSS. or most Edd.

That night he encamped upon the frontier, and the next day he sent the army and the money to Cyaxares; for he was near by, as he had promised to be. But Cyrus himself went hunting with Tigranes and the best of his Persians, wherever they came across game, and he was delighted with the sport.

Rewards for the meritorious

6. Now when he came back to Media he gave to each of his captains as much of the money as he thought sufficient, so that they in turn might be able to reward any of the men under them with whose conduct they were pleased; for he thought that if each one made his division worthy of commendation, he would find the whole army in fine condition. And whenever he himself saw anywhere anything calculated to improve his army, he always procured it and distributed it in presents from time to time among the most deserving; for he thought that everything that his army had that was beautiful and fine was an adornment to himself.

7. And when he was about to distribute a portion of what he had received, he took his place in the midst of the captains, lieutenants, and all whom he was about to reward, and spoke to this effect: "My friends, there seems now to be a kind of gladness in our hearts, both because some degree of prosperity has come to us and because we have the means of rewarding those whom we will and of receiving rewards, each according to his deserts. 8. But let us be sure to remember to what kind of conduct these blessings are due; for if you will consider, you will find that it is this—watching when occasion demanded, undergoing toil, making due haste, and never yielding to the enemy. Accordingly, we must

καὶ τὸ λοιπὸν ἄνδρας ἀγαθοὺς εἶναι, γιγνώσκοντα
ὅτι τὰς μεγάλας ἡδονὰς καὶ τἀγαθὰ τὰ μεγάλ
ἡ πειθὼ καὶ ἡ καρτερία καὶ οἱ ἐν τῷ καιρῷ πόνο
καὶ κίνδυνοι παρέχονται.

9. Κατανοῶν δὲ ὁ Κῦρος ὡς εὖ μὲν αὐτῷ εἶχο
τὰ σώματα οἱ στρατιῶται πρὸς τὸ δύνασθα
στρατιωτικοὺς πόνους φέρειν, εὖ δὲ τὰς ψυχὰ
πρὸς τὸ καταφρονεῖν τῶν πολεμίων, ἐπιστήμονε
δ' ἦσαν τὰ προσήκοντα τῇ ἑαυτῶν ἕκαστοι ὁπλί
σει, καὶ πρὸς τὸ πείθεσθαι δὲ τοῖς ἄρχουσι
ἑώρα πάντας εὖ παρεσκευασμένους, ἐκ τούτω
οὖν ἐπεθύμει τι ἤδη τῶν πρὸς τοὺς πολεμίου
πράττειν, γιγνώσκων ὅτι ἐν τῷ μέλλειν πολλάκι
τοῖς ἄρχουσι καὶ τῆς καλῆς παρασκευῆς ἀλ
λοιοῦταί τι.

10. Ἔτι δ' ὁρῶν ὅτι φιλοτίμως ἔχοντες, ἐ
οἷς ἀντηγωνίζοντο, πολλοὶ καὶ ἐπιφθόνως εἶχο
πρὸς ἀλλήλους τῶν στρατιωτῶν, καὶ τούτων
ἕνεκα ἐξάγειν αὐτοὺς ἐβούλετο εἰς τὴν πολεμία
ὡς τάχιστα, εἰδὼς ὅτι οἱ κοινοὶ κίνδυνοι φιλο
φρόνως ποιοῦσιν ἔχειν τοὺς συμμάχους πρὸ
ἀλλήλους, καὶ οὐκέτι ἐν τούτῳ οὔτε τοῖς ἐ
ὅπλοις κοσμουμένοις φθονοῦσιν οὔτε τοῖς δόξη
ἐφιεμένοις, ἀλλὰ μᾶλλον καὶ ἐπαινοῦσι καὶ ἀσπά
ζονται οἱ τοιοῦτοι τοὺς ὁμοίους, νομίζοντες συν
εργοὺς αὐτοὺς τοῦ κοινοῦ ἀγαθοῦ εἶναι.

11. Οὕτω δὴ πρῶτον μὲν ἐξώπλισε τὴν στρα
τιὰν καὶ κατέταξεν ὡς ἐδύνατο κάλλιστά τε κα
ἄριστα, ἔπειτα δὲ συνεκάλεσε μυριάρχους κα
χιλιάρχους καὶ ταξιάρχους καὶ λοχαγούς. οὗτο

[1] τούτων Breitenbach, later Edd.; τῶνδε xy, Dindorf, Sauppe; τούτων δὲ z.

ı future also be brave men, knowing that obedience, erseverance, and the endurance of toil and danger t the critical time bring the great pleasures and the reat blessings."

9. Cyrus now saw that his soldiers were in good hysical condition to endure the fatigue of military ervice, that their hearts were disposed to regard the nemy with contempt, that they were skilled each in he exercise adapted to his kind of armour, and that hey were all well disciplined to obey the officers; ccordingly, he was eager to undertake some move gainst the enemy at once, for he knew that generals ften find some even of their best laid plans brought o naught through delay.

Cyrus thinks of invading the enemy's country

10. And he further observed that, because they vere so eager to excel in those exercises in which hey vied with one another, many of the soldiers vere even jealous of one another; for this reason lso he wished to lead them into the enemy's ountry as soon as possible. For he knew that ommon dangers make comrades kindly disposed oward one another, and that in the midst of such langers there is no jealousy of those who wear lecorations on their armour or of those who are triving for glory; on the contrary, soldiers praise nd love their fellows even more, because they ecognize in them co-workers for the common ;ood.

11. Accordingly, he first completely armed his orces and marshalled them in the best and most mposing order possible; then he called together the ;enerals, colonels, captains, and lieutenants; for

He rouses his army to take the offensive

γὰρ ἀπολελυμένοι ἦσαν τοῦ καταλέγεσθαι ἐν τοῖ
τακτικοῖς ἀριθμοῖς, καὶ ὁπότε δέοι ἢ ὑπακούει
τῷ στρατηγῷ ἢ παραγγέλλειν τι, οὐδ' ὣς οὐδὲ
ἄναρχον κατελείπετο, ἀλλὰ δωδεκαδάρχοις κα
ἐξαδάρχοις πάντα τὰ καταλειπόμενα διεκοσμεῖτο

12. Ἐπεὶ δὲ συνῆλθον οἱ ἐπικαίριοι, παράγων
αὐτοὺς ἐπεδείκνυ τε αὐτοῖς τὰ καλῶς ἔχοντα κα
ἐδίδασκεν ᾗ ἕκαστον ἰσχυρὸν ἦν τῶν συμμαχικῶν
ἐπεὶ δὲ κἀκείνους ἐποίησεν ἐρωτικῶς ἔχειν τοῦ ἤδ
ποιεῖν τι, εἶπεν αὐτοῖς νῦν μὲν ἀπιέναι ἐπὶ τὰ
τάξεις καὶ διδάσκειν ἕκαστον τοὺς ἑαυτοῦ ἅπε
αὐτὸς ἐκείνους, καὶ πειρᾶσθαι αὐτοὺς ἐπιθυμία
ἐμβαλεῖν πᾶσι τοῦ στρατεύεσθαι, ὅπως εὐθυμό
τατα πάντες ἐξορμῷντο, πρῲ δὲ παρεῖναι ἐπὶ τὰ
Κυαξάρου θύρας. 13. τότε μὲν δὴ ἀπιόντες οὕτ
πάντες ἐποίουν. τῇ δ' ὑστεραίᾳ ἅμα τῇ ἡμέρ
παρῆσαν οἱ ἐπικαίριοι ἐπὶ θύραις. σὺν τούτοι
οὖν ὁ Κῦρος εἰσελθὼν πρὸς τὸν Κυαξάρην ἤρχετ
λόγου τοιοῦδε·

Οἶδα μέν, ἔφη, ὦ Κυαξάρη, ὅτι ἃ μέλλω λέγει
σοὶ πάλαι δοκεῖ οὐδὲν ἧττον ἢ ἡμῖν· ἀλλ' ἴσω
αἰσχύνει λέγειν αὐτά, μὴ δοκῇς ἀχθόμενος ὅτ
τρέφεις ἡμᾶς ἐξόδου μεμνῆσθαι. 14. ἐπεὶ οὖν σ
σιωπᾷς, ἐγὼ λέξω καὶ ὑπὲρ σοῦ καὶ ὑπὲρ ἡμῶν

[1] οἱ ἐπικαίριοι are literally "the most timely," "the mos
important," "the chief officers." It is consistently rendere
by "staff-officers" in this translation, though the word ma

hese had been exempted from enrolment in the ines of the regular battalions; and even when it vas necessary for any of them to report to the commander-in-chief or to transmit any order, no part of he army was left without a commanding officer, for he sergeants and corporals kept in proper order the livisions from which the superior officers had gone.

12. And when the staff-officers[1] had come together, e conducted them along the ranks, showed them in vhat good order everything was and pointed out to hem the special strength of each contingent of the uxiliaries. And when he had filled them with an ager desire for immediate action, he bade them hen go to their own several divisions and tell their nen what he had told them and try to inspire in hem all a desire to begin the campaign, for he vished them all to start out in the best of spirits; nd early in the morning they were to meet him at Cyaxares's gates. 13. Thereupon they all went their way and proceeded so to do. At daybreak on the following day the staff-officers presented themselves at the gates of the king. So Cyrus went in with them to Cyaxares and began to speak as follows:

He lays his plan before Cyaxares

"I am sure, Cyaxares," said he, "that you have this long time been thinking no less than we of the proposition that I am going to lay before you; but perhaps you hesitate to broach the subject for fear it should be thought that you speak of an expedition from here because you are embarrassed at having to maintain us. 14. Therefore, since you do not say anything, I will speak both for you and for ourselves.

be applied to all who are in authority, whether military or civil.

ἡμῖν γὰρ δοκεῖ πᾶσιν, ἐπείπερ παρεσκευάσμεθα, μὴ ἐπειδὰν ἐμβάλωσιν οἱ πολέμιοι εἰς τὴν σὴν χώραν, τότε μάχεσθαι, μηδ' ἐν τῇ φιλίᾳ καθημένους ἡμᾶς ὑπομένειν, ἀλλ' ἰέναι ὡς τάχιστα εἰς τὴν πολεμίαν. 15. νῦν μὲν γὰρ ἐν τῇ σῇ χώρᾳ ὄντες πολλὰ τῶν σῶν σινόμεθα ἄκοντες· ἢν δ' εἰς τὴν πολεμίαν ἴωμεν, τὰ ἐκείνων κακῶς ποιήσομεν ἡδόμενοι.

16. Ἔπειτα νῦν μὲν σὺ ἡμᾶς τρέφεις πολλὰ δαπανῶν, ἢν δ' ἐκστρατευσώμεθα, θρεψόμεθα ἐκ τῆς πολεμίας. 17. ἔτι δὲ εἰ μὲν μείζων τις ἡμῖν ὁ κίνδυνος ἔμελλεν εἶναι ἐκεῖ ἢ ἐνθάδε, ἴσως τὸ ἀσφαλέστατον ἦν αἱρετέον. νῦν δὲ ἴσοι μὲν ἐκεῖνοι ἔσονται, ἤν τε ἐνθάδε ὑπομένωμεν ἤν τε εἰς τὴν ἐκείνων ἰόντες ὑπαντῶμεν αὐτοῖς· ἴσοι δὲ ἡμεῖς ὄντες μαχούμεθα, ἤν τε ἐνθάδε ἐπιόντας αὐτοὺς δεχώμεθα ἤν τε ἐπ' ἐκείνους ἰόντες τὴν μάχην συνάπτωμεν. 18. πολὺ μέντοι ἡμεῖς βελτίοσι καὶ ἐρρωμενεστέραις ταῖς ψυχαῖς τῶν στρατιωτῶν χρησόμεθα, ἢν ἴωμεν ἐπὶ τοὺς ἐχθροὺς καὶ μὴ ἄκοντες ὁρᾶν δοκῶμεν τοὺς πολεμίους· πολὺ δὲ κἀκεῖνοι μᾶλλον ἡμᾶς φοβήσονται, ὅταν ἀκούσωσιν ὅτι οὐ φοβούμενοι πτήσσομεν αὐτοὺς οἴκοι καθήμενοι, ἀλλ' ἐπεὶ αἰσθανόμεθα προσιόντας, ἀπαντῶμέν τε αὐτοῖς, ἵν' ὡς τάχιστα συμμίξωμεν, καὶ οὐκ ἀναμένομεν ἕως ἂν ἡ ἡμετέρα χώρα κακῶται, ἀλλὰ φθάνοντες ἤδη δῃοῦμεν τὴν ἐκείνων γῆν. 19. καίτοι, ἔφη, εἴ τι ἐκείνους μὲν φοβερωτέρους ποιήσομεν, ἡμᾶς δ' αὐτοὺς θαρραλεωτέρους, πολὺ τοῦτο ἡμῖν ἐγὼ πλεονέκτημα νομίζω, καὶ τὸν κίνδυνον οὕτως ἡμῖν μὲν ἐλάττω λογίζομαι, τοῖς δὲ πολεμίοις μείζω. πολὺ γὰρ μᾶλλον, καὶ ὁ

Ve are all agreed that, inasmuch as we are quite eady, it is best not to sit down here in a friendly ountry and wait till the enemy have invaded your erritory before we begin to fight, but to go as uickly as possible into the enemy's country. 5. For now, while we are in your country, we do our people's property much injury quite against our vill; but if we go into the enemy's country, we hall do injury to theirs with all our hearts.

16. "In the second place, you support us now at reat expense; whereas, if we take the field, we hall get our support from the enemy's country. 17. And then again, if we were likely to be in any greater langer there than here, we should, perhaps, have to hoose the safer course. But their numbers will be he same, whether we wait here or whether we go nd meet them in their own territory. And our umbers in the fight will be just the same, whether ve engage them as they come hither or whether we go against them to join battle. 18. We shall, however, find the courage of our soldiers much better and tronger, if we assume the offensive and show that we are not unwilling to face the foe; and they will oe much more afraid of us, when they hear that we lo not sit down at home and cower in fear of them, out that, when we hear that they are coming, we dvance to meet them to join battle as soon as possible, and do not wait until our country is ravaged, but take the initiative and devastate theirs. 19. And surely," he added, "if we make them more afraid and ourselves more courageous, I think it would be a great gain to us and it would, as I reckon it, lessen the danger under such circumstances for us and increase it for the enemy. And my father

πατὴρ ἀεὶ λέγει καὶ σὺ φῂς καὶ οἱ ἄλλοι δὲ πάντες ὁμολογοῦσιν, ὡς αἱ μάχαι κρίνονται μᾶλλο
ταῖς ψυχαῖς ἢ ταῖς τῶν σωμάτων ῥώμαις.

20. Ὁ μὲν οὕτως εἶπε· Κυαξάρης δὲ ἀπεκρίνατο, Ἀλλ' ὅπως μέν, ὦ Κῦρε καὶ οἱ ἄλλο
Πέρσαι, ἐγὼ ἄχθομαι ὑμᾶς τρέφων μηδ' ὑπονοεῖτε
τό γε μέντοι ἰέναι εἰς τὴν πολεμίαν ἤδη καὶ ἐμο
δοκεῖ βέλτιον εἶναι πρὸς πάντα.

Ἐπεὶ τοίνυν, ἔφη ὁ Κῦρος, ὁμογνωμονοῦμεν
συσκευαζώμεθα καὶ ἢν τὰ τῶν θεῶν ἡμῖν θᾶττο
συγκαταινῇ, ἐξίωμεν ὡς τάχιστα.

21. Ἐκ τούτου τοῖς μὲν στρατιώταις εἶπον συ-
σκευάζεσθαι· ὁ δὲ Κῦρος ἔθυε πρῶτον μὲν Δι
βασιλεῖ, ἔπειτα δὲ καὶ τοῖς ἄλλοις θεοῖς, οὓ
ᾐτεῖτο ἵλεως καὶ εὐμενεῖς ὄντας ἡγεμόνας γενέσθα
τῇ στρατιᾷ καὶ παραστάτας ἀγαθοὺς καὶ συμμάχους καὶ συμβούλους τῶν ἀγαθῶν. 22. συμ-
παρεκάλει δὲ καὶ ἥρωας γῆς Μηδίας οἰκήτορα
καὶ κηδεμόνας.

Ἐπεὶ δ' ἐκαλλιέρησέ τε καὶ ἀθρόον ἦν αὐτῷ τ
στράτευμα πρὸς τοῖς ὁρίοις, τότε δὴ οἰωνοῖς χρη-
σάμενος αἰσίοις ἐνέβαλεν εἰς τὴν πολεμίαν. ἐπε
δὲ τάχιστα διέβη τὰ ὅρια, ἐκεῖ αὖ καὶ Γῆν ἱλά-
σκετο χοαῖς καὶ θεοὺς θυσίαις καὶ ἥρωας Ἀσ-
συρίας οἰκήτορας ηὐμενίζετο. ταῦτα δὲ ποιήσα
αὖθις Διὶ πατρῴῳ ἔθυε, καὶ εἴ τις ἄλλος θεῶν ἀνε-
φαίνετο, οὐδενὸς ἠμέλει.

23. Ἐπεὶ δὲ καλῶς ταῦτα εἶχεν, εὐθὺς τοὺς μὲ
πεζοὺς προαγαγόντες οὐ πολλὴν ὁδὸν ἐστρατο

always says, and so do you, and all the rest agree, that battles are decided more by men's souls than by the strength of their bodies."

20. Thus he spoke; and Cyaxares answered: "Do not let yourselves imagine, Cyrus and the rest of you Persians, that I am embarrassed at having to support you. As for invading the enemy's country at once, however, I too consider that the better plan from every point of view."

Cyaxares approves

"Well then," said Cyrus, "since we are agreed, let us make ready and, as soon as ever the gods give us their sanction, let us march out without a moment's delay."

21. Hereupon they gave the soldiers the word to make ready to break camp. And Cyrus proceeded to sacrifice first to Sovereign Zeus and then to the rest of the gods; and he besought them to lead his army with their grace and favour and to be their mighty defenders and helpers and counsellors for the common good. 22. And he called also upon the heroes who dwelt in Media and were its guardians.

And when the sacrifice was found to be favourable and his army was assembled at the frontier, then amid favourable auspices he crossed into the enemy's country. And as soon as he had crossed the boundary, there again he made propitiatory offerings to Earth with libations and sought with sacrifices to win the favour of the gods and heroes that dwelt in Assyria. And when he had done this he sacrificed again to Zeus, the god of his fathers; and of the other divinities that were brought to his attention he neglected not one.

Cyrus invades Assyria

23. And when these rites were duly performed, they at once led the infantry forward a short distance

πεδεύοντο, τοῖς δ' ἵπποις καταδρομὴν ποιησάμενο περιεβάλοντο πολλὴν καὶ παντοίαν λείαν. κα τὸ λοιπὸν δὲ μεταστρατοπεδευόμενοι καὶ ἔχοντε ἄφθονα τἀπιτήδεια καὶ δῃοῦντες τὴν χώραν ἀνέ μενον τοὺς πολεμίους.

24. Ἡνίκα δὲ προσιόντες ἐλέγοντο οὐκέτι δέχ ἡμερῶν ὁδὸν ἀπέχειν, τότε δὴ ὁ Κῦρος λέγει, Ὦ Κυαξάρη, ὥρα δὴ ἀπαντᾶν καὶ μήτε τοῖς πολε μίοις δοκεῖν μήτε τοῖς ἡμετέροις φοβουμένους μὴ ἀντιπροσιέναι, ἀλλὰ δῆλοι ὦμεν ὅτι οὐκ ἄκοντες μαχούμεθα.

25. Ἐπεὶ δὲ ταῦτα συνέδοξε τῷ Κυαξάρῃ, οὕτω δὴ συντεταγμένοι προῇσαν τοσοῦτον καθ' ἡμέραν ὅσον ἐδόκει αὐτοῖς καλῶς ἔχειν. καὶ δεῖπνον μὲν ἀεὶ κατὰ φῶς ἐποιοῦντο, πυρὰ δὲ νύκτωρ οὐκ ἔκαον ἐν τῷ στρατοπέδῳ· ἔμπροσθεν μέντοι τοῦ στρατοπέδου ἔκαον, ὅπως ὁρῷεν μὲν εἴ τινες νυκτὸς προσίοιεν διὰ τὸ πῦρ, μὴ ὁρῷντο δ' ὑπὸ τῶν προσιόντων. πολλάκις δὲ καὶ ὄπισθεν τοῦ στρατοπέδου ἐπυρπόλουν ἀπάτης ἕνεκα τῶν πολεμίων. ὥστ' ἔστιν ὅτε καὶ κατάσκοποι ἐνέπιπτον εἰς τὰς προφυλακὰς αὐτῶν, διὰ τὸ ὄπισθεν τὰ πυρὰ εἶναι ἔτι πρόσω[1] τοῦ στρατοπέδου οἰόμενοι εἶναι.

26. Οἱ μὲν οὖν Ἀσσύριοι καὶ οἱ σὺν αὐτοῖς, ἐπεὶ ἤδη ἐγγὺς ἀλλήλων τὰ στρατεύματα ἐγίγνετο, τάφρον περιεβάλοντο, ὅπερ καὶ νῦν ἔτι ποιοῦσιν οἱ βάρβαροι βασιλεῖς, ὅπου ἂν στρατοπεδεύωνται, τάφρον περιβάλλονται εὐπετῶς διὰ τὴν πολυχειρίαν· ἴσασι γὰρ ὅτι ἱππικὸν στρά-

[1] πρόσω z, Dindorf, Breitenbach, Marchant; πόρρω xy, Gemoll (*far from*).

nd pitched camp, while with the cavalry they made . raid and got possession of a large quantity of every ort of booty. And thenceforward they shifted heir camp from time to time, kept provisions upplied in abundance, and ravaged the country, vhile they awaited the enemy's approach.

24. And when rumours came that the enemy were dvancing and no longer ten days' march away, hen Cyrus said: "Now, Cyaxares, is the time for us o go to meet them and not to let either the enemy r our own men suppose that we fail to advance gainst them out of fear, but let us make it clear that ve are not going to fight against our will."

Cyrus and Cyaxares advance to meet the foe

25. As Cyaxares agreed to this, they advanced n battle order each day as far as they thought roper. Their dinner they always prepared by lay-light, and at night they never lighted a fire in amp. They did, however, keep fires burning in ront of the camp, in order that if any one approached n the dark, they might see him by the light of the ire but not be seen. And frequently also they kept ires burning in the rear of the camp for the purpose f deceiving the enemy; and so sometimes the nemy's scouts fell into the hands of the pickets; or because the fires were behind, they supposed hemselves to be still far in front of the camp.

A barbarian encampment

26. Then, when the two armies were near each ther, the Assyrians and their allies drew a ditch round their camp, as even to this day the barbarian ings do whenever they go into camp; and they hrow up such entrenchments with ease because of the nultitude of hands at their command. They take his precaution because they know that cavalry

τευμα ἐν νυκτὶ ταραχῶδές ἐστι καὶ δύσχρηστ
ἄλλως τε καὶ βάρβαρον. 27. πεποδισμένους γα
ἔχουσι τοὺς ἵππους ἐπὶ ταῖς φάτναις, καὶ εἴ τ
ἐπ' αὐτοὺς ἴοι, ἔργον μὲν νυκτὸς λῦσαι ἵππου
ἔργον δὲ χαλινῶσαι, ἔργον δ' ἐπισάξαι, ἔργον
θωρακίσασθαι, ἀναβάντας δ' ἐφ' ἵππων ἐλάσ
διὰ στρατοπέδου παντάπασιν ἀδύνατον. τούτ
δὴ ἕνεκα πάντων καὶ οἱ ἄλλοι καὶ ἐκεῖνοι τὰ ἐρ
ματα περιβάλλονται, καὶ ἅμα αὐτοῖς δοκεῖ τὸ
ἐχυρῷ εἶναι ἐξουσίαν παρέχειν ὅταν βούλωντ
μάχεσθαι.

28. Τοιαῦτα μὲν δὴ ποιοῦντες ἐγγὺς ἀλλήλα
ἐγίγνοντο. ἐπεὶ δὲ προσιόντες ἀπεῖχον ὅσ
παρασάγγην, οἱ μὲν Ἀσσύριοι οὕτως ἐστρατ
πεδεύοντο ὥσπερ εἴρηται, ἐν περιτεταφρευμέν
μὲν καταφανεῖ δέ, ὁ δὲ Κῦρος ὡς ἐδύνατο
ἀφανεστάτῳ, κώμας τε καὶ γηλόφους ἐπίπροσθ
ποιησάμενος, νομίζων πάντα τὰ πολέμια ἐξαί
νης ὁρώμενα φοβερώτερα τοῖς ἐναντίοις εἶνα
καὶ ἐκείνην μὲν τὴν νύκτα ὥσπερ ἔπρεπε προφ
λακὰς ποιησάμενοι ἑκάτεροι ἐκοιμήθησαν.

29. Τῇ δ' ὑστεραίᾳ ὁ μὲν Ἀσσύριος καὶ
Κροῖσος καὶ οἱ ἄλλοι ἡγεμόνες ἀνέπαυον τ
στρατεύματα ἐν τῷ ἐχυρῷ· Κῦρος δὲ καὶ Κυα
ξάρης συνταξάμενοι περιέμενον, ὡς εἰ προσίοιε
οἱ πολέμιοι, μαχούμενοι. ὡς δὲ δῆλον ἐγένετ
ὅτι οὐκ ἐξίοιεν οἱ πολέμιοι ἐκ τοῦ ἐρύματο
οὐδὲ μάχην ποιήσοιντο ἐν ταύτῃ τῇ ἡμέρᾳ
ὁ μὲν Κυαξάρης καλέσας τὸν Κῦρον καὶ τῶ
ἄλλων τοὺς ἐπικαιρίους ἔλεξε τοιάδε· 30. Δοκ
μοι, ἔφη, ὦ ἄνδρες, ὥσπερ τυγχάνομεν συντε

troops—especially barbarian cavalry—are at night prone to confusion and hard to manage. 27. For they keep their horses hobbled at the mangers, and if any enemy should make an attack, it is a difficult task to loose the horses in the darkness, it is difficult to bridle them, difficult to saddle them, difficult to put on a coat of mail, and utterly impossible to mount and ride through camp. For all these reasons and also because they think that if they are behind fortifications they are in a position to choose their time for fighting, the Assyrians and the rest of the barbarians throw up breastworks.

28. With such tactics the armies were approaching each other; but when, as they advanced, they were only about a parasang apart, the Assyrians encamped in the manner described in a place surrounded, indeed, by a ditch, but open to view. Cyrus, on the other hand, encamped in a place as much out of sight as possible, keeping under cover behind the hills and villages, for he thought that if all one's equipment for war flashes suddenly into view, it inspires more terror in the enemy. And that night each side stationed advance guards, as was proper, and went to rest.

Cyrus and Cyaxares await an attack

29. And on the following day the Assyrian king and Croesus and the other commanders let their troops rest within the entrenchments; but Cyrus and Cyaxares awaited them in battle array, ready to fight if the enemy should come on. But when it was evident that the enemy would not come out from behind their breastworks nor accept battle that day, Cyaxares called Cyrus and the staff officers besides and spoke as follows: 30. "Men," said he, "I propose to march up to those fellows' breast-

ταγμένοι οὕτως ἰέναι πρὸς τὸ ἔρυμα τῶν ἀνδρῶν καὶ δηλοῦν ὅτι θέλομεν μάχεσθαι. οὕτω γάρ, ἔφη, ἐὰν μὴ ἀντεπεξίωσιν ἐκεῖνοι, οἱ μὲν ἡμέτεροι μᾶλλον θαρρήσαντες ἀπίασιν, οἱ πολέμιοι δὲ τὴν τόλμαν ἰδόντες ἡμῶν μᾶλλον φοβήσονται.[1]

31. Τούτῳ μὲν οὕτως ἐδόκει. ὁ δὲ Κῦρος, Μηδαμῶς, ἔφη, πρὸς τῶν θεῶν, ὦ Κυαξάρη, οὕτω ποιήσωμεν. εἰ γὰρ ἤδη ἐκφανέντες πορευσόμεθα, ὡς σὺ κελεύεις, νῦν τε προσιόντας ἡμᾶς οἱ πολέμιοι θεάσονται οὐδὲν φοβούμενοι, εἰδότες ὅτι ἐν ἀσφαλεῖ εἰσι τοῦ μηδὲν παθεῖν, ἐπειδάν τε μηδὲν ποιήσαντες ἀπίωμεν, πάλιν καθορῶντες ἡμῶν τὸ πλῆθος πολὺ ἐνδεέστερον τοῦ ἑαυτῶν καταφρονήσουσι, καὶ αὔριον ἐξίασι πολὺ ἐρρωμενεστέραις ταῖς γνώμαις. 32. νῦν δ', ἔφη, εἰδότες μὲν ὅτι πάρεσμεν, οὐχ ὁρῶντες δὲ ἡμᾶς, εὖ τοῦτο ἐπίστω, οὐ καταφρονοῦσιν, ἀλλὰ φροντίζουσι τί ποτε τοῦτ' ἔστι, καὶ διαλεγόμενοι περὶ ἡμῶν ἐγᾦδ' ὅτι οὐδὲν παύονται. ὅταν δ' ἐξίωσι, τότε δεῖ αὐτοῖς ἅμα φανερούς τε ἡμᾶς γενέσθαι καὶ ἰέναι εὐθὺς ὁμόσε, εἰληφότας αὐτοὺς ἔνθα πάλαι ἐβουλόμεθα.

33. Λέξαντος δ' οὕτω Κύρου συνέδοξε ταῦτα καὶ Κυαξάρῃ καὶ τοῖς ἄλλοις. καὶ τότε μὲν δειπνοποιησάμενοι καὶ φυλακὰς καταστησάμενοι καὶ πυρὰ πολλὰ πρὸς τῶν φυλακῶν καύσαντες ἐκοιμήθησαν.

34. Τῇ δ' ὑστεραίᾳ πρῲ Κῦρος μὲν ἐστεφανωμένος ἔθυε, παρήγγειλε δὲ καὶ τοῖς ἄλλοις ὁμοτίμοις ἐστεφανωμένοις πρὸς τὰ ἱερὰ παρεῖναι.

[1] φοβήσονται Dindorf, most Edd.; φοβηθήσονται MSS., Sauppe.

works, drawn up just as we are now, and show them that we are eager to fight. For," said he, "if we do that and they do not come out against us, our men will come back to camp more full of courage, and the enemy seeing our daring will be more frightened."

31. Such was his proposal. But Cyrus said: "No, by the gods, Cyaxares, let us not do that; never! For if we march out and show ourselves, as you suggest, the enemy will see us marching up but will have no fear, for they know that they are secure against any injury; and when we withdraw without having accomplished anything, they will furthermore see that our numbers are inferior to their own and despise us; and to-morrow they will come out with much stouter hearts. 32. But as matters stand now," said he, "as they know that we are here but do not see us, you may be sure that they do not despise us but inquire anxiously what in the world this means, and I am positive that they are talking about us all the time. But when they come out, then we must show ourselves and at once engage them hand to hand, when we shall have them where we have long since been wishing to have them."

33. When Cyrus had thus spoken, Cyaxares and the rest agreed with him. And then, when they had dined and stationed their sentinels and lighted many fires in front of the outposts, they went to rest.

Cyrus offers sacrifice and exhorts the peers

34. Early on the following day Cyrus crowned himself with a garland and prepared to sacrifice, and sent word to the rest of the peers to attend the

ἐπεὶ δὲ τέλος εἶχεν ἡ θυσία, συγκαλέσας αὐτοὺς ἔλεξεν· Ἄνδρες, οἱ μὲν θεοί, ὡς οἵ τε μάντεις φασὶ καὶ ἐμοὶ συνδοκεῖ, μάχην τ' ἔσεσθαι προαγγέλλουσι καὶ νίκην διδόασι καὶ σωτηρίαν ὑπισχνοῦνται ἐν τοῖς ἱεροῖς. 35. ἐγὼ δὲ ὑμῖν μὲν παραινῶν ποίους τινὰς χρὴ εἶναι ἐν τῷ τοιῷδε κἂν αἰσχυνοίμην ἄν· οἶδα γὰρ ὑμᾶς ταῦτα ἐπισταμένους καὶ μεμελετηκότας καὶ ἀκούοντας διὰ τέλους [οἷάπερ ἐγώ],[1] ὥστε κἂν ἄλλους εἰκότως ἂν διδάσκοιτε. τάδε δὲ εἰ μὴ τυγχάνετε κατανενοηκότες, ἀκούσατε·

36. Οὓς γὰρ νεωστὶ συμμάχους τε ἔχομεν καὶ πειρώμεθα ἡμῖν αὐτοῖς ὁμοίους ποιεῖν, τούτους δὲ ἡμᾶς δεῖ ὑπομιμνήσκειν ἐφ' οἷς τε ἐτρεφόμεθα ὑπὸ Κυαξάρου, ἅ τε ἠσκοῦμεν, ἐφ' ἅ τε αὐτοὺς παρακεκλήκαμεν, ὧν τε[2] ἄσμενοι ἀνταγωνισταὶ ἔφασαν ἡμῖν ἔσεσθαι. 37. καὶ τοῦτο δ' αὐτοὺς ὑπομιμνήσκετε ὅτι ἥδε ἡ ἡμέρα δείξει ὧν ἕκαστός ἐστιν ἄξιος. ὧν γὰρ ἂν ὀψιμαθεῖς ἄνθρωποι γένωνται, οὐδὲν θαυμαστὸν εἴ τινες αὐτῶν καὶ τοῦ ὑπομιμνήσκοντος δέοιντο, ἀλλ' ἀγαπητὸν εἰ καὶ ἐξ ὑποβολῆς δύναιντο ἄνδρες ἀγαθοὶ εἶναι. 38. καὶ ταῦτα μέντοι πράττοντες ἅμα καὶ ὑμῶν αὐτῶν πεῖραν λήψεσθε. ὁ μὲν γὰρ δυνάμενος ἐν τῷ τοιῷδε καὶ ἄλλους βελτίους ποιεῖν εἰκότως ἂν ἤδη καὶ ἑαυτῷ συνειδείη τελέως ἀγαθὸς ἀνὴρ ὤν, ὁ δὲ τὴν τούτων ὑπόμνησιν αὐτὸς μόνος ἔχων καὶ τοῦτ' ἀγαπῶν,

[1] οἷάπερ ἐγώ z, Dindorf, Marchant; ἅπερ ἐγώ y, Gemoll; ὥσπερ ἐγώ x; omitted by Pantazides; bracketed by Hug Breitenbach.

[2] ὧν τε Schneider, Edd.; ὥστε xy; παρακεκλημένων τε z.

service with chaplets on their heads. And when the sacrifice was concluded, Cyrus called them together and said: "Men, the gods announce, as the soothsayers say and also as I interpret it, that there is to be a battle; through the omens of the sacrifice they grant us victory and promise us no loss. 35. Now I should be ashamed indeed to suggest to you how you ought to conduct yourselves at such a time; for I know that you understand what you have to do, that you have practised it, and have been continually hearing of it just as I have, so that you might properly even teach others. But if you happen not to have had this other matter called to your attention, listen.

36. "Those whom we recently took as our comrades and whom we are trying to make like ourselves—these men we must remind of the conditions on which we have been maintained by Cyaxares, what we have been in training for, why we have invited them to join us, and what it is in which they said they would gladly be our rivals. 37. And remind them also that this day will prove what each one is worth. For when people are late in learning anything, it is not surprising that some of them actually need a monitor; and we may be content if they manage even with the help of a suggestion to prove themselves valiant. 38. And in doing this, you will at the same time be getting a proof of yourselves also. For he who on such an occasion can make others more valiant would naturally also gain the consciousness that he is himself a thoroughly valiant man; he, on the other hand, who keeps all to himself the admonition to such conduct and rests satisfied with

εἰκότως ἂν ἡμιτελῆ αὐτὸν[1] νομίζοι. 39. τούτου δ' ἕνεκα οὐκ ἐγώ, ἔφη, αὐτοῖς λέγω, ἀλλ' ὑμᾶς κελεύω λέγειν, ἵνα καὶ ἀρέσκειν ὑμῖν πειρῶνται· ὑμεῖς γὰρ καὶ πλησιάζετε αὐτοῖς ἕκαστος τῷ ἑαυτοῦ μέρει. εὖ δ' ἐπίστασθε ὡς ἢν θαρροῦντας τούτοις ὑμᾶς αὐτοὺς ἐπιδεικνύητε, καὶ τούτους καὶ ἄλλους πολλοὺς οὐ λόγῳ ἀλλ' ἔργῳ θαρρεῖν διδάξετε. 40. τέλος εἶπεν ἀπιόντας ἀριστᾶν ἐστεφανωμένους καὶ σπονδὰς ποιησαμένους ἥκειν εἰς τὰς τάξεις αὐτοῖς στεφάνοις.

Ἐπεὶ δ' ἀπῆλθον, αὖθις τοὺς οὐραγοὺς προσεκάλεσε, καὶ τούτοις τοιάδε ἐνετέλλετο· 41. Ἄνδρες Πέρσαι, ὑμεῖς καὶ τῶν ὁμοτίμων γεγόνατε καὶ ἐπιλελεγμένοι ἐστέ, οἳ δοκεῖτε τὰ μὲν ἄλλα τοῖς κρατίστοις ὅμοιοι εἶναι, τῇ δ' ἡλικίᾳ καὶ φρονιμώτεροι. καὶ τοίνυν χώραν ἔχετε οὐδὲν ἧττον ἔντιμον τῶν πρωτοστατῶν·[2] ὑμεῖς γὰρ ὄπισθεν ὄντες τούς τ' ἀγαθοὺς ἂν ἐφορῶντες καὶ ἐπικελεύοντες αὐτοῖς ἔτι κρείττους ποιοῖτε, καὶ εἴ τις μαλακίζοιτο, καὶ τοῦτον ὁρῶντες οὐκ ἂν ἐπιτρέποιτε αὐτῷ. 42. συμφέρει δ' ὑμῖν, εἴπερ τῳ καὶ ἄλλῳ, τὸ νικᾶν καὶ διὰ τὴν ἡλικίαν καὶ διὰ τὸ βάρος τῆς στολῆς. ἢν δ' ἄρα ὑμᾶς καὶ οἱ ἔμπροσθεν ἀνακαλοῦντες ἕπεσθαι παρεγγυῶσιν, ὑπακούετε αὐτοῖς, καὶ ὅπως μηδ' ἐν τούτῳ αὐτῶν ἡττηθήσεσθε, ἀντιπαρακελευόμενοι αὐτοῖς θᾶττον ἡγεῖσθαι[3] ἐπὶ τοὺς πολεμίους.

[1] αὐτὸν Edd. ; αὑτὸν MSS.
[2] πρωτοστατῶν Dindorf, later Edd. ; προστατῶν MSS.
[3] ἡγεῖσθαι Stephanus, Edd.; ἡγεῖσθε MSS.

hat might properly consider himself but half valiant. 9. The reason why I do not speak to them but bid ou do so is that so they may try to please you, for ou are in touch with them, each in his own division. nd remember this, that if in their eyes you prove ourselves courageous, you will teach not only your omrades but many others also, not by precept erely but by example, to be courageous." 40. In oncluding, he told them to go with their chaplets n and take luncheon and when they had poured he libation to go, still wearing the chaplets, to their osts.

He exhorts also the rear-guard officers

And when they had gone away, he called in the fficers of the rear-guard and gave them the following instructions: 41. "Men of Persia, you also ave now taken your places among the peers, and ou have been selected for your positions because ou are considered in every way equal to the bravest, nd by virtue of your years even more discreet than hey. And so you occupy a place not at all less onourable than that of our front-rank men. For s you are behind, you can observe those who are aliant and by exhorting them make them still more aliant; and if any one should be inclined to hang ack and you should see it, you would not permit it. 2. And because of your years and because of the eight of your armour it is more to your advantage han to any others' that we should be victorious. nd if those in front call to you and bid you follow, bey them and see that you be not outdone by them ven in this respect but give them a counter cheer o lead on faster against the enemy. Now go and

καὶ ἀπιόντες, ἔφη, ἀριστήσαντες καὶ ὑμεῖς ἥκετ
σὺν τοῖς ἄλλοις ἐστεφανωμένοι εἰς τὰς τάξεις.

43. Οἱ μὲν δὴ ἀμφὶ Κῦρον ἐν τούτοις ἦσα
οἱ δὲ Ἀσσύριοι καὶ δὴ ἠριστηκότες ἐξῆσάν τ
θρασέως καὶ παρετάττοντο ἐρρωμένως. παρέταττ
δὲ αὐτοὺς αὐτὸς ὁ βασιλεὺς ἐφ' ἅρματος παρε
λαύνων καὶ τοιάδε παρεκελεύετο· 44. Ἄνδρε
Ἀσσύριοι, νῦν δεῖ ἄνδρας ἀγαθοὺς εἶναι· νῦ
γὰρ ὑπὲρ[1] ψυχῶν τῶν ὑμετέρων ἀγὼν καὶ ὑπὲρ
γῆς ἐν ᾗ ἔφυτε καὶ[2] οἴκων ἐν οἷς ἐτράφητε, κα
ὑπὲρ[1] γυναικῶν τε καὶ τέκνων καὶ περὶ πάντω
ὧν πέπασθε ἀγαθῶν. νικήσαντες μὲν γὰρ ἁπάν
των τούτων ὑμεῖς ὥσπερ πρόσθεν κύριοι ἔσεσθε
εἰ δ' ἡττηθήσεσθε, εὖ ἴστε ὅτι παραδώσετε ταῦτ
πάντα τοῖς πολεμίοις. 45. ἅτε οὖν νίκης ἐρῶντε
μένοντες μάχεσθε. μῶρον γὰρ τὸ κρατεῖν βου
λομένους τὰ τυφλὰ τοῦ σώματος καὶ ἄοπλ
καὶ ἄχειρα ταῦτα ἐναντία τάττειν τοῖς πολεμίοι
φεύγοντας· μῶρος δὲ καὶ εἴ τις ζῆν βουλόμενο
φεύγειν ἐπιχειροίη, εἰδὼς ὅτι οἱ μὲν νικῶντε
σώζονται, οἱ δὲ φεύγοντες ἀποθνήσκουσι μᾶλλο
τῶν μενόντων· μῶρος δὲ καὶ εἴ τις χρημάτω
ἐπιθυμῶν ἧτταν προσίεται. τίς γὰρ οὐκ οἶδε
ὅτι οἱ μὲν νικῶντες τά τε ἑαυτῶν σώζουσι κα
τὰ τῶν ἡττωμένων προσλαμβάνουσιν, οἱ δὲ ἡττώ
μενοι ἅμα ἑαυτούς τε καὶ τὰ ἑαυτῶν πάντ
ἀποβάλλουσιν;

[1] ὑπὲρ z, Dindorf, Breitenbach, Marchant; περὶ xyn Gemoll.

[2] καὶ Hug; καὶ περὶ MSS., Dindorf; [καὶ περὶ] Breitenbach Marchant, Gemoll.

get your luncheon and then go with your chaplets on your heads with the others to your posts."

43. Thus Cyrus and his men were occupied; and the Assyrians, when they had lunched, came out boldly and bravely drew up in line. And the king in person rode along in his chariot and marshalled the lines and exhorted them as follows: 44. "Men of Assyria, now is the time for you to be brave men; for the struggle now impending is one for your lives, for the land in which you were born, for the homes in which you were bred, for your wives and children and all the blessings you enjoy. For if you are victorious, you will have possession of all that, as before; but if you are defeated, be well assured that you will surrender it all to the enemy. 45. Therefore, as you desire victory, stand and fight; for it would be folly for men who desire to win a battle to turn their backs and offer to the enemy the side of their body that is without eyes or hands or weapons; and any one who wishes to live would be a fool if he tried to run away, when he knows that it is the victors who save their lives, while those who try to run away are more likely to meet their death than those who stand their ground. And if any one desires wealth, he also is foolish if he submits to defeat. For who does not know that the victors not only save what is their own but take in addition the property of the vanquished, while the vanquished throw both themselves and all they have away?"

The king of Assyria exhorts his troops

46. Ὁ μὲν δὴ Ἀσσύριος ἐν τούτοις ἦν. ὁ
δὲ Κυαξάρης πέμπων πρὸς τὸν Κῦρον ἔλεγεν
ὅτι ἤδη καιρὸς εἴη ἄγειν ἐπὶ τοὺς πολεμίους
Εἰ γὰρ νῦν, ἔφη, ἔτι ὀλίγοι εἰσὶν οἱ ἔξω τοῦ
ἐρύματος, ἐν ᾧ ἂν προσίωμεν πολλοὶ ἔσονται
μὴ οὖν ἀναμείνωμεν ἕως ἂν πλείους ἡμῶν γένωνται. ἀλλ' ἴωμεν ἕως ἔτι οἰόμεθα εὐπετῶς
ἂν αὐτῶν κρατῆσαι.

47. Ὁ δ' αὖ Κῦρος ἀπεκρίνατο, Ὦ Κυαξάρη, εἰ
μὴ ὑπὲρ ἥμισυ αὐτῶν ἔσονται οἱ ἡττηθέντες, εὖ
ἴσθι ὅτι ἡμᾶς μὲν ἐροῦσι φοβουμένους τὸ πλῆθο
τοῖς ὀλίγοις ἐπιχειρῆσαι, αὐτοὶ δὲ οὐ νομιοῦσιν
ἡττῆσθαι, ἀλλ' ἄλλης σοι μάχης δεήσει, ἐν ᾗ
ἄμεινον ἂν ἴσως βουλεύσαιντο ἢ νῦν βεβούλευνται
παραδόντες ἑαυτοὺς ἡμῖν ταμιεύεσθαι ὥσθ' ὁπόσοις ἂν βουλώμεθα αὐτῶν μάχεσθαι.

48. Οἱ μὲν δὴ ἄγγελοι ταῦτ' ἀκούσαντες ᾤχοντο.
ἐν τούτῳ δὲ ἧκε Χρυσάντας ὁ Πέρσης καὶ ἄλλοι
τινὲς τῶν ὁμοτίμων αὐτομόλους ἄγοντες. καὶ ὁ
Κῦρος ὥσπερ εἰκὸς ἠρώτα τοὺς αὐτομόλους τὰ ἐκ
τῶν πολεμίων. οἱ δ' ἔλεγον ὅτι ἐξίοιέν τε ἤδη
σὺν τοῖς ὅπλοις καὶ παρατάττοι αὐτοὺς αὐτὸς ὁ
βασιλεὺς ἔξω ὢν καὶ παρακελεύοιτο μὲν δὴ τοῖς
ἀεὶ ἔξω οὖσι πολλά τε καὶ ἰσχυρά, ὡς ἔφασαν
λέγειν τοὺς ἀκούοντας.

49. Ἔνθα δὴ ὁ Χρυσάντας εἶπε, Τί δ', ἔφη, ὦ
Κῦρε, εἰ καὶ σὺ συγκαλέσας ἕως ἔτι ἔξεστι
παρακελεύσαιο, εἰ ἄρα τι καὶ σὺ ἀμείνους ποιή-
σαις τοὺς στρατιώτας;

50. Καὶ ὁ Κῦρος εἶπεν, Ὦ Χρυσάντα, μηδέν

46. Thus the Assyrian was occupied; and Cyaxares sent to Cyrus to say that now was the time to advance upon the enemy. "For," said he, "although those outside the fortifications are as yet but few, they will become many while we are advancing; let us therefore not wait until their numbers are more than our own, but let us go while yet we think we could defeat them easily."

Cyaxares proposes an immediate attack

47. "But, Cyaxares," Cyrus answered, "if it is not more than half of them that are defeated, you may rest assured that they will say that we attacked only a few because we were afraid of their main body, and they will maintain that they have not been defeated; the result will be that you will find another battle necessary; and then they may perhaps plan better than they have now in delivering themselves so completely to our disposal that we may fight as many or as few of them as we please."

Cyrus wisely counsels delay

48. The messengers received this answer and were gone. And at this juncture Chrysantas, the Persian, and certain other peers came up with some deserters. And Cyrus, as a matter of course, asked the deserters what was going on among the enemy; and they said that the troops were already coming out under arms and that the king was out in person marshalling them and addressing them with many earnest words of exhortation as they came out in succession. So, they said, those reported who heard him.

49. "How would it do, Cyrus," Chrysantas then asked, "for you to get your men together, too, while yet you may, and exhort them, and see if you also might make your soldiers better men."

The value of exhortations to valour

50. "Do not let the exhortations of the Assyrian

σε λυπούντων αἱ τοῦ Ἀσσυρίου παρακελεύσεις· οὐδεμία γάρ ἐστιν οὕτω καλὴ παραίνεσις ἥτις τοὺς μὴ ὄντας ἀγαθοὺς αὐθημερὸν ἀκούσαντας ἀγαθοὺς ποιήσει· οὐκ ἂν οὖν τοξότας γε, εἰ μὴ ἔμπροσθεν τοῦτο μεμελετηκότες εἶεν, οὐδὲ μὴν ἀκοντιστάς, οὐδὲ μὴν ἱππέας, ἀλλ' οὐδὲ μὴν τά γε σώματα ἱκανοὺς πονεῖν, ἢν μὴ πρόσθεν ἠσκηκότες ὦσι.

51. Καὶ ὁ Χρυσάντας εἶπεν, Ἀλλ' ἀρκεῖ τοι, ὦ Κῦρε, ἢν τὰς ψυχὰς αὐτῶν ἀμείνονας παρακελευσάμενος ποιήσῃς.

Ἦ καὶ δύναιτ' ἄν, ἔφη ὁ Κῦρος, εἷς λόγος ῥηθεὶς αὐθημερὸν αἰδοῦς μὲν ἐμπλῆσαι τὰς ψυχὰς τῶν ἀκουόντων, ἢ ἀπὸ τῶν αἰσχρῶν κωλῦσαι, προτρέψαι δὲ ὡς χρὴ ἐπαίνου μὲν ἕνεκα πάντα μὲν πόνον, πάντα δὲ κίνδυνον ὑποδύεσθαι, λαβεῖν δ' ἐν ταῖς γνώμαις βεβαίως τοῦτο ὡς αἱρετώτερόν ἐστι μαχομένους ἀποθνήσκειν μᾶλλον ἢ φεύγοντας σώζεσθαι; 52. ἆρ' οὐκ, ἔφη, εἰ μέλλουσι τοιαῦται διάνοιαι ἐγγραφήσεσθαι ἀνθρώποις καὶ ἔμμονοι ἔσεσθαι, πρῶτον μὲν νόμους ὑπάρξαι δεῖ τοιούτους δι' ὧν τοῖς μὲν ἀγαθοῖς ἔντιμος καὶ ἐλευθέριος ὁ βίος παρασκευασθήσεται, τοῖς δὲ κακοῖς ταπεινός τε καὶ ἀλγεινὸς καὶ ἀβίωτος ὁ αἰὼν ἐπανακείσεται;

53. Ἔπειτα διδασκάλους οἶμαι δεῖ καὶ ἄρχοντας ἐπὶ τούτοις γενέσθαι οἵ τινες δείξουσί τε ὀρθῶς καὶ διδάξουσι καὶ ἐθιοῦσι ταῦτα δρᾶν, ἔστ' ἂν ἐγγένηται αὐτοῖς τοὺς μὲν ἀγαθοὺς καὶ εὐκλεεῖς εὐδαιμονεστάτους τῷ ὄντι νομίζειν, τοὺς

trouble you in the least, Chrysantas," Cyrus answered; "for no speech of admonition can be so fine that it will all at once make those who hear it good men if they are not good already; it would surely not make archers good if they had not had previous practice in shooting; neither could it make lancers good, nor horsemen; it cannot even make men able to endure bodily labour, unless they have been trained to it before."

51. "But, Cyrus," answered Chrysantas, "it is really enough if you make their souls better with your words of exhortation."

"Do you really think," returned Cyrus, "that one word spoken could all at once fill with a sense of honour the souls of those who hear, or keep them from actions that would be wrong, and convince them that for the sake of praise they must undergo every toil and every danger? Could it impress the idea indelibly upon their minds that it is better to die in battle than to save one's life by running away? 52. And," he continued, "if such sentiments are to be imprinted on men's hearts and to be abiding, is it not necessary in the first place that laws be already in existence such that by them a life of freedom and honour shall be provided for the good, but that upon the bad shall be imposed a life of humiliation and misery which would not be worth living?

53. "And then again, I think, there must be, in addition to the laws, teachers and officers to show them the right way, to teach them and accustom them to do as they are taught, until it becomes a part of their nature to consider the good and honourable men as really the most happy, and to look upon

δὲ κακοὺς καὶ δυσκλεεῖς ἀθλιωτάτους ἁπάντων ἡγεῖσθαι. οὕτω γὰρ δεῖ διατεθῆναι τοὺς μέλλοντας τοῦ ἀπὸ τῶν πολεμίων φόβου τὴν μάθησιν κρείττονα παρέξεσθαι. 54. εἰ δέ τοι ἰόντων εἰς μάχην σὺν ὅπλοις, ἐν ᾧ πολλοὶ καὶ τῶν παλαιῶν μαθημάτων ἐξίστανται, ἐν τούτῳ δυνήσεταί τις ἀπορραψῳδήσας παραχρῆμα ἄνδρας πολεμικοὺς ποιῆσαι, πάντων ἂν ῥᾷστον εἴη καὶ μαθεῖν καὶ διδάξαι τὴν μεγίστην τῶν ἐν ἀνθρώποις ἀρετήν. 55. ἐπεὶ ἔγωγ', ἔφη, οὐδ' ἂν τούτοις ἐπίστευον ἐμμόνοις ἔσεσθαι οὓς νῦν ἔχοντες παρ' ἡμῖν αὐτοῖς ἠσκοῦμεν, εἰ μὴ καὶ ὑμᾶς ἑώρων παρόντας, οἳ καὶ παραδείγματα αὐτοῖς ἔσεσθε οἵους χρὴ εἶναι καὶ ὑποβαλεῖν δυνήσεσθε, ἤν τι ἐπιλανθάνωνται. τοὺς δ' ἀπαιδεύτους παντάπασιν ἀρετῆς θαυμάζοιμ' ἄν, ἔφη, ὦ Χρυσάντα, εἴ τι πλέον ἂν ὠφελήσειε λόγος καλῶς ῥηθεὶς εἰς ἀνδραγαθίαν ἢ τοὺς ἀπαιδεύτους μουσικῆς ᾆσμα καλῶς ᾀσθὲν εἰς μουσικήν.

56. Οἱ μὲν ταῦτα διελέγοντο. ὁ δὲ Κυαξάρης πάλιν πέμπων ἔλεγεν ὅτι ἐξαμαρτάνοι διατρίβων καὶ οὐκ ἄγων ὡς τάχιστα ἐπὶ τοὺς πολεμίους. καὶ ὁ Κῦρος ἀπεκρίνατο δὴ τότε τοῖς ἀγγέλοις, Ἀλλ' εὖ μὲν ἴστω, ἔφη, ὅτι οὔπω εἰσὶν ἔξω ὅσους δεῖ· καὶ ταῦτα ἀπαγγέλλετε αὐτῷ ἐν ἅπασιν· ὅμως δέ, ἐπεὶ ἐκείνῳ δοκεῖ, ἄξω ἤδη.

57. Ταῦτ' εἰπὼν καὶ προσευξάμενος τοῖς θεοῖς ἐξῆγε τὸ στράτευμα. ὡς δ' ἤρξατο ἄγειν, ἤδη[1] θᾶττον ἡγεῖτο, οἱ δ' εἵποντο εὐτάκτως μὲν διὰ

[1] ἤδη Hug, Breitenbach, Marchant; ἔτι xy; ἐπεὶ z; αὐτί<κα> Gemoll; omitted by Dindorf.

the bad and the disreputable as the most wretched of all people. For such ought to be the feelings of those who are going to show the victory of training over fear in the presence of the enemy. 54. But if, when soldiers are about to go armed into battle, when many forget even the lessons oft learned of old, if then any one by an oratorical flourish can then and there make men warlike, it would be the easiest thing under heaven both to learn and to teach the greatest virtue in the world. 55. For even in the case of those whom we have kept and trained among ourselves, I, for my part, should not trust even them to be steadfast, if I did not see you also before me, who will be an example to them of what they ought to be and who will be able to prompt them if they forget anything. But I should be surprised, Chrysantas, if a word well spoken would help those wholly untrained in excellence to the attainment of manly worth any more than a song well sung would help those untrained in music to high attainments in music."

Cyaxares orders a charge

56. Thus they conversed. And again Cyaxares sent to Cyrus to say that he was making a serious mistake to delay instead of leading as soon as possible against the enemy. And then Cyrus answered the messengers saying: "Very well; but I want him to know that there are not yet as many of them outside the breastworks as we ought to have; and tell him this in the presence of all. Nevertheless, since he thinks best, I will lead on at once."

The charge of the Persians

57. When he had said this, he prayed to the gods and led out his army. And as soon as he began to advance, he led on at a double-quick pace and they

τὸ ἐπίστασθαί τε καὶ μεμελετηκέναι ἐν τάξ
πορεύεσθαι, ἐρρωμένως δὲ διὰ τὸ φιλονίκως ἔχε
πρὸς ἀλλήλους καὶ διὰ τὸ τὰ σώματα ἐκπεπ
νῆσθαι καὶ διὰ τὸ πάντας ἄρχοντας τοὺς πρωτ
στάτας εἶναι, ἡδέως δὲ διὰ τὸ φρονίμως ἔχειν· ἠπ
σταντο γὰρ καὶ ἐκ πολλοῦ οὕτως ἐμεμαθήκεσα
ἀσφαλέστατον εἶναι καὶ ῥᾷστον τὸ ὁμόσε ἰένα
τοῖς πολεμίοις, ἄλλως τε καὶ τοξόταις καὶ ἀκοντ
σταῖς καὶ ἱππεῦσιν.

58. Ἕως δ' ἔτι ἔξω βελῶν ἦσαν, παρηγγύα
Κῦρος σύνθημα Ζεὺς σύμμαχος καὶ ἡγεμώ
ἐπεὶ δὲ πάλιν ἧκε τὸ σύνθημα ἀνταποδιδόμενο
ἐξῆρχεν αὐτὸς ὁ Κῦρος[1] παιᾶνα τὸν νομιζό
μενον· οἱ δὲ θεοσεβῶς πάντες συνεπήχησα
μεγάλῃ τῇ φωνῇ· ἐν τῷ τοιούτῳ γὰρ δὴ
δεισιδαίμονες ἧττον τοὺς ἀνθρώπους φοβοῦντα
59. ἐπεὶ δ' ὁ παιὰν ἐγένετο, ἅμα πορευόμενοι
ὁμότιμοι φαιδροὶ [πεπαιδευμένοι][2] καὶ παρα
ρῶντες εἰς ἀλλήλους, ὀνομάζοντες παραστάτας
ἐπιστάτας, λέγοντες πολὺ τὸ Ἄγετ' ἄνδρες φίλο
Ἄγετ' ἄνδρες ἀγαθοί, παρεκάλουν ἀλλήλου
ἕπεσθαι. οἱ δ' ὄπισθεν αὐτῶν ἀκούσαντες ἀντ
παρεκελεύοντο τοῖς πρώτοις ἡγεῖσθαι ἐρρωμένως
ἦν δὲ μεστὸν τὸ στράτευμα τῷ Κύρῳ προθυμίας
φιλοτιμίας, ῥώμης, θάρρους, παρακελευσμοῦ, σω
φροσύνης, πειθοῦς, ὅπερ οἶμαι δεινότατον τοῖ
ὑπεναντίοις.

[1] αὐτὸς ὁ Κῦρος Hug, Breitenbach, Nitsche, Marchant
Gemoll; αὖ διοσκό(-ου y)ροις yC (*again to the sons of Zeu*
[Castor and Pollux]); αὖ ὁ Κῦρος zC²F², Dindorf; ὁ Κῦρος ἅμ
διοσκόροις E.

[2] πεπαιδευμένοι MSS., Dindorf, et al.; bracketed by Hug

followed in good order, for they understood marching in line and had practised it; moreover, they followed courageously, because they were in eager rivalry with one another and because their bodies were in thorough training and because the front-rank men were all officers; and they followed gladly, because they were intelligent men; for they had become convinced by long instruction that the easiest and safest way was to meet the enemy hand to hand—especially if that enemy were made up of bowmen, spearmen, and cavalry.

58. While they were still out of range, Cyrus passed the watchword, ZEUS OUR HELPER AND OUR GUIDE. And when the watchword came back and was delivered again to him, Cyrus himself began the usual paean, and they all devoutly joined with a loud voice in the singing, for in the performance of such service the God-fearing have less fear of men. 59. And when the paean was ended, the peers marched on cheerily [, well-disciplined], looking toward one another, calling by name to comrades beside them and behind them, and often saying: "On, friends," "On, brave fellows;" thus they encouraged one another to the charge. And those behind, hearing them, in their turn cheered the front line to lead them bravely on. So Cyrus's army was filled with enthusiasm, ambition, strength, courage, exhortation, self-control, obedience; and this, I think, is the most formidable thing an enemy has to face.

Breitenbach, Marchant; τε πεπ. z; <ἅ>τε πεπαιδευμένοι Gemoll.

60. Τῶν δ' Ἀσσυρίων οἱ μὲν ἀπὸ τῶν ἁρμάτω
προμαχοῦντες, ὡς ἐγγὺς ἤδη προσεμίγνυ τ
Περσικὸν πλῆθος, ἀνέβαινόν τε ἐπὶ τὰ ἅρματ
καὶ ὑπεξῆγον πρὸς τὸ ἑαυτῶν πλῆθος· οἱ δ
τοξόται καὶ ἀκοντισταὶ καὶ σφενδονῆται αὐτῶ
ἀφίεσαν τὰ βέλη πολὺ πρὶν ἐξικνεῖσθαι. 61. ὡ
δ' ἐπιόντες οἱ Πέρσαι ἐπέβησαν τῶν ἀφειμένω
βελῶν, ἐφθέγξατο δὴ ὁ Κῦρος, Ἄνδρες ἄριστοι
ἤδη θᾶττόν τις ἰὼν ἐπιδεικνύτω ἑαυτὸν καὶ παρεγ
γυάτω. οἱ μὲν δὴ παρεδίδοσαν· ὑπὸ δὲ προ
θυμίας καὶ μένους καὶ τοῦ σπεύδειν συμμῖξα
δρόμου τινὲς ἦρξαν, συνεφείπετο δὲ καὶ πᾶσα
φάλαγξ δρόμῳ. 62. καὶ αὐτὸς δὲ ὁ Κῦρο
ἐπιλαθόμενος τοῦ βάδην δρόμῳ ἡγεῖτο, καὶ ἅμ
ἐφθέγγετο· Τίς ἕψεται; Τίς ἀγαθός; Τίς πρῶτο
ἄνδρα καταβαλεῖ;

Οἱ δὲ ἀκούσαντες ταὐτὸ τοῦτο ἐφθέγγοντο, κα
διὰ πάντων δὲ ὥσπερ παρηγγύα οὕτως ἐχώρει
Τίς ἕψεται; Τίς ἀγαθός;

63. Οἱ μὲν δὴ Πέρσαι οὕτως ἔχοντες ὁμόσ
ἐφέροντο. οἵ γε μὴν πολέμιοι οὐκέτι ἐδύναντ
μένειν, ἀλλὰ στραφέντες ἔφευγον εἰς τὸ ἔρυμα
64. οἱ δ' αὖ Πέρσαι κατά τε τὰς εἰσόδους ἐφεπό-
μενοι ὠθουμένων αὐτῶν πολλοὺς κατεστρώννυσαν
τοὺς δ' εἰς τὰς τάφρους ἐμπίπτοντας ἐπεισπη-
δῶντες ἐφόνευον ἄνδρας ὁμοῦ καὶ ἵππους· ἔνια γὰρ
τῶν ἁρμάτων εἰς τὰς τάφρους ἠναγκάσθη φεύγοντα ἐμπεσεῖν. 65. καὶ οἱ τῶν Μήδων δ' ἱππεῖς
ὁρῶντες ταῦτα ἤλαυνον εἰς τοὺς ἱππέας τοὺς τῶν

60. But when the main body of the Persians began) get close to them, those of the Assyrians who dis- ıounted from their chariots and fought in front of heir army remounted their chariots and gradually rew back to their own main body, while the bow- ıen, spearmen, and slingers let fly their missiles long efore they could reach the enemy. 61. And when he Persians, charging on, set foot upon the missiles hat had been discharged, Cyrus shouted, "Bravest f men, now let each press on and distinguish him- elf and pass the word to the others to come on ıster." And they passed it on; and under the npulse of their enthusiasm, courage, and eagerness o close with the enemy some broke into a run, nd the whole phalanx also followed at a run. 2. And even Cyrus himself, forgetting to proceed t a walk, led them on at a run and shouted as ıe ran: "Who will follow? Who is brave? Who vill be the first to lay low his man?"

The Assyrians fail to withstand the charge

And those who heard him shouted with the same vords, and the cry passed through all the ranks as ıe had started it: "Who will follow? Who is rave?"

63. In such spirit the Persians rushed to the ncounter, and the enemy could not longer stand heir ground but turned and fled back into their ntrenchments. 64. And the Persians on their part, ollowing them up to the gates, mowed many of hem down as they were pushing and shoving one ınother; and upon some who fell into the ditches hey leaped down and slew them, both men and ıorses; for some of the chariots were forced in heir flight to plunge into the ditches. 65. And vhen the Median cavalry saw this, they also charged

They flee into their entrenchments

πολεμίων· οἱ δ' ἐνέκλιναν καὶ αὐτοί.[1] ἔνθα δ
καὶ ἵππων διωγμὸς ἦν καὶ ἀνδρῶν καὶ φόνος δὲ
ἀμφοτέρων.

66. Οἱ δ' ἐντὸς τοῦ ἐρύματος τῶν Ἀσσυρία
ἑστηκότες ἐπὶ τῆς κεφαλῆς τῆς τάφρου τοξεύει
μὲν ἢ ἀκοντίζειν εἰς τοὺς κατακαίνοντας οὔτ
ἐφρόνουν οὔτε ἐδύναντο διὰ τὰ δεινὰ ὁράματα κα
διὰ τὸν φόβον. τάχα δὲ καὶ καταμαθόντες τῶ
Περσῶν τινας διακεκοφότας πρὸς τὰς εἰσόδους το
ἐρύματος ἐτράποντο καὶ ἀπὸ τῶν κεφαλῶν τῶ
ἔνδον.[3] 67. ἰδοῦσαι δ' αἱ γυναῖκες τῶν Ἀσσυρία
καὶ τῶν συμμάχων ἤδη φυγὴν καὶ ἐν τῷ στρα
τοπέδῳ ἀνέκραγον καὶ ἔθεον ἐκπεπληγμέναι, α
μὲν καὶ τέκνα ἔχουσαι, αἱ δὲ καὶ νεώτερα
καταρρηγνύμεναί τε πέπλους καὶ δρυπτόμενα
καὶ ἱκετεύουσαι πάντας ὅτῳ ἐντυγχάνοιεν μ
φεύγειν καταλιπόντας αὐτάς, ἀλλ' ἀμῦναι κα
τέκνοις καὶ ἑαυταῖς καὶ σφίσιν αὐτοῖς.

68. Ἔνθα δὴ καὶ αὐτοὶ οἱ βασιλεῖς σὺν τοῖ
πιστοτάτοις στάντες ἐπὶ τὰς εἰσόδους καὶ ανα
βάντες ἐπὶ τὰς κεφαλὰς καὶ αὐτοὶ ἐμάχοντο κα
τοῖς ἄλλοις παρεκελεύοντο.

69. Ὡς δ' ἔγνω ὁ Κῦρος τὰ γιγνόμενα, δείσα
μή, καὶ εἰ βιάσαιντο εἴσω, ὀλίγοι ὄντες ὑπ
πολλῶν σφαλεῖέν τι, παρηγγύησεν ἐπὶ πόδ
ἀνάγειν ἔξω βελῶν [καὶ πείθεσθαι].[4]

70. Ἔνθα δὴ ἔγνω τις ἂν τοὺς ὁμοτίμους πεπαι

[1] αὐτοί Sauppe, Breitenbach, Marchant, Gemoll; τούτοις z
Dindorf; τούτους xy; οὗτοι Pantazides.

[2] δὲ Pantazides, most Edd.; ἐξ MSS., Dindorf.

[3] τῶν ἔνδον z, Edd.; ἔφευγον xy.

[4] καὶ πείθεσθαι MSS., Dindorf; bracketed by Wörner an
most Edd.

.pon the enemy's cavalry; but the latter gave way, ike the rest. Then followed a pursuit of horses and nen and slaughter of both.

The panic in the camp

66. And those of the Assyrians inside the fort who tood upon the rampart of the breastworks neither ıad the presence of mind to shoot arrows or hurl pears at the enemy who were mowing down their anks, nor had they the strength to do so because of he awful spectacle and their own panic fear. And resently, discovering that some of the Persians had ut their way through to the gates in the mbankment, they turned away even from the inner ampart of the breastworks. 67. And the women of he Assyrians and their allies, seeing the men in light even inside the camp, raised a cry and ran panic-stricken, both those who had children and the younger women as well, while they rent their garments, tore their cheeks, and begged all whom hey met not to run away and leave them but to lefend both them and their children and themselves as well.

68. Then even the kings themselves with their most trusty followers took their stand at the gates, mounted upon the ramparts, and both fought in person and encouraged the rest to fight.

Cyrus orders a retreat

69. But when Cyrus realized what was going on, he feared lest his men, even if they did force their way in, might be worsted by superior numbers, for his own men were but few; so he gave orders to retreat still facing the foe, until they were out of range.

70. Then one might have seen the ideal discipline

δευμένους ὡς δεῖ· ταχὺ μὲν γὰρ αὐτοὶ ἐπείθοντο
ταχὺ δὲ τοῖς ἄλλοις παρήγγελλον. ὡς δ' ἔξω
βελῶν ἐγένοντο, ἔστησαν κατὰ χώραν, πολὺ
μᾶλλον χοροῦ ἀκριβῶς εἰδότες ὅπου ἔδει ἕκαστον
αὐτῶν γενέσθαι.

›f the peers; for they themselves obeyed at once and ıt once passed on the word to the rest. And when .hey were out of range, they halted in their regular ›ositions, for they knew much more accurately than ı chorus, each the spot where he should stand.

BOOK IV

THE CAPTURE OF THE FIRST AND SECOND CAMPS OF THE ASSYRIANS

Δ

I

1. Μείνας δὲ ὁ Κῦρος μέτριον χρόνον αὐτο[ῦ] σὺν τῷ στρατεύματι καὶ δηλώσας ὅτι ἕτοι[μ]μοί εἰσι μάχεσθαι εἴ τις ἐξέρχοιτο, ὡς οὐδεὶ[ς] ἀντεξῄει, ἀπήγαγεν ὅσον ἐδόκει καλῶς ἔχει[ν] καὶ ἐστρατοπεδεύσατο. φυλακὰς δὲ καταστη-σάμενος καὶ σκοποὺς προπέμψας, στὰς εἰς τ[ὸ] μέσον συνεκάλεσε τοὺς ἑαυτοῦ στρατιώτας κα[ὶ] ἔλεξε τοιάδε·

2. Ἄνδρες Πέρσαι, πρῶτον μὲν τοὺς θεοὺ[ς] ἐγὼ ἐπαινῶ ὅσον δύναμαι, καὶ ὑμεῖς δὲ πάντες οἶμαι· νίκης τε γὰρ τετυχήκαμεν καὶ σωτηρίας τούτων μὲν οὖν χρὴ χαριστήρια ὧν ἂν ἔχωμε[ν] τοῖς θεοῖς ἀποτελεῖν. ἐγὼ δὲ σύμπαντας μὲ[ν] ὑμᾶς ἤδη ἐπαινῶ· τὸ γὰρ γεγενημένον ἔργο[ν] σύμπασιν ὑμῖν καλῶς ἀποτετέλεσται· ὧν δ' ἕκαστος ἄξιος, ἐπειδὰν παρ' ὧν προσήκει πύθω-μαι, τότε τὴν ἀξίαν ἑκάστῳ καὶ λόγῳ καὶ ἔργῳ πειράσομαι ἀποδιδόναι. 3. τὸν δ' ἐμοῦ ἐγγύτατα ταξίαρχον Χρυσάνταν οὐδὲν ἄλλων δέομαι πυν-θάνεσθαι, ἀλλ' αὐτὸς οἶδα οἷος ἦν· τὰ μὲν γὰρ ἄλλα ὅσαπερ οἶμαι καὶ πάντες ὑμεῖς ἐποιεῖτε· ἐπεὶ δ' ἐγὼ παρηγγύησα ἐπανάγειν καλέσας αὐτὸ[ν]

BOOK IV

I

1. Cyrus remained there for a while with his army and showed that they were ready to do battle, if any one should come out. But as no one did come out against him, he withdrew as far as he thought proper and encamped. And when he had stationed his outposts and sent out his scouts, he called together his own men, took his place in their midst, and addressed them as follows:

Cyrus withdraws

2. "Fellow-citizens of Persia, first of all I praise the gods with all my soul; and so, I believe, do all of you; for we not only have won a victory, but our lives have been spared. We ought, therefore, to render to the gods thank-offerings of whatsoever we have. And I here and now commend you as a body, for you have all contributed to this glorious achievement; but as for the deserts of each of you individually, I shall try by word and deed to give every man his due reward, when I have ascertained from proper sources what credit each one deserves. 3. But as to Captain Chrysantas, who fought next to me, I have no need to make enquiry from others, for I myself know how gallant his conduct was; in everything else he did just as I think all of you also did; but

His address to his troops

Chrysantas promoted

ὀνομαστί, ἀνατεταμένος οὗτος τὴν μάχαιραν, ὡς παίσων πολέμιον, ὑπήκουσέ τε ἐμοὶ εὐθὺς ἀφείς τε ὃ ἔμελλε ποιεῖν τὸ κελευόμενον ἔπραττεν· αὐτός τε γὰρ ἐπανῆγε καὶ τοῖς ἄλλοις μάλα ἐπισπερχῶς παρηγγύα· ὥστ'[1] ἔφθασεν ἔξω βελῶν τὴν τάξιν ποιήσας πρὶν τοὺς πολεμίους κατανοῆσαι ὅτι ἀνεχωροῦμεν καὶ τόξα ἐντείνασθαι καὶ τὰ παλτὰ ἐπαφεῖναι· ὥστε αὐτός τε ἀβλαβὴς καὶ τοὺς αὑτοῦ ἄνδρας ἀβλαβεῖς διὰ τὸ πείθεσθαι παρέχεται. 4. ἄλλους δ', ἔφη, ὁρῶ τετρωμενους, περὶ ὧν ἐγὼ σκεψάμενος ἐν ὁποίῳ χρόνῳ ἐτρώθησαν, τότε τὴν γνώμην περὶ αὐτῶν ἀποφανοῦμαι. Χρυσάνταν δὲ ὡς καὶ ἐργάτην τῶν ἐν πολέμῳ καὶ φρόνιμον καὶ ἄρχεσθαι ἱκανὸν καὶ ἄρχειν χιλιαρχίᾳ μὲν ἤδη τιμῶ· ὅταν δὲ καὶ ἄλλο τι ἀγαθὸν ὁ θεὸς δῷ, οὐδὲ τότε ἐπιλήσομαι αὐτοῦ.

5. Καὶ πάντας δὲ βούλομαι ὑμᾶς, ἔφη, ὑπομνῆσαι· ἃ γὰρ νῦν εἴδετε ἐν τῇ μάχῃ τῇδε, ταῦτα ἐνθυμούμενοι μήποτε παύεσθε, ἵνα παρ' ὑμῖν αὐτοῖς ἀεὶ κρίνητε πότερον ἡ ἀρετὴ μᾶλλον ἢ ἡ φυγὴ σῴζει τὰς ψυχὰς καὶ πότερον οἱ μάχεσθαι ἐθέλοντες ῥᾷον ἀπαλλάττουσιν ἢ οἱ οὐκ ἐθέλοντες, καὶ ποίαν τινὰ ἡδονὴν τὸ νικᾶν παρέχει· ταῦτα γὰρ νῦν ἄριστα κρίναιτ' ἂν πεῖράν τε αὐτῶν ἔχοντες καὶ ἄρτι γεγενημένου τοῦ πράγματος. 6. καὶ ταῦτα μέν, ἔφη, ἀεὶ διανοούμενοι βελτίους ἂν εἴητε.

Νῦν δὲ ὡς θεοφιλεῖς καὶ ἀγαθοὶ καὶ σώφρονες

[1] ὥστ' xy, Breitenbach, Marchant, Gemoll; ἔστ' z, Dindorf, Hug (*until*).

when I gave the word to retreat and called to him by name, even though he had his sword raised to smite down an enemy he obeyed me at once and refrained from what he was on the point of doing and proceeded to carry out my order; not only did he himself retreat but he also with instant promptness passed the word on to the others; and so he succeeded in getting his division out of range before the enemy discovered that we were retreating or drew their bows or let fly their javelins. And thus by his obedience he is unharmed himself and he has kept his men unharmed. 4. But others," said he, "I see wounded; and when I have enquired at what moment of the engagement they received their wounds, I will then express my opinion concerning them. But Chrysantas, as a mighty man of war, prudent and fitted to command and to obey—him I now promote to a colonelship. And when God shall vouchsafe some further blessing, then, too, I shall not forget him.

The lessons of the battle

5. "I wish also to leave this thought with all of you," he went on: "never cease to bear in mind what you have just seen in this day's battle, so that you may always judge in your own hearts whether courage is more likely to save men's lives than running away, and whether it is easier for those to withdraw who wish to fight than for those who are unwilling, and what sort of pleasure victory brings; for you can best judge of these matters now when you have experience of them and while the event is of so recent occurrence. 6. And if you would always keep this in mind, you would be more valiant men.

"Now go to dinner, as men beloved of God and

ἄνδρες δειπνοποιεῖσθε καὶ σπονδὰς τοῖς θεοῖς ποιεῖσθε καὶ παιᾶνα ἐξάρχεσθε καὶ ἅμα τὸ παραγγελλόμενον προνοεῖτε.

7. Εἰπὼν δὲ[1] ταῦτα ἀναβὰς ἐπὶ τὸν ἵππον ἤλασε καὶ πρὸς Κυαξάρην ἐλθὼν καὶ συνησθεὶς ἐκείνῳ κοινῇ ὡς εἰκὸς καὶ ἰδὼν τἀκεῖ καὶ ἐρόμενος εἴ τι δέοιτο, ἀπήλαυνεν εἰς τὸ αὑτοῦ στράτευμα· καὶ οἱ μὲν δὴ ἀμφὶ Κῦρον δειπνοποιησάμενοι καὶ φυλακὰς καταστησάμενοι ὡς ἔδει ἐκοιμήθησαν.

8. Οἱ δὲ Ἀσσύριοι, ἅτε καὶ τεθνηκότος τοῦ ἄρχοντος καὶ σχεδὸν σὺν αὐτῷ τῶν βελτίστων, ἠθύμουν μὲν πάντες, πολλοὶ δὲ καὶ ἀπεδίδρασκον αὐτῶν τῆς νυκτὸς ἐκ τοῦ στρατοπέδου. ὁρῶντες δὲ ταῦτα ὅ τε Κροῖσος καὶ οἱ ἄλλοι σύμμαχοι αὐτῶν ἠθύμουν· πάντα μὲν γὰρ ἦν χαλεπά· ἀθυμίαν δὲ πλείστην παρεῖχε πᾶσιν ὅτι τὸ ἡγούμενον τῆς στρατιᾶς φῦλον διέφθαρτο τὰς γνώμας. οὕτω δὴ ἐκλείπουσι τὸ στρατόπεδον καὶ ἀπέρχονται τῆς νυκτός. 9. ὡς δ' ἡμέρα ἐγένετο καὶ ἔρημον ἀνδρῶν ἐφάνη τὸ τῶν πολεμίων στρατόπεδον, εὐθὺς διαβιβάζει ὁ Κῦρος τοὺς Πέρσας πρώτους· κατελέλειπτο δὲ ὑπὸ τῶν πολεμίων πολλὰ μὲν πρόβατα, πολλοὶ δὲ βόες, πολλαὶ δὲ ἅμαξαι πολλῶν ἀγαθῶν μεσταί· ἐκ δὲ τούτου διέβαινον ἤδη καὶ οἱ ἀμφὶ Κυαξάρην Μῆδοι πάντες καὶ ἠριστοποιοῦντο ἐνταῦθα. 10. ἐπεὶ δὲ ἠρίστησαν, συνεκάλεσεν ὁ Κῦρος τοὺς αὑτοῦ ταξιάρχους καὶ ἔλεξε τοιάδε·

Οἷά μοι δοκοῦμεν καὶ ὅσα ἀγαθά, ὦ ἄνδρες, ἀφεῖναι, θεῶν ἡμῖν αὐτὰ διδόντων. νῦν γὰρ ὅτι

[1] δὲ Zeune, Edd.; τε z; not in xy.

brave and wise; pour libations to the gods, raise the song of victory, and at the same time be on the lookout for orders that may come."

7. When he had said this, he mounted his horse and rode away to Cyaxares. They exchanged congratulations, as was fitting, and after Cyrus had taken note of matters there and asked if there were anything he could do, he rode back to his own army. Then he and his followers dined, stationed their pickets duly, and went to rest.

The Assyrians decamp

8. The Assyrians, on the other hand, inasmuch as they had lost their general and with him nearly all their best men, were all disheartened, and many of them even ran away from the camp in the course of the night. And when Croesus and the rest of their allies saw this, they too lost heart; for the whole situation was desperate; but what caused the greatest despondency in all was the fact that the leading contingent of the army had become thoroughly demoralized. Thus dispirited, then, they quitted their camp and departed under cover of the night. 9. And when it became day and the enemy's camp was found to be forsaken of men, Cyrus at once led his Persians first across the entrenchments. And many sheep and many cattle and many wagons packed full of good things had been left behind by the enemy. Directly after this, Cyaxares also and all his Medes crossed over and had breakfast there. 10. And when they had breakfasted, Cyrus called together his captains and spoke as follows:

"What good things, fellow-soldiers, and how great, have we let slip, it seems, while the gods were

οἱ πολέμιοι ἡμᾶς ἀποδεδράκασιν αὐτοὶ ὁρᾶτε οἵτινες δὲ ἐν ἐρύματι ὄντες ἐκλιπόντες τοῦτο φεύγουσι, πῶς ἄν τις τούτους οἴοιτ' ἂν μεῖναι ἰδόντας ἡμᾶς ἐν τῷ ἰσοπέδῳ; οἵτινες δὲ ἡμῶν ἄπειροι ὄντες οὐχ ὑπέμειναν, πῶς νῦν γ' ἂν ὑπομείνειαν, ἐπεὶ ἥττηνταί τε καὶ πολλὰ κακὰ ὑφ' ἡμῶν πεπόνθασιν; ὧν δὲ οἱ βέλτιστοι ἀπολώλασι, πῶς οἱ πονηρότεροι ἐκείνων μάχεσθαι ἂν ἡμῖν ἐθέλοιεν;

11. Καί τις εἶπε, Τί οὖν οὐ διώκομεν ὡς τάχιστα, καταδήλων γε οὕτω τῶν ἀγαθῶν ὄντων;

Καὶ ὃς εἶπεν, Ὅτι ἵππων προσδεόμεθα· οἱ μὲν γὰρ κράτιστοι τῶν πολεμίων, οὓς μάλιστα καιρὸς ἦν ἢ λαβεῖν ἢ κατακανεῖν,[1] οὗτοι ἐφ' ἵππων ὀχοῦνται·[2] οὓς ἡμεῖς τρέπεσθαι μὲν σὺν τοῖς θεοῖς ἱκανοί, διώκοντες δὲ αἱρεῖν οὐχ ἱκανοι.

12. Τί οὖν, ἔφασαν, οὐκ ἐλθὼν Κυαξάρῃ λέγεις ταῦτα;

Καὶ ὃς εἶπε, Συνέπεσθε τοίνυν μοι πάντες, ὡς εἰδῇ ὅτι πᾶσιν ἡμῖν ταῦτα δοκεῖ.

Ἐκ τούτου εἵποντό τε πάντες καὶ ἔλεγον οἷα ἐπιτήδεια ἐδόκουν εἶναι ὑπὲρ ὧν ἐδέοντο.

13. Καὶ ὁ Κυαξάρης ἅμα μὲν ὅτι ἐκεῖνοι ἦρχον τοῦ λόγου, ὥσπερ ὑπεφθόνει· ἅμα δ' ἴσως καλῶς ἔχειν ἐδόκει αὐτῷ μὴ πάλιν κινδυνεύειν· καὶ γὰρ αὐτός τε περὶ εὐθυμίαν ἐτύγχανεν ὢν καὶ τῶν

[1] κατακανεῖν Dindorf, Edd.; κατακαινειν z; ἀποκτεῖναι xy.

[2] ὀχοῦνται Cobet, Breitenbach, Marchant; νέονται xF¹, Dindorf (*are moving off*); <κι>νοῦνται Gemoll; ἔσονται zDF².

delivering them into our hands! Why, you see with your own eyes that the enemy have run away from us; when people behind fortifications abandon them and flee, how would any one expect them to stand and fight, if they met us in a fair and open field? And if they did not stand their ground when they were yet unacquainted with us, how would they withstand us now, when they have been defeated and have suffered heavy loss at our hands? And when their bravest men have been slain, how would their more cowardly be willing to fight us?"

Pursuit proposed

11. "Why not pursue them as swiftly as possible," said one of the men; "now that the good things we have let slip are so manifest to us?"

"Because," he replied, "we have not horses enough; for the best of the enemy, those whom it were most desirable either to capture or to kill, are riding off on horseback. With the help of the gods we were able to put them to flight, but we are not able to pursue and overtake them."

12. "Then why do you not go and tell Cyaxares this?" said they.

"Come with me, then, all of you," he answered, "so that he may know that we are all agreed upon this point."

Thereupon they all followed and submitted such arguments as they thought calculated to gain their object.

13. Now Cyaxares seemed to feel some little jealousy because the proposal came from them; at the same time, perhaps, he did not care to risk another engagement; then, too, he rather wished to stay where he was, for it happened that he was

ἄλλων Μήδων ἑώρα πολλοὺς τὸ αὐτὸ ποιοῦντας· εἶπε δ' οὖν ὧδε· 14. Ἀλλ', ὦ Κῦρε, ὅτι μὲν τῶν ἄλλων μᾶλλον[1] ἀνθρώπων μελετᾶτε ὑμεῖς οἱ Πέρσαι μηδὲ πρὸς μίαν ἡδονὴν ἀπλήστως διακεῖσθαι καὶ ὁρῶν καὶ ἀκούων οἶδα· ἐμοὶ δὲ δοκεῖ τῆς μεγίστης ἡδονῆς πολὺ μάλιστα συμφέρειν ἐγκρατῆ εἶναι. μείζω δὲ ἡδονὴν τί παρέχει ἀνθρώποις εὐτυχίας ἢ νῦν ἡμῖν παραγεγένηται;

15. Ἢν μὲν τοίνυν [ἐπεὶ εὐτυχοῦμεν],[2] σωφρόνως διαφυλάττωμεν αὐτήν, ἴσως δυναίμεθ' ἂν ἀκινδύνως εὐδαιμονοῦντες γηρᾶν· εἰ δ' ἀπλήστως χρώμενοι ταύτῃ ἄλλην καὶ ἄλλην πειρασόμεθα διώκειν, ὁρᾶτε μὴ πάθωμεν ἅπερ πολλοὺς μὲν λέγουσιν ἐν θαλάττῃ πεπονθέναι, διὰ τὸ εὐτυχεῖν οὐκ ἐθέλοντας παύσασθαι πλέοντας ἀπολέσθαι· πολλοὺς δὲ νίκης τυχόντας ἑτέρας ἐφιεμένους καὶ τὴν πρόσθεν ἀποβαλεῖν. 16. καὶ γὰρ εἰ μὲν οἱ πολέμιοι ἥττους ὄντες ἡμῶν ἔφευγον, ἴσως ἂν καὶ διώκειν τοὺς ἥττους ἀσφαλῶς εἶχε. νῦν δὲ κατανόησον πόστῳ μέρει αὐτῶν πάντες μαχεσάμενοι νενικήκαμεν· οἱ δ' ἄλλοι ἄμαχοί εἰσιν· οὓς εἰ μὲν μὴ ἀναγκάσομεν μάχεσθαι, ἀγνοοῦντες καὶ ἡμᾶς καὶ ἑαυτοὺς δι' ἀμαθίαν καὶ μαλακίαν ἀπίασιν· εἰ δὲ γνώσονται ὅτι ἀπιόντες οὐδὲν

[1] τῶν ἄλλων μᾶλλον z, Dindorf, Breitenbach; κάλλιστα x, Marchant, Gemoll; μάλιστα y.
[2] [ἐπεὶ εὐτυχοῦμεν] bracketed by Hug.

busily engaged in making merry himself, and he saw that many of the other Medes were doing the same. However that may be, he spoke as follows: 14. "Well, Cyrus, I know from what I see and hear that you Persians are more careful than other people not to incline to the least intemperance in any kind of pleasure. But it seems to me that it is much better to be moderate in the greatest pleasure than to be moderate in lesser pleasures; and what brings to man greater pleasure than success, such as has now been granted us?

Cyaxares replies

15. "If, therefore [when we are successful], we follow up our success with moderation, we might, perhaps, be able to grow old in happiness unalloyed with danger. But if we enjoy it intemperately and try to pursue first one success and then another, see to it that we do not share the same fate that they say many have suffered upon the sea, that is, because of their success they have not been willing to give up seafaring, and so they have been lost; and many others, when they have gained a victory, have aimed at another and so have lost even what they gained by the first. 16. And that is the way with us; for if it were because they were inferior to us in numbers that the enemy are fleeing from us, perhaps it might be safe for us actually to pursue this lesser army. But, as it is, reflect with what a mere fraction of their numbers we, with all our forces, have fought and won, while the rest of theirs have not tasted of battle; and if we do not compel them to fight, they will remain unacquainted with our strength and with their own, and they will go away because of their ignorance

ἧττον κινδυνεύουσιν ἢ μένοντες, ὅπως μὴ ἀναγκάσομεν[1] αὐτούς, κἂν μὴ βούλωνται, ἀγαθοὺς γενέσθαι. 17. ἴσθι γὰρ ὅτι οὐ σὺ μᾶλλον τὰς ἐκείνων γυναῖκας καὶ παῖδας λαβεῖν ἐπιθυμεῖς ἢ ἐκεῖνοι σῶσαι. ἐννόει δ' ὅτι καὶ αἱ σύες ἐπειδὰν ὀφθῶσι, φεύγουσι, κἂν πολλαὶ ὦσι, σὺν τοῖς τέκνοις· ἐπειδὰν δέ τις αὐτῶν θηρᾷ τι τῶν τέκνων, οὐκέτι φεύγει οὐδ' ἣν μία τύχῃ οὖσα, ἀλλ' ἵεται ἐπὶ τὸν λαμβάνειν πειρώμενον. 18. καὶ νῦν μὲν κατακλείσαντες ἑαυτοὺς εἰς ἔρυμα παρέσχον ἡμῖν ταμιεύεσθαι ὥστε ὁπόσοις ἐβουλόμεθα αὐτῶν μάχεσθαι· εἰ δ' ἐν εὐρυχωρίᾳ πρόσιμεν αὐτοῖς καὶ μαθήσονται χωρὶς γενόμενοι οἱ μὲν κατὰ πρόσωπον ἡμῖν ὥσπερ καὶ νῦν ἐναντιοῦσθαι, οἱ δ' ἐκ πλαγίου, οἱ δὲ καὶ ὄπισθεν, ὅρα μὴ πολλῶν ἑκάστῳ ἡμῶν χειρῶν δεήσει καὶ ὀφθαλμῶν. προσέτι δ' οὐδ' ἂν ἐθέλοιμι, ἔφη, ἐγὼ νῦν, ὁρῶν Μήδους εὐθυμουμένους, ἐξαναστήσας ἀναγκάζειν κινδυνεύσοντας ἰέναι.

19. Καὶ ὁ Κῦρος ὑπολαβὼν εἶπεν, Ἀλλὰ σύ γε μηδένα ἀναγκάσῃς, ἀλλὰ τοὺς ἐθέλοντάς μοι ἕπεσθαι δός· καὶ ἴσως ἄν σοι καὶ τῶν σῶν φίλων τούτων ἥκοιμεν ἑκάστῳ ἄγοντες ἐφ' οἷς ἅπαντες εὐθυμήσεσθε. τὸ μὲν γὰρ πλῆθος ἡμεῖς γε τῶν πολεμίων οὐδὲ διωξόμεθα· πῶς γὰρ ἂν καὶ καταλάβοιμεν; ἢν δέ τι ἢ ἀπεσχισμένον τοῦ στρατεύματος λάβωμεν ἤ τι ὑπολειπόμενον,

[1] ἀναγκάσομεν Dindorf, Edd.; ἀναγκάσωμεν MSS.

and cowardice. But if they discover that they are in no less danger if they go away than if they remain in the field, beware lest we compel them to be valiant even against their will. 17. And let me assure you that you are not more eager to capture their women and children than they are to save them. And bethink you that even wild swine flee with their young, when they are discovered, no matter how great their numbers may be; but if any one tries to catch one of the young, the old one, even if she happens to be the only one, does not think of flight but rushes upon the man who is trying to effect the capture. 18. And now, when they had shut themselves up in their fortifications, they allowed us to manage things so as to fight as many at a time as we pleased. But if we go against them in an open plain and they learn to meet us in separate detachments, some in front of us (as even now), some on either flank, and some in our rear, see to it that we do not each one of us stand in need of many hands and many eyes. And besides," said he, "now that I see the Medes making merry, I should not like to rout them out and compel them to go into danger."

Cyrus answers his uncle's objections

19. "Nay," said Cyrus in reply; "please do not place anybody under compulsion; but allow those who will volunteer to follow me, and perhaps we may come back bringing to you and each of your friends here something for you all to make merry with. For the main body of the enemy we certainly shall not even pursue; for how could we ever overtake them? But if we find any detachment of their army straggling or left behind, we shall bring them

ἥξομεν πρὸς σὲ ἄγοντες. 20. ἐννόει δ', ἔφη, ὅτι καὶ ἡμεῖς, ἐπεὶ σὺ ἐδέου, ἤλθομεν σοὶ χαριζόμενοι μακρὰν ὁδόν· καὶ σὺ οὖν ἡμῖν δίκαιος εἶ ἀντιχαρίζεσθαι, ἵνα καὶ ἔχοντές τι οἴκαδ' ἀφικώμεθα καὶ μὴ εἰς τὸν σὸν θησαυρὸν πάντες ὁρῶμεν.

21. Ἐνταῦθα δὴ ἔλεξεν ὁ Κυαξάρης, Ἀλλ' εἴ γε μέντοι ἐθέλων τις ἕποιτο, καὶ χάριν ἔγωγέ σοι εἰδείην ἄν.

Σύμπεμψον τοίνυν μοί τινα, ἔφη, τῶν ἀξιοπίστων τουτωνί, ὃς ἐρεῖ ἃν σὺ ἐπιστείλῃς.

Λαβὼν δὴ ἴθι, ἔφη, ὅντινα ἐθέλεις τουτωνί.

22. Ἔνθα δὴ ἔτυχε παρὼν[1] ὁ φήσας ποτὲ συγγενὴς αὐτοῦ εἶναι καὶ φιληθεὶς [παρ' αὐτοῦ].[2] εὐθὺς οὖν ὁ Κῦρος εἶπεν, Ἀρκεῖ μοι, ἔφη, οὑτοσί.

Οὗτος τοίνυν σοι ἑπέσθω. καὶ λέγε σύ, ἔφη, τὸν ἐθέλοντα ἰέναι μετὰ Κύρου.

23. Οὕτω δὴ λαβὼν τὸν ἄνδρα ἐξῄει. ἐπεὶ δ' ἐξῆλθον,[3] ὁ Κῦρος εἶπε, Νῦν δὴ σὺ δηλώσεις εἰ ἀληθῆ ἔλεγες, ὅτε[4] ἔφης ἥδεσθαι θεώμενος ἐμέ.

Οὔκουν ἀπολείψομαί γέ σου, ἔφη ὁ Μῆδος, εἰ τοῦτο λέγεις.

Καὶ ὁ Κῦρος εἶπεν, Οὐκοῦν καὶ ἄλλους προθύμως ἐξάξεις;

Ἐπομόσας οὖν ἐκεῖνος Νὴ τὸν Δί', ἔφη, ἔστε γ' ἂν ποιήσω καὶ σὲ ἐμὲ ἡδέως θεᾶσθαι.

24. Τότε δὴ καὶ ἐκπεμφθεὶς ὑπὸ τοῦ Κυαξάρου

[1] παρὼν Schneider, Edd.; ὢν MSS.

[2] παρ' αὐτοῦ x, Hug, Gemoll; omitted in z, Dindorf, Marchant, Breitenbach.

[3] ἐξῆλθον Hug, Marchant, Gemoll; ἐξῆλθεν MSS., Dindorf, Breitenbach.

[4] ὅτε MSS., all Edd. except Hug, who writes ὅτι.

› you. 20. And remember," he added, "that we
.so, when you asked us, came a long journey to do
ou a favour; and it is therefore only fair that you
ıould do us a favour in return, so that we may not
ave to go home empty-handed nor always be look-
ıg to your treasury here for support."

21. "Very well," said Cyaxares then; "if indeed
ıy one will volunteer to follow you, I for my part
ıould be really grateful to you."

Cyaxares accepts Cyrus's proposal

"Well, then," said he, "send with me some one
f these notables in positions of trust to announce
our commands."

"Take any of them you wish," said the other,
and go."

22. Now it happened that the man who had once
retended to be a kinsman of his and had got a kiss
om him was present there. Cyrus, therefore, said
t once: "This man will do."

I. iv. 27–28

"Let him follow you, then," said Cyaxares. "And
o you," he added to Artabazus, "say that whoever
ill may go with Cyrus."

23. So then he took the man and went away.
ınd when they had come out, Cyrus said: "Now
hen, you shall prove if you spoke the truth when you
ıid that you liked to look at me."

"If you talk that way," said the Mede, "I shall
ever leave you."

"Will you do your best, then, to bring others also
ith you?" asked Cyrus.

"Yes, by Zeus," he answered with an oath, "to
ıch an extent that I shall make you also glad to
ok at me."

24. Then, as he had his commission from Cyaxares

τά τε ἄλλα προθύμως ἀπήγγελλε τοῖς Μήδο
καὶ προσετίθει ὅτι αὐτός γε οὐκ ἀπολείψοι
ἀνδρὸς καλλίστου καὶ ἀρίστου, καὶ τὸ μέγιστο
ἀπὸ θεῶν γεγονότος.

II

1. Πράττοντος δὲ τοῦ Κύρου ταῦτα θείως π
ἀφικνοῦνται ἀπὸ Ὑρκανίων ἄγγελοι. οἱ δὲ Ὑρκ
νιοι ὅμοροι μὲν τῶν Ἀσσυρίων εἰσίν, ἔθνος δ'
πολύ, διὸ καὶ ὑπήκοοι ἦσαν τῶν Ἀσσυρίω
εὔιπποι[1] δὲ καὶ τότε ἐδόκουν εἶναι καὶ νῦν ἔ
δοκοῦσιν· διὸ καὶ ἐχρῶντο αὐτοῖς οἱ Ἀσσύρι
ὥσπερ καὶ οἱ Λακεδαιμόνιοι τοῖς Σκιρίταις, οὐδ
φειδόμενοι αὐτῶν οὔτ' ἐν πόνοις οὔτ' ἐν κινδύνοι
καὶ δὴ καὶ τότε ὀπισθοφυλακεῖν ἐκέλευον αὐτο
ὡς χιλίους ἱππέας ὄντας, ὅπως εἴ τι ὄπισθ
δεινὸν εἴη, ἐκεῖνοι πρὸ αὐτῶν τοῦτ' ἔχοιεν. 2.
δὲ Ὑρκάνιοι, ἅτε μέλλοντες ὕστατοι πορεύεσθα
καὶ τὰς ἁμάξας τὰς ἑαυτῶν καὶ τοὺς οἰκέτ
ὑστάτους εἶχον. στρατεύονται γὰρ δὴ οἱ κατ
τὴν Ἀσίαν ἔχοντες οἱ πολλοὶ μεθ' ὧνπερ κ
οἰκοῦσι· καὶ τότε δὴ ἐστρατεύοντο οὕτως
Ὑρκάνιοι.

3. Ἐννοηθέντες δὲ οἷά τε πάσχουσιν ὑπὸ τ
Ἀσσυρίων καὶ ὅτι νῦν τεθναίη μὲν ὁ ἄρχ
αὐτῶν, ἡττημένοι δ' εἶεν, φόβος δ' ἐνείη τ
στρατεύματι, οἱ δὲ σύμμαχοι αὐτῶν ὡς ἀθύμ
ἔχοιεν καὶ ἀπολείποιεν, ταῦτα ἐνθυμουμένοις ἔδ

[1] εὔιπποι Fischer, Edd.; ἔφιπποι MSS. (*on horseback*).

also, he not only gave his message to the Medes with enthusiasm, but he added that, for his part, he himself would never leave the noblest and best of men, and what was more than all, a man descended from the gods.

II

1. While Cyrus was thus occupied, messengers came as if providentially from the Hyrcanians. Now the Hyrcanians are neighbours of the Assyrians; they are not a large nation; and for that reason they also were subjects of the Assyrians. Even then they had a reputation for being good horsemen, and they have that reputation still. For this reason the Assyrians used to employ them as the Spartans do the Sciritae, sparing them neither in hardships nor in dangers. And on that particular occasion they were ordered to bring up the rear (they were cavalrymen about a thousand strong), in order that, if any danger should threaten from behind, they might have to bear the brunt of it instead of the Assyrians. 2. But as the Hyrcanians were to march in the very rear, they had their wagons also and their families in the rear. For, as we know, most of the Asiatic peoples take the field accompanied by their entire households. So in this particular campaign, the Hyrcanians had taken the field thus attended.

The Hyrcanians

3. But as they reflected how they were being treated by the Assyrians, that the Assyrian monarch was now slain and the army defeated, that there was great panic throughout the ranks, and that the allies were discouraged and deserting—as they thought

ξεν αὐτοῖς νῦν καλὸν εἶναι ἀποστῆναι, εἰ θέλοιε
οἱ ἀμφὶ Κῦρον συνεπιθέσθαι. καὶ πέμπουσι
ἀγγέλους πρὸς Κῦρον· ἀπὸ γὰρ τῆς μάχης τ
τούτου ὄνομα μέγιστον ηὔξητο. 4. οἱ δὲ πεμ
φθέντες λέγουσι Κύρῳ ὅτι μισοῖέν τε τοὺς Ἀσσυ
ρίους δικαίως, νῦν τ᾿, εἰ βούλοιτο ἰέναι ἐπ᾿ αὐτούς
καὶ σφεῖς σύμμαχοι ὑπάρξοιεν καὶ ἡγήσοιντο
ἅμα δὲ πρὸς τούτοις διηγοῦντο τὰ τῶν πολεμίω
ὡς ἔχοι, ἐπαίρειν βουλόμενοι μάλιστα στρατεύε
σθαι αὐτόν.

5. Καὶ ὁ Κῦρος ἐπήρετο αὐτούς, Καὶ δοκεῖτ
ἄν, ἔφη, ἔτι ἡμᾶς καταλαβεῖν αὐτοὺς πρὶν ἐ
τοῖς ἐρύμασιν εἶναι; ἡμεῖς μὲν γάρ, ἔφη, μάλ
συμφορὰν τοῦτο ἡγούμεθα εἶναι ὅτι ἔλαθον ἡμᾶ
ἀποδράντες. ταῦτα δὲ ἔλεγε βουλόμενος αὐτοὺ
ὡς μέγιστον φρονεῖν ἐπὶ σφίσιν.

6. Οἱ δὲ ἀπεκρίναντο ὅτι καὶ αὔριον, ἕωθε
εἰ εὔζωνοι πορεύοιντο, καταλήψοιντο· ὑπὸ γὰ
τοῦ ὄχλου καὶ τῶν ἁμαξῶν σχολῇ πορεύεσθα
αὐτούς· καὶ ἅμα, ἔφασαν, τὴν προτέραν νύκτα
ἀγρυπνήσαντες νῦν μικρὸν προελθόντες [1] ἐστρα
τοπέδευνται.

7. Καὶ ὁ Κῦρος ἔφη, Ἔχετε οὖν ὧν λέγετ
πιστόν τι ἡμᾶς διδάσκειν ὡς ἀληθεύετε;

Ὁμήρους γ᾿, ἔφασαν, ἐθέλομεν αὐτίκα ἐλάσαντε
τῆς νυκτὸς ἀγαγεῖν· μόνον καὶ σὺ ἡμῖν πιστὰ
θεῶν [πεποίησο] [2] καὶ δεξιὰν δός, ἵνα φέρωμε
καὶ τοῖς ἄλλοις τὰ αὐτὰ ἅπερ ἂν αὐτοὶ λάβωμε
παρὰ σοῦ.

[1] προελθόντες Zeune, Edd, ; προσελθόντες z ; πορευθέντες xy
[2] [πεποίησο] Cobet, Breitenbach ; πεποίησο z, Dindorf, Marchant ; ποίησον xy.

over these conditions, they decided that now was a good opportunity to revolt, if Cyrus and his followers would join them in an attack. So they sent envoys to Cyrus; for in consequence of the battle his name had been very greatly magnified. 4. And those who were sent told Cyrus that they had good reason to hate the Assyrians and that now, if he would proceed against them, they would be his allies and his guides as well. And at the same time they also gave him an account of the enemy's plight, for they wished above all things to incite him to push the campaign.

They send envoys to Cyrus

5. "Do you really think," Cyrus enquired, "that we could still overtake them before they reach their strongholds? For we," he added, "consider it hard luck that they have run away from us when we were not watching." Now he said this to make them think as highly as possible of his troops.

6. They answered that if Cyrus and his army would start out at daybreak in light marching order, he would come up with them the next day: for because their numbers were so vast and so encumbered with baggage, the enemy were marching slowly. "And besides," they said, "as they had no sleep last night, they have gone ahead only a little way and are now encamped."

They report the enemy within striking distance

7. "Have you, then, any surety to give us," Cyrus asked, "to prove that what you say is true?"

"Yes," they answered, "we are ready to ride away and bring you hostages this very night. Only do you also give us assurance in the name of the gods and give us your right hand, that we may give to the rest of our people, too, the same assurance that we receive from you."

8. Ἐκ τούτου τὰ πιστὰ δίδωσιν αὐτοῖς ἦ μην ἐὰν ἐμπεδώσωσιν ἃ λέγουσιν, ὡς φίλοις καὶ πιστοῖς χρήσεσθαι αὐτοῖς, ὡς μήτε Περσῶν μήτε Μήδων μεῖον ἔχειν παρ' ἑαυτῷ. καὶ νῦν ἔστιν ἔτι ἰδεῖν Ὑρκανίους καὶ πιστευομένους καὶ ἀρχὰς ἔχοντας, ὥσπερ καὶ Περσῶν καὶ Μήδων οἳ ἂν δοκῶσιν ἄξιοι εἶναι.

9. Ἐπεὶ δ' ἐδείπνησαν, ἐξῆγε τὸ στράτευμα ἔτ φάους ὄντος, καὶ τοὺς Ὑρκανίους περιμένειν ἐκέλευσεν, ἵνα ἅμα ἴοιεν. οἱ μὲν δὴ Πέρσαι, ὥσπερ εἰκός, πάντες ἐξῆσαν, καὶ Τιγράνης ἔχων τὸ αὑτοῦ στράτευμα· 10. τῶν δὲ Μήδων ἐξῇσαν[1] οἱ μὲν διὰ τὸ παιδὶ ὄντι Κύρῳ παῖδες ὄντες φίλοι γενέσθαι, οἱ δὲ διὰ τὸ ἐν θήραις συγγενόμενοι ἀγασθῆναι αὐτοῦ τὸν τρόπον, οἱ δὲ διὰ τὸ καὶ χάριν εἰδέναι ὅτι μέγαν αὐτοῖς φόβον ἀπεληλακέναι ἐδόκει, οἱ δὲ καὶ ἐλπίδας ἔχοντες διὰ τὸ ἄνδρα φαίνεσθαι ἀγαθὸν καὶ εὐτυχῆ καὶ μέγαν ἔτι ἰσχυρῶς ἔσεσθαι αὐτόν, οἱ δέ, ὅτε ἐτρέφετο ἐν Μήδοις, εἴ τι ἀγαθόν τῳ ἔπραξεν, ἀντιχαρίζεσθαι ἐβούλοντο· πολλοῖς δὲ πολλὰ διὰ φιλανθρωπίαν παρὰ τοῦ πάππου ἀγαθὰ διεπέπρακτο· πολλοὶ δ', ἐπεὶ καὶ τοὺς Ὑρκανίους εἶδον καὶ λόγος διῆλθεν ὡς ἡγήσοιντο ἐπὶ πολλὰ ἀγαθά, ἐξῇσαν καὶ τοῦ λαβεῖν τι ἕνεκα.

11. Οὕτω δὴ ἐξῆλθον σχεδὸν ἅπαντες καὶ οἱ Μῆδοι πλὴν ὅσοι σὺν Κυαξάρῃ ἔτυχον σκηνοῦν-

[1] ἐξῇσαν Hug, Breitenbach, Marchant, Gemoll; ἔξω ἦσαν MSS., Dindorf, et al.

8. Thereupon he gave them his solemn promise that, if they should make good their statements, he would treat them as his true friends, so that they should count for no less in his esteem than the Persians or the Medes. And even to this day one may see the Hyrcanians holding positions of trust and authority, just like those of the Persians and Medes who are thought to be deserving.

The volunteers to follow Cyrus

9. When they had dined, he led out his army while it was still daylight, and he bade the Hyrcanians wait for him that they might go together. Now the Persians, as was to be expected, came out to a man to go with him, and Tigranes came with his army; 10. while of the Medes some came out because as boys they had been friends of Cyrus when he was a boy, others because they liked his ways when they had been with him on the chase, others because they were grateful to him for freeing them, as they thought, from great impending danger, and still others because they cherished the hope that as he seemed to be a man of ability he would one day be exceedingly successful and exceedingly great besides; others wished to requite him for some service he had done for them while he was growing up in Media; many, too, owed to his kindness of heart many a favour at the hands of his grandfather; and many, when they saw the Hyrcanians and when the report spread that these would lead them to rich plunder, came out (apart from other motives) for the sake of getting some gain.

11. The result was that almost all came out—even the Medes, except those who happened to be feasting in the same tent with Cyaxares; these and

τες· οὗτοι δὲ κατέμενον καὶ οἱ τούτων ὑπήκοοι, οἱ δ' ἄλλοι πάντες φαιδρῶς καὶ προθύμως ἐξωρμῶντο, ἅτε οὐκ ἀνάγκῃ ἀλλ' ἐθελούσιοι καὶ χάριτος ἕνεκα ἐξιόντες.

12. Ἐπεὶ δ' ἔξω ἦσαν, πρῶτον μὲν πρὸς τοὺς Μήδους ἐλθὼν ἐπῄνεσέ τε αὐτοὺς καὶ ἐπηύξατο μάλιστα μὲν θεοὺς αὐτοῖς ἵλεως ἡγεῖσθαι καὶ σφίσιν, ἔπειτα δὲ καὶ αὐτὸς δυνασθῆναι χάριν αὐτοῖς ταύτης τῆς προθυμίας ἀποδοῦναι. τέλος δ' εἶπεν ὅτι ἡγήσοιντο μὲν αὐτοῖς οἱ πεζοί, ἐκείνους δ' ἕπεσθαι σὺν τοῖς ἵπποις ἐκέλευσε· καὶ ὅπου ἂν ἀναπαύωνται ἢ ἐπίσχωσι τῆς πορείας, ἐνετείλατο αὐτοῖς πρὸς αὐτὸν παρελαύνειν τινάς, ἵνα εἰδῶσι τὸ ἀεὶ καίριον. 13. ἐκ τούτου ἡγεῖσθαι ἐκέλευε τοὺς Ὑρκανίους.

Καὶ οἳ ἠρώτων, Τί δέ; οὐκ ἀναμενεῖς,[1] ἔφασαν, τοὺς ὁμήρους ἕως ἂν ἀγάγωμεν, ἵνα ἔχων καὶ σὺ τὰ πιστὰ παρ' ἡμῶν πορεύῃ;

Καὶ τὸν ἀποκρίνασθαι λέγεται, Ἐννοῶ γάρ, φάναι, ὅτι ἔχομεν τὰ πιστὰ ἐν ταῖς ἡμετέραις ψυχαῖς καὶ ταῖς ἡμετέραις χερσίν. οὕτω γὰρ δοκοῦμεν παρεσκευάσθαι ὡς ἢν μὲν ἀληθεύητε, ἱκανοὶ εἶναι ἡμᾶς εὖ ποιεῖν· ἢν δὲ ἐξαπατᾶτε, οὕτω νομίζομεν ἔχειν ὡς οὐχ ἡμᾶς ἐφ' ὑμῖν ἔσεσθαι, ἀλλὰ μᾶλλον, ἢν οἱ θεοὶ θέλωσιν, ὑμᾶς ἐφ' ἡμῖν γενέσθαι. καὶ μέντοι, ἔφη, ὦ Ὑρκάνιοι, ἐπείπερ φατὲ ὑστάτους ἕπεσθαι τοὺς ὑμετέρους, ἐπειδὰν ἴδητε αὐτούς, σημήνατε[2] ἡμῖν ὅτι οἱ ὑμέτεροι[3] εἰσιν, ἵνα φειδώμεθα αὐτῶν.

[1] ἀναμενεῖς Dindorf, later Edd.; ἀναμένεις MSS., Dindorf, Sauppe.
[2] σημήνατε Dindorf, later Edd.; σημάνετε z; σημαίνετε xy.
[3] ὑμέτεροι Brodaeus, Edd.; ἡμέτεροι MSS.

heir subordinates remained behind. But all the rest ıastened out cheerily and enthusiastically, for they ame not from compulsion but of their own free will nd out of gratitude.

12. And when they were out of the camp, he went irst to the Medes and praised them and prayed the ·ods above all things graciously to lead them and his ›wn men, and he prayed also that he himself might ›e enabled to reward them for this zeal of theirs. n concluding, he stated that the infantry should go irst, and he ordered the Medes to follow with their avalry. And wherever they were to rest or halt rom their march, he enjoined it upon them that ome of their number should always come to him, hat they might know the need of the hour. .3. Then he ordered the Hyrcanians to lead the vay.

He assigns the order of marching

"What!" they exclaimed, "are you not going to vait until we bring the hostages, that you also may ıave a guarantee of our good faith before you ›roceed?"

"No," he is said to have answered; "for I :onsider that we have the guarantee in our own ıearts and hands. For it is with these, I think, that ve are in a position to do you a service, if you speak he truth; but if you are trying to deceive us, we hink that, as things are, we shall not be in your ›ower, but rather, if the gods will, you shall be in ›urs. And hark you, men of Hyrcania," said he, "as ‚ou say that your people are bringing up the enemy's ear, inform us, as soon as you see them, that they ıre yours, that we may do them no harm."

14. Ἀκούσαντες δὲ ταῦτα οἱ Ὑρκάνιοι τὴν μὲν ὁδὸν ἡγοῦντο ὥσπερ ἐκέλευε, τὴν δὲ ῥώμην τῆς ψυχῆς ἐθαύμαζον· καὶ οὔτε Ἀσσυρίους οὔτε Λυδοὺς οὔτε τοὺς συμμάχους αὐτῶν ἔτι[1] ἐφοβοῦντο, ἀλλὰ μὴ παντάπασιν ὁ Κῦρος μικράν τινα αὐτῶν οἴοιτο ῥοπὴν εἶναι καὶ προσόντων καὶ ἀπόντων.

15. Πορευομένων δὲ ἐπεὶ νὺξ ἐπεγένετο, λέγεται φῶς τῷ Κύρῳ καὶ τῷ στρατεύματι ἐκ τοῦ οὐρανοῦ προφανὲς γενέσθαι, ὥστε πᾶσι μὲν φρίκην ἐγγίγνεσθαι πρὸς τὸ θεῖον, θάρρος δὲ πρὸς τοὺς πολεμίους. ὡς δ' εὔζωνοί τε καὶ ταχὺ ἐπορεύοντο, εἰκότως πολλήν τε ὁδὸν διήνυσαν καὶ ἅμα κνέφᾳ πλησίον γίγνονται τοῦ τῶν Ὑρκανίων στρατεύματος. 16. ὡς δ' ἔγνωσαν οἱ ἄγγελοι, καὶ τῷ Κύρῳ λέγουσιν ὅτι οὗτοί εἰσιν οἱ σφέτεροι· τῷ τε γὰρ ὑστάτους εἶναι γιγνώσκειν ἔφασαν καὶ τῷ πλήθει τῶν πυρῶν. 17. ἐκ τούτου πέμπει τὸν ἕτερον αὐτῶν πρὸς αὐτούς, προστάξας λέγειν, εἰ φίλοι εἰσίν, ὡς τάχιστα ὑπαντᾶν τὰς δεξιὰς ἀνατείναντας· συμπέμπει δέ τινα[2] καὶ τῶν σὺν ἑαυτῷ καὶ λέγειν ἐκέλευσε τοῖς Ὑρκανίοις ὅτι ὡς ἂν ὁρῶσιν αὐτοὺς προσφερομένους, οὕτω καὶ αὐτοὶ ποιήσουσιν. οὕτω δὴ ὁ μὲν μένει τῶν ἀγγέλων παρὰ τῷ Κύρῳ, ὁ δὲ προσελαύνει πρὸς τοὺς Ὑρκανίους.

18. Ἐν ᾧ δ' ἐσκόπει τοὺς Ὑρκανίους ὁ Κῦρος ὅ τι ποιήσουσιν, ἐπέστησε τὸ στράτευμα· παρελαύνουσι δὲ πρὸς αὐτὸν οἱ τῶν Μήδων προεστη-

[1] ἔτι xy, Dindorf, Gemoll; omitted in z, Hug, Breitenbach, Marchant.
[2] τινα Zeune, Edd.; τινὰς MSS.

14. When the Hyrcanians heard this, they led the way, as he ordered. They wondered at his magnanimity; and they no longer had any fear of either the Assyrians or the Lydians or their allies, but they feared only lest he should think that it was not of the slightest moment whether they joined him or not.

He comes up with the Hyrcanians

15. As they proceeded, night came on, and it is said that a light from heaven shone forth upon Cyrus and his army, so that they were all filled with awe at the miracle but with courage to meet the enemy. And as they were proceeding in light marching order with all dispatch, they naturally covered a great distance, and in the morning twilight they drew near to the army of the Hyrcanians. 16. And when the messengers recognized the fact, they reported to Cyrus that these were their own people; for they said that they recognized them both by the fact that they were in the rear and by the number of their fires. 17. Upon hearing this report he sent one of the two messengers to them with orders to say that if they were friends, they should come to meet him with their right hands raised. And he sent along also one of his own men and ordered him to tell the Hyrcanians that he and his army would govern their conduct according to the way in which they should see the Hyrcanians behave. And thus it came to pass that one of the messengers remained with Cyrus, while the other rode away to the Hyrcanians.

18. While Cyrus was watching to see what the Hyrcanians were going to do, he halted his army. And Tigranes and the officers of the Medes rode up

κότες καὶ ὁ Τιγράνης καὶ ἐπερωτῶσι τί δεῖ ποιεῖν. ὁ δὲ λέγει αὐτοῖς ὅτι τοῦτ' ἔστι τὸ πλησίον Ὑρκανίων στράτευμα καὶ οἴχεται ὁ ἕτερος τῶν ἀγγέλων πρὸς αὐτοὺς καὶ τῶν ἡμετερων τις σὺν αὐτῷ, ἐροῦντες, εἰ φίλοι εἰσίν, ὑπαντιάζειν τὰς δεξιὰς ἀνατείναντας πάντας. ἢν μὲν οὖν οὕτω ποιῶσι, δεξιοῦσθέ τε αὐτοὺς καθ' ὃν ἂν ᾖ ἕκαστος, καὶ ἅμα θαρρύνετε· ἢν δὲ ὅπλα αἴρωνται ἢ φεύγειν ἐπιχειρῶσι, τούτων, ἔφη, εὐθὺς δεῖ πρώτων πειρᾶσθαι μηδένα λιπεῖν.

19. Ὁ μὲν τοιαῦτα παρήγγειλεν. οἱ δὲ Ὑρκάνιοι ἀκούσαντες τῶν ἀγγέλων ἥσθησάν τε καὶ ἀναπηδήσαντες ἐπὶ τοὺς ἵππους παρῆσαν τὰς δεξιάς, ὥσπερ εἴρητο, προτείνοντες· οἱ δὲ Μῆδοι καὶ Πέρσαι ἀντεδεξιοῦντό τε αὐτοὺς καὶ ἐθάρρυνον.

20. Ἐκ τούτου δὴ ὁ Κῦρος λέγει, Ἡμεῖς μὲν δή, ὦ Ὑρκάνιοι, ἤδη ὑμῖν πιστεύομεν· καὶ ὑμᾶς δὲ χρὴ πρὸς ἡμᾶς οὕτως ἔχειν. τοῦτο δ', ἔφη, πρῶτον ἡμῖν εἴπατε πόσον ἀπέχει ἐνθένδε ἔνθα αἱ ἀρχαί εἰσι τῶν πολεμίων καὶ τὸ ἁθρόον αὐτῶν.

Οἱ δ' ἀπεκρίναντο ὅτι ὀλίγῳ πλέον ἢ παρασάγγην.

21. Ἐνταῦθα δὴ λέγει ὁ Κῦρος, Ἄγετε δή, ἔφη, ὦ ἄνδρες Πέρσαι καὶ Μῆδοι καὶ ὑμεῖς, ὦ Ὑρκάνιοι, ἤδη γὰρ καὶ πρὸς ὑμᾶς ὡς πρὸς συμμάχους καὶ κοινωνοὺς διαλέγομαι, εὖ χρὴ εἰδέναι νῦν ὅτι ἐν τοιούτῳ ἐσμὲν ἔνθα δὴ μαλακισάμενοι μὲν πάντων ἂν τῶν χαλεπωτάτων τύχοιμεν· ἴσασι γὰρ οἱ πολέμιοι ἐφ' ἃ ἥκομεν· ἢν δὲ τὸ καρτερὸν ἐμβαλόμενοι ἴωμεν ῥώμῃ καὶ θυμῷ ἐπὶ τοὺς πολεμίους, αὐτίκα μάλ' ὄψεσθε ὥσπερ δούλων ἀποδιδρασκόν-

o him and asked what they should do. And he said o them: "What you see there not far away is the Iyrcanian army; and one of their envoys has gone o them, and one of our men with him, to tell them ll, if they are our friends, to come to meet us with heir right hands upraised. Now, if they do so, give o them the right hand of fellowship, each of you to he man opposite himself, and at the same time bid hem welcome. But if they raise a weapon or ttempt to run away, we must lose no time in trying iot to leave a single one of these first alive."

19. Such were his commands. And the Hyrcanians vere delighted when they heard the report of the envoys, and leaping upon their horses they came at once with right hands upraised, as directed, and the Medes and Persians gave the right hand of fellowship and bade them welcome.

They all join his army

20. "Men of Hyrcania," Cyrus said presently, "we trust you now, as you see; and you also ought to feel the same way toward us. But tell us first how far it is from here to the headquarters of the enemy and the main body of their army."

"Not much more than a parasang," they answered.

21. "Come on, then, Persians and Medes," Cyrus cried; "and you Hyrcanians—for now I speak with you also as confederates and allies—you must know that we are in a position where we shall meet with nothing but disaster if we betray a lack of courage; for the enemy know what we have come for. But if we go into the attack upon the enemy with might and main and with stout hearts, you will see right soon that, just like a lot of slaves caught in an attempt to run away, some of them will beg for mercy, others

Cyrus outlines plans for a second attack

των ηὑρημένων τοὺς μὲν ἱκετεύοντας αὐτῶν, τοὺ
δὲ φεύγοντας, τοὺς δ' οὐδὲ ταῦτα φρονεῖν δυναμέ
νους. ἡττημένοι τε γὰρ ὄψονται ἡμᾶς καὶ οὔτ
οἰόμενοι ἥξειν οὔτε συντεταγμένοι οὔτε μάχεσθα
παρεσκευασμένοι κατειλημμένοι ἔσονται. 22. εἰ οὖ
ἡδέως βουλόμεθα καὶ δειπνῆσαι καὶ νυκτερεῦσα
καὶ βιοτεύειν τὸ ἀπὸ τοῦδε, μὴ δῶμεν αὐτοῖ
σχολὴν μήτε βουλεύσασθαι μήτε παρασκευάσα
σθαι ἀγαθὸν αὑτοῖς μηδέν, μηδὲ γνῶναι πάμπαν ὅτ
ἄνθρωποί ἐσμεν, ἀλλὰ γέρρα καὶ κοπίδας κα
σαγάρεις ἅπαντα καὶ πληγὰς ἥκειν νομιζόντων.

23. Καὶ ὑμεῖς μέν, ἔφη, ὦ Ὑρκάνιοι, ὑμᾶ
αὐτοὺς προπετάσαντες ἡμῶν πορεύεσθε ἔμπρο
σθεν, ὅπως τῶν ὑμετέρων ὅπλων ὁρωμένων λαν
θάνωμεν ὅτι πλεῖστον χρόνον. ἐπειδὰν δ' ἐγ
πρὸς τῷ στρατεύματι γένωμαι τῶν πολεμίων, παρ
ἐμοὶ μὲν καταλίπετε ἕκαστοι τάξιν ἱππέων, ἡ
ἄν τι δέῃ, χρῶμαι μένων παρὰ τὸ στρατόπεδον
24. ὑμῶν δὲ οἱ μὲν ἄρχοντες καὶ οἱ πρεσβύτεροι ἐ
τάξει ἀθρόοι ἐλαύνετε, εἰ σωφρονεῖτε, ἵνα μήποτ
ἀθρόῳ τινὶ ἐντυχόντες ἀποβιασθῆτε, τοὺς δὲ νεω
τέρους ἐφίετε διώκειν· οὗτοι δὲ καινόντων· τοῦτ
γὰρ ἀσφαλέστατον, νῦν ὡς ἐλαχίστους τῶ
πολεμίων λιπεῖν.

25. Ἢν δὲ νικῶμεν, ἔφη, ὃ πολλοῖς δὴ κρα
τοῦσι τὴν τύχην ἀνέτρεψε, φυλάξασθαι δεῖ τ
ἐφ' ἁρπαγὴν τραπέσθαι· ὡς ὁ τοῦτο ποιῶν οὐκέτ
ἀνήρ ἐστιν, ἀλλὰ σκευοφόρος· καὶ ἔξεστι τῷ
βουλομένῳ χρῆσθαι ἤδη τούτῳ ὡς ἀνδραπόδῳ.

26. Ἐκεῖνο δὲ χρὴ γνῶναι ὅτι οὐδέν ἐστ
κερδαλεώτερον τοῦ νικᾶν· ὁ γὰρ κρατῶν ἅμ
πάντα συνήρπακε, καὶ τοὺς ἄνδρας καὶ τὰ

will try to escape, others still will not even have presence of mind to do either. For they will see us before they have recovered from their first defeat, and they will find themselves caught neither thinking of our coming, nor drawn up in line, nor prepared to fight. 22. If, therefore, we wish from this time forth to eat well, to sleep soundly, and to live comfortably, let us not give them time either to take counsel or to provide any defence for themselves, or even to recognize at all that we are human beings; but let them think that nothing but shields, swords, bills, and blows have descended upon them.

23. "And you, Hyrcanians," said he, "spread yourselves out in the van and march before us, in order that only your arms may be seen and that our presence here may be concealed as long as possible. And when I come up with the enemy's army, then leave with me, each of you, a division of cavalry for me to use while I remain near their camp. 24. But you, officers and men of years, march together in close order, if you are wise, so that if you fall in with any compact body you may never be forced back; and leave the pursuit to the younger men, and let them kill all they can; for this is the safest measure—to leave now as few of the enemy alive as possible.

25. "And if we win the battle," he continued, "we must be on our guard against an error which has lost the day for many in the hour of victory—turning aside to plunder. For the man who does this is no longer a soldier but a camp-follower; and any one who will is free to treat him as a slave.

How to conserve the results of victory

26. "You should realize this also, that nothing is more enriching than victory. For the victor has swept together all the spoil at once, the men and

γυναῖκας καὶ τὰ χρήματα καὶ πᾶσαν τὴν χώραν
πρὸς ταῦτα τοῦτο μόνον ὁρᾶτε ὅπως τὴν νίκην
διασῳζώμεθα· ἐὰν γὰρ κρατηθῇ, καὶ αὐτὸς ὁ
ἁρπάζων ἔχεται. καὶ τοῦτο ἅμα διώκοντες μέ-
μνησθε, ἥκειν πάλιν ὡς ἐμὲ ἔτι φάους ὄντος· ὡς
σκότους γενομένου οὐδένα ἔτι προσδεξόμεθα.

27. Ταῦτ᾽ εἰπὼν ἀπέπεμπεν εἰς τὰς τάξεις
ἑκάστους καὶ ἐκέλευεν ἅμα πορευομένους τοῖς
ἑαυτοῦ ἕκαστον δεκαδάρχοις ταὐτὰ σημαίνειν·
ἐν μετώπῳ γὰρ ἦσαν οἱ δεκάδαρχοι, ὥστε
ἀκούειν· τοὺς δὲ δεκαδάρχους τῇ δεκάδι ἕκαστον
κελεύειν παραγγέλλειν.

Ἐκ τούτου προηγοῦντο μὲν οἱ Ὑρκάνιοι, αὐτὸς
δὲ τὸ μέσον ἔχων σὺν τοῖς Πέρσαις ἐπορεύετο·
τοὺς δὲ ἱππέας ἑκατέρωθεν, ὥσπερ εἰκός, παρ-
έταξε.

28. Τῶν δὲ πολεμίων, ἐπεὶ φῶς ἐγένετο, οἱ μὲν
ἐθαύμαζον τὰ ὁρώμενα,[1] οἱ δ᾽ ἐγίγνωσκον ἤδη,
οἱ δ᾽ ἤγγελλον, οἱ δ᾽ ἐβόων, οἱ δ᾽ ἔλυον ἵππους,
οἱ δὲ συνεσκευάζοντο, οἱ δ᾽ ἐρρίπτουν τὰ ὅπλα
ἀπὸ τῶν ὑποζυγίων, οἱ δ᾽ ὡπλίζοντο, οἱ δ᾽
ἀνεπήδων ἐπὶ τοὺς ἵππους, οἱ δ᾽ ἐχαλίνουν, οἱ δὲ
τὰς γυναῖκας ἀνεβίβαζον ἐπὶ τὰ ὀχήματα, οἱ δὲ
τὰ πλείστου ἄξια ἐλάμβανον ὡς διασωσόμενοι,
οἱ δὲ κατορύττοντες τὰ τοιαῦτα ἡλίσκοντο, οἱ δὲ
πλεῖστοι εἰς φυγὴν ὥρμων· οἴεσθαι δὲ δεῖ καὶ
ἄλλα πολλά τε καὶ παντοδαπὰ ποιεῖν αὐτούς,
πλὴν ἐμάχετο οὐδείς, ἀλλ᾽ ἀμαχητὶ ἀπώλλυντο.

29. Κροῖσος δὲ ὁ Λυδῶν βασιλεύς, ὡς θέρος

[1] ὁρώμενα xy, most Edd.; δρώμενα z, Dindorf (*the doings*).

the women, the wealth and all the lands. Therefore have an eye to this alone—that we may conserve our victory; for even the plunderer himself is in the enemy's power if he is conquered. And remember even in the heat of pursuit to come back to me while it is yet daylight; for after nightfall we shall not admit another man."

27. When he had said this he sent them away to their several companies with orders to issue, as they marched, the same directions each to his own corporals (for the corporals were in the front so as to hear); and they were to bid the corporals each one to announce it to his squad.

Then the Hyrcanians led the way while he himself with his Persians occupied the centre as they marched. The cavalry he arranged, as was natural, on either flank.

The panic flight of the Assyrian army

28. And when daylight came, some of the enemy wondered at what they saw, some realized at once what it meant, some began to spread the news, some to cry out, some proceeded to untie the horses, some to pack up, others to toss the armour off the pack-animals, still others to arm themselves, while some were leaping upon their horses, some bridling them, others helping the women into the wagons, and others were snatching up their most valuable possessions to save them; still others were caught in the act of burying theirs, while the most of them sought refuge in precipitate flight. We may imagine that they were doing many other things also—all sorts of other things—except that no one offered to resist, but they perished without striking a blow.

29. As it was summer, Croesus, the king of Lydia,

ἦν, τας τε γυναῖκας ἐν ταῖς ἁρμαμάξαις προαπ
επέμψατο τῆς νυκτός, ὡς ἂν ῥᾷον πορεύοιντ
κατὰ ψῦχος, καὶ αὐτὸς ἔχων τοὺς ἱππέας ἐπ
κολούθει. 30. καὶ τὸν Φρύγα τὰ αὐτὰ ποιῆσ
φασι τὸν τῆς παρ' Ἑλλήσποντον ἄρχοντα Φρ
γίας. ὡς δὲ παρῄσθοντο τῶν φευγόντων κα
καταλαμβανόντων αὐτούς, πυθόμενοι τὸ γιγν
μενον ἔφευγον δὴ καὶ αὐτοὶ ἀνὰ κράτος.

31. Τὸν δὲ τῶν Καππαδοκῶν βασιλέα καὶ τὸ
τῶν Ἀραβίων ἔτι ἐγγὺς ὄντας καὶ ὑποστάντα
ἀθωρακίστους κατακαίνουσιν οἱ Ὑρκάνιοι. τ
δὲ πλεῖστον ἦν τῶν ἀποθανόντων Ἀσσυρίων κα
Ἀραβίων· ἐν γὰρ τῇ αὑτῶν ὄντες χώρᾳ ἀσυντο
νώτατα πρὸς τὴν πορείαν εἶχον.

32. Οἱ μὲν δὴ Μῆδοι καὶ Ὑρκάνιοι, οἷα δ
εἰκὸς κρατοῦντας,[1] τοιαῦτα ἐποίουν διώκοντες.
δὲ Κῦρος τοὺς παρ' ἑαυτῷ ἱππέας καταλειφθέντα
περιελαύνειν ἐκέλευε τὸ στρατόπεδον, καὶ εἴ τινα
σὺν ὅπλοις ἴδοιεν ἐξιόντας, κατακαίνειν· τοῖς δ
ὑπομένουσιν ἐκήρυξεν, ὁπόσοι τῶν πολεμίω
στρατιωτῶν ἦσαν ἱππεῖς ἢ πελτασταὶ ἢ τοξόται
ἀποφέρειν τὰ ὅπλα συνδεδεμένα, τοὺς δὲ ἵππου
ἐπὶ ταῖς σκηναῖς καταλείπειν· ὅστις δὲ ταῦτα μ
ποιήσοι, αὐτίκα τῆς κεφαλῆς στερήσεσθαι· τὰ
δὲ κοπίδας προχείρους ἔχοντες ἐν τάξει περιέ
στασαν.[2] 33. οἱ μὲν δὴ τὰ ὅπλα ἔχοντες ἐρρί
πτουν, ἀποφέροντες εἰς ἓν χωρίον ὅποι ἐκέλευε
καὶ ταῦτα μὲν οἷς ἐπέταξεν ἔκαον.

34. Ὁ δὲ Κῦρος ἐνενόησεν ὅτι ἦλθον μὲν οὔτ

[1] κρατοῦντας Castalio, Edd. ; κρατοῦντες MSS.
[2] περιέστασαν Fischer, Edd. ; περιίστασαν MSS.

ad had his women sent on by night in carriages, hat they might proceed more comfortably in the ool of the night, and he himself was following after vith his cavalry. 30. And the Phrygian king, the uler of Phrygia on the Hellespont, they say, did the ame. And when they saw the fugitives who were vertaking them, they enquired of them what was appening, and then they also took to flight as fast s they could go.

31. But the king of Cappadocia and the Arabian ing, as they were still near by and stood their ground hough unarmed, were cut down by the Hyrcanians. But the majority of the slain were Assyrians and Arabians. For as these were in their own country, hey were very leisurely about getting away.

How the victors behaved

32. Now the Medes and Hyrcanians, as they pursued, committed such acts as men might be expected o commit in the hour of victory. But Cyrus ordered he horsemen who had been left with him to ride around the camp and to kill any that they saw coming out under arms; while to those who remained nside he issued a proclamation that as many of the enemy's soldiers as were cavalrymen or targeteers or bowmen should bring out their weapons tied in bundles and deliver them up, but should leave their horses at their tents. Whoever failed to do so should soon lose his head. Now Cyrus's men stood in line around them, sabre in hand. 33. Accordingly, those who had the weapons carried them to one place, where he directed, and threw them down, and men whom he had appointed for the purpose burned them.

34. Now Cyrus recollected that they had come

σῖτα οὔτε ποτὰ ἔχοντες, ἄνευ δὲ τούτων οὔτ
στρατεύεσθαι δυνατὸν οὔτ' ἄλλο ποιεῖν οὐδέι
σκοπῶν δ' ὅπως ἂν κάλλιστα καὶ τάχιστα ταῦτ
γένοιτο, ἐνθυμεῖται ὅτι ἀνάγκη πᾶσι τοῖς στρα
τευομένοις εἶναί τινα ὅτῳ καὶ σκηνῆς μελήσει κα
ὅπως τἀπιτήδεια παρεσκευασμένα τοῖς στρατιώ
ταις εἰσιοῦσιν ἔσται. 35. καὶ τοίνυν ἔγνω ὅτ
τούτους εἰκὸς μάλιστα πάντων ἐν τῷ στρατοπέδ
νῦν κατειλῆφθαι ἣν διὰ τὸ ἀμφὶ συσκευασία
ἔχειν· ἐκήρυξε δὴ παρεῖναι τοὺς ἐπιτρόπου
πάντας· εἰ δέ που μὴ εἴη ἐπίτροπος, τὸν πρεσ
βύτατον ἀπὸ σκηνῆς· τῷ δὲ ἀπειθοῦντι πάντ
τὰ χαλεπὰ ἀνεῖπεν. οἱ δὲ ὁρῶντες καὶ τοὺ
δεσπότας πειθομένους ταχὺ ἐπείθοντο. ἐπεὶ δ
παρεγένοντο, πρῶτον μὲν ἐκέλευε καθίζεσθα
αὐτῶν ὅσοις ἐστὶ πλέον ἢ δυοῖν μηνοῖν ἐν τ
σκηνῇ τἀπιτήδεια. 36. ἐπεὶ δὲ τούτους εἶδεν
αὖθις ἐκέλευεν ὅσοις μηνὸς ἦν· ἐν τούτῳ σχεδὸ
πάντες ἐκαθίζοντο. 37. ἐπεὶ δὲ ταῦτα ἔμαθεν
εἶπεν ὧδε αὐτοῖς·

Ἄγετέ νυν,[1] ἔφη, ὦ ἄνδρες, οἵ τινες ὑμῶν τ
μὲν κακὰ μισεῖτε, μαλακοῦ δέ τινος παρ' ἡμῶ
βούλοισθ' ἂν τυγχάνειν, ἐπιμελήθητε προθύμως
ὅπως διπλάσια ἐν τῇ σκηνῇ ἑκάστῃ σῖτα καὶ
ποτὰ παρεσκευασμένα ᾖ ἢ τοῖς δεσπόταις καὶ
τοῖς οἰκέταις καθ' ἡμέραν ἐποιεῖτε· καὶ τἆλλα
δὲ πάντα ὁπόσα καλὴν δαῖτα παρέξει ἕτοιμα
ποιεῖτε, ὡς αὐτίκα μάλα παρέσονται ὁπότεροι ἂν
κρατῶσι, καὶ ἀξιώσουσιν ἔκπλεω ἔχειν πάντα

[1] Ἄγετέ νυν Edd.; ἄγετε νῦν z; ἄγετε τοίνυν xD.

with neither food nor drink, and without these it was not possible to prosecute a campaign or to do anything else. And as he was considering how to procure the best possible supplies with the greatest possible dispatch, it occurred to him that all those who take the field must have some one to take care of the tent and to have food prepared for the soldiers when they came in. 35. So he concluded that of all people these were the ones most likely to have been caught in the camp, because they would have been busy packing up. Accordingly, he issued a proclamation for all the commissaries to come to him; but if a commissary officer should be lacking anywhere, the oldest man from that tent should come. And to any one who should dare to disobey he threatened direst punishment. But when they saw their masters obeying, they also obeyed at once. And when they had come, he first ordered those of them to sit down who had more than two months' supply of provisions in their tents. 36. And when he had noted them, he gave the same order to those who had one month's supply. Hereupon nearly all sat down. 37. And when he had this information he addressed them as follows:

Cyrus organizes his commissariat

"Now then, my men," said he, "if any of you have a dislike for trouble and wish that you might receive kind treatment at our hands, be sure to see to it that there be twice as much food and drink prepared in each tent as you used to get ready every day for your masters and their servants; and get everything else ready that belongs to a good meal; for whichever side is victorious, they will very soon be here and they will expect to find plenty of every

τἀπιτήδεια. εὖ οὖν ἴστε ὅτι συμφέροι ἂν ὑμῖν ἀμέμπτως δέχεσθαι τοὺς ἄνδρας.

38. Οἱ μὲν δὴ ταῦτ' ἀκούσαντες πολλῇ σπουδῇ τὰ παρηγγελμένα ἔπραττον· ὁ δὲ συγκαλέσας τοὺς ταξιάρχους ἔλεξε τοιάδε· Ἄνδρες φίλοι, γιγνώσκω μὲν[1] ὅτι νῦν ἔξεστιν ἡμῖν προτέροις τῶν ἀπόντων συμμάχων ἀρίστου τυχεῖν καὶ τοῖς μάλιστα ἐσπουδασμένοις σίτοις καὶ ποτοῖς χρῆσθαι· ἀλλ' οὔ μοι δοκεῖ τοῦτ' ἂν τὸ ἄριστον πλέον ὠφελῆσαι ἡμᾶς ἢ τὸ τῶν συμμάχων ἐπιμελεῖς φανῆναι, οὐδ' ἂν αὕτη ἡ εὐωχία ἰσχυροτέρους τοσοῦτον ποιῆσαι ὅσον εἰ δυναίμεθα τοὺς συμμάχους προθύμους ποιεῖσθαι. 39. εἰ δὲ τῶν νυνὶ διωκόντων καὶ κατακαινόντων τοὺς ἡμετέρους πολεμίους καὶ μαχομένων, εἴ τις ἐναντιοῦται, τούτων δόξομεν οὕτως ἀμελεῖν ὥστε καὶ πρὶν εἰδέναι πῶς πράττουσιν ἠριστηκότες φαίνεσθαι, ὅπως μὴ αἰσχροὶ μὲν φανούμεθα, ἀσθενεῖς δ' ἐσόμεθα συμμάχων ἀποροῦντες. τὸ δὲ τῶν κινδυνευόντων καὶ πονούντων ἐπιμεληθῆναι ὅπως εἰσιόντες τἀπιτήδεια ἕξουσιν, αὕτη ἂν ἡμᾶς ἡ θοίνη πλείω εὐφράνειεν, ὡς ἐγώ φημι, ἢ τὸ παραχρῆμα τῇ γαστρὶ χαρίσασθαι. 40. ἐννοήσατε δ', ἔφη, ὡς εἰ μηδ' ἐκείνους αἰσχυντέον ἦν, οὐδ' ὣς ἡμῖν νῦν προσήκει οὔτε πλησμονῆς πω οὔτε μέθης· οὐ γάρ πω διαπέπρακται ἡμῖν ἃ βουλόμεθα, ἀλλ' αὖ τὰ πάντα νῦν ἀκμάζει ἐπιμελείας δεόμενα. ἔχομεν γὰρ ἐν τῷ στρατοπέδῳ πολεμίους πολλαπλασίους ἡμῶν αὐτῶν, καὶ

[1] γιγνώσκω μὲν an otherwise unknown MS. of Valckenaer (cited as O by Dindorf), Breitenbach, Gemoll; γιγνώσκομεν xyz, Marchant.

sort of provisions. Let me assure you, then, that it would be to your advantage to entertain those men handsomely."

38. When they heard this, they proceeded with great alacrity to carry out his directions, while he called together his captains and spoke as follows: "I realize, friends, that it is possible for us now to take luncheon first, while our comrades are away, and to enjoy the choicest food and drink. But I do not think that it would be of more advantage to us to eat this luncheon than it would to show ourselves thoughtful for our comrades; neither do I think that this feasting would add as much to our strength as we should gain if we could make our allies devoted to us. 39. But if we show ourselves to be so neglectful of them that we are found to have broken our fast even before we know how they are faring, while they are pursuing and slaying our enemies and fighting any one that opposes them, let us beware lest we be disgraced in their eyes and lest we find ourselves crippled by the loss of our allies. If, on the other hand, we take care that those who are bearing the danger and the toil shall have what they need when they come back, a banquet of this sort would, in my opinion, give us more pleasure than any immediate gratification of our appetites. 40. And remember," said he, "that even if we were under no obligation to show them every consideration, even so it is not proper for us as yet to sate ourselves with food or drink; for not yet have we accomplished what we wish, but, on the contrary, everything is now at a crisis and requires care. For we have enemies in camp many times our own number, and that, too,

Cyrus exhorts the Persians to self-denial and consideration of others

τούτους λελυμένους· οὓς καὶ φυλάττεσθαι ἔτι προσήκει καὶ φυλάττειν, ὅπως ὦσι καὶ οἱ ποιήσοντες ἡμῖν τἀπιτήδεια· ἔτι δ' οἱ ἱππεῖς ἡμῖν ἄπεισι, φροντίδα παρέχοντες ὅπου[1] εἰσι· κἂν ἔλθωσιν, εἰ παραμενοῦσιν.

41. Ὥστ', ὦ ἄνδρες, νῦν μοι δοκεῖ τοιοῦτον σῖτον ἡμᾶς προσφέρεσθαι δεῖν καὶ τοιοῦτον ποτὸν ὁποῖον ἄν τις οἴεται μάλιστα σύμφορον εἶναι πρὸς τὸ μήτε ὕπνου μήτε ἀφροσύνης ἐμπίμπλασθαι.

42. Ἔτι δὲ και χρήματα πολλά ἐστιν ἐν τῷ στρατοπέδῳ, ὧν οὐκ ἀγνοῶ ὅτι δυνατὸν ἡμῖν κοινῶν ὄντων τοῖς συγκατειληφόσι νοσφίσασθαι ὁπόσα ἂν βουλώμεθα· ἀλλ' οὔ μοι δοκεῖ τὸ λαβεῖν κερδαλεώτερον εἶναι τοῦ δικαίους φαινομένους ἐκείνοις τούτῳ πρίασθαι ἔτι μᾶλλον αὐτοὺς ἢ νῦν ἀσπάζεσθαι ἡμᾶς. 43. δοκεῖ δέ μοι, ἔφη, καὶ τὸ νεῖμαι τὰ χρήματα, ἐπειδὰν ἔλθωσι, Μήδοις καὶ Ὑρκανίοις καὶ Τιγράνῃ ἐπιτρέψαι· καὶ ἤν τι μεῖον ἡμῖν δάσωνται, κέρδος ἡγεῖσθαι· διὰ γὰρ τὰ κέρδη ἥδιον ἡμῖν παραμενοῦσι. 44. τὸ μὲν γὰρ νῦν πλεονεκτῆσαι ὀλιγοχρόνιον ἂν ἡμῖν τὸν πλοῦτον παράσχοι· τὸ δὲ ταῦτα προεμένους ἐκεῖνα κτήσασθαι ὅθεν ὁ πλοῦτος φύεται, τοῦτο, ὡς ἐγὼ δοκῶ, ἀεναώτερον ἡμῖν δύναιτ' ἂν τὸν ὄλβον καὶ πᾶσι τοῖς ἡμετέροις παρέχειν.

45. Οἶμαι δ', ἔφη, καὶ οἴκοι ἡμᾶς τούτου ἕνεκα ἀσκεῖν καὶ γαστρὸς κρείττους εἶναι καὶ κερδέων

[1] ὅπου xD, most Edd.; ποῦ AH, Dindorf, Hug.

nder no confinement. We not only must keep vatch against them but we must keep watch over hem, so that we may have people to look after our rovisions. Besides, our cavalry are gone, making us nxious to know where they are and whether they vill stay with us if they do come back.

41. "And so, my men," said he, "it seems to me hat we should take only such meat and such drink s one would suppose to be least likely to overcome s with sleep and foolishness.

42. "Besides, there is also a vast amount of reasure in the camp, and I am not ignorant of the act that it is possible for us to appropriate to our-elves as much of it as we please, though it belongs ust as much to those who helped us to get it. But do not think it would bring us greater gain to take t than it would to show that we mean to be fair and quare, and by such dealing to secure greater affection rom them than we have already. 43. And so it eems best to me to entrust the division of the reasure to the Medes and Hyrcanians and Tigranes when they come; and if they apportion to us the smaller share, I think we should account it our gain; for because of what they gain, they will be the more glad to stay with us. 44. For to secure a present advantage would give us but short-lived riches. But to sacrifice this and obtain the source from which real wealth flows, that, as I see it, could put us and all of ours in possession of a perennial fountain of wealth.

45. "And if I am not mistaken, we used to train ourselves at home, too, to control our appetites and to abstain from unseasonable gain with this in view, that,

ἀκαίρων, ἵν', εἴ ποτε δέοι, δυναίμεθα αὐτοῖ συμφόρως χρῆσθαι· ποῦ δ' ἂν ἐν μείζοσι τῶ νῦν παρόντων ἐπιδειξαίμεθ' ἂν τὴν παιδείαν ἐγὼ μὲν οὐχ ὁρῶ.

46. Ὁ μὲν οὕτως εἶπε. συνεῖπε δ' αὐτῷ Ὑστάσπας ἀνὴρ Πέρσης τῶν ὁμοτίμων ὧδε Δεινὸν γάρ τἂν εἴη, ὦ Κῦρε, εἰ ἐν θήρᾳ μὲ πολλάκις ἄσιτοι καρτεροῦμεν, ὅπως θηρίον τ ὑποχείριον ποιησώμεθα καὶ μάλα μικροῦ ἴσω ἄξιον· ὄλβον δὲ ὅλον πειρώμενοι θηρᾶν εἰ ἐμπο δών τι ποιησαίμεθα γενέσθαι ἡμῖν ἃ τῶν μὲ κακῶν ἀνθρώπων ἄρχει, τοῖς δ' ἀγαθοῖς πείθεται οὐκ ἂν πρέποντα ἡμῖν δοκοῦμεν[1] ποιεῖν.

47. Ὁ μὲν οὖν Ὑστάσπας οὕτως εἶπεν· οἱ δ ἄλλοι πάντες ταῦτα συνῄνουν. ὁ δὲ Κῦρος εἶπεν Ἄγε δή, ἔφη, ἐπειδὴ ὁμονοοῦμεν ταῦτα, πέμψατ ἀπὸ λόχου ἕκαστος πέντε ἄνδρας τῶν σπουδαιο τάτων· οὗτοι δὲ περιιόντες, οὓς μὲν ἂν ὁρῶσ πορσύνοντας τἀπιτήδεια, ἐπαινούντων· οὓς δ' ἂ ἀμελοῦντας, κολαζόντων ἀφειδέστερον ἢ ὡς δε σπόται.

Οὗτοι μὲν δὴ ταῦτα ἐποίουν.

III

1. Τῶν δὲ Μήδων τινὲς ἤδη, οἱ μὲν ἁμάξας προωρμημένας καταλαβόντες καὶ ἀποστρέψαντες προσήλαυνον μεστὰς ὧν δεῖται στρατιά, οἱ δὲ

[1] δοκοῦμεν Dindorf[4], Marchant, Hug; δοκοίημεν zE[2], Dindorf[3], Breitenbach; δοκοῖεν E[1]; δοκοῖμεν CD.

if occasion should ever demand it, we might be able to employ our powers of self-control to our advantage. And I fail to see where we could give proof of our training on a more important occasion than the present."

The Persians ready to put their training to the proof

46. Thus he spoke; and Hystaspas, one of the Persian peers, supported him in the following speech: "Why, yes, Cyrus; on the chase we often hold out without a thing to eat, in order to get our hands on some beast, perhaps one worth very little; and it would be strange indeed now, when the quarry we are trying to secure is a world of wealth, if we should for a moment allow those passions to stand in our way which are bad men's masters but good men's servants. I think, if we did so, we should be doing what does not befit us."

47. Such was Hystaspas's speech, and all the rest agreed with it. Then Cyrus said: "Come then, since we are of one mind on this point, send each of you five of the most reliable men from his platoon. Let them go about and praise all those whom they see preparing provisions; and let them punish more unsparingly than if they were their masters those whom they see neglectful."

Accordingly, they set about doing so.

III

The cavalry bring in spoils

1. Now a part of the Medes were already bringing in the wagons which had been hurried forward and which they had overtaken and turned back packed

καὶ ἁρμαμάξας γυναικῶν τῶν βελτίστων τῶν μὲν γνησίων, τῶν δὲ καὶ παλλακίδων διὰ τὸ κάλλος συμπεριαγομένων, ταύτας εἰληφότες προσῆγον. 2. πάντες γὰρ ἔτι καὶ νῦν οἱ κατὰ τὴν Ἀσίαν στρατευόμενοι ἔχοντες τὰ πλείστου ἄξια στρατεύονται, λέγοντες ὅτι μᾶλλον μάχοιντ' ἂν εἰ τὰ φίλτατα παρείη· τούτοις γάρ φασιν ἀνάγκην εἶναι προθύμως ἀλέξειν. ἴσως μὲν οὖν οὕτως ἔχει, ἴσως δὲ καὶ ποιοῦσιν αὐτὰ τῇ ἡδονῇ χαριζόμενοι.

3. Ὁ δὲ Κῦρος θεωρῶν τὰ τῶν Μήδων ἔργα καὶ Ὑρκανίων ὥσπερ κατεμέμφετο καὶ αὑτὸν καὶ τοὺς σὺν αὑτῷ, εἰ οἱ ἄλλοι τοῦτον τὸν χρόνον ἀκμάζειν τε μᾶλλον ἑαυτῶν ἐδόκουν καὶ προσκτᾶσθαί τι, αὐτοὶ δ' ἐν ἀργοτέρᾳ χώρᾳ ὑπομένειν. καὶ γὰρ δὴ οἱ ἀπάγοντες καὶ ἀποδεικνύντες Κύρῳ ἃ ἦγον πάλιν ἀπήλαυνον, μεταδιώκοντες τοὺς ἄλλους· ταῦτα γὰρ σφίσιν ἔφασαν προστετάχθαι ποιεῖν ὑπὸ τῶν ἀρχόντων.

Δακνόμενος δὴ ὁ Κῦρος ἐπὶ τούτοις ταῦτα μὲν ὅμως κατεχώριζε· συνεκάλει δὲ πάλιν τοὺς ταξιάρχους, καὶ στὰς ὅπου ἔμελλον πάντες ἀκούσεσθαι τὰ βουλευόμενα λέγει τάδε· 4. Ὅτι μέν, ὦ ἄνδρες φίλοι, εἰ κατάσχοιμεν τὰ νῦν προφαινόμενα, μεγάλα μὲν ἂν ἅπασι Πέρσαις ἀγαθὰ γένοιτο, μέγιστα δ' ἂν εἰκότως ἡμῖν δι' ὧν πράττεται, πάντες οἶμαι γιγνώσκομεν· ὅπως δ' ἂν

full of what an army needs; others were bringing in the carriages that conveyed the most high-born women, not only wedded wives but also concubines, who on account of their beauty had been brought along; these also they captured and brought in. 2. For even unto this day all who go to war in Asia take with them to the field what they prize most highly; for they say that they would do battle the more valiantly, if all that they hold dearest were there; for these, they say, they must do their best to protect. This may, perhaps, be true; but perhaps also they follow this custom for their own sensual gratification.

3. When Cyrus saw what the Medes and Hyrcanians were doing, he poured reproach, as it were, upon himself and his men, because during this time the others seemed to be surpassing them in strenuous activity and gaining something by it, too, while he and his men remained in a position where there was little or nothing to do. And it did seem so; for when the horsemen brought in and showed to Cyrus what they brought, they rode away again in pursuit of the others; for, they said, they had been instructed by their officers so to do.

Though Cyrus was naturally nettled at this, still he assigned a place to the spoil. And again he called his captains together and standing where they would all be sure to hear his words of counsel, he spoke as follows: 4. "Friends, we all appreciate, I am sure, that if we could but make our own the good fortune that is now dawning upon us, great blessings would come to all the Persians and above all, as is reasonable, to us by whom they are secured. But I fail to see how we are to establish a

αὐτῶν ἡμεῖς κύριοι γιγνοίμεθα, μὴ αὐτάρκεις ὄντες κτήσασθαι αὐτά, εἰ μὴ ἔσται οἰκεῖον ἱππικὸν Πέρσαις τοῦτο ἐγὼ οὐκέτι ὁρῶ. 5. ἐννοεῖτε γὰρ δή, ἔφη· ἔχομεν ἡμεῖς οἱ Πέρσαι ὅπλα οἷς δοκοῦμεν τρέπεσθαι τοὺς πολεμίους ὁμόσε ἰόντες· καὶ δὴ τρεπόμενοι πῶς[1] ἢ[2] ἱππέας ἢ τοξότας ἢ πελταστὰς ἄνευ ἵππων ὄντες δυναίμεθ' ἂν φεύγοντας ἢ λαβεῖν ἢ κατακανεῖν; τίνες δ' ἂν φοβοῖντο ἡμᾶς προσιόντες κακοῦν ἢ τοξόται ἢ ἀκοντισταὶ ἢ ἱππεῖς, εὖ εἰδότες ὅτι οὐδεὶς αὐτοῖς κίνδυνος ὑφ' ἡμῶν κακόν τι παθεῖν μᾶλλον ἢ ὑπὸ τῶν πεφυκότων δένδρων; 6. εἰ δ' οὕτω ταῦτ' ἔχει, οὐκ εὔδηλον[3] ὅτι οἱ νῦν παρόντες ἡμῖν ἱππεῖς νομίζουσι πάντα τὰ ὑποχείρια γιγνόμενα ἑαυτῶν εἶναι οὐχ ἧττον ἢ ἡμέτερα, ἴσως δὲ νὴ Δία καὶ μᾶλλον; 7. νῦν μὲν οὖν οὕτω ταῦτ' ἔχει κατ' ἀνάγκην. εἰ δ' ἡμεῖς ἱππικὸν κτησαίμεθα μὴ χεῖρον τούτων, οὐ πᾶσιν ἡμῖν καταφανὲς ὅτι τούς τ' ἂν πολεμίους δυναίμεθα καὶ ἄνευ τούτων ποιεῖν ὅσαπερ νῦν σὺν τούτοις, τούτους τε ἔχοιμεν ἂν τότε μετριώτερον πρὸς ἡμᾶς φρονοῦντας; ὁπότε γὰρ παρεῖναι ἢ ἀπεῖναι βούλοιντο, ἧττον ἂν ἡμῖν μέλοι, εἰ αὐτοὶ ἄνευ τούτων ἀρκοῖμεν ἡμῖν αὐτοῖς. εἶεν. 8. ταῦτα μὲν δὴ οἶμαι οὐδεὶς ἂν ἀντιγνωμονήσειε μὴ οὐχὶ τὸ πᾶν διαφέρειν Περσῶν γενέσθαι οἰκεῖον ἱππικόν· ἀλλ' ἐκεῖνο ἴσως ἐννοεῖτε πῶς ἂν τοῦτο γένοιτο. ἆρ' οὖν σκεψώμεθα, εἰ βουλοίμεθα καθιστάναι ἱππικόν, τί ἡμῖν ὑπάρχει καὶ τίνος ἐνδεῖ; 9. οὐκ-

[1] πῶς Jacob, Gemoll; ποίους MSS., most Edd.
[2] ἢ z; not in xy or most Edd.
[3] εὔδηλον yzE, most Edd.; ἔνδηλον C, Hug.

valid claim to the spoil if we cannot gain it by our own strength; and this we cannot do, unless the Persians have cavalry of their own. 5. Just think of it," he went on; "we Persians have arms with which, it seems, we go into close quarters and put the enemy to flight; and then when we have routed them, how could we without horses capture or kill horsemen or bowmen or targeteers in their flight? And what bowmen or spearmen or horsemen would be afraid to come up and inflict loss upon us, when they are perfectly sure that they are in no more danger of being harmed by us than by the trees growing yonder? 6. And if this is so, is it not evident that the horsemen who are now with us consider that everything that has fallen into our hands is theirs no less than ours, and perhaps, by Zeus, even more so? 7. As things are now, therefore, this is necessarily the case. But suppose we acquired a body of cavalry not inferior to theirs, is it not patent to us all that we should be able even without them to do to the enemy what we are now doing with their aid, and that we should find them then less presumptuous toward us? For whenever they chose to remain or to go away, we should care less, if we were sufficient unto ourselves without them. Well and good. 8. No one, I think, would gainsay me in this statement, that it makes all the difference in the world whether the Persians have their own cavalry or not. But perhaps you are wondering how this may be accomplished. Well then, supposing that we wished to organize a division of cavalry, had we not better consider our resources and our deficiencies? 9. Here, then, in camp are numbers

The Persians handicapped without cavalry of their own

Cyrus proposes to have Persian cavalry

οὖν ἵπποι μὲν οὗτοι πολλοὶ ἐν τῷ στρατοπέδῳ κατειλημμένοι καὶ χαλινοὶ οἷς πείθονται καὶ τἄλλα ὅσα δεῖ ἵπποις ἔχουσι χρῆσθαι. ἀλλὰ μὴν καὶ οἷς γε δεῖ ἄνδρα ἱππέα χρῆσθαι ἔχομεν, θώρακας μὲν ἐρύματα τῶν σωμάτων, παλτὰ δὲ οἷς καὶ μεθιέντες καὶ ἔχοντες χρῴμεθ' ἄν. 10. τί δὴ τὸ λοιπόν; δῆλον ὅτι ἀνδρῶν δεῖ. οὐκοῦν τοῦτο μάλιστα ἔχομεν· οὐδὲν γὰρ οὕτως ἡμέτερόν ἐστιν ὡς ἡμεῖς ἡμῖν αὐτοῖς.

'Αλλ' ἐρεῖ τις ἴσως ὅτι οὐκ ἐπιστάμεθα. μὰ Δί' οὐδὲ γὰρ τούτων τῶν ἐπισταμένων νῦν πρὶν μαθεῖν οὐδεὶς ἠπίστατο. ἀλλ' εἴποι ἄν τις ὅτι παῖδες ὄντες ἐμάνθανον. 11. καὶ πότερα παῖδές εἰσι φρονιμώτεροι ὥστε μαθεῖν τὰ φραζόμενα καὶ δεικνύμενα ἢ ἄνδρες; πότεροι δὲ ἃν μάθωσιν ἱκανώτεροι τῷ σώματι ἐκπονεῖν, οἱ παῖδες ἢ οἱ ἄνδρες; 12. ἀλλὰ μὴν σχολή γε ἡμῖν μανθάνειν ὅση οὔτε παισὶν οὔτε ἄλλοις ἀνδράσιν· οὔτε γὰρ τοξεύειν ἡμῖν μαθητέον ὥσπερ τοῖς παισί· προεπιστάμεθα γὰρ τοῦτο· οὔτε μὴν ἀκοντίζειν· ἐπιστάμεθα γὰρ καὶ τοῦτο· ἀλλ' οὐδὲ μήν, ὥσπερ τοῖς ἄλλοις ἀνδράσι τοῖς μὲν γεωργίαι ἀσχολίαν παρέχουσι, τοῖς δὲ τέχναι, τοῖς δὲ ἄλλα οἰκεῖα· ἡμῖν δὲ στρατεύεσθαι οὐ μόνον σχολή, ἀλλὰ καὶ ἀνάγκη. 13. ἀλλὰ μὴν οὐχ ὥσπερ ἄλλα πολλὰ τῶν πολεμικῶν χαλεπὰ μέν, χρήσιμα δέ· ἱππικὴ δὲ οὐκ ἐν ὁδῷ μὲν ἡδίων ἢ αὐτοῖν τοῖν ποδοῖν πορεύεσθαι; ἐν δὲ σπουδῇ οὐχ ἡδὺ ταχὺ μὲν φίλῳ παραγενέσθαι, εἰ δέοι, ταχὺ δέ, εἴτε ἄνδρα εἴτε θῆρα δέοι διώκεσθαι, καταλαβεῖν;

f horses which we have taken and reins which they
bey, and everything else that horses must have before
ou can use them. Yes, and more, all that a horse-
ıan must use we have—breastplates as defensive
rmour for the body and spears which we may use
ither to hurl or to thrust. 10. What then remains?
)bviously we must have men. Now these above all
ther things we have; for nothing is so fully ours as
e ourselves are our own.

"But perhaps some one will say that we do not
now how to ride. No, by Zeus; and no one of
hese who now know how to ride did know before he
earned. But, some one may say, they learned when
hey were boys. 11. And are boys more clever in
earning what is explained to them and what is
hown them than are men? And which are better
ble with bodily strength to put into practice what
hey have learned, boys or men? 12. Again, we
ave more time for learning than either boys or other
ıen; for we have not, like boys, to learn to shoot,
r we know how already; or to throw the spear, for
e understand that, too. No; nor yet again are we
situated as other men, some of whom are kept
usy with their farming, some with their trades, and
ome with other domestic labours, while we not only
ave time for military operations, but they are forced
pon us. 13. And this is not like many other
ranches of military discipline, useful but laborious;
ay, when it comes to marching, is not riding more
leasant than tramping along on one's own two feet?
nd when speed is required, is it not delightful
uickly to reach a friend's side, if need be, and
uickly to overtake a man or an animal, if occasion
hould require one to give chase? And is this not

ἐκεῖνο δὲ οὐχὶ εὐπετὲς τὸ ὅ τι ἂν δέῃ ὅπλο
φέρειν τὸν ἵππον τοῦτο συμφέρειν; οὔκουν ταὐτ
γ' ἐστὶν ἔχειν τε καὶ φερειν.

14. Ὅ γε μὴν μάλιστ' ἄν τις φοβηθείη, μ
εἰ δεήσει ἐφ' ἵππου κινδυνεύειν ἡμᾶς πρότερο
πρὶν ἀκριβοῦν τὸ ἔργον τοῦτο, κἄπειτα μήτ
πεζοὶ ἔτι ὦμεν μήτε πω ἱππεῖς ἱκανοί, ἀλλ' οὐδ
τοῦτο ἀμήχανον· ὅπου γὰρ ἂν βουλώμεθα, ἐξέστα
ἡμῖν πεζοῖς εὐθὺς μάχεσθαι· οὐδὲν γὰρ τῶ
πεζικῶν ἀπομαθησόμεθα ἱππεύειν μανθάνοντες.

15. Κῦρος μὲν οὕτως εἶπε· Χρυσάντας δὲ συν
αγορεύων αὐτῷ ὧδε ἔλεξεν· Ἀλλ' ἐγὼ μέν, ἔφη
οὕτως ἐπιθυμῶ ἱππεύειν μαθεῖν ὡς νομίζω, ἢ
ἱππεὺς γένωμαι, ἄνθρωπος πτηνὸς ἔσεσθαι. 16
νῦν μὲν γὰρ ἔγωγε ἀγαπῶ ἤν γ' ἐξ ἴσου τῳ θεῖ
ὁρμηθεὶς ἀνθρώπων μόνον τῇ κεφαλῇ πρόσχω, κἂ
θηρίον παραθέον ἰδὼν δυνασθῶ διατεινάμενος φθά
σαι ὥστε ἀκοντίσαι ἢ τοξεῦσαι πρὶν πάνυ πρόσω
αὐτὸ γενέσθαι. ἢν δ' ἱππεὺς γένωμαι, δυνήσομα
μὲν ἄνδρα ἐξ ὄψεως μήκους καθαιρεῖν· δυνήσομα
δὲ θηρία διώκων τὰ μὲν ἐκ χειρὸς παίειν καταλαμ
βάνων, τὰ δὲ ἀκοντίζειν ὥσπερ ἑστηκότα· [κα
γὰρ ἐὰν ἀμφότερα ταχέα ᾖ, ὅμως ἐὰν πλησίο
γίγνηται ἀλλήλων, ὥσπερ τὰ ἑστηκότα ἐστίν.]
17. ὃ δὲ δὴ μάλιστα δοκῶ ζῴων, ἔφη, ἐζηλωκένα
ἱπποκενταύρους, εἰ ἐγένοντο, ὥστε προβουλεύε

[1] καὶ . . . ἐστίν MSS., Dindorf, Breitenbach, et al. bracketed by Hug, Marchant, Gemoll.

convenient, that the horse should help you to carry whatever accoutrement you must take along? Surely, to have and to carry are not quite the same thing.

14. "What one might have most of all to fear, however, is that in case it is necessary for us to go into action on horseback before we have thoroughly mastered this task, we shall then be no longer infantrymen and not yet competent cavalrymen. But not even this is an insurmountable difficulty; for whenever we wish, we may at once fight on foot; for in learning to ride we shall not be unlearning any of our infantry tactics."

Chrysantas supports the proposition

15. Thus Cyrus spoke; and Chrysantas seconded him in the following speech: "I, for one, am so eager to learn horsemanship, that I think that if I become a horseman I shall be a man on wings. 16. For as we are now, I, at least, am satisfied, when I have an even start in running a race with any man, if I can beat him only by a head; and when I see an animal running along, I am satisfied if I can get a good aim quickly enough to shoot him or spear him before he gets very far away. But if I become a horseman I shall be able to overtake a man though he is as far off as I can see him; and I shall be able to pursue animals and overtake them and either strike them down from close at hand or spear them as if they were standing still; [and they seem so, for though both be moving rapidly, yet, if they are near to one another, they are as if standing still.] 17. Now the creature that I have envied most is, I think, the Centaur (if any such being ever existed), able to reason with a man's intelligence and to

σθαι μὲν ἀνθρώπου φρονήσει, ταῖς δὲ χερσὶ τὸ δέο παλαμᾶσθαι, ἵππου δὲ τάχος ἔχειν καὶ ἰσχύι ὥστε τὸ μὲν φεῦγον αἱρεῖν, τὸ δ' ὑπομένον ἀνα τρέπειν, οὐκοῦν πάντα κἀγὼ ταῦτα ἱππεὺς γενό μενος συγκομίζομαι πρὸς ἐμαυτόν. 18. προνοεῖ μέν γε ἕξω πάντα τῇ ἀνθρωπινῃ γνώμῃ, ταῖς δ χερσὶν ὁπλοφορήσω, διώξομαι δὲ τῷ ἵππῳ, τὸν δ ἐναντίον ἀνατρέψω τῇ τοῦ ἵππου ῥύμῃ,[1] ἀλλ' ο συμπεφυκὼς δεδήσομαι ὥσπερ οἱ ἱπποκένταυροι 19. οὐκοῦν τοῦτό γε κρεῖττον ἢ συμπεφυκέναι τοὺς μὲν γὰρ ἱπποκενταύρους οἶμαι ἔγωγε πολλοῖ μὲν ἀπορεῖν τῶν ἀνθρώποις ηὑρημένων ἀγαθῶ ὅπως δεῖ χρῆσθαι, πολλοῖς δὲ τῶν ἵπποις πεφυκό των ἡδέων πῶς αὐτῶν χρὴ ἀπολαύειν. 20. ἐγὼ δὲ ἢν ἱππεύειν μάθω, ὅταν μὲν ἐπὶ τοῦ ἵππο γένωμαι, τὰ τοῦ ἱπποκενταύρου δήπου διαπρά ξομαι· ὅταν δὲ καταβῶ, δειπνήσω καὶ ἀμφιέσο μαι καὶ καθευδήσω ὥσπερ οἱ ἄλλοι ἄνθρωποι ὥστε τί ἄλλο ἢ διαιρετὸς ἱπποκένταυρος κα πάλιν σύνθετος γίγνομαι;

21. Ἔτι δ', ἔφη, καὶ τοῖσδε πλεονεκτήσω τοῦ ἱπποκενταύρου· ὁ μὲν γὰρ δυοῖν ὀφθαλμοῖν ἑώρα τε[2] καὶ δυοῖν ὤτοιν ἤκουεν· ἐγὼ δὲ τέτταρσι μὲν ὀφθαλμοῖς τεκμαροῦμαι, τέτταρσι δὲ ὠσὶν αἰσθή σομαι· πολλὰ γάρ φασι καὶ ἵππον ἀνθρώπῳ[3] τοῖς ὀφθαλμοῖς προορῶντα δηλοῦν, πολλὰ δὲ τοῖ

[1] ῥύμῃ B (Dindorf), Edd.; ῥώμῃ xyz.
[2] ἑώρα τε Hug, Marchant, Gemoll; προ(-σ D)εωρᾶτο MSS. Dindorf, Breitenbach.
[3] ἀνθρώπῳ Pantazides, Marchant, Gemoll; ἀνθρώπου MSS. Dindorf, Breitenbach.

nanufacture with his hands what he needed, while
ıe possessed the fleetness and strength of a horse so
s to overtake whatever ran before him and to knock
lown whatever stood in his way. Well, all his
dvantages I combine in myself by becoming a
ıorseman. 18. At any rate, I shall be able to take
orethought for everything with my human mind, I
hall carry my weapons with my hands, I shall
ursue with my horse and overthrow my opponent by
he rush of my steed, but I shall not be bound fast
o him in one growth, like the Centaurs. 19. Indeed,
ny state will be better than being grown together in
ne piece; for, in my opinion at least, the Centaurs
nust have had difficulty in making use of many of
he good things invented for man; and how could
hey have enjoyed many of the comforts natural to
he horse? 20. But if I learn to ride, I shall, when
I am on horseback, do everything as the Centaur
loes, of course; but when I dismount, I shall dine and
lress myself and sleep like other human beings; and
so what else shall I be than a Centaur that can be
aken apart and put together again?

21. "And then," he added, "I shall have the
ıdvantage of the Centaur in this, too, that he used to
see with but two eyes and hear with but two ears,
while I shall gather evidence with four eyes and
earn through four ears; for they say that a horse
ıctually sees many things with his eyes before his
rider does and makes them known to him, and that
he hears many things with his ears before his rider

ὡσὶ προακούοντα σημαίνειν. ἐμὲ μὲν οὖν, ἔφη, γράφε τῶν ἱππεύειν ὑπερεπιθυμούντων.

Νὴ τὸν Δί', ἔφασαν οἱ ἄλλοι πάντες, καὶ ἡμᾶς γε.

22. Ἐκ τούτου δὴ ὁ Κῦρος λέγει, Τί οὖν, ἔφη, ἐπεὶ σφόδρα ἡμῖν δοκεῖ ταῦτα, εἰ καὶ νόμον ἡμῖν αὐτοῖς ποιησαίμεθα αἰσχρὸν εἶναι, οἷς ἂν ἵππους ἐγὼ πορίσω, ἤν τις φανῇ πεζῇ ἡμῶν πορευόμενος, ἤν τε πολλὴν ἤν τε ὀλίγην ὁδὸν δέῃ διελθεῖν; ἵνα καὶ παντάπασιν ἱπποκενταύρους ἡμᾶς οἴωνται ἄνθρωποι εἶναι.

23. Ὁ μὲν οὕτως ἐπήρετο, οἱ δὲ πάντες συνῄνεσαν· ὥστ' ἔτι καὶ νῦν ἐξ ἐκείνου χρῶνται Πέρσαι οὕτω, καὶ οὐδεὶς ἂν τῶν καλῶν κἀγαθῶν ἑκὼν ὀφθείη Περσῶν οὐδαμῇ πεζὸς ἰών.

Οἱ μὲν δὴ ἐν τούτοις τοῖς λόγοις ἦσαν.

IV

1. Ἡνίκα δ' ἦν ἔξω μέσου ἡμέρας, προσήλαυνον μὲν οἱ Μῆδοι ἱππεῖς καὶ Ὑρκάνιοι, ἵππους τε ἄγοντες αἰχμαλώτους καὶ ἄνδρας· ὅσοι γὰρ τὰ ὅπλα παρεδίδοσαν, οὐ κατέκαινον.[1] 2. ἐπεὶ δὲ προσήλασαν, πρῶτον μὲν αὐτῶν ἐπυνθάνετο ὁ Κῦρος εἰ σωθεῖεν πάντες αὐτῷ· ἐπεὶ δὲ τοῦτ' ἔφασαν, ἐκ τούτου ἠρώτα τί ἔπραξαν. οἱ δὲ διηγοῦντο ἅ τ' ἐποίησαν καὶ ὡς ἀνδρείως ἕκαστα ἐμεγαληγόρουν. 3. ὁ δὲ διήκουέ τε[2] ἡδέως πάν-

[1] κατέκαινον HG, Marchant, Gemoll; κατέκανον Dindorf, Breitenbach, Hug; κατέκαιον A; ἀπέκτεινον xD.

[2] διήκουέ τε Schneider, Dindorf, Breitenbach, Marchant; διηκούετο z; διήκουε Gemoll.

does and gives him intimation of them. Put me down, therefore," said he, "as one of those who are more than eager to become cavalrymen."

"Aye, by Zeus," said all the rest, "and us too."

The captains are unanimous

22. "How would it do, then," Cyrus asked, "since we are all so very well agreed upon this matter, if we should make a rule for ourselves that it be considered improper for any one of us whom I provide with a horse to be seen going anywhere on foot, whether the distance he has to go be long or short, so that people may think that we are really Centaurs?"

23. He put the question thus and they all voted aye. And so from that time even to this day, the Persians follow that practice, and no Persian gentleman would be seen going anywhere on foot, if he could help it.

Such were their discussions on this occasion.

IV

The allies return with prisoners of war

1. And when it was past midday, the Median and Hyrcanian horsemen came in, bringing both horses and men that they had taken. For they had spared the lives of all who had surrendered their arms. 2. And when they had ridden up, Cyrus asked them first whether his men were all safe. And when they answered this in the affirmative, he asked how they had fared. And they narrated to him what they had accomplished and proudly told how gallantly they had behaved in every particular. 3. And he listened with pleasure to all they wished

των ἃ ἐβούλοντο λέγειν· ἔπειτα δὲ καὶ ἐπῄνεσει αὐτοὺς οὕτως·

Ἀλλὰ καὶ δῆλοί τοι, ἔφη, ἐστὲ ὅτι ἄνδρε ἀγαθοὶ ἐγένεσθε· καὶ γὰρ μείζους φαίνεσθε κα καλλίους καὶ γοργότεροι ἢ πρόσθεν ἰδεῖν.

4. Ἐκ δὲ τούτου ἐπυνθάνετο ἤδη αὐτῶν καὶ ὁπόσην ὁδὸν διήλασαν καὶ εἰ οἰκοῖτο ἡ χώρα. οἱ δ᾽ ἔλεγον ὅτι καὶ πολλὴν διελάσειαν καὶ πᾶσα οἰκοῖτο καὶ μεστὴ εἴη καὶ οἰῶν καὶ αἰγῶν καὶ βοῶν καὶ ἵππων καὶ σίτου καὶ πάντων ἀγαθῶν.

5. Δυοῖν ἄν, ἔφη, ἐπιμελητέον ἡμῖν εἴη, ὅπως τε κρείττους ἐσόμεθα τῶν ταῦτα[1] ἐχόντων καὶ ὅπως αὐτοὶ μενοῦσιν· οἰκουμένη μὲν γὰρ χώρα πολλοῦ ἄξιον κτῆμα· ἐρήμη δ᾽ ἀνθρώπων οὖσα ἐρήμη καὶ τῶν ἀγαθῶν γίγνεται. 6. τοὺς μὲν οὖν ἀμυνομένους, ἔφη, οἶδα ὅτι κατεκάνετε,[2] ὀρθῶς ποιοῦντες· τοῦτο γὰρ μάλιστα σώζει τὴν νίκην· τοὺς δὲ παραδιδόντας αἰχμαλώτους ἠγάγετε· οὓς εἰ ἀφείημεν, τοῦτ᾽ αὖ σύμφορον ἄν, ὡς ἐγώ φημι, ποιήσαιμεν· 7. πρῶτον μὲν γὰρ νῦν οὐκ ἂν φυλάττεσθαι οὐδὲ φυλάττειν ἡμᾶς τούτους δέοι, οὐδ᾽ αὖ[3] σιτοποιεῖν τούτοις· οὐ γὰρ λιμῷ γε δήπου κατακανοῦμεν[4] αὐτούς· ἔπειτα δὲ τούτους ἀφέντες πλείοσιν αἰχμαλώτοις χρησόμεθα. 8. ἢν γὰρ κρατῶμεν τῆς χώρας, πάντες ἡμῖν οἱ ἐν αὐτῇ οἰκοῦντες αἰχμάλωτοι ἔσονται· μᾶλλον δὲ τούτους ζῶντας ἰδόντες καὶ ἀφεθέντας μενοῦσιν οἱ ἄλλοι

[1] ταῦτα Hug, Marchant, Gemoll; αὐτὰ MSS., earlier Edd.
[2] κατεκάνετε Dindorf, later Edd.; κατεκαίνετε z; ἀπεκτείνετε xD. [3] αὖ Castalio, Edd.; ἂν MSS.
[4] κατακανοῦμεν Zeune, Edd.; κατακαινοῦμεν z; ἀποκτενοῦμεν. xD.

o tell him, and then he praised them in these vords:

"It is quite evident that you have conducted your-elves as brave men; and any one can see it, for you ppear taller and handsomer and more terrible to look ıpon than heretofore."

4. Then he enquired of them further how far hey had ridden and whether the country was nhabited. And they replied, first, that they had idden a long way, and second, that all the country vas inhabited and that it was full of sheep and goats, attle and horses, grain and all sorts of produce.

What to do with these prisoners

5. "There are two things," said he, "that it were vell for us to look out for: that we make ourselves nasters of those who own this property, and that hey stay where they are. For an inhabited country s a very valuable possession, but a land destitute of people becomes likewise destitute of produce. . Those, therefore, who tried to keep you off, you lew, I know; and you did right. For this is the est way to conserve the fruits of victory. But hose who surrendered you have brought as prisoners f war. Now, if we should let them go, we should, I hink, do what would be in itself an advantage. . For, in the first place, we should not have to keep watch against them nor should we have to keep watch over them, nor yet to furnish them with food; for, of course, we do not mean to let them starve to leath; and in the second place, if we let them go, we shall have more prisoners of war than if we do not. 8. For, if we are masters of the country, all they that dwell therein will be our prisoners of war; and the rest, when they see these alive and set at liberty, will stay in their places and choose to

καὶ πείθεσθαι αἱρήσονται μᾶλλον ἢ μάχεσθα
ἐγὼ μὲν οὖν οὕτω γιγνώσκω· εἰ δ' ἄλλο τις ὁρ
ἄμεινον, λεγέτω.

Οἱ δὲ ἀκούσαντες συνῄνουν ταῦτα ποιεῖν.

9. Οὕτω δὴ ὁ Κῦρος καλέσας τοὺς αἰχμαλω
τους λέγει τοιάδε· 10. Ἄνδρες, ἔφη, νῦν
ὅτι ἐπείθεσθε τὰς ψυχὰς περιεποιήσασθε, τ
τε λοιποῦ, ἢν οὕτω ποιῆτε, οὐδ' ὁτιοῦν καινὸν
ἔσται ὑμῖν ἀλλ' ἢ οὐχ ὁ αὐτὸς ἄρξει ὑμῶν ὅσπε
καὶ πρότερον· οἰκήσετε δὲ τὰς αὐτὰς οἰκίας κα
χώραν τὴν αὐτὴν ἐργάσεσθε καὶ γυναιξὶ ταῖ
αὐταῖς συνοικήσετε καὶ παίδων τῶν ὑμετέρω
ἄρξετε ὥσπερ νῦν. 11. ἡμῖν μέντοι οὐ μαχεῖσθ
οὐδὲ ἄλλῳ οὐδενί· ἡνίκα δ' ἄν τις ὑμᾶς ἀδικῇ
ἡμεῖς ὑπὲρ ὑμῶν μαχούμεθα. ὅπως δὲ μηδ' ἐπαγ
γέλλῃ μηδεὶς ὑμῖν στρατεύειν, τὰ ὅπλα πρὸς ἡμᾶ
κομίσατε· καὶ τοῖς μὲν κομίζουσιν ἔσται εἰρήν
καὶ ἃ λέγομεν ἀδόλως. ὁπόσοι δ' ἂν τὰ πολεμικ
μὴ ἀποφέρωσιν ὅπλα, ἐπὶ τούτους ἡμεῖς καὶ δ
στρατευσόμεθα. 12. ἐὰν δέ τις ὑμῶν καὶ ἰὼν ὡ
ἡμᾶς εὐνοϊκῶς καὶ πράττων τι καὶ διδάσκω
φαίνηται, τοῦτον ἡμεῖς ὡς εὐεργέτην καὶ φίλον
οὐχ ὡς δοῦλον περιέψομεν. ταῦτα οὖν, ἔφη, αὐτο
τε ἴστε καὶ τοῖς ἄλλοις διαγγέλλετε. 13. ἢν δ
ἄρα, ἔφη, ὑμῶν βουλομένων ταῦτα μὴ πείθωντα
τινες, ἐπὶ τούτους ἡμᾶς ἄγετε, ὅπως ὑμεῖς ἐκείνων
μὴ ἐκεῖνοι ὑμῶν ἄρχωσιν.

Ὁ μὲν δὴ ταῦτ' εἶπεν· οἱ δὲ προσεκύνουν τε κα
ὑπισχνοῦντο ταῦτα ποιήσειν.

[1] καινὸν xD, later Edd.; κακὸν z, Dindorf (*harm*).

submit rather than to fight. This, then, is my proposition; but if any one else sees a better plan, let him speak."

But when they heard his proposal they agreed to adopt it.

9. Accordingly, Cyrus called the prisoners together and spoke as follows: 10. "My men," said he, "you have now saved your lives by your submission; and in the future also, if you continue to be obedient, no change whatever shall come to you except that you shall not have the same ruler over you as before; but you shall dwell in the same houses and work the same farms; you shall live with the same wives and have control of your children just as now. 11. But you shall not have to fight either us or any one else; but when any one injures you, we will fight for you; and that no one may even ask military service of you, bring your arms to us. And those that bring them shall have peace, and what we promise shall be done without guile. But as many as fail to deliver up their weapons of war, against these we ourselves shall take the field immediately. 12. But if any one of you comes to us in a friendly way and shows that he is dealing fairly with us and giving us information, we shall treat him as our benefactor and friend and not as a slave. Accept these assurances for yourselves, and convey them to the rest also. 13. But if," said he "while, you are willing to accept these terms of submission, some others are not, do you lead us against them that you may be their masters and not they yours."

Cyrus offers them their liberty

Thus he spoke and they did obeisance and promised to do what he directed.

V

1. Ἐπεὶ δ' ἐκεῖνοι ᾤχοντο, ὁ Κῦρος εἶπεν, Ὥρα δή, ὦ Μῆδοι καὶ Ἀρμένιοι, δειπνεῖν πᾶσιν ἡμῖν· παρεσκεύασται δὲ ὑμῖν τἀπιτήδεια ὡς ἡμεῖς βέλτιστα ἐδυνάμεθα. ἀλλ' ἴτε καὶ ἡμῖν πέμπετε τοῦ πεποιημένου[1] σίτου τὸν ἥμισυν· ἱκανὸς δὲ ἀμφοτέροις πεποίηται· ὄψον δὲ μὴ πέμπετε μηδὲ πιεῖν· ἱκανὰ γὰρ ἔχομεν παρ' ἡμῖν αὐτοῖς παρεσκευασμένα.

2. Καὶ ὑμεῖς δέ, ὦ Ὑρκάνιοι, ἔφη, διάγετε αὐτοὺς ἐπὶ τὰς σκηνάς, τοὺς μὲν ἄρχοντας ἐπὶ τὰς μεγίστας, γιγνώσκετε δέ, τοὺς δ' ἄλλους ὡς ἂν δοκῇ κάλλιστα ἔχειν· καὶ αὐτοὶ δὲ δειπνεῖτε ὅπουπερ ἥδιστον ὑμῖν· σῷ μὲν γὰρ ὑμῖν καὶ ἀκέραιοι αἱ σκηναί· παρεσκεύασται δὲ καὶ ἐνθάδε ὥσπερ καὶ τούτοις.

3. Καὶ τοῦτο δὲ ἴστε ἀμφότεροι ὅτι τὰ μὲν ἔξω ὑμῖν ἡμεῖς νυκτοφυλακήσομεν, τὰ δ' ἐν ταῖς σκηναῖς αὐτοὶ ὁρᾶτε καὶ τὰ ὅπλα εὖ τίθεσθε· οἱ γὰρ ἐν ταῖς σκηναῖς οὔπω φίλοι ἡμῖν.

4. Οἱ μὲν δὴ Μῆδοι καὶ οἱ ἀμφὶ Τιγράνην ἐλοῦντο, καί, ἦν γὰρ παρεσκευασμένα, ἱμάτια μεταλαβόντες ἐδείπνουν, καὶ οἱ ἵπποι αὐτοῖς εἶχον τἀπιτήδεια.

Καὶ τοῖς Πέρσαις δὲ ἔπεμπον τῶν ἄρτων τοὺς ἡμίσεις. ὄψον δὲ οὐκ ἔπεμπον οὐδ' οἶνον, οἰόμενοι ἔχειν τοὺς ἀμφὶ Κῦρον ἔτι ἄφθονα ταῦτα.[2] ὁ δὲ

[1] πεποιημένου Zeune, Edd.; πεπονημένου MSS.

[2] ἔτι ἄφθονα ταῦτα Dindorf[4], Hug, Marchant, Gemoll; ὅτι ἔφη ἄφθονα ταῦτα ἔχειν xD, Dindorf[3], Breitenbach (*for he said they had an abundance of that*); ὅτι ἄφθονα ταῦτα z.

V

1. When they were gone, Cyrus said: "Medes and Armenians, it is now high time for us all to go to dinner; and everything necessary has been prepared for you to the best of our ability. Go, then, and send to us half of the bread that has been baked —enough has been made for all; but do not send us any meat nor anything to drink; for enough has been provided for us at our own quarters.

General orders for dinner

2. "And you, Hyrcanians," he said to these, "lead them to their several tents—the officers to the largest (you know which they are), and the rest as you think best. And you yourselves also may dine where it best pleases you. For your own tents also are safe and sound, and there also the same provision has been made as for these.

3. "And all of you may be assured of this, that we shall keep the night-watches for you outside the camp, but do you look out for what may happen in the tents and have your arms stacked conveniently; for the men in the tents are not yet our friends."

4. Then the Medes and Tigranes and his men bathed, changed their clothes (for they were provided with a change), and went to dinner. Their horses also were provided for.

Of the bread, half was sent to the Persians; but neither meat for relish nor wine was sent, for they thought that Cyrus and his men had those articles left in abundance. But what Cyrus meant was that

Κῦρος ταῦτα ἔλεγεν, ὄψον μὲν τὸν λιμόν, πιεῖ
δ' ἀπὸ τοῦ παραρρέοντος ποταμοῦ.

5. Ὁ μὲν οὖν Κῦρος δειπνίσας τοὺς Πέρσας
ἐπεὶ συνεσκότασε, κατὰ πεμπάδας καὶ κατ
δεκάδας πολλοὺς αὐτῶν διέπεμψε καὶ ἐκέλευσ
κύκλῳ τοῦ στρατοπέδου κρυπτεύειν, νομίζων ἅμ
μὲν φυλακὴν ἔσεσθαι, ἄν τις ἔξωθεν προσίῃ, ἅμ
δέ, ἄν τις ἔξω φέρων χρήματα ἀποδιδράσκῃ
ἁλώσεσθαι αὐτόν· καὶ ἐγένετο οὕτω· πολλοὶ μὲ
γὰρ ἀπεδίδρασκον, πολλοὶ δὲ ἑάλωσαν. 6. ὁ δ
Κῦρος τὰ μὲν χρήματα τοὺς λαβόντας εἴα ἔχειν
τοὺς δὲ ἀνθρώπους ἀποσφάξαι ἐκέλευσεν· ὥστ
τοῦ λοιποῦ οὐδὲ βουλόμενος ἂν ηὗρες ῥᾳδίως τὸ
νύκτωρ πορευόμενον.

7. Οἱ μὲν δὴ Πέρσαι οὕτω διῆγον· οἱ δὲ Μῆδο
καὶ εὐωχοῦντο καὶ ἔπινον καὶ ηὐλοῦντο καὶ πάση
εὐθυμίας ἐνεπίμπλαντο· πολλὰ γὰρ καὶ τὰ τοι
αῦτα ἥλω, ὥστε μὴ ἀπορεῖν ἔργων τοὺς ἐγρη-
γορότας.

8. Ὁ δὲ Κυαξάρης ὁ τῶν Μήδων βασιλεὺ
τὴν μὲν νύκτα ἐν ᾗ ἐξῆλθεν ὁ Κῦρος αὐτός τ
ἐμεθύσκετο μεθ' ὧνπερ ἐσκήνου ὡς ἐπ' εὐτυχίᾳ
καὶ τοὺς ἄλλους δὲ Μήδους ᾤετο παρεῖναι ἐ
τῷ στρατοπέδῳ πλὴν ὀλίγων, ἀκούων θόρυβο
πολύν· οἱ γὰρ οἰκέται τῶν Μήδων, ἅτε τῶ
δεσποτῶν ἀπεληλυθότων, ἀνειμένως ἔπινον καὶ
ἐθορύβουν, ἄλλως τε καὶ ἐκ τοῦ Ἀσσυρίο
στρατεύματος καὶ οἶνον καὶ ἄλλα πολλὰ εἰληφότες.

9. Ἐπεὶ δὲ ἡμέρα ἐγένετο, καὶ ἐπὶ θύρας οὐδεὶ
ἧκε πλὴν οἵπερ καὶ συνεδείπνουν, καὶ τὸ στρα-

hunger was their relish and that they could drink from the river that flowed by.

5. Accordingly, when Cyrus had seen that the Persians had their dinner, he sent many of them out, when it was dark, in squads of five and ten, with orders to lie in hiding round about the camp; for he thought that they would serve as sentinels, in case any one should come to attack from the outside, and at the same time that they would catch any one who tried to run away with his possessions. And it turned out so; for many did try to run away, and many were caught. 6. And Cyrus permitted those who effected the capture to keep the spoil, but the men he bade them slay; and so after that you could not easily have found, had you tried, any one attempting to get away by night.

How the night was spent by the Persians

7. Thus, then, the Persians employed their time; but the Medes drank and revelled and listened to the music of the flute and indulged themselves to the full with all sorts of merry-making. For many things that contribute to pleasure had been captured, so that those who stayed awake were at no loss for something to do.

by the Medes

8. Now the night in which Cyrus had marched out, Cyaxares, the king of the Medes, and his messmates got drunk in celebration of their success; and he supposed that the rest of the Medes were all in camp except a few, for he heard a great racket. For inasmuch as their masters had gone off, the servants of the Medes were drinking and carousing without restraint, especially as they had taken from the Assyrian army wine and many other supplies.

by Cyaxares

9. But when it was day and no one came to his headquarters except those who had been dining with

τόπεδον ἤκουε κενὸν εἶναι τῶν Μήδων καὶ τῶν ἱππέων, καὶ ἑώρα, ἐπειδὴ ἐξῆλθεν, οὕτως ἔχοντα ἐνταῦθα δὴ ἐβριμοῦτό τε τῷ Κύρῳ καὶ τοῖς Μήδοις τῷ καταλιπόντας αὐτὸν ἔρημον οἴχεσθαι καὶ εὐθύς, ὥσπερ λέγεται ὠμὸς εἶναι καὶ ἀγνώμων τῶν παρόντων κελεύει τινὰ λαβόντα τοὺς ἑαυτοῦ ἱππέας πορεύεσθαι ὡς τάχιστα ἐπὶ τὸ ἀμφὶ Κῦρον στράτευμα καὶ λέγειν τάδε·

10. Ὤιμην μὲν ἔγωγε, οὐδ᾽ ἂν σέ, ὦ Κῦρε, περὶ ἐμοῦ οὕτως ἀπρονοήτως βουλεῦσαι, εἰ δὲ Κῦρος οὕτω γιγνώσκοι, οὐκ ἂν ὑμᾶς, ὦ Μῆδοι, ἐθελῆσαι οὕτως ἔρημον ἐμὲ καταλιπεῖν. καὶ νῦν, ἂν μὲν Κῦρος βούληται, εἰ δὲ μή, ὑμεῖς γε τὴν ταχίστην πάρεστε.

11. Ταῦτα δὴ ἐπέστειλεν. ὁ δὲ ταττόμενος πορεύεσθαι ἔφη, Καὶ πῶς, ὦ δέσποτα, ἐγὼ εὑρήσω ἐκείνους;

Πῶς δὲ Κῦρος, ἔφη, καὶ οἱ σὺν αὐτῷ ἐφ᾽ οὓς ἐπορεύοντο;

Ὅτι νὴ Δί᾽, ἔφη, ἀκούω ἀφεστηκότας τῶν πολεμίων Ὑρκανίους τινὰς καὶ ἐλθόντας δεῦρο οἴχεσθαι ἡγουμένους αὐτῷ.

12. Ἀκούσας δὲ ταῦτα ὁ Κυαξάρης πολὺ μᾶλλον ἔτι τῷ Κύρῳ ὠργίζετο τῷ μηδ᾽ εἰπεῖν αὐτῷ ταῦτα, καὶ πολλῇ σπουδῇ μᾶλλον ἔπεμπεν ἐπὶ τοὺς Μήδους, ὡς ψιλώσων αὐτόν, καὶ ἰσχυρότερον ἔτι ἢ πρόσθεν τοῖς Μήδοις ἀπειλῶν ἀπεκάλει· καὶ τῷ πεμπομένῳ δὲ ἠπείλει, εἰ μὴ ἰσχυρῶς ταῦτα ἀπαγγέλλοι.

13. Ὁ μὲν δὴ πεμπόμενος ἐπορεύετο ἔχων

im, and when he heard that the camp was forsaken y the Medes and the cavalry, and when he iscovered on going out that such was really the ase, then he fumed and raged against both Cyrus nd the Medes because they had gone off and left im deserted. And straightway, in keeping with is reputation for being violent and unreasonable, he rdered one of those present to take his own cavalry orps and proceed at topmost speed to Cyrus's army nd deliver the following message:

10. "I should think that even you, Cyrus, ould not have shown such want of consideration oward me; and if Cyrus were so minded, I should hink that at least you Medes would not have onsented to leave me thus deserted. And now, f Cyrus will, let him come with you; if not, do you t least return to me as speedily as possible."

The king's message to Cyrus

11. Such was his message. But he to whom he ave the marching order said: "And how shall I nd them, your majesty?"

"How," he answered, "did Cyrus and those with im find those against whom they went?"

"Why," said the man, "by Zeus, I am told that ome Hyrcanians who had deserted from the enemy ame hither and went away as his guides."

12. Upon hearing this, Cyaxares was much more ngry than ever with Cyrus for not even having told im that, and he sent off in greater haste to recall he Medes, for he hoped to strip him of his forces; nd with even more violent threats than before, he rdered the Medes to return. And he threatened he messenger also if he did not deliver his message n all its emphasis.

13 Accordingly, the officer assigned to this duty

τοὺς ἑαυτοῦ ἱππέας ὡς ἑκατόν, ἀνιώμενος ὅτι οὐ καὶ αὐτὸς τότε ἐπορεύθη μετὰ τοῦ Κύρου. ἐν δὲ τῇ ὁδῷ πορευόμενοι διασχισθέντες τρίβῳ τινὶ ἐπλανῶντο, καὶ οὐ πρόσθεν ἀφίκοντο ἐπὶ τὸ φίλιον στράτευμα πρὶν ἐντυχόντες ἀποχωροῦσί τισι τῶν Ἀσσυρίων ἠνάγκασαν αὐτοὺς ἡγεῖσθαι· καὶ οὕτως ἀφικνοῦνται τὰ πυρὰ κατιδόντες ἀμφὶ μέσας πως νύκτας. 14. ἐπεὶ δ' ἐγένοντο πρὸς τῷ στρατοπέδῳ, οἱ φύλακες, ὥσπερ εἰρημένον ἦν ὑπὸ Κύρου, οὐκ εἰσέφρηκαν[1] αὐτοὺς πρὸ ἡμέρας.

Ἐπεὶ δὲ ἡμέρα ὑπέφαινε, πρῶτον μὲν τοὺς μάγους καλέσας ὁ Κῦρος τὰ τοῖς θεοῖς νομιζόμενα ἐπὶ τοῖς τοιούτοις ἀγαθοῖς ἐξαιρεῖσθαι ἐκέλευε. 15. καὶ οἱ μὲν ἀμφὶ ταῦτα εἶχον· ὁ δὲ συγκαλέσας τοὺς ὁμοτίμους εἶπεν, Ἄνδρες, ὁ μὲν θεὸς προφαίνει πολλὰ κἀγαθά· ἡμεῖς δὲ οἱ[2] Πέρσαι ἐν τῷ παρόντι ὀλίγοι ἐσμὲν ὡς ἐγκρατεῖς εἶναι αὐτῶν. εἴτε γὰρ ὁπόσα[3] ἂν προσεργασώμεθα, μὴ φυλάξομεν, πάλιν ταῦτα ἀλλότρια ἔσται· εἴτε καταλείψομέν τινας ἡμῶν αὐτῶν φύλακας ἐπὶ τοῖς ἐφ' ἡμῖν γιγνομένοις, αὐτίκα οὐδεμίαν ἰσχὺν ἔχοντες ἀναφανούμεθα. 16. δοκεῖ οὖν μοι ὡς τάχιστα ἰέναι τινὰ ὑμῶν εἰς Πέρσας καὶ διδάσκειν ἅπερ ἐγὼ λέγω, καὶ κελεύειν ὡς τάχιστα ἐπιπέμπειν στράτευμα, εἴπερ ἐπιθυμοῦσι Πέρσαι τὴν ἀρχὴν τῆς Ἀσίας αὑτοῖς[4] καὶ τὴν κάρπωσιν γενέσθαι. 17. ἴθι μὲν οὖν σύ, ἔφη,

[1] εἰσέφρηκαν Cobet, later Edd.; εἰσαφῆκαν MSS., Dindorf, et al.
[2] οἱ Bothe, Edd.; ὦ MSS.
[3] ὁπόσα Poppo, Edd.; ὁποῖα xz; ὅσα D.
[4] αὑτοῖς Gemoll; αὐτοῖς MSS., earlier Edd.

set out with his cavalry, about a hundred in number, vexed with himself for not having gone along with Cyrus when he went. And as they proceeded on their journey, they were misled by a certain by-path and so lost their way and did not reach the army of their friends, until they fell in with some deserters from the Assyrians and compelled them to act as their guides. And so they came in sight of the camp-fires sometime about midnight. 14. And when they came up to the camp, the sentinels, following the instructions of Cyrus, refused to admit them before daylight.

Now at peep of day the first thing that Cyrus did was to call the magi and bid them select the gifts ordained for the gods in acknowledgment of such success; 15. and they proceeded to attend to this, while he called the peers together and said: "Friends, God holds out before us many blessings. But we Persians are, under the present circumstances, too few to avail ourselves of them. For if we fail to guard what we win, it will again become the property of others; and if we leave some of our own men to guard what falls into our possession, it will very soon be found out that we have no strength. 16. Accordingly, I have decided that one of you should go with all speed to Persia, present my message and ask them to send reinforcements with the utmost dispatch, if the Persians desire to have control of Asia and the revenues accruing therefrom. 17. Do you, therefore, go, for you are the senior officer, and

Cyrus sends to Persia for reinforcements

ὁ πρεσβύτατος, καὶ ἰὼν ταῦτα λέγε, καὶ ὅτι οὓ ἂν πέμπωσι στρατιώτας, ἐπειδὰν ἔλθωσι παρ ἐμέ, ἐμοὶ μελήσει περὶ τροφῆς αὐτοῖς. ἃ δ ἔχομεν ἡμεῖς, ὁρᾷς μὲν αὐτός,[1] κρύπτε δὲ τούτω μηδέν, ὅ τι δὲ τούτων ἐγὼ πέμπων εἰς Πέρσα καλῶς καὶ νομίμως ποιοίην ἂν τὰ μὲν πρὸς τοὺ θεοὺς τὸν πατέρα ἐρώτα, τὰ δὲ πρὸς τὸ κοινὸ τὰς ἀρχάς. πεμψάντων δὲ καὶ ὀπτῆρας ὧ πράττομεν καὶ φραστῆρας ὧν ἐρωτῶμεν. καὶ σὺ μέν, ἔφη, συσκευάζου καὶ τὸν λόχον προπομπὸ ἄγε.

18. Ἐκ τούτου δὲ[2] καὶ τοὺς Μήδους ἐκάλει, καὶ ἅμα ὁ παρὰ τοῦ Κυαξάρου ἄγγελος παρίσταται, καὶ ἐν πᾶσι τήν τε πρὸς Κῦρον ὀργὴν καὶ τὰς πρὸς Μήδους ἀπειλὰς αὐτοῦ ἔλεγε· καὶ τέλος εἶπεν ὅτι ἀπιέναι Μήδους κελεύει, καὶ εἰ Κῦρος μένειν βούλεται.

19. Οἱ μὲν οὖν Μῆδοι ἀκούσαντες τοῦ ἀγγέλου ἐσίγησαν, ἀποροῦντες μὲν πῶς χρὴ καλοῦντος ἀπειθεῖν, φοβούμενοι δὲ πῶς χρὴ ἀπειλοῦντι ὑπακοῦσαι, ἄλλως τε καὶ εἰδότες τὴν ὠμότητα αὐτοῦ. 20. ὁ δὲ Κῦρος εἶπεν, Ἀλλ' ἐγώ, ὦ ἄγγελέ τε καὶ Μῆδοι, οὐδέν, ἔφη, θαυμάζω εἰ Κυαξάρης, πολλοὺς μὲν πολεμίους τότ' ἰδών, ἡμᾶς δὲ οὐκ εἰδὼς ὅ τι πράττομεν, ὀκνεῖ περί τε ἡμῶν καὶ περὶ αὑτοῦ· ἐπειδὰν δὲ αἴσθηται πολλοὺς μὲν τῶν πολεμίων ἀπολωλότας, πάντας δὲ ἀπεληλαμένους, πρῶτον μὲν παύσεται φοβούμενος, ἔπειτα γνώσεται, ὅτι οὐ νῦν ἔρημος γίγνε-

[1] αὐτός Cobet, most Edd.; αὐτά MSS., Dindorf.
[2] δὲ D, most Edd.; δὴ xz, Gemoll.

when you arrive tell them this; and say also that for whatever soldiers they send I will provide maintenance after they come. Conceal from them nothing in regard to what we have, and you see for yourself what there is. And what portion of these spoils honour and the law require that I should send to Persia—in regard to what is due the gods, ask my father; in regard to what is due to the State, ask the authorities. And let them send men also to observe what we do and to answer our questions. And you," said he, "make ready and take your own platoon to escort you."

18. After this he called in the Medes also and at the same moment the messenger from Cyaxares presented himself and in the presence of all reported his king's anger against Cyrus and his threats against the Medes; and at the last he said that Cyaxares ordered the Medes to return, even if Cyrus wished to stay.

The king's message is received

19. On hearing the messenger, therefore, the Medes were silent, for they were at a loss how they could disobey him when he summoned them, and they asked themselves in fear how they could obey him when he threatened so, especially as they had had experience of his fury. 20. But Cyrus said: "Well, Sir Messenger and you Medes, inasmuch as Cyaxares saw in our first encounter that the enemy were numerous and as he does not know how we have been faring, I am not at all surprised that he is concerned for us and for himself. But when he discovers that many of the enemy have been slain and all have been routed, in the first place he will banish his fears and in the second place he will

ται, ἡνίκα οἱ φίλοι αὐτοῦ τοὺς ἐκείνου ἐχθροὺ ἀπολλύασιν.

21. Ἀλλὰ μὴν μέμψεώς γε πῶς ἐσμὲν ἄξιοι εὖ τε ποιοῦντες ἐκεῖνον καὶ οὐδὲ ταῦτα αὐτομα τίσαντες; ἀλλ' ἐγὼ μὲν ἐκεῖνον ἔπεισα ἐᾶσα με λαβόντα ὑμᾶς ἐξελθεῖν·[1] ὑμεῖς δὲ οὐχ ὡ ἐπιθυμοῦντες τῆς ἐξόδου ἠρωτήσατε εἰ ἐξίοιτ καὶ νῦν δεῦρο ἥκετε, ἀλλ' ὑπ' ἐκείνου κελευ σθέντες ἐξιέναι ὅτῳ ὑμῶν μὴ ἀχθομένῳ εἴη. κα ἡ ὀργὴ οὖν αὕτη σάφ' οἶδα ὑπό τε τῶν ἀγαθῶ πεπανθήσεται καὶ σὺν τῷ φόβῳ λήγοντι ἄπεισι.

22. Νῦν μὲν οὖν, ἔφη, σύ τε, ὦ ἄγγελε ἀνάπαυσαι, ἐπεὶ καὶ πεπόνηκας, ἡμεῖς τε, ὦ Πέρσαι, ἐπεὶ προσδεχόμεθα πολεμίους ἤτοι μαχουμένους γε ἢ πεισομένους παρέσεσθαι, ταχθῶμεν ὡς κάλλιστα· οὕτω γὰρ ὁρωμένους εἰκὸς πλέον προανύτειν ὧν χρῄζομεν. σὺ δ', ἔφη, ὦ τῶν Ὑρκανίων ἄρχων, ὑπόμεινον προστάξας τοῖς ἡγεμόσι τῶν σῶν στρατιωτῶν ἐξοπλίζειν αὐτούς.

23. Ἐπεὶ δὲ ταῦτα ποιήσας ὁ Ὑρκάνιος προσῆλθε, λέγει ὁ Κῦρος, Ἐγὼ δέ, ἔφη, ὦ Ὑρκάνιε, ἥδομαι αἰσθανόμενος ὅτι οὐ μόνον φιλίαν ἐπιδεικνύμενος πάρει, ἀλλὰ καὶ σύνεσιν φαίνει μοι ἔχειν. καὶ νῦν ὅτι συμφέρει ἡμῖν ταὐτὰ δῆλον· ἐμοί τε γὰρ πολέμιοι Ἀσσύριοι, σοί τε νῦν ἔτι[2] ἐχθίονές εἰσιν ἢ ἐμοί· 24. οὕτως οὖν ἡμῖν ἀμφοτέροις βουλευτέον ὅπως τῶν μὲν νῦν παρόντων μηδεὶς ἀποστατήσει ἡμῖν συμμάχων, ἄλλους δέ,

[1] ἔπεισα . . . ἐξελθεῖν D, Breitenbach, Marchant, Gemoll; πείσας . . . ἐξελθεῖν τάδε ποιῶ xz, Dindorf, Sauppe.

[2] ἔτι D, Marchant, Gemoll; not in xz, other Edd.

ealize that he is not deserted now, when his friends re annihilating his enemies.

21. "But further, how do we deserve any blame, ince we have been doing him good service and have ot been doing even that on our own motion? But I, or my part, first got his consent to march out and ake you with me; while you did not ask whether ou might join the expedition and you are not here ow because you desired to make such an expedition, ut because you were ordered by him to make it—vhoever of you was not averse to it. This wrath, herefore, I am quite sure, will be assuaged by our uccesses and will be gone with the passing of his ear.

22. "Now, therefore, Sir Messenger," said he, "take some rest, for you must be fatigued, and since ve are expecting the enemy to come either to surender, or possibly to fight, let us, fellow-Persians, get into line in as good order as possible; for if we present such an appearance, it is likely that we shall better promote the accomplishment of what we desire. And you, king of Hyrcania, be pleased to order the commanders of your forces to get them under arms, and then attend me here."

Cyrus's plans to meet the crisis

23. And when the Hyrcanian had done so and returned, Cyrus said: "I am delighted, king of Hyrcania, to see that you not only show me your friendship by your presence, but also that you evidently possess good judgment. And now it is evident that our interests are identical. For the Assyrians are enemies to me, and now they are still more hostile to you than to me. 24. Under these circumstances, we must both take counsel that none of the allies now present shall desert us, and also

ἐὰν δυνώμεθα, προσληψόμεθα. τοῦ δὲ Μήδο
ἤκουες ἀποκαλοῦντος τοὺς ἱππέας· εἰ δ' οὗτ
ἀπίασιν, ἡμεῖς μόνοι οἱ πεζοὶ μενοῦμεν. 25. οἱ
τως οὖν δεῖ ποιεῖν ἐμὲ καὶ σὲ ὅπως ὁ ἀποκαλῶ
οὗτος καὶ αὐτὸς μένειν παρ' ἡμῖν βουλήσετα
σὺ μὲν οὖν εὑρὼν σκηνὴν δὸς αὐτῷ ὅπου κάλ
λιστα διάξει πάντα τὰ δέοντα ἔχων· ἐγὼ
αὖ πειράσομαι αὐτῷ ἔργον τι προστάξαι ὅπε
αὐτὸς ἥδιον πράξει ἢ ἄπεισι· καὶ διαλέγου δ
αὐτῷ ὁπόσα ἐλπὶς γενέσθαι ἀγαθὰ πᾶσι τοῖ
φίλοις, ἢν ταῦτ' εὖ γένηται· ποιήσας μέντοι αὐτ
ἧκε πάλιν παρ' ἐμέ.

26. Ὁ μὲν δὴ Ὑρκάνιος τὸν Μῆδον ᾤχετο ἄγω
ἐπὶ σκηνήν· ὁ δ' εἰς Πέρσας ἰὼν παρῆν συνε
σκευασμένος· ὁ δὲ Κῦρος αὐτῷ ἐπέστελλε πρὸ
μὲν Πέρσας λέγειν ἃ καὶ πρόσθεν ἐν τῷ λόγῳ
δεδήλωται, Κυαξάρῃ δὲ ἀποδοῦναι τὰ γράμματα
ἀναγνῶναι δέ σοι καὶ τὰ ἐπιστελλόμενα, ἔφη
βούλομαι, ἵνα εἰδὼς αὐτὰ ὁμολογῇς, ἐάν τί σ
πρὸς ταῦτα ἐρωτᾷ.

Ἐνῆν δὲ ἐν τῇ ἐπιστολῇ τάδε·

27. Κῦρος Κυαξάρῃ χαίρειν. ἡμεῖς σε οὔτ
ἔρημον κατελίπομεν· οὐδεὶς γάρ, ὅταν ἐχθρῶ
κρατῇ, τότε φίλων ἔρημος γίγνεται. οὐδὲ μὴ
ἀποχωροῦντές γέ σε οἰόμεθα ἐν κινδύνῳ καθι
στάναι· ἀλλὰ ὅσῳ πλέον ἀπέχομεν, τοσούτῳ
πλείονά σοι τὴν ἀσφάλειαν ποιεῖν νομίζομεν
28. οὐ γὰρ οἱ ἐγγύτατα τῶν φίλων καθήμενοι

hat, if we can, we may secure other allies besides. Now you heard the Mede recalling the cavalry; and f they go away, we only, the infantry, shall be left. 25. Accordingly, it is necessary for you and for me to do all we can to make this man also who is recalling them desire to remain with us himself. Do you, therefore, find and assign to him a tent where he will have the best kind of a time, with everything he wants; while I, for my part, will try to assign him some post that he himself would rather fill than go away. And do you have a talk with him and tell him what wealth we have hopes that all our friends will obtain, if we are successful in this; and when you have done this, come back again to me."

26. Accordingly, the Hyrcanian took the Mede and went away to a tent. And then the officer who was going to leave for Persia presented himself ready to start. And Cyrus commissioned him to tell the Persians what has been set forth in the foregoing narrative and also to deliver a letter to Cyaxares. "Now," said he, "I wish to read my message to you also, that you may understand its contents and confirm the facts, if he asks you anything in reference to them."

Now the contents of the letter ran as follows:

Cyrus's answer to Cyaxares

27. "My Dear Cyaxares:

We have not left you deserted; for no one is deserted by his friends at a time when he is conquering his enemies. We do not even think that we have brought you into any danger through our departure; but we maintain that the farther away we are, the greater the security we provide for you. 28. For it is not those who sit down nearest to their

μάλιστα τοῖς φίλοις τὴν ἀσφάλειαν παρέχουσι
ἀλλ' οἱ τοὺς ἐχθροὺς μήκιστον ἀπελαύνοντ
μᾶλλον τοὺς φίλους ἐν ἀκινδύνῳ καθιστᾶσι.

29. Σκέψαι δὲ οἵῳ ὄντι μοι περὶ σὲ οἷος ὢ
περὶ ἐμὲ ἔπειτά μοι μέμφει. ἐγὼ μέν γέ σ
ἤγαγον συμμάχους, οὐχ ὅσους σὺ ἔπεισας, ἀλλ
ὁπόσους ἐγὼ πλείστους ἐδυνάμην· σὺ δέ μ
ἔδωκας μὲν ἐν τῇ φιλίᾳ ὄντι ὅσους πεῖσαι δυνα
σθείην· νῦν δ' ἐν τῇ πολεμίᾳ ὄντος οὐ τὸν θέλοντ
ἀλλὰ πάντας ἀποκαλεῖς. 30. τοιγαροῦν τότε μὲ
ᾤμην ἀμφοτέροις ὑμῖν χάριν ὀφείλειν· νῦν δὲ σ
μ' ἀναγκάζεις σοῦ μὲν ἐπιλαθέσθαι, τοῖς δὲ ἀκο
λουθήσασι πειρᾶσθαι πᾶσαν τὴν χάριν ἀποδ
δόναι.

31. Οὐ μέντοι ἔγωγε σοὶ ὅμοιος δύναμαι γενέ
σθαι, ἀλλὰ καὶ νῦν πέμπων ἐπὶ στράτευμ
εἰς Πέρσας ἐπιστέλλω, ὁπόσοι ἂν ἴωσιν ὡς ἐμέ
ἤν τι σὺ αὐτῶν δέῃ πρὶν ἡμᾶς ἐλθεῖν, σο
ὑπάρχειν, οὐχ ὅπως ἂν ἐθέλωσιν, ἀλλ' ὅπω
ἂν σὺ βούλῃ χρῆσθαι αὐτοῖς.

32. Συμβουλεύω δέ σοι καίπερ νεώτερος ὢ
μὴ ἀφαιρεῖσθαι ἂν δῷς, ἵνα μή σοι ἀντὶ χαρίτω
ἔχθραι ὀφείλωνται, μηδ' ὅντινα βούλει πρὸς σ
ταχὺ ἐλθεῖν, ἀπειλοῦντα μεταπέμπεσθαι, μηδ

iends that provide them with the greatest security; ıt it is those who drive the enemy farthest away ıat help their friends most effectually out of ınger.

29. "And consider how I have acted toward you ıd how you have acted toward me, and yet in ›ite of all, you are finding fault with me. At all vents, I brought you allies—not merely as many as ›u persuaded to come, but as many as ever I had it ı my power to bring; whereas you gave to me, hen I was on friendly soil, as many as I could ersuade to join me, and now when I am in the nemy's territory you are recalling not merely those ho may be willing to leave me, but all my men. 0. Indeed, I thought at that time that I was under bligation both to you and to your men; but now ou are acting so as to force me to leave you out of onsideration and to try to devote all my gratitude › those who have followed me.

31. "However, I cannot on my part treat you in he same spirit as you treat me, but at this very ıoment I am sending to Persia for reinforcements, ith directions that as many as shall come to join ıe shall be at your service, if you need them for nything before we return, not as they may be leased to serve, but as you may wish to employ hem.

32. "Furthermore, although I am a younger ıan than you, let me advise you not to take back hat you have once given, lest ill-will be your ue instead of gratitude, nor to summon with threats hose whom you would have come to you quickly; nd again let me advise you not to employ threats gainst large numbers, while at the same time you

φάσκοντα ἔρημον εἶναι ἅμα πολλοῖς ἀπειλεῖ
ἵνα μὴ διδάσκῃς αὐτοὺς σοῦ μὴ φροντίζειν.

33. Ἡμεῖς δὲ πειρασόμεθα παρεῖναι, ὅτι
τάχιστα διαπραξώμεθα ἃ σοί τ' ἂν καὶ ἡμ
νομίζομεν πραχθέντα κοινὰ γενέσθαι ἀγαθ
ἔρρωσο.

34. Ταύτην αὐτῷ ἀπόδος καὶ ὅ τι ἄν σε τούτ
ἐρωτᾷ, ᾗ γέγραπται σύμφαθι. καὶ γὰρ ἐγὼ ἐπ
στέλλω σοι περὶ Περσῶν ᾗπερ γέγραπται.

Τούτῳ μὲν οὕτως εἶπε, καὶ δοὺς τὴν ἐπιστολ
ἀπέπεμπε, προσεντειλάμενος οὕτω σπεύδειν ὥσπ
οἶδεν ὅτι συμφέρει ταχὺ παρεῖναι.

35. Ἐκ τούτου δὲ ἑώρα μὲν ἐξωπλισμένους ἤδ
πάντας καὶ τοὺς Μήδους καὶ τοὺς Ὑρκανίους κ
τοὺς ἀμφὶ Τιγράνην· καὶ οἱ Πέρσαι δὲ ἐξωπλ
σμένοι ἦσαν· ἤδη δέ τινες τῶν προσχώρων κ
ἵππους ἀπῆγον καὶ ὅπλα ἀπέφερον. 36. ὁ δὲ τ
μὲν παλτὰ ὅπουπερ τοὺς πρόσθεν καταβάλλει
ἐκέλευσε, καὶ ἔκαον οἷς τοῦτο ἔργον ἦν ὁπόσων μ
αὐτοὶ ἐδέοντο· τοὺς δ' ἵππους ἐκέλευε φυλάττει
μένοντας τοὺς ἀγαγόντας ἕως ἄν τι σημανθ
αὐτοῖς· τοὺς δ' ἄρχοντας τῶν ἱππέων καὶ Ὑρκα
νίων καλέσας τοιάδε ἔλεξεν·

37. Ἄνδρες φίλοι τε καὶ σύμμαχοι, μὴ θαυ
μάζετε ὅτι πολλάκις ὑμᾶς συγκαλῶ· καινὰ γὰ

sert that you are deserted, for fear you teach
em to pay no attention to you.

33. "We shall try, however, to come to you just
soon as we have accomplished what we think it
ould be a common benefit to you and to us to have
one.

Farewell.

CYRUS."

34. "Deliver this to him and whatever he asks
ou in regard to these matters, answer him in
eeping with what is written. And you can do this
ith perfect truth, for my instructions to you in
egard to the Persians correspond exactly with what
written in my letter."

Final directions to his envoy

Thus he spoke to him and giving him the letter
ent him away, adding the injunction that he should
ake haste as one who knows that it is important to
e back again promptly.

35. At this moment he observed that all—both
he Medes and the Hyrcanians and Tigranes's men—
ere already under arms, and the Persians also
tood under arms. And some of the natives from
ear by were already delivering up horses and arms.
6. And the javelins he commanded them to throw
own in the same place as in the former instance,
nd they whose task this was burned all that they
id not themselves need. But as for the horses, he
ommanded those who brought them to keep them
nd wait until he sent them word. Then he called
n the officers of the cavalry and of the Hyrcanians
nd spoke as follows:

IV. ii. 33

37. "Friends and allies, do not wonder that I call
you together so often. For our present situation is

ἡμῖν ὄντα τὰ παρόντα πολλὰ αὐτῶν ἐστι
ἀσύντακτα· ἃ δ' ἂν ἀσύντακτα ᾖ, ἀνάγκη ταῦτ
ἀεὶ πράγματα παρέχειν, ἕως ἂν χώραν λάβῃ.

38. Καὶ νῦν ἔστι μὲν ἡμῖν πολλὰ τὰ αἰχμάλωτ
χρήματα, καὶ ἄνδρες ἐπ' αὐτοῖς· διὰ δὲ τὸ μήτ
ἡμᾶς εἰδέναι ποῖα τούτων ἑκάστου ἐστὶν ἡμῶι
μήτε τούτους εἰδέναι ὅστις ἑκάστῳ αὐτῶν δε
σπότης, περαίνοντας μὲν δὴ τὰ δέον ταοὐ πάν
ἔστιν ὁρᾶν αὐτῶν πολλούς, ἀποροῦντας δὲ ὅ τ
χρὴ ποιεῖν σχεδὸν πάντας. 39. ὡς οὖν μὴ οὕτω
ἔχῃ, διορίσατε αὐτά· καὶ ὅστις μὲν ἔλαβε σκη
νὴν ἔχουσαν ἱκανὰ καὶ σῖτα καὶ ποτὰ καὶ τοὺ
ὑπηρετήσοντας καὶ στρωμνὴν καὶ ἐσθῆτα κα
τἆλλα οἷς οἰκεῖται σκηνὴ καλῶς στρατιωτική
ἐνταῦθα μὲν οὐδὲν ἄλλο δεῖ προσγενέσθαι ἢ τὸν
λαβόντα εἰδέναι ὅτι τούτων ὡς οἰκείων ἐπιμέλε
σθαι δεῖ· ὅστις δ' εἰς ἐνδεόμενά του κατεσκή
νωσε, τούτοις ὑμεῖς σκεψάμενοι τὸ ἐλλεῖπον
ἐκπληρώσατε· 40. πολλὰ δὲ καὶ τὰ περιττὰ οἶδ
ὅτι ἔσται· πλείω γὰρ ἅπαντα ἢ κατὰ τὸ ἡμέτερον
πλῆθος εἶχον οἱ πολέμιοι. ἦλθον δὲ πρὸς ἐμὲ καὶ
χρημάτων ταμίαι, οἵ τε τοῦ Ἀσσυρίων βασιλέως
καὶ ἄλλων δυναστῶν, οἳ ἔλεγον ὅτι χρυσίον εἴη
παρὰ σφίσιν ἐπίσημον, δασμούς τινας λέγοντες.
41. καὶ ταῦτα οὖν κηρύττετε πάντα ἀποφέρειν
πρὸς ὑμᾶς ὅπου ἂν καθέζησθε· καὶ φόβον ἐπιτί-
θεσθε τῷ μὴ ποιοῦντι τὸ παραγγελλόμενον· ὑμεῖς
δὲ διάδοτε λαβόντες ἱππεῖ μὲν τὸ διπλοῦν, πεζῷ δὲ

novel, and many things about it are in an unorganized condition; and whatever lacks organization must necessarily always cause us trouble until it is reduced to order.

The Medes and Hyrcanians directed to divide the spoils

38 "We now have much spoil that we have taken, and men besides. But, as we do not know how much of it belongs to each one of us, and as the captives do not know who are their several masters, it is consequently impossible to see very many of them attending to their duty, for almost all are in doubt as to what they are expected to do. 39. In order, therefore, that this may not go on so, divide the spoil; and whoever has been assigned a tent with plenty of food and drink and people to serve him, and bedding and clothing and other things with which a soldier's tent should be furnished so as to be comfortable—in such a case nothing more need be added, except that he who has received it should be given to understand that he must take care of it as his own. But if any one has got into quarters that lack something, do you make a note of it and supply the want. 40. And I am sure that what is left over will be considerable, for the enemy had more of everything than is required by our numbers. Furthermore, the treasurers, both of the Assyrian king and of the other monarchs, have come to me to report that they have gold coin in their possession, by which they referred to certain payments of tribute. 41. Notify them, therefore, to deliver all this also to you, wherever you have your headquarters. And give that man reason to fear who shall not do as you command. And do you take the money and pay it out to the cavalry and infantry in the proportion of two to one, in order that you may all

τὸ ἁπλοῦν, ἵνα ἔχητε, ἤν τινος προσδέησθε, καὶ ὅτου ὠνήσεσθε.

42. Τὴν δ' ἀγορὰν τὴν οὖσαν ἐν τῷ στρατοπέδῳ κηρυξάτω μὲν ἤδη, ἔφη, μὴ ἀδικεῖν μηδένα, πωλεῖν δὲ τοὺς καπήλους ὅ τι ἔχει ἕκαστος πράσιμον, καὶ ταῦτα διαθεμένους ἄλλα ἄγειν, ὅπως οἰκῆται ἡμῖν τὸ στρατόπεδον.

43. Ταῦτα μὲν ἐκήρυττον εὐθύς. οἱ δὲ Μῆδοι καὶ Ὑρκάνιοι εἶπον ὧδε· Καὶ πῶς ἄν, ἔφασαν, ἡμεῖς ἄνευ σοῦ καὶ τῶν σῶν διανέμοιμεν ταῦτα;

44. Ὁ δ' αὖ Κῦρος πρὸς τοῦτον τὸν λόγον ὧδε προσηνέχθη· Ἦ γὰρ οὕτως, ἔφη, ὦ ἄνδρες, γιγνώσκετε ὡς ὅ τι ἂν δέῃ πραχθῆναι, ἐπὶ πᾶσι πάντας ἡμᾶς δεήσει παρεῖναι, καὶ οὔτε ἐγὼ ἀρκέσω πράττων τι πρὸ ὑμῶν ὅ τι ἂν δέῃ, οὔτε ὑμεῖς πρὸ ἡμῶν; καὶ πῶς ἂν ἄλλως πλείω μὲν πράγματα ἔχοιμεν, μείω δὲ διαπραττοίμεθα ἢ οὕτως; 45. ἀλλ', ὁρᾶτε, ἔφη· ἡμεῖς μὲν γὰρ διεφυλάξαμέν τε ὑμῖν τάδε, καὶ ὑμεῖς ἡμῖν πιστεύετε καλῶς διαπεφυλάχθαι· ὑμεῖς δ' αὖ διανείματε, καὶ ἡμεῖς πιστεύσομεν ὑμῖν καλῶς διανενεμηκέναι. 46. καὶ ἄλλο δέ τι αὖ ἡμεῖς πειρασόμεθα κοινὸν ἀγαθὸν πράττειν. ὁρᾶτε γὰρ δή, ἔφη, νυνὶ πρῶτον ἵπποι ὅσοι ἡμῖν πάρεισιν, οἱ δὲ προσάγονται· τούτους οὖν εἰ μὲν ἐάσομεν ἀναμβάτους, ὠφελήσουσι μὲν οὐδὲν ἡμᾶς, πράγματα δὲ παρέξουσιν ἐπιμέλεσθαι· ἢν δ' ἱππέας ἐπ' αὐτοὺς καταστήσωμεν, ἅμα πραγμάτων τε ἀπαλλαξόμεθα καὶ ἰσχὺν ἡμῖν αὐτοῖς προσθησόμεθα. 47. εἰ μὲν οὖν ἄλλους ἔχετε

have the wherewithal to buy whatever you still may need.

42. "Further," he added, "let the herald proclaim that no one shall interfere with the market in the camp, but that the hucksters may sell what each of them has for sale and, when they have disposed of that, get in a new stock, that our camp may be supplied."

43. And they proceeded at once to issue the proclamation. But the Medes and Hyrcanians asked: "How could we divide this spoil without help from you and your men?"

44. And Cyrus in turn answered their question as follows: "Why, my good men, do you really suppose that we must all be present to oversee everything that has to be done, and that I shall not be competent in case of need to do anything on your behalf, nor you again on ours? How else could we make more trouble and accomplish less than in this way? 45. No," said he; "you must look to it, for we have kept it for you and you must have confidence in us that we have kept it well; now for your part, do you divide it, and we shall have the same confidence in your dividing it fairly. 46. And there is something more that we, on our part, shall try to gain for the common advantage. For here, you observe, first of all, how many horses we have right now, and more are being brought in. If we leave them without riders, they will be of no use to us but will only give us the trouble of looking after them; but if we put riders upon them, we shall at the same time be rid of the trouble and add strength to ourselves. 47. If, therefore, you have others to whom you would rather

Cyrus asks for the horses for his Persians

οἷστισιν ἂν δοίητε αὐτούς, μεθ' ὧν ἂν καὶ κινδυνεύοιτε ἥδιον, εἴ τι δέοι, ἢ μεθ' ἡμῶν, ἐκείνοις δίδοτε· εἰ μέντοι ἡμᾶς βούλεσθε παραστάτας ἂν μάλιστα ἔχειν ἡμῖν αὐτοὺς δότε. 48. καὶ γὰρ νῦν ὅτε ἄνευ ἡμῶν προσελάσαντες ἐκινδυνεύετε, πολὺν μὲν φόβον ἡμῖν παρείχετε μή τι πάθητε, μάλα δὲ αἰσχύνεσθαι ἡμᾶς ἐποιήσατε ὅτι οὐ παρῆμεν ὅπουπερ ὑμεῖς· ἢν δὲ λάβωμεν τοὺς ἵππους, ἑψόμεθα ὑμῖν. 49. κἂν μὲν δοκῶμεν ὠφελεῖν πλέον ἀπ' αὐτῶν[1] συναγωνιζόμενοι, οὕτω προθυμίας οὐδὲν ἐλλείψομεν· ἢν δὲ πεζοὶ γενόμενοι δοκῶμεν καιριωτέρως ἂν παρεῖναι, τό τε καταβῆναι ἐν μέσῳ καὶ εὐθὺς πεζοὶ ὑμῖν παρεσόμεθα· τοὺς δ' ἵππους μηχανησόμεθα οἷς ἂν παραδοίημεν.

50. Ὁ μὲν οὕτως ἔλεξεν· οἱ δὲ ἀπεκρίναντο· Ἀλλ' ἡμεῖς μέν, ὦ Κῦρε, οὔτ' ἄνδρας ἔχομεν οὓς ἀναβιβάσαιμεν ἂν ἐπὶ τούτους τοὺς ἵππους, οὔτ' εἰ εἴχομεν, σοῦ ταῦτα βουλομένου ἄλλο ἂν ἀντὶ τούτων ᾑρούμεθα. καὶ νῦν, ἔφασαν, τούτους λαβὼν ποίει ὅπως ἄριστόν σοι δοκεῖ εἶναι.

51. Ἀλλὰ δέχομαί τε, ἔφη, καὶ ἀγαθῇ τύχῃ ἡμεῖς τε ἱππεῖς γενοίμεθα καὶ ὑμεῖς διέλοιτε τὰ κοινά. πρῶτον μὲν οὖν τοῖς θεοῖς, ἔφη, ἐξαιρεῖτε ὅ τι ἂν οἱ μάγοι ἐξηγῶνται· ἔπειτα δὲ καὶ Κυαξάρῃ ἐκλέξασθε ὁποῖ' ἂν οἴεσθε αὐτῷ μάλιστα χαρίζεσθαι.

52. Καὶ οἳ γελάσαντες εἶπον ὅτι γυναῖκας ἐξαιρετέον εἴη.

Γυναῖκάς τε τοίνυν ἐξαιρεῖτε, ἔφη, καὶ ἄλλο ὅ

[1] ἀπ' αὐτῶν Cobet, Edd.; ἐπ' αὐτῶν xz; ἐπὶ τῶν ἵππων D.

give them and with whom you would rather go into danger, if need should be, than with us, offer them the horses. If, however, you should wish to have us as your comrades in preference to others, give them to us. 48. And I have good reasons for asking; for just now when you rode on into danger without us, you filled us with apprehension lest something should happen to you and made us very much ashamed because we were not at your side. But if we get the horses, we shall follow you next time. 49. And if it seems that we are of more use to you by fighting with you on horseback, in that case we shall not fail for want of courage. But if it seems that by turning footmen again we could assist to better advantage, it will be open to us to dismount and at once stand by you as foot soldiers; and as for the horses, we shall manage to find some one to whom we may entrust them."

50. Thus he spoke, and they made answer: "Well, Cyrus, we have no men whom we could mount upon these horses; and if we had, we should not choose to make any other disposition of them, since this is what you desire. So now," they added, "take them and do as you think best."

He suggests suitable gifts for others

51. "Well," said he, "I accept them; may good fortune attend our turning into horsemen and your dividing the common spoils. In the first place, set apart for the gods whatever the magi direct, as they interpret the will of the gods. Next select for Cyaxares also whatever you think would be most acceptable to him."

52. They laughed and said that they would have to choose women for him.

"Choose women then," said he, "and whatever

τι ἂν δοκῇ ὑμῖν. ἐπειδὰν δ' ἐκείνῳ ἐξέλητε, τοὺς ἐμοί, ὦ Ὑρκάνιοι, ἐθελουσίους τούτους ἐπισπομένους πάντας ἀμέμπτους ποιεῖτε εἰς δύναμιν.

53. Ὑμεῖς δ' αὖ, ὦ Μῆδοι, τοὺς πρώτους συμμάχους γενομένους τιμᾶτε τούτους, ὅπως εὖ βεβουλεῦσθαι ἡγήσωνται ἡμῖν φίλοι γενόμενοι. νείματε δὲ πάντων τὸ μέρος καὶ τῷ παρὰ Κυαξάρου ἥκοντι αὐτῷ τε καὶ τοῖς μετ' αὐτοῦ· καὶ συνδιαμένειν δὲ παρακαλεῖτε, ὡς ἐμοὶ τοῦτο συνδοκοῦν, ἵνα καὶ Κυαξάρῃ μᾶλλον εἰδὼς περὶ ἑκάστου ἀπαγγείλῃ τὰ ὄντα. 54. Πέρσαις δ', ἔφη, τοῖς μετ' ἐμοῦ, ὅσα ἂν περιττὰ γένηται ὑμῶν καλῶς κατεσκευασμένων, ταῦτα ἀρκέσει· καὶ γάρ, ἔφη, μάλα πως ἡμεῖς οὐκ ἐν χλιδῇ τεθράμμεθα ἀλλὰ χωριτικῶς, ὥστε ἴσως ἂν ἡμῶν καταγελάσαιτε, εἴ τι σεμνὸν ἡμῖν περιτεθείη, ὥσπερ, ἔφη, οἶδ' ὅτι πολὺν ὑμῖν γέλωτα παρέξομεν καὶ ἐπὶ τῶν ἵππων καθήμενοι, οἶμαι δ', ἔφη, καὶ ἐπὶ τῆς γῆς καταπίπτοντες.

55. Ἐκ τούτου οἱ μὲν ᾖσαν ἐπὶ τὴν διαίρεσιν, μάλα ἐπὶ τῷ ἱππικῷ γελῶντες· ὁ δὲ τοὺς ταξιάρχους καλέσας ἐκέλευσε τοὺς ἵππους λαμβάνειν καὶ τὰ τῶν ἵππων σκεύη καὶ τοὺς ἱπποκόμους, καὶ ἀριθμήσαντας διαλαβεῖν[1] κληρωσαμένους εἰς τάξιν ἴσους ἑκάστοις.

56. Αὖθις δὲ ὁ Κῦρος ἀνειπεῖν ἐκέλευσεν, εἴ τις εἴη ἐν τῷ Ἀσσυρίων ἢ Σύρων ἢ Ἀραβίων στρατεύματι ἀνὴρ δοῦλος ἢ Μήδων ἢ Περσῶν ἢ Βακτρίων ἢ Καρῶν ἢ Κιλίκων ἢ Ἑλλήνων ἢ ἄλλοθέν ποθεν βεβιασμένος, ἐκφαίνεσθαι. 57. οἱ δὲ ἀκού-

[1] διαλαβεῖν Hug Marchant, Gemoll; λαβεῖν MSS., earlier Edd.

else you please. And when you have made your choice for him, then do you Hyrcanians do all you can to see that all those who volunteered to follow me have no cause to complain.

53. "And do you Medes, in your turn, show honour to those who first became our allies, that they may think that they have been well advised in becoming our friends. And allot his proper share of everything to the envoy who came from Cyaxares and to those who attended him; and invite him also to stay on with us (and give him to understand that this is my pleasure also), so that he may know better the true state of things and report the facts to Cyaxares concerning each particular. 54. As for the Persians with me," he said, "what is left after you are amply provided for will suffice for us; for we have not been reared in any sort of luxury, but altogether in rustic fashion, so that you would perhaps laugh at us, if anything gorgeous were to be put upon us, even as we shall, I know, furnish you no little cause for laughter when we are seated upon our horses, and, I presume," he added, "when we fall off upon the ground."

The Persians will be content with what is left

55. Hereupon they proceeded to the division of the spoil, laughing heartily at his joke about the Persian horsemanship, while he called his captains and ordered them to take the horses and the grooms and the trappings of the horses, and to count them off and divide them by lot so that they should each have an equal share for each company.

The spoils are divided

56. And again Cyrus ordered proclamation to be made that if there were any one from Media or Persia or Bactria or Caria or Greece or anywhere else forced into service as a slave in the army of the Assyrians or Syrians or Arabians, he should show himself. 57. And

Cyrus finds squires for his Persians

σαντες τοῦ κήρυκος ἄσμενοι πολλοὶ προυφάνησαν·[1] ὁ δ' ἐκλεξάμενος αὐτῶν τοὺς τὰ εἴδη βελτίστους ἔλεγεν ὅτι ἐλευθέρους αὐτοὺς ὄντας δεήσει ὅπλα ὑποφέρειν ἃν αὐτοῖς διδῶσι· τὰ δ' ἐπιτήδεια ὅπως ἂν ἔχωσιν ἔφη αὐτῷ μελήσειν.

58. Καὶ εὐθὺς ἄγων πρὸς τοὺς ταξιάρχους συνέστησεν αὐτούς, καὶ ἐκέλευσε τά τε γέρρα καὶ τὰς ψιλὰς μαχαίρας τούτοις δοῦναι, ὅπως ἔχοντες σὺν τοῖς ἵπποις ἕπωνται, καὶ τἀπιτήδεια τούτοις ὥσπερ καὶ τοῖς μετ' αὐτοῦ Πέρσαις λαμβάνειν, αὐτοὺς δὲ τοὺς θώρακας καὶ τὰ ξυστὰ ἔχοντας ἀεὶ ἐπὶ τῶν ἵππων ὀχεῖσθαι, καὶ αὐτὸς οὕτω ποιῶν κατῆρχεν, ἐπὶ δὲ τοὺς πεζοὺς τῶν ὁμοτίμων ἀνθ' αὐτοῦ ἕκαστον καθιστάναι ἄλλον ἄρχοντα τῶν ὁμοτίμων.

VI

1. Οἱ μὲν δὴ ἀμφὶ ταῦτα εἶχον. Γωβρύας δ' ἐν τούτῳ παρῆν Ἀσσύριος πρεσβύτης ἀνὴρ ἐφ' ἵππου σὺν ἱππικῇ θεραπείᾳ· εἶχον δὲ πάντες τὰ ἐφίππων ὅπλα. καὶ οἱ μὲν ἐπὶ τῷ τὰ ὅπλα παραλαμβάνειν τεταγμένοι ἐκέλευον παραδιδόναι τὰ ξυστά, ὅπως κατακάοιεν ὥσπερ τἆλλα. ὁ δὲ Γωβρύας εἶπεν ὅτι Κῦρον πρῶτον βούλοιτο ἰδεῖν· καὶ οἱ ὑπηρέται τοὺς μὲν ἄλλους ἱππέας αὐτοῦ

[1] προυφάνησαν Edd. ; προ(-σ D)εφάνησαν MSS.

when they heard the herald's proclamation, many came forward gladly. And he selected the finest looking of them and told them that they should be made free, but that they would have to act as carriers of any arms given them to carry; and for their sustenance he himself, he said, would make provision.

58. And so he led them at once to his captains and presented them, bidding his men give them their shields and swords without belts, that they might carry them and follow after the horses. Furthermore, he bade his captains draw rations for them just as for the Persians under him. The Persians, moreover, he bade always ride on horseback with their corselets and lances, and he himself set the example of doing so. He also instructed each one of the newly-mounted officers to appoint some other peer to take his place of command over the infantry of the peers.

VI

The arrival of Gobryas

1. Thus, then, they were occupied. Meanwhile Gobryas, an Assyrian, a man well advanced in years, came up on horseback with a cavalry escort; and they all carried cavalry weapons. And those who were assigned to the duty of receiving the weapons ordered them to surrender their spears, that they might burn them as they had done with the rest. But Gobryas said that he wished to see Cyrus first. Then the officers left the rest of the horsemen there,

κατέλιπον, τὸν δὲ Γωβρύαν ἄγουσι πρὸς τὸν Κῦρον. ὁ δ᾽ ὡς εἶδε τὸν Κῦρον, ἔλεξεν ὧδε·

2. Ὦ δέσποτα, ἐγώ εἰμι τὸ μὲν γένος Ἀσσύριος· ἔχω δὲ καὶ τεῖχος ἰσχυρὸν καὶ χώρας ἐπάρχω πολλῆς· καὶ ἵππον ἔχω εἰς χιλίαν, ἣν τῷ τῶν Ἀσσυρίων βασιλεῖ παρειχόμην καὶ φίλος ἦν ἐκείνῳ ὡς μάλιστα· ἐπεὶ δὲ ἐκεῖνος τέθνηκεν ὑφ᾽ ὑμῶν ἀνὴρ ἀγαθὸς ὤν, ὁ δὲ παῖς ἐκείνου τὴν ἀρχὴν ἔχει ἔχθιστος ὢν ἐμοί, ἥκω πρὸς σὲ καὶ ἱκέτης προσπίπτω καὶ δίδωμί σοι ἐμαυτὸν δοῦλον καὶ σύμμαχον, σὲ δὲ τιμωρὸν αἰτοῦμαι ἐμοὶ γενέσθαι· καὶ παῖδα οὕτως ὡς δυνατόν σε ποιοῦμαι· ἄπαις δ᾽ εἰμὶ ἀρρένων παίδων. 3. ὃς γὰρ ἦν μοι μόνος καὶ καλὸς κἀγαθός, ὦ δέσποτα, καὶ ἐμὲ φιλῶν καὶ τιμῶν ὥσπερ ἂν εὐδαίμονα πατέρα παῖς τιμῶν τιθείη, τοῦτον ὁ νῦν βασιλεὺς οὗτος καλέσαντος τοῦ τότε βασιλέως, πατρὸς δὲ τοῦ νῦν, ὡς δώσοντος τὴν θυγατέρα τῷ ἐμῷ παιδί, ἐγὼ μὲν ἀπεπεμψάμην μέγα φρονῶν ὅτι δῆθεν τῆς βασιλέως θυγατρὸς ὀψοίμην τὸν ἐμὸν υἱὸν γαμέτην· ὁ δὲ νῦν βασιλεὺς εἰς θήραν αὐτὸν παρακαλέσας καὶ ἀνεὶς αὐτῷ θηρᾶν ἀνὰ κράτος, ὡς πολὺ κρείττων αὐτοῦ ἱππεὺς ἡγούμενος εἶναι, ὁ μὲν ὡς φίλῳ συνεθήρα, φανείσης δὲ ἄρκτου διώκοντες ἀμφότεροι, ὁ μὲν νῦν ἄρχων οὗτος ἀκοντίσας ἥμαρτεν, ὡς μήποτε ὤφελεν, ὁ δ᾽ ἐμὸς παῖς βαλών, οὐδὲν δέον, καταβάλλει τὴν ἄρκτον.

but Gobryas they conducted to Cyrus. 2. And when he saw Cyrus, he spoke as follows:

His story

"Sire, I am by birth an Assyrian; I have also a castle, and wide are the domains which I govern. I have also about a thousand horse which I used to put at the disposal of the Assyrian king, and I used to be his most devoted friend. But since he has been slain by you, excellent man that he was, and since his son, who is my worst enemy, has succeeded to his crown, I have come to you and fall a suppliant at your feet. I offer myself to be your vassal and ally and ask that you will be my avenger; and thus, in the only way I may, I make you my son, for I have no male child more. 3. For he who was my son, my only son, a beautiful and brave young man, Sire, and one who loved me and paid me the filial reverence that would make a father happy—[1] him this present king—[1] when the old king, the father of the present ruler, invited my son to his court purposing to give him his daughter in marriage—and I let him go; for I was proud that, as I flattered myself, I should see my son wedded to the king's daughter—then, I say, the man who is now king invited him to go hunting with him and gave him permission to do his best in the chase, for he thought that he himself was a much better rider than my son. And my boy went hunting with him as his friend, and when a bear came out, they both gave chase and the present ruler let fly his javelin but missed. Oh! would to God he had not! Then my son threw (as he should not have done) and brought down the bear.

[1] The grief-stricken father's recital is broken with sobs; the sentences begun are never finished.

4. καὶ τότε μὲν δὴ ἀνιαθεὶς ἄρ' οὗτος κατέσχεν ὑπὸ σκότου τὸν φθόνον· ὡς δὲ πάλιν λέοντος παρατυχόντος ὁ μὲν αὖ ἥμαρτεν, οὐδὲν θαυμαστὸν οἶμαι παθών, ὁ δ' αὖ ἐμὸς παῖς αὖθις τυχὼν κατειργάσατό τε τὸν λέοντα καὶ εἶπεν, Ἆρα βέβληκα δὶς ἐφεξῆς καὶ καταβέβληκα θῆρα ἑκατεράκις, ἐν τούτῳ δὴ οὐκέτι κατίσχει ὁ ἀνόσιος τὸν φθόνον, ἀλλ' αἰχμὴν παρά τινος τῶν ἑπομένων ἁρπάσας, παίσας εἰς τὰ στέρνα τὸν μόνον μοι καὶ φίλον παῖδα ἀφείλετο τὴν ψυχήν. 5. κἀγὼ μὲν ὁ τάλας νεκρὸν ἀντὶ νυμφίου ἐκομισάμην καὶ ἔθαψα τηλικοῦτος ὢν ἄρτι γενειάσκοντα τὸν ἄριστον παῖδα τὸν ἀγαπητόν· ὁ δὲ κατακανὼν ὥσπερ ἐχθρὸν ἀπολέσας οὔτε μεταμελόμενος πώποτε φανερὸς ἐγένετο οὔτε ἀντὶ τοῦ κακοῦ ἔργου τιμῆς τινος ἠξίωσε τὸν κατὰ γῆς. ὅ γε μὴν πατὴρ αὐτοῦ καὶ συνῴκτισέ με καὶ δῆλος ἦν συναχθόμενός μοι τῇ συμφορᾷ. 6. ἐγὼ οὖν, εἰ μὲν ἔζη ἐκεῖνος, οὐκ ἄν ποτε ἦλθον πρὸς σὲ ἐπὶ τῷ ἐκείνου κακῷ· πολλὰ γὰρ φιλικὰ ἔπαθον ὑπ' ἐκείνου καὶ ὑπηρέτησα ἐκείνῳ· ἐπεὶ δ' εἰς τὸν τοῦ ἐμοῦ παιδὸς φονέα ἡ ἀρχὴ περιήκει, οὐκ ἄν ποτε τούτῳ ἐγὼ δυναίμην εὔνους γενέσθαι, οὐδὲ οὗτος ἐμὲ εὖ οἶδ' ὅτι φίλον ἄν ποτε ἡγήσαιτο. οἶδε γὰρ ὡς ἐγὼ πρὸς αὐτὸν ἔχω καὶ ὡς πρόσθεν φαιδρῶς βιοτεύων νῦν διάκειμαι, ἔρημος ὢν καὶ διὰ πένθους τὸ γῆρας διάγων.

7. Εἰ οὖν σύ με δέχει καὶ ἐλπίδα τινὰ λάβοιμι τῷ φίλῳ παιδὶ τιμωρίας ἄν τινος μετὰ σοῦ τυχεῖν, καὶ ἀνηβῆσαι ἂν πάλιν δοκῶ μοι καὶ οὔτε ζῶν ἂν

4. And then that man was vexed, to be sure, as it proved, but covered his jealousy in darkness. But when again a lion appeared, he missed again. There was nothing remarkable in that, so far as I can see; but again a second time my son hit his mark and killed the lion and cried, 'Have I not thrown twice in succession and brought an animal down each time!' Then that villain no longer restrained his jealous wrath but, snatching a spear from one of the attendants, smote him in the breast—my son, my only, well-loved son—and took away his life. 5. And I, unhappy I, received back a corpse instead of a bridegroom, and, old man that I am, I buried with the first down upon his cheeks my best, my well-beloved son. But the murderer, as if he had slain an enemy, has never shown any repentance, nor has he, to make amends for his wicked deed, ever deigned to show any honour to him beneath the earth. His father, however, expressed his sorrow for me and showed that he sympathized with me in my affliction. 6. And so, if he were living, I should never have come to you in a way to do him harm; for I have received many kindnesses at his hands and I have done him many services. But since the sceptre has passed on to the murderer of my son, I could never be loyal to him and I am sure that he would never regard me as a friend. For he knows how I feel toward him and how dark my life now is, though once it was so bright; for now I am forsaken and am spending my old age in sorrow.

The murder of his son

7. "If, therefore, you will receive me and I may find some hope of getting with your help some vengeance for my dear son, I think that I should find my youth again and, if I live, I should no longer

ἔτι αἰσχυνοίμην οὔτε ἀποθνήσκων ἀνιώμενος ἂν τελευτᾶν δοκῶ.

8. Ὁ μὲν οὕτως εἶπε· Κῦρος δ' ἀπεκρίνατο, Ἀλλ' ἤνπερ, ὦ Γωβρύα, καὶ φρονῶν φαίνῃ ὅσαπερ λέγεις πρὸς ἡμᾶς, δέχομαί τε ἱκέτην σε καὶ τιμωρήσειν σοι τοῦ παιδὸς σὺν θεοῖς ὑπισχνοῦμαι. λέξον δέ μοι, ἔφη, ἐάν σοι ταῦτα ποιῶμεν καὶ τὰ τείχη σε ἔχειν ἐῶμεν καὶ τὴν χώραν καὶ τὰ ὅπλα καὶ τὴν δύναμιν ἤνπερ πρόσθεν εἶχες, σὺ ἡμῖν τί ἀντὶ τούτων ὑπηρετήσεις;

9. Ὁ δὲ εἶπε, Τὰ μὲν τείχη, ὅταν ἔλθῃς, οἶκόν σοι παρέξω· δασμὸν δὲ τῆς χώρας ὅνπερ ἔφερον ἐκείνῳ σοὶ ἀποίσω καὶ ὅποι ἂν στρατεύῃ, συστρατεύσομαι τὴν ἐκ τῆς χώρας δύναμιν ἔχων. ἔστι δέ μοι, ἔφη, καὶ θυγάτηρ παρθένος ἀγαπητὴ γάμου ἤδη ὡραία, ἣν ἐγὼ πρόσθεν μὲν ᾤμην τῷ νῦν βασιλεύοντι γυναῖκα τρέφειν· νῦν δὲ αὐτή τέ μοι ἡ θυγάτηρ πολλὰ γοωμένη ἱκέτευσε μὴ δοῦναι αὐτὴν τῷ τοῦ ἀδελφοῦ φονεῖ, ἐγώ τε ὡσαύτως γιγνώσκω. νῦν δέ σοι δίδωμι βουλεύσασθαι καὶ περὶ ταύτης οὕτως ὥσπερ ἂν καὶ ἐγὼ βουλεύων περὶ σὲ φαίνωμαι.

10. Οὕτω δὴ ὁ Κῦρος εἶπεν, Ἐπὶ τούτοις, ἔφη, ἐγὼ ἀληθευομένοις δίδωμί σοι τὴν ἐμὴν καὶ λαμβάνω τὴν σὴν δεξιάν· θεοὶ δ' ἡμῖν μάρτυρες ἔστων.

Ἐπεὶ δὲ ταῦτα ἐπράχθη, ἀπιέναι τε κελεύει τὸν Γωβρύαν ἔχοντα τὰ ὅπλα καὶ ἐπήρετο πόση τις ὁδὸς ὡς αὐτὸν εἴη, ὡς ἥξων. ὁ δ' ἔλεγεν, Ἢν αὔριον ἴῃς πρῴ, τῇ ἑτέρᾳ ἂν αὐλίζοιο παρ' ἡμῖν.

11. Οὕτω δὴ οὗτος μὲν ᾤχετο ἡγεμόνα καταλι-

live in shame; and if I die, I think that I should die without a regret."

Cyrus and Gobryas make a compact

8. Thus he spoke; and Cyrus answered: "Well, Gobryas, if you prove that you really mean all that you say to us, I not only receive you as a suppliant, but promise you with the help of the gods to avenge the murder of your son. But tell me," said he, "if we do this for you and let you keep your castle and your province and the power which you had before, what service will you do us in return for that?"

9. "The castle," he answered, "I will give you for your quarters when you come; the tribute of the province, which before I used to pay to him, I will pay to you; and whithersoever you march I will march with you at the head of the forces of my province. Besides," said he, "I have a daughter, a maiden well-beloved and already ripe for marriage. I used once to think that I was rearing her to be the bride of the present king. But now my daughter herself has besought me with many tears not to give her to her brother's murderer; and I am so resolved myself. And now I leave it to you to deal with her as I shall prove to deal with you."

10. "According as what you have said is true," Cyrus then made answer, "I give you my right hand and take yours. The gods be our witnesses."

When this was done he bade Gobryas go and keep his arms; he also asked him how far it was to his place, for he meant to go there. And he said: "If you start to-morrow early in the morning, you would spend the night of the second day with us."

11. With these words he was gone, leaving a guide

πών. οἱ δὲ Μῆδοι παρῆσαν, ἃ[1] μὲν οἱ μάγοι ἔφασαν τοῖς θεοῖς ἐξελεῖν, ἀποδόντες τοῖς μάγοις, Κύρῳ δ' ἐξῃρηκότες τὴν καλλίστην σκηνὴν καὶ τὴν Σουσίδα γυναῖκα, ἣ καλλίστη δὴ λέγεται ἐν τῇ Ἀσίᾳ γυνὴ γενέσθαι, καὶ μουσουργοὺς δὲ δύο τὰς κρατίστας· δεύτερον δὲ Κυαξάρῃ τὰ δεύτερα· τοιαῦτα δὲ ἄλλα ὧν ἐδέοντο ἑαυτοῖς ἐκπληρώσαντες, ὡς μηδενὸς ἐνδεόμενοι στρατεύωνται· πάντα γὰρ ἦν πολλά.

12. Προσέλαβον δὲ καὶ Ὑρκάνιοι ὧν ἐδέοντο· ἰσόμοιρον δὲ ἐποίησαν καὶ τὸν παρὰ Κυαξάρου ἄγγελον· τὰς δὲ περιττὰς σκηνὰς ὅσαι ἦσαν Κύρῳ παρέδοσαν, ὡς τοῖς Πέρσαις γένοιντο. τὸ δὲ νόμισμα ἔφασαν, ἐπειδὰν ἅπαν συλλεχθῇ, διαδώσειν· καὶ διέδωκαν.

[1] ἃ Stephanus, Edd.; τὰ MSS.

behind. And then the Medes came in, after they had delivered to the magi what the magi had directed them to set apart for the gods. And they had selected for Cyrus the most splendid tent and the lady of Susa, who was said to be the most beautiful woman in Asia, and two of the most accomplished music-girls; and afterward they had selected for Cyaxares the next best. They had also supplied themselves with such other things as they needed, so that they might continue the campaign in want of nothing; for there was an abundance of everything.

How the spoils were divided

12. And the Hyrcanians also took what they wanted; and they made the messenger from Cyaxares share alike with them. And all the tents that were left over they delivered to Cyrus for the use of his Persians. The coin they said they would divide, as soon as it was all collected; and this they did.